THE LOST BOOK

The Quest for Deliverance

Atwiine Igonor

Archway Publishing books may be ordered through booksellers or by contacting:

Archway Publishing
1663 Liberty Drive
Bloomington, IN 47403
www.archwaypublishing.com
844-669-3957

ISBN: 978-1-6657-5112-4 (sc)
ISBN: 978-1-6657-5113-1 (e)

Library of Congress Control Number: 2023918999

Print information available on the last page.

Archway Publishing rev. date: 10/11/2023

1

The Sovereignty of Evil

THUS BEGINS: THE GREAT ACCOUNT
OF THE EVENTS AND TALES
THAT WOULD RESHAPE THE WORLD

IN THE TIME WHEN the Earth was corrupted by evil, there arose a ruler from the kingdom of Fozturia. Maguspra Intepar inherited the throne during the year 4850, after his father Titan's death. He stroked ghastly fear over the fellow countrymen he ruled over, reigning as a lion among lambs and as a snake slithering near doves. He held dominion over the far western land full of hills and valleys and resided in a grand palace in the chief city of Centero, along with his wife Elizabeth and their two sons Michael and David, and daughter Ruth. The palace was constructed by his ancestor Adumal, the first King of Fozturia, six hundred years before Maguspra began his reign.

In the early years of Maguspra's reign, there was hardly any war or conflict on Earth. Occasionally, threats and brief scares would come from distant kingdoms, but they would never amount to any serious conflicts. Nonetheless, he strengthened his kingdom's security by training and stationing seven thousand soldiers throughout the land. Thus, Fozturia experienced protection from the threat of any outside forces.

Within the kingdom, Maguspra held absolute authority over everyone and everything in the land. With this control, he could free the innocent and shower righteousness and justice on the land. He could prevent his citizens from living as peasants and they could instead live free lives spreading their joy and wisdom for all to see. Their joyful light could shine brighter than the stars during the night, far outnumbering any of the trials and hardships they might endure. The men and women of Fozturia could shine their lights brightly throughout the kingdom, spreading their joy and wisdom for all to see.

But none of this would happen under the reign of Maguspra. For he did what was right in his own eyes, according to what his forefathers had done in the past. He placed heavy yokes on his people, making their lives miserable and forcing them to give up what rightfully belonged to them. He bribed his many followers and advisors into believing his lies, and whoever dared speak against him would immediately be caught by his ever-watchful glare. The poor lost everything they possessed as he continually robbed them of their justice and freedom.

And while he would make many alliances with the other kingdoms of the Earth and showered his blessings on them, he in turn despised his people and ignored their desperate needs.

But there still existed many individuals throughout the kingdom of Fozturia who lived comfortable lives under his rule. Many of these became followers and advisors of him, benefitting from his rule of terror. He would bribe them with promises of wealth and security, and they in turn would remain loyal to their king. And so they too followed in the direction of Maguspra's evil, living their lives in identical ways to him. They robbed the poor of the meager things they owned, spreading further darkness throughout the kingdom.

Meanwhile, the rest of the population lived in constant fear under the shadow of Maguspra's terrible might. Many dreamt of a coming revolution that would overthrow him from power, but they remained afraid to express these hopes of theirs in public. But others grew increasingly weary as the suffering months and years went by, wishing to see a change in their lifetime even if it meant enduring the wrath and persecution of Maguspra.

Throughout Fozturia, from its town and city streets to its many farmlands, there existed a select few individuals who would proclaim their desire for freedom out in the open. They cared not what others would say, nor did they fear being caught by the king. They were tired of living lives of constant fear and desired to be free from their chains of bondage.

In one local town, an elderly beggar would shout his hopes out into the open square day after day, and hour after hour. Many walked passed him, but to those who made eye contact with him, he would plead all the more for them to listen to him.

"Listen to me!" he cried aloud in a voice stricken with grief. "Men and women of Fozturia, we must free ourselves from the slavery of this tyrant! Let us start a revolution and get rid of this black-hearted, corrupt brute!"

"You always say the same thing every day, old man," scoffed a man strolling by. "Just give up your fantasies and make the best of your own life. Or else you'll just be another victim of the king's wrath."

"I would rather die for freedom than spend life in captivity!" shouted the beggar. "Please, let us reason together! My intentions are for the best of us!" The old man reached out his hand to the man walking by, who swiftly slapped it away, glaring at the old beggar and shaking his head as he continued walking on.

A woman came by the beggar. "You better close your mouth," she whispered. "Because you never know whether or not the king has sent spies to capture those who speak out against him."

The woman went by, but the beggar found himself too weak even to try and argue with her. He sat silently to himself, with tears filling his eyes as he quietly watched the birds flying through across the sky. He listened to the songs they sang, observing the joy that filled their hearts and allowed them to freely glide through the air with no fear.

He sighed to himself. "When will I ever be like them?" he asked himself. "Who will liberate me from this terrible bondage?"

That question filled the hearts of those living in Fozturia, but no answer had the power to satisfy their hearts. Months and years passed by, but the king's oppressive shadow only continued to cover the land in spreading darkness. During the first four years of Maguspra's reign, he had already imprisoned thousands and executed a couple of hundreds of people who spoke out against him.

For those who tried to start a rebellion against him, their efforts were quickly squashed. But many more continued to try and lead more efforts in the hopes of gathering a great number of people to rebel against the king. One such person was a young man named Sam, who in the fourth year of Magusrpa's reign as king, shared his months of ideas with some of his friends. They immediately began working and spreading their ideas with as many people as they could, with those who joined them meeting together in underground locations to remain hidden.

And so as the days went by they continued to discuss and spread their ideas throughout Fozturia. Many supported Sam and met with him as they discussed what further action they could take to grow their movement even more. Many hundreds of people secretly met with each other, but the numbers would soon rise to a couple thousand. However, the majority of people were largely unaware that this growing group of people even existed since they remained fearful of getting caught by the king.

Unfortunately for Sam, many of Maguspra's spies had been scattered throughout Fozturia. And as his movement increased in numbers and strength, they soon discovered his plots and immediately reported them to the king.

When Maguspra heard the news, he arose from his throne in burning anger. He swiftly ordered his spies to find Sam, not even bothering to worry about the rest of those who had joined in on the rebellion. Hundreds of the king's spies were thus sent forth from the king, under the command of capturing Sam and bringing him to him.

The news was brought to Sam that Magusrpa desired to find and capture him, to execute him in his palace. Upon hearing the news, Sam quickly went into hiding in many underground locations, going from place to place as his friends and followers continued informing him where the spies were traveling throughout Fozturia.

But after many weeks of hiding, the king's spies soon became untraceable for Sam's followers to find, and they eventually managed to find the young man. After chaining him up, they led him to the Golden Mountains, and atop the mountains was the great brown palace of the king. The palace itself was shaped like a wide rectangle and surrounding it were many sturdy gray pillars and stone walls. A wide stone staircase led to the entrance, where two large brown flags displaying white birds stood proudly on each side of the door entrance. Many guards steadfastly held their ground, clothed in their gray uniforms and carrying both swords and shields. The spies led Sam inside the palace, snickering as they soon approached the king.

They made their way through the stone courts of the palace, with light brown walls and gray pillars all around them. Many carved figures were engraved into the walls, displaying the kings that had come long before the current king's lifetime. Windows hung just below the brown roof, but not much light came reflecting inside. Dark statues and images were scattered along the long hall, some displaying men and others different animals.

Sam stared longingly at the sights around him, engrossed by the vastness of the palace, yet trembling with fear as he knew that his doom was fast approaching. A tremendous uneasiness stirred within his heart as the many reflecting shadows and dark images and statues surrounded him. He knew that at any moment he would see the king, and he despaired at the imagination of what the fullness of his wrath would be like.

And then, under an image carved into the wall of a gray bird spreading its wings, was placed a black marble throne. Seated on it was the presence of an imposing man with a fierce glare in his eyes that would make even the proudest men whimper in fear. Once seeing Sam, he stood up from his seat and grinned from ear to ear.

For a moment, Sam stood in terror at the sight of Maguspra. Placed on the king's head was a silver crown designed and shaped in the figure of a bird. Even in the darkness of the hall, his eyes shone brightly with pure dread, but everything else about him was dark; from his clothing to his jet-black hair. And even as he smiled, Sam for a brief moment could see a heavy darkness that seemed to cover his face as a black shadow. Once he stood face to face with the king, the spies left the room, leaving Sam alone with Maguspra.

Sam's knees and legs trembled as Maguspra stared at him with his dark eyes, seeming to examine every twitching movement of his. After the long silence, Maguspra laughed aloud and spoke in a voice that echoed loudly throughout the space.

"Who are you, a mere man to come against the lion of lions?" he asked, taunting Sam with his deep and sinister voice. "Do you not know who I am? But tell me now, who are you? For you seem nothing to me but a weak and cowardly boy, especially because of where my spies found you."

Sam's eyes widened with uneasiness and his hands began shaking. He gulped to himself, not even daring to look into Maguspra's face as he responded to him. "I am Sam," he said quietly and fearfully. He looked up at Maguspra, waiting for a response from the king.

But the king only laughed, finding amusement in Sam's response to him. Then in a flash, his laughter subsided, and his face hardened. "Is that how you answer your king?" he asked in growing frustration. "You have been led all the way here to speak with the mighty King of Fozturia and yet you idly stand here with weakness and fear. I tell you, Sam, the King of Fozturia knows no fear and that is why the throne belongs to him. But who are you but a weak-minded and weak-willed boy who hides in underground locations, only to be caught by my spies? I would let you go if you didn't amuse me so much."

The king sat back in his seat, staring at the young man with his fierce and watchful glaring eyes. Sam thought to himself what he would do and whether or not the king would be willing to spare him. He thought of asking for the king's mercy in the hope of being let go, or even running away and escaping from him. But at that moment, Sam could feel a strong tugging on his heart, urging him to stand courageously against the king, speaking nothing but the truth. And so he lifted his head to the king, staring right back at him.

"I am not fearful of you, my king," he firmly said. "For I can boldly tell you that I and my many friends have firmly stood against you. And this I say to you, Maguspra son of Titan, you are the one filled with fear! For if you didn't know fear then you would have no cause to bring here before your throne. But because you are terrified of those willing to oppose you, you have no choice but to inflict pain on them with your hand. But this I say to you, I am not afraid of what you may do to me, for I know that what I have done is right! No wicked thing that you can do to me will ever be able to keep me on the ground. And for those whose spirits have been awakened, they shall cause you to fear them even more than you do me."

Even as he spoke in that long dark hall, a light seemed to surround Sam, while a black darkness covered Maguspra. The king immediately stood up from his seat, stepping forward closer to Sam.

"All that you say is a lie!" he shouted, filled now with great wrath. "You are one without wisdom, speaking words that you do not understand and have not considered before blurting them out. You are weak and afraid, but I am strong and full of confidence!"

"You speak great lies, my king," responded Sam, refusing to back down. "You should look at yourself and see the great fear and anger that covers your face now. I have remained calm in your presence, while you have reacted unjustly in response. And see how foolish you have become, ruling as a tyrant and not as a king."

With that, the king had heard enough. His eyes popped open with ferocious rage and he slapped Sam across the face. "I have heard enough from this mouth of yours!" he growled. "None of those filled with such foolish and lying words deserve to live!"

He immediately called upon two of his guards, who each carried swords with them. "Put this weakling to death," he ordered. "For none like him deserve to live in my kingdom."

The guards grabbed Sam's neck and arms, tying his hands and feet with ropes so that he couldn't escape from them. But even as they tied him up, Sam neither screamed nor said anything, instead calmly yielding to all that the guards did to him. He stared at Maguspra for many long minutes, not bothering to respond to his hate-filled curses put on him. And then once the time had come, Sam glared at the king for one last time before he cried out in excruciating pain. The sound of his final cries echoed like the mighty blasts of trumpets throughout the dark hall, and all that heard it thought that they could hear the sound of victory coming from those cries of pain.

Meanwhile, Maguspra stared longingly at the dead body of Sam, neither smiling nor laughing. But speaking to his spies he gave them a strong warning. "Let this serve as a reminder that anyone who dares oppose me will be struck down," he told them. "These flies cannot continue to thrive without any consequences. We have work to do, to ensure that those living in Fozturia are worthy of each breath of theirs."

The guards bowed their heads to Maguspra and departed from his presence. For several more hours, the eyes of the king were fixed on the body of Sam, thinking of all those like him who still lived in Fozturia. He then stood up from his throne and picked up his dead body, then came outside the palace after walking for some distance through the mountains, and threw his body into a covered space where none would ever see him again.

For several more months, a vast silence hovered over the kingdom of Fozturia. Hardly anyone came together secretly or openly in opposition to the king, as a number of his spies and guards went throughout the land, searching for anyone who spoke words against the king. A great hush fell on all the people, and they mostly lived their lives quietly and humbly.

But that would soon all change. For as the spies of Maguspra went through the whole land of Fozturia, they reported to him a beautiful and undiscovered land that existed. And so the king was sent information about the land, and he learned much about the rich fertile land.

He learned that only one man lived there, a young middle-class man named Augustus Latore who had lived a life of seclusion for many years. He discovered that the countryside was called Lerme, and was a beautiful land of rich fertile grass filled with many farms and plots of land. It was located to the northeast of Fozturia and was a place of peace where nature dwelled freely and securely.

As Maguspra learned about this, greed consumed his heart as he yearned to have more possessions and riches for himself. He desired to flaunt his glory to the other kings of the kingdoms of the Earth, impressing them with his riches and gaining even more allies in the process. And so with no warning he walked into Augustus' homeland and commanded the man to leave his home and relinquish all that he possessed to him. Augustus had no choice but to submit, as the king had brought with him many hundreds of soldiers to punish the man if he went against his order. And so Augustus said his final farewell to the land and was forced to follow the king's soldiers as they led him away from his home.

He followed them for many long miles far away from his home, before returning to Maguspra not before giving Augustus one last warning of the terrible things we would endure if he chose to return to his home. And so with great fear seizing his heart, he continued the long journey away from his home, eventually arriving in a local town square bustling with many people.

While walking around, an idea came to his mind. He knew that many people were infuriated with the king and desired to see him suffer the same pain that he inflicted on many others. He would use this frustration of the people and gather as many as he could to march in great numbers and protest against him. But he knew that he needed to garner as much support as he could manage, in the hopes of possibly overthrowing him entirely. He discussed his plans with as many of those as he could talk to, but they all mostly brushed his ideas aside.

"I'm sorry that you've lost your entire home, Augustus, but I don't think this plan of yours will work," said a fruit seller. "The king is way more powerful than all of us combined. His army will completely sabotage and wipe us out. What is the point of wasting our time for this, only to be killed like the many others who tried doing what you're planning?"

"But this is different," insisted Augustus. "With thousands of people, we could become a powerful enough force to be reckoned with. And imagine the great number of people who would join us while seeing what we're fighting for. And besides, to die for freedom is the noblest cause that any man could do. We are not wasting our time. Rather, to suffer under this tyrant's hand without stepping up for our rights is wasting our time."

The fruit seller dwelled on Augustus' words for a while. "You speak very well, young man," he said at last. "But I am too old and have seen too much to join you on this noble cause. I wish you the best in your pursuits, but I'm afraid that I can't join you."

Augustus was grieved to see the man give in to fear and doubt but continued to try and convince many others to join him. And very soon, with his convincing and wise words, a couple hundred of his fellow countrymen agreed to join his cause. And they all spread the same convincing words and information with as many as they could, talking with many others and spreading pamphlets everywhere they went.

Thus, a great number of people flocked to the movement in excitement to at least see a small glimmer of hope coming to the oppressed of Fozturia. They all did their parts as well, explaining all that had happened to Augustus, explaining their desires, and managing to impress many more people who agreed to join them. In time to come, a large number of thousands of people gathered together in a great crowd, voicing their support for the movement and especially for Augustus.

"I will support you in this mission!" cried a woman. "The time has come for justice to reign in our homes! Count me in!"

"Count me in as well!" shouted a man.

"I will join as well!" said another man. "Augustus is our hero! If we succeed in all that we have concocted, then we must make him king!"

"Yes, Augustus for King! Augustus for King!" chanted the people. "He stands courageously even in the presence of a dragon!"

Hour by hour and day by day, the movement that Augustus had started continued to grow and gain further traction. And it came to pass that they expressed their desire to begin marching to the palace of the king and protest against him. They were determined to fight for their cause of liberty, fearing neither the wrath of Maguspra nor death itself. If those in the past had given up their lives in the search of freedom with barely any support, then they believed that they had no choice but to fight for their cause even unto serious persecution.

From then on, they referred to themselves as 'the nobles,' because of their courageous fight for freedom.

Eventually, the big day of their protest arrived on a chilly November morning, with the wind blowing at moderate speed. It just so happened to be November 14th, the day when all the people of Fozturia reflect and honor the king and their monarchial history. The Nobles all arose early in the morning and were ready to walk many miles to the king's palace. In total at least ten thousand men and women walked side by side on the streets as they marched toward the Golden Mountains to protest against the king. They wished to lead peaceful, yet bold protests that would last for many days or even weeks and months before the king would feel weakened and overwhelmed. And they dreamed that the king would be completely overthrown, or at least repent and change his evil ways.

Thus the Nobles walked for many miles through the town streets and the Golden Mountains. They arrived in the chief city of Centero and ahead of them, they could see the king's palace on top of the great Golden Mountains. They made their way outside the palace's entrance and prepared to peacefully demonstrate their cause in front of the king.

But what Augustus didn't know was that many of the men and women had secretly been armed with weapons, and prepared to attack whoever would forcefully try and stop them. Once they climbed the stairs and stood by the door just outside the palace, they openly proclaimed what they had been planning for.

"Arise! Let us slaughter the king and his family!" shouted a man. "For the great day of our justice has come!"

Augustus stood stunned at the unexpected twist. He shook his head in disapproval that they had completely gone against what they had planned all along, by now seeking violence rather than a peaceful demonstration.

With great perplexity at the sudden change in the people's intentions, he tried to stop them from carrying out their desires. "What are you doing?" he asked, shouting and trying to grab the people's attention. "We planned to peacefully rebel and protest against the king, not try and start a war! Why are you abandoning our plan?"

But by then it was too late. The people had stormed through the entrance, yelling and screaming as they flocked inside the long and dark hall in great numbers. Armed with their swords and many other weapons they began striking down many guards and other servants of Maguspra that stood in their way.

Augustus tried restoring peace and order with the people, but their vengeful hearts were unconcerned to hear him. And so they continued their violent attack, attacking and striking as many as they could, while several others smashed and destroyed the many items that filled the hall.

Amidst the violence, one of the king's bodyguards managed to flee the scene and rushed to the king's room. He opened the door, breathing heavily as he spoke. "My king, a great number of rebels have stormed the palace," he said. "They have injured a number of your guards and servants, and many others have likely been killed. You and your family must exit from the back exit of the palace and enter the carriage to escape before these rebels manage to get to you."

Maguspra sat stunned and angered at all he heard but had no time to express his thoughts, as he, his wife, and his children were swiftly escorted by a dozen or so guards to the back exit of the palace, and taken to a carriage. Once inside, Maguspra ordered the driver to start moving, telling him to travel down the mountain and flee southwards.

But just as they began moving, a man armed with a sword suddenly appeared before them and jumped into the carriage. He leaped toward the king to strike him with his sword, but Maguspra managed to quickly move out of the way. But as he evaded the situation, his eldest son Michael was left unprotected and the momentum of the man's jump led him to strike Michael's chest with his sword. Streams of blood immediately came forth from the boy's chest, and he collapsed to the ground.

The family paused for a moment, with a wind of horror falling on them all as they watched the blood pour from Michael's chest. The king's wife let out a guttural cry of horror as she watched the blood cover her son's body.

At that moment, great fear such as he had never experienced before fell upon Maguspra as a vast cloud. His mouth dropped to the ground and his eyes widened as he watched his son cry out in pain. And then, great anger came over him as he began processing the sudden events that had just occurred.

Amidst his shock and anger, he soon came to his senses, hoping that his son could still be healed even with the deadly stabbing in his chest. He called out to one of his guards to bring him help. "Quick, one of you call the doctor!" he cried. "My son is dying!"

A few of his guards ran inside the palace, in search of the family's doctor. They waited for some time before the doctor would arrive at the carriage, staying aware of their surroundings in case anyone would try and attack them again.

Eventually, the doctor finally came to the carriage, and once safe they continued moving down the mountain and away from the palace. Just then a few rebels saw the king and swiftly attacked, but they were immediately put down by a number of the king's guards. For several minutes, the king and his family covered their heads and bodies while the guards protected them from any attacks, all the while they continued going down the Golden Mountains. Once they fled from the palace and mountains, any trace of the rebels attacking them was gone, and the doctor finally spoke to them.

"Well that was a frightening experience," he remarked, breathing a sigh of relief. "I'm glad that's over and done with. Those rebels were quite the scary bunch. But anyways, what has happened to your son, my king? Why is he unresponsive and why is blood stained all over his clothes?"

"He was stabbed by one of the rebels!" exclaimed Maguspra. "Which is why I called for you to help us. I need you to heal him!"

"My king, I will try my best to heal him," said the doctor. "But please understand that this will be difficult."

"Enough with the talking, just get to work!" shouted the king, growing frustrated with the doctor.

In great haste and fear of the king's wrath, the doctor quickly began to extract blood from Michael, only making him more fragile. He continued working for the next several minutes, trembling as the king and his family closely watched and examined everything that he did.

Elsewhere, the violence only continued in the king's palace with much blood being spilled and stained all over the halls and rooms. One man ran up the stairs to the second floor, seeking to enter the king's room before being forced out by several guards. Some others tore down and destroyed as many paintings and other images as they could. One woman even managed to cut off a guard's ear with a club. The chaos and disorder continued to ensue for at least half an hour, with the sounds of screams and the destruction of objects echoing throughout the halls. Many of those both injured and dead from both sides covered the ground, with streams of blood staining the floors of just about every side of the palace.

In all the fighting lasted for just under an hour, before many of Maguspra's guards and soldiers managed to overwhelm the rebels with great numbers, forcing them away from the palace. A few tried to remain fighting, but the majority of individuals immediately fled from the sight of thousands of the king's guards and soldiers arriving to strike them down. They ran down from the mountains, fleeing to whatever part of Fozturia they could.

Meanwhile, the king and his family continued their way down the mountains, fleeing as far south as they could down through Fozturia. As they escaped, Maguspra found himself in a state of madness as he repeatedly vowed to bring revenge onto the rebels. In great wrath and ignorance that the rebels had escaped from his palace, he ordered the rider of the carriage to go back to his palace.

"Are you sure though, my king?" asked the rider. "How will you and your family remain safe in your palace amidst all of the anarchy taking place?"

"Just do what I have told you!" sharply commanded Maguspra with rage. "I am the King of Fozturia, and I meant to dwell in my palace with my family, not at some random place away from my dwelling place!"

So in fear of the king's wrath, the rider swiftly turned the carriage around, going back northwards in the direction of the mountains. Maguspra's anger for many more long minutes, but as he looked at the doctor's efforts in trying to heal his son, he began to weep bitterly at the realization that he would soon die. Filled with desperation, he began shouting at the doctor and blaming him for not doing a good enough job of healing his son.

The doctor hastily continued his work, but nothing that he did would heal the king's son. Great fear covered his face as the king silently watched him working, and he hoped that they would soon arrive at the palace so that the king's attention and anger wouldn't be directed toward him.

The sun soon began to sink into the darkened sky as evening approached. In around an hour they had managed to make their way up the Golden Mountains, but as they made their way close to the palace, the king suddenly ordered the doctor and rider of the carriage to go back to the palace with his dying son, leaving him and the rest of the family alone.

The doctor was greatly surprised at the king's order. "Are you sure about this, my king?" he asked. "Don't you want to see the work that

I'm doing on your son? And how will you and your family come back to the palace"

"Just do as I have told you," sharply responded Maguspra. "I can't bear to see the work you're doing on my son even as he is dying. We will walk back to the palace since the distance is not very far. I need to spend time alone with my family."

"Very well, then, my king," obeyed the doctor. The king and his family jumped out of the carriage, leaving the rider, doctor, and Michael as the only ones inside.

As the carriage left, the king and his family stopped by a nearby cave to spend time alone and talk with each other. They shared their thoughts and worries for many minutes, with many tears being shed, particularly with the king's wife, Elizabeth, and their two other children. After a while, Elizabeth and her two children left the cave to silently gaze into the distance and breathe some fresh air outside. The king remained in the cave, sitting silently as thoughts of anger and bitterness filled his heart.

He thought to himself for a while, imagining how Michael was doing and whether the rebels were still fighting. He then stood up, wishing to speak some more with his family, but just then, coming forth behind him was a shadow.

As he turned around, Maguspra saw an elderly man clothed in a dark blue cloak and appearing to be in his sixties. The king stared at him in both confusion and shock at how he had suddenly appeared. The old man had a long white beard and long white hair, and walked toward the king, holding a long gray walking stick in his hand. He was rather tall and for a brief moment gave the king slight fear as he approached him.

Then suddenly as he stood face to face with the king, the elderly man spoke to him. "Maguspra, I am here to proclaim the truth to you," he said, speaking in such a bold voice that Maguspra shuddered for a second. "Because of your evil, you have lost your som. Despite the efforts of your doctor, he is now dead. After you head back to your palace and bury him, you must then repent of your evil and ask the people of Fozturia for forgiveness. For it is because of your wickedness that all of this disaster has fallen upon you and your family."

Maguspra didn't move, stricken with both fear and bewilderment at the words that the old man spoke. But as he processed his words, his countenance soon fell and anger and pride were stirred within his heart.

"Do you realize who you are talking to?" he asked, taunting the elderly man. "Who are you to speak such things against me, the mighty King of Fozturia? Why should I heed your words and repent? I do not need to listen to your words of lunacy! I will neither change my ways nor ask forgiveness from the people of Fozturia. Get away from my presence!"

The king turned away from the elderly man, shaking his head in disbelief that the man had felt entitled to speak to him in such a way. But just as he turned away, the elderly man suddenly raised his hand to the air and after dropping it down, Maguspra stopped dead in his tracks, having been struck blind and mute. He remained that way for half an hour until the elderly man raised his hand again and brought it down. Instantly Maguspra regained his sight and was able to speak. The king's eyes widened with horror at what had happened, and he once again saw the elderly man staring at him with great authority.

With a hate-filled heart, he tried attacking the old man. But just as he made his move, the old man vanished away from his sight. Maguspra collapsed to the ground in shock at what he had just witnessed and for a moment thought of taking notice of the man's words. But he laughed to himself as he thought about this, refusing to admit his wrongdoing.

Just then Elizabeth and the two children walked back into the cave. They were alarmed to see the king on the ground, breathing heavily, and wondered what had happened.

"Is everything alright?" asked Elizabeth. "Why are you lying on the ground breathing heavily? I hope you weren't attacked by anyone. I could even hear a faint voice coming from inside the cave unless my ears have failed me."

The king rose to his feet, filled with panic. "Your ears have failed you, Elizabeth," he said lying, being too afraid to admit all that had happened. "I am fine. I was just thinking of Michael and I guess grief took hold of me. We should go back to the palace now to see how he is doing, and if those rebels have finally fled away."

Elizabeth stared longingly at her husband, examining him to see if he was telling the truth. But eventually, she shook her head and let it go. "Fair enough," she conceded. "I guess my ears were failing me, probably because of how much I've been thinking of Michael. Let's go and see how he's doing."

So the king and his family departed from the cave, making their way to the palace. In all of this, Maguspra neither told them of his encounter with the elderly man nor of the words that were spoken to him. He expected to see that his son was dead but kept hoping that a miracle would happen.

But as they came near the palace's entrance, the doctor stood just outside with tears filling his eyes. He spoke to them before they could even ask him questions.

"I am sorry," he said, pausing and casting his head to the ground before continuing. "Your son Michael has died."

Immediately, the king and his family were stricken with grief at the announcement. Maguspra said nothing, but instead clenched his fists together and stared at the sky with a hardened face. His wife and children wept aloud in deep sorrow, refusing to accept any words of comfort that were offered by those around them. For many hours it seemed, they stood outside the palace doors, grieving over Michael's death. Many words of comfort and encouragement were shared with them, as well as promises to bring vengeance on the rebels, especially the ones who had killed their son. But they took no comfort in knowing this, and instead only focused on their son's life that had been taken away.

Once ready to bury him, the king's guards carried Michael's coffin and went outside of the palace. Coming to a spacious yard just behind the palace, they dug into the ground and after gazing at the coffin for one last time, they buried it into the ground.

For the rest of the day, the king and his family sat silently in their rooms, refusing anyone to enter inside. They privately grieved over Michael's death, with Elizabeth and her children crying all night, while Maguspra stared at the walls in his room.

But the next day, Maguspra felt in the mood to bring an announcement to all of his servants. He called for a meeting to be held and for a long table to be set in the hall where his throne was. As he walked to his throne with his family following him, everyone from his many servants and advisors, to his guards and soldiers clapped for him and his family. He then sat on his throne, and everyone immediately became silent and fixed their attention on him.

Once all had become silent, Maguspra spoke. "My loyal friends and family, the events that occurred yesterday were tragic and will never be forgotten in our history," he said. "However, we will rise above that and will strengthen ourselves, ensuring that a day like that never happens again. We will defend and secure our palace and will find the culprits of this attack. We will execute them and ensure that everyone respects the palace and the king. My son Michael has perished due to this barbarous plot of these filthy rebels and I will punish them for their wicked treachery!"

The people all cheered in response to the king, glad to see that he would bring revenge on the rebels.

The king continued. "And so I have declared November 14th as a precedent to be a day of mourning for my son," he said. "Meanwhile, I have changed today to be the day where we respect and honor the king and our monarchial history. I have also sent my spies and soldiers to find anyone accused of participating in the rebellion, to be executed publicly in my sight. Today will be a great day of vengeance and justice. That is all that I have to deliver to you today."

The people applauded the king and celebrated with one another. "Hooray! The king will punish the rebels for the evil they have brought on him!" they exclaimed.

For the rest of the day, there was much cheering and celebration for the king and his family. Many of his servants offered words of advice and praise for them, mainly for how they had held their heads high even amidst their grief. They promised to be with them for as long as they could and offered their help in bringing vengeance against those who had rebelled against the king.

And so it came to pass that in the days and weeks ahead, Maguspra's spies managed to find hundreds of the rebels and brought them to the king's palace. And there in the king's sight, they were all executed. It was great mourning for the families who lost their loved ones, but for the king and his family, it was great rejoicing as they were glad that the day of their revenge for Michael's death had finally come.

Throughout all of this, Maguspra's servants and followers celebrated what he had done, believing that the rebels' deaths were well deserved. Even as they watched the many people being executed, not in the very slightest did their hearts give them doubts that the king was going too far. Their minds had been completely enamored with the king, and they felt no sympathy for those who suffered in his reign of terror.

Now to understand how Maguspra managed to deceive his servants and followers, something must first be understood. Though he had been able to persuade his many servants and followers to follow him by spreading deceptive and cunning lives there was also a greater force at work that controlled their hearts and minds. And though he believed that he influenced them with his power and crafty words, in reality, there was much more going on behind the scenes.

The one who had caused the king's servants and followers to become completely devoted to him was an evil and dark being named Natugura. He was the Dark Lord of the world who controlled all the evil and injustice that came to the whole of Earth, including the kingdom of Fozturia. Yet all the people living on Earth never knew this, for they didn't understand the many things that happened outside their land. So with their limited knowledge, Natugura spread disaster throughout the land of the Earth. He did this by corrupting the hearts of men and influencing the minds of kings for thousands of years. Everyone on Earth was already corrupted by nature, so Natugura made them even more corrupted. Many of the people living in Fozturia were also evil and committed grievances against their neighbors. And so Natugura made them all even worse. However, Natugura wasn't able to completely control humans so that they would be able to fulfill all his evil desires. And for thousands of years, he desperately hoped and tried to control the race of humanity for them to become slaves to his will.

Now Natugura dwelled in the land of Nangorid, a land to the west of the Earth which no man had ever seen or heard of before. He lived with his corrupted race of creatures that served him, called wuzlirs. Other than the wuzlirs, other creatures were slaves to him, some being walking beasts and others winged creatures providing a foul presence that filled the air. But to Natugura, his most important servants were his wuzlirs, who were his slaves and mighty fighters that pledged their allegiance to him. They mostly dwelled in mountains and forests, while some of the more powerful ones dwelled in cities that they had built. But no matter where they dwelled, they all resided outside of the great black walls that surrounded the tall black tower of Wuzinch Torgol, where Natugura himself dwelled and reigned from his dark iron throne. But at times some of them would be called by the Dark Lord to work in his tower of residence and carry out the many tasks that he had for them.

Now the appearance of wuzlirs was that of physical beings with traits of extreme cunningness. They were filled with great physical strength, but their weakness was their extreme hideousness which forced Natugura to be completely clothed and mask them in black armor and masks.

But unlike the physical creatures of the world, Natugura was instead a dark and bodiless spirit who spent his time roaming around in his tower, thinking of ways to corrupt others to his will. Though he didn't have a physical body, he was still filled with tremendous cunningness and knowledge to force all that beheld him to submit under his control. He used this power of his to influence and control the Earth, even with all of humanity unaware of his existence. However, the power that he had was not of his own. He remained a created being who had been given many of his attributes. His knowledge and power could be taken away from him in an instant, and though it was a pain for him to admit, he was not the one with supreme authority over the world.

For the Dark Lord Natugura was formed and created by Jangart, the most powerful and glorious being to ever exist. Jangart created eight different lands to fill his created world and he populated each of the lands with its unique race of creatures. Jangart lived outside of his created world, and long before he had even begun his work of creation, Natugura dwelled with him.

The Dark Lord was created by Jangart to be a righteous and non-corrupted spirit full of great glory and perfection. For thousands of years, Natugura was just this, as during this time he lived as a righteous spirit being of light and perfection.

He was one of three spirit beings who were the great and ancient firstborns of Jangart who reflected his glory. The other two had been fashioned in the same way as Natugura by Jangart, and the three of them were in charge of organizing all of the creatures of the different worlds. Among the creatures were the wise and powerful gamdars.

Long before they fell under the shadow of Natugura, the wuzlirs once used to be gamdars themselves. The gamdars were created by Jangart as beautiful creatures with green bodies and faces and beautiful appearances. They had majestic clothing which was the most beautiful of all the creatures that existed and were the wisest and most skilled creatures of them all.

For some time, Natugura and the other two spirit beings were close friends who shared everything that was on their hearts and minds. They would never dare ponder on betraying each other or worse, rebelling against Jangart, even with their ability to do so. They remained loyal servants and sons of Jangart who faithfully executed their work with joy.

They all lived outside of the realm containing the lands created by Jangart, dwelling in Starlight, an unseen and endless place containing a vast and rich land of unsurpassed splendor and unfading glory.

Meanwhile, the gamdars dwelled in Watendelle, Jangart's most precious and beautiful creation outside of Starlight. But all of Jangart's created lands remained beautiful in their unique ways, and all of them were formed in perfection with evil and corruption not even in the hearts of Jangart's creatures. Thus they all lived eternal lives for a while, free from the curses of corruption and death.

During this time of peace and perfection, the three spirit beings of Jangart would fly over to different lands and watch the different creatures of Jangart. And when they did fly over, their spirits would fill the different lands with glory, wisdom, and perfection. The creatures of the lands gladly accepted their words of wisdom and continued their growth in knowledge and righteousness.

The three beings were also students who learned under Jangart's guidance, with the words that he spoke unto them dwelling richly in their hearts and minds. They learned many things about the process of his creation and the wisdom he used to bring everything into existence. He guided them to faithfully follow and obey him, assuring them that it was for their good that they served him for their good.

And so the more they learned under Jangart's direction, the wiser and more powerful they became. Yet they still had questions and didn't understand the deep secrets that Jangart knew. Their power was still limited and everything they did, first had to be approved by Jangart. Nonetheless, they continued to joyfully serve Jangart, admiring him as their creator and father.

But as time progressed, one of the three high beings of Jangart began to plant seeds of doubt and pride within his own heart. At times he would gaze at himself for a while, admiring his wisdom, glory, and power. And he started believing that he deserved to know the deep secrets of Jangart, growing in equal or even greater power than his creator.

Natugura was that being, and the seeds of pride continued to stir deep within his heart. Slowly over time, he became more envious of Jangart, with seeds of jealousy growing within him as he questioned Jangart's ways of withholding information from him. He began to wonder whether Jangart was anxious about revealing too much to him, in fear that he would overtake him in wisdom and power.

So it came to pass that Natugura said within himself that he couldn't keep his desires to himself, and he decided to meet with his two friends and discuss the intentions of his heart. By now he had already begun to think of a plot to rebel against Jangart, and he believed that they could help him in doing that.

But the two beings, perceiving Natugura's deceptive intentions, firmly rejected his plan. And so Natugura departed from them, and from that day forward was filled with intense hate against them. He knew that if he wished to succeed he would need others to fall under his sway and help him. So, his next plan was to talk with the gamdars and convince them of his plans.

Thus began Natugura's great rebellion. He went over to the gamdars in Watendelle and tried to convince them to follow him. The gamdars at first rejected Natugura, but when his words grew more cunning and attractive, some agreed to join him in his rebellion. Eventually, a great number of gamdars joined Natugura's plot, with Natugura having successfully deceived some of the wisest created creatures of Jangart, other than the volviers.

As Natugura continued to spread his planned revolt to many other gamdars, more and more began to understand his perspective and wanted to join him. There were tens of millions of gamdars who were created by Jangart, and they all pledged their allegiance to him and would've never thought of betraying him. However, Natugura's words were as sweet as honey to them, and their minds were influenced by his cunningness. Thousands began to follow him, and the numbers continued to grow and rise. Finally, it came to the point where one-third of the total gamdarian population decided to participate in Natugura's rebellion. Not only did Natugura want power and wisdom like Jangart, but he also wanted to completely overthrow Jangart from his throne.

The time came when Natugura along with his many gamdar followers came to Starlight. Now the gamdars had never seen Jangart up close and they were filled with awe and amazement as they saw his glory as he sat on his throne. They still weren't able to perceive the form of his face, but they were able to gaze upon his glorious presence and his great power.

Jangart, having seen all the deception and evil that Natugura had brought to his creation, urged him to repent from his ways. Natugura refused to turn from his wicked plans, and so he, along with his gamdars, tried to fight against Jangart and the two beings. Natugura armed with his armor and a deadly sword tried to strike the two spirit beings, but they were armed with the armor of Jangart which was far stronger than Natugura's own deadliest armor. They fought against each other while the other gamdars scratched and crawled against the two spirit beings along with Natugura. The battle went on for a long time until Natugura did something so terrible that words cannot possibly utter the wicked thing he did.

Immediately after he committed his one terrible act above all else, a great and thick wind that was dark black, spread across the air. The wind was strong and violently made its way across the air. However, the wind was evil and had a mind of its own, bringing with it evil, temptation, and disaster. The two beings and gamdars were able to understand what had happened, and Natugura knew what he had done. But being filled with pride and anger, he refused to admit his mistake and he continued to try and fight on in the battle.

Jangart knew that he had to punish Natugura for his evil, and he had to make sure that the black wind didn't cause any more damage. So with the snap of his finger, Natugura and his gamdars were sent flying down at an uncontrollable speed. As they were sent flying down, the gamdars began to change. The once beautiful faces they once had began to vanish away, and their faces now became hideous. The color of their skin changed from green to red, and the once beautiful clothing that they had, was now lost. They were now naked and hideous red creatures who had fallen. The good gamdars remained beautiful, while Natugura's gamdars became ugly. Even Natugura was greatly appalled after he saw his gamdars change from beautiful creatures to ugly beasts.

However, Natugura also began noticing changes in himself. His once glorious and beautiful spirit form was now dwindling, as he began to slowly transform into a dark entity without a form. He was now an evil and dark force, without a spirit form, but rather a bodiless spirit full of great cunningness and evil.

As the wind went flying down with them, it also spread across all the lands. And when the creatures on four of the eight created lands saw the wind and the evil that it had brought, they gladly accepted it despite the evil and disaster that came with it. The enticement of the wind was so powerful that their minds became completely numb to the evil and disaster that it had brought. They accepted the wind without any questions, for the wind had a mind of its own and managed to twist its evil into sweet words promising them power and greatness.

However, when the wind reached the four other lands the remaining creatures all rejected the wind, perceiving that its promises were empty and devious.

But for the creatures that chose to accept the evil of the wind, very soon their nature became evil in and of itself. Once new creatures were born, their nature was automatically evil as passed down from their corrupted parents. And so half of the total number of the once perfected lands had fallen under the corruption of the wind. And once corrupted, they quickly fell under the influence of Natugura.

Yet for the humans, though they had been corrupted by the wind creatures, they remained resistant to falling under Natugura's control. At different moments of their lives, they were capable of making choices of high virtue, even with their corrupted nature. And unlike the creatures of the different worlds around them, the entire race of humanity lost all knowledge of all that resided outside of their world. While the other creatures had either pledged their allegiance to Natugura or Jangart, the humans instead chose to do what pleased them, for good or ill since they had lost all memory of who Jangart or Natugura was.

And so all of the world's problems and evils were conceived on that very day. And death came to all of the creatures of the world, even those who had rejected the wind. Yet Natugura continued to live on for many long years, and none knew whether or not the curse of death would fall on him.

Meanwhile, after being cast away from the presence of Jangart, Natugura and his gamdarian followers continued to fall ever deeper while Jangart was in the process of creating a world for them to dwell in. Jangart was still full of everlasting love towards Natugura even after his rebellion and desired to see him repent from his ways and experience the restoration that would freely be rewarded to him.

But Natugura had no thoughts of regret, and after falling for many long and dark hours, he and his gamdars finally collapsed on flat ground. They rose and gazed upon the new land. They called the land Nangorid, for they proclaimed that it would be their home from where they had authority over the whole world. It was a cold and mysterious new world, with endless mountains, valleys, and forests all around them. All was dark and slightly unsettling, yet they knew that they had all made their choices and could only hope for the best in their new lives.

Natugura gazed all around at Nangorid and spoke to his followers. "My gamdars, this is our new home," he said. "We must make ourselves comfortable with Nangorid, for this shall be the place where we hold the ultimate power over the world."

Even as he spoke, great pride filled his heart that he could now live in a world separate from Jangart. And the thoughts of the great power he would possess from his new world ran through his mind.

However, these thoughts didn't run through the minds of the gamdars, as they were freezing from the cold weather. "I'm freezing!" exclaimed one of them with chattering teeth.

"We will get used to it very soon my friend," said Natugura. "Together we will rule all of the worlds." His attention was then brought to some clothes that were laid on the ground. There were black cloaks covered in heavy black armor along with black masks.

"Here put on these clothes and masks. It should warm you all up," said Natugura, leading the gamdars to the clothes.

The gamdars then put on the clothes and were deeply satisfied. Their nakedness had been covered, and their ugly faces were now hidden behind their masks. The clothes with armor also gave them great protection.

"These clothes are warm," said a gamdar. "I can get used to these."

All the gamdars agreed with him and immediately became used to the clothes which Natugura had given them.

Natugura then announced all the gamdars. "My loyal gamdars, together we will have dominion over all the lands of the world!" he boldly proclaimed. "Now to separate ourselves from Jangart and the other gamdars who refused to join us, you all will have new identities. Your new clothes and masks will be a symbol of your allegiance to me. And now that your identity has been changed, I will also be changing your names. You shall no longer be called gamdars, but you shall now be called wuzlirs, for you will be much greater than the gamdars who refused to join me!"

Immediately the newly named wuzlirs celebrated the announcement of their new title. "Yes! Our new names will signify our superiority over the gamdars!" exclaimed one of the wuzlirs. "They should've joined us with Natugura! For we shall rule over all the lands of the world!"

After this, Natugura filled his wuzlirs with his dark, tempting, and evil spirit, stirring great and evil power in their bodies. He then assigned them jobs to build a great black tower for him, where his dark and roaming spirit would reside. This tower would be massively tall and black. It would be his dwelling place and the location where his most important wuzlirs would work to discuss strategies and plans with the Dark Lord.

After many years of hard work, the wuzlirs successfully built the tower, named by Natugura as Wuzinch Torgol, "The Unshakable Fortress," and they also built a strong and vast black wall that would protect the tower. And for the next several years, the wuzlirs continued to be busy at work, building themselves many cities where the most important and powerful among them would dwell. The other less important wuzlirs would settle in the many mountains, forests, and wildernesses scattered throughout the land of Nangorid.

Now in power, Natugura's first step was to control all the creatures that he had corrupted, so that they would become completely devoted to him. He successfully achieved this with them, as they became enslaved to his will and purposes, but with the humans that dwelled on the Earth, he failed in accomplishing this goal of his. While he was able to corrupt them and influence them to commit evil deeds, they remained free from his total dominion and could also reject his tempting influence, choosing to do good things.

But all the more Natugura desperately tried turning the humans into his slaves, desiring to wholly control them as the Earth was the key that would help him succeed in his evil purposes. He believed that if he completely held the humans of the Earth in his hands, then he would have the ability to do the same thing to the creatures that remained non-corrupted.

However, controlling the entire human race proved a difficult task, so as the years went by he decided to use a different strategy to make them his slaves. He would first influence the kings on Earth to his evil, and once they became unknowingly yet completely controlled by him, the rest of the people would follow suit in the king's lead.

And so the Dark Lord tried his best to turn the kings of the Earth into his slaves so that the rest of the people would follow suit. Yet as time would prove, many of the humans of the Earth would follow in the footsteps of their king's evil, and an even greater amount would reject his evil, primarily for having suffered at his hands. And so Natugura's plans of having complete dominion over the Earth were thwarted. But as the years went by, he would all the more continue tirelessly working behind the scenes for his dreams of world domination to come true.

From that day forth, though the Earth hadn't fallen to the shadow of the Dark Lord, they nevertheless remained under his corrupting influence. As a result, evil, death, and injustice spread throughout the different kingdoms, particularly Fozturia. And even with the good kings who ruled righteously over their people, their kingdoms remained bound to evil and imperfection. So as Natugura continued to spread his dark and hidden presence over the Earth, much to the people's unawareness, he continued holding onto and working towards his goal of seeing the humans eventually succumb to his dominion. And since Fozturia was the evilest and corrupt of all the kingdoms on the Earth, Natugura kept an especially close eye on them. And with Maguspra's ascension to the throne, the Dark Lord was ready to unleash a fresh wave of his influence on the Earth, such as the land had never before experienced in all of its histories.

2

The Great Escape

IN THE FIRST FEW years of Maguspra's reign, Fozturia had largely experienced peace from any outside threats on the Earth. The majority of people living in the kingdom were furious at the king for the injustice and evil that he brought to the land, but none of their anger would pose a serious threat to the king. As the years progressed and as the people of Fozturia gradually became more silent in their criticism of the king, Maguspra began to rule with slightly more leniency. For he began to perceive that the rebellions of the people had mostly been wiped away, and he had no cause to worry himself over them. And though he remained unjust and corrupt toward the people, his acts of terror would slowly dwindle.

But in the eighth year of his reign, a kingdom from the east called Eletan would sweep its way westward and come close to approaching Fozturia. Led by their mighty warrior king Mboshkuleh Olutate, known as Meboku, they had attacked the kingdom of Qehat, a valuable alliance to Fozturia. They continued their swift charge through the west and slowly began threatening the safety and well-being of Fozturia.

Many heads were turned as Eletan rode through the Earth in war, and the knees of even the bravest souls began to tremble. For they knew that Eletan was the most powerful kingdom on Earth at the time, filled with a vast and powerful army and teeming with even more life in its great palaces and cities. It stood high above the rest of the kingdoms of the Earth, as the pinnacle of total might and control.

However, though Eletan was the most powerful kingdom on Earth in those days, there would be kingdoms that came long before it that would overpower its army in a heartbeat. One such kingdom was the ancient and mighty kingdom of Blumanad, the ancestral kingdom of Eletan. And as the Eletans remembered the ancient kingdom that their ancestors had lived in, they desired to see those glory days returned in their lifetimes. Meboku would desire that dream that dwelled in many of the Eletan peoples' hearts, conquering his way westward to bring back the glory days of his ancient ancestors.

Now the kingdom of Blumanad was far more powerful and splendid than Eletan was, standing as strong as iron for over a thousand years. From everywhere within it, from its many cities and smaller towns, everywhere overflowed with riches, beauty, and life. None dared to oppose the kingdom in a conflict, fearing the terrible repercussions that would fall on them. And so Blumanad stood proudly for many long centuries as an example of what the pure might and wisdom of men could achieve.

Yet as Blumanad grew in its power and riches, its kings and mighty men grew increasingly vain and vile. Evil was stirred within their hearts, and they slowly began spreading these vain intentions of theirs throughout the kingdom. In time to come, the kings and mighty men would pay more attention to their glory and riches than they did to the many people who lived among them. They continued building and decorating great palaces and cities for the wealthy, while the poor were left to suffer by themselves. These kings and powerful men of the kingdom acted as though the poor didn't exist, and held onto their riches tightly, taking great pride in themselves and declaring that nothing could take their possessions and power away.

In their hubris, they began to desire more riches and more beauty to add for themselves and for those who benefited from them. And so they cast their attention westward to the kingdoms of the west, wondering what more riches and power they could add to themselves. Yet for a while they held back from their desires, knowing that these Western kingdoms would unite under one banner if they were to attack them.

But it came to pass that in the days of King Bahlamar, the mightiest and most self-willed of all the Kings of Blumanad, he ordered many of his spies to travel westward and examine the western kingdoms of the Earth. Yet in response to the king's order, many of his spies expressed their doubts, fearing the downfall of their kingdom if they were to stir conflict in the west by their desire to expand westward.

But Bahlamar was unwilling to back down from his lust for the expansion of his kingdom and instead ordered his spies to travel on great ships across the wide sea so that the western kingdoms wouldn't be able to find them on land.

So his spies obeyed his edict and a great number totaling many thousands of spies were sent that day under the king's command. The first few days of their voyage were peaceful, but as they traveled through the wide sea, terrible blasting winds and roaring waves almost devoured their ships. And because of the pervasive torrents of the sea, their ships were led off course from their destination.

They eventually landed on a wide land, one that was filled with an atmosphere unlike that of the Earth. They felt greatly uncomfortable and fearful, as though heavy darkness covered the land, and after exploring it for only a few hours, they quickly went back onto their ships to return to Blumanad.

Though they remained concerned and confused at the new land, the spies nonetheless reported to the king all that they had discovered, neither telling him of how uncomfortable they felt nor of the darkness that covered the land. When the king heard about this, he was greatly pleased with his spies' discoveries and desired to possess this new and unseen land for himself. Yet the spies warned the king about the difficult passages and torrents of the sea that had led them off course in the first place and expressed their worries about a potential disaster that could occur on the sea.

Bahlamar heeded the warnings of his spies, and from that day forth thought of traveling on land westward, to find this land that he desperately yearned to have. He began strengthening and mobilizing his army, turning them into a mighty force to be reckoned with.

So it came to pass that when the army of Blumanad had garnered their full strength, they began riding westward across the Earth, in hopes of finding this never before seen land. And though Bahlamar had hoped to avoid confrontation with the western kingdoms, he was now more than willing to go to battle with them in his great ride westward.

As he and his army marched on, the civilians looking on from their western kingdoms stood in astonishment as they observed how the army's soldiers and battle horses completely covered every blade of grass that they stomped through. Great fear fell on them all as they watched the mighty king and his army make their way through, clothed in heavy armor of gold and black and carrying thick swords and broad shields.

At this sight, the people of the west fled from their kingdoms, in great fear of the army of Blumanad. When Bahlamar saw this, he laughed aloud, greatly pleased in himself and resting assured that no one and nothing would stand in his way. As he thought about this, he suddenly became confident that along with the land that his spies had seen, he would also be able to conquer all the kingdoms of the West.

His face suddenly shone with great pride as he imagined himself ruling over all the kingdoms of the world as the King of the Earth. And it seemed to all his soldiers and generals that his stature suddenly rose, and he towered over them as his fantasies of world domination ran wildly through his mind.

Yet even as he imagined all of this, the sky suddenly grew dark, and great clouds slowly covered the sky as the sound of thunder rumbled across the Earth. Flashes of lightning illuminated the night sky, and there came a mighty earthquake, such as had never before been experienced on Earth. It struck the ground where Bahlamar and his army were gathered, and at that moment, hundreds of thousands of the men of Blumanad, including Bahlamar himself were struck dead.

But even as the earthquake struck them, the kingdoms of the west remained safe. Many of the people of the west who had fled from the sight of the army of Blumanad, witnessed their obliteration from a far distance. And even amidst their horror at the terrible sight, confidence was restored to them and they immediately came running back to their kingdoms.

And the mighty earthquake struck the very heart of the kingdom of Blumanad with many more thousands perishing as the once great kingdom crumbled into ashes. And so it was that the great riches, cities, histories, and tales of the kingdom of Blumanad were swallowed up by the Earth, and the once-great iron kingdom of the Earth had fallen into permanent ruin.

But the peoples and cultures of Blumanad were not lost. Even as the earthquake struck the kingdom, it also split the massive land into three different and smaller lands. As the survivors of Blumanad saw this, they each migrated to these different lands, bringing their culture and memories along with them.

Though the surviving Blumanadians that had fled to the three different lands remained united under one banner for a while, as time progressed, they slowly began differing from one another, before completely breaking off their attachment to each other.

What followed was the formation of three distinctive kingdoms conceived from the ruins of Blumanad. Even at their conception, these kingdoms were mighty because of the deep roots of their ancestors. But they remained as shadows of what had once existed during the elder days of their great and ancient kingdom of Blumanad.

The most powerful of all these kingdoms was Eletan, and for many centuries it stood as the most powerful kingdom on Earth, a representation of what Blumanad had once been. And though they were vastly smaller and less populated than their ancestors, the kingdom of Eletan nonetheless teemed with life and stood as a shining beacon of glory throughout the Earth. Their army was filled with strong and bold men, led by their mighty kings. Yet even with all this power of theirs, Eletan stood alone by themselves, not any threats to the other kingdoms of the Earth.

However, in the days of King Meboku, all of that would change. Ever since his childhood growing up as the son of the great King of Eletan, he had heard many tales of the once great kingdom of his ancestors that had stood strong for over a thousand years, covering the face of the Earth in its glory. The young Meboku was greatly enthralled by these stories and he became king, he desired to bring back the glory of the fallen kingdom of Blumanad.

And so in his first move as King of Eletan, he first tried to convince the other two twin kingdoms to join Eletan and become one kingdom under one banner. He reminded them of the glory days of Blumanad and persuaded them with confident words explaining the great power, wealth, and wisdom they would possess if they became one kingdom.

And so the king and the people of the twin kingdom of Eletan, Rundol, were greatly enthralled by Meboku's words and agreed to join Eletan in becoming one kingdom. Once Rundol had joined, Meboku then came to the other twin kingdom of Yandur, spreading the same message to them. The king and the people, filled with excitement and joy, also joined with Eletan and Rundol, and these three kingdoms now became united under one kingdom, all desiring to restore the glory days of their ancient ancestors.

As these three kingdoms became one, the other western kingdoms of the Earth let them do as they wished, since they believed that they were only trying to restore the kingdom of their ancestors.

But all of this would change when Meboku and his Eletan army decided to attack the kingdom of Qehat. The people's worst fears which they had brushed aside, had suddenly come true as they now knew that Meboku wished to take over all the kingdoms of the Earth. Great terror fell on all the people and kings of the Western kingdoms, and they wondered what steps they would take to ensure their safety.

One such king who would grow increasingly worried about Meboku was Maguspra, and he knew that he had to take a bold risk in ensuring the safety of not only his kingdom but also of his allied kingdoms. But Meboku was a valiant man, refusing to surrender to anyone and striking fear in the hearts of his enemies.

And so the King of Fozturia found himself in a dilemma of what to do, whether to stay back or take a daring risk to hold the Eletans back in check. For many long weeks, he sat in his palace, thinking to himself and speaking with his advisors about what to do. They either told him to stay back or send his soldiers to Qehat and help their allies in fighting back against Eletan. But Maguspra knew that his meager amount of seven thousand soldiers would do nothing to turn the tide for the Qehatians against the fifty thousand soldiers that they came up against in the mighty and dark-skinned Eletans.

Thus the King of Fozturia surrendered in despair, losing all hope that the world as they knew it would survive against the might of the

Eletans. Yet even as hope had seemed to vanish from sight, an idea suddenly came to his mind of what to do.

The time came that nearing the end of August in the year 4858, Maguspra gathered together his advisors at a large table by his throne to discuss his plans with them. Hope was restored to him, and his advisors could see it on his face.

"I can sense that you're feeling good about your idea, my king," observed one of his advisors. "So what will you now do against the threat of Eletan? What plan have you concocted together from your vast wisdom?"

The king sat proudly to himself, grinning from ear to ear. "I have decided to order a conscription for all men between the ages of 20 and 45," he revealed. "Though I do not doubt the strength and valor of my soldiers, they will simply not be enough to bring any serious damage to the Eletans. But with a large number of these men, perhaps we will be able to save Qehat from falling to Eletan and ensure our safety in the process."

His advisors dwelled on his words for a moment, nodding their heads in approval. But one of his advisors was filled with doubt and objected to him. "But how are we sure that the people will obey your command, my king," he asked. "And even if they were to obey, would they strike any fear into the hearts of the Eletans? Many of the men of Fozturia are farmers and workers, not used to fighting or handling weapons."

"They will go through hard and intense training to ensure that they do cause the Eletans to recoil back and despair," responded the king. "And they will have no choice but to obey my commands, for if they disobey, they will suffer severe consequences. And after they have trained and turned into strong men, I will pick the best ones among them, numbering at least ten thousand men to go to Qehat and fight against the Eletans. And if I ever need more men, then I will send any number of the remaining men to help. In this way, we will ensure the defense of Qehat and the protection of Fozturia from any attacks of the crazy man Meboku. For he shall surrender to me in fear of standing in the presence of the true King of the Earth!"

His advisors sat impressed and filled with confidence in the king's plan. "That is a great idea, my king," said the once doubtful advisor. "I now cannot see how your plan will ever fail. We will force the Eletans to crawl back to their homes, and indeed their king shall be humbled and see who the true King of the Earth is!"

And so on the 27th day of August in the year 4858, Maguspra issued his military conscription requiring all men between the ages of 20 and 45 to go through training that would last for weeks and even months. Many of his advisors and spokesmen were sent throughout Fozturia, informing people of the king's decree.

"This training will ensure that we are ready and prepared to defend our ally from the enemy," said one of his spokesmen. "And as a result, we will also ensure our safety from the threats of the enemy."

Throughout all of this, every Fozturian living in the land united together in patriotism for their homeland. From the king's followers and advisors to the farmer and peasant who stood opposed to the king, no Fozturian wanted to see the downfall of their home, and all stood ready to sacrifice everything to ensure the preservation of their kingdom.

However, some people weren't as eager as others were, as they remembered how the king had ruled with injustice and corruption, causing misery and suffering in their lives. They tried reminding people of this reality, and as a result, many of them changed their views and now stood opposed to going through training to fight against the Eletans.

As days turned into weeks, many thousands of people soon held the same views as one another, being fiercely opposed to the king and anti-war. Their numbers only continued to swell and they eventually formed a large group, naming themselves the Resistants, for they resisted the royal edict of the king. Many more thousands joined this group, and they would grow to become not only a strong rival to the king but also to the many other Fozturians who were pro-war.

What soon came was distrust and hostility among the people of Fozturia, with many people viewing the Resistants as traitors. Even those who had hated the king for his evil and injustice, now found themselves defending his decree. They became hostile and filled with bitterness toward their fellow countrymen whom just a few months ago they would've referred to as good neighbors or friends. Even families weren't spared from the great divide, as children, siblings, and parents held opposing views of each other.

But all the more, the Resistants would grow in numbers and power. And as their members soon grew into the hundreds of thousands, there would be a select few among them who would hold positions of prominence.

One such individual was Steven Loubre, an ordinary and chubby man in his early thirties who came from the village of Frosh. He lived for over a decade as a shepherd, enjoying a tranquil and comfortable life as he took over his father's work when he grew old. He was the firstborn child among his two brothers and happily lived his life with them in peace.

However, as he learned of the king's decree that required him and his two brothers to go through training, he knew that he couldn't just accept the king's command. He had always disliked the king for his evil and was proud of the many attempted rebellions that had been made to overthrow him.

While his brothers left their homeland to go through their training, Steven remained living alone with his father and mother, despite their urging him to join his brothers. Then one day, he was informed that the king's soldiers had been alerted of his disobedience and that they would force him to submit to the king's order. Great fear fell upon him and his parents, who all the more implored him to just go through the training, which he refused to do.

The king's soldiers made their way close to his homeland, but even as he worried himself over this, he soon heard the news of the new movement of people called the Resistants. And so he immediately left his parents and life as a shepherd to flee south to the town of Varm, to live in safety with the Resistants.

After joining the group, he quickly rose in prominence, impressing everyone with his leadership and speaking. Eventually, in a swift turn of events in his life, he was chosen to be the Resistants' leader and spokesman. As days went by, he and the Resistants would travel throughout the many towns of Fozturia, giving passionate speeches and encouraging many more to join the group and stand against the king.

One early morning in a local town, the Resistants gathered together in their many meetings, and Steven spoke to them in a passionate speech. All eyes were fixed on him, as they eagerly awaited the hope-filled words that he would comfort their hearts with.

"My fellow brothers and sisters," he said. "The king has openly violated our rights by requiring us to serve a cause that we don't support. And many of our fellow brothers and sisters have been blinded by the fact that he has breached our freedoms. But we the Resistants will refuse to live our lives blinded by this truth. We have formed this group to openly and proudly reject serving in the military under this wicked king. And if the king continues to stand against us, then we will separate ourselves from his rule and form a new government based on what has been placed on our hearts. We will not be sheep led to the slaughter, for we will continue to speak our minds regardless of what the king says or does."

The people erupted into applause for Steven's words with faces and hearts overflowing with joy and confidence. Steven looked on at the great number of people with great joy, but also humility covering his face. For he had never received such attention before, even in his life as a leader of his sheep's flock. But all the more, his face beamed with a bright light of joy, and he even joined in the chants of the people, celebrating loudly with them in great happiness.

However, the people's excitement was quickly halted when suddenly, a man part of the group came dashing to Steven bringing news with him.

"Mr. Loubre, I'm afraid that I'm not the bearer of good news today," said the man. The people all stopped their celebrations, becoming silent and turning toward the man. "The king has declared today that anyone a part of this group who refuses to renounce their association with them within a month will be thrown into the harshest prisons of Fozturia. He declared that those prisons ought to fix them, and he would allow them to once again turn away from this group and accept their military service. But if they refuse for the last time and reject the king's warning, harsher punishments will be inflicted on them."

The people all gasped in shock upon hearing this, and much chattering broke out. Their faces of despair looked on at the man bearing the ill news, with thoughts of fear and anger of the king plaguing their minds. Many of them even thought of leaving the group altogether, fearing the terrible authority that the king possessed.

"Oh, this is horrible!" exclaimed a distressed woman. "How will our fate now be any different than that of the Nobles a few years ago?"

"I don't think our fate will be any different than theirs," said a young man. "Every movement that has arisen in Fozturia against the king has always been swiftly brought down to the ground. Why should we think that we'll be any different? We never should've formed this group, and now we're hopeless against the king's threats!"

The crowd of people continued to noisily chat amongst themselves, sharing the same feelings of despair and hopelessness that seized their hearts. Many of them began doubting their association with the group, losing all hope and believing that they would suffer the same fate as the many resistant groups and movements that had come years before them. A possessive cloud of terror reached out its claws to grasp them tightly, with no way of escape or hope seeming to be in sight.

But even as the people began losing all hope, Steven managed to intervene and pleaded for them to remain calm and patient.

"My friends, are we seriously surprised that this day has come?" he asked them. "We know that the king rules by tyranny and injustice, as that has been displayed by his ruthless iron hand that has struck down every movement that has come against him. But we cannot lose hope and surrender ourselves by saying our fate will be the same as theirs. There is a new age of hope and light coming, and we must hold onto that belief of ours. No movement like ours has ever arisen in the history of Fozturia, and we have the potential to do something so special that we could never imagine it in our wildest dreams."

"I suppose that this is true Mr. Loubre," said a young man. "But we should also be realistic and understand that the king holds great dominion over this land. And because of that, it will be nearly impossible for us to escape our plight."

"Yes, that is true," confessed Steven. "But we must nonetheless stand courageously and believe that we will succeed. And besides, even if the king persecutes us, why can't we just form our government without worrying about the king's evil? If worst comes to worst, we will travel to a hidden part of Fozturia or even to a new land where the king won't be able to find us. And there will set up a new government based on our ideals and hopes that we have closely held onto this whole time."

The people began to calm down in response to Steven's words, as his idea of forming a new government was like music to their ears. Hope sprung into their hearts and faint smiles even broke out on some of their faces. Yet many were still filled with doubt and many questions.

"But how will we manage to escape and form our government?" asked a man. "Have you forgotten that the king has thousands of spies and soldiers everywhere throughout Fozturia? And besides, there are many people throughout the land who are pro-war, and they will also manage to find and report us to the king."

Steven thought to himself for a while, with doubt of his idea seeming to take hold of him. But suddenly, a new idea sprang into his mind.

"There is still a region of Fozturia westward where nobody has inhabited," he said. "I have heard that the land there is rich, plentiful, and spacious for many people to permanently settle. Perhaps we should travel underground for the first few days, before coming up to the surface and finding this undiscovered land."

"What if there are deadly animals or people already inhabiting the land though?" objected a woman. "That will make it unbearable for us and we will be trapped right in the middle of an unknown region. I have even heard stories of dragons who occupy and live in the many unknown lands throughout Fozturia."

"Those are only rumors," responded Steven. "Dragons and any deadly creatures like them are not here in Fozturia and have never existed throughout our history. Have you forgotten that nearly two hundred years ago, it was King Louie who started those rumors to prevent the Fozturian people from exploring the many rich and glorious lands found throughout this kingdom? But they defied his order and secretly went to inhabit the many secret lands, and eventually found rich and beautiful lands where they dwelled and lived securely. What if we have the same opportunity as they did? Will we just avoid exploring there all because of the threats that the king may send our way?"

Suddenly all the people's hopes were restored, and they confidently assured themselves in Steven's words. "You are correct Mr. Loubre," conceded the woman. "All that you say is true and without falsehoods. I agree that we shouldn't avoid exploring just because of the king's threats."

"Good, that's what I like to hear," said Steven with a broad smile coming on his face. He directed his attention to the rest of the people. "Now what about the rest of you? Will you let fear define you, or will you boldly migrate to a new land where we shall live new lives free from the wickedness of the king?"

"We shall not let fear define us!" shouted a number of the people. "For we shall stand confidently with you every step of the way!"

At that moment, a wind of hope and courage rushed over the people, and they continued chanting and proclaiming all the more about how they would remain hopeful and not give in to despair. And in the days to come, the numbers of those a part of the Resistants only continued to grow, as they declared their beliefs and confident words with all those throughout Fozturia.

Meanwhile, the news was brought to the king of the growing progress that they made, and he began to worry about their growing influence over the men and women of Fozturia. He tried all the more to make them give up in fear, sending more messages of the consequences they would endure if they continued their opposition to them. But the Resistants had let go of their fears and concerns and continued multiplying and growing stronger even amid the adversity surrounding them.

So the king was greatly enraged and ordered a great number of his spies as had not been seen in Fozturia for many years, to arrest and throw as many as they could into his harsh prisons. Many of his spies managed to succeed, and several Resistants were thrown into harsh prisons and endured great suffering. But because of their growing numbers and the courage that consumed them, the Resistants continued to stand firm and assemble. All the more, the king grew increasingly infuriated with them, seeing that they wouldn't be as easy to deal with as the many resistant movements that had come against him years before

It was also around this time that the king sent a little over twenty thousand able-bodied men to join his soldiers and battle in Qehat, with his military generals and officers leading them. As he sent them, he quickly turned his focus back to the Resistants, thinking of ways in which he could strike great terror in them that would make them quiver and flee completely from their pursuits.

And so the king, feeling as though he had no other choice, decided that he would inflict such great punishments on the Resistants as had never before been seen in the history of Fozturia. He announced that any more individuals a part of the group would be captured and executed at once, declaring that he had no other choice and that they had gone too far in their rebellion.

Even in their growing fervor and hope, great fear fell on the Resistants as they heard of the king's announcement. As a few more days went by, they knew that they had no choice but to migrate westward, and Steven urged them to pack all their belongings and move quickly. They assembled in an underground location where the king's spies and soldiers wouldn't find them, as he discussed the plans for their departure with them.

"We must migrate westward and flee from the king's wrath," he said. "He is growing incredibly frustrated with us, and though I would've liked for more people to join us, it's for our safety and benefit that we migrate now."

"But what if the king finds us along the way, or even if he finds us in the new land westward?" asked a woman. "We will then be doomed for destruction and wiped away from existence."

"We will then have to move quicker than the king's spies and soldiers so that they don't catch us," answered Steven. "And if we travel underground through the many networks provided for us, then after a few days we'll be able to come back to the surface in safety from evading their pursuit of us. But we must continue to hold on to the growing hope we've experienced in these past few days, because if we lose hope, then we'll be more likely to be caught."

Amidst the tense discussions, an elderly man interrupted Steven to share all that was placed on his heart. "Men and women, as Steven has told us, we must remain strong and courageous," he said. "Throughout all my years living here in Fozturia, I have never seen such a bold resistance group as I see now. Are we just going to let go of all the hope that has been growing in our hearts, just because our situation has become even more difficult? My friends, we must rise and stand boldly as valiant soldiers against the king!"

"Very well said my friend," said Steven. "Will we heed these man's words and continue our bold stand against the king!"

"Yes, we will!" roared back the people.

"Very good," said Steven. "Since we are all ready then, at first light tomorrow morning, we will begin traveling underground through the many paths and locations, and once the path on the surface is clear, we will climb up and continue our march westward to live in our new homes."

"Very well Mr. Loubre," said the man. "That sounds like a good plan, and I am more than ready to get started!"

The people rested well that night, filled with high spirits and assurance of Steven's confident words. And the next morning, they all woke up early and gathered together in an underground location to begin their great escape west. Many hundreds of thousands of people gathered together, each bringing an abundant number of supplies including food, clothing, and other items that they would find useful in their great migration. Besides the traveling Resistants were many others who supported their cause secretly, but refused to associate and travel with them, fearing being caught and punished by the king. But they nonetheless supported and helped the Resistants, providing them with many supplies and assurance that they would be watching out for any of the king's spies and soldiers.

And so it was that on the 26th day of September, the great exodus of the Resistants began. They began by secretly traveling through underground locations, making their way through the many towns and villages of Fozturia. After three days had passed, they became convinced that they were far enough from the king and his servants that they no longer had to travel underground. They climbed their way up to the surface, discovering rocky paths surrounded by wide forests.

They found themselves now in the Fehborn Forest, a forest of Fozturia that was hardly populated, save only a few animals and creatures that roamed around. The people breathed the fresh air with gladness that they no longer had to migrate underground.

"Ah, it's so good to finally travel on the surface without worrying about getting caught by the king's servants," remarked a man, gazing all around at the wide forest. "And this place looks pretty safe. I can only see a few animals walking around this forest."

The mood of the people was one of relief and peace as they passed through the wide forest. They continued traveling through more woodland areas and rocky paths mainly populated with small creeping beasts. Tree trunks of innumerable sizes stood silently all around the people with plants and flowers beaming with life as many birds chirped songs of joy high above in the sky. The people felt such comfort as they had never known before, and not even the slightest fear of ever being caught by the king crossed their minds.

Over the next few days, they continued journeying along the path of the endless woodlands, stopping many times throughout the days to rest and recharge. Eventually, they finally came to the end of the woodland region and entered into a vast space of grassland plains.

Steven grew excited at the sight of the new land. "Well, now we've completed the first stage of our journey," he said. "We've made our way through the forest and now we'll continue our migration by going through these grasslands. This could only mean that we are advancing greatly in our journey. Let's continue!"

The people joyfully followed Steven as they merged their way onto a path with the rich and endless plains of grass surrounding them. There were only a few scattered trees and plants around them, but no other living beings were in sight. The atmosphere was dead silent, almost too silent for the as they became greatly surprised that no other Fozturians dwelled in these lands.

"Where are all the other Fozturians?" asked a man.

"I suppose that not even one of them dwells here," responded Steven. "I wouldn't blame them for not living here, because this only seems like a vast plain of grass and nothing else."

As the evening wore on, the people rested in the open plains of grass with hardly any coverings of trees or plants. The next morning they arose early to continue their traveling, walking for many miles under the burning heat of the sun. All that day they continued their laborious movement through endless grasslands where not a living thing was in sight again. The people grew bored at the same plain old sight, but kept their complaints to themselves, hoping that they would soon see a change in the landscape.

And in their wish would be granted. As another week of the people's westward migration passed by, they eventually made their way through the grasslands and into a hilly region covered in trees and bushes. They breathed sighs of relief to see the change in the landscape and became even more glad when they discovered several animals that dwelled in the region.

"Now that I think of it, we are so far away from the king that I don't even think these lands have names," remarked Steven. "The grasslands we went through were incredibly boring, but thank goodness we made our way through them because we would've never discovered all these unknown regions of Fozturia."

"You are right, Mr. Loubre," said a woman. "We've advanced farther on this journey than I ever could've imagined, and now look at where we are. We've found these peaceful regions of Fozturia that we never would've thought ever existed if we weren't bold enough to even go on this journey. How about we just settle down and live in these lands? Surely the king won't be able to find us here."

"No we must not do that," responded Steven. "The king is likely still relentlessly searching for us and we can't risk anything. We must continue to remain one step ahead of him and his many spies and soldiers. Let's just continue to make our way as far westward as we possibly can, and then we can settle down there in our new homes."

The people agreed with Steven's advice, believing it to be the wisest choice and in their best interests to continue migrating west as far as they could. So in the next couple of days, they continued to make their way through vast and beautiful hilly regions and even entered into mountainous regions populated only by animals.

After traveling through the mountains for some days, they began making their way downhill before arriving in a forest. Deep in the forest was a long river, and they continued their journey on a path that lay to the side of it.

As they walked they couldn't help but gaze intently at the rich blue water that sparkled in the sun's light. The streams of the river peacefully swayed as the cool wind silently blew on it. Serenity filled the people's hearts and they halted by the river's bank to rest and drink some of its cool and fresh water.

After about a half hour of resting and drinking their share of water, the people all arose to continue on their journey. They made their way along the paths of the wood with the river beside them, traveling a great deal through the forest.

The next day they journeyed their way through sloping hills and deep valleys through the rich and unknown regions of Fozturia. They found themselves gazing at the landscapes in admiration of the scope and beauty of the newly discovered lands. The wind breezed through the air, providing a gusting breeze that cooled the warm day. Their walking soon turned into small skips, and voices of singing flowed from their mouths in response to the chirping birds that flew above them. They stretched their arms as far and wide as they could in unrestricted freedom, knowing that their lives had become vastly different than what it was just a few weeks before.

They continued to migrate westwards through the rich and beautiful sight of the hills and valleys populated by no one but themselves and animals. They felt great peace and protection as they journeyed on. However, all of those feelings would come to a sharp halt as they suddenly realized that they were missing three members of their group. They didn't know how and why they only realized at that moment, but they nonetheless turned back around to search for the three missing people.

Assuming that they had lost them along the way, they came back to the valleys, mountains, and forests that they had traveled through, journeying and searching through the region to find them. But no sight of the missing Resistants could be seen. Filled with despair, the people made a stop by the mountains, gathering together in a cave to rest from their long hours and days of searching.

They sat to themselves for a couple of hours, not speaking with each other and instead dwelling on the fear that suddenly possessed their hearts. But eventually, one man who had received news of what had happened to the missing people came to report it to Steven.

"Mr. Loubre, I'm afraid that we have bad news," he said. "The two men and woman who we lost along the way, had lost track of us soon after we started our journey and were hiding in an underground bunker to remain safe before catching up with us. Unfortunately, the king's spies found them and they were executed weeks ago by the king."

Immediately, after Steven and the people heard the news, their mood suddenly changed. Their long silence turned into cries of grief that echoed throughout the cave, with faces of terror covering the people's faces as they wondered whether the king would also manage to find them.

"I knew it wasn't ever a good idea to go on this journey!" exclaimed a man, throwing his arms into the air in distress. "Now the king will find us and execute us all!"

"Mr. Loubre, let's just go back and submit to the king so we won't have to deal with any more problems like this," pleaded a woman.

"But there's no way that the king will just forgive us," remarked an old man. "He has given us many chances to turn to him, yet we have still gone against him. He will punish us ruthlessly for our rebellion against him."

The arguments and discussions ensued for a while, as the people grew increasingly chaotic and terrified. At that moment, many of them desired to turn their back on their entire cause and go back to their former homes to admit all that they had done to the king. But others knew that the king wouldn't graciously accept them back without first punishing them. But among the hysterical fear, others including Steven remained hopeful that they could continue on their journey without fear of being captured by the king and his servants.

After many minutes of chaos, Steven managed to get the people's attention as he spoke to them in the cave.

"My brothers and sisters, I can see the uncontrollable fear that has taken control of your hearts," he said. "Many are speaking of betraying our cause altogether and going back to the place where we escaped from. But you must understand that nobody who succeeds in life does so under the hand of a tyrant. If you decide to return to your old life, I can assure you that you will never again experience the true freedom we want. So you have a choice, either to rise above these difficult circumstances we find ourselves in, or to fearfully surrender under the hand of this tyrant and suffer miserably under his rule.

"But my brothers and sisters, let me challenge you with a question. How will future generations view us? Will they remember us as brave heroes who were willing to die for liberty and justice, or will they remember us as cowards who fled from the hope of freedom? We must not give up on what we've started, for we still have many more goals to fulfill. But you must not give in to fear and fill your hearts with courage. And if any one of you notices a brother or sister lacking courage, then you must encourage them and lift them. If they are injured or hurt, then lift them on your backs, and if their arms are weak, then hold their arms to give them strength. Whatever you do, don't neglect the sufferings of your brothers and sisters, for let their spirits will be lifted because of what you do. You all have the power to strengthen those who are weak, so we must not turn our backs on what we hope to accomplish, just because of this difficult situation that we're in. Arise my brothers and sisters, and let us stand boldly no matter what we face!"

Even as he spoke, a strong and calming wind breezed throughout the cave and filled the people's hearts with faith and reassurance. A joyful light came onto their faces and their spirits were lifted in response to Steven's words. Many of those who had expressed their doubts about continuing their cause, were now greatly encouraged. They expressed their gratitude to Steven, for the wise and bold words he had shared with them.

"Mr. Loubre, your words have returned the peace and joy that we were lacking," remarked a man. "Thank you for the encouraging words you have shared with us even amidst our great anxiety."

"Yes, this is why you are our leader," added a young woman. "Anyone else would've succumbed to the adversity, but you have chosen to rise and uplift us. We are grateful for you, Mr. Loubre."

"Well the least we can do is show Mr. Loubre how grateful we are for him," said a man. "How about we appreciate him for a moment?"

A roar of applause for Steven soon followed, as all the people thanked him for the reassurance that he had filled their hearts with. At that moment, their moods had completely changed from one of despair to one of hope after they had listened to Steven speak to them.

After the people had given thanks to Steven, he then spoke again to them, full of gratitude for their words of recognition toward him and their restored hope.

"Brothers and sisters," he said, gazing in admiration at the people. "My words right now simply can't do justice in explaining to you how grateful I am for the love that you've shown me. Thank you for having faith in me, and especially for not giving up on me or yourselves in this pivotal moment of our journey."

"It's only what you deserve, Mr. Loubre," said a man, grinning from ear to ear. "You've helped us reflect on the importance of our journey and why we can't give up now. Your words have restored the hope that we had lost for a brief moment."

The people continued to praise and thank Steven, with faces lit up with joy. But amidst their talking, a young boy with wavy brown hair and healthy blue eyes came forth to Steven, bringing everyone's attention to himself. Even as he walked, the people observed how he had a healthy and innocent appearance on his face, yet also a mature look, as though his heart contained words of wisdom that would benefit them all.

"May I say something that's been placed on my heart?" he asked, standing next to Steven. The people remained silent for a second, with shocked faces that were fixed on the young boy's peering blue eyes.

"You know better than to interrupt adults, young boy," suddenly said an old man with a disgusted look on his face. "Haven't your parents taught you not to do such a thing as this? I'm sure that you know that when adults speak, children are meant to remain silent and listen to us."

Many of the people agreed with the old man, telling the young boy to leave Steven alone and instead listen to him. The young boy cast his head toward the ground, full of disappointment that his voice wouldn't be heard. But even as he began walking away from Steven to return to where he was, Steven suddenly placed his hand on his shoulder, stopping him from moving any further away from him.

"Come back here, young man," he said, motioning for the boy to come back to him. The young boy slowly came back to Steven, with his eyes filled with fear as the people stared at him, filled with disbelief that Steven would ask him to stand next to him.

"What is Mr. Loubre doing?" whispered a woman. "Does he not know the customs of Fozturian culture of how children are not meant to interrupt adults when they speak?"

"I don't know what he's doing," responded a man. "But let's first watch and see what he says to this young boy. Perhaps we're all wrong and he's going to give him a strict admonition to never do what he did again."

The people stared intently at the young boy, wondering what Steven would say or do to him. Even as he walked back to Steven, the short distance felt like an eternity to the young boy because of all the watchful gazes of the people that were fixed on him. Once he finally came back to Steven, a vast silence came on the people as they watched to see what would happen.

"What is your name, young man and how old are you?" asked Steven, looking directly at the boy with keen eyes. "And where are your parents?"

"My name is Peter Mocon, and I'm sixteen years old," responded the boy. He turned toward the people, who continued staring at him with glaring eyes. "My parents are near the middle of the crowd," he said, pointing to where all the people stood in the middle, but to no particular people that Steven or the people could see.

"Very well," said Steven. "Whoever is Peter's parents, would you please make yourselves known?"

Just then, a tall slender man and a short woman both hesitantly raised their hands in the air. Immediately, the people turned their faces toward them and stared at them with intense disgust. The two of them stood as still as statues, with their faces covered in shame as the rest of the people's eyes remained fixed on them.

"Have you two not raised your boy to respect adults?" suddenly asked a woman. "And why would you let him escape from your grasp to bring this disgrace upon yourselves?"

Many of the people agreed with the woman and began attacking the couple. But their talking was quickly halted, as Steven once again got their attention.

"Quiet everyone!" he said in a loud voice. "When did I ask you to make the young boy and his parents feel ashamed of themselves? Let me speak with Peter."

The people became dead silent, and brought their attention back to Steven and Peter, much to the parents' relief.

Steven spoke once again with Peter. "Peter, what was it that you wanted to say?"

"Well, I first must say that I didn't mean to disrespect anyone," said Peter, gazing at the crowd of people who listened intently to him. "But all I wanted to share with these people was that we must not only say that we agree with you with our words, but we must also agree with you in the way that we live our lives. We can't just say that we're filled with hope and reassurance only to give into fear and despair the very next moment. We must act upon your words and prove that we will no longer submit to our worrying thoughts anymore."

Steven shook his head in approval of the young boy. "Those are wise words, Peter," he said. "I'm sure that many of these people here could dwell on your words and let them shape the ways they live their lives. You are full of wisdom, Peter, far more than what I ever contained at your age. Who else agrees that Peter has great wisdom beyond his years?"

"I sure do," said a man. "And on behalf of myself and the rest of the people here, I would like to apologize to Peter for disrespecting him, even before we gave him a chance to speak. And to his parents, I am deeply regretful that I along with these people judged them wrongly. I can now see that my eyes have been opened, and I thank Peter for sharing his wise and true words with us."

"Yes, I agree," remarked a woman. "All of this proves why we should let go of our wrong preconceived ideas of others, especially children. Because if we hadn't let this young man speak, then we would've never learned the importance of all that he's told us."

"I'm very pleased to hear all of you saying this," said Steven. "However, just as Peter has taught us, we must not only agree with him with our words but also in the way that we live now. We must put these words of his into action and let them transform our way of living and thinking."

"Yes, this has especially taught me valuable lessons that I can implement in my own life," remarked a man. "Lessons of not judging someone before they have a chance to speak, but rather judging them based on what the words they say and the people they prove to be. I'm thankful for this reminder, Mr. Loubre, and especially for the wise words that you, Peter have taught me."

Several more people added their comments, expressing how Peter's words had exposed how much change they still needed in their lives. Steven stood with Peter as they listened to the people's words, smiling with gladness to see their changed perspective.

"All that you've said is good, my friends," eventually said Steven. "I'm glad to see that many of you have understood the point of Peter's words and have let them bring change into your hearts and lives. And just to make sure that all of you have gotten the point, will you only agree with all that has been spoken of today, or will you let your agreement change your way of living?"

"We will let it change our way of living!" roared back the people, in a thunderous mixture of collective voices.

Steven smiled in excitement to see all the people agreeing with each other. "Very well then," he said. "You all have brought reassurance to my own heart because of your responses."

Steven then turned his back and spoke privately with Peter, as the rest of the people spoke amongst themselves. From that day forth, they all agreed to let the words that had been shared with them change how they conducted themselves and lived their lives.

And so with hope and confidence being restored to the people, they departed from the cave and continued their journey by migrating westwards. Fear of the king and his servants no longer plagued their minds, and they continued traveling through the vast unknown lands of Fozturia as they neared the very edge of the kingdom.

Meanwhile, back east in the king's palace, Maguspra could only wonder where the Resistants were. He had imagined that the beheading of the three Resistants would've led to the group turning back eastwards and confessing their rebellion against him, but to his astonishment, not a single one came back to betray their cause.

As the king sat on his throne on the morning of the 24th day of October, he wondered where the Resistants could've possibly gone. As he thought of many possibilities, one of his advisors came forth to his throne and spoke to him.

"My king, I was just thinking about the Resistants," he said. "And I was wondering, what if they escaped to some distant kingdom? They can't possibly still be in Fozturia."

The king didn't even look at his advisor, instead staring in the direction of one of his windows. "No, you are wrong," he said. "They are hiding somewhere in my kingdom which is why Nocolius managed to find three of them hiding in an underground location here in Fozturia.

And besides, those rebels wouldn't ever be able to survive the perils that migration entails."

"You are correct, my king," responded the advisor. "I am sorry for presenting such a foolish suggestion to you. Would you like me to send more spies to search for the rebels?"

"No," said the king. "All of my spies have been useless in their searches, except for Nocolius. And so I will search for the rebels with him. Arrange my carriage outside the palace so that Nocolius and I can search the country for any rebels that are hiding in my kingdom."

"At your word, my king," said the advisor, bowing his head to the king. "The carriage will be ready shortly."

The king's advisor swiftly arranged his carriage, bringing it just outside the palace for the king and his spy, Nocolius. But before Maguspra would jump in the carriage, he first decided to disguise himself as an ordinary man of Fozturia, so that no one would be able to recognize him and hide any of the rebels from his presence. One of his servants brought him an old shirt covered in dirt, plain rugged pants, and a mask to wear so that no one would see his face.

The king stared at the clothing presented to him with a disgusted look on his face. "Is this what the men of Fozturia wear?" he asked. "I have never known how undignified and dirty they are."

"Yes, my king. This is what most of the men living in Fozturia wear," answered the servant. "Most of them are too poor to afford dignified clothing that the rest of us own."

"Perhaps if they worked harder like me they could afford to wear some dignified clothes," remarked the king.

"Perhaps so, my king," said the servant.

After some time dressing up, the king made his way into the carriage that had been prepared for him and his most trusted spy right outside the palace. Nocolius was already seated in the carriage and nearly fell over when the figure wearing the mask and poor clothing came in. But his fears were swiftly brushed aside once he recognized that it was the king.

He breathed a sigh of relief and smiled at the king. "Greetings, my king," he said. "I didn't recognize you at first because of the clothing that you're wearing. Why have you decided to not wear your royal attire?"

"Because I must keep my identity a secret," responded Maguspra. "I am traveling with you around my kingdom to find where the remaining rebels are hiding. And to do that, they must not notice who I truly am."

"Ah yes I understand now, my king," said Nocolius. "Those rebellious folks must be punished for their crimes against you. Which direction are we going to travel in to search for them?"

"Let us travel eastward through the valley of Mofton," said the king. "The valley is filled with many towns, and is a fairly populated region filled with many dwelling places that could have many of those rebels hiding in them."

"Great idea, my king," said Nocolius. "I'm ready to find those rebels and see their petrified faces once they realize who you are."

And so the king and Nocolius went away eastward, first making their way down the Golden Mountains surrounding the palace, and through the vast glade of the Rockless Forest. Once they got past the forest, they went down sloping grass hills where they saw many animals roaming around the region.

As they went down the hills, they also made their way through a large and beautiful garden, where tall and colorful trees resided. The trees' leaves sparkled under the sun in a blooming mixture of red, orange, and pink. Maguspra and Nocolius made a stop by the garden, taking in a moment to gaze at and speak of the beauty of the garden's trees.

"Just look at those great trees," remarked the king, staring at them with fascination. "Aren't these Hoplo trees the most wonderful trees of all the kingdoms on Earth? Where else can trees like these be found?"

"They are remarkable, my king," said Nocolius. "No other kingdom on Earth can compare to the wonderful trees that are found in the kingdom of Fozturia."

The two of them continued observing the wonderful nature of the garden, silently listening to the chirps of the birds flying above them and examining the different colored trees and flowers that grew in full blossom.

The king walked over to one of the trees, grabbing a piece of its fruit. He observed the fruit for a moment, staring at its blue color and cubical shape that just fit into the palms of his hand. Tiny purple flowers grew around its side, giving it a unique and sweet taste to it. The king took a bite of the fruit and smiled as he chewed it slowly.

"This fruit is wonderful," he remarked. "Nothing in this world can come to the taste of the Hoplo trees' fruits. You should eat one as well, Nocolius."

Nocolius took a piece of fruit hanging from the tree's branch and took a large bite for himself. His eyes closed in amazement as he chewed on the fruit and he even took another for himself to eat.

"That is wonderful indeed, my king," he said, still chewing the fruit in his mouth. "Do you have any idea what the name of this fruit is called?"

"It is called a grajo," responded the king. "My father and I used to go to a garden that he owned and he would spend time eating this fruit. This reminds me of the joy that I felt in my childhood days."

For a moment, the king fell silent and pondered the life he once had as a child. He brought to his memory the special moments that he shared with his father as a child, remembering the joyful pleasure he once experienced. He thought of what life was once like in his younger days without the responsibility of being king, and he wondered how and when the innocent joyfulness of his childhood vanished from his grasp.

But just as these thoughts ran through his mind, Maguspra laughed aloud and assured himself that his current life as king was far better than anything he experienced as a child. He threw the remainder of the fruit he was eating to the ground and went back into the carriage.

Maguspra and Nocolius departed from the garden, journeying their way through regions of hills and valleys. They eventually arrived in the Mofton Valley, and as they went through it, they soon reached a village full of both many people and small houses. The two of them inspected rode through the village streets, inspecting everything that they could lay their eyes on. But all they found was a great crowd of people minding their own business and others staring at the two of them as though they were out of their minds.

But Maguspra and Nocolius remained persistent, making their way through as many streets and corners as they could to find any one of the Resistants. All the while, the eyes of the people remained fixed on them, as they wondered what the two of them were looking for.

After an hour of long and mindless searching, Maguspra decided to jump out of the carriage, ordering Nocolius to remain inside. He began walking through the streets, asking as many people as he could if they knew where the Resistants were. Yet almost all of the time responded in the same manner, telling him that they didn't where they were.

"I'm not sure, sir," said one man, staring at the masked man with great perplexity. "They are either really good hiders, or they've managed to migrate somewhere far from here."

Another woman chimed in. "Yes, I don't know where they could be," she said. "I've heard rumors that they are hiding in some underground place, but I'm not completely sure what to make of them. You might want to travel near the border of the kingdom if you want to find them. But why are you so devoted to searching for them?"

"Because I must," responded the king. "You don't need to know my reasons, but I promise you that I have no ill intentions for them. In which direction do you suggest I should travel to find them?"

The woman looked longingly at the king, wondering what the true purpose of this masked man was. But she brushed her worries aside and answered his question. "I would recommend that you go westward," she suggested. "Hardly anyone lives in the western regions of Fozturia and much of it is still unknown. It would make sense for them to go there."

The king processed the woman's words for a moment, before devilishly smiling under his mask as he concocted a question for her. "But have you not heard of the stories of dragons and other creatures that dwell in the West?" he asked. "It is said that all those who have journeyed there have never been heard of again."

The woman laughed to herself. "Those are lies, my friend," she said. "The ideas of dragons and other terrifying creatures like them existing in this kingdom, are only made-up stories that the Kings of Fozturia created since they didn't want people moving to those regions of Fozturia and enjoying the benefits of the land for themselves."

The king's face under his mask changed as he listened to the woman. "All that you say is a lie," he suddenly and passionately said. "The kings were telling the truth and wanted to protect the people from the dangers they would've faced if they defied their orders."

"I hate to break it to you, but the kings have never protected us," responded the woman. "Especially the current king, who is the worst of them all. He has inflicted tremendous suffering on many of those living in this kingdom all because of his evil deeds. Not only that but he's also executed hundreds, if not thousands of people who have spoken out against his tyrannical rule."

Even as she spoke, Maguspra could feel streams of smoke coming forth from his head. He stepped closer to the woman and clenched his hands, breathing heavily with intense rage against her. "How dare you speak such evil things against the king!" he angrily screamed in her face. "How can your life go unpunished for these heinous words you've proclaimed!"

The woman stepped back, shaking with both fear and confusion. "Sir, why are you so angry with me?" she asked. "All that I've said is simply the truth. Maguspra is the most wicked of all the kings in Fozturian history. If you were to see half of the things he did, I'm sure you wouldn't find a way to disagree with me."

Maguspra couldn't hide his identity anymore as he listened to the woman speak. He threw off the mask on his face, staring fiercely at the woman. "I am the King of Fozturia," he revealed. "I am the one to whom you have spoken these rebellious and disgusting words. And as king of this land, I will severely punish you for all you have said."

The woman's eyes widened with shock at this sudden revelation and she suddenly started crying bitterly to herself. "Oh, why did I have to let my tongue babble on?" she exclaimed. "Oh king, please have mercy on me! I will accept whatever punishment you inflict on me, but please don't take my life!"

Maguspra stared at her with a disgusted and wrathful look covering his face. "I must punish you for your rebellious words," he said. "But I will not execute you. At least you haven't decided to openly rebel against me as some others have done. But you will be thrown into harsh prisons for the words you have said."

The woman sighed to herself but felt relieved that she wouldn't be executed. Filled with anger, Maguspra grabbed onto her shoulder and dragged her to his carriage, with many fearful eyes staring at the two of them as the people realized that it was the king who was searching for the Resistants. They quickly hid from his presence, not wishing to face his wrathful side. Maguspra threw her in the back seat of the carriage, while he sat at the front with Nocolius. Nocolius at the king and the woman with a puzzled look on his face.

"My king, why is there a woman in the carriage with us?" he asked. "And why are you so angry?"

Maguspra's face grew hardened and he pointed his finger into the woman's face. "This woman spoke rebellious words against me and my ancestors," he responded. "Because of that I will I will throw her into the harshest prisons of Fozturia where she will suffer miserably until she learns her lesson never to speak such things against me ever again."

"Ah I see, my king," said Nocolius. "It is important that no one that disrespects you remains unpunished. You are doing the right thing."

"I know I am," proudly said Maguspra. "These rebels must see that I will rule over them with a strong iron arm. Our search in finding the rebels is done. Let's go back into the direction in which we came so that we can take this repulsive woman to where she belongs."

The woman squirmed as she listened to Maguspra, with her entire body from head to toe shaking uncontrollably. Maguspra and Nocolius turned the carriage around, making their way out of the village and into the same direction in which they had come from. Maguspra sat silently to himself, grinning and occasionally turning around to delight himself in the terror that covered the woman's face. The woman sat quietly to herself, imagining how terrible and ruined her life would now become in prison. She began to accept her fate, blaming herself for her lack of good judgment in speaking openly against the king.

But just as she slowly began to give into despair, an idea suddenly came to her mind. As the carriage made its way through the Mofton Valley, she began to observe how the king had forgotten about her and instead focused his attention on the beauty of nature outside. She saw his eyes beginning to fall half shut, with Nocolius' eyes completely shut. She smiled and laughed silently to herself as she realized that a way of escape for her was possible, and quickly pounced on it so that wouldn't escape from her grasp.

And so, finding a small opening to the side of the carriage, the woman swiftly slipped herself from the carriage and quietly hid in a bush as the carriage went on. Once the coast was clear, she quickly wandered off in the opposite different direction of the carriage and started running back to her village.

Once she made it back to her village, she collapsed to the ground, laughing to herself in amazement that she had managed to escape. She then stood up and began singing to herself as she joyfully began skipping her way through the village streets:

I foolishly mistook you as a stranger,
And became trapped under your hand.
But I have used my keen senses to escape the danger,
And come back to my homeland!

I shall never stop singing for joy,
Nor cease my shouts of celebration.
For I have successfully used my ploy,
To flee from my terrible isolation!

The woman continued to joyfully sing and shout to herself, with all those who saw her celebrating with relief to see that she had escaped.

Elsewhere, Maguspra finally opened his eyes, bringing his attention back to the carriage. He turned around, smiling even as he pictured what the woman's face was like. But to his horror, he found that she was gone. He frantically began looking in all directions of the valley to see if she was hiding anywhere, but not even a trace of her footsteps could be seen. He tapped Nocolius on the shoulder, waking his spy up from his sleep.

"Nocolius! What have you done?" he exclaimed. "The woman has escaped! Why did you go to sleep and not pay attention to what she was doing?"

Nocolius' mouth dropped to the ground as he turned around and discovered the woman missing from their carriage. Sweat came down from his forehead and his body started shaking as the king stared at him in anger.

"My king, I am so sorry," he said in a trembling voice. "I don't know how that woman managed to escape, but she must be pulling tricks on us somehow. Perhaps, she's hiding behind some of these bushes and trees, waiting for our carriage to pass from her sight. But please forgive me, my king. I had no idea she slipped away from us."

"Nocolius, what you have done is very disappointing," said Maguspra. "But you are my most trusted spy, so I have no other choice but to continue to trust in you. But understand that this must never happen again or else you will be dismissed from my service."

Nocolius gulped to himself in fear of the king's wrath against him but managed to respond to him. "I understand, my king," he said, with terror still covering his face.

The king looked longingly at him but accepted his response. "Very good," he said. "Perhaps luck is not on my side today. Let's go back to my palace and search for these rebels another time. Perhaps we will find them then."

The two men continued in the same direction, now heading back to the palace. They made their way through the vast hills and valleys around them and made a quick stop by the same garden they had gone through. They stepped outside of the carriage and picked the fruit that hung on the tree's branches, delighting themselves in the sweet taste of the fruit.

Once they had eaten their fair share of fruit, they came back to the carriage with the Golden Mountains in the far distance ahead of them. But just as they soon began to get themselves ready to move on, they noticed an unusual sight that caught their attention.

An elderly man, appearing to be in his sixties came walking towards them, holding a brown walking stick with him. Maguspra and Nocolius initially dismissed him as an insignificant old man, observing his long white beard, the plain brown cloak he wore, and his unusually long pointed nose. Yet as he approached them they noticed that he was quite tall and even slightly imposing in his stature, with his long pointed brown hat making him appear even taller than he already was. Maguspra and Nocolius came out of the carriage, staring at the old man in bewilderment at who he was and why he was approaching them.

As the old man came close to Maguspra and Nocolius, the two men couldn't help but observe how he walked. While gazing at him, they felt as though great authority oozed from his presence, and his eyes seemed to have contained an ancient vigor to them.

He stopped walking once he came to a close distance with the two men, who found themselves feeling humbled by his imposing stature. The old man locked eyes with Maguspra and Nocolius, and before they could ask questions, he suddenly opened his mouth.

"Listen to my words today, Maguspra, King of Fozturia," he said, with great authority issuing forth from his voice. "I know the purpose of your coming to these lands today. You have traveled here to search for the Resistants to punish them with your cruel hand. But they are not here, something you have only now realized after your search grew vain."

Maguspra stood terrified in front of the old man, enchanted by the boldness of his voice and the unknown authority he seemed to possess. But just as the fear of the man took hold of him, he reminded himself of the authority that he possessed, and as he stared at the old man he found himself suddenly laughing aloud.

"Ah, so you've been spying on me because you fear the great power that I have," he said, laughing at the old man. "Well, that's good to know. Since you already know so much about me and fear me, maybe you could now reveal to me where you know the Resistants are."

The old man shook his head, glaring at Maguspra with intense eyes. "That is not the reason why I have come to you today," he said.

"Oh really?" said Maguspra, now feeling relaxed and in the mood for jest. "So what is the reason that you've come to me today? Is it because you want to have great power for yourself just like I do? Or maybe you're just jealous of me and want to try and make me feel fearful of you, a trap that I nearly fell into."

"Maguspra, your pride is unlike anything that has been seen on the face of the Earth," said the old man. "You are not as mighty as you think you are, because everything that you think you have does not truly belong to you. I am here today to issue you a warning. It is for your good that you listen to my words and heed my warning."

The cunning smile on Maguspra's face quickly subsided, and a look of disgust now covered his face. He grew increasingly impatient with the old man. "Go ahead then! Speak quickly!" he demanded.

"Listen very closely to me," said the old man. "You, Maguspra, son of Titan, must publicly apologize to the people of Fozturia for all the evil that you've committed against them during your reign as king. You must also never go to search for the Resistants and cruelly punish them. For in the time that you do search for them to commit a terrible crime against them, disaster shall fall upon you, your family, and on the entire kingdom of Fozturia."

Maguspra for a split second felt something like a sharp knife piercing his heart as he listened to the old man. His face turned aghast and his heart was filled with both fear and confusion. But filled with pride and a hardened heart he rejected these feelings of his, despising the old man's words.

"You don't know what you're talking about, you fool," he sharply replied. "I will do whatever I desire to do when I want to do it. Who are you, an old man to speak such pompous words against the King of Fozturia?"

"I have handed you the chance to repent, Maguspra," responded the old man. "I have given you the option to either do good and prosper or to do evil and suffer. But it's your choice. It's now up to you to heed my warning and change how you rule over this great kingdom."

Maguspra stared at the old man with his face and body shaking with anger. "Why should I heed your stupid warning?" he asked. "Why are you here only to question my ways? You are just a madman who doesn't know what he's talking about. Get away from my presence!"

Disappointment covered the old man's face. "Very well then, Maguspra," he softly said. "Do as you, please. But you will suffer consequences if you refuse to heed my warning."

Maguspra reached his boiling point and stepped closer toward the old man, yelling in his face. "You have no idea what you're talking about!" he screamed in great wrath. "Your needless warning is just a tool you're using to try and intimidate me. But I will refuse to be intimidated by you!" He turned toward Nocolius, whose face was covered in terror. "Nocolius, let's get away from this old fool. I am tired of hearing his doom-filled words."

Nocolius bowed his head to Maguspra, and with that, the two of them hopped onto their carriage and began going back in the direction of the palace. But as they went through the garden, turning around they found that the old man was still there, staring at Maguspra with fixed eyes. Maguspra brushed this aside, focusing on the path ahead of him. But as he turned around again to see if the old man was still there, he found him standing in the same spot, glaring at Maguspra.

Deeply disturbed and filled with anger, Maguspra expressed his intention to confront the old man. "Nocolius, let's turn around," he said. "This weird old man is continuing to stare at me as if he's begging for trouble."

The two of them turned around, expecting to see the old man glaring at Maguspra. Yet the second they turned around, any sight of the man completely vanished

Maguspra laughed to himself and shook his head in disbelief. "That crazy man is still pulling tricks on us, Nocolius," he said. "Let's stop this mindless wandering. Perhaps a good night's rest will keep my senses in tack."

"He's nothing more than a troublemaker, my king," said Nocolius. "And we might just be imagining things that aren't happening. A good night's rest would be nice for us after this long day."

And so, Maguspra and Nocolius convinced themselves that their strange encounter with the old man was nothing more than a phantom of their imagination. Brushing everything they had experienced throughout the day they made their way out of the garden, nearing their way to the palace. The sky grew dark as the evening fell on them, with the orange setting sun illuminating the darkened sky. Maguspra and Nocolius stared at the wonderful sight for a moment, admiring it for its beauty.

"Isn't that a glorious sight, Nocolius?" remarked Maguspra. "The sun is shining on us as we ride back to the palace."

"Indeed, my king," said Nocolius, gazing at the sight. "It only makes sense that it would shine on us because you as the King of Fozturia, have illuminated and strengthened this great land."

"Yes, I have indeed, Nocolius," said Maguspra, filled with great pride. "But I don't understand how people could rebel against me. I have reinforced this great kingdom and protected it from its enemies. What more could I possibly do for them?"

"You have done all that you can do, my king," assured Nocolius. "You are the greatest king in all of this kingdom's history. No king has ever given us such great protection as you have. You have also strengthened and improved our military ensuring that the Eletans don't advance to complete their goals of world domination. You have done more than we could ever hope for, and I hope those rebels learn this one day."

A proud smile came on Maguspra's face as he listened to Nocolius, and he took his words to heart, assuring himself that he had done the best he could ever do in his reign as king.

The two men continued for another hour, making their way now through the vast Rockless forest that lay just outside the Golden Mountains. They soon made their way to the mountains and came up its rocky paths, catching a glimpse of the palace that stood atop it.

Once they reached the palace, the two men breathed sighs of relief, having been glad that they had survived the long and strange day. The king's guards stood outside the palace, and the doors were opened for the two men as they made their way inside. Maguspra and Nocolius wished each other a good night as the king went up the stairs to his room. The king jumped onto his bed and covered himself with his sheets, closing his eyes as he dozed off into sleep. But even as he slept, a large and proud smile covered his face as he continually assured himself even in his dreams that the rest of his days as king would be problem free.

3

Revelations Unmasked

The Resistants could practically see their new homes ahead of them as they walked the final steps of their journey. Steven was unable to hide the broad smile on his face, as he eagerly anticipated what the people's reactions to their new homes would be. They had finally arrived at the western coast of Fozturia in the afternoon of the 27th day of October after a month-long journey that tried them with many setbacks and difficulties. But they had managed to endure their long and tiring migration and were ready to enjoy the fruits of their labor alongside each other.

Ahead of them was a wide sea, but they first began examining the trees and plants that populated the land around them. They had expected to discover endless and rich hills and valleys, but to their surprise, found them nowhere in sight. The sea threw them off guard, and they found the land to be strange and exotic. They had never lived beside a large body of water, and they began fearing and wondering if they would ever get used to the new land.

"Where are the hills and valleys?" asked a man, gazing at the new land with both wonder and skepticism.

"There are none in this region," responded Steven. "This is our new home which just so happens to be a new and different land from what we have seen. We will have to get used to this land and adapt to the new environment we find ourselves in."

"But why though? Aren't we still in the kingdom?" asked a woman. "There should be hills and valleys in this land."

"I'm not certain for sure whether or not we are still in the kingdom," said Steven. "This is an unknown and uninhabited land, so it wouldn't surprise me if we are not currently standing in the land of Fozturia."

"Well, in that case, I think we should turn back around and go to a different land," suggested a man. "A land full of hills and valleys would be much preferred because this region is so much more different than what I'm used to seeing. Look how close the sea is to us! What if its waves manage to overpower and devour this land?"

"You're not wrong," remarked another man. "And I agree with you. I think we should go back and search for a land with hills and valleys to permanently settle in."

Much talking soon ensued amongst the people, and they all agreed that it would be best for them to go back in the opposite direction and find a familiar land where they could dwell. They expressed their concerns about the strange and exotic land they found themselves in, sharing their fears of the large sea right beside them.

Steven could only sigh to himself as he listened to the people. He shook his head in disappointment with the fear that seized their hearts, and desperately tried to urge them to remain optimistic about their new homes.

"Brothers and sisters, we can't now just decide to go back in the same direction in which we came from," he said. "We've traveled for four and a half weeks to finally get to the point where we are today, and yet you are all now deciding to give up because this land isn't what you expected it to be? Where is the courage that you said you would live your lives with?"

"We're not afraid, Mr. Loubre, rather we just want to go and find a land that reminds us of our former homes," responded a young man. "This new place is vastly different from what we were expecting, and I don't think we'll survive here long."

The people agreed with the young man, expressing their desire to turn back and go in the same direction from where they came. But even with the majority of them wishing to go to a different land, a few of them remained optimistic and listened to Steven, among whom was the young boy Peter. They tried convincing the people that staying where they were was the wisest choice to make in protecting themselves from the king and his spies, yet the majority of people stubbornly refused to listen to their pleas.

Eventually, after seeing that the people would be unwilling to waver from their opinion, Steven threw his arms up in the air and conceded to the people's wishes. "Fine, then you rebels. I will let you have it your way," he angrily said. "But understand that if anything bad happens to you, all the blame will rightfully be placed on your heads."

"Nothing bad will happen to us, Mr. Loubre," confidentially remarked a man. "We just want to go back and find a land of hills and valleys and then we will be satisfied. And we will still make sure that we're a good distance from the king's spies so that they are unable to find us."

Steven listened to the people with growing irritation, frustrated that they were refusing to listen to him. Yet he knew that he could do nothing to change their minds, and fearing what they would do to him if he refused to concede to their request, he decided to give up his protests and agreed to let them have their wish.

"Alright then, we will turn around and find a different area of land full of hills and valleys," he said, sighing to himself. "But even as we go back, we must still make sure that we are far enough from the king's spies. We have worked for so long trying to evade them, and it would be terrible of us to hand ourselves right to them."

"Of course, it would be foolish of us to do that," agreed a woman. "We don't want to be captured by the king's spies, we just want to see hills and valleys and live there peacefully."

"Very well then," responded Steven. "I will let you have your way. Since we've already had a long day, let's turn around and travel first thing tomorrow morning."

The people agreed to migrate in the morning, spending the rest of their day on the land by the sea. As they slept that night, the overwhelming majority of them were in a good mood, except for Steven and a small minority of them. Steven was especially anxious about the risk they were now taking, and whether the king's spies would manage to find them. Throughout the night, he spent his time twisting and turning, with worrying thoughts plaguing his mind.

But during that very night amidst his constant worries, Steven fell into a vivid dream. All was clear to him in the dream, and not even the smallest concealed truth was hidden from him. What looked like an elderly man with a dark blue cloak and white beard came forth to him, holding a large white spherical globe in one hand, and a walking stick in the other. He held the large globe out front where Steven could gaze at it in clarity, and as he stared at it, Steven noticed that inside the globe was a fire that seemed to sparkle and reflect a dark blue color. He stared at the strange sight for a moment, with his eyes moving back and forth as he tried capturing every detail he could manage.

Then suddenly, as though a veil had been removed, Steven noticed how the globe changed into a pure white light, and inside the object, he saw various events being played out before his very eyes. As he stared at the images of the globe, the old man began to speak, telling Steven that he and the people should remain where they were. He told them that if they turned back in the opposite direction, all would seem to go well at first, but that it would soon prove to be a deadly mistake of theirs. He ordered Steven to not give in to the people's pressure to turn around, and instead wait patiently wait and stay in the land they were currently in.

Steven became greatly worried and confused at the old man's words, but just before he could ask questions, the old man suddenly vanished from his sight, leaving the globe behind on the ground. The images of the globe ended, and Steven saw that it now burned with a blue fire all around it again. He reached over to pick it up, but just as he touched it, his dream suddenly ended.

Steven woke up, breathing heavily under the dark morning sky. Frantic thoughts ran through his mind, and standing up from where he was lying down, he started walking away from where the rest of the people were sleeping. He came to the seashore, silently listening to the sounds of the waves as he wondered what the meaning of his dream could be. He pondered the question of whether his dream was a warning for him to remain where he was, or if it just happened to be some strange coincidence.

After a half hour of thinking to himself, Steven became convinced that the dream was a warning for him and the people to stay in the land where they were. He started walking back to where the rest of the people were still sleeping in the early morning, ready to tell them all that he had just experienced.

But just as he started walking back, he suddenly felt a hand touch him on the shoulder from behind. Turning around he became terrified as he saw a tall and dark figure standing behind him. The figure quickly shushed him and stood face-to-face with Steven. As Steven stared at him with petrified eyes, he noticed that the figure seemed to be completely masked in black, with even his face hidden from him.

Suddenly there came a blinding light, and Steven quickly covered his eyes to avoid the bright light. Slowly removing his hand from his face, he now got a clear picture of what the figure looked like. Steven lifted his chin to look at the figure, who stood towered above him, standing well over a foot taller. He was completely masked and clothed in black, wearing heavy black armor. He was an imposing figure as he silently stared at Steven, appearing to be a strong soldier of some sort.

Steven stumbled back in fear, as the intimidating figure continued staring at him through his black mask. Questions and worries filled Steven, but he could barely say a word because of the great fear he felt. Eventually, with his entire body shaking, he managed to make out a few words as he stared at the dark figure with wide and terrified eyes.

"Who...who are you?" he asked, stammering.

The figure took a step closer to Steven, who immediately took a step back. The figure laughed to himself as he took a step back himself.

"I am Moneshob," he said in a deep and bold voice that threw Steven off guard for a moment. He paused for a moment, staring at Steven through his black mask before he spoke again.

"Steven, I am here to tell you that you must not stay here in this land," he said. "Instead you must go back on the path from which you came, for I can assure you that all will go well and you will not experience any dangers or threats from the king's spies. If you listen to me, you and the people will find a land of hills and valleys where you will safely dwell in."

Steven stood trembling in the presence of Moneshob, not only struck with fear by his deep voice and intimidating stature, but also that he knew what his name was, and what the purpose of his and the people's migration was.

"How do you know who I am and that I'm here trying to escape from the king?" he asked. "I have never seen you before, yet you know so much about me."

"You do not need to fear, Steven," responded Moneshob, perceiving the concern on Steven's face. "You may not know how I know you, but what I can assure you is that you can trust me. And when I say that you must go back in the same direction from where you came, you can rest assured knowing that I am full of wisdom far beyond what you could ever contain."

Fear and wonder fell upon Steven as a vast shadow, and he stood in awe of this formidable figure. But as he looked at Moneshob, more questions ran through his mind which he desired answers for.

"But I had a dream just now," he remarked. "And in the dream, an old man told me of all the terrible things that would happen if I left this place. Why did the dream have a contradictory opinion to that of yours?"

Moneshob suddenly laughed hysterically to himself, with a shrill sound coming forth from his throat. Steven's legs shook with fear as he stared at him in confusion.

"Those are only fallacies, Steven," said Moneshob. "Dreams can be deceitful at times, and they are usually the works of your imagination. You must not let your dreams impact you from making bold decisions, Steven. And just for your protection, I will personally lead you and the people back from where you came from, and I will direct you to a land of hills and valleys to ensure your satisfaction and safety."

Even as he listened to Moneshob, Steven could feel a tingling sensation of confidence entering his bones. Though he remained fearful and skeptical of the figure, he now stood uprightly and no longer trembled in his presence. He dwelled on his words for a moment, processing what it would be like for him to help him and the people in their journey. But even as he thought these things, doubt ran through his mind about whether the figure could be trusted.

"I do feel better just by listening to you," he eventually said. "But I am still having a difficult time believing all that you are telling me. Unless you prove yourself to me, then I might just have to stay here in this land."

Moneshob paused for a moment, staring at Steven and processing his words. Steven looked back at Moneshob, with newfound fear covering his face, as he started worrying that he had angered him. But just as he thought of apologizing to Moneshob, the figure suddenly spoke.

"That's fine, Steven," he said, speaking slowly and then falling silent for a moment once again.

Steven's face twisted with confusion at what Moneshob had meant. The dark figure continued staring at him, as though he was waiting for Steven to respond to him. Steven inched his way closer to Moneshob, ready to ask him what he truly meant.

But just as he was about to question him, Moneshob suddenly lifted his hand to the sky, and as he blinked, he saw a black horse standing beside Moneshob. The horse was incredibly large, far bigger than any mere horse he had ever seen, and it was covered in black armor, appearing to have been used in battle.

Steven stood stunned at the sudden sight that appeared before him but found no strength to speak or ask questions. As he silently stared at the black horse, Moneshob suddenly jumped onto it and unsheathed a large sword that had been hidden in his side.

As he lifted the sword to the sky, Steven beheld that it started to glow with a burning fire. He nearly collapsed to the ground as his knees violently trembled at the sight, and his mouth dropped to the ground. As Moneshob spurred his horse into action, it suddenly neighed loudly, and he started dangling his flaming word in the air. Great terror fell upon Steven at this sight, and as he stared at him, a sudden flash came before him where he beheld Moneshob as a mighty soldier king, leading a vast army of his into battle.

But just as quickly as he saw Moneshob in his full might, the black figure just as quickly stepped off his horse and sheathed his flaming sword back into his side. With that, the large black horse vanished from sight, and Steven stood as still as a statue, full of disbelief at all that he had just witnessed.

Moneshob stepped closer to Steven, towering over the ordinary man. "Now do you believe what I'm saying?" he asked.

Even as Moneshob directed a question to him, Steven didn't move an inch, instead continuing to stare at the black figure without a blink of an eye. Yet as he continued to stare at Moneshob with terror and confusion, a sudden change fell upon him. He felt a tugging in his heart and at that moment, all thoughts of fear were suddenly erased from his memory. He now looked at Moneshob differently, picturing him as a wise and mighty person who could be trusted.

"Yes, I believe you," he eventually said, with a strange sense of assurance coming upon his heart and mind. "I am at your command. Show me how you want me to lead these great people."

Moneshob took a step back. "Good, I'm glad that you trust me," he said. "If you follow me, I will protect and satisfy your and the people's desires."

"I trust you," responded Steven, gazing at Moneshob in admiration. "Thank you for the confidence with which you've filled my heart. I can't wait to share with the people my encounter with you, once they all wake up."

"Good," said Moneshob. "Once they wake up, come back here so that I can walk with you as I approach them."

Steven agreed to all that Moneshob said, and thanked him many times for the help that he offered him. He walked back to where the rest of the people were, lying on the ground to go back to sleep. He couldn't believe what he had just witnessed and pinched himself many times to ensure that he wasn't dreaming. But sure enough, what he had just experienced was very much real.

He slept peacefully for the rest of that early morning and woke up at the first rising of the dawn. Many of the people stood up, ready to continue their travels in the opposite direction. But before they could start going, Steven quickly stopped them, telling them that he had just had a remarkable encounter with a figure clothed and masked in black. He told them in great confidence that the figure would help lead and guide them in their travels and protect them from any potential dangers along the way.

Yet as he shared this with the people, many of them remained suspicious of the figure that Steven talked about. "Are you sure that this man is not a spy?" asked a man. "What if he's deceiving you to trap us here?"

"I promise you that he's not deceiving us," said Steven with complete assurance. "He can be trusted. When I first saw him, I trembled in terror at his intimidating presence, but as I listened to his words, I suddenly felt at ease and grew in confidence that he would help and protect us. With him leading us, we will be able to rest assured that he will guide us into safety."

The people listened to Steven with fascination, but with suspicion as well over the mysterious figure. They expressed their desire to see him for themselves so that they would feel the same confidence that Steven did.

And so Steven urged them on to meet the figure for themselves. "Follow me then, and you'll see him with your own eyes," he said, waving them on to follow him.

So the people followed Steven as he led them to the sandy coast by the sea, and there standing in the same spot where Steven met him was Moneshob. He stood as still as a statue with his back turned from Steven and the people, watching the waves of the sea. The people gazed at him in both wonder and fear, because of his imposing stature and his black clothing from head to toe.

Steven pointed toward the figure. "Here is the man that will lead us in the right direction into a land full of hills and valleys," he said

Suddenly Moneshob turned, facing Steven and the people. The people gazed at him in wonder, petrified of his heavy black armor and the black mask that covered his face.

"There is no need to fear him," continued Steven "His name is Moneshob, and I am confident in saying that we can all trust him as a friend and leader of our group. And not only will he guide us into safety, but he will also offer us great protection. As I was speaking to him this morning, a large black horse and a flaming sword that he wielded suddenly appeared before my very eyes! I am sure that he will use these weapons if we are ever in danger."

The people gasped in astonishment at Steven's words, and to their amazement, they found that their fears of him suddenly vanished. They now found themselves staring at him in wonder and admiration, wishing to surrender themselves to his guidance and protection.

They expressed their desire to see what Steven had witnessed himself. "We want to see this for ourselves!" they all said. "Show us your black horse and flaming sword!"

All eyes became fixed on Moneshob as the people eagerly awaited a response from him. Immediately after expressing their wish, Moneshob lifted his hand to the sky, and appearing before their eyes was a large black horse. They all gasped in shock, but their mouths dropped to the ground when they watched him unsheath the sharp flaming sword from his side. But as quickly as he had made the horse and sword appear, Moneshob placed his hand down from the sky, and with that, the horse and sword disappeared.

The people stood silently, filled with both terror and awe at the sight. But even as they felt fear at that moment, a wind of peace passed through their midst, and their hearts and minds were suddenly filled with confidence in Moneshob. They sprang to life with awe-inspiring looks covering their faces.

"I trust in you," remarked a man, gazing at Moneshob with newfound wonder. "All that you have revealed to us, is enough for me to place my hope in you."

The people agreed with the man, expressing the confidence that they now felt in the presence of Moneshob. They urged him to lead them on their journey and to protect them from any potential foes.

Moneshob stood motionless as the people beckoned for him to take control of their situation, not even speaking a single word to them. But all the more, the people continued urging him to help them in their situation, with many even begging him to become their new leader. Then, amidst their talking and requesting, the people suddenly broke out into a loud chant of celebration, dancing with joy as they lifted their collective voices together:

We celebrate all we have seen with our eyes,
For Moneshob will lead us on the way to go!
Dark and black is his guise,
But his sword shall protect us with a single blow!

Black is his horse and flaming is his weapon,
Black is his raiment, and tall is his height.
Though his unseen face is a strange sight to mention,
His presence shall lead us to the light.

Today we shall walk in full confidence,
While our enemies tremble before his sight!
For his wonders have given us evidence,
Of why we can trust in his great might!

The people roared in collective adoration of Moeshob, as he stood watching them in silence. They continued singing and dancing for some time before Moneshob suddenly placed out his hand in a gesture telling them to stop. They all froze, and patiently awaited the words that Moneshob would share with them.

"Your words of praise for me are admirable," he said. A vast silence fell upon the people as they stood entranced by his deep and commanding voice. "I see that you trust me to lead you into a land of hills and valleys. But the next step you must be willing to take if you wish to see your dreams come true is to follow and obey me. Will you heed my voice and follow me in every step I lead you?"

"Yes, we will!" declared the people in unison. "We will follow you until we reach our destination!"

Moneshob stood silently, processing the people's declaration. "Good," he said. "Now that you are ready to entrust yourselves under my hand, I can now reveal to you which paths I intend to guide you through. You do not know this, but there is a shortcut to the east that will take you to the land in which you are seeking in a short time. And if you listen to my voice, you will remain a good and safe distance away from your enemies, under my close protection. But will you obey me in all I tell you to do?"

"Of course, we will obey you!" responded a man from the crowd of people. "You've performed great wonders in our sight! It would be foolish of us to disobey you!"

"Good, all that you say is true," said Moneshob, placing his hand on his chin. "Now that you have all agreed to heed my voice, I will now lead you in departing from where you currently are and start traveling eastward. Are you all ready to start moving?"

"Yes we are all ready to begin moving," responded Steven, who found himself completely convinced by Moneshob along with the people.

"Well let us travel then," said Moneshob, responding to Steven and the people's resounding answer. "We don't have any time to waste, so let's start moving toward your final destination."

And so in the early morning hours of the day, the people hastily and eagerly gathered their many possessions and started following Moneshob along the path away from the coast. Steven remained close behind Moneshob but made sure that he didn't overtake him. He breathed a sigh of relief that he didn't have to lead the people anymore and thanked Moneshob for lifting the burden of guiding the great number of people off of his shoulders.

He came to Moneshob's side and whispered into his ear. "I would just like to thank you for leading these people," he said. "These people have exhausted me with all their complaining and bickering, but you've seemed to bring a halt to that."

Moneshob turned toward Steven, staring longingly at him for a moment. "I know that you've been through a lot, Steven," he eventually said. "And I can see the relief that covers your face. But you must continue to understand and trust that is for your good that you let me lead these people. The people have made wise decisions in heeding my advice and letting me lead them. You must continue to do the same, and not let your doubts or other outside forces change that."

Even as he spoke, Steven sensed the desperate urging that filled Moneshob's voice as he tried convincing Steven never to stop trusting in him. And so Steven took his words to heart and continued to grow in his trust for Moneshob.

As Moneshob continued leading the people, they soon arrived at an area of grasslands filled with many trees and bushes, where the people looked all around at the unfamiliar place. They inhaled the fresh and exotic air, making their way through the paths of the grassland, and silently observing the strange trees and bushes that were on the sides around them. A chilly gushing wind suddenly came upon them, as the sun hid its bright light just behind the clouds in the sky. They continued for another couple of hours through the vast grassland, curiously staring at the sights around them as Moneshob continued leading them along the path.

Eventually, they came to a sudden halt as the people soon learned that the path they were walking on would soon be separating into two different paths. Staring at the different paths, they found themselves in a dilemma in deciding which way to go, as both paths looked directly identical to each other. Much arguing and bickering soon ensued amongst the people as they debated where they should go.

"We should go on the path to the right," argued a young man. "Besides we all know how the old saying goes: '*To go right is to go the right way, but to go left is to go the wrong way.*' It's obvious that going to the right is usually the best choice to make, and so we should do the same as well."

Many people agreed with the man, but others expressed their disagreement. "No, we must not choose to go on the path to the right," remarked another man. "Have you not realized now that that old saying is one that the kings of Fozturia have used for many long years? Even Maguspra has uttered those words. Perhaps the king's spies are waiting for us to fall into that trap so that they can capture us. I think we should go onto the left path instead."

Some of the people nodded their heads in agreement with the man, thinking deeply about all that he said. Yet a sharp divide remained among the people as they continued arguing their cases of why they should go right or left. Steven and Moneshob shook their heads as the quarreling when on for many long minutes and started thinking of stepping in between the people before Peter suddenly managed to get all of the people's attention.

"Let's stop with all of the arguings," he said. "And since we can't seem to agree as to which way we should go, why don't we let Mr. Loubre or Moneshob have the final say?"

"That's a fantastic idea, young man," responded a woman, with many more of the people expressing their agreement with Peter's words.

Convinced by the people's compliance with his suggestion, Peter directed his attention to Steven and Moneshob. "So what direction do you two think we should go?" he asked.

Steven looked up at Moneshob, who remained standing silently. "I have my own opinions, but I think it will be best if I let Moneshob have the final say," he said. "After all, he is the wisest man that we have in this group of people, and he is the one who has been directing us in these past couple of hours."

The people agreed with Steven and humbly decided to let Moneshob have the final say in the decision they would make. And so they all turned their attention toward him, hesitantly waiting for his answer.

For a moment, Moneshob continued to stand silently among the people, staring at the many faces that gazed upon his imposing stature. But after a brief pause, he opened his mouth and announced where he would next them in their journey.

"Men and women, I see that you all are ready to trust me with your very lives," he said, gazing upon them with great pride in his heart. "And so I can boldly tell you that going on the path to the left will be in our best interest. If you went right, you would encounter wild animals and perilous paths, but going left will be a smooth journey."

Many of the people gasped in shock as soon as Moneshob uttered those words, while others started applauding him. Steven stood flabbergasted by his answer, and for a sudden moment felt as though it would be a bad idea to go on the left path. But he trusted Moneshob's leadership, though some of the people continued to express their doubts.

"Alright then, we shall go on the left path to continue in our journey," Steven said eventually. "We have already seen how much he has proven his leadership to us, so why should we not trust in his word? He knows what's best for us, and so we should continue to obey him, just as he has told us to."

At once the people who had expressed their worries ceased their arguing and stood convinced by all that Steven said. All of them agreed to follow Moneshob's direction, with growing confidence lighting up their faces. Assured by the people's response, Moneshob started walking onto the path to the left, and the people instantly followed in his guidance.

The path they journeyed on felt flat and smooth, and looks of joy covered their people's faces as their hearts continued warming to Moneshob's direction over their lives. The sun shone brightly just behind the clouds, and the people continued to gaze in wonder at the many trees and bushes that were around them. The leaves growing on the trees were unlike everything they had ever seen, as they were spiky and long. Yet they found them far more splendid than any of the trees that they had seen in their former homes.

Eventually, after an hour of walking along the path, the people grew tired, and listening to their grumblings of exhaustion, Moneshob led them to a small pond where they could fill their bottles with water and rest for some time. They rested for some time, but the sun began to hide behind the clouds and a chilly wind breezed throughout the air. They started complaining about how cold they were and how miserable they felt.

Steven sighed to himself and grew frustrated with the people. "When will you learn to stop complaining?" he asked. "Not everything is going to go your way. Just look around at this rich area of land with all of its trees and bushes, and at this pond full of fresh water. Moneshob is leading us into a rich land of hills and valleys, and so we have no right to start complaining."

The people became silent and ceased their talks of grumbling and complaining. Yet their faces were still covered in unhappiness, which Moneshob silently observed.

"Don't worry, Steven," he suddenly said. "The people will soon learn to trust in me no matter what they experience. Besides, this cold wind isn't very pleasant. You all just stay here and I'll find go into the trees and bushes to find some sticks, leaves, and stones to make a large fire to warm ourselves up. But don't come looking for me, just wait for me patiently."

Moneshob stood up and disappeared from the people's sight as he walked through a bushy area surrounded by tall trees. Smiles of relief covered the people's faces, and they thanked Moneshob within their hearts many times. They waited for a few minutes before they found him walking forth to them, carrying several sticks, leaves, and stones.

Yet as they looked closer, their eyes widened with both astonishment and horror as they noticed a strange-looking creature that walked by Moneshob's side. From a far distance, they could only see the bottom of the creature's body which to their shock was that of a giant green snake. They couldn't even see the head of the snake as even it towered over Moneshob's imposing stature.

The people gathered around together to pay closer attention to this strange sight and wondered what a snake could be doing walking with Moneshob. But as the snake slithered closer to them, the people nearly collapsed to the ground in horror as they saw a full picture of what it was. They suddenly saw its upper body and head, and to their bewilderment, they discovered that it had the body and face of a woman. Gazing at the strange sight, they observed the face and upper body of the woman. They saw that she had long silver hair which came down to the side of her sparkling silver dress, and they couldn't help but gaze at her glowing blue eyes that shined like blue stars from the far distance.

They all stood in terror at the bizarre creature that approached them, frightened by the bottom half of her body but equally entranced by the beauty of her face and dress. Some of them came running forth to the creature, full of questions for her and Moneshob.

Among the crowd of rushing people sprinting through the woods, was Steven as his eyes remained fixed on the creature by Moneshob's side. As they came within a short distance of Moneshob and the creature, the people suddenly stopped dead in their tracks, gazing up at the woman in fear of her colossal size. They stood speechless in front of her, and all of their attention was drawn away from Moneshob as they stared at her.

"Who...who are you?" asked Steven, managing to utter a few stammering words as he stood in fear at the presence of the creature.

For a moment, the creature stared at Steven with piercing eyes, as though she was examining every thought that filled his heart and mind. And then she suddenly spoke, in a soft yet authoritative voice.

"Who am I?" she said, as though she were questioning herself. "I have many titles that belong to me, Steven. I am the Queen of the Hzarves, and I hold rightful dominion over all the lands of the east. How you do not know me is beyond my understanding, but perhaps today you will learn to trust in my power, just as you have full confidence in Moneshob.

Steven and the people trembled in the presence of the creature, full of fear as they gazed into her discerning eyes. She stared at them for a while, as though disappointment filled her heart that they didn't know who she was. All remained silent, before speaking in a low voice, Moneshob suddenly began to silently murmur a few words. Yet as the people heard him, his voice grew louder. Silently listening to him, the people suddenly perceived that he was singing a song of remembrance for the creature that stood before them:

Londriel is the queen of the far East.
But has left her realm of rest,
To set out on a quest,
And spread her presence to the West.

Let none doubt her power,
Nor mistake that she is a queen,
For her servants were awakened by their founder,
And trained to become keen.

Let the queen of the Hzarves protect you,
For her servants trust in her,
As one speaking words more true,
Rather than one whose sight begins to blur.

A sudden revelation as it seemed fell on the people as they listened to the words that came forth from Moneshob's mouth. Their minds were instantly transformed and they suddenly felt a deep urging that the strange creature named Londriel was one who they could trust as a leader along with Moneshob.

Seeing the change in the people's attitude toward the creature, Moneshob continued to urge them to trust in her. "Londriel is a great light who can protect you from the dangers that you may face during the night," he said. "Not only that, but her mighty presence alone can illuminate a bright light for you in the dark so that you know where you came from and where you are going. She will give you light in the darkness of your journey, so I hope you will all learn to trust in her just as you trust in me."

Gazing at Londriel, the people felt as though their hearts warmed to her presence and they continued to grow in their respect and trust for her. Among them was Steven, whose heart was glad that he and the people would receive even more help for their journey.

He turned his attention toward Londriel, smiling and speaking to her. "Londriel, I along with this great group of people agree to let you guide us along the path of our journey alongside Moneshob," he said. "And if we do not fail in doubting your power, I ask for you to show us how we should go, just as Moneshob has done for us."

Londriel stared at Steven for a moment, saying nothing and suddenly turning away from him. But even as she turned away, Steven could see the slightest hint of a smile on the corner of her mouth.

Moneshob walked alongside Londriel as she slithered back to where the rest of the people were, with Steven and the others following the two of them. As Moneshob and Londriel came near to the other people who had stayed behind, astonished and frightened looks covered their faces at the sight of Londriel, with many of them slowly backing away from her presence. But their fears were quickly subsided by Steven and many of the people's explanations on how Londriel would be a great help and leader for them just like Moneshob. And so they all breathed sighs of relief that Londriel could be trusted, even though they still viewed her as a strange and fearsome creature.

Placing the sticks, leaves, and stones that he had gathered in a large pile, Moneshob started a large fire for all the people to gather around and warm themselves. For many long minutes, the people enjoyed themselves as they huddled by each other's side; joking, laughing, and conversing about all sorts of things that were on their minds. Joyful looks covered their faces, as they were glad to finally have some rest after a long and tiring day.

But amidst their talking, Moneshob and Londriel sat motionless among them, instead minding their own business and staring at the large fire. Steven tapped Moneshob on the shoulder but ignored Londriel, fearing the piercing look that she gave him. But he felt confident in talking with Moneshob and was full of questions for him, many of which he wondered from the first moment he met him. Once Momeshob turned toward him, he gazed at him for a moment with widened eyes of wonder before asking his questions.

"Moneshob, who exactly are you and where do you come from?" he asked. "And why are you completely covered in black from head to toe? I mean, I don't even know what you look like either because of your mask, yet you've been such a great help to us. I think it would be helpful if I and all the people knew a little more about you."

Moneshob stared at Steven for a moment, sighing to himself before answering him. "Your curiosity is a sight to behold, Steven," he said. "But some things are meant to remain secret. Perhaps when I lead you safely to your homes I might share with you more things about me. But you must first trust in me, Steven. Do you not see all the good that I have brought to you and these people? Do you still trust me even though you do not know what I look like?"

Steven's face was covered in anxiety as he sat speechless in front of Moneshob. He thought of how he would respond to him, before finally mustering the courage to respond to him. "I trust in you, sir," he eventually said. He paused for a moment before looking up again at Moneshob with a renewed set of curious eyes. "But I'm still really interested in knowing more about you and having a better understanding of who you truly are. Would you at least tell us where you are from and how you found us here?"

Steven eagerly awaited a response from Moneshob, but he remained silent. Londriel stared at Steven with piercing eyes, making him stare toward the ground in embarrassment. Steven then looked up, wishing to apologize to Moneshob for his foolish questions as he thought they were, but just as he was about to speak, Moneshob suddenly lifted his hand, preventing him from speaking.

Steven stared at Moneshob in wonder, and to his surprise, he spoke to him. "Well, Steven, I must say that your persistence is very interesting," he said. "And because of that, I will reward your persistence and tell you a few things about me, though I will still not reveal anything specific to you."

Steven breathed a sigh of relief, feeling as though a great weight of shame had suddenly been lifted from his shoulders. He and the people drew closer to Moneshob, waiting patiently for all that he would say.

After a long silence, Moneshob finally told the people more about him. "All of you dwell in the land of the Earth," he said. "But I come from another land, one that is close to your own yet farther than you could ever get to. The reason why I have come to you is that I have seen how much you all have suffered, as sheep without a shepherd, and I have to help guide you to your homes. Though I do not doubt Steven's leadership of these great people, you must also understand that it will take much more for you to arrive at your new homes in safety. Thus I came from my home to the west, and have also brought Londriel from her land to the east to help lead and protect you along the path you should go on. We have come to bring goodness and guidance to you all so that you will be safe and succeed in arriving in your new homes."

The people sat silently in response to Moneshob, amazed by the revelation that he and even Londriel came from another land other than the Earth. They were filled with even more questions and started directing them toward Moneshob.

"Tell us Moneshob, what is your home like?" asked a man, filled with great wonder. "Are the animals there still like those on the Earth, and what about the humans? Are there more humans that live there than we have ever before seen? How can we even be sure that you are a human and not some other creature."

The people gasped in astonishment at the man's last question and started talking among themselves if Moneshob even looked like them behind his mask. But they quickly quieted down once Moneshob and Londriel ordered them to be silent.

"I see that you all are full of many questions, but it is not the appointed time yet to answer all of your questions," responded Moneshob. "I have come to guide you to your new homes, and perhaps once I lead you there, then I can reveal more to you about myself and my land. But for now, you must remain content with what you currently know about me."

With that, no more questions filled the people's minds as they sat silently by each other, satisfied by all Moneshob had told them. They spent the rest of their time sitting quietly by the large fire, not daring to look at Moneshob or Londriel.

As the sky grew dark, the people stood up from where they were seated and continued their migration through the vast area of grasslands. In time the sky became pitch black during the night and their sight became dim, but just as they thought about complaining, Londriel's silver dress suddenly illuminated the night sky as the bright moon shone down upon her. The people trembled in awe at the sight, seeing Londriel manifested to them in such a way that they hadn't seen in her all day. While staring at her in wonder, they were suddenly reminded of Moneshob's words about her; how she was a great light that would help protect and guide them during the night.

For the rest of the night, as they followed Londriel's bright light and presence, they found themselves gazing at her in growing admiration in the same way that they gazed at Moneshob. Fear for her no longer consumed them as they grew increasingly confident in her guidance over their lives. After a couple of hours of walking through the dark, Londriel and Moneshob stopped by a sheltered place in the grassland where they and the people would sleep for the night. They all slept peacefully that night, with not even the slightest sound of an animal affecting their rest.

The next few days went, for the most part, the same way, as Moneshob and Londriel continued directing the people through the wide area of grasslands. As they journeyed, made their way away from the flat grasslands, and into a region of valleys, where in the far distance ahead of them they could faintly see the sight of green rolling hills. They were led toward this direction and were filled with wonder at what magnificent area of land lay before them.

On the morning of the fifth day since Moneshob and Londriel had led them, the people woke up to the bright sun shining on them. They had journeyed through a forested area during the previous day and rested for the evening there where they now found themselves gathered together. Yawning and stretching as they stood up, they gazed into the far distance filled with hills and valleys and staring longingly at the area of land ahead of them, they could also faintly see a cliff that hung just above a long river.

Steven went out to see the delightful sight for himself, going into a distance far away from the rest of the people's sight. He gazed in growing wonder at the scenery, imagining what his new home would look like. A calming and peaceful wind fell on him, as he closed his eyes for a few minutes, enjoying the warm sun and assuring himself that Moneshob and Londriel were leading him and the people in the right direction.

After some time had passed and feeling a renewed sense of confidence, Steven started to walk back toward the people, wishing to share with them the great peace that he felt at the moment by himself. But just as he started walking back, two men suddenly appeared before him, standing in front of him and nearly causing him to bump into them. Shock and fear filled Steven's heart at the sight of the two men, who both had long white beards and held walking sticks. But as he started to stare closely at them, he suddenly began to recognize one of them.

Trembling in their presence, Steven managed to speak to them, first directing his attention to the familiar-looking man. "I think that I've seen you before," he said, pointing toward the old man on the right. He was clothed in a dark blue cloak and had a long white beard. He thought to himself for a moment, before he suddenly remembered where he had seen the old man before. "Yes, I know where I've seen you before. You are the same man who I saw yesterday morning in my dream. Who are you and who is this other man standing to your left?"

The old man on the right inched his way closer to Steven, still clothed in the same dark blue cloak that Steven had seen him wearing in his dream. "Steven, you did indeed see me in the dream you had yesterday morning. My name is Mataput, and I came to you in that dream to warn you to stay where you were, and not go back in the same direction where you came from. Yet you refused to listen to my warning and listened to Moneshob, who has deceived you and all of the people."

A sharp sting as it felt inflicted Steven with shock, and his mouth dropped to the ground in disbelief at what Mataput had told him. But amidst his shock, his face suddenly changed and he became defensive of Moneshob.

"I don't think that you know what you're talking about," he said, laughing at Mataput and the other old man. "Moneshob is helping us and has given us a renewed sense of confidence in him. Even Londriel has proven to be a great help and leader for us as well, so how could we possibly betray them and decide not to follow them anymore?"

Mataput remained silent, but the other old man now walked closer to Steven. Steven stared at him in curiosity, observing the brown cloak and tall pointed brown hat he wore, and the brown walking stick that he held in his right hand.

He spoke to Steven. "Steven, I did not appear to you in the dream you had, but I can assure you that all that Mataout has told you is true," he said. "My name is Orieant, and along with Mataput we have both seen and observed how Moneshob and Londriel have tried convincing you and the people to trust in them. And though it is tempting to listen to their voices, Mataput and I are urging you today to stop trusting in them. I promise you that if you continue to let them lead you, they will direct you into the path of destruction, and there will be no escape for you. They are not leading you eastward into a land of hills and valleys, but northward, in the direction of the cliff that you have seen to destroy you and all the people with you."

Steven stared at Orieant with horror and confusion. But as he processed his words, his face soon grew hard with suspicion at the two old men. "And why should trust what you two are telling me?" he asked. "How exactly do you know that Moneshob and Londriel have malicious intentions and are desiring to destroy me and the people?"

The two elderly men looked intently at Steven for a moment, before Mataput responded to him. "Steven, there are many things hidden from you that must be uncovered now," he said. "All that Orieant and I wish to tell you are things that no man or woman has ever heard before on the face of the Earth. What we will tell you will be hard for you to believe, but is the truth nonetheless. We need you to listen to us with an open mind so that you and the people can be protected from the danger Moneshob and Londriel are leading you into.

Steven sighed to himself and crossed his arms. "Alright then, if what you want to tell me is so serious, then go ahead," he said. "I want to know why you two are so insistent on making me change my mind about them."

The two old men looked at each other, before Orieant nodded his head toward Mataput, assuring him all he would say would be in Steven's best interest. And so with a deep breath, Mataput began to explain to Steven all that he and Orieant had wanted to speak to him about.

"Steven, you must understand that Moneshob is an evil creature called a wuzlir," he said. "Londriel is also an evil and strange creature, but Orieant and I will wait before we share more about her. But what you need to know is that Moneshob serves an evil Dark Lord named Natugura, who has brought evil and destruction to the Earth for thousands of years. But before all of this, there was a time on the Earth when there was absolute perfection where not even death, evil, pain, or suffering was inflicted on its inhabitants. And it wasn't just in this land only, for you must understand that many other lands exist outside of the land of the Earth, and they too once existed in perfection. All of the creatures of these lands lived with each other in perfect harmony and peace, and I with Orieant and Natugura also lived in harmony and joy together. Yet we didn't dwell or even exist within the lands of this world for we were once the great spirit beings of Jangart, the high and mighty being who created this entire world. Within his created world, he fashioned eight individual and different lands each with its unique creatures and ways of life, to reflect his very glory.

"Meanwhile, myself, Orieant, and Natugura, dwelled outside of Jangart's created world, in a place called Starlight where we served and dwelled in peace with Jangart, working together and enjoying the fruit of his glory. However, as time progressed Orieant and I started to notice a change in Natugura. His countenance slowly changed and his spirit of light grew darker, as he became more envious of Jangart, even beginning to blame him rather than thank him for his service to him. And it came to the point that Natugura planned to lead a great rebellion against Jangart, and he even tried to sway us to join him in his pursuit. But we resisted him, sensing the lies and evil that consumed his heart. Yet he was still able to convince some of Jangart's created creatures to join him in his rebellion, and they were the gamdars, the wisest and most powerful of all of Jangart's created creatures. But most of the gamdars managed to reject Natugura's cunningness, with only a minority of them falling for his shadow of evil.

"And so with the gamdars he had deceived, Natugura mounted a great war against me, Orieant, but most importantly, Jangart as his heart burned with passion to usurp him of his authority and take his place as the one holding the entire world in his hands. But his plan failed as he and the deceived gamdars stood no chance against the might of Jangart, yet even in his defeat, Natugura managed to break the one commandment of Jangart, a commandment we have since forgotten of what it was. But once he did commit this terrible act of destruction, a great and terrible black wind full of evil and temptation was suddenly released throughout the air. The wind had a mind of its own, and with its presence combined with Natugura's wickedness, it brought evil, disaster, and death to all of the lands of the world that it spread to. Because of this, Jangart had no choice but to banish Natugura and his gamdars from his presence as they were sent flying down at terrible speed.

"Now the wind came to all eight of the lands of the world, and the creatures of those lands either had the choice to accept the wind and indulge in its evil, or to reject it and remain pure. Unfortunately, not all of the creatures of these lands passed the great test, as half of them decided to accept the wind with its evil, and the other half rejected it. Among those who fell to the shadow of the wind, were the humans of the Earth, and from that day four of the lands of Jangart's created world fell to evil and corruption, while the other four lands remained free from its presence, continuing to dwell in freedom and perfection. As they were sent flying down, Natugura and his gamdars landed in a land which they named Nangorid, 'The Key of the World' which Jangart had created specifically for them to dwell in. Thus, Jangart had now created the ninth and final land of the world, with five now being corrupted, and four remaining non-corrupted.

"Once landed in Nangorid, Natugura noticed how his gamdars had become hideous and vile beings, no longer the noble and beautiful creatures they once were. And so he renamed them the wuzlirs and gave them black armor and black masks to hide their ugliness. From that day forth, they became his servants and immediately began building strong fortresses and iron cities to populate their new homes. One such building of theirs would be a vast and impenetrable black tower of iron that they named Wuzinch Torgol, and it would be where Natugura would dwell from that day forth. And so from his Black Tower, Natugura began working on controlling the many other creatures of the lands that had fallen for the wind and its evil, and almost all of them became his servants.

"Yet, he found himself unable to control the humans of the Earth, for, unlike the other corrupted creatures of the world, they can either choose to do good or to do evil. They were made unaware of the other lands that existed outside of their own, or the presence of Jangart and Natugura. And so for thousands of years, Natugura has desired to make the humans of the Earth aware of his presence and power, in the hopes that he can completely corrupt them so that they have no other choice but to serve him and reject doing good.

"But his plans have not prevailed, and seeing the justice and righteousness that you have desired to bring to your people since fleeing from King Maguspra of Fozturia, Orieant and I have decided to give you this revelation. Steven, you are the first human to have ever discovered this revelation from us, and it is for your benefit that you listen to us and reject Moneshob's leading of the people. It is for this reason that Natugura sent Moneshob, the leader of the army of the wuzlirs and a very cunning and imposing creature, to try and lead you astray. He is merely a trap sent by Natugura to destroy you all and to try and corrupt the hearts of men to become completely surrendered and devoted to him. And if Natugura succeeds in corrupting the humans of the Earth, he believes that he will also be able to corrupt the non-corrupted creatures of the free lands of the world. You must heed our warning Steven, and send the people away from Moneshob. But it doesn't end there, as Orieant and I have even more important matters to share with you and the people, but you must first lead them in the opposite direction toward the coast and wait for us there so that we can bring more important revelations to you."

With that, Mataput ceased speaking, leaving Steven with wide eyes and a mouth dropped to the ground in shock at everything he had heard. He shook his head in astonishment, wondering whether Mataput's warnings and revelations of the Dark Lord and the many corrupted and non-corrupted lands of the world were true. But after much thinking, his face grew hard, and as he stared at Mataput and Orieant, he began to look at them with contempt, refusing to believe everything that had been revealed to him.

"None of this can be true," he eventually said. "Moneshob has been such an incredible help to us, and there is no way that your long tale is factual. How can so many other lands exist outside of our own, besides, if there ever was a Dark Lord who brought evil and suffering to this world, then I'm sure that I would have known about it from my birth."

The two elderly men shook their heads in disappointment at Steven's response, but Orieant persisted in trying to change his mind. "Steven, sometimes the truth is harder to believe than a lie," he said. "But you must believe us because this is not just some creative tale of our imagination, but is the reality of what this entire world is like. And if you are not careful, Natugura will catch you off guard for he is planning on doing something extremely dangerous to you and to the entire land of the Earth. And he is using Moneshob to at least fulfill the first part of his wicked schemes."

The two men hoped that this would convince Steven to heed their warning, but he instead stepped back from them and crossed his arms. "If all of this is true, then why are you only telling me about this?" he asked, growing in suspicion and fear toward the old men. "Why not tell someone else about this, or even tell a whole group of people? Do you not know that humans have been living on the Earth for thousands of years? Why then have you waited all this time to only share this now with me of all people?"

The two men pondered to themselves for a moment of Steven's questions, before Orieant again responded to him.

"We have waited all this time because it was not yet the appointed time to share this with anyone," he said. "Mataput and I waited for a group of humans who could help change their homes, yet we deemed that no one's hearts were in the right place to depart from their corrupted ways. But you, Steven, have been chosen by Jangart to be a light to the other kingdoms and peoples of the Earth. We have seen how you and the people following you have fled from the King of Fozturia, wishing to live free lives marked with justice and peace. And with this understanding, Jangart has now finally seen a group of people on the Earth who can model to the other peoples of the Earth how to live their own lives. And he wants you to lead your people in righteousness so that the other kings of the Earth will lead their people in the same way. The Earth can be completely changed through you, Steven, you only need to trust in what we say, and turn away from Moneshob in the opposite direction with the people before we share more things with you and the people."

For a moment, Steven dwelled on Orieant's words, thinking of what his life and the people's lives would be like if he lead them in truth and righteousness. He imagined how vastly different the Earth would become, and if all wars would finally cease as kings learned to change their way of ruling. Yet even as he pondered on all this, he laughed silently to himself, refusing to believe that the many kings of the Earth, both good and evil, would be willing to change their ways just because of some former shepherd who demonstrated how to lead a people properly. He chuckled to himself at the prospect of such a vast world with many different lands even existing.

And so Steven shut his ears to what the old men had told him, deciding to continue following Moneshob. "You two are speaking lies to me," he said, glaring at them with intense eyes. "And I can now see that you're only trying to discourage me from trusting in Moneshob, a trustworthy man who has proven to be a great leader for myself and the people. I have had enough of listening to your long stories. Maybe you can share it with someone else who is gullible enough to believe in what you say. In the meantime, it was good talking with you, but I hope I never have to deal with you two again. Goodbye!"

With that, Steven turned his back on the old men and began walking away from their presence, while they only watched dismally as he walked back toward the people, sighing to themselves before they too turned away.

While laughing to himself as he walked back toward the people, Steven found both Moneshob and Londriel ready to greet him. "Good morning, Mr. Loubre," he said, in an excited mood. "While you were absent, I was sharing with the people that today will be a big day that you all will never forget."

"Yes, and I also shared that you and the people are very close to arriving at your new homes," chimed in Londriel, with a faint smile on her face. "And I can't wait to see what your reactions will be like."

"I can only imagine the joy I will feel," said Steven. "The joy of finally being able to dwell in peace and security, free from the wrath of Maguspra and the fear of his spies constantly tracking our every move. I'm ready to see what our new homes will be like."

The people chatted among themselves for a while, enjoying the warmness of the sun as its light shone throughout the rich forests, giving the trees a golden color in certain patches. A light breeze flowed throughout the air, with the trees swaying from side to side in the wind's presence. Gazing into the land of hills and valleys just ahead of them, the people wondered what gift Moneshob and Londriel would have in store for them, and what the delightful nature would be like in their new homes.

Amidst their wondering, Moneshob and Londriel brought all of the people together, with Moneshob announcing something to them. "I can see the joy that is on all of your faces," he said. "And I can assure you that today will be the day that you will never forget in your lifetimes."

He then paused for a moment, before pointing in a certain direction. "Do you all see the cliff that is ahead of you?" he asked them.

The people looked closely into the distance ahead of them, before finding the sight of the cliff. "Yes we can see the cliff," they all said.

"Good, that is very good," responded Moneshob. "Londriel and I are going to lead you to your new homes, but while we travel, we are going to make a quick stop by that cliff so that we can share many important things with you.."

And so the people agreed to all that Moneshob said, and immediately started following him and Londriel as they traveled through the forest they were in. Very soon, they entered the region filled with lush valleys, and they enjoyed the warm sun and cool wind that tingled through their bones. A deep sense of serenity fell on the people, as they trusted in Moneshob and Londriel's protection and leadership for the rest of their journey.

After a few hours had passed, the people came to a hilly region and arrived at the cliff, where a long river of water hung just below them. Moneshob and Londriel gathered them together, with Moneshob speaking to them.

"I want to tell you all something extremely important," he said. "But before I do that, I want you all to line yourselves up side by side, while Londriel and I discuss important matters with each other. After that, we will also share these important matters with all of you.."

The people obeyed what Moneshob told them to do, gathering themselves side by side with each other. They directed their attention back to him waiting for another command or the important announcement that he promised to tell them.

Once they were organized, Moneshob and Londriel both quickly made their way away from the people, walking off into a far distance where none of the people could see them. Meanwhile, the people patiently stood and watched the two of them as they disappeared into a vast area of trees and bushes. Smiles covered the people's faces as they eagerly awaited what Moneshob and Londriel would tell them, but as time slowly began to pass, they grew discouraged and worried that they still hadn't come back. Half an hour passed, and the people began to fear that something bad had happened to Moneshob and Londriel.

Eventually, with the growing sense of fear wrapping its arms around him, Steven made the first move and decided to check on them. He ran off into the trees and bushed which Moneshob and Londriel had disappeared into, leaving the people behind to silently watch him. For many long minutes, he longingly searched for Moneshob and Londriel, filled with mounting desperation that consumed his innermost being. He ran through an area of trees in search of them, climbing down hills and making his way through vast areas of grasslands.

But even as he searched for them, no trace of Moneshob or Londriel could be found. Filled with despair, he ended his search and turned around in preparation of letting the rest of the people know of the sad news of Moneshob and Londriel's disappearance.

Yet even as he started walking back, Steven felt as though he could hear a slight movement of feet following him from behind. He instantly turned around, but even as he did, the sound stopped and gazing at the area around him, he couldn't locate a single trace of a living being. He continued walking, convinced that his ears were deceiving again, but once again the faint sound returned to him, and this time it seemed as though a greater number of footsteps were now marching right behind him. He turned around as his heart started to beat rapidly, seeing nothing but grass and trees behind and all around him. Drops of sweat dripped down his forehead, but he continued walking again.

But the sound of the footsteps refused to cease, instead growing louder in number and intensity, before they soon turned into the noise of rushing gallops coming from behind. Steven refused to turn around, not wanting to participate in the silly games of whoever was trying to deceive and scare him, but fear gripped his heart, and even as he continued making his way back to the people, his walk soon turned into a slow jog. The sound of footsteps and gallops suddenly grew louder as Steven started jogging, and before he knew it, he found himself running at full speed in great terror.

As he ran, he felt a sharp hand touch his back that made him stumble to the ground. Slowly rising to his feet, Steven almost cried out in horror when he saw into the far distance, Moneshob mounting towards him on a fearsome black horse, and carrying a large, flaming sword in his right hand. Closely following him from behind were around two dozen or so large black horses and on them were equally intimidating masked figures clothed in black armor and wearing black masks, just like Moneshob. They carried large, sharp swords as well, though theirs were not flaming like Moneshob's.

They violently rushed forward to attack Steven in full wrath, and coming from the rear of the group was Londriel, slithering toward Steven at great speed as she hissed and showed off her fearsome fangs to him. A terrible evil and darkness were revealed in Londriel, that Steven would have never imagined even existed in her amidst her great beauty and glory. But Steven had no time for thinking, as Moneshob, Londriel, and the group of masked riders continued to advance toward him in great wrath and speed.

Feeling a sudden compulsion to action, Steven started running back toward the people, now sprinting at the fastest speed he could. Even as he ran, he screamed at the top of his lungs, hoping that the people would become alerted to the plight he was in.

"Somebody help me!" he screamed. "Moneshob, Londriel, and many others are trying to kill me! I need help!"

He continued sprinting as fast as he could while Moneshob, Londriel, and the figures continued to stride closer to him. His cries for help were soon heard by the rest of the people, as his echoing words brought shock and terrible fear to them. They all started running in Steven's direction, hoping to provide help to him in any way.

But at this point, Steven could now see the people from a distance, and they all breathed sighs of relief when they saw him. But their relief quickly turned into frightened gasps of horror as they saw Moneshob, Londriel, and several black riders chasing Steven down.

Questions lurked through their heads, as they were filled with both confusion and horror as to why Moneshob and Londriel had now betrayed them and were trying to lead an assault upon them. Their attention, however, was quickly brought back to Steven, as he continued running toward them for his dear life. The people also ran toward him, and very soon they were mere hundreds of meters away from each other.

All the while, Moneshob, Londriel, and the riders continued their advance toward Steven and the people. And as they grew closer to the people, a hideous and troubling shrill could be heard coming from the mouths of the black riders. The people immediately covered their ears in terror and disgust, collapsing to the ground in response to the terrible sound. Steven and the people became paralyzed with fear even as the black riders mounted toward them. They began to think of accepting the doom that was now laid before them, giving up all hope of surviving the terrible assault brought upon them.

But just when Moneshob, Londriel, and the riders were ready to strike the people down in their terrible fury, two great blinding lights suddenly came crashing down from the sky. A dividing wall of bright light separated the people and the riders, and the people found protection from the attacks brought on them.

The people stood up, peering at the blinding lights and yet hardly being able to see and discern what they were. Yet as they looked closely, the lights appeared to have the shape of certain figures, and by their sides, the people could dimly see large fiery swords and shields that were blocking Moneshob, Londriel, and the black figures from attacking them.

In great anger, Moneshob tried charging through the wall of the two blinding lights, but he was immediately repelled back with great force. Londriel and the rest of the black figures then backed up and attempted to charge their way through the two lights with the collection of their brute force. But they were once again repelled by the two lights who remained standing firmly in their positions.

A shrilling and ear-piercing cry came from the black riders as they tumbled back, with Londriel hissing at the two lights with intense hate and anger. But then suddenly, they were immediately sent cowering to the ground in fear and humility, as a commanding voice resembling that of a man came forth from the presence of one of the lights. And in a rumbling voice like the sound of thunder, he spoke to Moneshob, Londriel, and the black riders.

"Go back to where you came from!" he said. "You have no right to bring destruction on these people!"

As soon as he uttered those words, the people stepped back in shock and fear at his commanding voice. They dared not stare at the two blinding lights, and instead remained where they were, standing as still as statues.

Once they realized they wouldn't be able to attack the people anymore, Moneshob, Londriel, and the black figures quickly began retreating in the opposite direction and disappeared in the distance through the many trees and bushes.

The people breathed a sigh of relief that they were gone, and brought their attention back to the two lights which had protected them. Their hearts were filled with gratitude for them, yet fear struck their hearts just by staring at them. Many questions lingered through their mind of whether the lights were actual people, or whether they were just some force of power that happened to speak. They shook with fear and stood silently among each other, not daring to speak or make a move toward the lights.

Yet eventually, Steven gained the boldness to go forward and softly touched the two lights. Suddenly, as soon as he touched them, a great boom and rumbling shook the ground, with him and the people immediately collapsing to the ground. They lay on the ground for some time, with their faces covered and hidden from the two lights. Yet even as they looked up and peered at them from the corner of their eyes, they noticed a change in them. The two lights began to grow dimmer, and very soon the people could faintly see the appearance of two men with long beards.

At first, Steven along with the people was shocked to see the change, wondering what was going on and who the men were. But as Steven looked closer at their faces, a sudden sense of familiarity struck him. Great shock and regret filled his heart as he realized that the two old men standing in front of him and the people, were the same ones who had warned him earlier not to trust in Moneshob and Londriel.

Steven was pierced to the heart at this understanding and suddenly began to roll all over the ground, crying bitterly in the presence of the people and even pleading for the forgiveness of the two men. "Oh! Oh! Why didn't I listen to you two?" he cried aloud. "I was such a fool to deny your warnings! Have mercy on me for my foolishness!"

The people around him were left staring at him with shocked and confused faces having never before seen Steven act in such a way in front of them. And they were left even more confused by the words that he cried out to the two men, and they wondered who they were and how he knew them. But before they could ask their questions, one of the old men came forth to Steven and lifted him to his feet.

"Steven, your stubbornness caused this attack on you and the people," he said. "You put yourself and these people in danger by refusing to listen to our warning, and your situation would've ended in disaster if it were not for us. But I am glad to see that have understood the error in your ways. Perhaps you will now listen to us."

Steven wiped the tears from his eyes, and a faint smile of gratitude came to his face. "Yes, I have no choice but to listen to you now," he responded. "I am deeply sorry for my foolishness of choosing to reject your warning. I and all of these people would've been wiped from the face of the Earth if it wasn't for your mercy. Please, direct me and these people in what we should do from here."

The two men pondered on what Steven said for a moment, staring at him with searching eyes. Meanwhile, the rest of the people stood in bewilderment at Steven's conversation with the old man.

"I'm sorry to interrupt, but what are you two even talking about?" asked a man. "Everything is spinning through my mind, but what I do remember is suddenly seeing Moneshob, Londriel, and a whole bunch of figures similar to Moneshob's appearance attacking us out of nowhere. Why did they turn on us, and why was Mr. Loubre crying in regret when he saw you two? Who are you two and did Steven know that Moneshob and Londriel would eventually betray us?"

The other old man who hadn't spoken to Steven, now stepped forward to respond to the man. "Those are important questions that all of you deserve to know," he said. "I am Orieant and standing to my right is Mataput. A couple of days ago, Mataput had come to Steven in a dream urging him to stay on the coast, where all of you were before. But after the dream, Moneshob appeared to him and deceived him and all of you into believing that he was someone whom you could trust. But earlier this morning, Mataput and I again came to Steven and gave him another warning to back in the opposite direction towards the coast, and we also told him the truth of Moneshob, that he was a deceiver whose intentions were to destroy you all. We revealed to him that Moneshob is an evil creature named a wuzlir that comes from another land far from the Earth and almost managed to obliterate you all from existence because of his deception and cunningness. He brought with him, Londriel, another evil creature who decided to join in with Moneshob to bring destruction to you all. Rather than leading you eastward to find regions of hills and valleys, they instead led you northward in the direction of this cliff, intending to kill or drown you in this river. And they nearly succeeded in their plans, all because Steven refused to listen to our warning."

The people all collectively gasped in horror upon hearing Orieant and were filled with even more questions.

"How can these things be though?" asked a woman. "How were Moneshob and Londriel so easily able to deceive us, and not only that but how are there other creatures and other lands that dwell outside of the Earth?"

"Steven had those very same questions when we came to him this morning," remarked Orieant. "And it was because of all that we explained to him, that he refused to listen to our warning, instead choosing to believe that we were making up false tales of our own. But everything that we told him is the truth, and perhaps if he explains all that we told him to you, then you would all believe us and become informed of the truth."

The people immediately turned their attention toward Steven, eagerly and yet nervously anticipating all that he would explain to them in further depth. Steven looked at Mataput and Orieant, who nodded him on to provide an answer for the great number of people who stared at him with curious eyes.

Then with a deep breath, he told them the long tale in full, explaining everything that Mataput and Orieant had told him in the morning. He spoke of Jangart and his creation of the world, how Mataput, Orieant, and Natugura were once the spirit beings of Jangart, the great rebellion of Natugura, and the tempting wind of evil which had brought evil and corruption to many of the lands of the world, including the Earth.

The people stared at him attentively as he spoke, fearfully trying to process all that he said. At the end of his explanation, many of the people were left trembling in fear, horrified of everything that had been revealed to them, especially on how Natugura had brought corruption to their lands. Yet, many others were left with even more questions, especially on why Jangart hadn't decided to stop Natugura during his rebellion.

The young boy Peter stepped forward to Mataput and Orieant, gazing at them with great interest. "Forgive me for asking," he said. "But if all that Steven has said is true, why didn't Jangart just stop Natugura from his rebellion? Couldn't he have just destroyed Natugura and prevented all of the evil that we now see in this world?"

Mataput and Orieant looked keenly at the boy, with a smile coming onto Mataput's face as he responded to him. "That is a very good question," he said. "And all that Steven has told you are correct, for he has hidden nothing from you all that Orieant and I didn't already share with him this morning. But with Jangart, one thing that you must understand about him is that he does and allows things that we may not always comprehend. And while Orieant and I don't know the full truth of why he didn't stop Natugura from his rebellion, one thing that we have learned is that Jangart loves his creations with everything that consumes him, and part of that love is allowing them to have the freedom in choosing to make their own decisions, no matter how malicious that may be. But despite this, he warned Natugura of the dangers of his evil ways and urged him to repent and be restored to his former state. Yet filled with bitterness and wickedness, Natugura refused to listen to Jangart and was allowed to do as he wished; corrupting and influencing many of the creatures of the world into his slaves."

"I suppose that's true," responded Peter. "I can see why Jangart allowed Natugura to go on with his ways. But what about the non-corrupted creatures that remained free from Natugura's influence? Why didn't they do something to combat his evil?"

For a moment Mataput stared at Peter with raised eyebrows, as though he was struck with amazement at his many questions. "What is your name, young man?" he asked.

"My name is Peter," replied Peter, looking at Mataput with wide eyes as he wondered why he even cared to know his name.

A broad smile came on Mataput's face. "Peter, your questions and observations are both very important and wise," he remarked. "And I can assure you that the knowledge you have for such a young age will be put to good use. Now to answer your question, something was done to combat the evil that Natugura had brought to the world. Many years after Natugura and his wuzlirs had dwelled in Nangorid for some time, the gamdars along with all of the free creatures of the world united with each other to go to war against the wuzlirs and the corrupted creatures. This war is now known as the War of Great Alliances as all of the creatures of the world, both good and evil garnered their full strength to war against each other in the land of Nangorid. Such a war like that has never since arose in the history of the world, and it is remembered in many songs and tales."

"What happened then?" asked Peter, filled with great wonder as he listened to Mataput.

Mataput sighed but responded to Peter. "A lot happened during the War of Great Alliances," he said. "So much happened during the days of the great war, that not even all the books of the world would be able to contain the many great and terrible events that occurred during that time. But what you need to know is that when the non-corrupted creatures of the world went to battle in Nangorid against the corrupted creatures, they were still immortal beings since they had not fallen from Natugura's corruption. But since they had now decided to go to war, many of them perished in battle, and because of that, their nature was changed from immortal to mortal beings. Yet, even with the terrible fate brought on them, they still courageously fought on, doing everything they could to ensure that Natugura wouldn't dominate the entire world. They very nearly succeeded in overthrowing Natugura, and after the ten-year war had finally ended, the non-corrupted creatures believed that they had successfully weakened Natugura and his servants so much that their influence would no longer be felt in the world.

"But unfortunately, because they had left their lands to fight in

Nangorid, their homes were left vulnerable for Natugura's servants to attack. And while they were fighting, Natugura specifically ordered his wuzlirs to attack the land of the gamdars because of his fear of them. Once the gamdars returned to their home, they discovered that a golden book written by their king had been stolen by the wuzlirs. Now, this wasn't just any regular book, for it was a book full of wisdom and truth about how kings should rule over their people, and how people should live righteous lives within their kingdoms. The gamdars grieved over their loss, and all efforts that they had made during the war, suddenly vanished before their very years. Ever since that fateful day, many wars and battles have been fought in Nangorid to bring back their lost golden book. But all of their attempts have proven futile, with many lives of brave gamdars being dashed away from the world. Many more wars and battles have been fought between the non-corrupted creatures and corrupted creatures of the world, all of which have resulted in neither side gaining any real influence or freedom."

Peter and the people fell silent, pondering on all that Mataput had said. Yet more questions still lingered through their minds, which another man brought forth to Mataput.

"Well that's good and all, but what about you and Orieant?" he asked. "I can now see how much non-corrupted creatures went through to try and defeat Natugura but didn't Steven also mention that you two along with Natugura were once the great spirit beings of Jangart, full of unimaginable power and wisdom? Did you two do anything to fight against Natugura? Because I'm sure that he and his servants would've been no match for the collective power you both possess."

Mataput and Orieant dwelled on the man's words for a moment, before Orieant decided to respond to him. "Since Mataput has responded to all of your questions, I will now answer yours," he said. "Mataput and I were indeed the spirits beings of Jangart at one time, and after seeing the destruction that Natugura had brought to the world, we wishes to help the free creatures that remained free from his dark shadow. But as we explained our wish to Jangart, he told us that we couldn't become involved in the fight, since it now belonged to the creatures of the world, and not to us who still dwelled in Starlight. Yet because of our desperate yearning to help the free creatures of the world, Jangart granted us our wish, yet in the process, we had to give up our spirit forms to now appear in physical form just as you see us now.

"Much of our power and the memory of our former lives in Starlight were lost, but with the remaining knowledge and power we had, we used this to help protect and guide the free creatures of the world. Thus we received new names and became known as the volviers, the great helpers of the free world. With our new forms, we are not meant to fight the battles of the creatures of the world, but to instead guide the free creatures and instruct them to make the right choices. But there are times when we have no choice but to use our power to fight against the desires of Natugura, such is the case of which we did today in protecting you all."

The people ceased asking any more questions, satisfied and encouraged by all that they had heard from Mataput and Orieant. Wide smiles of gratitude and peace covered their faces knowing that their lives had been protected from impending destruction by two mighty beings, and they all grew increasingly fond of the two of them.

Yet even with the peace that covered their hearts, a matter which had been heavily on their hearts would soon be revealed by a woman, who couldn't hold her question anymore to herself. "I am grateful for all that you two have revealed to us," she said. "But one thing that I've been wondering, is why have you two specifically come to us to explain to us these things? Aren't there many other peoples and kingdoms on this Earth to whom you could reveal these things to them? And why have you waited for all this time to only now reveal these matters to us, when many crucial events and weighty matters have taken place outside of the Earth?"

Orieant paused, nodding his head almost out of approval of the woman's questions. "Those are questions which Mataput and I have pondered on for ourselves," he responded. "But even with our many questions and worries, our purpose is to do the will of Jangart, no matter how much we may not fully understand what that may entail. But one thing that we have come to understand is that Jangart's timing remains perfect, and when we sense his urging to do something, we listen to him and enthusiastically do that thing to help the free creatures of the world. And today, Jangart has shown us how he wants to use all of you to become a light for the other kingdoms of the world, and to demonstrate to them what it truly means to live lives of righteousness and justice.

"And though you may not know it, it was his plan all along for Steven to become the leader of this group, and not Moneshob or Londriel. This is why Natugura has been closely watching you since he had now begun to see in broken veiled fragments the perfect will of Jangart that will be accomplished in the world. For this very reason, Natugura has tried leading you off his course, sending his most trusted and cunning servants to deceive and destroy you all. Yet, throughout your foolishness, Jangart has had mercy on you all and has led us to reveal to you all the truth about what the world is truly like. He sent us to remove the veil from your eyes, and for you to finally see the truth in the hopes that you and all the peoples and kingdoms of the world resist the influence of Natugura and become non-corrupted creatures."

Orieant fell silent, and the people stood flabbergasted and greatly humbled in knowing that such a great and powerful being would choose them to complete his incredible purpose. Yet, doubts and worries still consumed many of their hearts, as they wondered how exactly they would still manage to withstand the wrath of Natugura now finally revealed to them. And they were especially confused about how they could become a light to the other kingdoms of the world, especially the one from which they had just escaped from.

Another man stepped forward to present his objections to the volviers. "I am incredibly grateful to know this, but how exactly are we going to become a light to the kingdoms of the world?" he asked. "Do you not see how evil and corrupt many of the kings are, especially Maguspra, the king whom we suffered under for many years?"

"Trust me, my friend, Mataput, and I saw your years of suffering and sorrow under Maguspra," responded Orieant. "And though you may not fully understand everything yet, I can assure you that the will of Jangart is far stronger than all of the corrupt hearts that fill the Earth. Jangart will help you to fulfill his will, and you all will become a new kingdom where goodness and freedom will dwell in peace. And when all of the kingdoms of the world see your light, they will also become inspired by you and choose to follow in your direction. But before all of this comes to pass, you must continue to listen to us, and our first order for you all is to travel back to the coast from whence you came. From there, we will be able to discuss more things with you, things that will shape the very foundation of your lives."

The people grew excited at all that Orieant had said, wishing to hear of all the other things that he and Mataput would share with them.

"Well I can't wait to hear what you two still have in store to share with us," remarked Steven. "Which way then should we go in the direction of the coast?"

"You must travel back in the opposite direction from which Moneshob and Londriel led you," answered Orieant. "Since they led you northward, you will now go southward in the direction of the coast. But I must warn you that Natugura will not give up on trying to create more ways to deceive and trap you all. He will send an even greater number of his evil and cunning servants to deceive you, so to combat this you need to not only be alert and discerning but also armed with weapons for your protection."

As the people attentively listened to Orieant, he and Mataput took out swords from their cloak pockets; swords that were small but still sharp enough to do serious damage to anyone who tried to attack them. The two of them handed the weapons to hundreds of men, including Steven.

"We don't have enough weapons for all of you," said Mataput, after he and Orieant handed them out. "But the ones we have given to some of your men are more than enough for your protection."

The people gazed at the swords and approved them for their effectiveness. "Thank you for providing us with these swords," remarked a young man holding his weapon. "I can see that these are very sharp even to the tiniest point, and will help us slay any evil servants that Natugura throws our way. But what about you two? Will both of you travel with us to the coast?"

"We will not," responded Mataput. "You must now put our words into practice, and stand your ground no matter what attack or deception you may face. Do not become ignorant of Natugura's devices, and once you reach the coast, Orieant and I will appear to you again and speak of even more important matters with you all. But for now, we are going to depart from you and allow you all to show us what you are capable of.

And no matter what you face while traveling, remain encouraged since you will all very soon arrive at your new homes. Make sure to use your swords if ever needed, and remember to stay on the path in the direction of the coast, not taking any shortcuts or flattering paths that may appear to be smooth and clear but are just deceptions of the enemy."

With that, the people agreed to all that Mataput and Orieant instructed, and thanked them many times for their help. After the people said their final goodbyes to them, the two volviers walked away from them before disappearing into a far distance. Once out of their sight and reach, the people gathered their remaining items and excitedly started their long march back in the direction of the coast.

4

Prince Lelhond

STEVEN GAZED AT THE great number of people who followed him, sensing the great responsibility that he bore on his shoulders for leading them. As he remained deep in thought to himself as he walked alone, he was reminded of the nearly costly mistake that he had made in trusting in Moneshob. He now encouraged himself not to make that same choice, and to lead the people in the right direction, free from the deceptions of the enemy. Yet he understood that the situation he and the people found themselves in wasn't an easy one with the revelation that Natugura was still trying to desperately hunt them down.

Yet even with these worries placed on his heart, Steven comforted himself in knowing that even amid his and the people's difficulties, Mataput and Orieant promised to be with them on the other side. With this truth deeply ingrained into his heart, he suddenly stopped walking to turn around to the people and express how he felt.

"My brothers and sisters," he said. "As I was thinking to myself just now, anxious thoughts came to my mind with what Mataput and Orieant had told us. But even despite these worries, I now know that we do not need to fear, for if we stick together and continue to do what the two of them have told us to do, then we will arrive in our new homes before we even realize it."

Broad smiles came on the people's faces and they all stood in agreement with Steven. "All that you say is true, Mr. Loubre," remarked an old man. "I am glad to see the confidence in your heart, despite the many worries we are all facing. I feel greatly encouraged and strengthened just by your reminder."

All of the people agreed with the old man, thanking Steven for his leadership over their long journey and for the courage he had displayed to them. Sensing a wind of peace and comfort fall upon him, Steven breathed a deep sigh of relief and continued walking on forward as the people followed them.

As he led the people, they were led down the cliff and began journeying through the same region of hills which they had come from. Walking along the rocky path surrounded by the same area of land that their feet had formerly stepped on, they continued to gaze in wonder at the vastness of the area of land around them.

Steven inhaled the fresh cool air and turning around, he gazed at the high rocky cliff which they had now left behind. Staring at the cliff from the distance, he observed how it seemed a small insignificant rock, yet deep down he knew that it would be the site that would become deeply ingrained into his memory.

He turned around again, choosing to move on from the things of the past and focus on what the future would have in store for him and the people. He and the people continued descending the hills, before soon merging onto a rich area of valleys that sparkled with glimmers of gold as the sun shone upon the ground.

The atmosphere was silent as the only sound that filled the air was the people's feet brushing across the ground. Peter closely followed Steven from behind, and all of the people's spirits were lifted as they joyfully strolled across the ground.

The rest of their afternoon was spent journeying through the region of valleys, as they gave themselves enough time to rest and recover during the evening.

They woke up the next morning determined to continue and complete their long journey. For the first hour, they continued going through valleys and grasslands, before they soon found themselves going entering a deep and dense forest. Darkness covered the forest and was unfamiliar to the people, with only a few small glimmers of the sun providing the people with enough light to continue on the path they walked on Eerie sounds came from all around the dark forest, yet no creature could be seen or heard. As they went on, the path they walked became rockier and narrower, causing many of the people to stumble as they walked.

Keeping their complaints to themselves, the people journeyed on this way for a few more miles. But as they walked in the half-veiled darkness of the forest, a sudden misty fog rushed around them, turning the forest even darker than it already was.

The people cried out in fear, wondering what was going on and whether or not Natugura was sending a vast blindness to prevent them from knowing where they were. Yet with the remaining light they had, they turned to their right and saw another path where there was a bit more light and less fog. Immediately the people urged Steven to lead them in that direction.

"Mr. Loubre, I don't think we can continue in this way," remarked a man. "This doesn't look like the same forest we were in yesterday morning, and it's dark, foggy, and mysterious. But look! If we turn to the path on our right, we will have more light and less fog to see where we are going. Why don't we go that way?"

Steven sighed to himself as he listen to the man. "What did Mataput and Orieant tell us?" he asked. "Did they not instruct us to go in the direction toward the coast? And is that not what we are doing? The land we have traveled in yesterday and today is the same in which we came from, and this forest is no different. Just because it looks different, that doesn't mean that it is not the same place that he journeyed through. Besides, perhaps the path on the right is a trap that Natugura is trying to use to further attack us. So why should we open ourselves to the risk of falling again to his deception? Let's just continue going on the path that we are now so that we can reach the coast as soon as possible."

Immediately the man along with the rest of the people agreed with Steven and knew that no matter how difficult the path would be, they would have to continue in the direction where they were going.

And so the people went on again through the dark and foggy forest. For many long minutes that felt like enduring hours, the people laboriously and cautiously took each step, not wanting to trip over in the dark. Anxious thoughts clouded their minds as they wondered how long they would have to endure the darkness and fog that hovered over their sight like vast cloudy shadows.

Yet, as the people continued staring straight ahead into the fog, they could faintly see several strange and large stones gathered together in a circle. Coming to the sight, they counted seven stones in total, with one that was placed in the middle. Even with the fog clouding their vision, they were able to see the stones which quickly garnered their attention. Steven halted the people for a moment, as they all sensed a strange tugging and desire to examine the stones for themselves.

While gazing at them, they observed that the stones were dark black, yet they seemed to faintly shine even in the darkness. They were each irregularly shaped which they closely noted. They couldn't help but stare longingly at the stones with wide eyes, as all other thoughts of their journey swiftly subsided.

Steven bent down to further inspect the stones. "I've never seen stones like these before," he muttered. "They are all strangely shaped and though they are black, they seem to be glinting with brightness amidst this terrible fog. And they all seem to be in perfect alignment with each other, as though they were specifically placed like this for a certain reason."

Steven and the people were all drawn to the stones, unable to resist their pull on them or focus on anything else. As they all stared at them, Steven suddenly noticed that on the middle stone, there was an engraving written in white. He pointed at the sight, drawing the people together to read what it said.

"It is an engraving," remarked Steven. "And the words are written for us to see what it says."

Steven and the people gathered together around the middle black stone, and leaning over to get a closer look at it, they found words deeply engraved on it:

GORMOPIR THE SERVANT OF LONDRIEL
WHO IS THE QUEEN OF THE EAST

"Ah, so I guess that Londriel is some queen in a land to the east," remarked Peter. "Now I have a better understanding of who she truly is; at least a small facet of her being."

"Yes, this is good to know," commented Steven. "And now I understand what she meant when she remarked, *'I am the Queen of the Hzarves, and I hold rightful dominion over all the lands of the east.'* This indeed gives us a bit of understanding of who she is."

"But what about this Gormopir person?" asked a man, switching the subject. "We now understand a little more about Londriel, but what about this servant of hers? Could he possibly be one of those hzarves that she mentioned she was the queen over?"

"That is likely the case," said Steven, pausing and thinking to himself for a moment. "But now that I think about it, we should probably move on and ignore these stones. Now that we know that it's Londriel, it's likely another trap of hers to lead an attack upon us. Quick, we must be on our way!"

"You're right, Mr. Loubre," agreed the man, as frantic thoughts ran through his mind. "Why should we be paying attention to any devices that Londriel is trying to trap us with? Enough is enough. We can't keep on blindly falling for the traps of the enemy. We have already been warned about this by Mataput and Orieant, and so we should put their words of cautioning into practice."

The people agreed with Steven and the man, ignoring the stones which they had spent so much time staring at and continuing to walk straight ahead on the path they were on. The fog was still heavy, and as they could barely see anything, many of them began wondering if going on the path to the right which they had seen earlier wouldn't have been a bad idea.

Even Steven began having these thoughts and doubts cloud his mind, as he wondered if he had led the people in the wrong direction. As his doubts grew stronger, he felt like addressing them to the people, yet he kept it to himself as he sensed a tugging on his heart to not share it with the people.

But with each step that he took in the foggy dark forest, he grew gradually weaker and more tired. His eyes started closing in sleepiness, and he felt as though the path he was leading the people on was to blame.

At any time, he felt it would be the appropriate decision to turn around and find the path to the right and go in that direction.

But just as he was about to turn around, there came the noise of a loud screeching horn that vibrated through the air behind him and the people. The people suddenly became as silent as mice and turned around in shock and fear of the terrible noise. The sound of the horn came again, this time even louder and causing the people to cover their ears in horror at its ear-piercing noise. The people turned in every direction to see where the sound was coming from, but all remained dark and foggy around them.

Suddenly, they saw a dark shadow that silently came creeping from behind, slowly advancing toward the people. The shadow grew larger and before they knew it, the people suddenly saw the body of a large snake appear before them. They all became paralyzed with fear and screamed in horror when they saw the face of Londriel as she slithered toward them.

Many of the people dropped to the ground in terror of Londriel, as she smiled slyly at them while approaching them. Steven and the people trembled in her presence, with their mouths dropped to the ground. They stared at her with wide eyes, as though they were confused and terrified of what to do next.

Suddenly there came a cry from a man, who charged toward Londriel with his sword. "Those who have swords, attack her!" he cried. "What are you doing standing here?"

Some of the men took out their weapons and charged toward Londriel to attack her, but with the expansive fog, they found themselves helplessly flailing their weapons into the air. Some almost struck their fellow friends by accident in the dark and foggy sky, and Londriel couldn't help but laugh at the sight of the people trying to attack her.

"It's funny seeing you all trying to attack me when you can barely even see me." she snickered. "But at least I have a better vision than all of you combined."

Then with great ferocity, she suddenly charged toward the people at great speed and began whipping some of them were her large tail. Many tumbled backward across the ground as a result of her great force, while the others who had been spared from her wrath, immediately began running wildly across the forest.

Londriel continued whipping more people and snarling at them in intense wrath. “You foolish people!” she hissed at them. “You couldn’t help but fall for the bait. I was hoping that you would’ve gone on the other path so that we could see each other better. That would have been a much more entertaining fight. But I guess I can manage to finish you all off right now.”

Hundreds more were sent crashing to the ground by the strong whip of her tail, with many others recoiling back in fear at the sight of her sharp fangs. Others continued running around in circles throughout the forest, while other men helplessly tried using their swords to strike her. The battle went on for a few more minutes, and the people lost all hope that any of them would survive the wrath of Londriel.

But then suddenly, there came the sound of a swift arrow flying across the air and striking Londriel on the side of her face. She immediately let out a hideous yell and tumbled to the ground in great force. Turning to their side, the people stared in astonishment at the faint sight of a man hiding behind a tree and holding a bow and many arrows. They all wondered who it was that had saved them, but as they looked upon the man, they noticed that his face was green and that he was towering in height. Sudden fear and bewilderment came upon them, yet they inched their way closer to the creature, filled with a great fascination with who it was.

But just as they drew closer to the creature, Londriel suddenly sprung to her feet and started hissing toward them. Then turning around, she cried in a loud and terrifying voice. “Arise my hzarves and attack these people!” she cried. “You must destroy them all!” And then she started slithering away, before disappearing from everyone’s sight through the dark and foggy forest.

Turning around, the people stared with widened eyes of shock when with their very own eyes, they witnessed the seven black stones they had seen earlier, transform into living creatures. Staring with great fear at the creatures, they observed that they appeared slightly shorter than them, though they looked much bigger in build. In the dark, their skin color looked to be dark gray and they appeared to have brown armor. They had thick ears and noses and hideously laughed at the people, showing off their yellow fangs which glinted in the dark and foggy air.

They came charging toward the people with large spears in their hands, laughing and speaking in a strange and alien language. The people grimaced and screamed in fear and disgust at the ugly creatures, recoiling backward and having no courage to take out their weapons.

But just then, the creature that had struck Londriel with his arrow sprung from the tree he was hiding behind and positioned his arrow toward the charging hzarves. He turned aside to the people and urged them to fight.

"Quick! Gather your swords and strike these cursed beasts!" he cried. "There is no place to give in to fear now!"

The men who had swords obeyed the creature, including Steven as they began charging toward the hzarves.

The creature loosened his arrow, staring at the hzarves with sharp eyes. "Lelhond is here you cursed beasts!" he said, revealing his name. For a moment, as if struck by lightning, the hzarves slowed down and nearly stopped as they gazed at the creature named Lelhond with fear in their eyes. Then suddenly, he fired another one of his arrows, striking one of the hzarves in the eye and causing him to collapse to the ground.

Now feeling greatly roused, the hzarves continued running and came rushing toward the people with an even greater speed, roaring and yelling at them in the process. Then with giant leaps, they came crashing down on the people, but the men who had their weapons quickly came to defend those who were attacked. Steven came charging toward one of the hzarves and struck his heart with his sword, resulting in the hzarf thumping to the ground in great force and lying there dead. Steven stared longingly at the dead hzarf, hardly able to believe what he had just done.

The remaining hzarves were all attacked and pierced with the many sharp and bright swords that came against them, leaving almost all of them dead. Wielding his strong spear, he would've killed many people if the men hadn't come against him with their swords.

As he fought the people, he suddenly cried out in a hideous voice. "Today you shall learn to fear the great Gormopir!" he cried. "I am the servant of Londriel and you shall not prevail over me!" He continued swinging his spear into the air and mocking the people as he fought them.

But just then, Lelhond rose to his full stature, with what seemed like a mighty wind surrounding him. Then with a sudden radiance of white light that flashed around him like lightning, he spoke in a loud voice that rumbled like thunder.

"*Reh un o edgheyoth numdraith!*" he cried in a strange native tongue.

A sound of lightning came and then with a great boom, one of the trees of the forest collapsed to the ground, and Gormopir was sent wildly tumbling over at uncontrollable speed. Finally coming to his feet, the hzarf gnashed his teeth in anger toward Lelhond, before running away from his presence and disappearing into the forest through the thick fog.

For a moment, the eyes of the people were drawn toward Lelhond as he stood tall and motionless in their presence. Suddenly, the heavy fog and darkness of the forest vanished away, and the people trembled in awe at the sight of Lelhond now made clear to them. They stared in fascination at him not only for his green face and body but also for his towering and impressive stature, as he appeared to be at least seven feet in height. He was bearded and had a strikingly handsome, yet firm look on his face. The people couldn't help but gaze in wonder at him, staring at his piercing brown eyes which looked keenly upon each of them.

The people noted his strong build and wondered if he was some sort of soldier. Now looking closely at his clothing, they observed in great curiosity his silver breastplate which covered a silverish robe he wore. Looking a little higher up at him, their mouths dropped to the ground at the beauty of his hair; which was long and brown and had a few streaks of gold in it. Across his forehead was a silver circlet that glimmered with many diamonds and gems, and in his right hand he held the golden and silver bows and arrows which he had used. The people continued to stare longingly at him for a while in utter silence, observing his young yet mature and royal face and body with great fascination.

Eventually, Steven broke through the long moment of silence. "Who are you, and what just happened?" he asked, trembling with both fear and awe.

Lelhond turned to Steven, with a smile coming on the corner of his face. "I am Lelhond, son of Erundil," he answered. "I come from the land of Watendelle and was brought by Mataput and Orieant to help protect you when they saw you stopping your journey to stare longingly at the black stones. The stones were traps from Londriel and were disguised as her servants called hzarves. They could have done serious damage to you all, but luckily I came just in time to help you."

The people continued gazing in wonder at Lelhond, wondering what his land was like. They were also filled with bewilderment at how the hzarves had transformed from the black stones and wanted more understanding of that. But before they could ask any more questions, the sound of footsteps suddenly could be heard walking from behind them. Some of the men immediately drew out their swords, fearing that they would suffer more attacks from either Londriel or Gormopir.

But once they saw who it was, they instantly put their swords down. They breathed sighs of relief when they saw Mataput and Orieant coming forth to them, and all of the people had broad smiles on their faces. They came towards the volviers to greet them, yet the two of them both had stern looks on their faces.

The two of them stood on either side of Lelhond, while the people spoke to them. "Well, it's wonderful to see you both," said Steven, smiling with relief and gladness. "I never would've imagined that you two would've come to us before we reached the coast."

"We had no choice but to come to you," responded Mataput, with a disappointed look covering his face. "You were going in the right direction, yet you decided to look at the black stones which you soon realized was a trap of Londriel's. Yet when the hzarves attacked you, you all stood like statues and refused to attack. If it wasn't for Lelhond urging you on, many of you would've perished and many more would've been left injured."

The people shrunk back in fear of Mataput's stern rebuke of them, while Steven spoke up to try and appease their frustration. "But we killed all but one of the hzarves," he remarked. "I even killed one with my sword which pierced right through his heart."

Mataput shook his head to the side. "Yes, and I am glad that you did that, but that was only after Lelhond urged you on to attack them," he responded. "You must understand that there will be times when Orieant and I won't always be here to help protect you from attacks, so you must be willing to use the swords we gave you and fight bravely. Besides, once you attacked them you almost completely wiped out every last one of the seven hzarves. You just have to be willing to trust in yourself and not give in to the fear which the enemy has tried to consume your hearts with."

Regret covered the people's faces, and they dared not to look into the two volviers' faces. "I apologize, Mataput," remarked Steven. "All that you have said is true, and we should have been bolder in attacking the hzarves. Not only that, but we shouldn't have fallen for the bait Londriel tried to lead us into, and should've instead avoided even looking at the stones altogether."

A smile came on Mataput's face as he listened to Steven. "You speak well, Steven," he said. "Do not stand condemned even though I rebuked you and the people, for you especially have done a remarkable job in leading these many people throughout the entirety of your journey. There is still work to be done, however, so you and the people must be willing to take the big steps laid before you to reach your new homes in complete safety."

The people felt reassured and comforted by Mataput's words and found the courage to look upon the faces of the volviers, now seeing smiles rather than stern looks cover their two faces. For a moment, all was silent, as the people gazed in the direction of the bright sun glimmering through the leaves of the forest. But seeing the arrays of bright light shining down upon him, the people's attention was brought once again to Lelhond.

Steven scratched his head as he stared at Lelhond. "Can you tell us more about Lelhond?" he asked turning toward the volviers. "Who exactly is he and how were you able to take him from his own home to help us here."

"He's already told you all you need to know about him," answered Orieant. "He comes from the land of Watendelle which is far away from the Earth and we brought him here since he is a mighty soldier in his land. It was not an issue in bringing him here, because Mataput and I were already planning on introducing you all to him once you reached the coast. But since we saw that you would be attacked, we decided to bring him here early so that he could help you."

"That's interesting," remarked Steven. "But can we not know more about him and the history of his home and of what type of creature he is? I have never seen a tall, green-faced creature like him before, yet he seems so alike to us, though he is much taller and more dignified."

"That is a discussion for another time, Steven," responded Orieant. "Mataput and I were going to answer all of your questions once you reached the coast, and we are not going to depart from our plan. In the meantime, you must move on quickly in the direction of the coast. And just so it goes quicker, all three of us are going to lead you there, and once we get there, we will answer your questions and reveal to you many more important matters that we have wished to share with you."

The people sighed and dropped their heads in disappointment. They wished to hear what Mataput and Orieant had to tell them and didn't want to wait to hear what the two of them had to say until they reached the coast. Yet, they knew their pleading would do nothing to change their minds, and so they all began slowly walking onto the path they were on, wishing that the next few days of their journey toward the coast would end quickly.

Yet, before they got anywhere far, Lelhond suddenly stopped them. "Wait," he said. "I could see the great joy and wonder that came over the people when I told them a little bit about me, and so if Mataput and Orieant are willing, I can tell them much more about myself and of the history of my people and kingdom."

The people's spirits were suddenly lifted, especially at the mention of a kingdom. "Yes, that would be wonderful!" exclaimed a woman. "I would love to hear from you about yourself, your people, and your kingdom in full detail Please, Mataput and Orieant, let us hear from Lelhond!"

The people urged the volviers to allow them to hear from Lelhond, with some of them even getting down on their knees in desperation. Mataput and Orieant at first refused, but as they observed the people's growing excitement and constant pleading, broad smiles came to their faces and they soon granted the people their wish.

"We will allow Lelhond to speak to you more about himself and his home," said Mataput. "We were already going to allow him to share this with you all once you reached the coast, but since you are filled with such great fervor, we will allow Lelhond to tell the people all that they desire to hear."

The people thanked the volviers many times for allowing them the opportunity to hear from Lelhond and became silent once they turned toward him. Lelhond smiled in amazement at the people's great interest in him, and with a deep breath began telling them more about himself and his people.

"The volviers have told me that you have heard of gamdars and even seen wuzlirs who attacked you a few days ago," he began. "Those were indeed wuzlirs that attacked you since they were completely clothed and masked in black and rode on black horses. You have seen wuzlirs before your very eyes, and now I am glad to tell you that you are all looking upon the face of a gamdar! I am a gamdar and long ago during the rebellion of Natugura when the great tempting wind of evil spread throughout the lands of the world, my people rejected it and remained non-corrupted creatures. As I have told you, the land where I come from is called Watendelle, and it resides to the south of the Earth.

"But Watendelle is not only a land but also a great kingdom full of remarkable splendor and strength. My father, Erundil, has been the King of Watendelle for the last 25 years ever since his father Tutlandil died, and after my father dies, I will become the next king in his place since I am the eldest of my three brothers. But for now, I am the Prince of Watendelle and also a soldier in the army along with my brother Karandil, while my brother Forandor is a great musician and a learner of the history and lore of our people and kingdom. I also have a sister named Glowren, and my mother is Aradulin, and together we are the royal family of Watendelle.

"Now besides myself and my family, my people are mighty soldiers, musicians, and poets full of great wisdom. Our ancient history cannot be compared to anywhere else in the world, and if I were to tell you our full history in one sitting, I'm sure it would take many weeks or even months. But we are a people full of mighty kings and heroes of renown, and we record all of our histories in our many books, poems, legends, tales, and songs so that we do not forget about the great stories of our predecessors who provided our kingdom with such great pride and glory. We are also intelligent creatures who can speak in many tounges, among which includes our native Tuntish language and the language of the humans as well. But along with our many joys and delights, our people have suffered many sorrows as a result of our many long wars and battles with the wuzlirs that dwell in Nangorid. Nonetheless, our kingdom has stood proudly and firmly despite the many attacks we have faced from the evil slaves of Natugura."

Lelhond ceased speaking, and the people were left stunned and amazed by all that he had said. Wonder consumed their hearts of the rich history and lore he had spoken of about his people, and they were even more fascinated by the fact that his father was the king of his people, while he was a prince.

After a long silence, Steven shared his amazement at all he had heard. "That is incredible," he remarked, smiling in awe of Lelhond. "I now finally know about gamdars, and I would've never imagined that they were this powerful. I am even more amazed by the fact that you are a mighty prince and soldier, while your father is the king over your people. I am humbled to be in the presence of such a mighty creature as you," he paused for a moment before another thought came into his mind. "But now that you've spoken of the gamdars, I'm also wondering about the wuzlirs," he added. "How could such a powerful and beautiful race of creatures like gamdars turn into such ugly creatures to the point where they need black masks and black clothing to hide?"

Lelhond thought to himself before responding to Steven. "I admit, that I don't know the true answer to that question," he eventually said, with a look of sorrow in his eyes. "It is a tragic tale of how a great number of our people were deceived by Natugura and transformed into such evil and vile creatures. The wuzlirs were once beautiful gamdars, yet I guess that it was because of the terrible shadow of Natugura's corruption that they were turned into such hideous creatures. Their smooth green faces were turned into crooked and crumpled red faces, and their beautiful and dignified clothing was stripped from them. They were left so bare and ugly that even Natugura himself couldn't bear looking at them, so he changed their names and gave them black clothing and masks to cover their shame. Ever since then, that has been the way they have appeared for the past thousands of years."

The people were left astonished by what Lelhond had said, but while listening to him speak, they were filled with even more questions.

Peter brought his question before Lelhond. "We also heard from Mataput that you and all the non-corrupted creatures of the world united with each during a great long war," he remarked. "And you almost overthrew Natugura from his seat of power, yet even as you severely weakened him, the wuzlirs managed to steal an important golden book of wisdom that you had used. How were they able to steal it then? And why was it so devastating to you all?"

Lelhond sighed to himself as he listened to Peter. "All that you say is sadly correct," he said grimly. "Such a war like that has never since arisen in the world, a great long war in which the free creatures of the world banded together and nearly defeated Natugura in entirety. It was the War of Great Alliances, and though it ended in tragedy, we gamdars remember it in our songs, books, and tales for the great courage our people displayed. Alas! The great golden book of Ulohendel, who was the first King of Watendelle was stolen from us by the crooked wuzlirs! It is so devastating to us for it formed the very foundation of our lives. We knew not how to live our lives besides what was written in the wise book of Ulohendel. The wuzlirs stole it because we failed to guard our own home properly while we went to fight in Watendelle. I will forever blame the wuzlirs, but even more, I will also blame the smalves. For though the smalves are non-corrupted creatures like us gamdars are, all they know what to do is mess around rather than fight alongside us. Natugura used their foolishness to his advantage and I am sure that it was they who gave away the location of the golden book of Ulohendel. If it wasn't for them, our book would've never been stolen, and Natugura would've been defeated once and for all."

The people stared at Lelhond, sensing a feeling of sorrow that came into their hearts. They wished to comfort him, though they knew not what to say or how to express it.

However, the volviers looked on Lelhond with anything but sorrow. "That is not true, Lelhond," suddenly interrupted Orieant. "The smalves did not betray the location of Ulohendel's book to Natugura nor are they the lazy no good creatures you and your people have portrayed them to be. Even if they were great and mighty soldiers like the gamdars, that still would've likely not turned the fate of the great war."

The people stared at Orieant in amazement and found themselves filled with even more questions. "Who are smalves?" asked a woman. "They seem to have caused a lot of division for the gamdars. Can we learn more about them?"

The volviers said nothing, but a look of disdain could be seen on Lelhond's face at the mention of smalves. "The smalves are small lazy creatures who contribute nothing," he harshly answered. "They come from the east in the land of Laouli, and though they are non-corrupted creatures just like my people are, they've done nothing to help the free creatures of the world in their many wars and battles against Natugura and his servants. All they are good for is eating, joking, and singing silly songs with no real meaning or history behind them."

The people stared in amazement at Lelhond, shocked by the sudden change of frustration that he displayed toward the smalves. They turned toward the volviers, wondering how the two of them would respond.

Then suddenly, the people saw Mataput and Orieant's eyes seemingly turning into coals of fire as they glared at Lelhond. They all stepped back in fear, even Lelhond. Then inching a step closer to him, Mataput spoke in a thunderous voice toward Lelhond.

"You have no right to speak such things against the smalves, Lelhond!" he said in a mighty voice, striking terror into the hearts of Lelhond and the people. "You have spoken wrongly in saying that the smalves are lazy and no good, for they are skilled farmers and gardeners in their own homes, with no other race of creatures in the world being worthy enough to even find the comparison with the smalves. As for their love of food and joking around, they were fashioned by Jangart to have such personalities and habits, so why should you decide how they should act or be? Besides, just as you could teach them a thing or two about fighting or matters of knowledge, they could also teach you a thing or two about their crafts such as farming, cooking, and enjoying your life."

Even in his great stature, Lelhond seemed to shrivel in response to Mataput. He stared at the ground in embarrassment. "I apologize,

Mataput," he said. "It's just that my people and I have been through times of great sorrow and the smalves always seem to be working against us rather than for us. I am especially frustrated by the events of the great war when the wuzlirs succeeded in stealing the great book of my forefather."

Mataput sighed to himself in response to Lelhond, but a look of pity came on Orieant's face as he responded to Lelhond. "You have every right to be frustrated, Lelhond," he said, speaking in a soft tone. "But it is not good to blame the smalves for doing things that they would've never dreamed of doing. They have never joined the enemy in his evil pursuits, nor will they ever do so in the future. Yet your people have held a strong grudge against the smalves for the past thousands of years ever since the days of the great war. Though your people are the wisest and most powerful of all of Jangart's created creatures of the world, this one matter has been one that you all must fix. The smalves themselves have tried to mend their relationship with your people, yet they have stubbornly refused to let go of their bitterness."

Lelhond grew silent, thinking to himself and processing all that Orieant said before he spoke to him. "What you say is interesting," he admitted. "And I never thought of that before either. Perhaps it is for that very reason that you and Mataput prophesied that the humans, not the gamdars will bring back the lost book of Ulohendel from the clutches of Natugura in his Black Tower of Wuzinch Torgol."

"You are correct, Lelhond," responded Orieant. "The grudges that you and your people have held against the smalves have been one of the main reasons why you have been unable to bring back the lost book of Ulohendel to Watendelle. But we revealed this prophecy to you some hundred years ago, because your people don't need the book of wisdom anymore. Your people have lived righteous lives while your kings have ruled with goodness and justice, but the kings and peoples of the Earth have been the complete opposite. To prevent Natugura from holding dominion over them, the humans must bring back your ancestor's lost book of wisdom so that they can become non-corrupted creatures just like your people are."

The people listened in great fascination, amazed and overwhelmed by all they were hearing. Before Lelhond could respond to Orieant,

Steven quickly interrupted to ask a question that lingered through his mind.

"All that I am hearing is beyond anything that I would have imagined," he remarked. "And now I wonder, was this the very thing that you and Mataput wanted to tell us once we reached the coast? Now I see how I and these people will be able to form a kingdom where righteousness and goodness reign. This book of Ulohendel will be the key indeed. But how are we going to get it back from Natugura? Haven't the gamdars gone through many wars and battles over the years, all of which have proven futile?"

Orieant smiled as he listened to Steven. "Yes, Steven," he said. "Mataput and I wanted to wait until you and the people reached your new homes so that we could share these important matters with you. But now that you have already discovered the purpose of us coming to you and these people, I guess we can reveal the plan we have for you," he paused for a moment, smiling as the people earnestly watched and listened to what he would next say.

"Now to answer your question, Steven," he continued. "The gamdars have indeed endured many long wars and battles against the slaves of Natugura, though not all of them have ended in futility. For though the lost book of Ulohendel is still with the enemy in his Black Tower, the gamdars have brought much destruction to his land and people. But as Mataput and I have observed over the years, we knew that war was not the way to bring back the lost book of Ulohendel. For though war is crucial in defending your homes and standing boldly against the wrath of the enemy, it will not bring deliverance and salvation to those who most need it.

"And so, while we were wandering throughout the different regions of Watendelle, a vision from Jangart suddenly appeared to us where we saw how the lost book of Ulohendel could be delivered. We learned that the humans, not the gamdars would bring it back, and that stealth and secrecy, not large numbers and open war, would be the key to freeing the humans from the growing shadow of Natugura over their land. And so while we shared this with the gamdars, we have waited many hundreds of years to share this with the humans. But now, the appointed time has finally come and though you all may shut your ears in disbelief to this,

I can confidently say that it is appointed for Steven Loubre to go on a quest through the land of Nangorid, and to the tower of Wuzinch Torgol to get the lost book of Ulohendel and to use it in his role as a leader over these people."

The people gasped in both shock and amazement at all that Orieant had revealed, greatly astonished that Steven would be so entrusted on a great mission. Yet, even as his mouth dropped to the ground, Steven found himself shaking his head in doubt and disbelief at all Orieant had said.

"I am sorry, but I am not the one to complete such a great task," he said, still finding it hard to process all he had learned. "If the gamdars have tried so hard in bringing this book for thousands of years, why then would I make any difference? Maybe a strong soldier like Lelhond or someone wiser like you and Mataput complete such a mission."

"Steven, you have been chosen by Jangart himself to go on this quest," responded Orieant. "This is a journey on which a human is meant to go on. But do not be afraid, for Mataput and I will go with you on this quest along with a few several creatures to help you."

Steven breathed a sigh of relief in the comfort of knowing that Mataput and Orieant would go with him, though strong fear and worry still tingled through his bones. "So who are the other creatures that will go with me?" he asked. "And when are we going to begin this quest?"

"We will not start yet," responded Orieant. "And Mataput and I still don't quite know who will be joining you on this quest. So to decide on this, we have planned on introducing you to the gamdars. Myself, Mataput, and Lelhond will lead you to the kingdom of Watendelle where you will learn more about the land and history of the gamdars so that you can appreciate the importance of your quest even more. There, you will see the perfection and bliss in which they live, even amidst the many sorrows and difficulties that they have endured over the years as a result of many wars and battles. There you will meet Lelhond's father, Erundil, and by learning from him, you will get a better understanding of how you should lead your people to perfection. And it is there where we will decide who we want to join you on your quest to bring back the great golden book of Ulohendel."

Steven could hardly believe what Orieant revealed to him. His body was filled with a rush of emotions that he couldn't control, and he began jumping around in pure joy. "Yes! This is more than I could have ever dreamed of!" he exclaimed. "I shall go to Watendelle and see the kingdom of the gamdars for myself!"

Smiles of delight covered the rest of the people's faces as they grew excited for Steven. Yet many of them wondered if they could also go along with him.

"But what about us though?" asked Peter. "Can we go to Watendelle with Mr. Loubre as well? And who will lead the rest of the people to the coast when Steven is gone?"

The volviers looked on with Steven with smiles on their faces. "You impress me very much with your practical and wise reasoning, Peter," remarked Mataput. "But this tour through Watendelle is meant to be Steven only, while you and the rest of the people will stay where you are. And you do not need to fear. For if you remain in this forest you will be protected from any attacks from the enemy. Londriel and the hzarves have returned to their land, and I am sure that the wuzlirs will not bring any danger to you if you remain in this forest. We will only be gone for a few days, so you will not need to worry about anything. And perhaps some time in the future, we will bring all of you to Watendelle to see the beautiful land for yourself."

Many of the people, including Peter were disappointed that they would not see Watendelle, though they took Mataput's words of seeing it sometime in the distant future to heart. They felt assured knowing that they would be shielded from any attacks of the enemy while they remained in the forest, and an inner peace dwelled richly in their hearts.

Eventually, the volviers directed their attention back to Steven, announcing that they would soon be departing. "It is now the time to make our way to Watendelle," said Mataput. "It will not be a long journey there, in fact, it will only take a few minutes. We will be traveling to Watendelle on winged creatures, ones that Orieant and I command."

Steven grew excited at the mention of flying on winged creatures and was even more ready to go to Watendelle "Alright then, I'm ready to go!" he said with great excitement and joy.

With that, Steven along with Mataput, Orieant, and Lelhond said their goodbyes to the people as they began departing through the wide forest. They asked Steven to tell them of all the delightful wonders he would see in Watendelle, to which Steven promised to do so. Then as they grew farther from the people's sight, Orieant suddenly turned around to give the people some final instructions before they departed from them.

"As Mataput already told you all, we will only be gone for a few days," he said. "But even if our return happens to be delayed for some reason, you must remain in this forest. I know that you are all desperate to reach your homes, but it is for your good and protection that you stay here and wait for us to return to you. Here, you will not become susceptible to any attacks from the enemy and before you know it, we will be back. So do you agree to remain where you are?"

"Yes, we agree to remain here," replied the people in unison.

For a while, looked into each of the people's eyes, examining them and shaking his head in approval. "Very well then," he said at last. "It is up to you now to keep your word."

With that, he turned around, and he, Mataput, Lelhond, and Steven soon vanished from the people's sight into the vast thicket of the forest. With the afternoon sun shining on the path that the four of them walked on, the people silently turned away, as each of them was filled with great curiosity.

5

Into the Gamdarian Realm

THE FOUR OF THEM walked for a few miles through the forest, when suddenly, Mataput and Orieant began to whistle. Pure and beautiful whistling it was that came forth from their mouths, like the bubbling of clear water amidst the bright sunshine of summer. They then stopped their whistling, and immediately, the sound of rushing wings came flapping through the sky. They all gazed toward the sky, observing in wonder the remarkable winged creatures which came down.

Once they came down, the four of them stood silently in awe of the beauty and dignity which was displayed in the winged creatures. Four giant winged creatures with faces of eagles and bodies of white birds appeared before them. They stood proudly before them as four giant white birds, yet as the company gazed at them, they knew that they were no ordinary birds.

For within the winged creatures was strength as strong as iron, great power hidden underneath their wings, white feathers of wisdom covering their majestic bodies, and the glory as that of high and lofty crowns of stars covering their heads. They were glorious and beautiful beyond measure, shining with pure white light and shimmering with majesty and power. They couldn't stop gazing at them out of awe and amazement.

Mataput turned toward Steven. "These are the muenwos, the lords of all winged creatures," he said. "These are the winged creatures that will direct us to Watendelle. Are you ready to see the land of Watendelle?"

Steven was silent for some time, still gazing at the beauty and splendor of the four muenwos. At last, as if being awakened from a dream, he finally spoke. "Well, yes of course. I am ready," he said. "I am sorry for not answering you sooner, I was just drawn to the glory of the muenwos. But I can't wait to fly on these beautiful creatures to Watendelle."

Mataput smiled at Steven. "I am glad to hear that, Steven," he said. "Hope on then, and you will very soon delight yourself in the land of the gamdars."

At once Steven hopped onto one of the muenwos, with Mataput, Orieant, and Lelhond making their way onto the three remaining ones. Steven couldn't help but smile with joy and gaze in wonder toward the muenwos. And then, amidst the delight he felt, the four muenwos suddenly began to slowly elevate into the air, flapping their wings in the soft wind. Then, as they reached a high above the ground, the muenwos picked up their speed, and suddenly began dashing through the sky at lightning speed.

At first, Steven yelled in unexpected fear, but as the winged creatures glided across the sky, he began to laugh and shout for joy.

"Oh yeah! This is incredible!" he exclaimed. "This is the best day of my life!"

He continued shouting and laughing as the muenwos flapped their great wings across the sky, passing many areas of land and bodies of water below them. As they glided through the sky, Steven closed his eyes for a moment, delighting himself in the beautiful sounds that illuminated his ears as the wind blew upon him. A broad smile covered his face, and he felt as though he could spend the rest of his life just flying on one of the muenwos across the sky.

But after a few minutes had passed, he suddenly felt that they were now slowly descending, and as he opened up his eyes he found that they were close to landing on the surface below them. The muenwos began slowing down as they neared the surface, before they finally landed on the ground, and found themselves amid an open cave.

Steven jumped off the muenwo, patting the great winged creature on the back. But before he could anything, the volviers suddenly whistled again, and he saw all four of the muenwos ascending upward and disappearing through the sky. Steven turned toward Lelhond and the volviers with a booming smile, unable to hide the joy which covered his face.

But as he looked toward the volviers, he suddenly noticed a change in them. Instead of wearing their cloaks, they were instead clothed in bright white robes that sparkled in the sunlight, with many designs and patterns scattered across the piece of clothing. Orieant's brown pointed hat was now instead white, and even the staffs they held were white. Across their foreheads were golden circlets, and as he gazed at them, Steven couldn't help but notice how they appeared before him as glorious kings full of great power and wisdom.

All memory of his experience of flying with the muenwos was lost, as he now instead focused on the volviers as they and Lelhond led him away from the cave. Inside the cave, they slowly descended what felt like an endless amount of stairs, with many water fountains along the stone walls to their sides. They eventually came to the end of the cave, where ahead of them they saw a large waterfall with what looked like water which was poured along a silver glass. Steven gazed in wonder at the waterfall, wondering what lay in front of it.

As if answering the question in his mind, Mataput turned and spoke to Steven. "This right here is the border into the land of Watendelle," he said. "Though you may not see anything which lays in front of it, through this waterfall your eyes will be opened in seeing the land of the gamdars."

At once, he, Orieant, and Lelhond made their way through the waterfall, leaving Steven behind as the last one to cross. Closing his eyes and giving a deep breath, Steven crossed the waterfall, with a smile of peace coming onto his face as the warm water showered upon his head. Once he crossed the waterfall, he opened his eyes, and immediately his mouth dropped to the ground as he stood in awe of the glorious land of the gamdars.

Before him, he beheld a wide valley with a vast array of trees of all sorts of different colors; including leaves of green, red, orange, yellow, pink, and even more. Numerous waterfalls surrounded the trees of the valley, which all emptied into one great, long river. Along with the natural beauty of the land, he also saw an endless amount of beautifully decorated buildings and works of stone which surrounded the vastness of the trees and plants of the wide land. Ahead of him was a long golden bridge, and into the distance far distance ahead was a vast array of golden roads that sparkled under the bright light of the sun.

Turning to his right straight ahead, he saw a massive gray statue that stood around a vast array of trees. It was the statue of a figure who with outstretched arms held a large book in his right hand and a long scepter in his left hand. His hair was fairly long and on his head was a crown with what appeared to be many precious gems that sparkled like bright crystals in the sunlight. His piercing eyes glimmered in the bright light as sparkling stars, and the figure seemed to stare at Steven as it stood as a mighty tower of stone in the far distance.

The sun illuminated the whole land in great brightness, and amid the valleys, trees, buildings, and beautiful architecture that filled the land, there stood one palace, far above everything else in the land in its beauty and size. Steven gazed longingly at the structure for a while, struck in awe of it as he observed how it was unparalleled to any of the palaces that were on the Earth. Its bright white marble color sparkled with many crystals and reflected the light of the bright sun, and on its white and golden railings, and above its silver and bronze roof flew a multitude of birds, singing songs of praise of the kingdom of Watendelle.

Lelhond turned Steven. “What do you think of my home, Steven?” he asked. “Is it not beautiful to set your eyes on?”

Steven still gazed at the splendid land, soaking in all his eyes could take. “Yes, it is very beautiful, Lelhond,” he responded. “It is the best thing I have ever seen in my life.”

A smile came on Lelhond’s face. “I am glad to hear that, Steven,” he said. “There is still more beauty and wonder to delight your eyes with, so let us walk across this bridge and make our way to the great palace of the king. There, Mataput, Orieant, and I will introduce you to my father, King Erundil.”

Following Lelhond, Mataput, and Orieant, Steven made his way onto the long golden bridge and found himself staring at it in great wonder. While gazing upon it, he noticed that he could see his reflection staring back at him, as though he were looking at a clear mirror. As they walked Lelhond talked about how the bridge was made by hundreds of gamdarian craftsmen, builders, and artists, and that it took them many years to complete it.

Below the bridge, Steven could see the beautiful and colorful array of trees that filled the valley, and he watched as the animals leaped and enjoyed themselves. Peace consumed Steven's heart as he gazed upon the great serenity that filled the land of Watendelle, and he felt as though he could walk across the long bridge for hours, just staring at the delightful land.

Once the company of four made their way across the bridge, they could faintly see the great palace of the king in the far distance. They found themselves standing on golden roads, surrounded by a multitude of gamdars, some of whom were working, while others laughed and smiled with each other. Mataput and Orieant went to talk with some of the gamdars, while Steven and Lelhond stood by each other. Steven silently stood in awe as he observed everything which surrounded him, and he couldn't help but smile with joy at the land of great happiness and peace.

Gazing toward his right, his attention was then brought back to the massive statue that lay just ahead on the right side. He turned toward Lelhond. "What person is that statue displaying?" he asked. "I can't help but imagine that he is an important figure with great authority."

Lelhond gazed at the statue with a glimmer of pride that shone in his eyes. Steven then watched as he bowed his head to the ground, presumably out of respect for the figure.

"That is my ancestor Ulohendel," he responded, with the light on his face growing noble and proud. "He was the first King of Watendelle and it was he who filled his great golden book with wisdom on how kings should rule rightly over their people, how the people should live together in peace and righteousness, and he also added many words of prophecy and foresight. If you look closely, it is that great book of wisdom that he is holding in his right hand. In his left hand, he is holding the Scepter of the King, a symbol of the authority and power of the King of Watendelle that has been passed down through the line of the kings, all the way to my father who currently wields it. Ulohendel was the master of wisdom and foresight during his time, and we remember him as the wisest and greatest gamdar to have ever lived. He ruled with righteousness and unparalleled knowledge, setting the precedent for our line of kings to follow during their reigns. But it is a sad fate that his great golden book of wisdom was stolen by the wuzlirs toward the end of the War of Great Alliances. It is said that he died of a broken heart once he discovered that his book had been stolen, and this statue was constructed many years after he passed away. Nevertheless, we all look up to him for inspiration and honor him for the life he lived and for the memory that he passed onto us."

Steven gazed at Lelhond in amazement for all he said. "Our people have such a rich history," he remarked. "I can see why your people admire Ulohendel so much, and why I need to bring back his book of wisdom."

"Yes, it has been my people's dream to see the day in which the great book of Ulohendel is returned," replied Lelhond. "And you do not know how glad I am to see that you are the one who will bring it back, but not for my people to use, but for your people to use. But you will not be doing it on your own, for Mataput and Orieant will be going along with you on the journey, along with a few others, whom we will decide today."

Steven took Lelhond's words to heart, admiring the great care that he displayed toward him. After their talking, his attention was brought to the many gamdars that filled the golden streets. There was much talking, chattering, and laughing among the gamdars who fascinated Steven with their beautiful clothing and joyful faces.

Steven and Lelhond walked on through the streets for a while, observing the many structures, trees, and gardens that filled the golden roads on every side. As the two of them passed by, many gamdars smiled at them and bowed a knee out of respect for Lelhond. Lelhond stopped to speak with many of them in his native Tuntish language, while Steven listened on with great fascination. He stood amazed by the level of respect the gamdars showed Lelhond and wondered how amazing it was that the Prince of Watendelle was directing an ordinary human through the realm of the gamdars.

Amidst the bustling sounds and sights that filled the streets, Steven faintly hear several clear and delightful voices in the distance ahead. As he and Lelhond walked on, the voices grew louder, and before his eyes, Steven now saw three gamdarian women who sang by each other's side. The three of them were beautifully adorned with different color dresses;

one with white, the other green, and the other light blue. Beautiful gems covered their long dresses and the bright sun reflected glimmers of light through their long brown hair.

Steven gazed at them not only for the beauty and grace which they seemed to possess but also for the enchantment of their sweet soft voices. As he stared at them and listened to their singing, he noticed that smiles covered their faces when they saw him, and their eyes remained fixed on him. Though he couldn't understand a word that they sang in their native Tuntish language, Steven felt drawn and captivated to listen closely to them.

As he listened, he delighted himself in their beautiful and soothing voices, as they sang calmly and slowly. Yet it seemed to him that a deep underlying sorrow filled their voices as they sang, with their voices growing even more mournful as the song wore on. Yet toward the end of the song, it seemed as though a sense of hope and joy had been kindled within their hearts that was reflected in the sound of their voices and the light which covered their faces.

After they finished, Steven stood silently to himself for a moment, soaking himself in the beautiful voices of the women which illuminated the atmosphere. A river of emotions and feelings ran through his heart; among which included sadness, peace, and hope. Yet above everything else he felt, he experienced a certain level of joy that he was unable to describe. He turned to Lelhond to share all that he felt.

"I don't know how to explain it, but that song captivated my heart in such a strong way," he said. "Even though I was unable to understand a single word that they sang, I feel a rich tingling of hope and joy running through my bones right now."

Lelhond smiled at Steven. "I am glad that you feel that way, Steven," he responded. "And though it was sung in the native language of my people, all that hear it are captivated to their very core. Though you don't know it, the words that they sang were written down many hundreds of years ago, when Mataput and Orieant came to our land to share with us their prophecy which will be fulfilled in you."

Before he could ask any questions, Lelhond suddenly broke out into a song in the language that Steven understood, singing in a clear and soft voice. Steven listened on in amazement at the sweetness that flowed richly through Lelhond's mouth, and he noted how just like the three gamdarian women, his voice started off sounding sorrowful before echoes of hope and joy came forth from his mouth toward the end of the song:

Far back in the glorious days of old,
To the king far above the wise.
Words of stars from his book of gold,
To light our world from the sky.

The glory of Ulohendel was lost
And swept away by rushing winds.
Our years of war would pay the cost
When those words were erased from our minds.

The golden star was stolen from the bold,
By the beasts of everlasting shame.
To break our hearts from their faces of cold,
And proclaim the greatness of their name.

They stole our cherished book of words,
For our kings to use.
Refusing to be rescued by sharp swords,
Reserved for impending doom.

In endless days to come,
Our shame is drenched with fear.
In fear of what we will become,
And whether there would be cause to cheer.

The tears stream from our faces,
As watery crystals that shine from the sun.
Yet our tears meet no embraces,
For our days of sorrow have only begun.

Yet in the shadow of the dark,
We have seen a great light.
The great helpers have brought to us a spark,
For light to shine through the night.

The light shone as it ran,
For all those to see.
Yet the light was a man,
To set his people free.

The trees sang with words of hope,
As we saw the restored days of old.
We shall not withhold our helping rope,
For all shall turn back to gold.

Yet the glory shall not return here,
For it shall be lent as a gift.
To make the darkness clear,
And their corruption drift.

Our sorrow is met with joy,
And our lips utter songs of praise.
Our words of stars, the beasts shall not destroy,
For a man shall brighten our day.

Lelhond ceased his singing, and Steven was left staring at him in awe. He felt as though he were in a delightful dream that would never end, and imagined what more sources of wonder he would discover in this land.

Yet, as he reflected on the words he heard from the song, he was also left greatly confused. "All that you sang was lovely to my ears," he remarked. "But I still don't completely understand all that you sang about."

"I understand why you don't completely understand the words of this song," responded Steven. "But if you remember, I mentioned that these words were inspired by the prophecy that the volviers shared with our people many years ago. And as I said, that prophecy will be fulfilled in you. The words of this song are talking about you, Steven, and you are the one who has been chosen by Jangart to not only bring hope to the humans of the Earth but also peace to my people. For we gamdars have suffered many years not knowing when our book would ever come back, and we have shed many tears of sorrow. Yet, because of this prophecy brought to us by the volviers and the revelation that you are the man to brighten our day, we have never stopped singing this song for joy, even amidst our great sorrow."

Steven's mouth dropped to the ground in shock as he was beyond stunned to learn that the song was speaking about him. "This is unbelievable," he remarked. "I would have never imagined that this beautiful song was ever talking about me. Now I understand why those three women were smiling at me with joy as they sang, they must have known that I was the one to fulfill the prophecy of Mataput and Orieant!"

A broad smile came onto Lelhond's face, and he nodded his head in agreement with all that Steven had said. But as Steven thought of all he said, his smile began to slowly fade, and doubt suddenly seized his heart.

"But who am I to bring hope to the Earth and peace to Watendelle?" he asked, gazing at Lelhond with peering eyes. "Even if I do find this book, how will I be able to influence all of the kings and peoples of the Earth to transform into entirely new creatures? Have Mataput and Orieant forgotten the terrible evil of Maguspra, the king whom we fled from? How will his heart possibly be softened and changed to the point that he not only listens to me but also agrees to all I have to say?"

Lelhond listened to Steven's worries with great concern, thinking to himself for a moment about how he would respond to him. But before he could say anything, Mataput, and Orieant suddenly came forth to the two of them, having overheard their conversation.

"I understand your doubt, Steven," said Mataput. "Everything has come so quickly on you these past few days, and you have hardly had much time to process all that we have revealed to you. But you do not need to fear. For if Jangart has empowered you to flee from the King of Fozturia, he will also empower you to not only get the lost book of Ulohendel, but to also use it to rule righteously over your people, and to turn the hearts of people and kings, including Maguspra himself."

A sense of relief came over Steven as he dwelled on Mataput's words, letting them run deep through his heart and mind. Satisfied by all the heard, he continued walking through the golden streets filled with many gamdars, while the sight of the great palace of the king loomed just ahead.

As the company inched its way closer to the palace, Steven shook his head in disbelief as the great size of the structure began to dawn on him. Staring at it, he thought to himself that if it had been placed on the Earth, it would have been remembered as the largest structure to have ever been built.

Turning aside, his attention was diverted to the many gardens that filled the streets around him, containing beautiful flowers of red, green, blue, pink, yellow, and even purple colors. Large bushes engulfed the area of the road, along with large colorful trees, some of which reached high up to the sky. A calming breeze of peace and joy flowed through the air, providing Steven with great rest and comfort as he continued delighting himself in the land of Watendelle.

As they neared the palace, Steven noticed that just ahead of them lay a wide silver gate, which blocked them from the view of the palace. As they came to the silver gate, Steven stared at the figures which were carved into its large silver railings, and couldn't help but imagine the richness of the gamdars' history. Though the large gate blocked them, the company could faintly see the palace that lay on the other side and heard many voices talking.

Steven was eager to get inside and see the palace, though the gate remained locked. "What are we going to do?" he asked. "The gate seems to be locked.:

"Do not worry, I will open the gate," responded Lelhond. Then walking closer to the gate, he touched their silver railings, and speaking in a commanding voice, he said, "*Rahurrie ledo*!"

The gate began to open at once with a loud creaking sound slowly. Once it completely opened up, the company walked through, and in the opening could be seen thousands of gamdars shouting and singing for joy as the four of them walked through. Seeing the palace in its true scope and glory, Steven covered his mouth in awe of its immense size and design.

As the sun shone on the material of its white marble, glimmers of light seemed to radiate throughout the areas around it. The palace itself was shaped like a triangle, though several dome-shaped roofs lay on its top. Staring at the roofs that seemed to reach into the clouds, Steven stared in amazement at its precious gems and materials that sparkled with colors of silver, gold, and even hints of green. All around the palace, there seemed to be an infinite number of clear silver windows that sparkled from the bright radiance of the sun.

Casting his eyes away from the palace, Steven saw wide archways all of which provided many paths that led into or around the palace. Around the archways were an endless number of gardens along with many trees that provided shade from the heat of the sun. Within the gardens were waterfalls, all of which emptied into small ponds.

Turning again to the palace, Steven saw many statues of gold, silver, and bronze material that displayed great gamdarian figures. Some of the statues depicted mighty soldiers riding on their horses, while others displayed several musicians that either held harps or flutes, while other statues depicted some gamdars either writing or reading books.

Looking down, he observed how the road on which they now stood was a stone road with a pale amber color. In the area around the palace was an endless array of freshly cut green grass, where animals could be seen roaming around.

The company of four walked straight across the pale amber road, making their way toward the doors of the king's residence. As they walked on, a great number of at least a few thousand gamdars filled the lawn, cheering and singing as they made their way to the doors of the palace. In their hands, they waved leaves and flowers in celebration and gave some of them to the company of four.

Steven gazed around at the great crowd of gamdars in amazement at the attention he, Lelhond, and the volviers were receiving. "This is amazing," he remarked. "I would have never imagined that such a great crowd of people would be so excited to see me here," he then cast his attention to some of the flowers and leaves he had been given. "Now I wonder, why are they giving us these flowers and leaves?"

Lelhond looked at Steven's leaves and flowers closely. "These are no ordinary leaves and flowers, Steven," he responded. "For they are the special healing leaves of my people, reserved to only be eaten for those who are injured or ill and need healing and recovered strength."

Steven stared at the leaves and flowers in growing fascination. "Well that's very interesting," he remarked. "But they look so good to be eaten, and I wish I could only take one bite. But if you say they are for healing purposes only, then I will not eat them."

Lelhond smiled at Steven. "Good, I am glad that you understand," he said. "Come, and I will lead you to the palace to see my father."

At once, Steven followed Lelhond and the volviers as they walked across the pale umber road toward the doors of the great palace. Along the way they stopped many times to greet the many gamdars around them, receiving more flowers and leaves of healing and other gifts. One woman presented Steven with a white piece of gamdarian clothing, which he graciously accepted. They continued walking on until the volviers noticed the clothing which Steven had received.

"Wait," suddenly said Mataput coming to a halt. "You must change quickly, Steven. The clothing that you have received is an important gift from the gamdars because they recognize that you are about to meet the king in his royal abode. Go behind one of the bushes there to change your clothes. You can leave your other clothes behind the bushes and I will make sure to give them back to you."

Obeying Mataput, Steven quickly dashed off the road to hide behind one of the thick bushes of the gardens to change into his new outfit. Once he put it on, Steven nodded his head in approval, as it felt light and comfortable. Radiant sparkles of light seemed to reflect from his outfit, and its bright white color was a dazzling sight to behold.

He came back to Lelhond and the volviers, examining every spot of his outfit. "How do I look?" he asked, with a smile on his face.

Lelhond and the volviers stood impressed by his outfit. "You look like a real gamdarian prince, that is except for the green skin and tall height," remarked Lelhond with a laugh.

"But seriously, you look good, Steven," chimed in Orieant with a smile. "I am sure that the king will appreciate you for wearing a beautifully adorned gamdarian outfit."

Steven smiled and continued gazing at his new outfit, in awe of its splendor and design. The four of them continued walking on for a few minutes on the road, nearing the doors of the palace. Then as they neared the doors of the palace, two gamdars standing close together by the palace doors could be faintly seen in the distance ahead. As the four of them walked closer to the two gamdars, Steven was able to discern their appearance.

A bearded man wearing a golden crown on his head covered with red and green gems across its top stood before Steven. He was clothed in a gold-brownish robe that glittered in the sunlight, with many stripes and circles on it, depicting various symbols. Across his waist was a red and golden band with a green jewel in the center, and what appeared to be writing on the band. He had long dark hair coming down to his shoulders and healthy brown eyes. He appeared to be in his fifties and had a friendly, yet striking and proud look on his face. He appeared before Steven as a high and glorious king, unsurpassed in his regalness and splendor. Steven couldn't help but stare at him for a moment, having never seen the sight of such a mighty and kingly figure before, one who contained unparalleled grandeur to the kings of the Earth.

The woman standing to the right of the man was clothed in a light blue robe with many silver stripes and other symbols that sparkled in the sunlight. She wore a silver circlet across her head and on her wrists were many bracelets adorned with precious golden and silver jewels and gems. Her light brown hair, seeming to shine as gold, was much lighter and longer than the man's, and her eyes were light brown, yet seemed to shine like golden stars in the bright sun. She had a soft and welcoming smile on her face as she looked on toward the company, and had a slightly younger appearance than the man standing next to her. She appeared to Steven as a noble queen, full of beauty and dignity.

As the four of them came within talking distance to the two gamdars, Mataput stopped to turn toward Steven and tell him who they were. "Ahead of us is Erundil, the King of Watendelle, and his wife Aradulin, the Lady of Watendelle," he said.

Steven walked slowly, filled with amazement and wonder at the royalty that Erundil and Aradulin possessed. Coming close within the two gamdars' presence, Steven found himself unable to speak a word, as he was filled with awe to be in the presence of such figures containing great majesty and glory

Erundil smiled as the four of them stopped in front of him, and greeted his visitors. "Welcome Mataput and Orieant," he said. "I have seen you many times over these past few weeks and months, but it is always a pleasure to listen to the good tidings you have for us," he then cast his attention to Steven. "Welcome, Steven, to Kulendar, the chief city of Watendelle. I am Erundil, son of Tutlandil, the King of Watendelle. I am glad to finally see your face, as the volviers have told us much of the great deeds you are doing on the Earth, in leading your people even amid the attacks from the enemy's servants. I am well pleased that my son was able to help you and your people, and I am sure that he told you many things about our people."

Before Steven could respond, Aradulin stepped in to introduce herself. "I can say the same in that it is an honor to finally meet you, Steven," she said, smiling warmly at him with her brightly sparkling eyes. "I am Aradulin, the Lady of Watendelle, and I am glad that you are here in the kingdom of Watendelle."

Steven stood astounded to be introduced to such mighty figures and found himself bowing his head to the ground. "It is an honor as well to meet you, Lady Aradulin and King Erundil," he said.

"Mataput and I are always grateful to come to your wonderful kingdom," chimed in Orieant, speaking directly to Erundil. "The land of Watendelle has always given us memories of what Starlight was like when we once resided there. You are the embodiment of how to rule with truth and dignity over your people."

"I am grateful to hear that from you, Orieant," responded Erundil. "Any praise from the volviers is warmly received. But all of you, come inside the palace so that we can show Steven around and show you the rooms in which you will be staying."

Bowing their head once more to Erundil, Steven and the volviers followed the king and the lady as they led them to the tall golden doors of the palace. Two guards stood at the doors, and once they saw the king, they quickly stepped aside and opened the doors for the company.

Stepping through the doors, Steven found himself standing on a golden floor with depictions of gamdarian figures drawn on the ground.

Ahead of him lay a long and wide hall, which was surrounded by sturdy white walls with golden and silver pillars carved into them. Hanging on the walls were many paintings depicting different gamdars, some appearing as soldiers, others kings, others musicians, and even those learned in lore and history. Many statues filled the great hall of the palace with several overhanging lights on the roof shining upon the many stone depictions of gamdarian figures. Straight ahead and also to the right and left were crystal white stairs, where there could be seen many workers racing up and down.

Steven felt overwhelmed by all the beauty and luxury his eyes beheld and simply marveled to himself at the great creations made by the hands of the gamdars

After a while of staring at all their eyes could see, Erundil turned and spoke to Steven. “Welcome to the house of Yarwindil,” he said. “This is the great palace named after my ancestor and the eldest son of Ulohendel, who became king after his father’s death. It is he who first began the construction of this great palace and saw its completion during his lifetime. Come, there is still more you must see.”

And so Steven along with the volviers followed Erundil with Aradulin and Lelhond walking by his side, as he directed them through the palace. Steven observed the many depictions of figures and banners which covered the white walls. Seeing his great interest in the paintings and statues scattered throughout the palace, Erundil told Steven what the many statues and paintings were depicting. Steven listened on silently, being drawn into the rich lore and history of Watendelle.

Erundil then came to a specific painting, staring in great admiration at it. “This painting is of my son, Lelhond,” he said. “He is the second in command of the army of our soldiers, only behind me in his level of authority over them. In the painting, he is wearing his battle attire and holding his weapons.”

Staring at the painting, Steven first brought his attention to the armor that Lelhond wore. The armor appeared to be very heavy and was a mix of a golden and green color, with a shining golden tree that was placed on the center of the breastplate. Turning his sight from the armor,

Steven saw that he wore a large golden helm on his head, and held a large silver sword with green bows and arrows at his side. He was seated on a bronze throne with many different colored trees in the distance, and his eyes were fixed on a blue-colored bird that sat upon his right shoulder.

Steven turned to Lelhond after gazing at the painting for a while. "The painting is wonderful," he remarked. "You look like a mighty and royal soldier in this painting, but I guess that only fits who you are. After seeing how you rescued me and the people from Londriel and the hzarves, I do not doubt that you are a great soldier."

Lelhond could only smile at Steven, feeling greatly humbled. "Thank you, Steven, for your words of praise," he said. "But what I did for you and the people wasn't a big deal. All I did was defend you and the people from the attacks of the hzarves. Besides, even you managed to slay one for yourself."

"Well, I suppose that we humans are quite different than you gamdars," responded Steven with a laugh. "What we think is amazing, happens to be normal for you. But in all honesty, I am grateful for you coming to protect me and the people from the hzarves. If it wasn't for your urging we would have never done as well as we did in killing all but one of them."

"It is my duty, Steven," said Lelhond, with a firm expression now covering his face. "It is what a gamdarian soldier is meant to do. He must lead by example and not be overtaken by fear."

Steven processed what Lelhond said, amazed to be learning so much already from the gamdars. Sensing what he felt, Erundil spoke to Steven.

"All that my son has told you is true, Steven," he said. "A soldier of Watendelle is a leader in his way, and it is because of that, that our people have held such great power and might over these long years," he then turned to Mataput and Orieant. "But it's about time that I lead Steven and the volviers to their rooms. Perhaps I can fill Steven's mind with even more knowledge of the ways of my people, but for now, all of you should follow me up the stairs and to the great hallway of our rooms."

Erundil started walking up the stairs, with everyone else following me from behind. Staring at the stairs, Steven could see his reflection from its white crystal color. He and the company went up a long step of stairs, and after what felt like an eternity, they finally came to the second floor of the palace and found themselves standing on a long blue carpet. The walls around them were now golden instead of white, and along the sides were numerous doors, some open and others shut.

Being led by Erundil, the company walked across the blue carpet and through the long hall. They passed by doors and rooms to their sides, and in the ones that had their doors open could be seen many beautiful paintings, carpets, chairs, and other items. Inside the open doored rooms were gamdars who sat and spoke about different matters with each other. But when they saw the king along with his wife and son pass by, they all stopped what they were doing, and bowed their heads to the ground in front of them.

Eventually, after walking through the hall and observing the different doors and rooms around them, Erundil suddenly stopped at the sight of a bright red door. Written in white on the door was the name, *Steven Loubre.* Erundil opened the door and spoke to Steven about his room.

"Here is the room that you will be staying in," he said. "Come inside and I will show you around. The rest of you may be dismissed."

At once, Aradulin and Lelhond, along with the volviers departed from Erundil and Steven, while the two of them walked inside the room.

Finding himself in the room, Steven found it far more spacious and brilliant than he had seen from the distance by the door. Observing all that lay before his eyes, he found himself standing on a green carpet with numerous meticulous artistic designs on it. The walls were a bright golden color, and many paintings hung on them. Many lampstands and other lights stood on tables, along with a few small statues of renowned figures and heroes.

Turning to the bed, Steven thought that it must have been at least eight feet in length, long enough to fit a gamdar. The cover itself was a mix of green and gold color, and written on them was what looked like a poem in the Tuntish language of the gamdars.

After he had seen all he could, Steven turned to a large golden cabinet that stood to the right of the bed and asked Erundil what it was for.

"Inside this cabinet is specially made gamdarian clothing made just for you," he replied, walking to the cabinet.

Opening the cabinet, a wide array of clothing was revealed. Many different colored robes, cloaks, and trousers filled the cabinet, with the main color of clothing being brown, but also a fair number of clothes with light blue, green, white, and even red colors. Steven also saw three pairs of shoes that were each gray, blue, and black. Lying across the top of the shelf could be seen two circlets each gold and silver, and some different colored bracelets and necklaces filled the top as well.

While Steven examined the clothes and items in the cabinet, Erundil spoke to him. "Later today, you, Mataput, and Orieant, along with my three sons and other distinguished and trusted friends of mine, will be attending a council that I have set up," he announced. "Though I am impressed by the clothes you have on now, for this council you will need to wear the specific clothing provided for you in this cabinet. You may pick any of these clothes and shoes to wear, and you can decide whether you want to wear any of the circlets, necklaces, and bracelets as well."

Steven felt overwhelmed having been gifted with so much. "Thank you, Mr. Erundil, for providing me with all this wonderful clothing," he said. "I imagine that it took your people a long time just to make this clothing so that it would fit me. I am forever in debt for the great hospitality you have shown me, welcoming me into your great palace and gifting me such a wonderful room to stay in."

"It is my pleasure, Steven," responded Erundil. "And besides, this is how our people have always welcomed guests when they come to our palace. And I hope that you enjoy your stay here. But come, there is still more I want to show you, especially of the wonderful view that you have from this room's porch."

Being led by Erundil, Steven now came to a long sliding glass door covered in golden blinds. As Erundil opened up the blinds and door, a great radiance of sunshine was revealed, which shone brightly over the porch. By the porch were numerous plants which covered the area surrounding a small tree. Several chairs lay outside, with large canopies providing shade from the sun's heat.

Erundil motioned Steven forward to sit down. "Come here, Steven," he said. "Sit down and behold the wonderful nature of Watendelle that lies outside by your porch."

Steven came forward and sat on a white chair, filled with awe as he gazed upon the beautiful nature that lay just a short distance from where he sat. The same river which when entering Watendelle lay before him, with the bright light of the sun making the river shine with sparkling crystals. Surrounding the river was a vast garden full of all sorts of multicolored trees, and numerous plants, flowers, and bushes.

A gray walking path embedded with stones ran through the garden, where there could be seen many gamdars walking. Some of them seemed to sing as they walked on, while others simply talked with each other, and even others watered the plants and flowers of the garden. In the far distance were great and lofty structures and houses, and hovering in the bright blue sky were birds that refused to cease their singing. Steven let his mind wander in the beautiful nature that he witnessed.

Erundil turned and spoke to him. "Do you like the view, Steven?" he asked. "I wanted to give you a room that has the best view of nature outside of the palace."

No answer came from Steven as his eyes remained fixed on the beautiful sight of nature. For a moment, all memories and thoughts of the difficulties he had experienced were suddenly lost in time, as the beauty and glory of the land of Watendelle led him to remain fixated on a never-ending dream of peace and joy.

Then as one being roused from sleep, Steven felt the tap of Erundil's hand on his shoulder and suddenly remembered what he had said to him.

"Oh, yes, I love it," he said. "The beauty of this land nearly led me to fade in what felt like a dream. I could gaze at this sight for hours upon hours."

"I can see that, Steven," remarked Erundil with a smile. "I am glad to see how much you enjoy this view."

Steven went on to stare at the view for a few more minutes before Erundil stood up from his chair.

"I should be on my way now," he said. "I'll let you continue looking at the view, but just so you know, the council which I have invited you to will start in about three hours. There is a clock on the table near your bed, and if you look at it, you will see that it is two o'clock right now. The council will start at five o'clock, so in the meantime, you can get some rest if you wish. I have also asked my daughter to bring some lunch to you later this afternoon."

Erundil headed toward the door and turned back one last time. "I will see you later today, Steven," he said. "And don't forget to pick out any of the clothes which I showed you in the cabinet."

"I won't forget," replied Steven.

With that, Erundil exited the room and shut the room's door, leaving Steven seated alone by the porch. For many more minutes, Steven continued to silently observe the nature that lay before him. Delighting himself in the sun's warmness, he closed his eyes for a moment and thought of what life would be like in the land of Watendelle.

Opening his eyes, he stood up from his chair and sat on his bed. Lying on his bed, he stared at the golden headboard which had a gamdarian figure embedded in it, wondering who the figure was. He then cast his attention on the white ceiling, which was covered with several beautiful art designs carved into it. His eyes began to slowly shut as he relaxed in the comfort of his new room.

But after half an hour had passed, a sudden and large knock came on the door. He quickly rose from his bed and ran toward the door. "Come in!" he said.

As the door slowly opened, he beheld a tall and beautiful gamdarian woman clothed in a light bluish dress. A warm smile covered her face as her bright light brown eyes looked at Steven, and she had an elegant and graceful look on her face. Observing her appearance for a moment, Steven stared at her long flowing golden brown hair and noticed that across her forehead was a silver circlet with a blue gem at its center. Looking at her blue necklace and silver bracelet, Steven noticed that she held a large silver tray full of food in her hands. On the tray was bread, vegetables, and soup, but even as he looked at the food, Steven couldn't help but continue to gaze at the woman who stood before him, as he was drawn away by her remarkable beauty.

"Hello, Mr. Loubre," she eventually said in a soft voice. "I am Glowren, the daughter of Erundil. I imagine that you must be very hungry, so I have brought food for you to eat."

Steven continued gazing at her, being blown away by her glorious beauty. Then, after snapping himself out of his enchantment, he responded to her, stammering even as he spoke.

"Thank you, Glowren, for your great bb… beauty… I mean for your great generosity," he said, swiftly retracing his words. His face grew red in embarrassment. "Yes, thank you for your great generosity. That's what I meant to say."

Glowren laughed with a bright smile covering her face. "No worries, Mr. Loubre," she said. "All of this food is for you, so you can go ahead and take the tray away from me."

Taking the silver tray from her hands, Steven was unable to turn aside from her beauty and elegance. He nearly dropped the tray as he stared at her, and finally turned away from her sight as he took the tray and sat at a chair in his room.

He gave one last glance at her, as she turned away and shut the door of the room. Once she left, Steven brought his full attention back to the food.

He stared at the tray of food for a moment, wondering what he would eat first. Turning to the oval-shaped bread he observed five flat and thin pieces that were slightly smaller than his hands. Its color was light brown, but as he looked closer at it, Steven could see tiny green leaves that were sprinkled throughout each piece. Holding one of the pieces with his hand, he took a bite of it, and his eyebrows were instantly raised in pleasant surprise at its taste. As he chewed on it, he was surprised by how soft it was and by the level of sweetness it contained. He quickly moved on to the rest of the pieces and finished eating all five of them.

He turned now to the soup, which was a bright orange color, and made a silent bubbling sound. It was filled with some mushrooms and vegetables which included carrots, peas, and tomatoes. Picking up the silver spoon on the tray, he dug it into the soup and slurped a large portion of it. Before he knew it, he had finished the soup, and all that was left was a plate full of vegetables and a glass of water, which he quickly finished just as fast.

Once he had eaten his fill of lunch, Steven looked at the clock beside his bed and saw that it was two-forty. Feeling tired, he shut the window blinds and covered himself in the sheets of his bed. He instantly fell into a deep and peaceful sleep, as a broad smile covered his wide face.

After some time, a loud knock came on the door. Feeling greatly alarmed and annoyed, Steven uncovered himself from his sheets and remained on his bed. "Yes, who is it?" he asked. "You can come in!"

The door opened, and there standing outside of the room with a shocked expression on his face was Mataput. "Steven, what were you doing sleeping?" he asked, with his eyes widened in disbelief. "The council starts in eight minutes! You must get yourself ready so that you can make it in time. And here are your clothes that you hid behind the bush," he added, throwing Steven's clothes onto his bed.

Ignoring his clothes, Steven quickly glanced at the clock and saw that Mataput was indeed speaking the truth, as the time read four fifty-two, just eight minutes before the council would start. Filled with great shock that he had slept the two hours away, he quickly ran to grab some clothes by the golden cabinet, randomly grabbing a pair of brown shoes to wear. Once he had changed, he quickly dashed to the hall outside of his room, where he saw Mataput standing against the wall.

Upon seeing Steven, a smile came to Mataput's face. "Perfect, it's only four-fifty-five right now," he said. "At this rate, we will make it to the council in no time. Come, follow me downstairs and I will show you where Erundil is holding his council."

Steven followed Mataput as they descended the long step of stairs. He wondered what they would be discussing at the council, and what matters of wisdom Mataput would share with the group. But as he thought about Mataput, his focus was brought to Orieant, as he realized that he was not with him and Mataput.

"Where is Orieant?" he asked, bringing his concern to Mataput's attention. "I just realized that he is not with you. Will he be attending the council?"

"Yes, he will," responded Mataput. "Don't worry about him, Steven. Right now, he is inviting some special guests to the council and will be a few minutes late. But he has already alerted the king to this, and he has given him an exception to his tardiness."

The two of them continued to walk down the stairs, before reaching its end and stepping onto the golden ground of the first floor. Leading Steven through the long hall, Mataput gained pace as the start time of the council neared, before suddenly slowing down as with one minute to spare, they reached the sight of a door that led outside onto a porch.

6

The Council of Erundil

MANY HEADS TURNED WHEN Mataput and Steven made their way outside onto the porch where the council was being held. Looking around at the sights and sounds, Steven found himself standing on a wide stone courtyard, and surrounding him was a beautiful garden with a small pond. A silent stream of bubbling water coming from the pond delighted his eardrums, while the colorful flowers and plants of the garden which teemed with life, captured his gaze in bliss. A few birds chirped through the sky above, hovering over some statues spread throughout the area, many of them worn out over time, but still standing strong and proud.

Turning away from the garden area, Steven brought his attention to the porch area centered around the courtyard, where everyone was sitting. Gathered in a large circle and seated on brown chairs were twelve gamdars, with an extra five chairs left empty. The faces of those seated were covered with relief once they saw the arrival of Mataput and Steven. Erundil was present among them, clothed in a silver robe and wearing his crown on his head. Lelhond sat to his left and was clothed in a dark blue robe and had a silver circlet on his head. Staring at him, Steven couldn't help but perceive that Lelhond seemed to possess a certain level of importance that was unmatched by any of those seated in the circle, except for his father.

Looking now at the other gamdars who were seated, Steven beheld two young men seated to Lelhond's left, who had similar appearances to him and Erundil. Examining the one directly seated to Lelhond's left, Steven observed that he was beardless unlike many of those seated together, and was clothed in a light red robe. He had long light brown hair, and on his forehead was a silver circlet. Though he was less physically imposing than the rest of those seated, he appeared to contain a certain and powerful level of tender power.

Seated to the left of him was one who looked almost identical to him in his face, though he was bearded and appeared to be slightly older. He contained a strong build and was more physically imposing than all those seated together, even more so than Lelhond. He was clothed in a light brown robe and also had on a silver circlet across his forehead, though his hair was much darker than the one seated to the right of him. He had a noble face with a proud glance shimmering in his eyes.

The eight other gamdars seated together were all clothed in similar royal attires, and each held a level of high and noble looks on their face. Some were old, others young, and staring at them closely, Steven guessed which ones were soldiers, and which ones were those containing wisdom that helped spread counsel and advice.

Upon seeing Mataput and Steven, Erundil welcomed the two of them and introduced them to those seated with him. "Welcome to my council, Steven and Mataput," he said. He then turned toward the gamdars seated together. "I am sure all of you who Mataput is, but standing alongside him is, Steven Loubre, the man whom I have been speaking of lately. He has been brought to Watendelle, and to this council to learn many things about us and about the quest he will soon be embarking on."

Presenting Mataput and Steven to two open chairs to his right, the two of them sat down with the watchful eyes of the gamdars being fixed on Steven. The chair was tall for Steven, whose feet slightly brushed across the ground. He ignored this, however, and turned his attention to Erundil who had more to tell him.

"Before we begin, I would first like to introduce Steven to my other two sons seated to Lelhond's left," he said. "Seated to the left of Lelhond is Forandor, a musician greatly skilled in singing and the playing of stringed instruments. And to the left of Forandor is Karandil, a great soldier who is currently serving in our army of soldiers."

Steven smiled toward Forandor and Karandil, feeling greatly honored to be introduced to more members of the royal family of Watendelle. "It's a pleasure to meet you both," he said.

"It's a pleasure to meet you as well, Steven," responded Forandor. "My heart is filled with joy to see that the humans have hope because of you."

"Yes, I feel the same way about you as well, Steven," remarked Karandil. "For very long our people have suffered days of sorrow, not knowing when the great book of our forefather would come back. But it looks like you are the man to bring it back, and not for us, but for your people."

Steven continued smiling at them, feeling greatly humbled by their words. He wished to express his gratitude toward them, though he found no words to speak at that moment. At that instant, Erundil continued to speak to Steven.

"You have now met every one of my family, Steven," he remarked. "Now, as for the rest of those that you see here in this circle, they are either my advisors, friends, or workers, all skilled in many different areas. Some that you see now are mighty soldiers in our army, while others are important advisors of mine. I do not have time to tell you about all of them, but there is one who I would personally like to name, as I believe he is important for you to know."

Then, pointing to a particular gamdar seated directly across from him, Steven's attention was brought to a gamdar clothed in a dark blue robe. Slim he was in build, yet tall he appeared and looking keenly into his unwavering eyes, Steven beheld a sense of strength and wisdom that surrounded his presence. Advanced in age he looked, though not much older than Erundil, and great knowledge and keen judgment seemed to surround him like a vast cloud.

Now speaking, Erundil told Steven who he was. "This is Olindule, my chief advisor," he revealed. "I am telling you who he is because, without him, I am sure that I would have made many hasty and illogical decisions. I trust him to direct me to make the right decisions, and I am more than confident in saying that if my family line wasn't of the line of kings, he would make a great King of Watendelle."

Steven listened on in fascination and turned to Olindule, greeting the chief advisor of the king, who simply gave Steven a warm smile in return. Once he had finished telling Steven of all those who were seated in the council, Erundil then spoke to all those gathered together.

"Well, I suppose we can now begin," he said. "Today, on the 2nd day of November, I have scheduled a council to discuss many important matters that I wish to share with all those seated here, along with a few others who are yet to arrive. But just so we all know the significance of what I will be speaking of today, I would first like to provide the background of the ancient history of the world, especially that which affects our people. We all know that Jangart created eight distinct lands of this world, filled with their unique creatures. For a while, the creatures and lands of his creation lived in harmony and peace among each other, until the Dark Lord Natugura rose and rebelled against his creator. With his wicked act, he took with him many gamdars who were later transformed into hideous beasts now known as wuzlirs. They were banished from Jangart's presence because of their rebellion and found themselves in a new land, which they named Nangorid.

"With their terrible act of dissension, a terrible and luring wind of great evil was spread throughout the lands of the world, with some of the creatures either choosing to reject or accept it. Those who rejected it, which includes us gamdars, remained free creatures, while those who embraced its wickedness, fell under the corruption and influence of the Dark Lord. Among those who chose to accept the wind with all of its deception, were the humans, yet they remained free from the control of the Dark Lord. However, all knowledge of the other lands of the world and the opposing natures influenced by Jangart and Natugura were erased from their memory. Thus, evil, injustice, and foolishness have ruled over the peoples of the Earth for the past thousands of years.

"Meanwhile, the free creatures of the world have remained free from the shadow of Natugura's presence for all of these young years. And it came to pass that while my forefather Ulohendel ruled as King of Watendelle, he had created a great golden book full of wisdom, foresight, prophecies, and insight on how we should continue to flourish by living lives of truth, wisdom, and goodness. He wrote his book soon after many of the creatures of the world fell into decay and corruption, and he desired to share it with them so that they become free from the bonds of slavery to the destructive evil of the Dark Lord. Above anyone else, he desired most to share his creative work with the wuzlirs, for it was some of his closest friends and advisors who had fallen for the deception of the Dark Lord. It grieved his heart to see them transformed into such hideous creatures of madness, and he steadfastly dreamed of the day when they would be restored to their former condition of wisdom, beauty, and glory.

"But before his plan could prevail, we gamdars along with the free creatures of the world which included the dwarfs and giants, decided to unite and wage war against the Dark Lord, so that his swaying influence over the world would subside. War was declared on Natugura, and in response, his slaves which were the wuzlirs, along with the hzarves, goblins, and eliants, came to Nangorid to protect him and ensure his domination over the world. Though the free creatures of the world were still immortal at this time, they decided to surrender this gift of theirs to weaken the ever-spreading darkness covering many of the lands of the world.

"And so fighting broke out throughout the land of Nangorid, as Ulohendel led the free creatures of the world to battle against the slaves of the enemy. For six enduring years, the sound of marching and galloping horses rumbled across the ground, with shouts and cries trumpeting the tense air. Never before have we been so close to overthrowing the Dark Lord as was seen during the days of the War of Great Alliances, and I doubt that we will ever see a day like that in a long time. The free creatures led by Ulohendel had managed to force their way to the region of Parsuglin, and there before the very gates of the tower of Wuzinch Torgol, they laid siege to the stronghold of the enemy for over a year. Much blood was stained outside the fortress of Natugura, with many of our ancestors fighting courageously even to the point of death. But we came close to collapsing the very foundation of the Dark Lord's throne, and we could see the glory of victory from the reflections of our swords.

"While we laid siege to the Black Tower of our enemy, many of our soldiers returned home to Watendelle to let our people know how we were doing. But as they returned, to their terrible devastation and shock, they learned that the great golden book of Ulohendel had been stolen by the wuzlirs. At that moment, all hope of victory vanished, and when our forces at Nangorid were alerted to his news, they too broke down in frailty. All progress we had made against the Dark Lord was lost, and because their spirits were filled with pain and grief, they deemed that their sacrifices had been made in vain. The free creatures of the world ceased their long war against Natugura, who was left feeling satisfied in his dark abode.

"Soon after, Ulohendel died of a broken heart once he realized what had happened, and within the blink of an eye, all hope of overthrowing the enemy was lost. Ever since then, many wars and battles have been fought to try and bring back the book of our greatest king to our people, some of which have ended in minimal victories and others in utter defeats. But none of our attempts have managed to shake the very foundations of the Dark Lord's tower, and he has remained sitting on his throne in ease over these long years.

"Yet glimmers of hope have remained for our people, though we didn't know how much this hope would amount to. But when the volviers came to us two hundred years ago during the days of my great grandfather, King Onwandil, their words of prophecy sparked a newfound kindling of hope in our hearts. They told us that the lost book of Ulohendel would be returned, though it wouldn't be returned for us to use. A man of the Earth would accomplish this seemingly impossible task, and the humans of the Earth would use the words of wisdom from Ulohendel to become non-corrupted creatures just like us.

"And so we have eagerly held onto these words of Mataput and Orieant spoken to us long ago. To ensure that we wouldn't forget the hope that they had brought to us, we stored their words of prophecy in our many songs and scrolls. I grew up learning of their great prophecy and wondered whether it would come to pass during my lifetime. But I can now see that this man whom you see sitting among us, Steven Loubre, is the man prophesied by the volviers to bring back the lost book of Ulohendel. Hope and joy have been restored to our people, and the humans of the Earth no longer have to suffer under the abiding shadow of the Dark Lord. All we have to do now is discuss what our plan will be to best support Steven on this quest that he will soon be embarking on."

At that, Erundil ceased speaking and relaxed back into his chair. With his words, a calming wind of peace and comfort filled the hearts of all those who had listened to him, with Steven feeling especially confident about the quest he would be going on. Looks of calmness and satisfaction covered their smiling faces, as they thought of what comments they would add to what Erundil had said.

But at that instant, footsteps could be heard coming toward them. Turning their heads, they saw Orieant walking toward them. Gladness filled their hearts to see him, but as they looked closely, they saw two other creatures who came walking with the volvier. And once the gamdars had discerned their appearances, their moods suddenly changed.

To Orieant's left and right were creatures with a similar resemblance to that of humans, but very small as they only appeared to be about four feet in height. The two of them both wore baggy coats, one being dark green and the other gray. They had on short brown trousers which were slightly above the bottom of their hairy legs, and on their feet, they wore brown sandals. Curly brown hair covered their large round ears, and on their faces were bushy dark eyebrows along with round noses. The cheerful and innocent looks on their faces gave them the appearance of young children, but looking closer they looked to be in their late teenage years or even in their early twenties. The stocky little creatures were led to the courtyard by Orieant, where they sat in the chairs that were left open. All eyes were fixed on the two creatures whose feet didn't even touch the ground.

For a while, the gamdars simply stared at the two of them with faces of disgust. Confusion filled Steven's mind as he wondered what was going on and who the two creatures were. Suddenly, Erundil rose from his seat, with a look of disdain toward the two creatures glowing in his eyes.

"What are these smalves doing in Watendelle?" he asked, looking at Orieant. "When you said you would be bringing a couple of special guests to this council, I was expecting to see some noble gamdars, or even giants or dwarves. Yet I would have never imagined that you would shock me in this way. I am sorry, but you have brought disgrace upon us by inviting these smalves to my council."

He slumped back into his chair, crossing his arms in frustration and disbelief. Meanwhile, Steven observed the smalves from head to toe, greatly fascinated to see what they looked like. Yet he wondered why Erundil and the gamdars were so bitterly hostile to them, even though they looked like harmless little creatures.

Staring at Erundil, Orieant simply shook his head in grave disappointment. "I have not brought the smalves here just so they can listen to your complaining, Erundil," he responded. "But I am glad that they have been exposed to the views that you and your people have held against them. I know that your people hate the wuzlirs, but in all honesty, you seem to hate the smalves even more than the enemies of the gamdars. Let this be a warning for you and your people, that if you want to succeed on this quest of bringing back the lost book of Ulohendel, you must be willing to turn away from the stubborn animosity that you have unfairly held against the smalves."

Erundil thought of all that Orieant had said, but was unwilling to change his mind. "How can I trust them if they didn't help my people during the great war?" he asked. "While the gamdars, dwarfs, and giants fought hard in battle, what were the smalves doing to aid us in our long and desperate fight against Natugura? Even if we were to change our mind about them, how would they be of any help to us in our quest to bring back the lost book of my people?"

"They would be of great help to you, Erundil," responded Orieant. "Though you do not see it now, the smalves can be trusted to not only help you but to also give you a serious advantage over the enemy. And you must be willing to understand that the stories you have heard about the smalves during the Great War have been fabricated. Though they have never been the ones to fight in battle, they still managed to help the wounded soldiers that fought in battle by feeding them with their soups which helped strengthen and heal them. If it wasn't for this, many more soldiers would have perished and you would have never even been in the position to overthrow the Dark Lord from his throne."

Erundil remained insistent on his opinion of the smalves. "Maybe those wounded soldiers weren't as deathly ill as you think," he suggested. "Perhaps they just needed a warm meal to gain strength, which is something that anyone, not just smalves could do."

"Were you even born when the great war occurred, Erundil?" asked

Orieant. "How then can you claim what things were like when all you know about the events of this time are stories and tales passed on to you? The only ones seated here who can confirm what happened during those days are me and Mataput. And I can say in truth that though the gamdars tried to heal the many wounded soldiers of your people, only the smalves managed to restore their strength so that they were able to narrowly escape death."

Feeling humbled, Erundil remained silent for some time, before responding again to Orieant. "I suppose that you're right, Orieant," he said. "After all, you were there during that time so you must've known what happened. But by your same logic, how can I say for certain that it was because of the smalves that the soldiers were healed? If I wasn't there at that time, how can I reach the conclusion you are making?"

Orieant shook his head in astonishment. "I hope you are not calling me a liar," he said. "You know that Mataput and I will always speak the truth to you in all cases. So why would we lie to you about something that we witnessed with our very own eyes?"

"I'm not saying that you're lying," responded Erundil. "But I find it quite hard to imagine that the smalves were able to help our wounded soldiers in such a way like that, just as I am unable to imagine them being soldiers or great fighters."

"That is because you have always hardened your heart whenever something good is said of the smalves," replied Orieant. "Even if Jangart himself were to come down and speak in an audible voice to you about all the great things that the smalves have done, you would still not believe."

A smile came to Erundil's face, though it was one of annoyance and not happiness. "In that case, I would believe," he said. "But that doesn't mean that it would be easy to digest. What you are telling me is the same as if I were to tell you that the smalves were mighty soldiers, which I am sure you and Mataput would not believe."

"If you were speaking the truth I would believe it," firmly responded Orieant, not wishing to satisfy Erundil's way of thinking. "I would not ignorantly refuse to change my thinking just because I had always had a biased opinion against them."

Erundil shook his head in irritation, sensing that Orieant would not budge from his earnest point of view. Meanwhile, everyone else had been keenly listening to Erundil and Orieant's discussion with curious looks covering their faces. They wished to share all that was on their mind, but they remained silent and allowed them to finish speaking. Now that they were done, the gamdars, especially Erundil's sons, wished to swiftly come to their father's defense. However, before they could do so, one of the two smalves present among them spoke before they could utter a word.

"Well, Mr. Erundil, what you said about us smalves not being soldiers is simply not true," he said, crossing his arms. All attention was brought to him, the little creature clothed in a stained green coat. "I am Huminli Frauttins, and sitting next to me is my brother, Glophi Frauttins, and I can confirm that our great grandfather, Berry Frauttins, was a mighty soldier, greatly skilled in the wielding of the sword. Those skills came into handy use when as a young man he went on a great adventure with friends which included some dwarfs and giants, along with Mataput and Orieant, to travel through the evil lands of the goblins and hzarves so that they could recover lost treasures.

"Many times they went to fight in those lands, and my great grandfather slew many goblins and hzarves there. They then managed to find the lost treasures, returned home safely, and divided the treasure up along with the giants and dwarfs. Once we smalves received our share of the treasure, many of our people became very rich, with my great grandfather and his friends having many stories to tell in our home of Laouli. After our people gained great wealth, my great-grandfather trained many smalves to become mighty soldiers just as he was. And it is because of him that many of us smalves are very skilled and bold soldiers."

The smalf stopped speaking and glanced toward Erundil, who stared at him silently and intently. Curiosity filled his heart by all he had heard from the smalf, yet doubt quickly crept into his mind on whether or not what he was saying was true. He turned in the direction of the volviers.

"Is what this smalf saying, true?" he asked them. "Are the smalves mighty warriors as he claims, or is this just some lie he has concocted from his mind to make me change my mind? Not only that, but did you two accompany this smalf's great-grandfather along with dwarfs and giants on some adventure to reclaim lost treasures? Explain all of this to me, for all that I am hearing is alarming news."

All heads turned toward the volviers when Mataput spoke in response to Erundil. "Yes, I can confirm that what Huminli is saying is the truth," he said. "Orieant and I indeed go on an adventure with his great grandfather, Mr. Berry Frauttins, whose skills as a soldier and fighter were put on full display for us. Even with the dwarfs and giants among us, his ability as a fighter never failed to amaze us, nor did his humor and fun-loving nature which makes up a smalf's personality. There were times when he made me roll on the ground, unable to control my laughter, while other times he made me stand in awe of his great courage. Never before have I ever met such a unique creature in my life, one so small yet so fearless."

Erundil's eyebrows were raised in response to what he heard from Mataput. "I must admit, what you say about this smalf named Berry is impressive," he said. "But I would still have liked to see all that you are saying with my own eyes. Once I witness a smalf wielding a sword in his hand and boldly attacking our enemies, then I might consider changing my view on them. But for now, my mind is set on them and I will not waver from that just because of a few stories of this smalf's great-grandfather."

Mataput shook his head in amazement. "Your lack of faith in the smalves is making itself evident, Erundil," he said. "How much longer will you let your stubborn pride prevent the success of this quest we are here to discuss."

Many of those present and listening closely gasped in shock to hear Mataput speaking in such a way to Erundil. Some of the gamdars voiced their opinions of defense for Erundil, mainly his three sons and his chief advisor, Olindule. Others, however, wished to allow the smalves to have a chance to prove themselves, though they too remained doubtful whether the smalves would manage to completely change their minds about them. Steven remained silent, as he watched and listened to the spectacle with widened eyes. He wished to stop the arguments, though he knew that he had no right to prevent the gamdars from voicing their opinions.

But after several minutes of arguments, Orieant managed to intervene and subside the many opposing arguments voicing their views against each other. "That is enough," he said, standing up from his seat. "We have heard what you all think of the smalves, and I'm sure that Huminli and Glophi are not feeling any better than you are. Now regarding other important matters, we haven't even gotten into the main part of our discussion on who else we will send, besides Mataput and I, to support Steven on his quest through Nangorid."

At once, Erundil spoke his idea openly. "I suggest that my three sons accompany Steven on his journey through Nangorid," he said. "That way, Steven will not only find protection from you and Mataput, but my three sons will also provide the group with courage and strength, especially Lelhond and Karanduil who will use their skills as soldiers to good use."

Many of the gamdars voiced their agreement to Erundil, though Olindule took his suggestion one step forward. "Why should we only send three gamdars to accompany Steven?" he asked. "Why not send our army of gamdarian soldiers to help Steven on his quest that way you have enough protection and safety as he seeks to bring back the lost book of Ulohendel. Not only that, but if major fighting happens to break out, we will be prepared to go to battle."

Many gamdars voiced their agreement with Olindule, and even Steven found himself nodding his head in approval. However, an annoyed look seemed to cover the volviers' faces, especially Mataput's as he listened to what Olindule had to say.

"The purpose of our quest is in stealth and secrecy," he said. "Not in open war. Orieant and I have already made ourselves clear on this, so I am surprised to hear you, Olindule, suggesting this idea. It would be foolish of us to gather the whole army of gamdarian soldiers to bring back the lost book, especially since attempts like that had been made for thousands of years, all of which have ended to no avail. Erundil's idea of sending his sons with us is a good one, we will just need a few more to go with us, and then our group will be complete."

Once Mataput had spoken, all became silent, as though a vast lock in their mouths had prevented those in the council from arguing with the volvier. Erundil sat back with a smile on his face, glad that his sons would be allowed to accompany Steven and the volviers on their quest.

Yet, he wondered who else would accompany them, and though ideas filled his mind, he ultimately decided to remain quiet.

Meanwhile, Steven who had remained silent during the entire time thus far had had many questions lurk through his mind. Now that all was silent, he built up the courage to bring forth his objection into the open for all to hear.

"I must say that all I've heard today has brought me confidence in the quest I will be embarking on," he admitted. "Yet, I also have some questions as well. One thing that I've been wondering, is why can't I just fly to Nangorid rather than travel through the land for many weeks and months. When I arrived here in this land just a few hours ago, it was the muenwos who had flown me, Lelhond, and the volviers on a trip that took only just a few minutes. I don't get why no one has brought this up. It seems like the most logical choice we can make."

Feeling confident by what he had said, Steven sat back with ease. Yet, to his surprise, many of the gamdars broke out in laughter in response to his question. A puzzled look came onto his face, and he whispered into Mataput's ear for an explanation as to why they found his question to be amusing."

Speaking to Steven, Mataput spoke loud enough for all to hear his response to him. "You have brought up a good question, Steven," he said. "But you must also understand that though the muenwos were able to fly you safely to Watendelle, it wouldn't be that easy to do that in Nangorid. Natugura has many spies throughout his land, which includes a large number of winged beasts that patrol the sky. Sending the muenwos to fly us to Nangorid would both be foolish and dangerous since it would endanger our lives. We would immediately be recognized and struck down."

"Oh, I understand now," responded Steven, embarrassed that he had not thought his question through before asking it. "I should have known that Natugura wouldn't have allowed us to bring back the book that easily. If it was that easy, the gamdars would have already brought back the book long ago."

"That is right, Steven," replied Mataput. "But the good thing though, is that once we do get the book, we will then be able to call on the muenwos to fly us back as all attention will be brought to us and not to them. And from there, they will bring us back to safety with all speed before Natugura or his servants can recognize us or them."

A smile came to Steven's face. "Now that makes me feel glad," he remarked. "I was wondering what our return journey would be like, but I guess it will only take a few minutes."

"Yes, you are right again, Steven," said Mataput. "We will not have to worry about our return journey, rather the only thing that concerns us is our journey to the Black Tower of the enemy. And it is for that reason that we are here in this council so that we can discuss who will accompany you on your quest. Orieant and I will be going with you, and we are also willing to grant Erundil his suggestion of bringing his three sons, Lelhond, Karandil, and Forandor with you on this quest. The only question left is, who else will join us on this journey?"

A dead silence filled the atmosphere in response to Mataput's question. None of the rest of those seated wished to go on the quest through Nangorid, mainly because of the fear and doubt that consumed their hearts. Yet, they began thinking to themselves of who else they could suggest going on the quest. Mataput and Orieant watched on with crossed arms, as they observed the gamdars who were deep in thought imagining who else could support the company. During the long silence, Erundil had thought of a couple of people who could complete the small company and prepared to announce it to all those present.

But before he could even speak a word, Glophi, the smalf clothed in a gray coat suddenly sprang to his feet. "I will volunteer to go on the quest," he said, with all attention now fixed on him.

His brother, Huminli, likewise stood up from his seat and followed his brother's lead. "I will also join my brother and join the company in this quest," he said, standing close by his brother's side and observing the many eyes that stared at the two of them.

Many of the gamdars gasped in shock, feeling as though the air had been sucked from the atmosphere. Erundil couldn't believe what he said and looked on at Huminli and Glophi with both contempt and pity.

"I'm amused to see the two of you's boldness," he said, staring at the smalves with a scornful smile on his face. "You smalves are just small insignificant creatures yet you are willing to throw yourself into such an important quest. I would agree to let you two go, but I can't do that because of how important this journey is. You would both be left vulnerable and would not help us in any way."

Numerous individuals voiced their consent to what Erundil said, while the volviers looked on at him with grieved faces. Orieant sighed to himself and responded to Erundil.

"When will you ever learn to let the smalves have a chance?" he asked. "Huminli and Glophi have displayed great courage in recommending themselves to go on this quest, yet you will not even allow them to have a chance to prove themselves. Not only that, but you have failed to understand that if the smalves go with us, they will be of great help to us. Not only because of their boldness and many useful skills, but also because Natugura himself doesn't fear them, and would not send his servants to attack or trap them in any way. If Huminli and Glophi were to go with us, they would be underestimated by the Dark Lord, and because of that, we would have a great advantage of success."

Mataput voiced his agreement with Orieant. "What Orieant has said is true," he remarked. "I never expected Huminli and Glophi to volunteer themselves on this quest, but I am in full support of it. I have always known the smalves to be a brave and fun race of creatures, and though they are small, their bravery has always blown me away. And I believe that this courage of theirs will be put to good use for all to see once they went on us on this journey through Nangorid."

Erundil silently listened to the volviers' suggestions, greatly amazed by their faith in the smalves. Yet, the idea that he had had on who else could accompany Steven, the volviers, and his sons on their quest had not been erased from his mind. And he brought this plan of his for all to hear.

"I can see how much you want the smalves to accompany you on this quest," he said, turning toward Mataput and Orieant. "But before these two smalves endorsed themselves to go on this quest, I had another idea in mind. I can't think of many other gamdars who could join you on this journey, but what about having a dwarf and a giant join you? Didn't one of these smalves talk about how his great-grandfather went on an adventure with you two along with some dwarfs and giants to reclaim their lost treasures? Though they have remained silent for many long years, they were great allies of us in many wars long ago. Perhaps if a dwarf and a giant joined you on this quest, our people's ties with them will be both restored and strengthened."

Olindule chimed in to add to what Erundil said. "I believe that what Erundil has said is a wise suggestion," he said. "We have no proof that these smalves are as reliable as they claim to be, and on a quest this crucial, we can take no risks. Having a dwarf and giant join this quest would be wise and to this company's benefit. We know how much of good fighters they are, and though we have not heard from them in a long time, I still trust that they would do anything to help us, as was seen during the days of the great war.

The volviers thought deeply about all that was suggested before Mataput acknowledged Erundil and Olindule's idea. "What you two have both suggested is indeed reasonable and wise," he admitted. "But as you have already said, the dwarfs and giants as a people have remained secluded for many years by now. Why they have not decided to communicate with the outside world is beyond my understanding, but what I do know is that their homes have suffered increased attacks over the last hundreds of years. And since then, no matter how many times Orieant and I have tried to speak with them, their lands have remained shut from our entering. Because of that, we have no choice but to let Huminli and Glophi accompany us on this journey, as they are the last hope we have left to go with us on this quest. We have already agreed to let Erundil's sons join us, so you must be willing to let the smalves join us as well."

Erundil sighed to himself, before looking on at Huminli and Glophi with growing suspicion and thinking of another objection that came to his mind. "There must be something that these two smalves are hiding from us," he said. "This is the first time in a very long period that the smalves have been eager to partner with my people. I understand that you and Orieant brought them here, but how these two smalves have been so eager to go on this quest and to defend themselves, has been nothing short of strange. I'm now beginning to think that they are trying to take advantage of us and steal the great book of my forefather to keep it for themselves."

Before Mataput or Orieant could answer back, Huminli swiftly responded to Erundil's suspicion. "I can assure you, sir, that we smalves have nothing to hide," he confidently said. "Even if we tried to steal the great book of your wise forefather, I'm sure that your sons along with the volviers would immediately prevent us from succeeding in that goal. We are only going on this quest to help support the company and prove why we are great helpers for you."

Smiling at Huminli, Mataput added his comment toward Erundil. "As you can see, Erundil, you do not need to be questioning of the smalves," he said. "When Mataput and I went on the great adventure with these two smalves' great grandfather, we found no malicious intentions in his heart. And are you forgetting that the smalves are non-corrupted creatures just as the gamdars are? If they had malicious intentions in their hearts, wouldn't you think that Jangart would've revealed that to us a long time ago? I assure you, that you can trust in the smalves to go on this journey with us."

Glophi quickly chimed in to express his thoughts. "Yes, all that my brother and Mataput have said about us is true," he said. "Not only can you trust us, but we are willing to sacrifice everything to help make this quest a success. My brother and I grew up reading the stories of our great-grandfather and his adventures with the volviers, dwarfs, and giants, and we aspired to be just like him. The time to prove ourselves to be like him is now, and we can help save the fate of the Earth in the process. I assure you, Mr. Erundil, that if you let us join the company on this journey, the shadow of Natugura will be forced back and hidden from ever touching the Earth or the free lands of the world ever again. Perhaps then, you will see that the smalves are creatures whom you and your people can greatly respect and trust as your allies."

Glophi fell silent, leaving Erundil stunned by all he had heard. All was silent, as those in the council thought deeply to themselves, pondering everything they had just heard. Amid the silence, Orieant decided to add his comment toward Erundil, as he tried one last time to persuade him to let Huminli and Glophi join the company on the quest.

"You have heard for yourself how the intentions of the smalves are for good and not for evil, Erundil," he said. "And not only that, but I am persuaded that it is within Jangart's perfect will that these two smalves accompany myself, Orieant, Steven, and your sons on the journey through the land of Nangorid. So how are you to stand against the will of Jangart?"

A dagger as it felt, struck Erundil's heart at the mere mention of him possibly going against Jangart's will. He sighed to himself, before conceding to Orieant.

"I would hate to be going against the will of Jangart," he confessed. "And so if it's his will for these smalves to accompany you on this quest, then I can do nothing about it. But, I am still unable to trust the smalves, so before we make a decision, I would like to hear from my sons on what they have to say of the smalves accompanying them on this journey."

Orieant shook his head in amazement at Erundil's stubbornness but brought his attention to the king's three sons. Everyone else turned toward Lelhond, Karandil, and Forandor, wondering what the three gamdars would have to say regarding the smalves. Many of the gamdars, including Erundil and Olindule, sat with smiles covering their faces in confidence that the three of them would support them in mentioning their suspicions of the smalves. All eyes were fixed on the three sons of Erundil, as those present imagined what they would say.

Eventually, amid the many glances that the three brothers gave each other, Lelhond stood up from his seat and spoke to all those who stared at him.

"Well, I guess the time has come to express my thoughts of the smalves," he said. "I have remained silent this entire time out of respect for all my father has had to say, but now that I get to directly speak with Huminli and Glophi, I think that it's time that I speak the truth about all that I've been feeling on my heart over these past few minutes," he paused for a moment, with his father listening anxiously as he desperately hoped that his son would defend him his view.

Lelhond continued speaking, this time turning toward Huminli and Glophi with a smile on his face. "Who would have ever thought that two smalf brothers would ever find themselves in the kingdom of Watendelle?" he remarked. "I must admit, for the longest time I have held ill-fated views toward the race of smalves. All my life, I have believed that the smalves were nothing but small lazy creatures who were secretly working against my people. I was taught to be strong and courageous and to never work with the smalves, who I always believed to be weak and afraid. And when I saw you two walking to the council, I admit that I was shocked and holding bitter feelings against you two. But to my amazement, you two have greatly surprised me with the confidence and courage which you have displayed for all of us to see. Seeing how Mataput and Orieant have defended you and your people has been a sight for me to behold, and even now, I feel as though my heart is gradually warming toward you two. And even if you don't happen to be mighty soldiers, I am still impressed by all you two have shown me today. With that being said, though doubt is still creeping through my heart even now as I speak, if it's the will of Jangart for you two to join us on this great quest to find and bring back the lost book of Ulohendel, I will not stand in his way. I am open to you two joining us on this journey."

With his concluding statement, a rush of mixed emotions ran through the atmosphere. The air grew tense as many of those who had listened to Lelhond, chatted among themselves, either expressing their approval or disappointment by what he said. Erundil sat still and didn't speak a word, though his eyes widened with horror at what his son had said. The talking of those in the council went on for some time before Erundil managed to get their attention.

"Alright, we have heard what my son has said," he said, silencing everyone. He then turned toward Lelhond and spoke directly to him. "I am shocked to hear you saying this, Lelhond. But, now that I know what your position on the smalves is, I would now like to hear from Karandil and Forandor. What do you two have to say? Are you willing to let these two smalves join you on this great and perilous journey?"

Immediately, Forandor spoke in response to his father, sharing what felt to him like a heavy burden that had been placed on his heart.

"For too long I have held negative views of the smalves," he said, shaking his head as though he was disgusted with himself. "Just like Lelhond mentioned, growing up I was always told that the smalves were lazy creatures who were working against us rather than for us. While our people along with our allies which are the dwarfs and giants have fought many wars and battles together, I always believed that the smalves did nothing to help us. But I can boldly proclaim that my eyes have been open and I have seen the light. Even if the smalves may not be great warriors just as my people are, I now know that they are brave little creatures who have always helped us, and will prove their help for us if they join us on this quest. This journey will be a perilous one, but with Huminli and Glophi's help, I believe that it will go far smoother and become a success."

Mixed reactions soon followed Forandor's statement just as Lelhond's had caused, with Erundil finding himself gasping aloud. But before anything else could be said, Karandil swiftly followed his brothers' lead in his defense of the smalves.

"I agree with all that Lelhond and Forandor have said," he remarked. "Now is the time to allow the smalves a chance to prove themselves, and we can see how desperate Huminli and Glophi are to impress us. Even if they fail with their chance to prove themselves to us, at least we can rest assured that they tried to help us. But if they do succeed, which I hope and trust you two will, then my people as a whole will have no choice but to turn from our bitter feelings toward the smalves. And so it is in our best interest that they join us on this great journey through Nangorid to give us support in our desire to retrieve the lost book of Ulohendel."

At that, all grew silent once again, with Erundil slumping back into his chair and shaking his head in despair. Meanwhile, Mataput and Orieant's faces were covered in broad smiles as they were greatly appreciative of the words of support toward the smalves that Erundil's sons proclaimed in the open. Cheerful and excited looks covered Huminli and Glophi's faces as they started dreaming of what their new journey would be like.

Turning to Erundil, Orieant spoke to him despite how unhappy he was. "Well, Erundil, you have now heard the words that have come out of your own sons' mouths," he remarked. "They have made themselves quite clear that today is the day that your people turn from harboring bitterness and hate toward the smalves. And though you may not see it now, allowing Huminli and Glophi to go on this quest with us, is the best decision you could make as the King of Watendelle. So, what do you have to say, Erundil son of Tutlandil, King of Watendelle? Will you grant these two smalves to join us on the quest to restore the fortunes of not only your people but of the humans as well? Will you surrender your pride and stubbornness to allow the light to shine forth?"

Erundil remained sitting in silence, mumbling inaudible words of frustration to himself. But eventually, looking at the eager looks that covered the faces of many of those seated, including the smalves, his sons, the volviers, and even Steven, he knew that he had no choice but to grant them their wish. Yet he would ask for one final condition before letting Huminli and Glophi celebrate in joy. And so, after a long period of intense thinking, he finally responded to Orieant.

"I am surprised to hear myself saying this, but for the sake of my sons, I will allow these two smalves to accompany you on this journey," he said. "But, just so I can see the supposed greatness of the smalves for myself, I must join this company on this quest to the Black Tower of the Dark Lord to bring back the lost book of my forefather. If you allow me to join you on this journey, then I will no longer have any objections to the smalves joining us."

Many of the gamdars present in the council gasped in shock that Erundil had agreed to let the smalves join the journey. Yet, they were even more astonished that Erundil would be willing to go on the quest. Feeling greatly disappointed, Olindule brought this to his king's attention.

"My king, I am shocked to see you giving in to the volviers' demands," he said. "I would have never imagined the day in which you would allow the smalves a chance to prove themselves. They are still unproven and could be a dangerous risk to go on this quest. Not only that, but I am concerned to see you willing to go on this quest. Who will rule in your stead when you are gone? Have you not forgotten that the leaves of the golden tree become black when a king is absent from the throne? I do not think that it is a good idea for you to go on this quest, for I deem that much suffering will result from your absence."

Erundil pondered on what Olindule said, now feeling second doubts over his agreement of letting the smalves join the company on their quest. Yet, as he looked into the faces of the volviers and smalves, he sensed that whatever he would say in his approval of Olindule would instantly become overridden. And so, he sighed to himself as he responded to his chief advisor.

"I appreciate your concern, Olindule," he replied. "But I think that I have no choice but to let these smalves go on this quest, no matter how much I may oppose their going. With that, I must also go on this quest so that I can see whether or not these smalves are telling the truth of all that they have had to say about themselves today. And when I am gone, I will leave my wife Aradulin as the Ruling Queen of Watendelle. The leaves may grow black, but it will not be that way for long."

Olindule shook his head in response to Erundil, as he felt dismayed not only that the smalves would be joining the quest, but that the King of Watendelle would also be going on the quest with not even a son of his that is seated on the throne. Meanwhile, smiles covered the volviers and smalves' faces as they were overjoyed to finally see Erundil allowing them to have their purpose done. Speaking in response to Erundil, Mataput not only thanked him but also allowed him to join the company on their journey.

"I am glad to see that you have turned from your stubbornness, Erundil," he said. "Even if your heart may still be harboring bitterness against the smalves. But because you have allowed Huminli and Glophi to have their wish, I will also grant you your wish. You can join us on this quest. But understand that the purpose of our journey is in stealth and secrecy, not in battles and wars. And for us to succeed, you must be reconciled to Huminli and Glophi so that we have no inner turmoil in our group. You must be willing to become like your sons in completely accepting the smalves with open arms. Do you understand?"

Erundil grumbled to himself. "I understand," he said. "But don't expect me to go on and start becoming an ally with the smalves. Just because I have allowed them to go on this quest, doesn't mean that I am too fond of that idea. This quest is an incredibly risky journey that we are undertaking, and what if these two smalves do something terrible to ruin our secrecy? What would you say then, Mataput?"

Mataput shook his head in disbelief toward Erundil. "Why are you still hoping for the worst of the smalves, Erundil?" he asked, with a growing sense of frustration in his tone. "If they were to make a deadly mistake, then I would correct them, but just as I would do the same for you. Are you forgetting that you could easily do something to ruin the secrecy of the quest? Why then are you attempting to blame the smalves before taking a look at yourself?"

Erundil crossed his arms, yet said nothing in response, knowing that what Mataput had said was the truth. Eventually, however, he responded to him, but not to try to change the volvier's mind.

"I am humbled by what you have said, Mataput," he remarked. "It is the truth that any of us could make a horrible mistake on this journey, ruining the purpose of our journey," he then suddenly switched the topic and turned toward Steven. "You have been silent this whole time, Steven," he continued, now speaking to the man. "What do you have to say after hearing all that we have debated today? Do you trust these smalves to benefit this company on our quest, or do questions linger through your mind about them? I want to hear your response, Steven. After all, the purpose of this quest is to provide support for Steven in his attempt to find and bring back the lost book of Ulohendel, using it as a source of wisdom on how to rule righteously over his people. His opinion is the one that most matters in this regard, as I am sure we could all agree with."

Voices of approval rang forth in response to Erundil's statement, with even the volviers consenting to allow Steven to have his say. All attention was swiftly brought to Steven, who thoughtfully looked around at all the staring faces that were fixed on him. Then, with a deep breath, he revealed all that was on his heart.

"Well, today is the first time that I have come into contact with smalves," he said, with a smile covering his face. "And I have listened silently to all the discussions and debates that have taken place today, with keen ears. But, in my opinion, Huminli and Glophi seem to be really interesting and jolly creatures, which looks like they may reflect the smalves as a whole. I have also been pleasantly surprised by how bold and confident they have been, and I'm confident that I will need that on my quest, as I am still worried about this journey through the land of the enemy. But I know that with them, the volviers, Erundil, and his sons, I will have enough support and protection that I need. So, I am completely on board with the smalves accompanying the company and me on this most important quest."

The volviers and smalves smiled with gladness in response to Steven, while Erundil sat still with a hardened face. He knew that there was nothing he could now do to beat around the bush and that it was now inevitable that the smalves would be joining him and the company on their quest.

"Well, I guess that concludes our discussion for today," he said, with a clear look of dissatisfaction covering his face. "We have now heard from the volviers, my sons, and from Steven of whether they want the smalves accompanying them on this quest. And so, we have no choice but to let them have what they want. So, do we all agree that the nine of us going on this quest will be me, Steven, Mataput, Orieant, Lelhond, Karandil, Forandor, Huminli, and Glophi?"

Everyone responded to Erundil with a resounding yes, some of them being excited to see the smalves joining the company, while others including Erundil and Olindule remained doubtful. But those who remained suspicious over the smalves, let their feelings subside for a moment, as they knew that this quest would be a perilous journey, one that needed serious attention and focus.

After everyone agreed on who would be going on the quest, Karandil then directed another question to all those listening. "Well, now that we know who will accompany Steven on his quest to find the lost book of Ulohendel, we should now discuss the plans for our journey," he said. "I still want to know what our strategy for traveling through Nangorid will be. What places will we journey through to reach the region of Parsuglin and get the golden book that is stored in the Black Tower of the enemy?"

Erundil shrugged his shoulders. "I do not know what our plan is, my son," he responded. "The purpose of this council was only to discuss who would support Steven on this quest and what it would do to shape our world as we now know it. But perhaps the volviers have something to say regarding how we will journey through Nangorid to arrive at Wuznich Torgol, the very stronghold of the enemy, and to steal the great book of Ulohendel from his chains of darkness."

Clearing his throat, Mataput responded to Erundil and Karandil. "Yes, I have something to say regarding that," he said. "Orieant and I have thought deeply about this for a while now, and we were going to share a synopsis of what our journey would look like toward the end of the council. So, I guess that time is now," he paused, looking around at everyone to make sure they were paying attention before he continued speaking.

"This will be a long description, but a very useful one in mapping our way through the land of the enemy," he continued. "What Orieant and I have decided upon, is that once Steven leads his group of people to their new homes by the coast of Fozturia, this company of nine will then be gathered together to embark on our quest. We will travel westward across the sea since the land of the enemy lies directly west of the Earth, and once we arrive in Nangorid, we will begin our journey by first going through the plains of Meneth Gusgranil. Though the plains are hardly populated, there will be sights that may be hard for many of us to take, but we will have to endure them in order to pass through the region. From there, we will continue our journey westward by climbing upward in hilly regions and through the mountains of Lehu Shalank, where we will need to carefully move as the weather conditions there can be quite violent with lots of snow and bitterly cold wind speeds. But there are some caves there where no wuzlirs dwell, so we will be able to spend some time warming up in there while we endure the bitter weather outside.

"Once we manage to advance through and cross the mountains of Lehu Shalank, we will then find ourselves traveling through unnamed wildernesses and valleys where hardly any creature dwells except for a few roaming beasts and outcasted wuzlirs. Once we make our way through the valleys and wildernesses, we will then find ourselves in the Alinden forest, a dark woodland full of creeping beats. There may even be some wuzlirs in the forest, as a few of them usually reside there to keep everything in order. But if we can continue journeying in stealth, then we will be able to make our way through the forest. Once we make our way through there, we will continue traveling westward by making our way through more valleys and hilly regions which will take several more weeks. We will have to continue to remain focused and travel in secrecy as we near the region of Parsuglin.

"Eventually, after at least a couple of months of traveling, we will finally arrive in the region of Parsuglin, a dark and desolate land that is home to Wuzinch Torgol, the Black Tower of Natugura. The region itself is incredibly wide and is full of numerous black mountains and hills where hardly any grass grows on it. It is an expansive region covered in the Dark Lord's extensive shadow of uninviting darkness, but we will have to make our way through the dark land. For many days and perhaps weeks, we will journey through barren wastelands and abandoned settlements before finally arriving at the tower of Wuzinch Torgol. Now, getting inside the tower will not be an easy task, as the enemy's impenetrable fortress is surrounded and protected by iron strong black walls with a vast number of his wuzlirian forces. But the good thing is that there are many entrances into the tower, some of which are less heavily guarded. And once we quietly make our way through the walls and into one of the side entrances of the tower, we will climb up many winding steps before finally finding the lost book of Ulohendel.

"This task may seem impossible, but you must understand that the lost book isn't stored away in some secret chamber. Rather, the enemy has left it in the open in his black tower, largely because of his pride in knowing that all of the attempts of the gamdars to reclaim the ancient book have failed. Also, the atmosphere of the tower itself is covered in a shadow of heavy darkness, so if we make no sound we will be able to steal it just in time. Once we get the book, Orieant and I will call upon our muenwos to fly us back to safety. All attention will be brought to us, and because of that, the muenwos will be able to fly through Nangorid unharmed and take us away before the enemy can learn that we stole the book from his tower.

"From there, our quest will be complete. The muenwos will bring us back to Watendelle and to the Earth, to announce that the lost book of Ulohendel had been found and brought back. Our journey through the Dark Lord's land will be a long and perilous one, but I believe that we can succeed in bringing the ancient book of the gamdars to the Earth so that Steven will be able to rule over his people with perfection and righteousness. Thus, the other peoples and kingdoms of the Earth will see a bright light shining near the coast of Fozturia, and they will be drawn to that light and model themselves after Steven and his people. And they too shall also read the great book of Ulohendel and be filled with wisdom and the discernment to do that which is right rather than wrong. And with that, hope shall be restored to humanity, and Natugura's plan of total domination over the world shall fail."

With that, Mataput fell silent after giving the long synopsis of their journey. Those who had paid attention to all he said stared at him in amazement over the vast knowledge that he seemed to have of Nangorid. Steven was left shaking his head in astonishment, with a broad smile covering his face.

"Well, after hearing all that you have said, I am now convinced that this quest will end in victory for us," he confidently said. "Not that I wasn't assured before, since I knew that you, Orieant, and the rest of the company would support me, but the long description that you gave us over this quest has given me an even greater sense of protection. Tell me, how are you filled with such wisdom of the land of Nangorid?"

Mataput silently laughed to himself. "Steven, you must understand that Orieant and I have lived in this world for thousands of years," he said. "And we have gone to the land of Nangorid many times to investigate the enemy's whereabouts and tactics. But, this quest of ours is unlike anything we have ever been through, and I am sure that some of the regions we will be going through will either be unfamiliar or new to Orieant and me."

Steven gulped to himself. "Well, I hope these new regions we are going through won't be too different than what you and Orieant have seen," he hopefully remarked. "And understand why you and Mataput have such wisdom of Nangorid since you two are such mighty beings who have been around for thousands of years, while I am just a mere man who has lived for thirty-three years."

"Don't worry, Steven," said Mataput trying to assure him. "All will go well in our quest even if we encounter strange places which Orieant and I have never seen before. But, after hearing all I've had to say, do all of those sitting in this council agree with our plan of how this company of nine will be journeying through the land of Nangorid?"

"I certainly do!" hastily remarked Huminli. "I can't wait for my brother and I show to prove our usefulness in our great fighting skills."

A smile came across Orieant's face as he listened to Huminli. "I am glad to hear your excitement, Huminli," he said. "But understand that the purpose of this quest is in stealth, not in open fighting. But, if the time does come for us to protect ourselves from any threats, then we will have no choice but to fight."

"I understand," replied Huminli with a sigh. "I just want all of these gamdars to see what my brother and I are capable of doing."

"That time will come, Huminli," said Orieant. "And I am sure that the hearts of all gamdars will be completely altered to trust in the might of the smalves. But in an important and perilous journey that we find ourselves in, we must first trust in each other before we hastily make decisions that will not be to our benefit. The key to our success will be in our fellowship, which is why Mataput and I desired to gather all of these unique creatures to accompany Steven on his quest. And I am especially looking at you, Erundil, to learn to completely trust in the smalves, just as you have now decided to do. For if you turn from your ways, then perhaps this company will be wholly united."

Erundil's face hardened, but he conceded to Orieant. "I understand," he said. "But don't expect me to become friends with the smalves overnight."

"I understand that Erundil," replied Orieant. "But I hope that one day you will see how valuable the smalves are and how wrong you have thought of them, and I hope that realization would lead you to repentance. But for now, I can manage with your current view of the smalves, as long as it doesn't cause any division in our group."

Erundil didn't speak a word in response to Orieant but simply nodded his head. The sun began to slowly sink behind the clouds as the evening wore on. The wind silently bristled against the trees and plants of the garden, as the night cool began to set in. The sky was bright orange with the clouds reflecting golden patches of light everywhere throughout the stone courtyard. Those seated in the council stared at the sight in wonder, especially Steven, Huminli, and Glophi, who were growing increasingly fascinated by the land of Watendelle.

Then suddenly, all attention was brought away from the sunset as a loud rumbling sound could be heard coming from someone's stomach. The sound came again, and all attention was brought to Glophi whose face turned red in embarrassment.

"Well, I guess that means I'm really hungry," he said, wiping his stomach. He looked around in awkwardness at the staring faces that were fixed on him. "Well don't blame me. My brother and I are smalves, and we love to eat. That reminds me, will dinner be served soon?"

Erundil glared at Glophi with a disgusted look covering his face. Orieant eventually turned and spoke to Erundil.

"Well, you heard the smalf, Erundil," he said. He then turned toward Glophi. "There is no need to be embarrassed, Glophi. I am feeling quite hungry myself, and I'm sure that all of us are starving now."

He turned again to Erundil, who sighed to himself but now responded to Glophi and Orieant. "Well, I guess it is time to have dinner now," he said. "It's around seven-fifteen right now and I have prepared a great banquet dinner for you all to enjoy. Come, follow me and I will lead you all into the hall where our banquet will be served."

At once, everyone stood up from their seats and followed Erundil to the side doors to go back inside the palace. Huminli and Glophi came skipping in, wondering what type of food had been prepared and feeling excited to enjoy a dinner feast.

7

An Eventful Dinner

ONCE INSIDE THE PALACE, Erundil led everyone through the long royal hall full of decorated paintings and striking statues on every side. Passing through the hall were many of the king's advisors and workers, who greeted him and the company walking behind him. Yet, as they saw two smalves walking behind their king, they all collectively gasped in shock and began whispering among themselves.

"What business do smalves have in Watendelle?" asked one woman

"I do not know, and I do not wish to know," responded a man. "Let's just continue working and not bother ourselves with the meaning of all of this."

Regardless, many of the king's advisors and workers stopped what they were doing once they noticed the smalves walking around their palace. They stared longingly at the two young smalves both with the horror of seeing them, but also of growing intrigue. Yet, not wishing to disturb their king they eventually continued doing their work and minding their own business.

However, one such worker was all too curious about what was going on, and turning to the king, he brought his questions to his attention.

"My king, I apologize if I'm disturbing you in any way, but why are their smalves following you in the palace?" he asked. "I was informed that the kingdom would be having visitors in the volviers and the man named Steven, regarding the quest to bring back the lost book of Ulohendel from the enemy's tower, but I never imagined that smalves would be part of that discussion. I hope that they will not have anything to do with our upcoming plans."

For a moment, as a swift wind comes passing by, Erundil wished to agree with the worker in questioning why the smalves had been brought to his kingdom. Yet, as he looked into the watchful eyes of Mataput and Orieant, he knew that all had already been decided in the council, and with those many decisions came the choice of allowing the smalves to accompany the company on their great quest. And so, responding to the worker, he attempted to ease his worries.

"Do not worry about these smalves, Handar," he said. "A lot has happened today, with many things going against my wishes. It was the volviers who brought these two smalves here, and not me. That was one such thing I had to concede to their wishes, and as for the other things, I can explain all of it to you later. But come follow me with these people to the dining hall, and then I may have some time to answer your questions."

With a worrying scratch of his head, Handar followed Erundil with the rest of those with him through the hall and in the direction of the dining hall. Hearing what their king had said to Handar, some more of Erundil's workers and advisors all likewise jumped into the growing line of those following the king. All in all, it was about fifteen advisors and workers who had ceased doing their work out of strange interest in what Erundil would have to say regarding the two smalves that were with him once they reached the dining hall.

And so, Erundil led the growing crowd of gamdars, volviers, smalves, and the man who followed him; thirty-one individuals in total. Many more peculiar gazes and gossiping tongues met them as they made their way down the vast golden-floored hall of the palace, walking for what felt like an endless amount of time. They grew uncomfortable with the attention placed on them, especially Huminli and Glophi, who could sense the bitter tension flowing through the air once the gamdars saw them. But the two smalves continued walking on, proudly and with assurance knowing who they were and that they had the approval of not only the volviers but also of the king's sons and Steven.

After a while of walking, the crowd was finally led to a long blue curtain covered in drawings of white stars and words written in Tuntish.

"Through this curtain is the great dining hall of the palace," said Erundil. "This is a dinner which I have prepared for you all, though I did not expect all of these workers and advisors of mine to be here. But, there are many seats along the table, perhaps seventy in total, so there should be enough chairs for all of you to sit in. Seated at the table will be many of my other advisors, friends, and soldiers from the army, along with my wife Aradulin, and daughter Glowren. So, I will ask all of you to behave yourselves and act respectfully, especially you two smalves."

He gave Huminli and Glophi a sharp glance, yet the two of them seemed to be unconcerned by his warning.

"Yeah, yeah we'll behave ourselves," said Glophi. "I'm just really looking forward to eating the delicious food you have for us."

Erundil shook his head in growing frustration "I'm serious," he said. "This dinner conversation with my many other advisors and friends will be just as important as the council we just had. I need all of them to be on board for the plan we have agreed to take regarding our quest. So, you two must behave yourselves and act dignified."

Serious looks came onto Huminli and Glophi's faces. "I promise to behave myself, Mr. Erundil," remarked Glophi. "No matter how much I enjoy the food, I will still try to be aware of my surroundings."

"So will I," promised Huminli. "As the older brother, I will try my best to lead by example and restore confidence to your advisors and friends. But understand that we are smalves, and smalves love having fun."

A bewildered look came on Erundil's face after hearing Huminli, though he decided not to bring it up, and to brush it aside instead. Shaking his head, he doubted that the smalves would keep their promises, but he opened the curtain anyway.

Once the curtain was removed, a long and beautiful dining hall was revealed for every eye to dazzle in. There before them lay a vastly long table covered with a green tablecloth and set on the table were foods of all sorts; bread, meats, soups, fruits, and vegetables, along with numerous ornaments, flowers, and other items filling the lengthy table. Seated in chairs overlaid with silver could be seen many gamdars, perhaps twenty in total, all with healthy looks and smiles on their faces. Looking straight ahead, a large painting could be seen hovering over a window, depicting

Erundil and his wife Aradulin seated on silver thrones and wearing silver robes and dresses respectively. Many other paintings and statues filled the space surrounding the dinner table, with several flowers and plants providing a delicate inclusion of nature filling the palace's inside.

As they came to the middle of the table, Aradulin warmly greeted the company that came with Erundil. Seated to her left was her daughter Glowren, and to her right was an open seat that had the name *Erundil* written on it. The many other gamdars seated around the table greeted Erundil and the company with him, and they were especially delighted to see Steven. But once they noticed the two smalves standing in their presence, their moods immediately changed. Their mouths dropped to the ground, with even Aradulin's warm smile fading into an appalled look on her face.

But they said nothing as Erundil led the guests to the table, directing them to the open seats and showing which seats belonged to Steven and the volviers. The three of them were seated in respectable chairs close to the king and his family, on their chairs were their names written in them just like with Erundil. The king's many advisors and workers didn't have their names written on the chairs, but they found themselves seated in decent spots at the table. But when the time came for Erundil to show Huminli and Glophi where they would be seated, he pointed in the direction far into the corner of the long table.

"Since you two weren't even expected to be here, I guess you can sit in the empty seats at the end of the table," he said."

Huminli and Glophi dropped their heads, disappointed that they would be seated in the farthest seats away from the king's guests. They started making their long walk to the two open seats by the table's end, but just then, Mataput and Orieant suddenly stood up from their seats and stopped the two smalves in their tracks.

"Do not be ashamed, Huminli and Glophi," said Orieant. "You two can sit in the chairs where Mataput and I are right now, and we will instead move to the seats at the far end of the table."

"Yes, you two can sit here in these respectable seats," said Mataput. "We want all of Erundil's advisors and friends to see how important you two are for our quest so that they too could perhaps change their mind over your people, just as Lelhond, Karandil, and Forandor have managed to do."

Huminli and Glophi instantly turned around, filled with gratitude and excitement toward the volviers. Erundil, however, quickly intervened to speak to Mataput and Orieant. “What are you two doing?” he asked them. “You are the great volviers of Jangart and deserve to sit in these respectable seats. As for these two smalves, they are still yet to prove themselves to us, and for now, they can sit over there.”

“I understand, Erundil, but Mataput and I have made our choice” responded Orieant. “We have the right to choose wherever we want to sit, and what we want is to sit in that corner, and allow the smalves to sit here so that with the words that they share today, the hearts of those seated here will be touched.”

Erundil grumbled to himself but eventually gave in to the volviers' adamant wish. “Fine, they can take your seats,” he said.

At once, Huminli and Glophi made their way to Mataput and Orieant's seats, while the volviers began walking to the far end of the table. Once they had settled in, all attention was cast to the two smalves, with many of the gamdars staring at the two of them with shocked and outraged faces.

“Well, these two smalves have finally taken your seats,” remarked Erundil, speaking to the volviers. “Will you now explain yourselves in full as to why you have chosen them to sit here while you two have decided to sit over there?”

“And will you please tell us why these smalves are even here in Watendelle?” requested Aradulin. “I was told of Steven being invited to our kingdom, but the word of a smalf coming here was never even briefly mentioned to me.”

All attention was then brought to the end of the table, where Mataput and Orieant were seated. At once, Mataput responded to the gamdars' questions and worries.

“As you all know, just a few hours earlier, we attended the council which Erundil had called for,” he explained. “As you all expected, Steven was brought here to the kingdom of Watendelle to meet the king and his family and to see the lives which the gamdars live here in this land. The purpose of his coming was to see what it meant for a good king to rule over his people, which we hoped would provide him with the understanding of how important the quest is to bring back the lost book of Ulohendel from the enemy's hand. During the council, we discussed who would be joining him on the journey, which we agreed would include me, Orieant, Erundil, and his three sons.

"But we also agreed to bring these two smalf brothers with us on the journey, whose names are Huminli and Glophi. We picked them not only for their courage and boldness, which has been seen in their family line, but also so that the gamdars can see that they do not need to hold a grudge against them, but can instead accept them and become friends with them. And I hope that everyone seated here can learn to do this very thing which Orieant and I ask for."

A dead silence fell over the table at the revelation of the smalves joining the company on their journey. They were even more shocked that Erundil and his sons would be going on the quest as well.

"My king, is the news that Mataput has brought to us true?" asked Handar. "I hope that my worst fears aren't coming true, that these smalves will be involved in the great quest. And I was never told that you and your sons would be going on this quest. I can't lie to you, my king, I am greatly concerned by everything I have heard from Mataput."

"You have every right to be concerned, Handar," responded Erundil. "And I can assure you that my original plan was for our army to go to war against the wuzlirs, to provide a distraction for Steven on his quest. But my ideas have not been to any avail, as I have learned that the purpose of our quest will be in stealth and secrecy, not in open fighting. We have gathered a company of nine people to go on this quest, and against my wish, these smalves were recommended by the volviers to join us. Though I was against it, I had no choice but to submit to Mataput and Orieant's wish. And to my astonishment, I found that my sons were now defending the smalves, choosing to change from their previous views of them, which I still hold on to. And so, we decided that accompanying Steven on his quest would be the volviers, my three sons, and these two smalves. But, I let my sons and the volviers have their wish on one condition, that I would also go on the quest so that we could see what made the smalves so special. And so, everything that Mataput has said is true, and these smalves will be going on this important journey with us."

Handar sighed to himself and shook his head in disbelief. "I am surprised that you allowed this, my king," he said. "And I am even more shocked to hear that your sons have grown fond of the smalves. But my real concern is over who will rule in your stead while you and your sons are away."

"I have decided to allow my wife to be the Queen Regent of Watendelle in my place," revealed Erundil.

Aradulin along with many of those seated gasped in shock at this revelation. "I was never told of this," remarked Aradulin, with a bewildered look covering her face. "Will not the leaves of the golden tree grow black while you and our sons are away? I do not doubt my ability to rule over these people while you are gone, I only worry whether it will be to our benefit. I suggest that at least one of our sons stay behind so that we still have a king sitting on the throne."

"Our final decision has been made, Aradulin," replied Erundil. "I'm afraid that it's not in our power to reverse it now."

A tremor of fear fell over Aradulin as she listened to her husband, as she now found herself worrying over her husband and sons, now that she saw the full magnitude of the quest that lay ahead of them. Yet, even as she thought deeply to herself over all that Erundil and Mataput had said, a sharp twist as it felt struck the very core of her heart. As she let the thoughts race through her mind, she found herself warming to her sons' newfound opinions of the smalves, feeling as though it was the right thing to do. So, to her surprise she spoke in defense of the smalves, choosing to turn from her previous way of thinking.

"Maybe it's time for our people to turn put off our grudges against the smalves, just like our sons have done," she remarked, speaking to Erundil. "Though I was disgusted just a few moments ago to see these smalves sitting at our table, I must admit that I'm beginning to have second thoughts about all that I have ever known of the smalves. When have they ever fought against us? Or when have they ever betrayed us? And if Mataput and Orieant have endorsed them to go on this quest, then why should we stand in their way?"

Gasps of shock rang around the table. "Do you know the full weight of what you have just said, Lady Aradulin?" asked one horrified gamdar. "Do you now think that the smalves could be trusted?"

"I never said that the smalves can be trusted," responded Aradulin.

"We have not yet seen what they are made up of, and whether or not they are worthy to become our allies and friends. But perhaps now is the time for us to no longer view them as failures working against us, but as creatures desperately hoping to earn our approval."

Several of those seated could hardly believe the words which come out of Aradulin's mouth. The king's advisors and friends had always known the Lady of Watendelle to be a gracious yet determined woman, one who was unwilling to surrender her views, just like her husband. Yet, they now saw a change in her, which especially delighted her three sons, who were glad to see her so willing to turn from her bitter feelings against the smalves.

But before they could respond to Aradulin, her daughter Glowren quickly chimed in to agree with her mother. "I would have to concur with my mother," she said. "Though I have not completely processed my thoughts, I still think that now might indeed be the time when we allow the smalves to have a chance. I do not blame those who are still doubtful of what they are capable of, but I am more than willing to side with my brothers and mother on this matter."

Erundil and many others could only shake their head in disbelief, as they listened to Aradulin and Glowren expressing their desire to allow the smalves a chance to prove themselves. All was silent for some time before Lelhond stepped in to speak.

"I must confess that I am glad to hear what my mother and sister have had to say regarding the smalves," he said. "Today has been the day where I have had a change of heart toward them, mainly because of what Mataput and Orieant shared with us at the council. And I've come to realize that Huminli and Glophi could be more than great helpers for us on the journey through the land of Nangorid. They could be more than we had ever imagined them to be, and I will be the first person to support them. If they need to be trained with weapons when fighting, then I will train them, and if they need to learn the art of traveling in stealth, then I will do my best to teach them. If they need to become stronger, then I will build them up. Whatever they need help with, I am willing to be the first person to support them on this quest."

Erundil's face hardened with frustration as he listened to his son's growing fondness of the smalves. To many of the gamdars who had known Lelhond for years, he would've been the last person they would have imagined to say such things regarding the smalves. But for the volviers, they couldn't have been any more delighted by what the Prince of Watendelle had said.

A broad smile covered Mataput's face. "I am amazed by your transformation, Lelhond," he remarked. "Just earlier this morning you were not saying the best things about the smalves, yet ever since this council, you have been the first one to step in and defend Huminli and Glophi. Perhaps you are the spark that can ignite a change between the relationship of gamdars and smalves."

"Perhaps so," chimed in Orieant. "The Prince of Watendelle is proving himself to be a worthy candidate as the king. But let us also not forget about Aradulin and Glowren, as these two women have now had a change of heart toward the smalves. You two along with Lelhond and his brothers are leading by example of what is needed for this quest of ours to succeed. All we need is for the King of Watendelle to also see the light and change his attitude toward the smalves, and then nothing will be able to divide this company on our quest. The key to our quest is not only in skillful and secret traveling but also in friendship and unity, which will bring harmony to all of the free creatures of the world. This journey through Nangorid will be a turning point for many of you, and I am glad to see how so many hearts have already been transformed today."

Erundil sighed to himself. "I think that I've heard you well enough today, Orieant," he said with annoyance. "You have stressed how much you want my people to change their minds about the smalves, and because of you and Mataput, my entire family has now become fond of the smalves! Is it not enough that we have agreed to let the smalves join us on the quest? Must we now become their friends, rather than just minding our business from each other?"

Before Orieant could respond, Lelhond spoke in defense of the volvier. "Father, the volviers have done great things for us," he said. "And I think that today has been the turning point for our people, where we have now seen the truth about the smalves. There is no need for us to remain their bitter enemies, rather we can work with them and build friendships and alliances to our people and their people's good fortune."

A sick look could be seen on Erundil's face, as his body started shaking with horror. "Oh, my son! My son!" he suddenly exclaimed. "What spell has come of you? All my life I have known you to be the one closest to me in your opinions and hobbies, yet now you have decided to go against me and endorse these two smalves. And not only that but your siblings and mothers have decided to follow you in doing this abominable thing."

Gasps of shock came across the table. Fear could be seen on Lelhond's face, though he still found the boldness to stand up to his father.

"We are not doing an abominable thing, father," he responded. "And I have not become bewitched, neither has Karandil, Forandor, Glowren, or mother. If we want to succeed on this journey, we must choose to build our relationship with the smalves, and surrender our pride and stubbornness. For too long we have held unfair opinions against the smalves, which has been to our people's downfall. But now we have a chance to redeem ourselves and show why the alliance between the gamdars and smalves will be unlike anything ever seen before in the history of this world. Will you join us, father? Will you allow yourself to be exposed to the truth?"

Erundil sat silently, with visible frustration covering his hardened face. Knowing that he wouldn't respond to his son, Aradulin intervened to calm the growing tension.

"Well, I think we have heard enough of the opposing views dividing my husband and his family," she said. "Now that I think of it, we have hardly heard from these two smalves today. Why don't they tell us a little bit about their people and what they are like?"

With a sudden switch of enthusiasm covering his face, Glophi swiftly spoke of what his people were like. "Ah, I'm so glad that I can finally talk to you all about what my people are like," he excitedly said. "We smalves have had many important figures impact what our lives are like, but almost all of us live simple lives, mainly as farmers. My brother and I come from the land of Laouli, and throughout our homeland, we have many vast farms where we grow many different plants and vegetables in plentiful amounts, which we eat especially in our delicious soups. Speaking of food, we smalves are really good cooks who love to have merry meals as many times in a day as we can manage. Since we are small creatures, we live in undersized houses surrounded by forests, valleys, and hills. Almost all of the regions in our land are hill countries, where our governors ensure that all is going well wherever we live.

"We have governors since no king rules over us, and even our governors usually have nothing to do and live respectively and joyfully among all of us. As for our renowned figures, they are known for being famous and bold explorers who almost always come back to tell us of their many great deeds and adventures. One such adventurer, who is perhaps our greatest ever, would be my great-grandfather Berrliadon Frauttins, known as Berry Frauttins, who went on a great journey through the lands of the hzarves and goblins on a great quest with some of his friends, the volviers, the giants, and the dwarfs, to reclaim some lost treasures. His knack for skillful fighting made him a key component of the group on their journey, and he came back full of many tales of his celebrated experiences. He trained many smalves to become strong warriors for themselves, one of them being Mortin Joggulstan, probably the greatest warrior we have ever had, even surpassing my great grandfather. And I can say that my brother and I have learned many of our great grandfather's tricks and skills, which we hope to use in our quest."

Those at the table listened on with growing fascination of the smalves, especially Aradulin who found herself even more impressed by them. "Your kind seems to be interesting creatures who have the perfect balance of being both fun and also surprisingly courageous. I can see that you inherited those traits of determination from your great-grandfather, which I'm sure will be put to the test on your quest. But I wish nothing but success for you two, in all the ventures that lie ahead of you."

"I appreciate your kind words, Lady Aradulin," replied Huminli. "And I am glad to see how engrossed you are in my people, just by listening to what my brother had to say. But," he said, now bringing his attention to the food at the table. "Though my brother and I could talk for endless hours, are we just going to ignore all this food that is placed before us? Another thing that you should know about is, is that we smalves are always hungry, and we will never refuse to gobble up a full plate of food that is before us. Isn't that right, Huminli?"

"That is right," added Huminli, who had been staring at the food with an open mouth for some time. "I can sense that my stomach is grumbling in frustration that I have ignored it. I could use a good dinner right now, and this food sure looks delicious."

Aradulin laughed to herself. "Well, this is another thing of your kind that interests me," she said. "Your love for food seems like a strong foundation of your lives, and it would be unwise for me to neglect that."

Suddenly, she clapped her hands together and whistled in the direction where the blue curtain was.

At once, many gamdars, around thirty in total, sprang from the curtain and rushed to the dinner table. They carried plates, bowls, glasses, and utensils, and started serving those seated with the food that was placed before them. They filled the plates with bread, meat, fruits, and vegetables added soup into the bowls, and poured water into the glasses. They gave everyone seated an equal amount of food and bowed in front of the King and Lady of Watendelle once they served them their food. Once they had served everyone, they swiftly dashed away through the curtain.

Once they had gone, everyone started picking up their utensils and started eating the food that filled their plates and bowls. But while everyone ate, Huminli and Glophi looked around with confusion when they saw everyone using their utensils to eat. Shaking their head, they started eating by using their hairy hands to pick up the food that was on their plates, munching all of it down at once with large bites and licking off the remaining crumbs on their plates. They then grabbed their bowls of soup, which they swiftly slurped down in mere seconds. Once they had finished eating, they let out synchronized burps and wiped off the oil that was on their faces.

Everyone stared at them with open mouths, with Erundil and many of those seated close to him staring at the smalves with disgusted faces. "What are you two doing?" he asked, with his hands shaking in irritation. "Did you two not promise that you would behave yourselves by acting respectfully? Why then have you disgraced everyone seated here with your disgusting table manners?"

"I'm sorry, Mr. Erundil, but this is just the way we are," remarked Huminli. "I didn't realize that you wanted us to behave respectfully by eating the way your kind does. If you would have told us that, then we would have tried our best to eat with these utensils, or we would have just told you plainly that we wouldn't have been able to do that."

Erundil rolled his eyes in annoyance. "You two are getting on my nerves," he muttered under his breath.

"I'm sorry that we have made you unwell, Mr. Erundil," said Glophi, wishing to ease Erundil's frustration. "But if there is something that you should know about our kind, it's that we love to eat and have fun. Why then should we change our way of living?" he asked, turning to his brother, Huminli. "You know what, Huminli, why don't we show everyone what makes smalves so fun to be around?"

"I would love to," replied Huminli. "Let's put on a show for them, and demonstrate what makes even the most annoyed of people laugh in amazement."

Glophi agreed, and at once, the two brothers grabbed the utensils that were by their sides, and suddenly started banging them on their plates as if they were sticks on a drum. Standing up, they grabbed their plates and bowls and spun them around their head, and even on their feet. Those watching immediately stood up from their seats, trying to restore order.

But it was all to no avail as Mataput and Orieant prevented them from stopping the smalves. The two of them continued playing with their plates, bowls, and utensils, making musical sounds and balancing them as they danced. They continued ignoring Erundil and the many other gamdars' cries to restore order, showing no sign of stopping. Then, breaking off into a chant, the two brothers began singing a popular song of theirs, while everyone's attention remained fixed on them:

Balancing the bowl and dancing with the plate,
Spinning the glass and playing with the spike!
Don't withhold the food or else you'll witness our hate,
For it's what we smalves are like!

Chug down the water and gobble down the meat,
Then walk through the rolling hills on a great hike!
But don't leave us hungry and instead, let us eat,
For it's what we smalves are like!

Feed us some bread or else we will dread,
For we little creatures are not afraid to strike!
Yes, don't stop feeding us some bread,
For it's what we smalves are like!

Come to our farms and grow your plants,
For we will not block you as a dike!
Come and eat quickly, lest the food is eaten by the ants,
For it's what we smalves are like!

Come for yourselves and see why we sing with hype,
For we do not notice the difference between you and us alike!
Come and eat our food while it remains ripe,
For it's what we smalves are like!

Once they finished singing and dancing, Erundil, rose from his seat in great vexation. "What was the purpose of this dangerous performance of you two?" he asked.

"We just wanted to expose all of you to how fun smalves can be," answered Glophi. "What we just sang is a particularly famous song in our homeland of the Marn, that was written many hundreds of years ago by Gerrin Tokenmill. It tells us what our people are like and how those who have never stumbled upon us can still celebrate and enjoy themselves with us since we smalves don't hinder others from coming to our land."

"Well I for enjoyed listening and dancing along to your song," remarked Forandor. "It was good to enjoy myself by the passion and joyfulness which you two have warmed my heart with. But take it easy next time with the plates of bowls, as I feared that at least one of them would be broken. But good for you for not destroying any of our dinner items."

"I think that Huminli and Glophi deserve more than just our words of praise," commented Lelhond. At once, he started applauding the smalves, and in response, an endless noise of clapping hands filled the room.

With the applause for the smalves came an array of voices shouting, "bravo," as many of those seated continued celebrating the performance of

Huminli and Glophi. Broad smiles covered the faces of Erundil's family, while he and many others sat back with crossed arms and frowning faces.

In response to the roar of adoration they received, Huminli and Glophi bowed in the presence of all those that surrounded them.

"Thank you, everyone, thank you so much," said Huminli, overwhelmed by all the attention he and his brother were receiving. "It was a pleasure to delight all of you with our performance, and we hope to share many more with you all."

"I can't wait to see more of your performances," said Glowren, with a cheerful smile. "I am impressed by this most wonderful show of yours."

"I am not impressed," said Erundil, suddenly blurting out his opinion. "These two smalves could have nearly broken all of our valuable dinner items, just because of their cheap and foolish show! Not only that but I was left shocked by how disgustingly they were eating their food, with no care at all for table manners or the attention of those around them. I have had enough of you two. I must have time to rest and think for myself. I will see all of you tomorrow morning just outside the palace where I will give Steven a tour of my kingdom."

At once, Erundil stood up from his seat and left the dinner table. The volviers stared at him as he neared the red curtain, shaking their heads in disbelief. But just as he was about to depart, Huminli suddenly called out to him.

"Can my brother and I get a tour of your kingdom well?" he asked, with eager and curious eyes.

For a brief moment, Erundil thought of harshly rejecting the smalves' request. But as he looked at the keen eyes that stared at him, noting the looks that his family and the volviers gave him, he realized that he had no choice but to allow the smalves to have their wish.

"Fine, you can join me on the tour," he conceded. "But make no mistake, if you do anything else as foolish as you two have demonstrated tonight, then you will no longer have any part in the tour. Have I made myself clear?"

"Yes we understand, Mr. Erundil," replied Huminli and Glophi in unison, celebrating with joy that Erundil had allowed them to go on the tour.

Saying his final goodbyes to those at the table, Erundil made his way through the curtain, vanishing from everyone's sight and thought.

Aradulin turned to Huminli and Glophi with a grave look on her face. "I think that you two went a little too far in your show," she admitted. "I don't blame my husband for being upset over you two even though I believe he could have handled it in a better way. But don't be ashamed," she said, now with a gracious look returning to her face. "For I now understand that it's the way your kind is like and it's not my power to try and alter that. I found your performance to be quite amusing, and if I am honest, this has been one of the few times that I have had a reason to smile recently. Now that you two have brought a smile to my face and have taught me and all of us about your kind, I wish to tell you a bit about my people as well. But, it would take ages for me to explain all of that to you, which is why I am glad that you will be going on the tour tomorrow. And now that I know that you will be spending another day in Watendelle, it would be appropriate for me to allow you two to stay in some of the empty rooms of this palace."

Huminli and Glophi stared at Aradulin, full of gratitude and wonder at both her honesty and grace. While gazing at her, she once more clapped her hands together and whistled, bringing in many more gamdarian workers into the room. She called them forth to her and whispered into one of the workers' ears.

"I want you to prepare rooms for these two smalves to stay in," she said. "They will be staying with us for a short time, so it would be hospitable of us to make their stay in the palace a memorable one. Don't worry about showing them our clothing, as I am sure that they would rather stay clothed in what they are wearing right now."

A befuddled look came onto the young worker's face. "Are you sure, my lady?" he asked. "Have we not feared for many years that the smalves have sought to bring a curse upon our people rather than a blessing? Yet now you are willing to allow them to have a stay in our palace."

"I know what I am doing," responded Aradulin. "These smalves will not bring us a curse, as they have never sought to do in their entire existence. I do not have time to explain why this is, but you must do as I have ordered you and prepare them with rooms."

The worker bowed his head to Aradulin. "At your command, my lady," he said. He turned to the workers around him, whispering into their ears what the Lady of Watendelle had instructed him, and they all quickly departed from the dining hall to prepare rooms for Huminli and Glophi.

For the rest of the night, those remaining at the dinner table chatted among themselves. Mataput spoke to Aradulin, having been greatly impressed by the change he had witnessed in her during the night.

"I must say, Aradulin, that while your sons and daughter have impressed me by their change of opinion regarding the smalves, you are the one who is leading by example," he remarked. "I would have least expected you to turn from your resistance against the smalves, yet you have completely turned my preconceived idea of you upside down. Now it is only up for your husband to accept the smalves for who they are."

"That day will come," said Aradulin. "It is only a matter of time before he learns to trust in the smalves. If I have managed to make a complete turnaround regarding my judgment of the little creatures, then I am sure that Erundil will also."

Many more discussions continued into the late night, with Huminli and Glophi continuing to entertain everyone with their stories and jokes. Steven, who had mostly been silent all night, shared his heart with Erundil's sons and the many gamdars who listened to him, speaking of his underlying fear that Maguspra and his spies would catch up and find the people whom he was leading, and expressing his concerns over his quest into the land of the enemy. But, his fears were alleviated mainly by Lelhond and Karandil, who both talked about the many battles and wars that had been fought which had weakened the enemy's forces over the years and destroyed many of his cities and fortresses. The volviers hardly shared anything, instead listening intently to the discussions which took place and remaining seated at the far end of the table.

Eventually, having noticed that Huminli and Glophi had begun yawning out of tiredness, Aradulin decided to call it a night. "I think this is a good place for us to end our gathering," she said. "It is well into the night now, and several of you will need enough sleep before you go on the tour of the kingdom with my husband and sons. Just know that those of you going on the tour will be expected to come down to the first floor by nine o'clock so that you have enough time in the day to visit our many cities and towns."

Everyone stood up from their seats, speaking their final words to each other. "It was good talking with you, Lady Aradulin," said Huminli, bowing his head to her. "Thank you for being so generous and accepting of my brother and me."

"It is my pleasure," said Aradulin with a warm smile. "I am grateful to have been exposed to you and your brother's merry personalities and of the many stories of what your people are like. I hope to hear many more good things coming forth from both of your mouths."

Wishing their last goodnights to everyone, Huminli, and Glophi came to the curtain, where Steven and the volviers stood, and were led through the long hall of the palace and up the many steps of the staircase. Being shown their rooms by the gamdars around them, the smalves entered their rooms and at once collapsed onto their beds, dozing off into a deep sleep.

8

The Ancient Wanderer

STEVEN WAS ALERTED TO the sound of the door of his room bursting open. Standing by the door was Mataput, who was clothed in his regular blue cloak and held his gray walking stick. He shook his head while watching Steven scramble out of his bed.

"You've made me do it again, Steven," he said, crossing his arms. "I don't know how you've managed to sleep the morning away, but all I know is that you have eleven minutes to get ready in time for the tour Erundil is giving you of his kingdom.

Turning to the clock, Steven saw that the time read eight forty-nine, and he suddenly remembered what Aradulin and Erundil had said of the tour yesterday at the dinner table. He quickly sprung from his bed, running to the bathroom to wash his face and swiftly putting on the old clothes he had come to Watendelle with. Once ready, he opened his room, where Mataput and Orieant, who was now wearing his brown cloak with his pointed hat, were standing by the hall outside his room.

"Well, you've managed to get ready just in time again," said Mataput with a smile on his face. "We have five minutes before the king, his sons, and the smalves will depart for the tour of the kingdom, so we better catch up to meet with them."

At once, Steven followed the volviers as the three of them hastily made their way down the stairs and onto the main floor of the palace. They made their way through the golden palace doors, and standing under the bright sunlight, were Erundil and his sons along with Huminli and Glophi.

Erundil greeted Steven and the volviers. "Good morning," he said with a smile on his face. "Today is a great day for me to give you all a tour of the wonderful realm of my people."

"I can't wait to see the beauty of this land," remarked Steven. "Will I get to see numerous cities and towns today?"

"You will, Steven," replied Lelhond. "Though you have already seen part of our chief city of Kulendar, there are still many places to visit and stories to tell. Today, you will feast your eyes on vast structures, rest under the blissful nature of our homeland, and hopefully meet many more of my father's friends. You will see the fulfilled lives that we have managed to live, despite all of the attacks of the enemy against our people. You will be taught of our many traditions and practices which I hope will influence you in the way you interact with your people."

"Well, I'm even more excited to see all of this today," said Steven, growing with keen interest.

"Then let us get going then," said Erundil. "There are many places that we want Steven to see today, so we have no time to waste. And just so we can visit as many regions as we can, we are going to travel by horse, not by foot."

With that, the company began following Erundil as he led them through the long road away from the palace. Passing through the garden lawn which surrounded them, Steven and the smalves couldn't help but gaze in wonder at the delightful nature that lay to their sides, smiling with joy at the sight of rabbits and squirrels playing under the shadows of the trees and plants. Turning their attention to the many small statues that stood with pride, they couldn't help but stare at the famous figures with admiration at how much the gamdars respected their ancestors.

Leading the company through the vast silver gate that blocked the palace, Erundil came to the side of the golden streets where in the distance could be seen nine green horses, all greatly large and imposing in their size, though two of them were vastly smaller in size. For a moment, they all stood in awe of the majestic sight of the horses, captivated not only by the bright green color that covered their bodies but also by the majesty and strength that seemed to be contained within their bones.

Their faces were fierce, oozing off the feeling that they were mighty beings that none could resist admitting. The bright light of the sun reflected glitters of gold across their long black manes, and across their backs were green banners with the image of a large golden tree at its center, and the emblem of a golden crown across its top.

But even with their might and honor, one of the horses seemed to be head and shoulders above the rest both in his strength and presence. He stood proudly, with his head held high, but suddenly bowed when Erundil came to him. But the great king also bowed his head to the horse in reverence before jumping onto him.

Turning now to those who beheld him, Erundil explained who the horse was. "This is my battle horse," he explained. "His name is Linfast, and I have inherited him as the horse I use for battle from my father Tutlandil. His body is as strong as an iron wall and no other horse found throughout the kingdom of Watendelle can compare to him both in his great achievements and the respect he has earned. The rest of the horses you see are the battle horses of many of the soldiers in my army, including those of my sons Lelhond and Karandil. The smaller horses you see are our young ones, not yet ready for battle, though remaining strong and worthy of a level of respect."

Filled with fascination at the sight of the battle horses, Huminli and Glophi immediately jumped onto the two smaller ones.

"I don't think that I've ever ridden on a horse before," remarked Glophi, patting the horse's back. "Nor have I ever seen one that is green in color and so strong as these. These small horses are perfect for my brother and me. I wish we could take them back to our own homes and show them to our people."

"These horses belong to my people," responded Erundil, with a stern look on his face. "You will be able to enjoy them throughout your tour of my people's land, but you will have no right to take them to your people. Though the horses that you and your brother are sitting upon are not ready for battle yet, in just a few years they will have grown up to their full stature and strength. Enjoy your time with them now, but don't expect me to grant you your every wish."

With that, Erundil stirred his battle horse, Linfast, who began walking proudly through the golden streets just outside the silver gate of the palace. The king's sons, the volviers, the smalves, and Steven likewise got onto their horses, following Erundil from close behind. As they journeyed on, the many gamdars that beheld the king and Linfast, bowed in reverence to their great authority, wishing them the best in their future endeavors. A proud smile covered Erundil's face, as he thanked the many gamdars for the respect that they showed him and Linfast.

They traveled through the golden streets of the chief city of Kulendar, making their way through aisles of gardens and trees, that were surrounded by tall statues and vast structures on every side. As they went on in this direction for the next hour, Lelhond spoke with Steven and fascinated him with the many stories of the many famous figures that impacted his land.

"This silver statue is of one of our greatest soldiers ever," explained Lelhond, pointing to the statue of a figure holding a bow and arrow. "His name was Himalin, and nearly two thousand years ago, when a force of wuzlirs led an attack of a group of our people in the mountains, he led a force of thousands of gamdars to strike back at the enemy's forces. Thus it was that because of his courage, the enemy's forces didn't attack us for quite some time, and we endured a period of peace while he lived."

"Now what is that structure for?" asked Steven, pointing at the site of a large white house, which showed signs of decay though it remained standing firm.

"Ah yes, this is one of the many libraries that were built during the days of King Walandil, the grandson of King Ulohendel," answered Lelhond. "He was a master of the lore and wisdom of our people and was especially fond of the many books and poems that his grandfather wrote. Yet his heart still longed for the day when the great golden book of Ulohendel would be discovered and brought back to our people, though he doubted that that day would ever come. Still, King Walandil wrote many poems and laments during his time as king, wondering when the great days of our people under the blissful years of our first king would be restored. Many of his wonderful works are stored in this library, along with the many houses and structures that he built during his lifetime."

Even as he listened to him, Steven noticed a growing light that shone on Lelhond's face, as though a shade of the glory of his people reflected from his countenance. "All that you have told me is amazing, Lelhond," he remarked. "If this were all I witnessed today on the tour, then I would be satisfied."

"Yet there is still more to see, Steven," replied Lelhond. "There are many more stories of our people that must be told, and numerous statues and works of art that your eyes must be drawn to."

"Well, I can't wait to see it all then," said Steven with a smile, and he continued listening to the many stories that Lelhond shared with him."

For the next hour, they continued traveling through the golden streets of Kulendar, greeting the many gamdars that passed by, and gazing at the beauty of the land that surrounded them. Many gardens and pools lay to each side of them, where numerous animals could be seen frolicking in peace and joy. Birds flew high above them, singing songs of joy and praise as they hovered over the land of the gamdars. Lelhond continued sharing many stories of his people, while Karandil and Forandor each told Huminli and Glophi their own stories that filled the smalves with overwhelming fascination and joy.

Eventually, Erundil led them away from the path of the golden streets and into the direction of a forest, where a smooth stone path led them through the wide glade. Several flowers and plants covered the vast greenwood along with several animals of all different sizes, but most appealing to the eye were the towering trees that blossomed with every color imaginable. Staring at the majestic and colorful leaves that sprouted from the lofty trees, every single one of them couldn't help but pause and reflect on their beauty. To Steven, he couldn't help but imagine that the trees had been forged from the very hands of the gamdars themselves, just the as they had designed the many structures and houses that filled their great city.

Calling ahead to Erundil, Steven reflected on how beautiful the forest was. "I must say that I have never seen such a delightful forest as this one," he remarked. "I can't even see one single speck of dirt on these trees, and their leaves seem to be reflecting a rainbow of colors from the light of the sun. What is this place called?"

"My people call this forest, Palororen, meaning the Glory of Kings," responded Erundil. "For it is here in this forest that many of my relatives and ancestors grew up, including Ulohendel himself, before the great palace of his son Yarwindil was created. But it is also here in this blissful place where many of our soldiers came from, and some of the most important figures whose very words and actions shaped the lives we live today came from this region."

For the next few minutes or so, they all stopped where they were and listened as Erundil told them many stories about the forest and the famous figures that came from it. He told them the significance of the place, and why it was such an honor for them to travel through the forest.

"For here in this forest," he said. "Were the works of legend and stories of old created from the many gamdars that grew up here. Many times has the enemy tried to lay waste to this forest, yet a hidden power has lied upon it, protecting our people from his many attacks."

Listening to Erundil, Mataput spoke in response to all he said. "That is because Jangart himself has issued a protective veil over this forest," he explained. "No amount of armies that mount on this place will ever be able to tear down a tree or even a single branch. These trees that have grown from the foundation of the earth, are stronger than the most sturdy structures of metal that any work of the gamdars or even of the wuzlirs could concoct. It is here in this forest, that the blessing of Jangart most powerfully lies over your people."

Erundil listened to Mataput in astonishment for all he revealed. "You speak rightly so, Mataput," he said. "I believe in all you have had to say, though I was never told of all this. I am glad that we came here so that I could listen to these most wonderful words of yours."

"And I'm glad to be here as well," chimed in Glophi, laughing in cheerful joy at the wonderful sights that surrounded him. "Why don't we stop here to play with the animals over covering this most amazing forest?"

"Why would we play with the animals though?" questioned Steven. "Are you not afraid of the deer and bears that you see?"

"Why would we be afraid of them?" said Forandor. "All of the creatures and animals that dwell in the land of Watendelle live in perfect harmony with each other, not fearing being threatened or attacked by each other. We gamdars keep to ourselves while these animals also keep to themselves."

Steven shook his head in amazement. "That is incredible," he said with a broad smile. "Because we humans on Earth hardly ever interact with wild animals, fearing the wrath that they may inflict on us. We never know when they may attack or even try to eat us."

"I am sorry to hear that, Steven," responded Forandor with a sudden laugh. "I guess this is another thing that you have learned about our people, that the creatures and animals of our land do not live in tension with each other, but rather in harmony."

"So can we play with them then, if they live in harmony with each other?" asked Glophi again.

"No," firmly responded Erundil. "There is still more that I want to show you all of this land, and if we were to play with the animals of this forest, you would never want to depart from them."

Glophi shrugged his shoulders in disappointment but followed Erundil and the company as they continued their journey through the Palororen Forest. As they passed through the wide forest, they saw many soldiers training in the land, all of whom bowed their heads at the presence of their king. Many houses could be seen hiding behind the trees in the distance, where several gamdars lived in.

As noon soon approached, the company could suddenly feel the heat of the sun showering down on them, as they sensed that the trees grew shorted in size, though remained no different in their beauty and grandeur. Very soon the stony path they found themselves on suddenly became steep as a great long sloping path made them slowly descend through the forest. Once they reached the bottom of the steep path, they noticed a great long river that flowed to their side, remarkable in its bright blue color and sparkling crystals of light from the sun.

Turning to the company, Erundil told them of the river. "This is the Artla River," he said. "It is the longest river that flows through the land of Watendelle, and is so clean and clear, that you can see your reflection from it like a bright mirror."

Stepping off his horse, Erundil came to the bank of the river, with everyone else following him as well. Staring at the clear blue water, Steven was indeed able to see his reflection like a mirror and saw many fish that swam throughout the body of water.

After their short stop by the river bank, they returned to their horses and continued traveling through the forest, delighting themselves in the sights and sounds that gave them such great peace that stilled any worries that consumed their hearts. The vast and colorful trees of the forest still loomed high all around them, with many animals and creatures either resting under its shade or swimming in the water of the river. Steven wondered when the endless forest would end, or even when the sight of a different tree would come, one that was different from the rest of the crowd.

As if answering the questions that ran through his head, the company approached the sight of a specific tree, one whose leaves bloomed with gold, and stood as a vast tower, soaring over the rest of the trees. Coming to his tree, Erundil suddenly halted at it and stepped off his horse. Gazing at it, Steven knew that it was no ordinary tree, as it was the largest and most magnificent sight of nature that he had ever set his eyes upon. Its glittering golden leaves seemed to shine as bright stars under the light of the sun, with a sturdy and thick light brown trunk holding it together as a wide wall at its bottom. Staring at the base of the tree, he noticed that many weapons were on the ground; swords, spears, bows, and arrows. Several of the weapons were either gold or silver in color, while most of them were either black, brown, or gray. But, they all seemed to be sharp and effective, as though they were weapons made specifically for mighty warriors and kings.

Turning to Erundil, Steven asked him about the tree. "What is this tree?" he asked, gazing at it in wonder. "I have never seen such a glorious tree like this before?"

Erundil smiled in pride at the site of the great tree. "This is the golden tree of the Palororen forest," he answered. "It is the great tree of the King of Watendelle, and while there is still a king sitting upon the throne of Watendelle, its leaves remain golden. It was referenced yesterday by my chief advisor, Olindule, and by my wife, Aradulin, and as they remarked, when there is not a king on the throne, its leaves grow black. But that has not been the case for our people, and its golden leaves have continued to sprout on the ever-growing tree. This tree is the emblem of our people, being the image that is at the center of our flags, war banners, and the armor that our soldiers wear."

Touching the trunk of the golden tree, Erundil crouched down and placed his hand on a certain silver sword that was stumped into its roots.

"All of these weapons that you see are the weapons of the kings that have reigned in days before me," he explained. "This sword that I am touching was the weapon of my father, Tutlandil, and every year I come to this site just to reflect on the life he lived and the lives the kings lived before us. After each king dies we dig the weapons that they used in battle into the ground, as a way to remember and honor our great ancestors."

He then walked over to more weapons that were on the ground, before stopping at the site of a golden sword with green bows and arrows that lay beside it. "Now these were the weapons of Ulohendel," he said. "Though he is renowned for his wisdom and goodness, he was also a mighty man, one who fought tirelessly in battle, even when hope seemed to be swiftly fading for our people."

Coming to the site of many other weapons that were dug into the ground, Erundil spoke no more, instead silently observing all that lay before his eyes. His sons joined him as well, each touching the weapons that resonated with them the most, and allowing their hearts to be touched in that silent moment. They remained deep in thought, with everyone else quietly watching them out of respect.

Then suddenly, as the four gamdars stood still in the presence of that mighty tree, Forandor began lingering through the path of the forest, humming and murmuring inaudible words to himself. He seemed to be in a sweet dream, yet a look of distant sorrow, one that comes with having experienced many days of winter, covered his face like an overpowering shadow. Then as he sang, his voice grew louder, and all that listened to him could hear the words that came from his mouth, words that were as the enchanting sound of birds chirping above the gardens during the heat of a bright summer:

The ancient tree brings our memory of the glorious past,
Reminding us that not all that is gold will last.
It remains high above all else in the old land,
Yet it shall pass away one day and no longer stand.

Even the great Ulohendel who was wise,
As long as life continues, shall not rise.
For the fate of a gamdar is to eventually die,
No matter how hard he may try.

The sweetness of his voice faded, though to Steven, it was the most beautiful voice he had ever heard. Meanwhile, Forandor's brothers and father listened to what he sang with heavy hearts, as they brought their remembrance back to the days of their glorious past when Ulohendel reigned as king over the immortal gamdars. They wondered when those days would be restored and whether or not the quest they would be going on would be the very thing to completely shape their lives as they knew them.

Erundil departed from the tree, making his way back to Linfast with a face covered in sorrow and gloom. His sons followed him as well to their horses, staring at the ground with heavy hearts.

Erundil turned toward the volviers and spoke to them. "I will not lie in saying that as I have remembered what the days of our people used to be like, it has given me great sadness," he admitted. "I desperately hope that this quest will restore the pride and honor of my people and that our hearts full of pity will be replaced instead with joy. But I confess that I do not know what to do now in the tour of my people's kingdom. There was much I wanted to share with Steven today, though I am not in the mood for that right now. A place to relax would work well in easing the concerns of my heart."

A look of sympathy came to Mataput's face as he listened to Erundil. "I understand how you are feeling, Erundil," he said. "The gamdars have long been able to hold their heads high with honor, and even now your people are still full of dignity. And with this quest of ours, I am confident that the glory of your people will be restored, and that the glory of the humans will be revealed. But, if you are still not in the mood to lead us through the tour of your kingdom then I suggest that you lead us to the house of Dulanmidir. It has been years since Orieant and I spoke with him, and he always manages to lift our spirits and provide us with important insight. And it is about time that Steven, Huminli, and Glophi met him as well."

Erundil sighed to himself, but a glint of joy came to his face. “I have always been fond of the ancient wanderer,” he said. “Not only for the laughter that he provides to ease the worries of my heart but also for the great wisdom that he possesses. But, are you sure that now is the appropriate time to speak with him? I do not know if his many jokes will manage to lighten up my mood, nor do I feel like listening to him now.”

“I think that it would be best for us to listen to him, Erundil,” responded Mataput. “And I sense a longing in my heart, that it is the appointed time that we meet with him before we begin our quest. I feel as though that whatever he says to us, will be to the betterment of our understanding and the advancement of our quest.”

“Well if you feel it is right, then I guess we must go to the house of Dulanmidir,” conceded Erundil. “Perhaps we do need his jolliness and his words of wisdom in this solemn time of my family.”

Steven scratched his confusion while listening to Mataput and Erundil. “Who is Dulanmidir?” he asked. “And why would it be so important for us to visit him?”

“That is a good question, Steven,” remarked Orieant. “Though we do not know who he truly is, he has still been a good friend not only to Mataput and me but to all of the free creatures of the world. He has dwelled in his house in this forest for some time, but before this, he dwelled among the dwarfs, the giants, and even the smalves. He is a mysterious being, but a helpful one who has given us wisdom and insight in many of our times of need. He is called by many other names as well, but most know him as Dulanmidir, ‘The Ancient Wanderer.’ And just like Mataput, I sense it would be wise of us to visit him now, as I am sure he has many important things he wants to share with us all.”

Huminli suddenly sprang from the horse he was sitting on, as though a distant memory had been recalled to his mind. “Oh, I know who you are talking about, Orieant,” he said. “Glophi and I have heard many tales of this ancient wanderer. We smalves call him Wotalin, ‘The Mystery Friend.’ Though my people have heard much about him, it has been a while since he dwelled in our homeland, which has resulted in many of us wondering if he is only a myth.”

“He is far from a myth, Huminli,” replied Orieant. “And once you see him, you will be able to tell your people that he not only exists but lives to serve the free creatures of the world with his wisdom and jolly nature."

"Well, I can't wait to see him!" chimed in Glophi with excitement. "I am sure that his presence alone will benefit us in some way."

"Then let us get going," said Orieant, and with that, Erundil led the way through the path of the forest, with everyone else closely following him from behind.

As they traveled deep into the forest, the path grew rockier and winding, with no sign of life existing in this part of the woodland except for a few roaming animals. No houses of gamdars could be seen, as all that lay before them and around them were endless miles of vast colorful trees.

A chilly wind flowed through the air, as the first signs of the autumn season were finally felt in the land of Watendelle. Eventually, after a half hour of making their way through the spacious and colorful forest, the company noticed a strange sight in the far distance on their right. They saw an incredibly wide and thick tree branch with no leaves or branches ahead of them. As they drew closer to the sight, they noticed that the large tree branch was shaped like a small house, with a door carved into it, as well as many windows lying above the door. Once they came within walking distance of the house, Erundil turned around and spoke to the company.

"Well, we have made it to the dwelling place of Dulanmidir," he said.

"His house is strange, yet unique," remarked Glophi. "I have never seen anything like this before in my life."

"Nor have you seen the sight of such a strange yet wise creature like Dulanmidir," commented Mataput. "This is not the strangest thing you have seen today. Because once you meet Dulanmidir, everything else that you thought was strange, will be considered a trivial insult to the peculiarities of the ancient wanderer. Just looking at him will fill you with wonder. His height is that of a giant, his beard that of a dwarf, his wisdom that of a gamdar, and his personality that of the nature of a smalf."

"Well if his personality is anything like mine, then I want to meet this ancient wanderer of whom my people have many stories to tell," said

Glophi, and at once, he stepped off of his horse and came to the front of the house.

Everyone else followed the smalf, coming to the porch of the house and pondering its distinctive design. Then, as they all stared at the shape of the house, Mataput and Orieant reached out their hands and both gave three large knocks on the brown door. No answer came, and so after a few seconds, the volviers knocked on the door again. Yet no answer came once again.

Coming closer to the door, Mataput now spoke in a loud voice. "It's Orieant and I, Dulanmidir," he said. "We have also brought the king and his sons, along with the man Steven, and Huminli and Glophi, the two smalf brothers. We have come here to enjoy our time in your cheerful presence while listening to your words of knowledge."

Immediately, the door flung wide open, and there standing before the company was the most unusual sight of a man. Coming outside to greet his guests with a wide grin on his face was a large and imposing man in his stature, towering over Erundil and his sons as he appeared to be around eight feet in height. He was clothed in a thick green coat with a brown felt around his waist and had on thick brown boots on his massive feet. His head was covered in dirty and curly brown hair, and he had a long and thick red beard that came all the way down to his brown belt. On a few of his hairy fingers were golden rings, that were so tight on him that it seemed as though the rings themselves were unwilling to be removed from his fingers. Staring at his face, Steven observed how the man appeared neither old nor young, though he felt as though he had been around for many long years, dwelling as an ageless creature among the mortal creatures that covered the wide world.

The man came outside, with a broad smile and a cheerful look covering his face. "Welcome and welcome all of you!" he enthusiastically said. "I am glad that you have decided to stop by my temporary abode here in the Palororen Forest. I am sorry that I ignored you when I heard knocking on my door, I just assumed that it was those dreaded gamdars trying to busy me with all of their work. From houses and inns for them to dwell, then to stables to keep their horses, they are always trying to make me build something. When will it ever stop?"

"I don't know, Dulanmidir," replied Orieant with a laugh. "But perhaps those gamdars are just trying to enrich themselves with your vast wisdom."

Dulanmidir let out a loud and animated laugh, one that surprised Steven with how lighthearted it made him feel. "Perhaps so, Orieant," he said. "You and Mataput always ensure to make me feel better about myself. But please, enter my house so that all of you can make yourselves comfortable. I am sure that you have traveled for a while under the warm sun, though it is getting a bit cooler now."

Entering the house, the company found themselves standing in a wide living room with many candles, lights, and plants filling the house. A small fireplace could be in the distance, where a round table with brown chairs lying beside it. Dulanmidir led them to the table, where they all sat down.

Once they had made themselves comfortable, Dulanmidir suddenly turned toward Steven with an excited expression on his wide face. "Oh Steven, I am so glad to see you!" he said. "I have heard and seen much about you recently, and it is a very merry day to finally be meeting you!"

Steven stared in wonder at Dulanmidir since he knew who he was. "I am glad to meet you as well," he replied. "But how do you already know me, and what should I call you? It looks like the gamdars call you Dulanmidir, while the smalves name you Wotalin."

"You may call me Dulanmidir, Steven," responded Dulanmidir. "The smalves know me by the name they call me, while everyone else knows me by the name Dulanmidir. And what you must know, Steven is that the ancient wanderer of this world knows many things that would surprise many that came into contact with me. I have also spoken with the gamdars, who have told me all that I need to know about you."

A look of astonishment came over Steven's face. "Other than the volviers, I have never met someone with so great of a source of wisdom like you," he remarked. "But tell me, how is it that you have existed for thousands of years? I know that Mataput and Orieant once used to be the great spirit beings of Jangart before entering this world in physical form, but what of you? Were you once some spirit being like them?"

Dulanmidir's smile faded as he sighed to himself. "Unfortunately, my memory doesn't reach that far back, Steven," he said. "But what I do know and what you must know, is that ever since the days of the great war, I have been as you see me know. It was during that time that I first met Mataput and Orieant, who immediately began telling me stories about Jangart and of the rebellion of Natugura, tales that were yet unheard of and foreign to my young ears. But over time I began to believe the volviers before I formed a friendship with them and helped them in their purpose of aiding the free creatures of the world."

"But why are you a wanderer?" asked Huminli. "Do you not have a temporary home where you dwell in some faraway land that we have never heard of before? Do you not know more about yourself?"

Dulanmidir's smile returned to his face. "Ah, the curiosity of smalves never fails to amaze me," he said. "My good friend, Huminli, not even I know all the things about myself that I would rightly deserve to know. But all that would benefit you is knowing that I am Dulanmidir, he who has existed throughout the ages of the world alongside the volviers. I am he who belongs to himself and wanders through this world to provide support and direction for the free creatures that have managed to still hold back against the enemy. But we can talk about all of this later. I am sure that you all would enjoy a meal, and I am happy to say that I have already prepared one, as I sensed that I would be expecting some visitors today."

"Well a meal certainly sounds good enough for me!" remarked Huminli with eagerness.

"Same with me as well," added Glophi. "None of us have eaten anything yet today, which is not a good thing for smalves. We could sure use some food to fill our empty stomachs,"

Immediately, Dulanmidir rose from the table and walked away with a broad smile on his face, opening the door to his kitchen to bring out the food he had prepared for his guests. After a few minutes, he opened his kitchen door holding a large brown tray with gray plates, that was filled with slices of bread, vegetables, bowls of soups, and brown cups filled with water.

Dulanmidir placed the tray onto the table and brought out each plate and cup for everyone to have. Once their food had been served, Huminli and Glophi swiftly dug their faces into their plates of food, gobbling up their bread and vegetables, and slurping their bowls of soup. Dulanmidir couldn't help but laugh at the smalves, a laugh that was both deep yet had a cheerful ring to it.

Steven was impressed by how decent the food tasted, yet what surprised him the most was the water he drank from his cup. Staring at the liquid, he noticed that though it mostly resembled water, its color was deep blue, and it had a sweet taste to it which delighted him with every sip he took.

"Is this water?" he asked, picking up his cup and examining the liquid inside of it. "It is like water in every way imaginable, yet it is so sweet that I wouldn't be surprised if someone mistook it as juice."

"It is water, Steven," responded Erundil. "It is just that the water that flows from the Artla River is much sweeter and more pleasant to taste than that of any other regular type of water that you would come across in the land of Watendelle."

"Well, I am glad that I have come to settle in this great forest, where the Artla River flows for endless miles," remarked Dulanmidir. "And I can confidently say, that hardly any drink in this world can compare to the water that comes from the Artla River. Not even the beer of the smalves is worthy to even be mentioned next to this water, and that is saying a lot since the beer that the smalves make never fails to amaze me by its splendid taste!"

Glophi crossed his arms. "I would have to disagree with that, Wotalin," he said. "This water of the gamdars is very tasty, but you know how good our beer is. Even the mere smell of its delightful carbonation is enough for anyone to claim that our beer is the best drink that they have not only tasted but also smelled."

"Why yes, Glophi, I have not betrayed my thoughts on how pleasant your beer is," said Dulanmidir. "The plants that you grow on your farms give your beer a unique taste to it which no other type of beer can compare to. Every other beer I have tasted is not only bland but also makes me feel dizzy and tired. But that is not so with your people. The sweetness and flavor of your beer manage to fill me with much energy and joy that will help me last for many weeks without growing weary."

Glophi sat back in his chair with a satisfied look on his face. For several more minutes, the company at the table with Dulanmidir discussed many other matters that were on their minds. Huminli and Glophi talked more about their farms and many talents, while Erundil and his sons spoke of the lore and history of their people, which especially filled Steven with great fascination while only managing to bore out the smalves.

After much talking, Steven suddenly brought his attention to Dulanmidir. "You have shown us great hospitality in welcoming us into your home and setting a meal before us, Dulanmidir," he said. "My heart has been warmed by your very presence, and your jolly nature has filled me with joy. But, now that I have been thinking to myself, I would still really love to know more about you. Isn't there at least something about yourself that you could share with us and provide us with further happiness to experience?"

"Yes, I would love to know at least one more thing about you, Wotalin," chimed in Huminli. "I understand that your memory doesn't reach far back into the beginning of your days, but surely there are some details about yourself that could cause us to stare at you in awe."

"Ah my good friends," said Dulanmidir with a broad smile on his face as he looked at Steven and Huminli. "I appreciate your fond interest in me, but you must understand that not even I know everything about myself. All that you know about me is enough to give you comfort, and if you were to know how I was in my entirety, it would bring you down to your knees and shake your entire being."

"Why would it shake our entire being?" asked Huminli. "I'm sure we would be able to handle everything you told us about yourself."

"You smalves are very curious creatures, aren't you," said Dulanmidir with a wide grin at Huminli. "That is one thing that I enjoyed of your kind when I dwelled in Laouli. But I am afraid that your curiosity cannot be any more than just speculation, for there are things that only a few can know, and there is only one who is worthy to know all things, and that is Jangart. Not even I, Mataput, or Orieant know everything about ourselves, as the memories of what we once used to be like are as fading leaves during the transition of a season."

"Well, I suppose that's fair enough," mumbled Huminli, with a sense of disappointment, yet understanding as well. "If it is not our purpose to know everything that we want to know, then we can do nothing to change that. But I am glad to know that you, Wotalin, are filled with great wisdom that I am sure will be useful in our quest through the land of Nangorid."

"I am glad to see that you understand, Huminli," replied Dulanmidir. "And I am also pleased to see how much you understand the significance of your quest. I have held onto many things in my heart for many long years now, which I wished to share first with the volviers. But now that you are all gathered here and have decided how will be going on this great quest to aid Steven, I am now willing to share all that I have wished to reveal to you for some time now."

An uneasy feeling fell on the company, as they wondered what Dulanmidir had wished to share for many years. Yet, they desired to learn from him, knowing that it would most likely be to the benefit of their quest. Though he feared what Dulanmidir would tell them, Lelhond spoke first to give his approval of whatever Dulanmidir would say.

"I for sure need to listen to whatever wisdom you will share with us Dulanmidir," he said. "The only other time I met you was when I was a youth, and though I have heard many stories of your wisdom and jolly nature, I have always wanted to meet you once I was old enough to truly understand all you said. And now, it looks like that wish of mine will come to fruition, and I will not let that opportunity pass, no matter how fearful I may be of it."

"Perhaps Dulanmidir can even join us in our quest to the Black Tower of the enemy," remarked Erundil. "I can confirm that I have witnessed the wisdom of Dulanmidir, a knowledge so great that it could do wonders for us on our journey. Just imagine Mataput, Orieant, and Dulanmidir all aiding us on this seemingly impossible task. Our hope would be further enhanced and our worries would be subsided."

The company fell silent at Erundil's suggestion, thinking deeply of all he said. Steven especially felt like it was a great idea, one that would further ensure not only his protection but also the success of the company's quest. Though he had hardly heard or experienced Dulanmidir's wisdom yet, just what everyone had claimed of him was enough for him to endorse Erundil's idea.

However, before anyone could say anything, Dulanmidir quickly shut down Erundil's idea. "I understand why you wish for me to join you,

Erundil," he said. "But you must understand that though it is my purpose to aid you in whatever way I can, it is not my business to go with you on this great journey. It is enough that the volviers are going with you, and all you need from me is my words of wisdom and revelation."

"Then what are those words of wisdom and revelation that you can share with us?" asked Erundil. "You have said that you wished to share with us all that had been placed on your heart and that now it is the appointed time to do so."

Dulanmidir took a deep breath and looked longingly at Erundil with a serious look covering his face. "Well, as you know, Erundil, the volviers are the great helpers of this world," he said. "They have aided the free creatures of this world for thousands of years, and there are things that only they are worthy to set their eyes upon. But, there is a thing that I have long desired to show all of you, and that is the gorlinto."

Bewildered looks came onto the faces of the entire company. Most confused was Steven, who wondered what Dulanmidir was talking about.

"What is the gorlinto?" he asked. "I have never heard of such a thing in my life. Wouldn't Mataput or Orieant have shared with me what that is, if it's so important?"

Dulanmidir laughed to himself as he listened to Steven. "Steven, are you forgetting about the dream you had which completely altered the direction of your life?" he asked. "Mataput told me that you have already seen the gorlinto, as he showed it to you in the dream you had many days ago."

"Oh, yes, I remember Mataput showing me that white spherical globe that burned with blue fire inside of it," responded Steven. Then, as he thought to himself, a troubled look came onto his face as he remembered how he had been deceived by Moneshob right after he experienced his dream. "But I also remember how I was so foolish in not listening to Mataput's warning at the time," he said with a sigh. "Many terrible events happened so after I had that dream, and it if wasn't for the volviers' intervention, the people and I would've been headed to our doom."

"Yet Mataput and Orieant had mercy on you," replied Dulanmidir. "They could've left you for destruction after you refused to listen to their warning, yet it was because of their understanding of how important you would be in shaping this world that they continued to fight for you and the people you have left behind. And it is for that reason that they and everyone gathered here have decided to join you on this quest, so that deliverance from the shadow of Natugura can be brought to the humans of the Earth. And since everyone here is doing their part to bring your people hope, Steven, it would be wrong of me to disregard what has been weighing heavily on my mind for some time now."

Then, standing up from his seat, Dulanmidir opened the palms of his hands, with everyone staring at him with faces of wonder. He then raised his hands above his head and closed his eyes. Immediately, a large white spherical globe suddenly appeared in his lifted hands, burning with an intense blue fire that filled the object. But as they looked closely at the globe, the company noticed that some of the fire even burned outside of the object, yet it wasn't consumed.

Opening his eyes, Dulanmidir brought the globe down and set it on the table for everyone to have a closer look at it. Everyone sat silently for a moment, especially the smalves and gamdars who had never seen the object before.

"I have never seen any object like this before," remarked Erundil, staring at the globe with wide eyes. "It is burning with a strong blue fire inside and outside, yet the fire is not managing to consume it. This gorlinto is greatly enthralling, yet I wonder why in all my meetings with you, Dulanmidir, I have never heard you mention that this object existed. Now tell me, why is this globe so important for you to tell us about it? Does it hold some great source of power or will we be able to wield it to our advantage?"

"The former," responded Dulanmidir. "The gorlinto is indeed a source of power and wisdom unrivaled to any object in this world, yet it is not within your authority to wield it as a weapon. None of you, except for Mataput and Orieant are aware of the awesome yet terrifying power this object possesses. And it is for that reason that I withheld telling you about this Erundil, but now that you and this company are going on a long and tiring journey to alter the fate of the humans, it is in your best interest that I show you the force which this object carries with it."

"So what force does this object carry?" asked Erundil. "I want to know why it would be to our advantage to know the truth of this source of power."

For a moment, Dulanmidir stared intently at Erundil, as though he were examining the very depths of his heart with his discerning gaze. "Only those that are willing to accept the whole truth are worthy to view the great power of the gorlinto," he said after a while. "You and everyone here must promise me that no matter what I show you all, you will be willing to acknowledge all that is revealed to you as the truth."

"I am willing," responded Erundil, with everyone else quickly voicing their agreement with what Dulanmidir said.

"Good," said Dulanmidir, nodding his head in approval. "Now that you are willing to accept the truth, I shall now reveal to you the deep secrets that not even Mataput or Orieant know about."

With his last statement, concerned looks came over the faces of the company, especially over Mataput and Orieant's who wondered what those deep secrets which they didn't know could be. All was silent for a while, as everyone's faces were drawn to Dulanmidir.

And then, after the long silence, it seemed to those who beheld Dulanmidir that his piercing eyes were on fire. And as he stared at the white globe burning with an intense blue fire that sat on the table, it suddenly began floating in the air. As the object rose, it began to expand and grow larger, with its blue fire seeming to burn with even more intensity. Staring at the remarkable sight with astonished and fearful looks on their faces, the company could see their reflections through the gorlinto even amidst the blue fire burning at its very strongest.

Filled with curiosity, Glophi broke the long and terrified silence of all those who stared at Dulanmidir and the gorlinto. "What is going on, Wotalin?" he asked, in a voice filled with both interest and fear.

Dulanmidir turned to Glophi, and to everyone's surprise, spoke in a thunderous voice that radiated through his entire house. "Now is not the time to utter words as I summon the deep revelations of the gorlinto!" he cried in a mighty voice. Immediately, Glophi shrank back in dead silence, with everyone else seeming to cower down in pure terror. They would have never imagined witnessing such a change in the ever-so-merry Dulanmidir, and for the first time for many of them, they now saw the great and terrible power that the ancient wanderer possessed.

After some more time had passed, the globe slowly descended back down to the table, and once it had been set down, it revolved in a circular motion. As everyone stared at Dulanmidir with petrified faces, he finally spoke to the company as his eyes still burned with a bright and glowing fire.

"If anyone dares to come and learn of the revelations of the gorlinto, then come forth now," he said in a commanding voice.

Nobody moved an inch, as they were all filled with a terrible fear of all that they had just witnessed. They felt as though the very depths of their hearts had been struck with terror, and they all felt unworthy to look upon the gorlinto. Even the volviers seemed to be staring at Dulanmidir with frightened eyes, as they too had never seen Dulanmidir act in such an authoritative way before.

But, amid everyone's terrified faces, it was Lelhond who responded to Dulanmidir's call. He stood up from his seat and crept closer to Dulanmidir, as his eyes remained fixated on the revolving globe. However, as he drew closer to the gorlinto, Erundil placed his hand on his shoulder, staring at his son with widened eyes of horror.

"What are you doing, Lelhond?" he asked. "I do not know what has come over Dulanmidir, but I don't think it is the appropriate time to look at this globe. I fear for our wellbeing and I don't know what will happen to us once we discover these deep secrets which Dulanmidir has hidden from us."

With a dropped head, Lelhond began slowly walking back in the direction of his seat. But he was immediately stopped by Dulanmidir, who turned toward Erundil with his eyes still glowing with fire.

"Do not hinder your son from coming forth, Erundil!" he ordered. "Long have I wished to share these secrets with you all, and if he is the only one willing to accept these revelations, then that is better than nobody knowing about them. And if you are willing to let go of your fear, then come forth and follow your son to look upon the hidden truths of the gorlinto."

Erundil sighed to himself, but looking into the balls of fire that consumed Dulanmidir's eyes, he suddenly felt a strong desire to look at the gorlinto for himself. And so, hardly believing in what he was doing, he found himself standing up from his seat and joining Lelhond to have a close view of the white globe burning with blue fire. Following their father and brother's lead came Karandil and Forandor, and soon after, the smalves and volviers followed suit as well, wishing to see what Dulanmidir had in store for them to learn. But, the only one remaining seated was Steven, with his eyes cast to the ground in terrible anxiety of what he would discover if he looked upon that dreadful source of power.

Sensing his fear, a smile came to Dulanmidir's face and the fire burning inside of his eyes slowly began to subside. "Will you come and have a look at the gorlinto, Steven?" he asked. "There is nothing to fear, just follow everyone's lead and you will be glad that you were bold enough to allow your eyes to be opened."

Steven remained still, not moving an inch except in quivering with terror. "When Mataput showed me this object in the dream, it didn't possess me with a dreadful feeling," he said, with his voice shaking. "Yet now that I see this globe of revelation, it has not ceased to make me shake and tremble with great fear."

"That is because you were never shown the gorlinto in its full strength in your dream, Steven," responded Dulanmidir. "This great object of power not only has the power to show future events, but it has the poignant ability to strike and convict the heart, possibly causing fear for a moment but filling the observer's heart with wisdom which he would have never gained. Seemingly strange acts are only called upon in dangerous seasons, Steven, and the quest you find yourself now involved in leads you with no choice but to accept the deep secrets that have never been discovered before in the long ages of this world. If you heed my call, blind eyes and deaf ears will be opened, and though it may not work its effect upon you immediately, your courage and the fervent urging that you will experience to complete this task set before you will begin its long yet fulfilling work to save the destiny of those headed for destruction."

Steven could sense the growing persistence that filled Dulanmidir, yet he still found himself unwilling to let go of his fears. "And what if I still choose not to look at the gorlinto?" he asked. "Surely what everyone else sees will still work to the benefit of this company."

Dulanmidir laughed, though within his usual fun-natured and innocent laugh was a tinge of bitterness. Then, looking upon Steven, his eyes glowed once more with the bright flame of a ball of fire, and he spoke once more in a strong voice that pierced the room like the flash of lightning flickering through a gray and cloudy sky.

"I am the Ancient Wanderer!" he cried aloud in such a fearsome voice that the very foundation of his house shook with a mighty rumbling noise. "I am the Mystery Friend, and it is only I who has looked upon the gorlinto in its full glory! Yet now is the appointed time for me to share it with you, and so fear must flee before your eyes lest you fall into the doom of ignorance."

Then, raising his hands to the air, it seemed as though the blue fire that consumed the globe began to slowly spread throughout the room. And with another blink of an eye, the company so that their eyes indeed did not deceive them, as an expansive blue fire surrounded the house in a large ring. Dulanmidir's face glowed amid the fire, with his appearance so terrible and mighty to behold, the company trembled in his presence and dared not to look upon him, except for Mataput and Orieant who had witnessed Dulanmidir in the full weight of his splendor many ages ago. But the rest of the company remained to stare at the ground in terror of Dulanmidir.

But just as quickly as he had changed the atmosphere of the room, Dulanmidir once more brought everything back under control. With his command, the ring of fire that surrounded the room of the house vanished from sight, while the gorlinto remained burning with its blue fire. Standing up from his seat, Dulanmidir walked over to the fireplace by the table, carrying the flaming globe which seemed to not even scorch his hands in the very slightest way. Then, standing by the fireplace, he threw the globe into the furnace, to the company's confusion and fear of what would next take place.

Breathing heavy sighs of relief, the company felt that a sense of confidence had been restored to them, though they remained seated where they were, with knees continuing to shake and knock into each other under the table.

The same cheerful smile that they had seen covering Dulanmidir's face a moment ago, came onto his face once more. "Now is the time for your eyes to be opened," he said. "Many of you who have only met me for the first time today, have now seen a part of my glory unveiled. And with that understanding, I invite you to look upon the gorlinto for yourselves."

The company stared at the sight of the globe that had been thrown into the furnace, observing how its strong fire prevented it from melting in the flaming heat of the fireplace. Though many of them were still filled with their levels of doubts and fears, as though a strong impulsive desire took hold of their minds at that moment, they all stood up from their seats and steadily began approaching the fireplace.

But just as the company neared the sight of the gorlinto in the furnace, Mataput suddenly called them to a halt to question Dulanmidir. "Are you sure that what you are doing is for our good?" he asked. "I hope that you will not reveal to us something that Orieant and I already one, which we could easily share with this company without unnecessarily terrorizing them. Will you not tell us plainly what you wish to show us?"

The company turned in amazement at Mataput, shocked that he had questioned Dulanmidir's motives. They feared what Dulanmidir's response would be, but casting their worries aside, he instead simply chuckled to himself before looking intently at Mataput with a serious look on his face.

"There are things which you and Orieant will learn for the first time today," he responded. "Warnings of the vast and dangerous influence of the enemy will be revealed to you in its full entirety. The tidings I share with you will be hard to believe, but if you wish to succeed on this most important quest of yours, then you must know about the terrible and unimaginable authority which the Dark Lord Natugura holds within this world."

Mataput stepped back, as though he were stricken by a sudden flash of lightning. He glanced at Orieant, whose face was also covered in shock. "So there are things regarding the Dark Lord which you have specifically withheld from Orieant and me?" asked Mataput. "Never would I have imagined that I would be hearing these words coming forth from your mouth, Dulanmidir. I must admit that all that you have said is hard for me to take in."

"I understand," said Dulanmidir. "But just as I have trusted you and Orieant with your vast knowledge that helped me during the period of my ignorance, so you must also trust me with this matter. I have battled and struggled with this matter for many long years, striving to allow myself to share these revelations with you and with all of the free creatures of the world. Yet for all that time, I could sense an invisible force preventing me from revealing these things with you and Orieant. But now that you and this company have expressed your desire to go on this quest and rescue the great book of Ulohendel, it was as though the heavy veil forbidding me from achieving my desire had finally been removed."

"Perhaps the will of Jangart has now been made manifest," remarked Orieant. "And who am I to stand in his way? For I am only a servant of the Eternal One, and I will obey him no matter how much I may doubt if it is right."

Mataput sighed to himself, though it was the sound of one who knew that the truth had been spoken. "I am a servant of him also," he said. "And Orieant and I have both seen many events played out together, and it would be foolish of us to now betray listening to the direction of Jangart. Let your desire come to pass then, Dulanmidir! Show us all that you have wished to show us for these many years."

A broad smile came over Dulanmidir's face, and he cast his attention to the gorlinto which lay in the fireplace. The company gathered themselves close by the fireplace, waiting patiently to see what would happen. But for a few minutes, all remained silent, with Dulanmidir not even moving as he stared at the fireplace. Steven drew closer to him, wishing to touch him and perhaps rouse him from his supposed dreamlike state. But just as he was about to touch him, a blinding light suddenly appeared, and as it slowly began to grow dim, he could now see the gorlinto more clearly in the fireplace. The globe seemed to grow larger, and everyone could see not only their reflections through the object but everything else that surrounded them in the house as well.

As they stared at the globe, a twilight land suddenly appeared in the reflection with many stars illuminating the dark and cloudy sky. Towering mountains with snow-capped peaks loomed high in the distance, and a heavy downpour of rain could be seen crashing down. On the surface could be seen a long and dark river, where a few unrecognizable creatures like vast shadows piercing the gloomy night could be seen roaming along the bank.

The vision then changed to the setting of a large cave along the mountainside. Sturdy and rocky walls surrounded each side of the cave as great pillars, and scattered throughout the ground were dead bodies and blood-stained cloaks and pieces of armor. The skeletons of the dead creatures appeared to be tall and physically imposing ones, who appeared to have been involved in a small battle or skirmish.

Then, the wide space of the cave was zoomed in to a large stone, where the back of a certain creature, wrinkled and slumped over could be seen. Suddenly, the creature began to move, walking on its feet though with its arms and shoulders hung down as if it were a wild beast. Its shadowy face was cast to the ground, and climbing its way down the stone and onto the rocky ground of the cave, it began sniffing around the area as though it were trying to smell the stench that the dead bodies filled the atmosphere with. Finding insects crawling on the ground, the creature started nibbling and snacking on them. Staring at this sight, through the vision of the gorlinto, the company looked on at the sight with disgust and recoiled back.

Suddenly, lifting its head, the creature turned toward the company that stared at him with distasteful faces. The creature's face was dark though the company could faintly see that it had large peering eyes and pointy ears. It hideously grinned at them, with streams of blood coming down from its sharp teeth and onto its skinny body. Its body was a grayish color with hints of green and red on its chest like large dots, and it wore nothing except for torn brown shorts. Strands of brown hair mixed with dirt came down almost to its shoulders, with short strands of hair also seeming to grow from the long nails of its fingers and toes. The company looked on at the creature for some time, wondering what exactly it could be.

But at once, the vision ended, and the gorlinto reappeared in Dulanmidir's hands. The company stood still for a moment, filled with both fear and bewilderment at the strange sight that they saw. They wondered if they had seen what a wuzlir looked like without its black armor and mask, yet they were perplexed by how scrawny the creature seemed to be.

Erundil broke through the silence. "What was that hideous creature that we just saw?" he asked. "Have our eyes finally beheld the ugliness of a wuzlir, and was this all that you wanted to reveal to us, Dulanmidir?"

"No," answered Dulanmidir. "The creature you saw was not a wuzlir, and it would have been ill-advised of me to only reveal to you the faces of those cursed creatures," he paused for a moment, sighing to himself as a grave look came onto his face. "I have held onto this reality for too long, and now that I am sharing it with you, grief and regret are trying to gnaw at my heart. But I know that I have no choice but to reveal the truth to you, as such is the role of my existence in altering the fate of your quest for good. And so it is with great sorrow that I have to disclose to you that the creature whom you saw in the vision was Silindan."

At this sudden revelation, Erundil and his sons collapsed to the ground in disbelief, clutching onto their hearts as though a heavy inflicting cloud had sucked the life out of their bodies. Watery tears filled Forandor's eyes, as his brothers and father cast their heads to the ground in despair. A wind of anguish as it felt, filled the atmosphere of the entire house as the rest of the company could only shake their heads in pity for the gamdars. They knew not why they were filled with such sudden tormenting distress, but they knew that whatever Dulanmidir had revealed was more poignant than even the sharpest sword.

Being risen to his feet from Mataput, Erundil gasped to himself, as though the words which Dulanmidir had spoken were like poison darts to his throat. "How can these things be?" he cried. "Alas! These are bitter tidings that you have revealed to us, Dulanmidir! But how could such a mighty hero of my people fall into such mad vileness as you have shown us?"

"I am sorry, Erundil," said Dulanmidir, filled with remorse. "But it was the appointed time for this to be revealed to you. I know it is hard to believe, and though I do not yet know the full reason for Silindan's fall, I have much that I need to share with you. But, I am willing to spare some time, so that you and your sons can cope with your grief in what seems best to you."

"We have already coped with our grief and are continuing to do so," said Erundil. "But I must know why Silindan is now like this. For a gamdar of such great renown like him to now be filled with terrible foulness is a strange and grievous reality that I and my people must search out and try to discover why this is the case. And not only that but how is he even alive? It is well known that he died around 600 years ago, and even if he still lived on for some strange reason, a mortal creature can't live for such a long time as that."

Before Dulanmidir could respond, Steven chimed in. "I am sorry to interrupt during this time of great grief for Erundil and his sons, but who is Silindan?" he asked.

Erundil sighed to himself, yet managed to put his grief aside for a moment to explain to Steven all that he knew of the famous figure of his people. "Silindan was a mighty hero of my people, so much so that he is remembered as the greatest soldier in our long history," he said. "His time to become a legend of my people would happen 600 years ago, when during a time of peace for our people, the Dark Lord's forces led an attack upon our land, burning many of our forests and slaying many innocent gamdars. In immediate retaliation, our king at the time, Kolcratil, led our army of soldiers to lead a counterattack on the enemy by making their way to the land of Nangorid, to slay many wuzlirs in return for their despicable actions. Such a burning anger against the enemy hadn't been roused for many years, and our righteous wrath was so hot that many gamdars who weren't even soldiers decided to join the army to achieve revenge for our people who had been mercilessly attacked by the enemy. Among those inexperienced soldiers was Silindan, whose anger perhaps burned the hottest since his mother and brother had been among those whose lives had been taken away from the wuzlirs.

"And so it was that in those many centuries ago, war broke out, one that my people remember as the War of the Great Revenge. Such a great number of gamdarian soldiers had hardly been seen in our history, and you would have to go back to the days of the first and great war if you would want to find a greater number. Though he had never been a soldier in his life, Silindan became a natural learner in the ways of battle, becoming a hardy and strong man, unrelenting to surrender in fear to the enemy. He became very useful in the army and rose so much in rank that he eventually became second in command of all the soldiers, only behind King Kolcratil in authority.

"And while the Dark Lord and his forces knew that he would retaliate against them, they hadn't expected us to bring such a large number of angered soldiers. Our army greatly outnumbered the wuzlirian forces, and within months we had swiftly advanced through the land of Nangorid, destroying our enemies as well as laying bare to many accursed places. The joy of battle seized our hearts and it was during that time that our only wish was to see our enemies suffer under the terrible might of our slaying hand. But it was amid the time when broad smiles covered our faces, that a group of wuzlirs ambushed King Kolcratil and slew him. And to humiliate and discourage us, they attached his beheaded face onto a spear and presented it for all to see during our battle with them. So it was that the host of our people wailed aloud in terror, with many of them either falling on their swords or rushing back to Watendelle while being chased down by the enemy's forces.

"But it was during this time of grief and horror for our people, that Silindan, the mightiest captain of war that our people have ever had, took a stand and rallied our remaining soldiers to himself under the mighty sound of his great voice. So it was that in the hour of the death and disgrace of King Kolcratil, that Silindan sounded his booming trumpet while his face shone as the brightness of the sun even as he stood under the shadow of darkness that covered that accursed land. A clear wind blew upon his shining face, propelling him to fight courageously in the many battles against the wuzlirs that would soon follow. Such a great resolve to punish the forces of the enemy even during a time of tremendous suffering and sorrow had never before been seen, and under the leadership of Silindan, many crucial victories were won against the enemy.

"But even with our newfound courage and strength, our soldiers continued to dwindle in number before we soon became vastly outnumbered by the enemy's forces. And it was said that during this time, Silindan was slain by multiple wuzlirs who tossed his body into the river out of fear for our people's burning wrath that would be kindled against them once again. Our people fled back to Watendelle out of the despair of not only hearing of Silindan's death but also the realization of how outnumbered we were. Thus came the end of Silindan and the War of the Great Revenge. Silindan is forever remembered as a mighty hero of our people, one who was unrelenting to surrender to the enemy out of fear. But it now appears that all that I have ever known of him is a lie, as it looks like he has fallen from honor and grace into some sort of madness and decay if that was him whom we saw in that vision."

Erundil shook his head, still full of disbelief by all Dulanmidir had revealed to him and the company. An empathetic look covered Dulanmidir's face, as he went over to place his hand on Erundil's shoulder.

"I understand the shock and heartbreak you are feeling, Erundil," he said, trying to comfort the gamdar. "And I can assure you that the tale you told about Silindan was true, regarding his great courage and the successes that he led the army of your people to. But, I am afraid that the greatest soldier and captain of your people never perished in battle, nor has he ever perished. Soon after the war ended, he fled not only from the sight of his people but also from the enemy. And for some odd reason, he is still living today, dwelling in the caves of Nangorid and falling into a downward spiral of corruption and ugliness with each passing year."

A sick and troubling feeling twisted Erundil's stomach, yet growing doubt took root in his heart at that same moment. "How can that be him though?" he asked. "Did the wuzlirs not cast his body into the river, causing our soldiers to flee back to Watendelle in wild fear? And even if a mortal creature could live for over 600 years, wouldn't it have been known by now? And besides, it is impossible for such noble and beautiful creatures as we gamdars to degrade into such terrible hideousness. If I'm being honest, I'm not sure that I could ever believe that that was Silindan who you showed us, Dulanmidir."

"But it was, Erundil," replied Dulanmidir. "Why would I cause so much sorrow and horror in you and your sons by deceiving you in this way? It was not the body of Silindan that was thrown into the river, but rather the body of some other gamdarian soldier who looked similar to Silindan in his appearance. But Silindan managed to escape from the battle, but even as he fled, something strange came over him. In some way, either willingly or unwillingly he became corrupted by the shadow of Natugura which led to him falling into a state of madness as his appearance and likeness began to slowly change into a hideous condition."

Gasps of horror rang through the table. "These are terrible things you are revealing to us, Dulanmidir," remarked Lelhond. "But I'm finding these statements of yours regarding Silindan nearly impossible to believe, even though I know you would never delude us. How could such a mighty hero of my people, let alone a non-corrupted creature as a gamdar is, be corrupted by Natugura? Never before have I ever heard such horrifying revelations, and even now I feel like laughing them off in disgust. And why would he flee from the Dark Lord if he became corrupted by him? After all, all of the corrupted creatures of the world have gone on to become the Dark Lord's slaves. So why would this case be any different?"

Dulanmidir sighed to himself, placing his chin on his hand and thinking deeply to himself. "You make good and reasonable points, Lelhond," he replied. "But, as Mataput and Orieant would say, the truth is sometimes harder to believe than the lie. And the truth is that the corrupting shadow of the Dark Lord has the power to influence the free creatures of the world. Long have I kept this reality in the life of Silindan to myself, but I knew that no time would have been more appropriate to share it with you all than now. Though I do not know the full answer to this terrible riddle, I deem that he stole something valuable from the enemy."

A glimmer of hope, though a tiny one, gleamed through Lelhond's eyes. "Could he have taken the lost book of Ulohendel?" he asked. Yet as he thought to himself, his excitement subsided. "But how could he have taken the book and still fallen into corruption? All of this doesn't make sense to me."

"I understand, Lelhond," said Dulanmidir. "And no, Silindan did not take the lost book of Ulohendel. If he had, I am confident that the enemy would have already swiftly found him, for such an important relic would bring hope not only to Watendelle but to the whole world. But, I suspect that he stole something else from the enemy, something not less in importance than the book, but perhaps less consumed by the Dark Lord's attention. Whatever the case is, when Silindan took this important thing from the enemy, he quickly went into hiding, fearing Natugura's wrath or his slaves discovering him. He has lived as a fugitive in the caves of Nangorid for these past centuries, yet during the time of his many adventures of escaping from the chains of the wuzlirs, he discovered a group of wild wuzlirs who were outcasts within the Dark Lord's slaves. Who they were and where they came from, I do not know, but they along with Silindan have together lived in hiding for many hundreds of years, devouring themselves in reckless and foul ways that I do not fully understand.

"Natugura knows that Silindan is still living and that it was he who stole whatever he desperately seeks. Yet, I am sure that he also knows that Silindan doesn't pose a large enough threat for him to wage war in finding whatever the corrupted gamdar stole from him. Discovering this source of importance and possibly great power which had been stolen from the Dark Lord is the last piece of this great puzzle in truly understanding the intentions and doings of Natugura. Truly knowing what this is, would benefit your quest in unimaginable ways, though it may not appear to do so at first. But whether we discover it or not, all that you need to know is that the Dark Lord has the power to corrupt the non-corrupted creatures of the world, as was demonstrated in Silindan. And I am not even sure that he knows that hardly anyone, save the mightiest beings dwelling within this world, are safe and strong enough to withstand his tempting shadow."

Shocked and horrified looks covered the faces of the company, who trembled at the deep secrets that Dulanmidir had revealed to them. Most alarmed besides the gamdars were Mataput and Orieant, who knowing Dulanmidir for many years now began noticing a change in him, as though a serious urgency had taken hold of him.

"You have been a very wise and good friend to Mataput and me for many years now, Dulanmidir," remarked Orieant. "But what you have revealed to us today, is beyond anything we could have ever imagined. I will not lie in saying that a strong sense of doubt is weighing heavily on my mind, that would you say was a phantom of the enemy's deceiving guise, yet deep down in my innermost being, I trust that what you have told us is nothing short of the truth. This has added a significant burden to our journey, though I cannot blame you for doing so. It was only a matter of time before you would reveal this to us, and now that we finally know what is lurking behind the shadows in Nangorid, we will not be in for a rude awakening."

"Yet, this revelation remains nothing short of overwhelmingly difficult to take in," added Mataput. "What you have told us, Dulanmidir is a dangerous matter for us to picture in our minds. The fact that the Dark Lord of this world does not even know the full range of his dreadful ability to corrupt the creatures of this world, is a terrifying thought to ponder."

"It is indeed," said Dulanmidir. "Yet one that remains true nonetheless. And this is why the salvation of humans as well as all the free creatures of this world depends on this great quest of yours. This journey will be the most significant event in the history of the world, even more so than the creation of Jangart or even the affairs of the War of Great Alliances. If Natugura finally understands this undiscovered power that he owns, it will mean disaster and destruction for all the creatures of this world. All would become his slaves, whether willingly or unwillingly, and his dominion would have no end.

"But I know that all of you would hate to see that day coming, and would do all in your designated authority to prevent that from happening. As for myself, I know the part that I must play to alter the trajectory of your quest's success. I have labored for quite a while within this world, and my great pilgrimage throughout the free lands of Jangart's creation has introduced me to some of the proudest, most courageous, and most pure-hearted creatures of this world. Within the time that has been allotted to me, I have seen the endless podium of world control stretch in favor of the free creatures before being snatched by the Dark Lord. From the days of Ulohendel to this present time, I have witnessed events that cause joy and peace and others that signal defeat and grief for a certain time. I have seen the rise and fall of many things both good and evil within the days of my many adventures, which have not even affected my unfazed manner in the slightest.

"Yet now, learning about this reality has brought me out of my comfort zone. I am unwilling to allow the enemy to achieve his purposes and destroy the order of the world as we know it. For if the Dark Lord succeeds, he would become unassailable to the creatures of this world, and everything which we have ever considered noble and true would perish under his deceptive and corrupting hand. We must not let him achieve his goals but must instead work in every way possible to frustrate him in his plans, which could perhaps even signal the beginning warning signs of his downfall. Yet the Dark Lord Natugura is stubborn and cunning and will try all he can to thwart our plans. So we must be on the highest alert to all of his wicked schemes to ensure the survival of righteousness and goodness within this world."

A wind of fear rushed through the room, yet gushes of hope and boldness were returned to the hearts of the company. But imagining what would happen if all of the free creatures of the world fell to the shadow of Natugura was more than they could bear. Many of them could only continue shaking in terror, no matter how desperately they wished for the fearful thoughts to be erased from their minds.

"The success of our quest now lies between the thinnest of margins," remarked Karandil. "The completion of our journey will either lead to everlasting joy and peace or come to doom and despair. Yet I am not sure that Natugura would be able to gain control over all the lands of this world. To do so, he would need to overthrow Jangart and who is mighty enough to topple his unending authority?"

"None can do so," replied Mataput. "Jangart will forever be in charge of the fate of this world and I know that no matter how hopeless things may become, there is one who cares for us far beyond what we could ever imagine. And I know whom it is that I serve, for my life in this world along with Orieant is meant to serve the free creatures of this world, and by effect, demonstrate Jangart's will to those who honor him. Yet, with all this hope we may have, Natugura remains able to do more than we might've first believed. When he was a perfect and beautiful spirit being along with Orieant and me, thoughts of evil and pride never once came to our minds, before we listened to the divisive words he spoke which brought his fall. He rebelled against Jangart and brought about the corruption of many creatures and places that were once fair and noble. And who knows what other frightening devices the Dark Lord wields?"

"None know for certain," remarked Erundil. "But I assure you that our quest will ensure that the Dark Lord fails in his purposes. And even if he may triumph over us for a time, my people will never fall for his deception. Though the whole world may crumble under his shadow, we gamdars will always stand defiantly against him."

Dulanmidir smiled at Erundil. "It is refreshing to see your

confidence, Erundil," he said. "Such boldness hasn't been seen in a King of Watendelle for quite some time, and seeing it in you is healthy to my ancient bones. But be careful in the words you choose. For all of us are not fully aware of the scope of the Dark Lord's might, and saying that your people will never fall under his shadow is speaking pompous words which few of us can know for certain."

"You are right, Dulanmidir," responded Erundil, falling silent and dwelling on Dulanmidir's words for some time.

For many more minutes, a vast silence hovered over the table. Everyone seated had heavy hearts after everything Dulanmidir had revealed to them. A giant burden it felt had been placed on their shoulders, and they knew that their quest would determine the fate of the world. The thought alone made them place their faces in their hands, yet they knew that they had each other and they would never depart from the purpose that had been laid ahead of them.

But none of them dared to look into Dulanmidir's eyes, fearing he would reveal some new and terrifying secret to them. Yet, they imagined that even if he shared something with them, it would not be worth comparing to everything they had already heard.

Then suddenly, amid the deep stillness that filled the house, a loud gasp came from Dulanmidir. He immediately stood up from his seat, shaking his head in disbelief. His shocked eyes were drawn to the gorlinto he held in his hands, and great fear fell on the company as they stared at him.

"What is going on, Dulanmidir?" asked Orieant, standing up from his seat with a deeply concerned look on his face. "Have you just seen something that can answer the deep questions running through our minds? Tell us what has happened."

Dulanmidir paced back and forth throughout the house before finally standing still in one place. "The Resistants have just been attacked by a group of wuzlirs!" he blurted out. "Just now I saw through the gorlinto how out of boredom and disobedience to Mataput and Orieant's commands, many of them decided to leave the forest they were staying in, which resulted in a few of the enemy's slaves attacking the people. The wuzlirs have since fled, but the damage has already been done. A number of the people have perished and the Dark Lord and his slaves now certainly know where the Resistants are."

The company gasped in horror upon hearing this news, amazed by how many terrible things had been revealed to them in the space of an hour or so. But as they processed this, frustration and anger were stored in the hearts of Steven and the volviers, who knew that it was the people's fault that they had been attacked.

Mataput sighed to himself. "We warned the people to stay in the forest," he said. "They knew that we would be gone for a few days, yet they blatantly ignored our warning on the second day of our departure from them. When will they ever learn to trust in what we have to say?"

"I don't know," said Steven with irritation. "You would think they would learn their lesson having been attacked two times before, with you, Orieant, and Lelhond all rescuing us. I was even foolish enough to ignore you and Orieant's warning to stay at the coast, which I deeply regret. But why have they now thrown all these things upside down to only suffer great harm at the hand of the enemy? These people can be hard to manage sometimes."

Steven placed his head in his hands, as Dulanmidir came over to him and placed his hand on his shoulder. "Do not despair, Steven," he said. "There is still hope for you and the people's protection despite their foolishness. And understand that most of them remained behind, trying to convince the others to listen to Mataput and Orieant's warning they gave them before leaving to go to Watendelle. But I fear that the enemy will use this to launch a further and greater assault on the people. So I am afraid that you and the volviers must go back to lead the people back to the coast in safety."

"But this is only my second day in Watendelle," protested Steven. "And I will not spoil the great time I have enjoyed here in this beautiful land all because of a few people's thoughtless choices."

"I understand, Steven," responded Dulanmidir. "But you are the leader of your people, and you must fight for them and defend them, no matter how much at fault they may be. I can see that they are difficult people to deal with, and without your leading along with Mataput and Orieant, the end of their path would be destruction."

"Dulanmidir is right," remarked Orieant. "Though I am disappointed that our stay in the land of Watendelle has been cut short, we have no choice but to help the people. I am sure that many of them are regretting their choices, and the last thing we need is for them to give up on all we have ever told them. We must uplift their hearts and continue to guide them, so that their foolish ways may be no more."

"I guess you're right," conceded Steven with a sigh. "Hopefully I will be able to return to this glorious land and discover more of the treasures of the gamdars."

"I hope so as well because there is more for you to see in this land, Steven," said Lelhond. He then turned to Dulanmidir. "Should I also come to protect the people along the way?" he asked. "And maybe even my brothers, father, and a group of our soldiers can come to help them, in case a much larger force of wuzlirs come to attack the people."

"No, there is no use for that," replied Dulanmidir. "The people must peacefully make their way back to the coast, and only Steven, Mataput, and Orieant are needed to accomplish that. But the three of you must leave now, for the people desperately need your help."

With his concluding words, the company conceded to Dulanmidir's wishes, agreeing that Steven, Mataput, and Orieant leaving to help the people was the best option for them. Following Dulanmidir to the front door, they were led outside his house where they all gathered together with heavy hearts.

"Well much was revealed to us today," remarked Mataput. "And though this was the not way I imagined our departure from this delightful land would come to, we have a business that we must take care of. But don't worry, in several more days we will meet up once again to embark on our journey through the land of Nangorid, one which has been added further significance by the words of Dulanmidir. And farewell Dulanmidir, though I do not know when I will see you again, I hope to enjoy myself under your wise and cheerful presence, knowing that the lost book of Ulohendel has been rescued for the deliverance of the world."

"I dream for that day to happen," said Dulanmidir. "But for now, focus on the task which has been entrusted to you, to lead the Resistants back to their new homes by the coast in safety. And once you complete that, you will be able to gather these gamdars and smalves to begin the great mission that lies ahead of you. The fate of the world depends on all of you, yet I know that you will find support along the way, both expected and unexpected."

With that, the company said their goodbyes to Steven and the volviers. "Farewell, but not for long I reckon," said Forandor. "We will see each other very soon, and I can't wait to help you on this great quest that will save us from the shadow of the Dark Lord."

"As do I," chimed in Huminli. "My brother and I will ensure that our quest succeeds in its goal."

"My sons and I will also ensure that," said Erundil, with a sideways glance at Huminli. "But I am glad that I finally got to meet you, Steven, and that you got to see the wonderful kingdom of my people. Now, I must come to your land and home and help ensure that your kind becomes free. And once you do become free creatures, make sure to return to Watendelle so that I can continue to give you the tour of this land."

"I will certainly do so," responded Steven. "It was a delight to learn of the history of your great people and to soak in the wonderful nature of this land. And I can't wait to see what else you have to show me."

Erundil and his sons smiled at Steven, ensuring themselves that this would not be the last time he looked upon the fair land of Watendelle. Once they had all said their final goodbyes, Mataput and Orieant whistled through the windy air, and coming down from the sky came three majestic muenwos. The three of them then hopped onto the winged creatures, waving to Dulanmidir, the gamdars, and the smalves as they elevated into the air and left the land of Watendelle with all speed to the land of the Earth.

9
A New Friendship

A VAST SEA OF water was the only thing below Steven, Mataput, and Orieant as they traveled through the sky. They soared through the heavens on the backs of the muenwos, with the winged creatures cruising past the birds beside them as the wind propelled them to fly at lightning speed. But after a short time had passed, dry land began to appear below them, and as they spiraled down, the border of a wide forest. Steven instantly recognized this as the place where he had departed from the people to go to the land of Watendelle. The three of them continued coming down before landing just on the forest's outskirts.

Once they came down, the muenwos immediately flew away and disappeared through the sky, leaving Steven and the volviers to themselves. The three of them started walking to the forest, which was foggy as before, yet not very dark. They walked on through rocky paths with overhanging trees surrounding them, with no sight of the people coming in any direction. It went on like this for several more minutes, with the only sound of the forest coming from the chirps of birds or the trees bristling from the breeze of the wind. All was silent for a while, and they began to grow concerned that they would never find the people. But just as they started growing discouraged, they finally saw the people scattered into different groups.

Observing the faces of the people, the three of them couldn't see one single relieved face among them. Great sadness and regret covered all of their faces, with no words of hope seemingly being able to lift the feeling of defeat that filled their hearts. All of their eyes were filled with sorrow, and into the distance could be seen Peter, weeping as he sat on the ground and refusing to look up to Steven or the volviers. Many people could be seen trying to bring him to his feet or offer words of encouragement, but his deep mourning was too strong for anyone to change his circumstances. Not a word was spoken among the great group of people, and not even the presence of Steven, Mataput, or Orieant could cheer them up.

While looking at the despaired looks that covered the people's faces, an overflow of grief and pity filled Steven and the volviers' hearts. Though they remained greatly disappointed in many of the people's foolish decision to leave the forest, they still wished to see the joy that had covered their faces and hearts before they left them, return to them once again. Most sorrowful among the three of them was Steven, who couldn't bear watching the depressed people, most of all Peter, soak in their calamity.

Glancing over at Mataput and Orieant for a moment, Steven could see the great sadness that filled their eyes, even with the displeased looks that were on their faces. But what broke their hearts was the piercing sound of Peter's weeping, a sound which they couldn't ignore. They started noticing that the boy began rolling over the ground, with piles of dirt and leaves covering his face and hair. The sight of this horrified them, and they feared for the worst of him above even the rest of the people's depressed faces that filled the forest as vast clouds of gloom.

Looking on at Peter's distress, Steven's eyes enlarged with such a great sense of worry and horror that he had never experienced before. "Why is Peter crying?" he asked, whispering to Mataput and Orieant. "What great tragedy has fallen upon him that is worse than that of the rest of the people?"

"I don't know, Steven," responded Mataput. "But it would be wise of us to try and figure that out. I fear that he has suffered the most out of all these people."

So the three of them inched their way in Peter's direction, who continued rolling over the ground and wildly crying. As they made their way closer toward him, the sound of his cry boomed even louder in the heavy air. Goosebumps covered their arms and they started shuddering with fear. The trees began swaying violently as the chilly wind blew strongly on them, making the three of them wonder if even the trees were earnestly anticipating their talk with Peter.

Once they made their way to Peter, they immediately covered their opened mouths with their hands, staring in horror at the tears that drenched his face. His eyes were bright red and his whole body shook uncontrollably. He suddenly turned to Steven and the volviers once he saw them, with a look of relief coming onto his face for a short moment, but it instantly vanished as he continued to suffer under the devastation he expressed.

Steven and the volviers didn't say a word to the young boy, though their hearts were pierced with shock and anguish. Steven could barely recognize the bright and young boy that Peter was, instead seeing a person drenched with hopelessness. The three of them couldn't even look at Peter, and would occasionally block their ears from hearing the blaring wail that came forth from his mouth. They tried their best to ignore him, in the hopes that he would be able to calm himself down, despite the gushes of tears that flew from his eyes and soaked his face and neck. But out of nowhere, he began smacking himself in the face and trying to tear his shirt, while mumbling words of blame to himself.

Steven and the volviers became alarmed at this sight and immediately jumped in to prevent Peter from harming himself. The young boy tried to resist at first, but once he realized who it was that was trying to calm him down, he began yielding to them. Eventually, he managed to have completely calmed down so that he no longer was crying and hurting himself, though he refused to look up at Steven and the volviers.

The three of them looked at each other, as though waiting for one of them to make the first move. Eventually, Mataput stepped in to express his concern for the boy. "What has happened to you, Peter?" he asked. "I know that you and the people have suffered from many terrible things today, yet it seems as though you are the most distressed out of them all. How can we try to ease your pain?"

Peter didn't respond and instead stared in the opposite direction. The three of them tapped him on the shoulder and waited for him to speak, but he continued not saying a word. Their hearts began to sink as they worried about what imaginable and devastating thing had happened to Peter that had left him scarred.

Filled with desperation, Steven tried everything to get Peter to speak. “Peter, won’t you tell us what is hurting you?” he asked, touching the boy’s shoulder softly. “You and the people had joyful faces when Mataput, Orieant, and I left to go to Watendelle with Lelhond, yet now you are all grieving. I know that many of you left this forest and were attacked by a group of wuzlirs that has tragically left some of you dead, but I want you to know that we are here to support all of you. We want to comfort you, Peter, and fill you with brightness and joy once again.”

Peter suddenly looked up at Steven with wide eyes, as though he were roused by his words. For a moment, he stared in amazement at him, either because he had known what had happened to him and the people, or because of the pity and support he was trying to offer him. Then, as he continued pondering on Steven’s words, he suddenly spoke, hiding nothing from Steven and the volviers.

“I was so foolish to lead my parents to their deaths!” he blurted out with a trembling voice. “I listened to the rest of the people when they talked about leaving the refuge that this forest gave us, and I was the one to convince my parents to follow me even though they remained doubtful. Oh, why did I have to follow along with the terrible idea? I should have been the one slain by the swords of the wuzlirs, not my parents!”

He continued rambling on as his voice shook more violently, before completely breaking down into tears again. Steven and the volviers were pierced to the heart upon hearing the news of his parent’s deaths. They drew even closer to him, wishing to embrace and console him in his time of grief. Yet Peter only continued crying and rambling on, refusing to cease blaming himself.

“No, it is my fault that they are dead!” he cried. “And nobody can tell me otherwise! If only I had joined them in their wisdom and ignored what everyone else was saying, they would have still been alive. But I am left here alone to suffer in grief and pain for the rest of my life, all because I neglected wisdom and embraced foolishness.”

Steven and the volviers could do nothing but silently watch Peter fall deeper into despair with each passing moment. For a moment, they stared at him with pitied looks, though nothing else showing their sorrow for the boy covered their faces. Filled with immense weakness, Peter collapsed to the ground, letting out a great wail of grief once more, that seemed to still the breeze of the wind. Time wore on, yet Steven, Mataput, and Orieant found themselves remaining still as stone statues, with no word or touch seemingly able to comfort Peter.

Yet while he witnessed the depression and despair that covered Peter like a black shadow of gloom, tears began to flow from Steven's eyes. They started as small drops which he swiftly wiped off his face, but they soon turned into large gushes of streams that he could not contain. Then suddenly, as though he could do nothing to prevent himself from doing anything else, Steven collapsed to the ground next to Peter, crying aloud openly as he shared his grief for the boy. Mataput and Orieant looked on at the sight with confused looks on their faces, and even Peter began to calm down as he saw Steven weeping alongside him.

Hearing the sound of Steven's cries, the rest of the people who were seated in groups around the forest came and gathered close to Steven and Peter. As distressed as they were, a sense of intrigue suddenly took hold of them, as they wondered why such a sudden change had come over Steven. They had never seen him act in such a manner before, believing him to be their strong leader who would remain unafraid in the face of the darkness that touched them. But in that hour they saw a change in Steven, and they now finally saw him as a tested and broken man, yet one who would always do his part to rise above affliction to support and encourage them. A newfound respect for him filled their hearts, and even distant smiles flashed across a few of their faces for a brief moment.

Seeing that the people had been drawn to him, Steven rose to his feet and wiped off the tears on his face, not wishing for any attention to be placed on him. Many peering eyes met his gaze, and even as he stood, his knees began to shake and his eyes twitched frantically. He nearly fell over on the ground but was quickly saved by Peter, who seemed to finally be over his misery as he too had risen to his feet.

Deeply concerned looks came over Mataput and Orieant's faces as they looked on at Steven. "Are you fine, Steven?" asked Mataput. "Peter seems to be doing better now, yet you started weeping bitterly and nearly fell to the ground. Is there something that we should know so that we can help you?"

Steven was silent, with his hands shaking as he stared at the many intimidating faces of the people that surrounded him. But after a while, he finally confessed why he had reacted the way he did.

"There is nothing you need to know," he said. "But I admit that I am not fine. I do not know why, but as I began processing the deep and awful anguish that Peter was enduring with seemingly no hope, I found myself unable to contain my emotions. My heart was shattered into pieces as I watched him weep and roll on the ground, and I couldn't help but burst into tears and collapse to the ground. I am grieved for this young boy, whose very source of innocence and support has been rudely snatched from him. His life has forever changed, and I would hate myself if I tried my best to ignore that. So from this day forth, I will not try to distance myself from what Peter is suffering from. When he weeps, I shall weep, and when he laughs, I shall also laugh. And no matter what he has done, I promise to be by his side at all times so that I can be a firm foundation throughout his life, whether he may be feeling weak or strong."

The hearts of the people were softened as they listened to Steven. Looks of delight could be seen covering the faces of Mataput and Orieant, while small drops of tears fell from Peter's eyes and onto the beam of his smiling lip. He came over to Steven and tightly embraced him, with tears flowing from Steven's eyes as he kissed Peter's forehead. Tears of joy filled both of their eyes, and they continued hugging each other for a while, with Peter not wishing to depart from the assurance which Steven had warmed his heart with.

While they longingly embraced each other, Steven whispered in Peter's ear. "Just know that I will always be here for you, Peter," he said. "As long as I am alive I will be whatever you require of me to be, whether that may be a brother, a father, or even a hero. And I will always provide you with not only what you want, but what you need."

Peter couldn't hold back his tears, even as a broad smile covered his face. "Thank you, Mr. Loubre," he replied while sniffing. "You have given me far more than I could ever deserve, and I will always hold you dear into my heart."

"This is the least I could have done for you, Peter," said Steven. "How could I neglect all that you have suffered from, and still be a friend of yours?" He paused for a moment before a smile came to his face. "And another thing, there is no need to call me mister. I am your friend who will strengthen and encourage you more than even the best brother could, and I have promised to stick close to you. Call me Steven instead."

Upon hearing this from Steven, Peter looked on at him with a joyful look on his face and he couldn't hold back the beaming smile on his face or the tears of joy flowing from his eyes. The two of them continued to embrace each other, sharing their many mixed emotions.

After the long moment of embracing each other, Steven and Peter finally let go of one another and turned their attention towards the people around them. Much to the surprise of both of them, they noticed that almost all of the people had tears in their eyes, including Mataput and Orieant. They could sense that everyone's hearts were melting out of pure joy, and many of them flocked to the two of them, embracing Steven and Peter and ensuring that they would all support and encourage them.

After all of the people had expressed their emotions to each other, serious looks came to many of their faces as they cast their attention to Mataput and Orieant. They could sense that the volviers were still searching for answers and that they wouldn't be able to hide from the difficult conversations that would ensue.

Sure enough, Orieant was the first to speak to all of them. "I am glad to see how all of you have come together to provide comfort, especially to Peter in this grievous moment," he said. "But it would also be wrong of me if I ignored everything that forced me, Mataput, and Steven to leave Watendelle and come back to all of you. We would still like a full explanation as to what caused all of this trouble to be brought upon you all in the first place. One of you must take the responsibility of admitting your failure so that we can know what would be the best decision for us to take."

All was silent, as the people's moods instantly changed. A shadow of fear and hesitation filled their hearts, and none of them were willing to take the responsibility that Orieant was calling them to take. Their eyes were cast to the ground, much to the suspicion of the volviers and even Steven.

"Is there no one willing to be honest?" asked Mataput, as he eagerly awaited a response from at least one person. "Tell us what you are hiding so that we can help you navigate what the right choice will be for you to take."

Mataput waited for a response, yet still, the people remained silent with some of them trying to act as though they didn't hear what Mataput said. Frustration began to grow within Steven and the volviers as they wondered when the people would admit their faults. Yet a vast stillness hovered over the forest, with only the passing wind making a sound in that quiet place. Eventually, the three of them sighed to themselves, convinced that the people would remain unwilling to let go of their fears. But just when they were about to give up on the people, Peter suddenly stepped in to speak.

"Well, if nobody is going to confess the mistakes that we made, then I will," he said, with all eyes now glued upon him. "It started earlier this morning when because of our boredom, we began to complain about the impatience we felt on staying in this forest for the next few days while we waited for you three. Many of us desired action and movement once again, and we dreaded having to experience the dullness of this bleak forest. We didn't just want to stay here and do nothing, but we instead wanted to go to our new homes as soon as we possibly could.

"So it was that we hastily devised the foolish idea to leave this forest and explore the region that lay outside it. Many people agreed to join this plan and though I was wary at first, mainly due to my parents' concerns, I eventually gave in because of my restlessness and the pressure of everyone else. But it came to the point that I began persuading other people to join us, including my parents. Though they desired to stay back in the safety of the forest, my parents would in time decide to come with the many thousands of us who marched our way through the forest and onto a wide area of grasslands. Despite the chilly weather, the sun shone high and proud in the sky and we felt the freedom of not having to be locked in a caged woodland. Excitement filled our hearts, and many of us began to go back to the forest to bring many other people into the wide and rich grassland.

"But it was in the moment of our happiness, that the consequences of our ill-advised choices would catch up to us. At that moment, we came into contact with five wuzlirs, whose very presence made many of us collapse to the ground in terror. A terrible darkness covered them, that not even the sun could pierce with its bright light. They were all seated on their huge and frightening black horses, who stared at us with unrelenting eyes. At first, the wuzlirs didn't make a move and instead began communicating with each other in the most hideous and vile voices I have ever heard. Their voices were like the sound of an animal getting stabbed, and we all covered our ears to the grotesque words they spoke. But we instantly removed our hands from the side of our faces when we began hearing their terrible laughs that pierced even our covered eyes.

"And then, the five of them finally made their moves, attacking us violently with the sharp swords that they raised in the air. We all immediately retreated in the direction of the forest, and as we did, the wuzlirs continued pursuing us while they hideously laughed at us in a noise that sounded like penetrating screeches. Most of us had forgotten our weapons, but the few who had remembered them, attacked the black riders even though many of their eyes were filled with fear. Among them were my parents, and though many of us were vastly overwhelmed and outnumbered by the wuzlirs, they hardly seemed to be impacted by us for some reason. The five of them were incredibly swift and managed to evade our blows while they inflicted heavy blows upon us. Some of their large and sharp swords struck the people, which instantly left many of them dead, among whom included my brave parents.

"Yet some still bravely tried fighting back, even though our weapons only seemed to scratch the heavy armor of the wuzlirs. All hope seemed lost to us, and we began wondering if any of us would survive. But to our shock, the wuzlirs fled from the battle and into the direction where they had come from. Many people tried pursuing them, though they were no match for the speed of their battle horses. We watched them disappear into the far distance, before bringing our attention to the couple dozen or so bodies that they had left dead. For many long minutes, we stared at the slain bodies with clenched fists and tears filling our eyes, before we eventually broke down in grief and disbelief. We wondered how we would ever come back from this horrible event, but it was not long after we returned to the forest that you three came to us amid our moment of deep sorrow."

Peter breathed a sigh of relief once he finished speaking, feeling as though a heavy burden had been lifted from his shoulders. Though looking into the eyes of Steven and the volviers, he could see their sense of displeasure that was directed toward the people as a whole.

Mataput sighed to himself, though he was pleased with Peter. "I appreciate your honesty, Peter," he said. "Being willing to speak with such clarity and candor even despite the horrible things that have happened to you this morning is a beautiful sight for all to behold. Your boldness and honesty are admired, Peter, and I know that you will do great things in the long life that is ahead of you. But, none of this removes the present danger that is lurking on every side of you. The enemy now knows where all of you are at now, and that is only because many of you decided to disobey our orders and face the consequences of your actions. You have only brought this danger upon yourselves, and I hope that all of you see how protected you would have been if you remained where you were."

"I certainly see it now," said Peter. "And I admit that I was foolish to blatantly disobey your orders, which has only brought this destruction upon ourselves," he paused for a moment, deep in thought, before speaking again. "But I wonder, why were the wuzlirs hardly affected by the many weapons that seemed to crush them on every side? There must have been dozens of swords that struck them, yet they seemed to only be small trifles that filled them with even more hate against us."

"That is because those wuzlirs are likely among the strongest soldiers of the Dark Lord's forces," responded Mataput. "The weapons we gave you would hardly pierce through their heavy armor, and only the mightiest gamdarian soldiers would be an even match up for them. But do not fear; for not all of the enemy's servants are as strong as they. If he had randomly selected some of his weaker wuzlirs to attack you, then I am sure they would have either been seriously injured or even killed by the many weapons that would have come against them. But the Dark Lord Natugura is dangerously shrewd, and he knew that for his servants to discover where you were, he would need them to come back to him alive."

"That would have been good to know while we fought against those wuzlirs," remarked Peter. "Though we never should have even been in that position in the first place," he sighed to himself. "What are we going to do now then? The wuzlirs will certainly tell their master where we are now, and I am sure that a greater onslaught will soon come. All have turned for the worst, and I'm not sure how we will survive it now."

"Do not worry, Peter," said Mataput. "Though things have indeed turned for the worst, all of you will remain safe if we travel with all speed to the coast. The enemy will not be able to find us if we manage to move quickly before he can track us. And I sense that he will likely think that we will stay in the forest, so if we go now, you can escape from his wrath and successfully remain sheltered in your new homes."

"But how will we remain safe in our new homes?" asked a man, still full of worry and doubt. "Wouldn't Natugura's servants be able to track our steps to the coast?"

"They would but only if you linger here too long," answered Orieant. "Once you make it to the coast, Mataput and I will give all of you a hedge of protection so that the enemy will not be able to find and attack you. Such is the power that we hold, even though we are not the great spirit beings we once were. But haste is needed if you want to remain safe, and you must be willing to trust us. For if you can't learn to listen to what we have to say now, how will you listen to Steven once he brings back the lost book of Ulohendel, the source of wisdom and salvation that will free you from the approaching bondage of complete corruption? There is no time for you to argue, for the fate of humanity rests on your collective ability to heed our words and obey them."

At that, the people became dead silent, not wishing to argue or ask any more questions with Mataput and Orieant. They were filled with shame that they had ever doubted the volviers and that they had overtly rebelled against them. They were determined to shift their way of thinking, and they knew that it would have to start right now.

"I will trust in you," conceded the man at last, with everyone else immediately pledging their allegiance to the volviers and Steven.

"Very well then," said Orieant with a smile on his face. "We will take you for your word and hope that it lasts. But we should now be on our way, lest the enemy's servants find you before you arrive at your new homes."

"I'm ready to go," said Peter. "But I must mention that the last time we made it to the coast, we found ourselves in an unfamiliar land. All that lay ahead of us was the seashore, and we found ourselves staring at strange trees and plants. We wish to see hills and valleys, so I hope that my desire won't be in vain."

"It will not," responded Orieant with a laugh. "When all of you reached the coast, you only saw the land that lay by the edge of the Earth. If you had explored the land that was full of unrecognizable trees and plants, then you would have danced and sung through a rich and fertile land full of hills and valleys. The coast is not all the land you will inherit, for there is still much land for you to see south, east, and north."

The people celebrated for joy at Orieant's words, with a stream of excitement now flowing through their nervous hearts. But even amid their joy, a dark thought suddenly came to Peter's mind.

"But what about the dead bodies lying outside this forest?" he asked. "We can't just leave them rotting out there and allow their memories to be disgraced."

"You are right, Peter," responded Mataput. "And we will make sure that their bodies are not dishonored. Yet because haste is needed now, we will first have to lead you to your homes and show you the land you will dwell in. And once you become comfortable with the new sights that will surround you, then you may go back in the direction from which you came to bring back the dead bodies that the wuzlirs killed and give them the proper burial that they deserve. And do not worry; Orieant and I will ensure that those who go to bring back the dead bodies to your new homes are safe and protected along the way."

Instantly, the shadow of fear that had come over Peter passed from his mind, and his joy was restored. He breathed a sigh of relief. "Well, that takes care of things," he said. "I do not need to worry whether or not my parents will get a proper burial. But for the time being, I am excited to finally feast my eyes on a countryside of hills and valleys! Such is what makes the land of Fozturia a delightful sight to behold."

"You are right indeed," chimed in Steven. "I can't think of anything better than a landscape of rolling hills and valleys."

"And you shall soon see what your heart longs for," said Mataput. "So now that you are all filled with excitement, let us get going so that you can see the land that will soon become your home."

With that, the people set out from the forest with Mataput and Orieant leading the way, and Steven and Peter following them from behind. The two of them walked side by side with joyful faces. Not a trace of regret could be seen on their or the rest of the people's faces, as they were all eager to enjoy the freedom of their new lives. They began picturing what the land of hills and valleys would be like and what abundant crops they would grow on their farms. Still, they allowed their hopes to go to the back of their minds as they continued following the volviers. As they marched on, the wind began quieting down and a shadow of light seemed to illuminate the expansive forest. The trees became brighter as they neared the edge of the woodland region.

At last, they departed from the forest and made their way through an area of grasslands and low valleys. The sky was clear, though the gentle breeze of the wind reminded them that the summer season had long gone. They walked on through this region for a couple of miles, with a dozen or so scattered bodies lying dead on the ground. They dared not look at the sight of the deceased souls that had suffered from the violence of the wuzlirs and instead continued staring straight ahead.

Yet as he came to the sight of his dead parents, Peter suddenly stopped still, gazing at their bodies as a firm stone figure. But even as he silently stood there, tears began welling in his eyes and he crouched down to touch their deceased faces. Steven came to his side, linking his arm around the boy's arm and speaking words of encouragement to him.

"You have me now, Peter," he said, trying to offer comfort to him. "I will be by your side for as long as I live, and you will not need to feel lonely."

A faint smile came to Peter's face and he wiped the tears from his eyes. Regaining his composure, he kissed each of his parents' foreheads and stood up to his feet. He joined the rest of the people walking along the path, and they continued migrating in the direction of their new homes.

Not a single cloud could be seen under the bright sky, though the chilly breeze of the wind began to intensify. For the next couple of hours, the people made their way through the path with endless grasslands surrounding them. A few birds soared through the sky, chirping and singing as they went in the same direction as the people.

The evening soon approached as the day wore on, and the sun could be seen sinking beneath the darkening sky. Ahead of them, the people saw the same hills and valleys that they had been in several days before, and they decided to stop there and rest for the night. Several stars filled the pitch-black sky, and many of them gazed into the night sky before drowsing to sleep.

Steven and Peter lay next to each other while they stared at the stars. "Isn't that a sight to behold, Steven?" remarked Peter, as he lay on his back. "My father used to say that the number of stars in the night sky represented the endless dreams we have no matter how dark the future may seem to be."

"Your father was a wise man, Peter," said Steven. "We all have dreams, and my most important desire is to lead you all in righteousness and freedom, in the hopes that you will enjoy a joyful life to the fullest. I would hate to rule over you as a tyrant and cause you to endure times of misery. I do not want to be a ruler like Maguspra, but rather a servant of you all first. I wish to live my life as a brother to the only child and a father to the orphan, and I certainly believe that I have a decent job in doing that. But I fear that won't be enough, and whether or not power will corrupt and turn me into a selfish person. That would be a terrible thing, and it fills my heart and mind with dread."

A worried look came on Peter's face, though he tried reassuring Steven. "Do not worry about something that won't happen to you, Steven," he said. "You have been an incredible leader and friend to all of us, and we owe you our very lives. I do not think that power will corrupt you, because you have a pure heart, unlike the many other rulers on the Earth."

"But we can all possess pure hearts at times, Peter," responded Steven. "Even Maguspra has a soft spot in his hardened heart, though hardly anyone would say that he is a good man."

"But you are different, Steven," said Peter. "Your fate is far different than Maguspra could ever wish for. It is you who has been chosen to bring back that great book of wisdom from the land of Nangorid, which will supernaturally change our hearts and minds for the better. Your rule over us will signal the beginning of a conversion of humanity from impending corruption to true deliverance. I can only imagine the words of wisdom that are stored in that golden book, eagerly awaiting for us to read them."

Steven sighed to himself, staring at the bright stars that illuminated the black sky. "All that you say is true," he said. "But I still fear for the worst. What if I fail in my quest of bringing this lost book to the Earth, and what if the book doesn't even have the power to transform our hearts and lives?"

"Do not fear, Steven," responded Peter. "If you want to succeed on your quest, you must have the boldness to look ahead with optimism rather than with pessimism. My mother used to say that if you hope for the worst, you will get the worst, but if you hope for the best, you will get the best. So it is up to you, Steven, to hope for the best, and I know that we will all need it if we want to experience hope and joy in our new lives."

A broad smile came to Steven's face. "I can always learn a thing or two from Peter the Wise," he laughed. "Your words have not failed to encourage me, and I will certainly need your wisdom to benefit me whenever I rule over you all. I am so glad that we have formed this unshakable relationship with each other."

"So am I," said Peter, yawning as his eyelids started drooping. "I'm getting rather sleepy now, and I will need as much rest as possible before we go on the road again in the morning. It was great talking with you, Steven."

"It was great talking with you as well, Peter," said Steven. "Goodnight and we will talk more in the morning." With that, both of them fell asleep, with peaceful smiles covering their faces as they dreamt of the new and glorious homes that awaited them.

The next morning, everyone woke up in a great mood, warmly greeting each other and ready to begin another day of traveling. The sky was gray and cloudy, yet no one seemed to worry about this. Their joy was the only light that they needed to reach their new homes, and great excitement consumed their minds. All that day they journeyed through hilly regions and low valleys, and no matter how they wished to stop and dwell here, they knew that their true homes would be close to the coast. They only stopped a few times throughout that day to rest, and by the evening they rested for the night in an area surrounded by wide valleys.

The next day went the same, as the people continued walking through the same familiar land of valleys. Hardly any living creatures, besides a few birds and insects, could be seen or heard around them. But as the next couple of days passed, the people began noticing many deer and cattle that surrounded them as they began traveling through wide and flat grasslands. Tremendous eagerness welled in their hearts at this sight and they knew that they were soon about to arrive at the coast.

Then finally, in the morning of their fourth day of journeying, the people could see in the far distance ahead of them the familiar sight of a sandy coastline with the wide sea beyond it. Catching a glimpse of the coast, many of them started running over to it, shouting and celebrating for joy that they had finally reached their new homes in safety. They were glad that their endurance had paid off, and they wondered what would now lay in store for them to enjoy.

"Well this is what we have all been waiting for!" remarked Peter, gazing at the coast in all directions. "We can now dwell here in peace, free from the attacks of Natugura and his slaves."

"Yes indeed, Peter," said Orieant. "You will not have much to worry about while you dwell here for the time being. But do not forget that this coast is not all of the areas of land you will inherit. There is still much more land that Mataput and I need to take you to so that you will be able to enjoy your new homes in the fullness of joy you all deserve."

"Show us then!" said Peter in growing excitement. "I want to see all of the hills and valleys and fertile land that we will be able to dwell in. I can't wait to run and play in this new glorious land."

And so walking along the coastline, Orieant and Mataput led the people northward to show them all what their new homes would entail. Once they made their way through the long coastline, the people were led into a land of trees and plants, very much similar to the ones that they had thought to be strange. For the next half hour, they made their way through this region, with their excitement beginning to die down.

But then their joy would be restored once they were led through a different path. Walking through this way they found themselves surrounded by a prosperous land covered in rolling green hills and wide fertile valleys. The land was covered in an abundance of large trees with juicy fruits and numerous plants and flowers engulfing the healthy grass. All over the land was a plethora of living beings which included sheep, cattle, goats, deer, and rabbits populating the region in large numbers. At this blissful sight, the people could only frolic in joyful celebration as even their most hopeful dreams never amounted to what they now saw with their own eyes. The whole region was teeming with life, and they wondered if they were even still in Fozturia. Flowing along the valleys was a long river and several ponds, providing a healthy amount of watering for the land. For the next couple of hours, the people continued either dancing or skipping through this fertile land, listening to the volviers as they explained to them all that they would inherit as their new homes.

After the people's greatest desires had been fulfilled, Orieant stopped and turned to speak with them. "For the past few hours, Mataput and I have led you northward in the land you will inherit," he said. "All of this land you have seen is yours, but do not forget that there is still much to see to the south and the east. But for time's sake, we will allow you to enjoy what you have currently seen. As you have seen, many animals and creatures already dwell in this rich and spacious land. Your purpose is to share in the land with them, which includes building houses for you to dwell in, and growing the many plants of this land to harvest on your farms. There will be plenty of food for you to eat, as the cows will provide you with milk, cheese, and butter, the trees with numerous kinds of fruits and vegetables, and the many other animals with meats. And so we leave you to enjoy the land which now belongs to you, including all that lies to the south and east which you have not yet seen."

At this description, the people shouted for joy, greatly impressed, and filled with enthusiasm to further explore the land that would be their dwelling place. But before they could continue traveling through the land, Mataput quickly stopped them.

"Now before any of you goes running away from us," he said. "Orieant and I will first like to lead you all back to the coast and rest there. That way, tomorrow morning we will feel greatly rested before Steven and us, along with several others including Lelhond begin our journey over the sea through the land of Nangorid."

The people agreed to this plan, and so they followed the volviers back toward the coast and rested there for the night. The next morning, they woke up to the sound of waves, as they looked on at the majestic sight of the blue water of the wide sea.

After finding some fruits and vegetables to eat, they all chatted with one another, with the focus mainly being on Steven's big quest that was now before him. Steven could hardly believe that the time had finally come, but he was determined to bring deliverance to not only his people but to all the people of the Earth through his journey.

Eventually, the people were all gathered together by the seashore as Orieant made some remarks to them. "As you all know, Steven will soon be embarking on an important journey that will likely determine the fate of the world," he said. But he will not be alone, as I, Mataput, and six others will help support and guide him on this quest. I reckon that we will be gone for many long months, hopefully not longer, but you will have all of this land to enjoy. I hope you have all liked seeing your new homes and that you will continue to explore even more and settle down while we are away."

"It has been a great joy to finally see our new homes," remarked a man from the crowd. "And I know that I will certainly continue to explore all that will fill my heart with joy."

A broad smile came across Orieant's face. "Very well," he said, turning toward Mataput who nodded his head in response. "Now that you are all satisfied, Mataout and I are going to fly back to Watendelle to gather together the six other creatures that will be joining us on our journey through Nangorid."

"Who are these other creatures?" asked Peter. "I know Lelhond is joining, but are the rest of them also gamdars?"

"You will see, Peter," responded Orieant. "But we should be on our way now, that way we have enough time to journey through the land throughout the morning and afternoon today. We will come back to you all within a few minutes, and after introducing you to the six others who will be joining us on this quest, we will finally depart for our journey."

With that, Orieant and Mataput suddenly whistled into the air, and flying down from the sky came two muenwos. The people gazed in awe at the sight of the majestic creatures having never seen them before, but before they could ask any questions, the winged creatures had hardly carried the volviers into the sky and they glided through the morning sky, disappearing from the people's sight.

10

The Entry into Nangorid

JUST SOMETIME LATER AFTER the volviers had vanished through the sky on the backs of the muenwos, they heard a sudden crashing boom along the coastline. Turning to their left, they all gathered together to see what had happened. As they became silent, they could see in the far distance Mataput and Orieant walking toward them, wearing dark gray cloaks while carrying their walking sticks along with brown backpacks, swords, arrows, and other weapons. Behind them, the people could faintly see four tall green-skinned figures, one of whom they recognized to be Lelhond and two short figures beside them. All six of them were clothed in the same dark cloaks of the volviers and also carried brown backpacks with many weapons at their side.

Once the six of them came within a short distance of them, the people could only stare in astonishment at them. They instantly recognized that the four gamdars were related in some way, yet they couldn't make out who the two small creatures who seemed so alike to them could be. Yet as Steven looked on at Lelhond, his father, and his brothers, he found himself greatly surprised by their sudden change in appearance. Though he could still sense the high status they possessed, they seemed to have lost a touch of their regalness. They no longer were the glorious and royal figures of Watendelle that had filled Steven with so much wonder, they now instead appeared to be rangers out in the wild. Even Erundil, despite how mighty of a king Steven knew him to be, seemed to now be some chieftain of a wandering people. But to the rest of the people, their hearts were filled with a sense of awe just by seeing a portion of how distinguished the gamdars were.

Once they drew near to the people, Mataput spoke to them. "Gathered together alongside Orieant and I are the six creatures who will be joining us on our journey," he said. "The four gamdars that you see are all related to each other, with the one standing to Lelhond's left being his younger brother Karandil, a mighty gamdarian soldier, and the one to his right is his youngest brother Forandor, a great musician. In front of them is their father, Erundil, the King of the Gamdars who reigns in the kingdom of Watendelle. Now the other two creatures you see are called smalves, and they come from the land of Laouli. They are both brothers and the one to my left is Huminli Frauttins, while the one to my right is Glophi Frauttins. The smalves are non-corrupted creatures just like the gamdars, and though they may not seem like it, I can assure you that they are brave and stout-hearted creatures. They can be jokesters at times, but it is all to our benefit. All six of these creatures will support Steven on his quest and make our journey through the land of Nangorid a less burdensome one."

Broad smiles covered all of the people's faces, and they felt greatly honored to be standing in the presence of such great and mighty creatures. They were filled with many questions, mainly of the smalves.

"I would like to learn more about the smalves," remarked Peter. "I have already much about the gamdars from Lelhond, and I am sure that Steven has learned so much more about them from his stay in their land, but what about the smalves? What do they enjoy doing and what are they like?"

Glophi quickly jumped in to respond to Peter. "Well I for sure can let you know all about my people," he said enthusiastically. "We smalves are fun-natured creatures who love to laugh, eat, cook, and farm. Our food is the delight of all the free creatures of the world, especially our crumpo soup which contains some of the finest vegetables that are grown in the hill country of Londur, where Lobie Hashinger first grew them. However, they are also grown very well in Malhon, the country where we reside. Malhon has been the home of my family for many hundreds of years, and hopefully, once we finish this quest you all can visit my brother and I's home one day. I can assure you that our food and stories will never tire you, and our acts of bravery will give you much hope, no matter how little we may seem to be."

"Well, I can see how large the hearts of the little smalves are!" remarked a man. "You are indeed a fun-loving race of creatures, and I can't wait to visit your land and taste your food sometime soon!"

"Me too!" chimed in Peter, with a beaming smile on his face. "I for sure love food myself, which I guess makes me similar in a way to the smalves!"

"Everyone has at least a piece of a smalf in them," remarked Glophi. "Whether you love food or are brave, these are all traits that make up a smalf."

"That is true indeed," confirmed Lelhond. "I have witnessed these traits being put on full display with Glophi and his brother Huminli, and I know that these two smalves will be a valuable help for us on this long and difficult journey."

Karandil and Forandor both nodded their heads in agreement, except for Erundil, who nervously smiled at the people while trying to cover up his animosity toward the smalves.

For the next several minutes, the people continued chatting with the smalves and gamdars, being greatly intrigued to learn more about them. Their interest was especially sparked by hearing about the lore of the gamdars and learning about the many kings, soldiers, and heroes of their history, which filled them with great fascination. But what filled their hearts with the greatest feeling of reverence was the story of Ulohendel, as they dreamed of what such a wise and powerful figure would be like in their world today.

"Ulohendel must have been unfathomably wise if this book of his will make Steven rule over us in perfection," remarked a man, who had been listening to Erundil's stories with close attention. "You must contain a great deal of wisdom yourself, considering he is your ancestor."

"Just to possess a meager amount of Ulohendel's wisdom is an honor in itself," responded Erundil. "His knowledge is unparalleled to anyone who has ever existed in the history of Watendelle, and it is a blessing to have his wisdom passed down to myself and my family. Yet, it is not only to us who are related to him that his gift of insight has been passed down.

Even those who are not related to him have inherited his wisdom just by allowing his words to dwell richly in their hearts. A good example of this is through the line of Yarclanin, who was the chief advisor of King Emilasara. Yarclanin was thought to be so much wiser than the king, that during his lifetime fifteen hundred years ago, he was considered the wisest gamdar to be alive. Many gamdars even considered making him King of Watendelle, with even King Emilasara wanting to hand over his power to his chief advisor.

"Yet in his wisdom and out of humility, Yarclanin denied the request, knowing that no matter how sweet his life would be as king, it would only last for a season as he would face the bitter consequences of going against the divine order of our kingdom. For the rest of his life, he continued advising the king, and would even advise the next king named Resmandil after his father Emilasara died. Eventually, Yarclanin would die and his son Montalorn would follow in his footsteps and advise King Resmandil. And to this very day, the chief advisors of the Kings of Watendelle can be traced back to the days of Yarclanin, and even my chief advisor Olindule can trace his lineage back to him."

The people were left staring at Erundil with open mouths, amazed by all they heard of the wisdom of the gamdars. Most amazed of them all was Steven, who found himself never growing tired by the endless stories of the gamdars.

"So what you're saying is that all gamdars have great wisdom no matter who they are related to?" he asked. "That is an incredible thought to imagine. But how do you have so much knowledge about the history of your people, even those who lived thousands of years ago? We, humans, can barely even remember events that happened decades ago."

A confused look came upon Erundil's face. "Well that is a strange thing that your people can hardly remember events of your past," he responded. "It has been a long tradition of my people to write down just about everything that happens during our lifetime and what happened throughout our history, and then we store it in numerous safe places. Don't your people do something similar to this?"

Steven sighed to himself. "No, we don't do the wise things that you gamdars do," he replied. "I can't speak of the other kingdoms and peoples of the Earth, but we people of Fozturia hardly write down about the events of our predecessors. And even when we do, our books and tales either get lost or forgotten. But you gamdars are much wiser than we are, and besides, you are non-corrupted creatures, unlike us humans. I am glad that you and your sons are going to help me on this important quest."

"It is my pleasure to help you, Steven," said Erundil. "Perhaps the words of Ulohendel's great book will transform the humans from creatures fast approaching corruption from the Dark Lord to creatures who are free from his influence just like us gamdars are. But I know that this journey will determine the fate of humanity, so it is that much better Mataput and Orieant are joining us on this quest. Without them, I don't know who would hold this company together. But I know we will be fine no matter what trials we may have to endure."

"You are right," agreed Steven. "We will succeed on this quest no matter what difficulties we face. And we have no choice but to succeed, for if we fail, the land of humanity will forever be doomed under chains of darkness."

"That is a dark thought, yet one that will not happen while we remain true to the purpose of our quest," said Erundil. "We will succeed on this quest, and no matter how mighty the Dark Lord Natugura and his slaves may seem to be, they stand no chance against the authority of the volviers and the combined force of the free creatures of the world. And with this company, we will certainly bring back the lost book of Ulohendel for the people of the Earth to use."

"Well it is up to us to save the fate of the world," muttered Steven, with a sense of doubt slowly creeping through his mind. But he took comfort in knowing that he would have the company to support him even in the toughest of times he would experience.

He and Erundil distanced themselves from the rest of the people, walking down the long sandy coast as they continued talking. Then, they stood silently by each other as they observed the beautiful waves that crashed just on the edge of the sandy beach. A chilly gust of wind flowed in the air and the clouds hid the sun from their sight, but they knew that during the summer this location would be a delightful experience. Turning around they saw how all the people seemed to be filled with a great sense of joy, especially as Huminli and Glophi seemed to be telling them endless stories that filled them all with laughter. Mataput and Orieant stood alone by themselves, but broad smiles could be seen covering their wise faces as they watched the great happiness that filled the hearts of the people. For some more time, Steven and Erundil stood quietly, with their hearts warmed to see the joy that now consumed the people, as their present worries had been lifted away from their minds.

But then, Erundil turned toward Steven, with a grave look now suddenly masking his face like a vast cloud. His eyes seemed to be slightly enlarged as he looked up and down at Steven with peering gazes. Steven's face grew red with embarrassment, and he wondered if he had said or done something wrong that had brought Erundil's disapproval on him.

"Is everything fine, Erundil?" he asked, filled with discomfort and confusion. "Have I done something wrong?"

Erundil snapped out from staring at Steven. "Oh, no no, Steven," he quickly said. "You have done nothing wrong, I was just thinking to myself," he paused for a moment, staring at the wide sea ahead of him. Then with a sigh, he confessed what he had been worrying about to Steven. "But you know, Steven, there are times when I can't help but wonder what awesome words of wisdom were penned by Ulohendel in his great book. For many long years, my people enjoyed the full benefits of not only his presence but also the power of his living words. I wonder what incredible insights and revelations are contained in that golden book. Yet as I think of this, I can't help but fear that Natugura has somehow corrupted it in some way while keeping it secret in his Black Tower. But at the same time, if that were to be the case, wouldn't the volviers have known it and told us? Yet I know that even they are not all-knowing, and perhaps the Dark Lord managed to evade their vast knowledge in this one matter. Perhaps he is sitting on his dark throne and laughing at us while knowing that we are only walking to our doom in this courageous journey."

Steven was speechless, and looking into Erundil's eyes he saw a great fear that he had hardly seen in anyone before. Erundil's expressed doubts began to creep into Steven's heart, and he found himself sympathizing with his fears. Yet as he thought to himself for a while, Steven garnered the confidence to counter what Erundil said, by trying to assure him of the goal of their quest.

"Well, the Dark Lord is very crafty and cunning indeed, but I still think the volviers would have known if he corrupted the book in some way," he said. "Besides even if the book was ruined in some way, why would so many wuzlirs be sent here to deceive and destroy all of these people? Wouldn't Natugura watch us with mocking eyes while knowing that even if we brought back the book, we would only find it completely stained? I don't think that this is an issue that we need to fear, Erundil, and just the attacks we have faced from his slaves have shown us that the lost book of Ulohendel has not been corrupted."

A glow of newfound confidence flickered in Erundil's eyes as he listened to Steven. "What you say makes sense, Steven," he responded. "It makes perfect sense actually, and I now see why such a terrible thought can't be possible. But I suppose that why I have been worrying about that is because of the one desire I have held dearly to my heart. It has long been my dream to see the great book of Ulohendel, and I have worried about what has happened to it while it has been kept in bondage under the prison walls of the Dark Lord's fortress. But it is good to be reassured that the enemy has been unable to taint it over these long years and that it remains our valued possession, not his. And now I see that this book of my ancestors will deliver you and all of humanity from impending doom, and foster a great alliance between our people. But promise me, Steven, that once we do get the book, you will show it to me and my people for us to read and meditate on. Just a page of that glorious book will make my life complete."

Steven could see the dignity that covered Erundil's face, yet he sensed that behind his confidence was a deep longing to see peace and hope restored to the world. Even in his lofty stature, Erundil was willing to humble himself so that his and others' wishes would be accomplished at the same time. So after thinking to himself for a while, Steven answered the King of Watendelle in a soft and reassuring tone.

"I promise to allow your people to dwell on the words of your ancestor for as long as you wish," he said. Even as he spoke he could see the relief that came on Erundil's face. "I can only imagine how long your people suffered while wondering when you would bring back your lost book, and I hope to bring you joy once more."

"I am glad to hear your strong support for my people, Steven," said Erundil with a large smile covering his face. "I don't think I have felt as eager for our quest as much as I do now. Just by talking with you, I have been more convinced than ever that we must succeed in our goal."

"Yes, we must succeed," agreed Steven. "And if we continue to diligently believe in our goal, then we will deliver this book from the hands of the enemy."

The two of them then fell silent, as they watched the great waves of the sea and wondered what kind of land lay far beyond it. They knew that Nangorid was in that direction, and they wondered how much different the land would feel from what they had known their entire life. But as they walked along the vast coastline, a wind of peace fell upon them. Steven imagined what a life unbothered by the problems of the outside world would be like in his new home. But he knew that he had work to do ahead of him, and he would only be able to enjoy the fruits of his labor once he completed the destiny that was now not far from him.

His thoughts quickly vanished away as his attention was brought to the volviers who were calling his and Erundil's names. Turning to Erundil, the two of them made their way in the direction of the volviers, where all the rest of the people were gathered together by the coast. Once they came back, Mataput gazed at them with a peculiar look on his face.

"Why did you two spend so much time talking separately with each other?" he asked. "Orieant and I called you many times before you finally heard us. Is everything fine?"

"Yes, everything is fine, Mataput," responded Steven. "Erundil and I were just so busy talking and expressing our wishes and concerns with each other, that I guess all other voices other than our own were perceived with our ears. But we had a great chat, and walking down this long sandy coast and seeing the great waves of the sea ahead of us was a beautiful sight to behold. I am glad that my people and I have found a land for us to live in safety, and bringing back this lost book will make our lives perfect."

"That is correct," agreed Erundil. "Your people are blessed to have found a land that you can enjoy and dwell in complete safety, and I know that finding the great book of Ulohendel will only further complete your lives."

The strange look on Mataput's face now disappeared, as a smile of satisfaction could be seen upon him. "These people are indeed blessed," he said. "Which is something I am glad you two have discovered. With this knowledge, the full scope of our quest will be of the utmost significance if we want to preserve the protection that everyone here is enjoying. On that matter, two boats are lying in the distance ahead of us which we will use to travel across the sea before we land in Nangorid. Are we ready to depart from the Earth and allow everything we have learned to be put into practice in our journey?"

A sense of heaviness slumped onto Steven's shoulders, as the thought of leaving the fair land of his new home to enter an evil and troubling new land presented a dark thought in his mind that he was unable to shake off. But as he thought to himself for a while, and as he looked upon the strong and friendly faces of the volviers, gamdars, and smalves, he knew that he would never be alone. So, sighing to himself, he announced his desire to depart from his new home and travel through the land of Nangorid on his and the company's journey.

"I am ready to go," he said, with a deep breath. "The time for our departure is now, and the quicker we can bring deliverance to the peoples of the Earth, the more complete will our joy and fulfillment be."

"So be it then," said Orieant. "With your word, the final decision to embark upon our journey has been made. The nine of us will go on a quest through the land of Nangorid to the black tower of the Dark Lord to bring back the lost book of Ulohendel for the salvation of humanity. We must stick together throughout this journey, as we will encounter trials and setbacks that the enemy will try to use and discourage us. But if we remain true to our mission, then hope will never depart from our hearts. And as for the rest of you, we will leave behind, do not worry. Very soon we will return to you with the great and wise book of the gamdars which will further make your lives and the lives of the people around you free from the fear of corruption. While we are gone, make sure to make the most of your time in this land, for it is your new home, and from this land, a new light will signal hope to all the kingdoms of the Earth."

With Orieant's words, hope was stirred in the hearts of the people, though this didn't make the departure of the company, especially of Steven, less bittersweet. Tears welled up in the eyes of many of the people as Steven came to hug them and say his final goodbyes. Many of the children saluted Steven, wishing him the best on his quest. But the one who took his departure with the greatest sadness was Peter, who worried that this might be the last time he spoke with his newfound friend.

He held tightly onto Steven's arm, refusing to let go of his grasp. "I can't leave you, Steven," he said. "What if something bad happens to you? How will I be able to help you in that case?"

"Do not worry, Peter," responded Steven, with a smile on his face. "All will be fine. With Mataput and Orieant, along with these gamdars and smalves with me, whatever danger I may face will be faced by all of us. We will return to you in safety, and erase any fears from your mind."

"How long will you be gone for?" asked Peter, still filled with much worry and questions. "I need to know when I can expect you to return."

"Based on what Mataput explained of our journey in Watendelle, we will likely be gone for two or three months," answered Steven. "But that time will be over before you know it since you will be enjoying the full benefits of this land while we are gone."

Peter's eyes suddenly became enlarged as his eyebrows were raised with shock. "That is way too long!" he exclaimed. "Way longer than I was expecting. I can't dare to think how anxious I will feel in that time while you are away," he then paused, before nodding his head almost in agreement with the thoughts that came to his mind. "I will join you on this journey," he said, garnering the courage. "Where you go, I will go with you. I will support you on this great quest, and be there in every moment to calm my fears."

Boldness covered the young face of Peter, but fear hovered over Steven's face as a vast cloud. "Peter, I don't think you understand how perilous this journey will be," said Steven with a shake of his head. "I am the one who was chosen to go on this quest and to bring salvation to the whole Earth. Joining me would not be fair to anyone, not least yourself, as I worry about how dangerous this adventure would be for you. It will be best for you, Peter, to stay here in safety with the rest of the people."

"But I want to help you," responded Peter, unwilling to surrender his desire. "I know that this journey will be difficult every step of the way, but I am willing to do anything to help all of you. If I were to stay here, I would be so restless that I fear I would swim across the sea in search of you."

A smile came to Steven, as he shook his head in disbelief at how adamant Peter remained. Seeing that he wouldn't be able to discourage the boy, he distanced himself to talk privately with Mataput and Orieant. He expected the volviers to agree with his opinion, but to his surprise, they explained how allowing Peter to go with him could prove to be a decision that would alter both of their lives forever. And so taking their weighty words with seriousness, he finally gave in to Peter's request.

"Fine," he said with a heavy sigh. "You can join us, Peter. But understand that whatever we suffer in this journey, will be something that we all suffer together. We are going to Nangorid, the dark and foul land of Natugura. His slaves will surely be on high alert, so we must too remain on high alert and never forget how perilous this quest will be."

"I understand," responded Peter with confidence. "I hope to ease the burdensome weight of this journey, and give everyone causes to rejoice and celebrate in victory once we bring back this lost book to the deliverance of our people."

Steven couldn't help but laugh out of joy at the bold words which Peter proclaimed. "Well your confidence would certainly be a valuable addition to this company," he said. "And I know that I will need it."

"And so will I," chimed in Mataput. "Because no matter how great Orieant and I may seem to be, without a company like this, we would never succeed on this quest. Peter joining us will instill hope and confidence in all ten of us, and will help us further remain by each other's side, no matter what evil may befall us."

"That is very good," said Erundil. "Let this boy join us on this journey, and bring hope to all of our hearts."

So it was that the company of ten was formed, and they all spoke in accord with each other, agreeing that Peter would join them on the quest. They promised to remain by each other's side at every step of the journey and to encourage anyone who would endure suffering. Worry over what their imminent journey would entail struck their hearts, yet deep down they were filled with sturdy hope that would not fail them. And so after they had agreed with each other, they finally said their last goodbyes to the rest of the people who looked on. Peter joining the company was difficult for many of them to take, yet tears of joy and excitement filled many of their eyes.

"We have come a long way, Mr. Loubre," remarked an old man, as he said his final goodbye to Steven. "From escaping from the wrath of Maguspra, to narrowly escaping from the deception of Moneshob and Londriel, and unfortunately suffering the loss of many lives to the wuzlirs, we have endured many terrible events in this short time. But I know that you and Peter will restore hope to all of us and that with this book that you will retrieve in the land of the Dark Lord, we shall be a light to all the kingdoms of this Earth. And so I will not give in to fear, but I will continue to wait and anticipate the glorious day when you shall return and rule over us in justice and peace."

"I look forward to that day as well," said Steven, placing his hand on the old man's shoulder. "We have come a long way, and I can't wait to return to all of you and restore the hope and joy that we all deserve."

After Steven and Peter had said their final goodbyes to the people, they followed the volviers and the rest of the company as they led them to where the two boats were located. The rest of the people followed them, wishing to wave one last time to them. Once they jumped into one of the boats together, Steven and Peter both noticed two dark gray cloaks and two brown backpacks that were there for them. Shocked looks covered their faces as they wondered how two sets of each of the items had been prepared.

Sensing their great surprise, Orieant spoke to them. "Mataput and I could anticipate that one person among this group of people would join Steven on this quest," he explained. "And so we brought two cloaks and backpacks, being assured that this would happen. Now what you see are the cloaks and backpacks that you will bring on our journey through the land of Nangorid. The cloaks you see are not ordinary, for they are specially crafted gamdarian cloaks, and though they may seem soft they are still strong enough to withstand heavy damage from weapons.

Their dark color is meant to conceal our identities as best as we can. In the backpacks are swords, arrows, and bows if we ever need to do any fighting. It is also filled with a few more cloaks, along with a plentiful supply of food including bread, meat, and vegetables, which should last us for over a month. But I am sure that we will find plenty of more food in Nangorid, for though it is an evil place, it is still a land full of natural resources that the Dark Lord uses to feed and supply his slaves. Last, of all, you each have large bottles of water in your backpacks, which we will be able to fill throughout our journey because of the many rivers and ponds there are in Nangorid. With all of these items, our journey will be well prepared and we shouldn't ever be lacking in anything we need."

Steven and Peter stared in amazement at these items, and putting on their cloaks they sensed that they were both warm and sturdy, almost as armor yet far lighter in their feel. Grabbing their backpacks they were quite surprised by how light they were despite the great supply of food that filled them up. Taking out their weapons, they found them the right size for them to wield and were fascinated by their wonderful craftsmanship.

Seeing that Steven and Peter were pleased by all they saw, Mataput spoke to the crowd of people that surrounded them for one last time. "Our final decision has now been made," he said. "The ten of us will now be departing for our quest, and we promise to come back to you as soon as we can, hopefully as heralds of good news."

"Well, I can't wait for that day to come," remarked a woman with growing excitement and confidence. "But make sure that you safely travel through the land before laying your hands on that great book that will save us. We will be eagerly and patiently waiting for you in this beautiful land we can now call our home."

"I am encouraged to hear your support for us," said Steven. "Now at last I can wish you a final farewell before I return here and share all of my joys with you all."

And so with the people waving one last time and saying their farewells to Steven and Peter who sat in the boats, Mataput, Erundil, and Lelhond made their way onto the same boat with the two of them, while Orieant, Huminli, Glophi, Karandil, and Forandor went onto the other boat. At once, they began paddling down the long and wide sea that lay ahead of them, while Steven and Peter both continued gazing and waving at the people behind them.

The rest of the company paddled each of the two boats and started to flow down the sea slowly but surely. After half an hour or so, they found themselves far away from the coastline, as they began going deep across the sea. The people behind them could faintly be seen in the far distance, still gathered together and waving on as the company departed from them. With one final sight of the people, Steven and Peter waved one last time at them, before finally turning around as they were now ready to embark on their quest.

Steven felt a slight tingling sensation of anxiety for the people he left behind, though he brushed it aside and focused on what lay ahead of him now. Eagerness filled Peter's eyes and an elegance of peace seemed to surround him like a blanket. The two of them joined the company in paddling their boats through the sea, listening silently to the calm sound of flowing water that led them further away from the Earth and closer to Nangorid. Vast clouds covered the gray sky, as the whistles and flapping sounds of seagulls could be heard flying above them. A great expanse of sea and nothing else was all that they could see around them, with even the faint sight of the coast behind them no longer visible to their naked eyes.

A sense of peace fell upon them all, and they wondered if they would ever experience this level of calmness in Nangorid. Matuput's eyes were closed as he paddled through the wide sea, with a wide smile covering his face.

"I hope that this quiet feeling of tranquility will never disappear," remarked Peter. "I do not know what evil may lie in store for us in Nangorid, but all I know is that I'm going to enjoy this moment."

Mataput opened his eyes, with an even broader smile covering his face. "And so you should, Peter," he said. "This is the calm before the storm, though I do not know when the storm will come or in what form it will take. But we should all soak in this moment of peace, and allow our minds to be stilled in complete assurance that our journey will end in victory, no matter what setbacks we may have to endure."

The company took Mataput's words to heart, with many outstretching their arms as the cool flowing wind blew gently through their cloaks. They paddled their boats for several hours, and at times stopped paddling to rest and enjoy the still-flowing tide of water. Huminli and Glophi were the ones mainly doing the talking, sharing fascinating stories of how wonderful their home in the peaceful hill countryside of Laouli was like, and sharing numerous stories of their skill in cooking and farming. The four gamdars too shared a few stories, mainly of the tales of their mighty kings and heroes of old, which filled everyone listening with a sense of awe and wonder.

By now at least three hours had passed since the company had left the coast, but still, no sign of land could be seen anywhere around them. They began growing hungry, and Peter opened up his backpack to grab some bread to eat, but before he could take a bite, Mataput swiftly turned around and stopped him.

"Wait Peter," he said. "I understand that you are hungry, but we want to save as enough food as possible for our journey. Wait until we reach the dry ground to eat your food, that way we will ensure that we have enough food throughout this quest."

Peter sighed in disappointment but closed his backpack. "Are we almost there yet?" he asked, as he slowly started craving just a bite of food. "I'm starving, and all that I've seen over these few hours is nothing but a wide body of water. I hope that we get to Nangorid soon."

"Don't worry, Peter," reassured Mataput. "In just another or two we will be stepping on the land of Nangorid, and we will take a long rest where we will nourish ourselves with the food we have."

Over the next hour, the company continued to paddle its way through the wide sea, with still no sight of land. They began to grow increasingly uneasy, wondering when just a portion of dry land would appear before their eyes. Peter's stomach began grumbling in hunger, and Huminli and Glophi also began mumbling about how starved they felt. Yet, Mataput and Orieant continued ordering them to cease complaining, saying that in just any moment they would notice a prospect of land.

Sure enough, it was in that very moment where in the faint distance ahead of them, the company could see the thin outline of dry land. Immediately, their spirits were lifted, with many of them excited that they would soon be able to leave the boats they sat in for the last few hours. They suddenly began paddling with greater strength and fervor, desperate to make their way to the land as soon as possible. Growing closer, they noticed that the sea began to grow narrower as a long river, and around them were vast rocky sides protecting them as great walls. Their eagerness was now unparalleled, and they were now more determined than ever to begin traveling through the land that was just ahead of them.

But as they continued paddling through the body of water and nearing dry land, their joy was suddenly erased from their minds. For as a clear picture of the land lay before them, their eyes were first drawn to three huge pillars of rock whose foundations were built into the very bottom of the sea. They were carved in the likeness of figures who seemed to almost welcome the company into the land that lay before them, but growing closer to the gray pillars, the company's faces were repulsed by the figures' appearances.

The three gray pillars were colossal, striking fear and wonder in the hearts of the company as they stared at what looked like three stone towers that had been placed in the sea. But overwhelming fear and disgust filled their hearts as they began gazing at the faces of the three figures. Their attention was first brought to the figure in the middle, whose body was shaped like that of a horse, yet was covered in many wings and had three faces in total; that of a wolf, an elderly man, and an eagle. Each of its three faces grinned with crooked teeth, with vicious veins coming down to its neck. There was nothing desirable of the figure, as its many faces were all ugly and loathsome to look upon.

The other two figures on either side of the one in the middle sparked an even greater sense of revulsion in the company. Both of the figures' arms were crossed and their disfigured faces made the company think of them as nothing more than depictions of savage animals. They seemed to stare at the company with red glaring eyes, and large spiky horns grew on each side of their head and the tips of their sharp teeth. They appeared to be strong and muscular figures wearing heavy armor, and the large swords they carried seemed to have been drenched in dark blood. Yet despite the overwhelming sense of terror that lay upon both of the figures, there remained differences between the two.

For the figure to the right had on a large crown covered in spikes, and the large grin on his face gave him almost the appearance of a wolf. The figure to the left, terrifying in his way, still seemed to have been a level lower than the other figure in terms of the power he possessed. The figure with the crown appeared to have been a mighty being containing great authority, whereas the other one only held a sense of renown. But they both struck fear in the hearts of the company, making their stomachs twist with sickness just by glancing at them.

Coming now within a short distance of the pillars, Mataput spoke to the company. "Behold the terrible pillars of the Unorimal," he said while gazing at the massive figures of stone. "These three pillars mark our entrance into the land of Nangorid, as we have now officially passed the land of the Earth.."

Peter gulped as his eyes twitched uncontrollably. "Who…who are those figures?" he asked stammering. "We have finally made it to Nangorid, but these pillars aren't necessarily a warm welcome into this land."

"It is certainly not a warm welcome," said Mataput. "And I know for certain that the Dark Lord never intended for anyone to meet a friendly embrace while their eyes were fixed upon these stone pillars. But the figure whom you see in the middle is a depiction of Natugura himself, and though he is a dark and bodiless spirit, he contains many characteristics that his slaves admire. Each of the three faces you see is meant to represent his fierceness, knowledge, and cunningness, all of which surround his presence with a mighty wind of dread. The figure to his right with the crown depicts his most loyal servant named Raleshob, who was the king of the now deserted city of Tuwanor, and was the most powerful wuzlir to have ever lived. He led the wuzlirian armies during the time of the War of Great Alliances, and his most trusted and mighty soldier named Botalund, the figure to the left, was widely celebrated for being the one who led the charge of stealing the great book of Ulohendel, soon after the end of the great war. Both of these servants of Natugura have not failed in achieving the evil purposes of the Dark Lord, and it is for that reason that he ordered these monuments to be erected in the entrance toward his land."

The company's spirits were troubled as they listened to Mataput, and their bones shook with terror at the sight of the pillars. “So that is what wuzlirs look like,” remarked Erundil, staring at the pillars with a distasteful expression on his face. “The Dark Lord has certainly not failed in breeding such vile creatures to strike fear in the hearts of his enemies. But I know that my people will not back down to any challenge, and no ugly monuments of these beasts will prevent us from achieving our goals.”

“That is right,” agreed Lelhond. “But to think that these ugly creatures used to once be gamdars is completely unimaginable to me. I can now understand why they never show their faces, as I’m sure if their hideous nature were to be revealed in the open, it would disgust their master himself.”

“That is the very reason why their faces are masked,” said Orieant. “It is a tragic tale to recount the downfall of these once beautiful and wise creatures of glory, but I suppose that their fall to corruption should fill us all the more with greater fervor to save the land of men from the ever-expanding shadow of the Dark Lord.”

“I’m already sensing the strong pull that the enemy holds over his slaves,” said Steven, staring at the pillar with fearful and wide eyes. “And I certainly hope that his corruptive power will not spread to my people, resulting in our entire nature becoming depraved.”

“Let us not think of that, Steven,” responded Orieant. “As long as we continue walking on the path set before us, then none of your deepest worries will come to pass. But we must not stray off the course or fall into discouragement. Lift your head and hold on to the promises of hope and deliverance that will come to your people.”

Peter held onto Steven’s hand, trying to reassure him that the long journey ahead of them would end in victory. Steven continued gazing with concern at the pillars, but eventually took Orieant’s words to heart and cast his eyes away from the foul figures.

The company finally passed the pillars of the three figures of Natugura, Raleshob, and Botalund, with none of them daring to look back. For a moment, the dreadful presence that had seemed to cover them as a thick shadow was finally lifted from their shoulders as the feeling of ease that they had once experienced was restored to their hearts. For several more minutes, the sound of paddles brushing against the still waves of the river calmed down their minds. The memory of those hideous and terrifying faces of the wuzlirs was still present in their thoughts, but at the very forefront of their head was silent confidence.

But then suddenly, a sharp spark of tension seemed to have ignited and spread through the air. Out of nowhere, the air grew heavily thick as though a strong presence of wickedness had been exhaled from the Dark Lord's breath. The company's breathing grew heavy, and their hands and feet became numb. For many long minutes, the feeling of torment went on, and they wondered for how long they would experience this terrible enslavement on their journey. Their physical and mental strength was severely weakened, and what filled them with even more worry was the sight of the outskirts of the land of Nangorid.

Peter covered his nose with his hands, trying to save himself from breathing the polluting air. "What is this horrible feeling in the air?" he asked. "It's as though a presence of evil radiates everywhere throughout this defiled land."

"This is yet another tactic of the Dark Lord to discourage those who go against him," responded Mataput. "He pollutes the air of the entrance into his stronghold to make it seem as though they will have to endure this the whole time they journey through his land. But that is not so. Though this terrible spoiling of the air marks our entrance into the land of Nangorid, we will not have to suffer this horrible weight of evil throughout our quest. Once we near the land ahead of us, we will be able to normally breathe in this air once again."

"That is good," said Forandor, speaking as he covered his nose with his cloak. "I would have never been able to have experienced this dreadful feeling the entire time we were here, as I for one am very sensitive to anything foul."

"And so are all of us," said Erundil. "But once we manage to endure this terrible outpouring of evil enclosing the air, the Dark Lord will be forced to think of another tactic to use against us."

So it was that the company continued paddling on through the river, constantly assuring themselves that they would soon no longer have to cover their noses and mouths. They continued to endure the terrible smothering air, and they paddled on with even more desperation to reach the dry ground as soon as possible. Yet Steven remained still, covering his face with his cloak as his entire body began rapidly twitching and shaking. He was gasping for fresh air and felt as though he couldn't overcome the horrible subjection he was facing.

"I don't think I can continue like this," he grimly said, while curled up in a ball. "Maybe it wasn't good for me to come along on this journey, as I can already feel the horrible presence of evil that will surround us. Is it worth our time to suffer in this dreadful place just in the hopes of acquiring something that has been lost for thousands of years? I think it would be wise for us to turn around, or at least let Peter and I go back and stay with the people while the rest of you complete the quest, as you seem to be far stronger than I."

The company couldn't believe what they were hearing from Steven, and the most disappointed of them all was Peter. "Oh no you don't, Steven," he said, crossing his arms and shaking his head toward Steven. "After all the discussions and talks of motivation you have received, are you just going to give up and throw it all away? Yes, there will be perils and dangers we face on this journey, but hope grows the greatest even in those worries. I promised to join you on this great quest, and I refuse to abandon it before we have even started. Imagine the number of upset faces that would meet us if we came back to the people without even starting on our journey. No, Steven, there is no turning back now, we must embark on this quest as it is your destiny to bring deliverance to all the people of the Earth."

Steven could see the glinting light of hope that flashed in Peter's eyes, and just by staring at them, he felt as though a spark of courage had been rejuvenated in his bones. He suddenly stood up straight and dwelled on the boy's words for some time. The rest of the company watched on in amazement, waiting for a response from the man.

"You are right, Peter," he said. "I was dead wrong to have spoken such hasty and hopeless words. I will continue on this journey, to whatever end we may face."

Sighs of relief echoed throughout the two boats, with the company glad to have seen Steven change his mind so quickly. Peter placed his hand on Steven's thigh, with a tender smile coming onto Steven's face. His heart was warmed at the great fearlessness that possessed the boy's heart, and he was glad that he had joined him on the quest. Then as he thought to himself, picturing the defeated words he had spoken, he suddenly laughed aloud as though he was amazed by how delusional he had been. And it was at that very moment that the strong evil force that had taken ahold of the atmosphere vanished away as if it had been repelled by the hope and courage that oozed from the company's hearts. Then all of them laughed aloud too, and for the next half hour, broad smiles covered their once grim and despaired faces. A tingling sensation of joy fell upon them all, and any worrying thoughts that had plagued their minds suddenly disappeared as they focused on the hope and opportunity that awaited them in the land of Nangorid.

At last, they reached dry ground, finding themselves on the border of a wide and spacious area of plains ahead of them. The grass was dry and though its green color was mixed with brown, this was little to their concern. They were glad to have finally landed in Nangorid, just as the sun had begun to sink with the evening fast approaching. A great sense of serenity seemed to lie on the company's shoulders, and they all stood up tall and straight as they stared at the far land ahead of them. They left their boats by the edge of the land, and camping by the edge of the plains they all immediately dug into their backpacks, eating some of the bread, meat, and vegetables that filled them. After satisfying their hunger, they all felt exhausted after spending such a long day paddling through the water. Their arms felt weak and they were all ready to rest.

They all lay side by side on the ground, staring at the stars that illuminated the night sky. "Our journey now begins," said Orieant, while everyone laid down silently on their backs. "We have arrived just on the outskirts of the plains of Meneth Gusgranil, a relatively safe region to begin our quest. We will travel through this land tomorrow and prepare ourselves for the first stage of our journey."

With that, everyone closed their eyes, wondering what highs and lows they would soon encounter in this unfamiliar land. They hoped that they would be able to travel through safe regions like this for many more days, weeks, and even months to come, but they knew that their hopes were asking a bit too much. Still, they slept peacefully that night under the beaming moon and glittering stars and were ready to begin their journey in the heart of the plains ahead of them.

11

The Plains of Death

THE COMPANY AWOKE TO the silent sound of the grass rustling against the gentle breeze of the wind. Their sleep was like any other they had experienced, and they wondered how much they would encounter this feeling of peace in the new and foreign land they found themselves in. No sight or sound of living creatures could be found in the open space of the plains, and the only thing noticeable was the few trees and bushes that were scattered throughout the land.

After eating some of the food in their backpacks for breakfast, they all sat silently with each other under the light of the rising sun. They were surprised by how safe they felt on the land, even as they were out in the open with hardly any space for protection.

"Are we sure that we are in Nangorid?" asked Peter, gazing all around at the wide area of land. "I can hear nothing but the sound of the wind, and this land is very reminiscent of what I would normally see. I don't feel worried in any way, though I know that I won't always be feeling this way throughout our journey."

"I am glad to hear how assured you feel, Peter," remarked Mataput. "But as you said, our current state of affairs won't always be like this throughout our journey. Where we are right now, though it may seem like an area of land that is not vulnerable, we will still have to endure difficult obstacles that will test our strength of mind. And indeed we will encounter numerous troubles that may affect us physically or mentally.

But as long as we focus straight ahead and sit close to each other, we will overcome any obstacles that may come our way."

"Such is the hope that we will continue to hold onto," said Peter. "We will not be afraid of the schemes of the Dark Lord, as we have already passed every test that has come our way thus far. And I don't see why this quest should be any different than that."

"You speak true and bold words, Peter," said Mataput with a wide smile on his face. "I can already see that you will bring encouragement and bravery to this company, which will work wonders for us on this quest. So if we are ready to walk in boldness, let us get going on our long awaited journey through this land by first traveling through the plains of Meneth Gusgranil."

Standing up from where they were all gathered, the company packed their bags and immediately began the first stage of their journey by following Mataput and Orieant as the two of them led them through the flat area of grasslands. The sun shone high above them in the sky, giving the grass almost a golden color, but hidden under many blades of grass were tiny rocks that made walking slightly painful. And even as they traveled through the seemingly safe region they were in, underlying thoughts and fears of what they would face on their quest worried them. Still, they shook these thoughts off and continued marching on, refusing to let this halt the progress that they would soon begin to make on their journey.

They continued walking straight across the flatland region for the next hour, with what seemed to be no end to the area of grasslands. A few trees and bushes popped up here and there as the company was led through the plains, but still, no sight of living creatures other than themselves was seen. So they continued like this for another hour, and by now they began wondering when a change in the land would become observable. But as they continued through the miles of endless plains that lay before them, they could see that the land ahead of them was even less desirable. Hardly any trees or bushes could be seen ahead of them and the grass seemed dead as its color was now wholly brown without even a hint of green.

And just then, the atmosphere around them began to change. The breeze of the wind they had felt earlier in the morning suddenly increased in its intensity, with a bitter chill running through their bones. Many clouds began to fill up the sky, covering the sun as the land began to slowly descend into a dimmed light of gray shadows. A looming sense of gloom and darkness seemed to be surrounding them as their bodies grew tense. Great uncertainty filled their minds and the speed with which they were walking was greatly slowed down because of the strong wind which blew in their direction.

"What is going on?" asked Huminli, trudging along as the vicious wind blew upon his face. He covered part of his face with his cloak to try and warm himself up from the cold breeze. "Everything seems to be getting dark and it's so cold now! How did our condition of ease suddenly turn into misery?"

"I am surprised by this sudden change," confessed Orieant, with him and Mataput slowly leading the company across the wide plains. "But Mataput already told us that we would face difficulties that would test our strength of mind. And so our obstacles now begin in these plains of Meneth Gusgranil, but we can overcome these trials as long as we continue walking straight ahead, no matter how slow we may go."

"How long will we have to endure this cold weather?" asked Steven, as his teeth chattered. "It's not even winter yet, but this horrible wind makes me wonder if we will have to suffer through an early seasonal change."

"There will be many cold days which we will have to face in this land," admitted Orieant. "But if it were not for your cloaks, your bodies wouldn't even have cause to feel any warmth. But as hard as it may be to believe, this cold and spreading darkness isn't the worst thing we will face in these plains. There are many other things that we will have to pass through Meneth Gusgranil, things that may terrify you."

The faces of the company became pale with heavy fear, as they wondered what terrifying things Orieant could be describing. "What is the worst thing we will see here then?" asked Steven, staring at Orieant with wide eyes. But even as his question slipped from his mouth, his mind had been left unprepared for what lay ahead of him.

And as he grew closer to the sight, his sight and senses were instantly blurred and infected as the most horrifying of sights lay in front of him. Lying across the vast plains of dead grass were hundreds if not thousands of dead bodies and skeletons. A grotesque smell ran through the air, as the many bodies on the ground seemed to have been there for many years as they slowly decayed over time. An overwhelming shadow of terror fell upon the company, as they all stopped dead in their tracks, with many of them feeling as though they wanted to puke. Their hearts began to rapidly race, and with their limited sight, they couldn't see an end to the vast array of bodies that covered the blades of grass.

But as their eyesight began to clear and they looked more closely at the dead bodies that were around them, a sharp dagger, as it felt, was stabbed in their hearts. For as they observed the faces and clothing that the figures wore, they recognized that they had all been gamdars, evidently, soldiers who had clashed with wuzlirs on these battle plains. Their bodies and armor were stained with dried blood, and their hair had been torn. Everywhere they turned the company were met with piles of bodies that filled the vast area of plains, and much of the grass had been smeared with blood. For a moment, the company said and did nothing, not moving an inch while their mouths and eyes widened with horror. But as they dwelled on the clear picture that had been laid in the open before them, Erundil and his three sons finally reacted, collapsing to the ground and weeping bitterly over the slain gamdarian bodies that met their eyes. Their hearts were crushed and it felt as though a strong club had struck them and shattered their bones. The rest of the company watched on in grief, full of disbelief at what they were seeing.

"What is this horrible place?" asked Steven, gagging while he closed his eyes and tried not to look at any more dead bodies.

"Why have you brought us to this evil site?" cried Lelhond, turning toward the volviers while his eyes watered with tears. "Why did you not warn us that you would be leading us here in these plains full of our many dead soldiers? And could there not have been another way for you to lead us through this land, far away from these dead and decaying bodies?"

Mataput sighed to himself, casting his eyes to the ground. "If Orieant and I had told you the truth of where we were leading you through, then you would have never agreed to go this way," he said grimly. "And I am afraid that this was the best and safest way for us to go, as going around these plains would not have only added many more weeks onto our journey, but it would have potentially led us in the direction where many of the Dark Lord's spies and servants reside. But I am sorry for not thinking of how deeply you would have been affected by this. Orieant and I should have at least thought this out and at least given you blindfolds. But we failed to ponder this, and for that, I am truly sorry."

Orieant too followed Mataput in offering his apology to the company, mainly to the gamdars, but it did little to ease their pain. Even after the gamdars managed to compose themselves and stand up, their faces were still covered in deep anguish.

"But why are there so many dead bodies filling up these plains?" asked Glophi. "Just a moment ago all we could see was a wide expanse of dry grass, and in an instant, everything turned for the worst. I hope that this is only a terrible dream that we can wake up from."

"You are unfortunately not dreaming," said Mataput, almost in a regretful tone. "These are the plains of Meneth Gusgranil, and it is here where many wars and battles have been over the years between the gamdars and wuzlirs, most notably the War of the Great Revenge where Silindan led the army of gamdarian soldiers to battle. Many wuzlirs were slain on these battlefields as well, though their bodies were collected and buried, while the many dead bodies of the gamdars were never found and instead left to rot on these plains. It is a sorrowful reality that the bodies of so many brave and noble gamdarian soldiers were left in disgrace on these plains, never to be found or properly honored in burial."

"I will never forgive those nasty wuzlirs for the suffering they have caused my people to endure!" remarked Erundil, with hot anger instead of sadness now covering his face. "When will those ugly and nasty pawns of the Dark Lord be punished for the devastation that they have brought upon the world? I cannot wait for the day when they are repaid tenfold for all they have done to us!"

His sons watched on with wide eyes, horrified to see the great wrath that consumed their father's heart. "That day of justice will be brought to our people, father," said Forandor, trying to comfort and calm down his father. "But I fear that we may not see that day come within our lifetime. Though I would greatly desire to see their evil deeds come back on their heads, I would remain satisfied if justice would come after our deaths."

"But why should we not be the ones to punish them for their evil?"

asked Erundil, with his hands clenched up. "Those vile creatures have already done much damage to our people by burning our destroying our homes, burning our cities and forests, and leaving many of the brave bodies of our soldiers and heroes left to be disgraced throughout their land. They have brought fear to the whole world, yet this was never meant to be the case. So why should we not hope and work to destroy them once and for all, not allowing a trace of their memory to be left behind in this world?"

The company listened silently to Erundil, observing how his green face darkened with resentment while his face grew hard. With each dead body he saw it seemed as though its clenched fists became even tighter, and though they wished to calm him down, they feared what his reaction would be like.

But Mataput managed to step closer to the king and placed his hand on his shoulder while he stared into the bleak and cold eyes of Erundil. "I understand your frustration, Erundil," he said. "It is completely right for you to be angry when it comes to the horrible deeds which the wuzlirs have committed throughout the years under the command of Natugura. And I promise you that one day, whether you live to see the day or not, the servants of the Dark Lord will be repaid in full for all of their wicked actions. But, you must understand that the purpose of our quest is not to go to war against the servants of the enemy, nor is it to punish them all at once. Our purpose is to bring back the lost book of Ulohendel and deliver it to the humans of the Earth, and it is in that way that the fall of Natugura will be brought about. And though I do not doubt that war will come in the future to bring about the destruction of all that corrupts, I do not perceive that our specific quest will have anything to do with it. But, I do admit that I cannot see all ends, and perhaps something will come about within this very company that will surprise me."

Erundil's face softened up in response to Mataput, though he remained unwilling to completely let go of his opinion. "I do hope that those wuzlirs get punished sooner rather than later then," he remarked. "And I cannot think of any way that they will be paid back in full other than my people going to war against them, After all, for the past thousands of years war has been the only option we have taken to gain victory over them."

"You are correct in saying that war has been the choice with which your people have turned throughout your long history," agreed Mataput. "But you must know that war was never within the original design of Jangart when he created the world. And although corruption and darkness have come to the world, the ultimate plan to truly gain mastery over evil has been to overcome it with good. But, ever since the War of Great Alliances, war has been the primary tool to bring triumph over the enemy, though it has always remained temporary and not long-lasting. But if you wish to see true and lasting victory over the enemy, then you, Erundil, must be willing to submit to the purpose of this quest. This company can change the trajectory of where this world heads to, and through this quest, we can bring light even to the darkest of places."

"I like what you say, but I would be lying to you if I did not confess that one of my strongest desires is to see all evil eradicated from this world immediately," responded Erundil. "But I am willing to submit to the purpose of our quest, though I wonder whether or not it will prevent the Dark Lord from retaliating against us ever again."

"As I said, I cannot see all ends, Erundil," said Mataput. "But what I do know is that the Dark Lord, even in his vast and cunning knowledge will not expect us to ever do what we are doing right now. If he ever discovers this company and the purpose of our quest, this will surely catch him off guard and make him react in an untimely and rushed fashion. So why should we not hope and believe that what we are doing now will spell the end of the influence of the Dark Lord over this world?"

Erundil thought to himself for a while, before he gave in to Mataput. "I concede to you, Mataput," he said with a sigh. "Perhaps your way and reasoning are the wisest out of anyone within this company. I guess we shall see what the fruit of our labor becomes then."

A faint smile of satisfaction and relief came on Mataput's face, though he did not say anything in return to Erundil. By now Erundil's frustration had completely cooled down, and as the company continued their journey through the piles of bodies that filled the plains, a new perspective filled his mind.

For the next mile or so, the company trudged its way through the sea of dead bodies that still surrounded them in every step they took. They walked along with bowed heads, with no one feeling in the mood to speak with each other. But as they continued their long walk through the plains while desperately hoping that this miserable day would be erased from their minds, they began noticing the sweet sound of humming that came from behind them. As they all turned around, they observed that Forandor had fallen far back behind the group, and he seemed to be mumbling the words of a song to himself. He was walking in circles with his head bowed to the ground.

The company immediately turned around with concern for the gamdar. "Is everything alright, Forandor?" asked Orieant. Forandor remained silent, as though he was lost in thought and the world around him had grown silent. Growing concern covered Orieant's face. "Will you not answer us, Forandor? And what are you humming about?"

Eventually, Forandor lifted his head, and the company could see tears welling up in his eyes. A deep sadness could be seen covering his face, though, behind all of this, the company sensed that an underlying storeroom of beauty lay in his heart. He sighed to himself, as though a deep and troubling memory came to his mind.

"I am fine," he said in a soft voice. "I am just remembering a song that has deeply been ingrained in my mind throughout my life. As I was gazing at these many dead bodies, my memory was brought to the many brave heroes of my people's histories whose slain bodies were never recovered. Yet despite all of this, their memory has not failed to escape our minds, and so I will continue to remember and honor all of their brave pursuits which impacted our world for the better."

A light of nobility and honor suddenly shone on the gamdar's face, and as he continued humming to himself, his lips began to break off into the words of a long-remembered song. A beautiful and yet sorrowful song it was, and his soothing voice, touched the company's hearts as they gazed in wonder at Forandor:

From the mountains and forests of our heroic soldiers,
To the palaces and tombs of the glorious kings,
What news can you illuminate on us with your torches?
Share with us the joy that Silindan the Swift's body brings.

Lend to us the king's broken sword and shield of great weight,
And bring us tidings of where Belehorn the Bold's body has gone.
His face was brave and his stature was great,
And his memory shines on us like the light of dawn.

Tell us where the birds have taken Valfindil the Valiant's body,
And bring us his weapons and clothes drenched with blood.
For the arrival of his body has been tardy,
And we fear that he has been carried away in a flood.

But share with us the hope of Semoril the Strong's presence,
For the mighty soldier of old was dauntless in strength.
All of our soldiers honor him in reverence,
And the children dream of having a portion of his strength.

Recall to us the deeds which Damaril the Dashing has done,
And tell us if we can draw his body from the sea.
For his delightful face was brightened by the sun,
And he deserves to rest as free.

What tidings do you bring of our many victors?
Must we say share with them a final farewell?
We will continue to celebrate our honored brothers,
But must we wait to gather them until the last days of Watendelle?

Take us back to the ancient days of our immortality,
So that our glorious dead are not swept by the wind.
But even now their bodies rot on the battlefield for eternity,
With the bodies of kings and soldiers treated as a lesser kind.

He fell silent and sighed, with the company silently gazing at him having been enthralled by his beautiful voice. After some time he spoke again, explaining the significance of all he had sung about.

"What I just sang is a song that brings depressing yet important remembrance of the many heroes of my people, all of whose lives ended miserably," he said in a soft and sorrowful tone. "It is a long tale sung in my native Tuntish tongue, but I sang it in the common tongue so that you could all understand. It tells of many of my people's ancient kings and mighty soldiers whose dead bodies were never found and properly buried, and the tale is normally sung with stringed instruments and delightful melodies playing in the background. It first tells of Silindan, the bravest and most renowned of all of the soldiers in our history who led the army of our soldiers farther into the land of Nangorid after King Kolcratil died during the War of the Great Revenge around 600 years ago. For all this time Silindan's body was never discovered, although Dulanmidir's revelation of him still being alive and dwelling somewhere in this land as a lonely fugitive having been corrupted in some way is certainly grievous and shocking news that we have recently learned.

"But regardless, after Silindan the song shifts to the dealings of King Belehorn, who was not only the tallest gamdar to ever live standing at nearly eight and a half feet tall but was also one of our boldest kings to ever sit upon the great throne in the house of Yarwindil. It was he who led our army to the land of Grandul, the land where the giants reside during the War of the Hunriland nearly 1,500 years ago. After the home of the giants had been savagely by a coalition of goblins and hzarves, the giants had stood alone for some time as they tried to fight back and defend their homeland. Even the dwarfs, the giants' closest allies had never come to their aid as they had dire matters of their own to deal with. And so seeing how the giants had been left to suffer on their own, King Belehorn led a force numbering at least 50,000 soldiers to help defend the giants in their time of need. Thus, the sight of our army helped turned the tide of the war, bringing such great encouragement to the giants that as they gazed at the glory, might, and authority that reflected from our bodies as magnificent lights, they at first mistook the king as a god and his soldiers as angels who had descended upon their land to help deliver them from the presence of evil. We had long been forgotten among the giants as the last time we had fought with them had been during the days of the first war, events that had happened so long ago that the legends of my people's deeds had been erased from their minds. Yet, fighting alongside us renewed an outpouring of fire that rushed through the giants' veins, which helped drive back the goblins and hzarves from where they had come from, thus establishing peace for some time. But unfortunately, the body of King Belehorn had been ambushed and slain because his armor-bearer had lost sight of him, and to this day his body has never been found.

"The song then celebrates the great exploits of Valfindil, the valiant soldier who lived 3,000 years ago. He is celebrated for his bravery in bringing back the qazirans, the precious jewels belonging to our line of kings that had long been kept safe in a storehouse near the border of our kingdom, which the wuzlirs took advantage of by breaking into the building and stealing the precious items. He was the one who volunteered to go to Nangorid and rescue the stolen jewels, while the king at the time, Falfrindil, along with our army created a diversion for the courageous gamdar about to perform a mighty deed that has long been etched into our memory. And because King Falfrindil longed to see the light and beauty that covered the qazirans, he too joined Valfindil in searching for the jewels, while allowing the captain of his army to lead his forces in battle. Unfortunately, the quest went awry with even the king eventually losing all hope in finding the jewels. Yet, Valfindil still held on to hope and continued searching for the jewels, before he single-handedly discovered them and lent them to the king. But just as he found the jewels and gave them to King Falfrindil, he was discovered and interrogated by dozens of wuzlirs. He revealed nothing to them, and so they killed him, while the king ran off with the jewels and brought them back to Watendelle in safety. But every gamdars knows that none of that would have been possible without the brave feats of Valfindil, whose body was likely left to be disgraced by the slaves of the Dark Lord. And for that very reason, the rest of King Falfrindil's life was haunted by his failure to even attempt to rescue the young and daring gamdar who had restored hope and light to his kingdom.

"And now the song recounts the tale of the strongest gamdar to have ever lived, the mighty Semoril. Many stories and legends have been told of this impenetrable soldier who lived around 4,500 years ago during the days of the War of Great Alliances. It is said that with the strength of his bare hands alone he killed thirty wuzlirs at one time, and even Raleshob, who is known as the most powerful wuzlir to have ever lived, feared Semoril for a time just by witnessing his vast physical power. Wherever Semoril went into battle, the forces of the Dark Lord would know fear, and because of the deadly combination of his strength and the leadership of the great Ulohendel, our army would always win battle after battle during the great war. However, Semoril's weakness was his pride, and when he began taunting the armies of the Dark Lord by exhibiting his great might and calling them fragile, he was ambushed by a group of wuzlirs when he least expected it and was brutally killed. His words came back on his head, as the wuzlirs gouged out his eyes, cut off his ears, and left his body to be humiliated out in the open as they let it rot until all that was left was his bones decomposing in the grass. It was a terrible fate for such a strong and mighty soldier who had given the armies of the free creatures of the world much hope and victory whenever he fought in battle.

"And lastly, the song tells of King Damaril, the most beautiful gamdar to have ever lived who was renowned both for his handsome appearance and for the purity of his heart. In the days when he lived nearly 900 years ago, his long flowing golden hair and golden eyes along with his sparkling smile that glimmered majestically under the sun, struck great admiration in the hearts of those who beheld him. From the head of his fair and noble face to the bottom of his feet, not a fault could be seen in his appearance, and even as he grew advanced in years not a single wrinkle could yet be seen on his body. Yet even with his impressive beauty, he remained the most humble and kind gamdar of his time. And though he was the King of Watendelle, a figure who held great authority and influence within his kingdom, he secretly despised having such great power, and if it were not for the loyalty and respect he held for his ancestors and the customs of his people, he would have renounced his right to the throne and instead lived as any ordinary gamdar. Still, he remained king yet even with his position he brought many changes to the traditions of the kingship by allowing anyone throughout the kingdom, even those without noble lineages to come to the great palace of the king and even dine with the king and his advisors if they so wished. Such a change had never been seen in the kingdom of Watendelle, and everyone who lived under his rule wished his reign would go on forever. Unfortunately, his life would be cut short when deciding to go on a scouting mission to Nangorid to ensure that the enemy wouldn't pose a threat to Watendelle for the years and decades to come, he was discovered by a group of wuzlirs who chained him up and after brutally humiliating him because of their jealousy of his delightful appearance, beheaded him and left his body hidden under their dark chambers. When the news was brought to our people of his death, they were left so devasted that 40 days of mourning were issued throughout the kingdom, with such a length of mourning having never been seen since the death of Ulohendel.

"Out of all the figures of my people's long history, I find myself relating to King Damaril the most not because of my appearance, but because of his pure heart and kindly nature. Since my days as a youth, I have looked up to him for inspiration, especially as an example to remain humble in everything I do. But with all things considered, these tales of the many great heroes of old of my people, reflect the noble lives they lived but also the sad fates that came with them to their deaths. So many of our kings and soldiers of renown have had their lives cut short while they were in the prime of their lives either performing mighty deeds or touching the hearts of my people. Their bodies were either left as a disgrace or left hidden in Nangorid, but regardless, the many beautiful and glorious tombs and graves that would be built as an honorary remembrance for their service would never be completed. Still, we have never forgotten all they have done for the success of my people, as their memories still live on to this day. And as long as the kingdom of Watendelle stands, their names and many deeds of renown will continue to be celebrated in our songs and tales forever and ever."

With that, Forandor bowed his head to the ground, before falling on his knees and closing his eyes. The company who had been closely listening to all he had said, reflected deeply on the many heroic figures of Watendelle. Erundil, Lelhond, and Karandil were all filled with pride just by hearing a recounting of the many mighty figures of old who had helped strengthen the foundation of their kingdom's greatness. But as Forandor slowly opened his eyes, tears could be seen welling in his eyes as he imagined the many thousands of families who had fallen into grief and despair upon hearing the news that their sons had been killed while serving in battle. His attention was then shifted to his father and brothers, and he wondered what would happen if he lost even just one of them in battle. Would he too fall into despair, or would he be able to muster the strength to continue his purpose in life? As he thought to himself of the many rich glories that filled the history of his people, he also pictured how many of those glories had been blemished because of the terrible deeds of the Dark Lord and his servants. Thinking of the horrible things his people had endured and lost through their long history, Forandor began to bitterly weep as his face was covered in his hands.

The company didn't move an inch, as they allowed Forandor to have his time of grief. His father and brothers' faces were covered in heavy sorrow, while the rest of the company had their heads bowed to the ground. Eventually, after the long silence that had hovered over the vast expanse of land covered by a sea of dead bodies, Forandor managed to regain his composure, slowly rising to his feet as his eyes were fixed on the volviers.

"Forgive me for halting our journey, I was just unable to carry on without expressing my emotions," he said, with a look of great coldness filling his sad eyes. "I do feel much better now, though my mind is still clouded with many questions and concerns. For one, I have long wondered why it is that so many of our courageous heroes of beauty and pride, and the ones most often being the purest in heart always seem to be the ones taken away from my people in the prime of their lives. Why is it that when my people think of the glory of Watendelle, we have to always look back into the past, remembering things that once were and have since passed away? Our great halls and vast gardens are filled with the statues of our soldiers, kings, wise ones, pure ones, helpful ones, and even ordinary ones. Yet even though we remember them in our poems, songs, and tales, they all lie asleep in their tombs never to rise again, no matter how much we may hope that their spirits could still dwell among us. For we who are living are the ones who are fast approaching our deep sleep, a fate so mysteriously beautiful yet tragic as I imagine how it is something we must all await. And even now as I think of the shadow of death, I wonder why that must still be our fate. And not only that but why do so many of our young ones have to perish in battle and leave our old and wise ones alone to grieve in pain? Will we ever return to our days of immortality, in those days when it seemed as though Ulohendel would be our high king forever? The more I read and sing of the great tales of my people's history, the more I hope and pray that we are saved from this most terrible fate that will infect us all at some point in our lives."

All was silent for some time, with the company staring at the volviers, even though those two didn't know how to respond to Forandor. But after a deep sigh, Orieant stepped closer to Forandor, tenderly touching his arm as he looked directly at the gamdar in the eyes. "Forandor, the questions you ask are ones that I am sure we all desperately wish to know," he responded in a soft voice. "But I am afraid that the greater our questions are, the less likely it is that even the wisest will be able to figure them out in full. And I confess that I cannot see all ends to what you are asking, but what I do know from the divine revelation of Jangart is that there is a reason for everything. But although I wish I could confidently proclaim on the mountaintop that that reason is for the day when all of the perished bodies of your people are resurrected to live in immortality with those alive, I know that it is both unwise and at the worst misleading to promise you something that I do not understand wholly. But what I have seen, is that though death may seem to be a painful and troubling reality, there still resides a light of beauty hidden underneath its shadows. The sense of remembrance of that which once was and desperately trying to restore it is only possible because of the reality that we will not all reside in this world forever. For if it was not for this great passing shadow that falls on the creatures of this world, there would be no need for your people to write poems, tales, and songs in remembrance of the glorious kings, brave soldiers, wise elders, and many other heroes who built the very foundation of your people's history. Yet remembering them in this way seems to be the only appropriate way for us to conduct ourselves during the limited amount of time that has been offered to us."

For a moment, Forandor looked deeply into Orieant's eyes. Then as if being dazed by his profound words of wisdom, the slightest crack of a smile suddenly appeared on his face. A wind of peace as it felt breezed around the gamdar and a refilling of joy was restored to his body.

"I must confess that your words, Orieant, though bittersweet, are more sweet than they are bitter I suppose," he said. "What you have said is true, and it brings me great joy to know that the glory of my people which has been reflected in beautifully adorned halls, paintings, statues, monuments, and great palaces and buildings is all because of our desire to hold that which used to be in close memory within our hearts. I only wonder how other creatures such as the humans or smalves respond to the reality of death."

"Well, I certainly can say that we smalves are not as impressive as your people are, Forandor," suddenly remarked Huminli. "My people's history is not as rich or glorious as your people's is, nor have we endured many things that have either brought us significant pain or joy. But, we still have many things to celebrate in our simple lives, and when death comes to many of our close friends or inspirational figures, we accept that their time had come and we do our best to hold them in our memories. Yet, we hardly ever weep over their passing, nor do we record the memory of their lives in poems, books, or songs. Though we do bury them in tombs, our monuments are not as beautifully decorated and adorned as your people's are, and we usually only mourn for them for a few days at most. We grieve when we need to, and once we are finished, we return to our lives with broad smiles on our faces."

"It seems to me that you smalves live a satisfactory life," said Forandor, with a wider smile now covering his face. "I know that my people could implement a thing or two from the way your people enjoy your time in this world in such a free and joyful way."

"But the same could be said about my people when it comes to learning from your people, Forandor," remarked Steven. "We humans are similar when it comes to the smalves in mourning over long periods in remembrance of our dead, though our tombs and monuments are far less glorious and decorative as yours. Our beauty cannot compare to yours, nor is our writing and singing even worth comparing to the profound majesty found within your people's work. Nonetheless, we do our best to remember and honor our dead, though at times I wonder if we pay more respect to those who have passed away than the poor and suffering living among us. For so long my people in the kingdom of Fozturia have been forced to pay our respects to the kings who have ruled over us, most of whom have reigned with injustice and terror. In this way, I suppose death can be looked at as a terrible fate that can further divide rather than unite my people."

Forandor remained silent, pondering Steven's words. But as everyone else also closely considered Steven's words, a glimmer of pride could be seen shining in Erundil's eyes. "I suppose that my people are blessed to not deal with the issues of your people," he said with a wide grin. "Though we honor those who have passed on, especially the kings and heroes who have enriched our kingdom, we also pay even more attention to those living among us and we make sure that we respect them as well. But at least your people can be grateful that you even at least significant time honoring your dead, as it appears that such a thing is too noble for the smalves to appreciate. Death is indeed a terrible yet beautiful reality, and my people have made sure that we hold onto the beauty of the subject by magnificently honoring our dead, as can be seen with our kings by their beautiful adorned tombs and their weapons which lie on the ground by the great golden tree of Palororen. And I could spend hours describing the many tales and stories of our renowned figures all of whom are recorded in our books, poems, and songs. The more I think of it, the more I realize that many of the creatures of this world could learn a thing or two from my people, not least of whom are the smalves."

"Each creature of this world has the right to honor their deceased in the way they choose to, Erundil," responded Mataput amidst the company's speechlessness, with a sense of soft firmness coming forth from his voice. "Who are you to tell the smalves and humans how they must remember those who have passed on? Do they not have the right to decide how they want to process the deaths of their loved ones and the many heroes of their people? Erundil, you must understand that each creature of this world was uniquely created by Jangart, and you do not have the authority to change that."

Erundil fell silent, with the sense of pride in his eyes beginning to vanish as Mataput's echoing words had the effect of humbling him. He turned toward his sons, wishing that they would agree with him. Yet, as he stared deeply at them, he could see how emboldened they felt to stand up for the smalves because of what Mataput had said.

"Mataput is right," remarked Lelhond. "Each creature has the right to decide how they wish to remember their dead, and if we wouldn't want the smalves or humans commanding us to honor our heroes in a certain way, what makes us feel as though we can do the same to them?"

Once again, the company pondered these words, with many of them shaking their heads in agreement. Erundil, meanwhile, stared off into the distance, saying nothing without the slightest hint of movement. All remained silent before Mataput and Orieant once again led the way through the plains urging the company to continue going on in their journey.

Ready to shake off the heavy feeling that consumed their hearts, the company followed the volviers, with endless bodies still covering the blades of grass in the land of death. The stench of darkness seemed to go on forever through the vast plains, as the gray clouds of the dull sky provided a sense of gloom that radiated deeply within the company's hearts. A chilly gust of wind flew through the air, and the sound of flies and ants swarming the numerous dead bodies greatly annoyed the company. With heads bowed low, they endured the long and treacherous journey through the ghastly plains of death.

The company continued their journey through Meneth Gusgranil suffering what felt like many days of horror, though only just over an hour had passed. Endless rows of dead bodies still surrounded them, and doubt began to creep within their hearts whether part of the endless numbers of dead gamdarian bodies had to do with the evil machinations of the Dark Lord. Nonetheless, they brushed these thoughts aside, and with heavy sighs continued going on.

At last, the company found an area with a few bushes and trees where there weren't any dead bodies in sight, and they decided to stop there and rest for a while. Gathering some sticks and wood they started a fire to warm themselves in the cold land, as they all huddled close together. No one spoke a word to each other as their hearts remained heavy from all they had experienced, though they stared at one another with wide suffering eyes. They ate their food and drank their water in silence, hoping that as they continued their journey they wouldn't have to see another dead body. But they refused to share their concerns as all remained quiet in that land for nearly half an hour. Yet eventually, unable to remain silent forever, Glophi suddenly directed a question toward Forandor.

"Do you have any more songs or poems that you would like to share with us, Forandor?" he asked, with a light of eager expectation in his eyes. He waited awhile for a response from Forandor but was instead met by the cold eyes of the gamdar.

"Allow Forandor to have some time to think for himself," firmly said Mataput, though a slight smile could be seen on the corner of his mouth. "Now is not the appropriate time to bother the gamdars, Glophi, as they have suffered enough by all the terrible things their eyes have had to endure today."

Glophi slumped back in disappointment, but at that very moment, Karandil suddenly stood up with a broad smile covering his face. "Don't hold back the smalf from his desire, Mataput!" he suddenly said, with a vigor of energy reflecting from his face. "I understand why my brother wants to remain silent, but I know many songs and poems of my people which I wish to share with everyone, though I am no musician in any way."

"Go ahead then, Karandil!" said Mataput, laughing as he saw the yearning curiosity that came back on Glophi's face. "Share or sing with us whatever has been stored in your heart."

Looking at everyone and waiting for them to bring his attention to them, Karandil then explained what he wished to share with them. "What I will be sharing with you is a poem that recounts the majesty and glory that has been reflected in our kings, soldiers, and heroes of old," he explained. "It was written by the great chief musician, Zendileroh, nearly 2,500 years ago during the reign of King Pamail, and it is held in such great honor by my people that it is remembered as one of the greatest poems of our history, only behind the wise revelations of Ulohendel himself. It is stored in the Great Hall of Poems, where many of our kings and advisors have read and recited from it to receive knowledge and hope. I have always wanted to share this with the other creatures of this world as I believe it reflects the glory of my people. And though I will not be doing justice to it since Forandor has a much more pleasant voice than me, I hope that you learn something about my people just by the few verses I will be sharing with you."

Then pausing for a brief moment, Karandil broke off into a soft chant as he began reciting some of the verses of the poem of Zendileroh:

Hail the kings, the ones full of splendor from the ancient forests.
A light shines upon the summit where the lofty mountain exists,
The high peak of the Gered Mentuath,
Where our mighty ones come forth from the caves beneath.

Let the mighty ones of renown come forth,
And make an opening for the Himdaras and Landils residing in the north.
Remember the wisdom of the Fuendils and the beauty that the Amilos bring,
And let us honor the Xinlars that come from the forests of the king.

Decorate the tombs of the mighty ones of old,
Lest we forget their memories like the passing cold.
Adorn their gardens with splendid flowers,
And we shall not fail to remember their great powers.

Karandil ceased his chanting, with the company silently staring at him with wonder filling their eyes. Most glad over what they heard were his father and two brothers, and a smile could now be seen covering Forandor's face.

"Ah yes, the great poem of Zendileroh," remarked Erundil gazing at his son with great pride on his face. "Is it not remarkable how after all these long years of our people's history, the line of the Xinlarian kings has never faltered? Even since the very earliest days of our kingdom's history which goes back to the time of Ulohendel's reign, not one sign has appeared that our line will ever cease from existence."

Lelhond gazed at his father, and confidence seemed to surround him as a vast shield. "I cannot see how the line of our kings will ever be broken," he said with great boldness. "Just as you have always told us, as long as Watendelle still stands and succeeds with great glory and prosperity, we will never fail to have a king sit upon the throne. But even if the impossible were to happen and the line of the Xinlars were to perish, I am sure that the Fuendils and Amilos would still have a mighty figure among them to reign as king of Watendelle if they were ever called upon to do so."

"But I suppose that is why you have called it the impossible," replied Erundil. "I have never even worried about such a terrible thing happening to our people, and I don't see why it would ever happen anytime soon, as I have three strong and healthy sons. Even after my time to depart comes, which I hope will come a long time from now, I will still have no cause to be troubled in my long rest as I know that our kingdom will continue to endure. And though I do not mean to be presumptuous, I fail to see why our line will not go on forever, unless Jangart himself has other ideas of what he wishes to see in our people."

The two of them continued talking about the hope they had in their people because of the rich history of their kingdom, leaving the rest of the company staring at them in wonder. They were especially surprised to learn that there were different kinds of gamdars each unique to their kindreds.

"I may be misunderstanding you two, but are you saying that your people are divided up into different kindreds?" asked Peter, filled with curiosity. "I thought that the gamdars were all the same, but now that I am hearing such exotic names coming from both of your mouths, I would love for you to explain these things to me."

At once, Erundil and Lelhond stopped talking, looking on at Peter for a moment before Erundil responded to the boy. "I am glad to see how curious you are of my people, Peter," he said. "You have rightly observed that there are many kindreds of my people that dwell in the land of Watendelle, and you have heard the names of some of them spoken in the poem which my son chanted, though not all of our kindreds were recorded in that poem. But just so your curiosity may be satisfied, I will tell you the names of the kindreds that you heard of in the poem. My family extending back to the line of my family's ancestors is of the Xinlar kind, with all of our kings being of that kind. Our kind has dwelled for thousands of years in the ancient forests of Watendelle, with our main place of dwelling being the Palororen Forest. We are the most mighty and vigorous of all the kindreds of our people, as all of our kings have been of the same kin, along with many of our greatest soldiers. Our blood has been mingled before with other kindreds in the past, though we have remained pure Xinlar.

"Other kindreds of my people include the Fuendils and Amilos who also dwell in forests, though ones that are separate from us Xinlars. The Fuendils are known to be the wisest kindred of my people, as that is the kind where the line of our chiefest advisors have descended from, and the Amilos are widely regarded to be the most beautiful in the appearance of my people. The final two kindreds which were spoken of in Zendileroh's poem are the Himdaras and Landils. The Himdaras dwell in the mountains and are the most hardy of my people which is reflected in their rough faces and dark skin, while the Landils are the most gentle in mood, preferring to dwell by the shores of roaring seas or by the banks of swift rivers, with their love for swimming in the water making their skin the lightest of my people. These are the five main kindreds of my people that you may know about, though as I said before there are many other kindreds of my people that dwell in Watendelle, each unique in their way."

Peter shook his head in amazed fascination. "And all this time I thought that your people were alike," he remarked with a broad smile. "This is so incredible to learn of the many unique kindreds of your people that exist. And now I wonder whether this is the same case for the smalves."

"It is the same with us, Peter," immediately replied Glophi. "We smalves are no different than the gamdars when it comes to many kindreds existing within our people, though ours may not be as appealing for you to hear. But just so you know, my brother and I are Hanofines, the bravest and strongest of our people. Other kindreds include the Mafonds, who are the slimmest and kindest of our people, as well as the Rarions who are the largest ones in size, known for their keen appetite and love for exploring things found in seas, lakes, and rivers. There are a few more kindreds of my people that exist, though I must confess that they are very simple in all they do and say."

Peter listened on in great fascination by all that had been revealed to him of the smalves and gamdars. A broad smile covered Steven's face whose mind was equally as imaginative as Peter's. But just then as he pondered these things within his heart, a startling question about the gamdars arose within Peter's mind, which he directed toward everyone in the company.

"Now that I have learned of the many kindreds that exist within the gamdars, how is it that despite their many differences they are still united under one king?" he asked. "Wouldn't it be logical for each kindred to have their king based on their kind? I ask this only because we humans have many kings in different kingdoms that each reflect their group of people."

A long and deep silence ensued, with everyone, especially the gamdars pondering Peter's question for a moment, with Erundil and his sons being unsure themselves why this was the case regarding their people. But even as they thought of possible answers for Peter, Mataput stepped in to share his insight with not only the young boy but with everyone who would listen to what he had to say.

"You have asked a fair question, Peter," he said, looking keenly at the boy's eyes. "But to simply answer you, you must understand that the whole of humanity has experienced a great sundering ever since the day they fell into partial corruption. Your people are divided for this reason and because war and evil are realities within the Earth, there is no choice for your people but to form different kingdoms each united under their kings. But that is not the case either with the free creatures of the world or those who have fallen into complete darkness. The rest of those dwelling in their lands within this world have either pledged their allegiance to the Almighty Jangart or the Dark Lord Natugura. And because of this, the whole of their people are under the authority of one leader or king, who has either chosen to lead his people into the light or the darkness. Yet this is not the case for humans, as they neither serve Jangart nor Natugura, which leaves them left to themselves to choose how they wish to govern their groups of people."

"And this is the very reason why this quest must succeed in bringing back the lost book of Ulohendel to the Earth," added Orieant. "For the supernatural power of that book will turn the hearts of all humanity back to Jangart, and only then will there only need to be one king to shepherd the whole Earth. War and fighting within your many kingdoms will fade forever, and hope and love will be renewed not within the might of your armory or the sharpness of your weapons, but rather in the restoration of the endless peace and joy that once used to be yours to enjoy."

"A glorious day that will be," remarked Erundil, gazing into the distance with shining eyes as though he beheld a clear vision from afar off. "The whole of humanity will be saved from impending doom, and their strength and wisdom will be united with my people for both of our kinds to celebrate with no end in sight. I just hope that we are the ones to bring the fulfillment of Jangart's will into being."

"All of our hope lies within this quest," said Orieant. "And not least of which resides within the strength of Steven and Peter, who have remained steadfast in their goal thus far. Many more perils will await us, but I can see a glorious end in sight, no matter how blurry it may seem to be at times."

The company stared in amazement at Orieant, heeding his prophetic words and treasuring them closely within their hearts. After spending some time in their thoughts, thinking of all that had been discussed, the company then talked among each other, sharing the many hopes and fears they felt of the great journey that lay ahead of them. Then lightening the mood, they shifted the subject and spoke of the many towns and cities and other fascinating stories of their peoples and lands. Most fascinating to all of them were the many places that filled the land of Watendelle with great beauty, which filled Steven with the greatest sense of wonder, as he began picturing all that he could've seen in Watendelle if he had stayed there longer.

"Why have I never seen these many spectacular cities and places in Watendelle?" he asked, directing his question to Erundil. "My eyes were amazed by the many structures, buildings, places, gardens, and forests I saw, but if I'm not mistaken, we were only able to stay in one city."

"You are correct, Steven," responded Erundil. "All that your eyes saw were gathered in the chief city of Watendelle, and I am afraid that your stay was cut short while we spoke with Dulanmidir, which meant that we didn't have enough time for you to see the many other cities of my realm. But don't worry, sometime after this journey ends and we can breathe in peace without any signs of worry, I will make sure to lead you again through my kingdom and show you the many great cities, towns, and structures of my people's land."

"I cannot wait for this quest to end then," said Steven with growing excitement. "Your people and land have not failed to continually amaze me, and I am certain that if I were to see just a fraction of your spectacular land, I would pass out in overwhelming awe."

Erundil laughed and shared many more stories with Steven of the glorious things he could have seen if he had spent more time in Watendelle, which only filled Steven with even more regret for what he missed out on. But he was glad that his ears could enjoy the many tales he listened to, and he was especially fond of what Forandor had to say regarding the many famous poets and musicians who helped fill Watendelle with an aroma of bliss. Peter too was very fond of all he heard, and just sitting in the presence of the gamdars as he listened to all the rich things they had to say, evoked a sense of high respect that he generated toward them. He was most interested in Erundil's stories of the many grand places and strong cities that reflected all that Watendelle stood for. And after Erundil had finished sharing all that was on his mind, Peter asked him a question that had been lurking on his mind for some time.

"Excuse me for asking, but I was wondering what the chief city of your land is, Mr. Erundil," he said, gazing at Erundil with curious eyes. "Where I used to live in Fozturia, the chief city of that kingdom is Centero which is located by the palace of the king which sits atop the Golden Mountains. But now that I have a new home, I still don't know what my new chief city will be, or how long it will take to build a town or city for that matter."

Erundil turned toward Peter, looking intently at him for a moment as though he were examining. Then, Peter noticed a cold look that came to his eyes, and at length, the gamdar sighed to himself before responding to the boy.

"The chief city of Watendelle is Kulendar," he answered, before pausing as though he was remembering some terrible distant memory of the past. "But long ago that was not so. For though Kulendar is the city where the house of Yarwindil is located, many years ago the chief city of my people was the port city of Aglonil. Aglonil was once a glorious place that was valuable not only for being the primary location of our navy, but also for being a center of learning and unimaginable beauty, as its bustling streets, buildings, statues, libraries, and gardens would place anyone into an enchanted dream. It was a place of music, wisdom, and joy unended, and as the years passed our craftsmen continued to build the city into an impenetrable location.

"But in the height of its glory, there came an unexpected attack from a force of wuzlirs, who traveling through strong ships passed the vast sea before coming out of their fleets and scattering across the land. They carried torches and strange weapons with them, and though we courageously defended the city and were able to preserve many of our most important works and objects, the forces of the enemy managed to burn down the city, destroying buildings, homes, and statues. They defiled our gardens and sites of nature, transforming all of that land by the coast into a bleak and deserted wasteland. Yet my people have long held onto the memory of that once beautiful city, and now and again we travel there to sit and ponder what the former days of its glory were like."

A look of sorrow now covered his face with his lifeless eyes causing the company's hearts to be filled with pity. "I am sorry to hear this," said Peter, staring toward the ground. "Your people have such a rich history of courageous figures and glorious times, though it seems that you have also had to endure many difficult times."

"We have," remarked Lelhond, with all attention now cast onto him. "The splendor of our history whose foundation was built upon the awe-inspiring works of our ancestors can still be seen shining brightly today as the sun in its full strength during the noontide. Yet despite this, much of our former glory has been marred by the efforts of the Dark Lord and his slaves, who have not failed in bringing grief to our land by destroying many of our sacred places. So many wars have been fought upon in the land of Watendelle, and each time a battle takes place a portion of our kingdom's grandeur is taken away from us, leaving us left to honor a shadow of that which once existed, as distant wanderers looking up to the heavens for the twinkling of stars that once reflected the sun in its glory. Yet, as my people have always done, we have never failed to forget the praiseworthy acts of our ancient heroes, and we record our stories in writings, music, and art. And no matter how much those vile servants of the enemy might try to burn Watendelle to the very ground in a heap of ashes, we have continued to thrive in the present while holding onto our glorious past. And though they may succeed in burning parts of our mighty kingdom, they will be unable to erase the memory of our tales, songs, and books, things that we have long held dear to our hearts. Unless they have the power to rip open our hearts, they will utterly fail to ever defeat us."

Lelhond ceased speaking, and for a time the company stared in wonder and astonishment not only at the heartfelt words he had spoken but also in a change of his appearance which appeared before their eyes. For at that very moment, whether a vision appeared before their eyes or not, they pictured Lelhond before them as a great king of renown; tall and noble and unyielding in both the words he spoke and the great deeds he performed. And as Mataput and Orieant stared at him, broad smiles covered their faces for they saw a great crown covering even his hooded head, and they knew that great exploits awaited him, feats that they felt deep within their hearts he would succeed in every possible way. The darkness of the enemy would have no power over him, and he would restore hope in places that were once deemed to be lost.

But just then the vision faded, and all attention was brought back to Erundil, who gazed on at his son with great pride and gladness of heart. "Your words are more than true, my son," he said with a large smile. "They have not failed to gladden my heart and give me peace of mind, knowing that no matter what may come we will always have something to hold onto. Indeed I can already see you as a mighty King of Watendelle, who shall ever remind our people of the necessity of never allowing the Dark Lord and his minions to steal our joy. Though they may outnumber us, they will never be able to outperform us in acts of boldness."

"Yea, and though we may be surrounded as though by vast clouds of pitch blackness, still we will ever fight on and pierce the darkness with our light," added Forandor, with a fresh filling of life rejuvenating his body. "The fires and waters the enemy throws against us will not demolish us, though it may harm us for a time being. In the end, we will be the ones standing in victory with no plans of evil able to calm us down."

Steven and the rest of the company could only shake their heads in admiration of the sudden change that had come over the gamdars. "I wish that I had such great courage as you four," he said, referencing Erundil and his sons. "I always try to look on the bright side of things, though I always seem to be easily susceptible to falling into fear or failing in the presence of adversity. I dream of the day when I can say that I will remain standing with boldness no matter how many enemies may surround me."

"And that is why we are here with you, Steven," said Erundil, speaking in a soft voice. "You would be nowhere without every member of this company, not least of whom are Mataput and Orieant. But we are here to support you and strengthen you not only in preparation for the difficult times we will face but also in overcoming those challenges and having enough energy to endure even more hardships in the future. And though I cannot promise you that your mindset will be completely changed by my own words, I can assure you that we will provide you with a new perspective on things that you will hold dear for all of your life. Thus, the old saying of Ulohendel is true indeed when he wrote in his great golden book of wisdom, '*Wise counsel and company, heals the mind and strengthens the heart.*'"

"That is indeed a wise and true saying," remarked Huminli, filled with great fascination at the many conversations he was listening to. "But let none of you forget about the boldness of the smalves, as my people have a great history of many brave warriors even though many of you are unaware of this. We do not possess an army that is large or organized enough to compete with that of the gamdars but dare I say that individually we are just as strong and fearless as any gamdar. And because of that, I can boldly proclaim, long live the smalves!"

"Long live the smalves indeed!" remarked Mataput as he laughed. "The smalves certainly deserve to be celebrated for all the great things they have done and brought to this world. But someone who I would like to bring to our attention, is the young boy, Peter, sitting among us. It is because of his encouragement so far that Steven has found the motivation to begin this quest. And though he is only 16 years of age, Orieant and I have not even found many grown people with such boldness and wisdom."

"Sixteen! This boy is sixteen?" exclaimed Erundil, with an amazed expression on his face. "I would have assumed that this boy was in his thirties, but how can he be so young of age? I can barely even remember the first sixteen years of my life, as I was just a little gamdar at the time."

A confused look covered Peter's face as he listened to Erundil. "Why do you think that I'm older than sixteen?" he asked. "Does not my height, my young face and everything about me show that I'm young? After all, if I was in my thirties, I would probably be growing a beard by now. But I see that you think it's odd that I'm not older than you believe I am. So if you don't mind me asking, how old are you, Mr. Erundil?"

Erundil stared at Peter for a brief moment, in amazement at all he was saying. "Well, I find it odd myself that you claim to be younger than I would have imagined you to be," he said. "I cannot lie when I say that you humans are remarkable, yet strange creatures as well. Now to answer your question, Peter, I am one hundred and twelve years old. And if you wish to know about the rest of my family, Lelhond is my eldest son at sixty-two years old, Karandil is fifty-eight, Forandor is fifty-two, my daughter Glowren is forty-six, and my wife Aradulin is one hundred and four years old."

Peter gasped in shock upon hearing this, along with Steven who had a shocked expression on his face. Yet, to both of their amazement, everyone else listened to Erundil with straight faces, unfazed by all they heard.

"But how can this be?" exclaimed Peter, filled with a rush of amazement, wonder, and confusion. "In my opinion, you look around fifty years old, yet you happen to be well over one hundred years old. Very rarely do we humans live past ninety years, yet here you are thriving at one hundred and twelve! How can these things be?"

"I do not know why you find these things strange, Peter," said Erundil, with a bewildered expression covering his face. "And I am even more amazed that you think I am fifty years of age as if that were true my sons would still be babies. I am hoping that you can explain to me how you are supposedly only sixteen years old."

"Well I would first like to learn how you are one hundred and twelve years old," responded Peter. "These things that I am learning about your people are both wonderful yet strange."

The two of them continued going back and forth, refusing to let go of their desire to know more about each other's people. Eventually, Orieant intervened to answer both of their confusion. "I can see that both of you have a misunderstanding of the nature of the creatures of this world," he said, glancing at each of them with a smile on his face. "The reason why your ages are so vastly different is that the gamdars, as well as the smalves age twice as long as humans. All of the free and corrupted creatures of this world age at the same rate, and it is only humans who have the least amount of time to spend their lives. This is because each of the creatures of this world was rewarded either by Jangart or Natugura, depending on whom they serve. Yet because the humans serve neither of them, their lives are significantly shorter than everyone else's."

Peter laughed in amazement at what he heard. "So that means that Huminli and Glophi must be much older than I imagined them to be," he remarked. "I would have guessed them to be somewhere between seventeen and twenty years old, yet after learning this, I am likely very wrong."

"You are very wrong indeed, Peter," responded Huminli. "For I am thirty-nine years old and Glophi is thirty-five years old."

Peter sat stunned, staring at Huminli and Glophi with wide and curious eyes. "This day has been full of many strange things that I have learned for the first time," he said. "And now that I know how old many of you are, I can't help but wonder if my people will ever live as long as the other creatures of this world."

"That may so happen, Peter," remarked Orieant. "That is only if this company succeeds in the quest of bringing back the lost book of Ulohendel. For at the very moment when the entire human race becomes non-corrupted creatures, Jangart will look on them with favor and certainly reward them with long life, twice the span of that which you currently possess. Yet even if the land of men falls to the shadow of Natugura, the Dark Lord would make you his slaves and also reward you with long life, as he too has the power to distribute that gift. But let me not speak or hope for such evil things to occur, as that day of brooding darkness should not be the fate of your people. We must now focus on this great and perilous journey that we have just now undertaken, and we must make the most of every moment, making sure that we carefully take one step at a time before we begin worrying or imagining things that lie in the future."

"Your words of wise counsel are more than true, Orieant," said Erundil, nodding his head in agreement with the volvier. "Though I have many hopes and dreams of how our world would be much better without the threat of the Dark Lord, I concede in saying that I must first follow your advice and focus on the present, which is continuing this quest and completing the goal that has been set ahead of us."

"I too must do the same," added Steven. "Before I begin imagining the great things that I may bring to my people in our new homes, I must first focus on finishing this task. Yet I know that this task is anything but simple, though your wise words do ease my worry, Orieant."

"I am glad it does, Steven," replied Orieant. "All we can do is focus our attention and energy on that which we see, for it has been appointed to us in this very age and time to bring encouragement and light wherever we go."

The company agreed with Orieant and decided that they would focus on that which was given to them at the present, rather than imagining what the future would hold. They all sat together for some more time, huddled together as they shared all that was on their hearts and minds. They didn't fail in confessing their worrying thoughts, but amid all of this, they remained firm in standing boldly in their quest. Among those who spoke the most, were Mataput and Orieant, who spoke of how they had longed for the day when the humans of the Earth would be saved from the fear of falling into complete darkness. The company intently listened to them as they shared how Steven and Peter were sparks of hope to all that would behold them, and that the two humans were mighty instruments that would bring hope which hadn't been seen in the world for a long time.

"Steven and Peter have the power to reshape the world of men," they both said. "With their efforts, the Earth will forever be transformed." Along with this, they shared many more hope-filled words that had been laid on their hearts, with Steven and Peter gladly smiling at all they heard.

Meanwhile, the gamdars shared numerous stories of the lore of their people, with the rest of the company listening in wonder as they were taught many more tales of rich legends, individuals, and histories that were all reflected in the many kings, soldiers, heroes, writers, and musicians who helped shape the kingdom of Watendelle. Their eyes shone in keen amazement as mainly Erundil and Lelhond spoke of the many cities, towns, structures, buildings, forests, gardens, and mountains whose glittering splendor and firmness together made up the foundation of the rich land of the gamdars. Peter was left open-mouthed by everything that came out of the mouths of the gamdars, filled with awe as he desperately wished that he would one day be able to look upon the land of Watendelle.

The smalves too spoke of the lore of their people, telling stories of the most famous figures in their history, as well as sharing tales of their rich countryside, towns, farms, and of their people's gift in cooking. They couldn't stop talking about their food, which they claimed no creature, even those who were corrupted would ever reject having. They shared the many delicious recipes of their soups, breads, cakes, and other meals that they would have throughout the day, with the most special meal of theirs being a unique soup that they had packed with them in their backpacks, which they claimed could heal anyone of wounds or injuries. Yet though they managed to pack this one meal with them, they expressed their dissatisfaction about how they hadn't been able to pack their many other delightful delicacies that they wouldn't be able to enjoy eating or sharing with the company throughout their journey through Nangorid. Despite this, they continued to express their gratitude toward Mataput and Orieant for how they had welcomed them to take part in the quest, knowing that their efforts would forever change the way their people were looked at.

Steven and Peter didn't have much to say about their people, though they briefly mentioned their own lives and the hometowns where they grew up in the kingdom of Fozturia. Steven recalled the memory of his once peaceful life as a shepherd in the village of Frosh, while Peter talked about the fresh memories of his life in the village of Gahuyo, getting emotional as he spoke about how wonderful his parents were. Talking about their present condition, the two of them shared their fears about the King of Fozturia, Maguspra, who had brought much suffering and injustice to Fozturia. They also expressed their worries about the Eletans, the men of the East coming from the strongest kingdom of men, who seemed as though they couldn't be stopped in their goals of total domination over the Earth. They feared for the people they left back at their new homes if the Eletans ever managed to advance into Fozturia. But despite all their worries, the volviers continued to assure them that their purpose was to focus on their quest and trust that everything else would remain in safe hands.

Getting their worries and fears out of the way, the company then shifted to talking about more lighthearted matters, with the smalves being the ones full of the most jokes. The atmosphere changed and the company was filled with so much peace that all memory of the misery of the day vanished away. They forgot about the piles of dead bodies that had surrounded them in the open plains, and they savored the good time that they were enjoying in each other's presence.

But suddenly, amid their talking and joking around a violent rumble of thunder pierced the dark sky. Immediately they all looked up to the sky, staring at the gray clouds which covered the sun, which to their surprise refused to yield even the slightest drop of rain. Meanwhile, the music of rumbling continued to rock and vibrate throughout the air, which filled the company with confusion as to what was going on. Then as the thunder continued to growl, in the far distance could be heard the sound of rushing wings, as though a great company of birds would soon swoop past them faster than the wind. Yet to their amazement, no sight of living creatures could be seen, though the sound of flapping wings and vibrating thunder continued to sound an alarm around them.

The company fell silent, staring at each other with puzzled faces, as they all sat paralyzed with fear and confusion. Many questions ran through their minds, yet they found themselves unable to open their mouths, as though their only choice was to remain still and capture the moment. Nonetheless, great worry consumed their hearts and they feared that something terrible would soon happen.

Then to the company's alarm, the volviers suddenly sprang to their feet, as though a spark of lightning had struck their bodies. The two of them immediately began shouting, with widened eyes consumed with such a great fear that the company hadn't seen in them before.

"Quick! Put out the fire and hide in these bushes and trees!" they cried. The company jumped to their feet in response, putting out the fire and rushing to the nearby bushes and trees to hide behind them.

They waited silently for a couple more minutes, not daring to move or make a sound while Mataput and Orieant stared at each one of them. The sound of thunder began to cease, but the noise of flapping wings grew louder as they all anticipated some flock of loving creatures to soon fly past them. Many of them began to panic and while covering their ears they felt like crying out in horror. Yet, the volviers continued to shush them and ordered them to remain silent, saying that the living creatures would soon come and pass them by. And then as they continued to remain silent, the distant shape of figures could be seen coming toward them, and very soon the company's eyes could see the flying creatures passing on ahead of them.

There before their eyes were massively giant winged creatures appearing to be at least forty feet in length. They came flying across the sky as terrifying black gusts of winds, striking great terror and wonder in the hearts of the company. There were only five of the creatures, yet the hideous screeching noises they made and the terrible vibration of their massively flapping wings made it seem as though they covered the entire sky as the ground shook by their mere presence alone. Their bodies were drenched in the stain of black scales and though their faces had the appearance of birds, their sharp fangs and popping eyes made it seem as though they had come out of the pits of the earth rather than the heavenly skies. The company found themselves unable to escape gazing at the frightening creatures, though they were filled with overwhelming fear. The creatures glided across the sky at lightning speed, before vanishing from the company's sight as they traveled with such a terrible force that it seemed as though for a moment that flames of fire were chasing them from behind.

Once the coast was clear, the company breathed sighs of relief as Mataput and Orieant told them to come out of the trees and bushes they were hiding in. Once they all came to their feet, they all froze and stared at each other while shaking with terror.

"What in the world just happened?" asked Peter, managing to speak amidst the rushing emotions that raced through his mind. "What were those winged creatures that we just saw flying through the sky? Could they be dragons? And do they breathe fire as well? I hope that we won't have to see them ever again!"

"Calm down, Peter," said Mataput, placing his hand on the boy's tense shoulder. "Those creatures that you saw are not dragons neither can they breathe fire. They are the matis, the great winged spies of the Dark Lord who roam throughout the land of Nangorid to search the land and grab anyone or anything they deem to be strange and bring them to the Black Tower of Wuzinch Torgol, the abode of the Dark Lord. I must admit that I am shocked to see them here roaming the plains of Meneth Gusgranil, as Orieant and I understand that they usually roam toward the west of Nangorid and not the east. Perhaps the Dark Lord can smell something going odd in his land, and he is sending his servants just to make sure that what he senses isn't anything he needs to worry about. For this very reason, I don't think that it's safe for us to remain here in this open land. Come, let us continue going on in our journey by making our way to the mountains of Lehu Shalank where there should be many caves for us to remain safe."

The company pondered Mataput's words for a moment, while still shaking with great fright. Many thoughts raced through their mind, and they wondered whether or not the Dark Lord now knew that they were in his land. Yet, they kept all of this to themselves and remained silent.

Eventually, Huminli garnered the strength to speak his mind and expressed his worries and doubts to the volviers. "Do we have to leave already though?" he asked with disappointment. "I enjoyed spending time here huddled together by the warm fire while telling stories and tales of our people. But now it seems as though that everywhere we go, we will now encounter numerous dangers, while the servants of the enemy roam across this land. I fear that they may eventually discover us and all of the good times that we have enjoyed together in this short amount of time will end in vain. I don't even know whether or not we will experience these good times again anytime soon, but I sure hope we will get to."

"I am sure that we will have many more good times to enjoy together,

Huminli," responded Mataput. "But at the moment, your lives are the most precious thing that matters. How will we ever be able to enjoy spending time together in laughter and sharing stories if we first don't protect ourselves from any potential dangers, whether they are big or small? I never imagined that we would be laughing and having a good time while here on these plains of death, but all of that was taken away from us in an instant, as the reality of where we were and the challenge of our quest was made plain to us once again. But I am confident that we will have many more close moments to spend together, and our next time to experience that may very well be within the caves of the mountains of Lehu Shalank, though the bitterly cold weather and falling snow won't be anything to celebrate. Nonetheless, who am I to say that I know what the future holds, Huminli? Let us not speculate about that now, as we still have many more days and weeks and maybe even long months to journey through this land. But come, let us quickly make our way out of these plains, as I sense that it would be best for us to move on now."

With that, Huminli along with the rest of the company laid aside their opinions, and followed the advice of Mataput, allowing the volviers to lead them through the plains and to their next destination. They hurriedly trekked their way across the plains, which though were still scattered with many dead bodies, didn't seem to bother the company anymore. All that time that they marched on, not one single of them looked back, with all of them instead fixing their eyes on what was in front of them. Just under an hour soon passed, though the volviers seemed to have no plans of stopping any time soon, though the sun began to slowly sink beneath the gray sky.

But then suddenly, feeling worn out with weariness, Glophi came to a sharp halt, breathing heavily while leaning over and placing his hands on his knees. He stood still for some time, staring upward at the sky as though he expected more spies of the enemy to discover him and the company journeying their way across the land. The company continued going forward, unaware that Glophi had stopped walking. But turning around, Erundil saw him and quickly rushed back toward the smalf.

"What are you doing?" he exclaimed. "Are you here trying to allow the enemy to find and trap us? Come on, we don't have any time to waste!"

Picking up the smalf, he carried him and ran forward to the rest of the company. To his surprise, the smalf was quite heavy, and once the two of them caught up with the rest of the company, Erundil put him down to his feet, while closely watching to ensure that he wouldn't fall back behind again.

The company continued going on for another half-hour, refusing to take a rest as they desperately wished to escape the plains as soon as they could. They wondered how much longer they would have to continue like this, but as soon as they began thinking of this, the volviers suddenly came to a halt. They stopped and now realized that they weren't even in the area of plains anymore, but rather in a hilly region. The sky darkened as the evening approached, and a vicious wind strongly blew from behind them.

As they all gazed around at where they were, small flakes of snow abruptly dropped from the gray clouds, coming down softly though the company knew that plenty more flakes were coming. More clouds began to gather in the evening sky, and as they drew their attention westward, they were suddenly aware that great mountains covered in snow lay there. In that distance there seemed to be plenty more snow that came crashing down the sky and onto the snow-capped mountains, and they all stared in wonder at the sight, imagining how difficult it would be for them to tread those snowy paths. Then as they imagined all of these things, Orieant spoke to them, while he too stared in the direction of the mountains.

"There lie the great and terrible mountains of Lehu Shalank," he said. "We will rest here for the night, and begin our passage through the mountains in the morning." And with that, he and Mataput led the company deep into the hilly region that lay northward. Their eyes, however, remained fixed westward on Lehu Shalank.

12

Unbreakable Bonds

THE COMPANY FOLLOWED THE volviers into the hilly region, with a chilly breeze blowing through the dark sky as small drops of snow continued falling. Coming to a place surrounded by many trees and bushes, they gathered some sticks and rocks and made a fire to warm themselves. Digging through their backpacks they chugged down their bottles of water and ate some of their food. But even as they silently ate, their attention was fixed almost entirely on the massive mountains of snow that lay just west of them.

Steven looked on hesitantly at the mountains of Lehu Shalank. "Are you sure that it's a good idea that we travel through those mountains?" he asked, staring at the site with wide eyes. "It seems as though that far greater amounts of snow are being poured atop the mountains, and even now these small flakes falling from the sky aren't entirely pleasant. Just look at all of that snow! Can any of you see it?"

"Yes, I see it, Steven," responded Mataput. "But we must go through that way as this is the next stage of our journey that we must complete. None of us ever said that this quest would be easy, and this next challenge of ours journeying through the mountains of Lehu Shalank will certainly not be a quick breeze for us. The mountains will be a very difficult passage to go through, as there will be great piles of snow on the paths we go through, with some of the snow maybe even reaching our knees. Endless amounts of unrelenting snow come down at great force, and there has never been a day where Lehu Shalank hasn't had a drop of snow fall from the sky. It is a remarkable thing to imagine, and no matter how much I wished that the snow would halt for just a brief moment, I don't suppose that it will change any time soon."

Steven along with the rest of the company stared at Mataput with shocked faces and fearful eyes. They breathed heavily just by looking at the tremendous amount of snow that piled upon the mountains in the far distance, with frightened thoughts racing through their minds. They found themselves unable to utter a word and they wondered why they would have to continue their journey through that way. Yet looking upon the bold faces of Mataput and Orieant, they gazed in astonishment at how calm the volviers seemed and they desperately wished that they would experience such ease themselves.

Perceiving the overwhelming anxiety that consumed the company, Orieant turned toward them to offer words of encouragement. "None of you has to fear for the next challenge coming toward us through the mountain pass of Lehu Shalank," he said. "You can rest assured knowing that Mataput and I would never lead you through a path in which no hope resided. Though the cold weather and unrelenting snow may be a struggle both physically and mentally for you all, I am confident that we can manage and overcome the bitterness of Lehu Shalank."

The company took heart to Orieant's words though it lasted only for a brief moment, as their attention was brought back yet again to those high and terrible snow-filled mountains. "But why must we go through there?" asked Steven. "I understand there will be challenges awaiting us on this journey, but is there, not another way we can travel through? The plains of dead bodies that we just went through were difficult to endure, both those mountains will be a far more demanding task for us to manage."

"I understand your concern, Steven," replied Orieant. "But it is for your safety that we are leading you through those mountains, as it will be nearly impossible for any spy of the Dark Lord to find us there. Almost no creature dwelling in the land of Nangorid can call Lehu Shalank their home, as its terrible weather conditions make it almost unbearable for any of Natugura's spies or wuzlirs to remain there for an extended period. To avoid being caught by the enemy, we must be willing to take these bold risks knowing that someday they will eventually pay off."

Steven sighed to himself. "So be it then," he conceded. "Maybe those mountains will end up not being half as bad as I deem them to be. Regardless, I trust in you to lead us to safety as you have already demonstrated your ability to successfully do."

The rest of the company ceased thinking of the worrying thoughts that roamed through their minds, with many of them deciding that it was in their best interests to trust in the words of the volviers. As they stared at the night sky they could see the faint twinkling of stars, as though its light was a reminder for them to continue to allow even the dimmest gleams of hope to reside deeply within their hearts. Many of their eyes began to slowly close, with many more starting to yawn as the night now lay upon them.

"It is a good time for us to get some rest now," remarked Orieant. We will talk more about our journey in the morning, but for now, let's get some good sleep and wake up fresh for our travels through Lehu Shalank."

With that, the company all lay down on the hilly grass, hiding amid the trees and bushes and wrapping tightly themselves in their cloaks to stay warm. All was silent in the land as the company fell asleep peacefully that night, as though for just a brief time they forgot about all the perils and fears of their journey.

They woke up the next morning to the rising light of the sun, which pierced the gray sky with its awesome brightness. No clouds could be seen in the sky, and the chilly wind that had flowed the previous day seemed to have died down.

Peter awoke from his sleep, standing on his feet with an amazed expression on his face. "Now take a look at that view of the sun!" he excitedly remarked, while gazing up at the sky. "It's already a bright day, unlike the dark and gloomy day we had to endure just yesterday. I am amazed by this sudden change of our surroundings!"

Mataput smiled at Peter as he brought himself to his feet. "I am glad to see you are in a much better mood," he said. "And I can see from the bright faces of all of you that you feel much more relaxed and confident than you did the previous day. But I will warn you, that the weather atop those mountains will not be anything remotely akin to this, so you all better enjoy this weather before we make our way to those mountains.

But I agree that it is a nice day thus far, with the sun shining brightly in the cloudless sky, which is a sight I wouldn't have expected to see on the morning of the 8th day of November. Yet even despite this, looking on ahead I can see that the snow is pouring down and the wind whistling past and all around Lehu Shalank."

The company hesitantly looked westward toward the mountains, and they could see how endless piles of snow were being stacked upon each other. But turning now to each other, they enjoyed the rest of the relaxed morning by eating breakfast, and returning to telling stories amongst themselves. Huminli and Glophi were particularly in good spirits, creating lots of laughter and happiness among the company, by telling jokes and sharing the last bits of the soups they had brought on the journey.

"Wow this soup is incredible!" remarked Steven, after trying some of the soup for himself. "Why can't we humans ever grow such tasty vegetables and mix them so well in soups like these?"

"I'm sure your people could make great soups as well," responded Huminli. "As I've seen for myself when I came to the Earth, you humans seem to have many hilly countries where you can grow a variety of plants and vegetables. But I will be the first to say that the finest soups in the world can only be found in the land of Laouli!"

"And I can see why you say that, Huminli," said Lelhond, smiling in amazement at how delicious the soup was. "You should try some of this soup, father because it tastes very good and seems to strengthen the bones."

Erundil could only smile at his son but refused to have any association with the smalves' food. "No, no, my son," he said, with the smile on his face now turning to a smirk as he stared at the soup with a distasteful gleam in his eyes. "I am fine, and I don't feel like trying any of this soup of the smalves."

Lelhond shook his head but continued to eat more of the soup for himself, and once he and his brothers had taken each of their last spoonfuls, Peter joined in to taste some of the soup for himself.

"Now I see why you two won't ever stop talking about your delicious soups," he remarked with a broad smile toward Huminli and Glophi. "This is indeed the finest and most tasty soup I've ever had."

Even the volviers joined in the action, slurping a couple of spoonfuls of soup given to them from the smalves But after spending another half hour of eating and having fun, Mataput and Orieant bade them get ready for their journey.

"I hate to cut the fun time we are having," said Orieant. "But we can't delay any more time, as before we know it, the afternoon and evening will come and pass while we spend this time joking around. We must not forget about our goal in journeying through the mountains of Lehu Shalank, and so we should be on our way now."

The company sighed in disappointment but understood that they had to complete the purpose of their journey. "You are right in what you say, Orieant," remarked Steven. "We should be on our way now, after all, we didn't come all this way to this land just to laugh and joke around. There is a reason why you and Mataput have not ceased in warning us of all the perilous steps ahead of us on this quest."

"That is right," agreed Erundil. "All of this joking around and eating this food of the smalves will only distract us from our true purpose of coming to this land. Those mountains do look terrible and perilous, but no one said our journey would be a quick success, certainly not the volviers."

And so with that, the company packed everything in their bags and following the volviers began heading towards the direction of the snowy mountains. The sun remained shining brightly high up in the sky as they left the hilly region from behind, though a pack of clouds slowly started to form. Peter and Steven were directly behind the volviers, and beyond them came the gamdars and smalves. They journeyed through many hills and areas of flat grasslands, with rocks and thorns scattered throughout the ground. Many winding paths there were which they tread upon, all of which led them steeply and narrowly down as they slowly approached their destination.

As time passed more clouds began to swarm in the sky, with the sun still shining through them. The company could feel small drops of snow beginning to come down, though they didn't pay much attention to this. Yet as the minutes which soon became an hour passed, the intensity of the snow started increasing as they neared the foot of the mountains.

By now their cloaks were covered in flakes of snow and the sound of the wind could be heard growing louder and more intense with each step they took. By now they started feeling a lot more worried, and seeing the mountains of Lehu Shalank now clearly laid in front of them they shook their heads in astonishment at the great amount of snow that came pouring down from the sky. Looking to the ground they were shocked to see how large flakes of snow drenched the green grass, and as they walked on for the next couple of hours, the whole land around them was covered in a sea of snow.

At last, after the few hours that had passed since they departed in the morning, the company arrived at the base of the snow-capped mountains, with all of them looking up and staring in a mixture of awe and alarm at how massive the mountains were. They wondered how they would ever climb up and through the great and lofty mountains, but with no time to think they immediately began following the volviers as they led them up the snow-covered paths. By now tremendously large downpours of snow came crashing down upon them, and each step they took became increasingly difficult. Their shoes were drenched in snow, and with each hesitant and slow step they took, they gazed at the menacing appearance and height of Lehu Shalank. Suddenly, after a few minutes of climbing had passed, they came to a halt only to gaze at how much more distance they would need to cover within the next few days.

Amidst the company's silence, Mataput spoke to them. "So begins our long adventure through the mountains of Lehu Shalank," he said. "As I mentioned before, great amounts of snow come crashing down unto these mountains, and we have witnessed first-hand just how much the weather can change in an instant."

Urging the company on, Mataput and Orieant started moving again and led the way through the ground of snow and up the gigantic mountains. They gingerly made their way through the snowy and steep paths that led them up, going as slow as they could manage since they wished not to trip or take a serious fall. But as they watched the volviers ahead of them, it seemed as though the two of them were easily climbing their way through the snowy path, as if they had trekked the mountains multiple times before.

The company gazed at the volviers in amazement, shocked to see the smiles that covered their faces as they effortlessly made their way through the thick snow that covered the ground. While they had to carefully watch their steps to ensure they didn't trip, the volviers easily glided their way through the snow as if the weather was little more than a trivial concern to them. But once the two of them realized that they were way ahead of the rest of the company, they came to a stop and waited for the rest of the company to draw closer to them.

Once the company came close to the volviers, Huminli shook his head in disbelief at how far of a distance the two of them had covered in such a short time. "How are you two so easily able to travel through these piles of snow?" he asked. "It's as if you two are hiding some special material under your feet that makes you glide through the snow so smoothly. Won't you tell us if you are hiding something that we too can use to our advantage?"

Mataput and Orieant could only laugh at Huminli, even as the smalf continued to stare at them with wide and peering eyes. "No, no, Huminli, Orieant, and I are not hiding anything from you all," said Mataput with a broad smile on his face. "You must understand that we have traveled through the land of Nangorid many times before for many other purposes, and at times our fate has led us to these mountains, where we have had to endure this bitter weather for many days and weeks. If we chose to, we could run through these mountains with no problem, but for the sake of this company, we are slowing down our pace so that we remain together in all of the perils we face on this journey."

"That's good and all, but I'm afraid that you two may have to slow your pace even more," replied Huminli. "If you two had continued going at the rate you were, I wouldn't have been surprised if we would have eventually lost sight of you. Maybe it would be a good idea if you gave us a long head start so that way you two van travel at the lightning-quick pace you are used to through these snowy paths."

"Very well them, I hear you, Huminli," responded Mataput. "Orieant and I will travel slower for the sake of this company, that way we don't lose track of each other in these terrible weather conditions."

At this the company breathed sighs of relief, and as the volviers led the way they all continued making their way up the snowy paths of the great mountains. They all walked in close packs just behind one another, as they especially didn't want to be separated as heavy downpours of snow continued falling on them. The sun still shone proudly in the sky, but a windy mist blew in the company's direction.

As they journeyed on, the company could faintly notice small rocks beginning to appear on the snow-covered paths they walked on. With each step they took, the ground grew rockier, though the mounds of snow they stepped on provided a cushion for their feet. But the number of rocks continued increasing and they seemed to grow larger as the company made their way up the mountains. And as they continued, they noticed that large stones, almost as hard pillars stood on either side of them, though great piles of snow stacked upon them.

After a half hour had passed, the weather began to grow almost unbearable, as the wind quickly started growing in its intensity. Even as the snow continued crashing down on them, the company had gotten somewhat used to it, despite how uncomfortable it made them feel. But the increase in the wind's force provided a new challenge for them, making them feel cold and miserable under the terrible weather conditions. The freezing breeze nearly knocked them off their feet, and they now had to watch their steps even more carefully as any fall to the ground could potentially send them tumbling back, or even worse, make them collapse over the mountainside. And so as they desperately fought off the vicious breeze that blew in their faces, thoughts of what uncertain thing could happen to them slowly crept into their minds.

But even as their mind wandered, they were brought back to the reality of their current condition, which was reinforced by the misery they felt from the weather. By now the snow and wind had joined together, and were both screaming in the company's faces, causing them to cower down as they walked along. They started worrying what would happen if they tumbled over, and even began preparing themselves mentally for the worst event. Yet as they looked upon the way that Mataput and Orieant walked uprightly, a small measure of assurance, ever so small, was restored to the hearts of the company that if anything bad happened, the volviers would be able to save them.

But then suddenly, even as they began imagining the many different scenarios that could befall them, they were immediately called to action.

For as if the mighty force of the wind had taken a brutal toll on him, Steven was sent tumbling back over the snow-filled path at great speed. The company instantly turned around in shock and wondered how they could help him, but answering their question, Peter rushed down to come to his friend's aid. Now that the wind was blowing behind him, he moved with great speed down the snowy path, yet even as he went the company tried to get ahold of him so that he too wouldn't fall over. But he refused to take heed to their warnings, instead rushing down the sloping rocky path covered in snow as his one purpose in mind was to save Steven at all costs. At that moment, all memory of the miserable weather he had to endure vanished from his mind, and as he came rushing down to save his friend, it seemed to all who watched on that the boy was running on level ground. On he ran, with the mighty force of the wind propelling him forward as a mighty sprinter of old who remembered that he had wings on his back. His eyes widened with terrible fear, though he pushed on with bravery, as the company now began shouting and encouraging him on in desperate hope that he could save Steven.

At last, he came to Steven and grabbing ahold of his shirt, he lifted the man up from the ground. An overwhelming feeling of joy and relief filled the boy's heart, and being exhausted from running, he collapsed unto the soft bed of the heaps of snow.

He turned to Steven, laughing wildly as he couldn't believe what he had just done. "Are you all right, Steven?" he asked, with a relieved smile covering his face.

For a moment, Steven gazed at the boy in wonder at what he had just done. "Yes, Peter, I am just fine," he said, with a warmth of gratitude filling his heart. "I seemed to be in a dream while I was tumbling, and yet out of nowhere you appeared, and at that instant, I knew that I was indeed awake and was being saved by you."

Peter continued laughing. "Ah, I can hardly believe what I've done, Steven!" he said. "I feared for you when I saw you tumbling backward since it seemed as though you wouldn't ever come to a stop at the rate you were falling over. The wind was blowing with terrible momentum just behind you, but I'm glad that I was brave enough to come running after you before anything worse happened."

"I am glad as well, Peter," replied Steven with a smile of relief.

"Where would I possibly be without you in my life? Your acts of bravery and loyal commitment greatly inspire me to be bold in my own life. Thank you for saving me."

"It is my pleasure to help you in any way I can, Steven," responded Peter. "As I've said before, wherever you go I will be with you, and no matter what we go through together, I will always be there to fight with you. You can trust me to stick closer to you than even a dear friend, as I vow to follow you as if you were my very own big brother. And I promise that you can trust those words to be true and faithful."

Steven smiled at Peter, with the slightest drops of tears seen falling from his eyes and onto his cheeks. Sharing an embrace, the two of them started walking back to the rest of the company, and once they made their way to them, the company breathed heavy sighs of relief that the two of them were safe. Huminli and Glophi went to hug the two humans, while the rest of the company simply watched on with glad and relieved expressions on their faces.

Once they had finished embracing, Mataput came toward Peter, standing face-to-face with the young boy. "That was a close one," he said, with a smile on his face. "Oh but, Peter, Peter, Peter. Peter the Brave seemed to have other ideas of how we would overcome this sudden challenge that appeared before us. Where would this company be without your boldness? Even as Orieant and I urged you to stop running since we would have been able to save Steven ourselves, still, you ran on with no looking back, and you proved that you could do just the same as us, perhaps even better. You are a very brave young man, Peter, and I am glad that you insisted on joining this company on this journey, as we certainly need your brave soul to uplift our spirits even in difficult times."

Peter stared at the ground, finding himself unable to respond to the words of praise that he received from Mataput. But at that moment, words came to his mind, which he shared with all that heard him. "I have only done what is my duty," he responded. "Just now I made a vow to Steven to always follow him wherever he goes, and even before then, I have promised to remain by his side in all things. And I don't plan on breaking my vow anytime soon, as a true friend would remain faithful in all things, no matter the cost. I am confident that Steven would do the same thing for me if I were ever caught in a moment of danger."

Mataput gazed at Peter, with a light of gladness covering his wise face. "Never before have I heard such bold and loyal words come out of the mouth of a youth," he remarked. "Nothing indeed can separate the two of you, and I can see that both of your fates will be tied directly with each other. I admire you, Peter, and I am filled with satisfaction knowing that you will never leave Steven's side."

A warm smile came onto Peter's face, though a fire of boldness consumed his heart. "Only death could separate us," he proclaimed with no fear. "But even then I doubt if even the fate of mortality could cause us to become disconnected, as I am confident that our spirits would still find a way to reunite with each other. But let me not speak of such things yet, as I am still only a young boy of 16 years."

With these words, Steven could, at last, take no more. He felt as though his melting heart would fall out of his chest, and with tears streaming down his face, he found himself unable to hold back his words in silence anymore. "The words you speak are wise and faithful, Peter the Brave," he said, with tears continuing to flow down his face. "As you have said, even at death we shall remain by each other's side, with no thoughts of departure ever crossing our minds. You have been an unexpected, yet great and loyal friend, Peter, far greater than even my good friends who I grew up with in my hometown village of Frosh. And the fact that an orphan could be filled with such an unrelenting passion of his refusal to submit to fear, is something that I have found myself pondering and admiring of you as of late, Peter. I wish that I possessed even just half of the boldness that you have."

As Peter gazed at Steven with a shocked expression, his eyes began to water. "Yet I wouldn't even be here if it were not for you, Steven," he said. "I have had my fair share of weak and grievous moments, such as when I foolishly led my parents away from the forest, to their deaths. But even then you were there to comfort me and to fill the void in my life that my parents had left behind. Your wise words certainly encouraged my heart, Steven, and you remind me of how much we can look confidently ahead, has filled me with such boldness that I wouldn't have gained any other way."

"I am humbled to hear such praise coming out of your mouth, Peter," said Steven, gazing at the boy with watery eyes. "I know that my life wouldn't be complete without you, and I am glad that I have had the same effect on yours."

Just then Steven and Peter embraced each other, as the rest of the company silently watched on with lights of joy covering their faces. Some of their eyes began to water as they observed the two humans, and once the two of them had finished embracing, Erundil came forward to express his gratitude for how much the two of them stuck close by one another through everything they faced.

"Seeing the great commitment you two have for each other, truly touches my heart," he said with a broad smile. He then paused, pondering something deep in his mind before sighing to himself and speaking once more.

"I once had a friend," he continued. "One that stuck closer to me than even my brothers did. And just like you two, we had a deep devotion to each other, so deep that we made a vow never to leave one another's side. My friend's name was, Fohranil, and he was the son of one of my father's many wise advisors. The two of us grew up together from our childhood to our early adulthood, sharing stories of the many ancient histories and legends of our people, and training alongside each other as soldiers in the army. But our time as soldiers remained problem-free, as our time as young adults were mostly spent serving during peaceful times, which meant that we were never deployed to other lands other than our own. We enjoyed our time in Watendelle, and for many years grew in our close respect for each other.

"But then one day, while we were training in one of the many forests of our kingdom, the trees were suddenly set on fire. On that tragic day, Fohranil along with many other soldiers was caught in the middle of the forest, and hundreds of gamdars perished because of the fire. As we tried saving those who were caught in the fire, we could faintly see five wuzlirs riding on their black horses laughing in our faces before fleeing from our sight before we could do anything to them. That moment has stuck with me ever since, and my hate for the slaves of Natugura has only been rekindled in its growth. But at that moment, my thought was brought back to my best friend, and though I tried entering the forest to save him, I was repelled back as no one wanted me pointlessly surrendering my life, as they all recognized me as the heir of my father's throne. And so my friend was left to be consumed by the fires, and his body was shriveled up in pieces. So passed my friend, who was a brave and noble gamdar, one whom I learned much from, and was prevented from learning more from because of a disgusting act from those group of wuzlirs. In the days and weeks after this day, I along with many others tried urging my father to declare war upon the wuzlirs and march out to Nangorid in response to their terrible act of darkness. But he refused our desperate request, leaving us left to suffer the deaths of our friends in loneliness. Long have I desired to see the destruction of the wuzlirs, for all of the suffering and wickedness they have brought to this once fair world."

He ceased speaking, gazing up at the sky with great sorrow covering his proud face. Then suddenly, to the company's shock, the gamdar dropped his head and let out such a bitter cry of grief and regret that Steven felt as though a sword had pierced his heart. No tears streamed down his hardened face, though a terrible sound of wailing came forth from his mouth.

Orieant came forward, and placing his hand on Erundil's shoulder wished to comfort him. "I am sorry for your loss, Erundil, but even in your friend's death, you two had never left each other's side," he said, while the gamdar continued staring at the ground. "I am sure that a warm smile covered Fohranil's face as he watched on as his brave and noble friend tried saving him even as he might have worried that both of you wouldn't have escaped alive. You two remained loyal to one another, even at the point of death, and such a devoted friendship doesn't come too often."

"But only if we had spent more time together, I wouldn't be filled with so much regret of the past," responded Erundil, now coming to his full stature as he composed himself. "I only wish I had managed to save him because I still had many more things that I wanted to learn from his wise words. To this very day, the wuzlirs have not been avenged for the blood they spilled on that innocent day, all because my father refused to pay back what they deserved for their great evil. And it is because of my father that my righteous anger against the slaves of the Dark Lord has still not been quelled."

"It is in your complete right to hold righteous anger against the enemy, Erundil," responded Orieant. "But you must know that your father was only trying to help your people, as repaying the wuzlirs for their vile deeds would have only led to war, causing thousands of more pointless deaths of gamdars in a needless war of vengeance. Different times call for different measures in the way we respond to attacks from the enemy, and Tutlandil made a wise decision in holding back from going into battle, as he instead worked on restrengthening the army to secure the borders of your kingdom and make your people from resilient from any future attacks."

A sting of bitterness filled Erundil's heart as he listened to Orieant and a strained expression now covered his face. "A strong and bold king would have chosen to fight back," he responded. "Though I have much respect for my father in all of the good he brought to Watendelle, he remained weak in many more important matters."

"Weak? Your father was not a weak king, Erundil," argued Orieant. "He was wise not to fight back, for what gain would there have been if he had brought all of those thousands of soldiers to fight in battle upon this very land? Many wuzlirs would be killed, but would Natugura even need to lift his head in fear? He would have regarded your people as angry flies wishing to sting an army of bears, only to arouse them to anger and cause their fury to bring heavy destruction to your people. Your father was a man of keen judgment, Erundil, who could accurately see the consequences that would come with making hasty decisions."

"I do not doubt that my father was a wise man, I just wonder why he was so hesitant when we needed him most to be bold," replied Erundil. "As far as I'm concerned, all of the renowned kings of my people were known for their daring feats of heroism, where they stood up to the terrors brought about by our age-long foe. Was not Ulohendel, the wisest king of all, the one who made the decision to go to war against the Dark Lord, leading the armies of all of the free creatures of this world to battle in the days of that first and great war? If a wise king was one who never made hasty choices, why then did Ulohendel lead this army into battle in the land of Nangorid in hardly any time for our people or our allies to think our plan through?"

"As I said, different times call for different measures, Erundil," responded Orieant. "Such were the days this young world found itself in, that Ulohendel had no choice but to directly challenge the Dark Lord, as that was the time when Natugura had openly demonstrated his rebellion against all that was good. The free creatures of this world had no knowledge of what power their new foe might have gained, and besides, they had never seen the fruit of corruption and evil up until that point. The time called for them to display noble bravery in the fields of battle, lest the Dark Lord burn the world to the very ground. But that has not been our purpose for many years now. To go to war now, while seemingly a noble deed, would prove to be falling into a trap of the enemy. Maybe sometime later the fate of this world will call for the free creatures to arise and unite in war, but for now, it would be a foolish thing to challenge the Dark Lord so early."

Erundil sighed to himself, turning away from Orieant. "A foolish thing, though it remains an action that must be eventually taken," he muttered under his breath.

A blanket of regret came on Orieant's face, and he walked over to Erundil. "Erundil, please come back," he said, urging the gamdar to return to him. Erundil hesitantly turned back, with a weary and bitter expression on his face. "Please know that I am deeply sorry for what happened to your friend and the grief that it brought to you. And I understand why you desire to see the slaves of the enemy punished for their horrible feeds, as it is the right view to hold. But the time for complete justice has not come yet, but there will be a day when restoration will return to those who deserve it. A time may come when events will call all of the free creatures to go to war, but whatever happens, know that we can always hold onto the hope that what we are doing will bring lasting good to this world."

The bitter expression on Erundil's face began to fade away. "Your wise words always amaze me, even when I may dare to believe something else," he admitted. "I know that you and Mataput only hope for the absolute best of us, and I hope that if Fohranil were to see me today, he would be proud of the job I have done as the king over my people. His fearless face shall never depart from my memory, and I wish to be half as brave as he was."

A smile came onto Orieant's face. "The fact that your friend remains deeply ingrained in your mind, proves that he will forever be a friend of yours, never a former one. Nothing, not even death will be able to change that, as these are the unbreakable bonds that form and mold us into the people we desire to be."

A faint smile now came onto Erundil's face, as the sun glistened on his face as a bright light of undimmed joy. "I am grateful to listen to these words of yours, Orieant," he said. "Indeed these unbreakable bonds will never be able to separate my friend and me, as his memory in my mind proves that I will never forget about his life. You have spoken rightly, Orieant, and now I wonder, what about the unbreakable bonds of your own life? I have shared the deep secrets of my life with you, and now I desire to learn more about yours and Mataput's life as well if you don't mind."

The company all cast their attention toward Orieant, waiting for the volvier to share the secrets of his ancient life. But before he could speak, Mataput quickly interrupted to share all that was on his heart.

"If you don't mind, I would like to answer Erundil's question," he said, with all eyes now fixed upon him. "As you all know, Orieant and I are the great volviers of Jangart, which means we have lived for many long years, even in the days before time was when we dwelled in Starlight as spirit beings. We witnessed the ancient days of old that seem like yesterday to our mind, and this was the time when all of the creatures of this once-perfect world, were immortal, complete, and without shame. These were the days when Jangart would visit his many created lands, and the whole world would be filled with his glory and wisdom. These were the great and awesome elder days of perfection, and the memory of them has impacted the work that I have done since I left Starlight. Yet despite how much I have to hold onto the memories of the ancient past, these stories are still recorded in many books, poems, and songs of the free creatures of this world. But many other weightier and far more splendid matters have been kept hidden by Jangart, and he will only share the many tales of the elder days once all is made whole once again."

"But before we look ahead to that day in the future, I would like to mention that Orieant's words of the unbreakable bonds in our lives are completely true, and I can see that reflected in my existence as Orieant and I have held a deep and faithful bond with each other. But going even further back in the elder days, I once had an even closer bond with a friend whom I never imagined would have betrayed not only me but also Jangart himself in the most evil of ways. That friend of mine was Natugura and before his great rebellion, I was a close friend of his, including Orieant, with the three of us being so close that we shared our thoughts, words of wisdom, and laughs with each other. Nothing that we said or did was made unknown to one another, and the three of us held unbreakable bonds that could never be shattered, or so we thought. Because then the change came, as the shifting tide of a season that can be sensed by the chilly breeze of the wind. And I noticed this dark change that came upon Natugura, and I could sense that a heavy doom would fall upon the world if he failed to repent for his evil thoughts that soon turned into open words. A desire for power, authority, and worship consumed his crippling heart, and I could see just how triggered he was becoming whenever Orieant and I warned him against rebelling against Jangart.

"Soon after, the time of his rebellion came, and for the very last time, he came to us, revealing all that had been laid on his heart regarding the plans of his cataclysmic war upon his holy creator. Our hearts were crushed to hear the foul words that come from his mouth and seeing how dark his once pure and unadulterated spirit of glorious light had become, we firmly rejected his offer for us to join him. But as his closest friends and being yet new to the presence of evil, we pleaded with him to return to Jangart and seek his mercy, and all would be restored to goodness. But he cruelly laughed in our faces, calling us weak as he refused to seek the pardon of Jangart who would have restored him to his rightful place. And thus we had no choice but to end our friendship with him, and from that day forth we became his most bitter enemies as we wanted no part in the irreversible damage he had brought to this world."

A wind of sorrow flew all around the presence of the volviers, as Mataput recounted the memory of their once close friendship with the Dark Lord. The company stood still, with bowed heads and pale faces as they closely listened to hear what their time was like when they once dwelled with their enemy. Sympathetic expressions covered the company's faces as they were grieved to learn the tale of how Natugura, once a good friend of the volviers had betrayed his relationship with them.

Amidst the silence, Orieant spoke to the whole company, though his words were mainly directed toward his friend, Mataput. "Yet when we think deeply of it, even Natugura's rebellion has benefited this world," he said. "Because he departed from the light, the darkness that had been residing in his heart was finally revealed, and Mataput and I grew even closer with each other, as we knew that we had to stick closer than even the most faithful friends. We had lost our gold old friend to madness, but even despite his rebellion, good remained and while Mataput and I continued to walk by each other's side in every step of the new chapter of our lives, we would also be able to lead the free creatures of this world in defying the dark purposes of the Dark Lord."

Mataput's sorrowful face morphed into a faint smile. "All that you say is more than true, my friend," he said. "It is because of Natugura's rebellion that we have never done anything apart from each other's knowledge, such as when we appeared before Steven to reveal to him his great purpose designed by Jangart. All that the two of us have ever done has been done together, which is what we have modeled for the rest of you to follow, as can be seen with Steven and Peter."

"And the two of them have certainly proved how powerful friendship can be," remarked Orieant. "And now that we continue demonstrating the great deeds we can perform while we remain faithful to each other, let's continue going on in our journey. Besides, the snow doesn't seem to be slowing down any time soon."

The company brought their attention back to the snowy-covered paths they found themselves on and were reminded of just how miserable the weather was. As if they had snapped out of a dreamlike state, they suddenly began shivering as they felt the cold wind blowing in their faces. And wiping the piles of snow that covered their cloaks, they were ready once more to continue their journey and escape the bitter weather for some time."

"So what are we waiting for then?" asked Huminli, while his body shivered and teeth chattered from the tormenting blast of the wind and downpour of snow. "I'm glad to be learning about how important friendship is, but I imagine that if we had continued making our way through these mountains a long time ago, we would have found ourselves a cave where we would be able to warm ourselves by a large fire."

The sound of a warm cave alerted the company, and they were determined all the more to find a place to avoid the terrible weather outside by the mountains. “Huminli is right,” remarked Lelhond. “Why are we wasting our time sharing stories in this cold when we could be in a warm cave? Let us make our way there and that way we can share all the stories we want without having to bear these miserable weather conditions.”

“I can’t argue with any of you,” said Orieant, smiling as he looked upon the company. “But let none of you take all that you learned about friendships lightly. For it was as if when you listened to the stories of the unbreakable bonds that have shaped all of our lives, the memory of this cold weather disappeared from your minds. But now that you have been reminded of this weather, we should continue on our journey before any of you lingers behind.”

And so, Mataput and Orieant turned their attention back to the snowy paths that lay ahead of them and slowly began their march through the bitter mountains. Immediately the smalves jumped behind them, eager to find a warm place to enjoy and share more stories. The rest of the company followed them from behind, not wishing to spend any more extended time in the snowy and windy weather that began to weigh heavily on their minds.

Upon walking behind the volviers, Huminli turned around and directed some playful words toward Steven. “Now you better not go tumbling over again,” he said with a smile. “Because I don’t want to waste any more time in this miserable cold.”

Steven laughed as he heard the smalf. “I promise I won’t,” he said. “But perhaps I should rather say that I hope I won’t. For I do not know how much worse this powerful wind might become.”

“Well let’s hope that the wind’s intensity begins to calm down,” responded Huminli. “Because we don’t want anyone else falling facedown in this freezing snow. But as long as we watch where we’re going, we’ll arrive in a warm cave in no time.

Steven agreed with the smalf, and turning his face forward once more, Huminli braced himself to endure the perilous march through the snowy and rocky paths of the mountains. The snow continued to tumble down at rapid speeds, as the vicious wind continued to blow in their faces without a sign of slowing down. The company's cloaks hardly kept them warm in the chilly weather, but the hope of a warm cave hidden somewhere deep within the mountains was a constant reminder of what they would be rewarded with once they finished enduring the bitter cold.

But even with their hopeful thoughts, the weather only seemed to grow worse in its intensity. The wind continued its rampaging effect on them, and they started to walk even more slowly as the snowy paths they walked along began to get icy. Worries about slipping on the ice now came to their minds, which only added more issues to the ones they were already facing. Some of them grabbed ahold of each other, hoping that they wouldn't slip on the ice, or even worse, fall and crack their heads on the icy and rocky ground. Both Steven and Peter grabbed ahold of each other's shirts, refusing to let go of one another as the two of them fell back to the rear of the company.

Huminli was growing rather frustrated with himself, as he had a few slips along the way. "Right when I thought that the snow and wind were the worst things we would have to face, this snowy path has now decided to become slippery and icy," he said, shaking his head in perplexity. "How much longer do we have to suffer through this madness?"

"Not much longer," responded Mataput. "Huminli, I plead with you to not give up. We are almost near a cave, so I would advise you to grab a hold of someone next to you that way you don't slip anymore. We don't need any cracked heads or sliding bodies going down this snowy and icy winding path with the unrelenting wind blowing in our direction."

Huminli sighed to himself, but taking Mataput's advice he refused to give up just yet and decided to brace for the challenge ahead of himself. He knew that he had to continue, reminding himself that the purpose of a smalf was to be brave no matter what challenge he may face. Though the snow was beginning to freeze his toes, turning to his brother, Glophi who seemed to be doing just fine, he knew that he too could walk confidently amidst the blistering wind and pouring snow. He kept on speaking to himself in his head, saying that in just a little more time he would be able to rest in a warm and safe cave.

And so the rest of the company advanced their way up the winding snowy paths, slowly but surely making their way through the mountains as the blasting wind continued blaring in their faces. They deliberately fell silent, not saying a word to one another as they didn't want a conversation to distract them from advancing on their journey. They trudged their way around and through the piles of snow that stood as firm walls all around them, constantly warming their numb hands and trying to avoid freezing their already lifeless feet. They knew not when they would find a cave, and thoughts of giving up began to well in their minds, especially with Steven. For not only was the weather a challenge to endure, but the winding paths up the mountains made their heads dizzy, and Steven nearly collapsed at one moment if it were not for Peter holding onto him.

"Thank you, my friend," he said, turning to Peter. "I don't know where I would be without your support, but all I know is that I will use this as motivation to endure and press on forward because all will end up just fine in the end."

Peter said nothing in return but continued holding onto his friend, with Steven regaining his strength just by receiving support in his weak and cold body.

About half an hour passed as the company endured the bitter weather, and by now many of them were freezing, exhausted, and filled with doubts and worries. They wondered when their difficult maze through the bitter mountains of Lehu Shalank would end, or at least come to a brief halt in the form of a warm place to abide away from the cold. Steven thought deeply of coming to a halt to ask Mataput and Orieant the many questions that plagued his mind, but sensing what he wanted to do, Peter quickly intervened without saying a word by placing his hand on his friend's shoulder and nodding him on to continue enduring the pain. The two of them walked together, hand in hand with a broad smile covering Peter's frozen face. The young boy along with the volviers seemed to be the only ones unaffected by the weather, as smiles were spread across all three of their faces. Even the strong gamdars seemed to be showing signs of weariness, as they desperately wished for a place where they could rest for a while. But they too pushed forward, knowing that they could still hold onto the promise of a warm cave where they could finally break their silence and share all that was on their mind.

Another half-hour passed, and by now serious doubts lingered through the minds of everyone, even Peter. Thoughts of Mataput and Orieant abandoning their promise to them briefly came to them, though they laughed and brushed those imaginations of nonsense aside. But they felt that they couldn't hide their growing discontent anymore and that they had to share what they were feeling with the ones who had led them in this direction. And especially with Steven, though he had felt encouraged and strengthened by Peter, he was now beginning to wonder whether or not it would be enough to completely remove the doubts that crept ever so cunningly deep in his heart. He soon started thinking of a formal way he could present his concerns to the volviers, and feeling encouraged that they would listen to him and yield to his worries, a rejuvenating sense of energy seemed to be restored to his body. He now walked with more speed through the snowy paths, quickly passing by Peter before passing the gamdars and eventually the smalves, which left him directly behind Mataput and Orieant. And once he came within touching distance of the volviers, he debated with himself for a while, wondering whether or not it would be the best idea to announce his worrying thoughts to them. But at length, he decided that it would be the best choice for him to make, for perhaps they would have some grace and allow the company to take a break and descend their way down the mountain, or so he thought.

For just as he began raising his hand to tap Mataput on the shoulder, the most remarkable of sights appeared in the corner of his eye. Looking up ahead and turning his head toward the right, he could see the slightest of a small rocky opening, and he instantly held back his hand and gazed in relief and amazement at the sight for some time.

The rest of the company caught up and continued their way up the path before they all breathed heavy sighs of relief once the opening became clear before their eyes. Tremendous excitement welled within their hearts and the feeling of hope starting to dwindle vanished into thin air. Smiles of joy covered their faces, and turning to Mataput and Orieant they noticed that the volviers too had delighted expressions on their faces. Walking a few more steps toward the opening, they came to a halt, as they all gathered together with exceeding gladness that they had finally arrived at what they had long hoped for.

13

The Caves of the Melondairs

THE COMPANY STOOD THERE silently, soaking in what lay in front of them. A wide and open cave provided a haven for them from the bitter weather, though it was uninviting because of its darkness and strange formation of stone pillars. But they celebrated that they had finally reached the cave, with the doubts that had long been gnawing at their minds finally being erased from their memory. They looked on at the site laid before them with relief, and entering the dark cabe their cold and tired bodies were filled with comfort and strength.

Steven's anxious and fatigued face was now replaced by a refreshment of hope and energy as he breathed a sigh of relief that he could finally take a break from all the walking he had done outside.

Sensing the peace and strength that had returned to Steven's face, Peter turned and spoke with him. "Well, we have come here at last," he said. "The hope that we have been holding onto for this entire time, has finally been manifest to us. And I can see the peace and joy that you are experiencing right now, Steven, just by looking at your face."

Steven turned toward Peter, amazed by the boy's keen observation. "I am indeed filled with such peace that has restored relief and confidence to my heart," he remarked. "And I am glad that we no longer have to worry about that blistering wind or those cold drops of snow, at least for the present time. But I do need to spend some time to rest and relax, as

I know that my body needs it, and I imagine that you feel the same way as well."

"Well I for sure need this time to relax," responded Peter. "But more than that, I am glad to see the strength and joy on your face."

The rest of the company gathered together, speaking and laughing with each other as they felt free to finally let go of all their anxieties. Though they could only faintly see one another's faces in the dark cave, they knew that everyone had broad smiles on their faces with the darkness seeming to not affect their mood. Several minutes passed by, and though many of them had first thought of lying on the ground to close their eyes, to their amazement they felt more awake than ever as though they could talk for hours on end.

But while they chatted amongst each other, Mataput and Orieant tried getting their attention, waving their hands in the air and tapping their shoulders since they knew that no amount of shouting would be able to raise their voices above everyone else's. No one paid attention to the volviers, with the noise of their chatter overwhelming all other things the volviers were trying to tell the company. Then suddenly, amid their talking and laughter, a bright light shone from the middle of the cave, reflecting its white hue in every direction. The company collapsed to the ground in shock, and they instantly fell noiseless. They all covered their eyes from the intensity of the shining light, but as they slowly staggered up to their feet, the light began to grow dim, and uncovering their hands from their eyes, they stood in amazement at how the once dark cave was now lit all around by a clear and brilliant glowing.

Observing the cave which was now revealed plainly to them, they gazed in amazement at the vast and wonderful sights they beheld. Looking in all directions of the shimmering cave, they stared at the great stone pillars and walls with awestruck faces and opened mouths. The stone walls themselves seemed to be as hard as iron, and their color was so magnificent that for a moment the company believed they were staring at silver walls. Many writings, markings, and drawings engraved in white covered the bright walls, and there seemed to be no end to the many images of tall figures riding on great ships across the wide sea and coming to some large and distant unknown land. Many of the images seemed to be worn out by age with many of the different markings and writings also diminishing over time, yet despite the many seemingly long years that had passed, the abode of this vast cave seemed as though it would fill any new visitor with a sense of awe.

The company gazed in wonder at these marvelous yet strange sights for many more minutes, before Peter broke the silence. "What is this place?" he asked. "It is so huge and there seems to be no end to these bright stone walls with all of its drawings and writings."

"These are some of the most well-known caves throughout Nangorid, though I forget the name of them," answered Orieant. "But what I do recall is that these are the caves of the melondairs, where the mighty sea-raiders and pirates of old belonging to the creatures of the eliants once dwelled long ago. The eliants come from the farthest point west of Jangart's created world, where they dwell in the land of Canlodar. And in the decades after the War of Great Alliances had ended, the Dark Lord decided to arouse his slaves to another war, but this time a much different one. This time he called upon the eliants and gathered them to attack the gamdars by sea, and what followed was the Great Sea War, where many of the eliants worked as pirates, earning their name of the melondairs which means, '*The Mighty Commanders of the Sea.*' During this time the melondairs raided the ships of the gamdars, and many great battles both strategic and bloody were fought throughout the boundless sea.

"But at the last, the gamdars using their wisdom managed to learn the tactics of the melondairs, and using their strategies against them they chased the pirates eastward across the sea before forcing them to land here in Nangorid. And it was here in these caves where the melondairs dwelled for many long years, filling these caves with many writings and drawings, reflecting their pride and their skill in sailing across the sea for battle. They strengthened the foundation of these stone walls by overlaying the soft rocks, with a hard and bright material that they used for their swords, shields, and armor, which had helped them tremendously to their advantage whenever fighting in direct combat. They abode long in these caves, and as the years went by they desired to form a great kingdom in these halls as they labored and continued building more marvelous things in these caves as well as sprinkling their hard work with many precious gems, treasures, and riches which they extravagantly boasted of in secret.

"But the time came when the bitterness of Lehu Shalank caught up with them, and being at that time unprepared of the full effect the cold weather would have on them, swelling numbers of their population began perishing due to terrible sickness caused by the freezing wind and snow. Many more froze to death, and before long all of them had perished in these caves. And noticing that they had been quiet for many years in these caves, the Dark Lord sent his wuzlirs to search out this place, and seeing their dead bodies that filled these caves, they gathered the bodies of the eliants and sent them on large ships back westward across the sea back to their home of Canlodar so that their people could bury them in honor. And ever since that day when the eliants recovered the dead bodies of the melondairs, they have remained hidden from all sight, staying out of every war and battle that has fallen and living secretly among themselves, though still full of corruption."

The company listened in fascination to Orieant's account of the melondairs, filled with amazement and curiosity. "The melondairs seem to be mighty creatures, but I wonder why this is only the first time I am learning about them," remarked Peter. "But I guess it's because they live far away from the rest of the lands of this world, dwelling among themselves in secret as you said. But I can only wonder how frustrated Natugura must be in knowing that they have not fought for him over the past thousands of years."

"The eliants as a whole have been a cause of great annoyance for the Dark Lord," responded Orieant. "In the years after the melondairs mighty deeds performed on the seas and their subsequent exile in these caves, Natugura has tried to rouse them to fight many more battles, especially ones that would bring damage to the coasts of Watendelle. But the eliants have remained quiet, refusing to heed the Dark Lord's calls for war and instead choosing to live in peace among themselves. Yet, their hearts remain wicked as they still pledge allegiance to the Dark Lord, and their intentions against the free creatures remain dark. Nonetheless, the eliants have vanished from all sight, and none have dared to enter their land not only because of their sturdy walls and iron bars but also of the presence of darkness that at times can be more uninviting than even the vilest places in Nangorid. Dark and strange images both of unusual beasts and of some of their most mighty and renowned pirates cover their land, rising as mighty towers shimmering with lights of silver under the pale moon. It is said that one wuzlir dared to set sail to the land of the eliants, for he was a mighty captain and one of the most trusted slaves of the Dark Lord under his servitude. But coming to the coast of the dark land and seeing the ghastly images and horrifying structures that covered the gray hills, it is believed that he passed out and died from shock by how foul the place was. And thus, none have ever ventured to set sail to the westernmost land of Canlodar, either of the creatures that are free or in slavery."

The company's eyes widened in fear, with many of them gulping as they listened to Orieant. But Erundil had a proud expression on his face, and laughing silently to himself he spoke in response to Orieant.

"It is plain to see that the eliants are foul creatures if even the wuzlirs are shocked by how repulsive they are," he said. "But surely the eliants can't be all that terrifying if they have chosen to live in solitude among themselves, unbothered by the troubles of the outside world. Surely it must have been because of my people's strength in battle which was surprisingly made manifest with our skill of navigating ships across the sea that the eliants fled in terror from the splendor of our wise and shining faces. I have heard tales and stories of how our great sea captains kept the eliants at bay for many months, before finally chasing them across the vast sea until they fled to Nangorid. And as you said, it was here in these caves where the melondairs perished, and with the eliants having received their dead bodies from the wuzlirs, an overwhelming foreboding of fear must have terrorized their hearts from that day forward. And the more that I learn of these supposed mighty sea raiders and pirates, the more I laugh in amazement at my own people's vast might and wisdom."

Orieant remained unmoved by what Erundil had said. "I am glad to see the boldness you possess, Erundil," he said. "And indeed, your people performed valiant and awesome deeds during the Great Sea War, defending their homeland from the attacks of the eliants. And much of the peace that came to the free creatures soon after this war, comes down to the bravery and wisdom of your people. But be careful by how confidently you speak, and don't let that lead you down a path of presumptuous pride. Much of the reason why the eliants have not fought for the Dark Lord since this time, is because of the lasting impression his land had on them. Many of them feared that the Dark Lord had himself caused the bitter weather of these mountains to result in the perishing of the melondairs. Silent broodings of rebellion against the Dark Lord rose among the eliants, but their hate for all that was pure in the world ultimately led most of them to remain loyal to Natugura in thought. But they have only chosen to serve him in their thoughts, and for many years they have not been troubled to act out their thoughts in acts of war in service of the Dark Lord."

Erundil fell silent, seeing that his argument with Orieant would amount to nothing. The rest of the company listened on both with wonder and a slight sense of concern as they imagined what the eliants could be up to now.

But at length, while the company remained silent in their thoughts, Forandor suddenly murmured something in a low voice, as he walked around and gazed at the vast caves. The company's attention was turned toward him, and listening quietly to his voice they perceived that he was reciting the words of a poem of some past event:

The battle rages, deep across the vast sea,
Where our captains and heroes defend our land.
The tall ones clad in gray and on large ships are forced to flee,
Into an unknown land, led by their fearful hand.

Our banner is raised high on our ship,
With the glorious light shining from the sun.
We have steered the sea with our tight grip,
As our new troubles are suddenly undone.

"Now I understand the meaning of this poem," remarked Forandor, with the company gazing at him with fascination. "For very long I had never understood why my people would ever need to defend ourselves on ships across the sea, but now all has been made clear. All my life I heard tales and listened to songs about our renowned sea captains and soldiers, fighting battles with iron-clad and giant creatures across the sea. I disregarded these stories, believing them to be nonsensical tales devised by our loremasters to make us young ones dream of doing such mighty things as well. I had always known that my people fight on land, but fighting in tall ships across the broad sea was a new thought that I could not yet grasp. Even the eliants were a brief thought of mine, creatures taller than us with a skill in steering ships and devising strong weapons. But now I have seen the truth that the eliants do exist, and they dwell in the far land to the west where no gamdar has ever ventured to."

Lelhond turned towards Forandor, pondering everything that his brother had admitted. "I have seen the truth as well, though I confess that all still seems strange to me," he said, now turning toward the volviers. "I find it hard to believe that the eliants are still alive today, though they have not fought in any battles or wars for many years now. How could they still pledge their allegiance to the Dark Lord even though they have done nothing to prove their loyalty to him?"

"It is indeed a strange thought to consider, Lelhond," responded Mataput. "But it is true that the eliants are still alive, dwelling in the land of Canlodar as Orieant said. But if I may add, as I have long considered the fate of the eliants, I have wondered if some curse may have been put over them that explains why they no longer fight for the Dark Lord. But more than anything, the fear of seeing what happened to the melondairs likely led the eliants to dwell by themselves unconcerned by the troubles of the outside world, though deep within their hearts they are still under the corruption of Natugura."

A distasteful look as a shadow came over Erundil's face. "And they better continue to mind their own business," he remarked. "Whether or not they have fought on the side of the Dark Lord in the years that followed the Great Sea War, they remain no different than the wuzlirs. They are corrupted creatures, slaves to the will of the Dark Enemy who guided them to attack my people and contribute to bringing death, destruction, and despair to the kingdom of Watendelle. And though I admit that the wuzlirs have brought much more destruction to Watendelle than any other creature of this world has, I still treat the eliants as a foe of mine since they are corrupted creatures and shall remain that way forevermore. I am glad that they were driven force from the sea and left to rot in these bitter mountains."

The company listened silently to Erundil, observing the disgust and hardness that covered his face. But when they turned to Mataput, they marveled at the sight of his face for a look of pity was on him, and they all wondered what had brought this change over him.

"Erundil, the eliants are not a great foe of your people as the wuzlirs are," he responded. "I know that they fought many battles against your people across the wide sea, but since then they have not fought in any battle or war, nor formed any alliance with any creature of this world in league with the Dark Lord. Yes, they are corrupted creatures who are still under the influence of the Dark Lord, but the only reason why they are slaves to him is because they believe they have no other choice but to remain under his authority. I imagine if someone were to offer them a new way of thinking and living, they would gladly receive it."

Erundil's countenance fell as he listened to Mataput. "Why do you speak with such pitiful words for the eliants?" he asked. "Was it not their choice to join the side of the enemy which has been proven by the battles they have fought against my people across the sea, resulting in the deaths of many of our soldiers and captains? How then could they be willing to turn aside from the darkness all because you wish to show mercy toward them? No, I do not support us showing mercy toward the eliants, as it would be far more just for them to suffer under the consequences of their actions. And I hope and pray that the wuzlirs and for that sake, all the corrupted creatures of this world will experience the same fate for their wicked actions as well."

Mataput remains silent for some time, thinking of what Erundil had said. "I hear you," he eventually said. "As King of Watendelle, it is your duty to defend your people, and I believe that it is right for you to hold onto this righteous anger. But I have only one wish for you, Erundil, and that is to not let your anger stop the will of Jangart from being accomplished. Though the eliants remain stricken under the bondage of slavery to the Dark Lord, they have still lived their lives in seclusion, choosing not to fight for him. Explain to me if a wuzlir could ever choose to do something like that. Why then should we have no hope that the eliants can repent from their dark ways and become new creatures?"

Erundil shook his head and laughed within himself. "No hope remains for the eliants because if there was any hope for their redemption, then they would have chosen to fight on our side long ago," he said in response. "Mataput, it is clear that the eliants are corrupted creatures, and even if they have chosen not to fight for the Dark Lord, the memory of what their ancestors did against my people's ancestors will surely never be forgotten. And besides, they have had thousands of years to attempt to rectify these deeds by joining us and fighting against the enemy, which they have also chosen not to do. For this reason among many others, it is evident that the eliants are cursed and corrupted creatures, and some things such as those can never be altered."

Mataput looked on at Erundil with a straight face. "You are stubborn, Erundil, and though that may work in your favor at times, I just wonder when you will be willing to embrace other opinions, especially from those who have lived hundreds of your lifetime," he said, gazing at the gamdar for a moment. "Will you not tell me what these words of Ulohendel the Wise mean when he says:

Not all those in exile are lost,
Not all those bound by evil shall we hate.
Those who have set sail to that cross,
Shall not forever remain in their state.

In days to come, the king shall open the gate
And shall set the captives free.
Those forgotten shall be awoken from their place,
To be rescued from bondage with the one key.

"Who could've Ulohendel spoken of when he wrote these words, Erundil?" he asked. "The words he has written in this poem were bold ones that no man can take back. And so it is either that while writing these words, Ulohendel was the wisest gamdar to have ever lived, gifted with unimaginable foresight to prophecy great things to come, or he was the most foolish gamdar to ever live, devising hopeful phantoms from his imagination."

A zealous fervor like that of a rushing wind suddenly came over Erundil. "The Great Ulohendel was certainly not a fool," he confidently said. "That I know for sure since no gamdar has ever struck such great fear into the heart of the Dark Lord as the first king of my people has.

His wisdom was infinite and in his vast knowledge, I know that he would have never treated the eliants in any other way than they are deserving of. And for that reason, he couldn't have been talking about the eliants in that poem, instead, he might've been speaking of our many prisoners of war who throughout history have longed for freedom from the king."

"Then tell me, Erundil, why did Ulohendel proclaim: '*Not all those bound by evil shall we hate.*'" asked Mataput. "How could he have referred to prisoners of war being bound by evil as though their sacrifices weren't enough proof that their ways were noble? And why would your people ever need to worry about hating your brave heroes? When you consider all of these sayings of Ulohendel, it makes no sense for him to be speaking of gamdars, let alone any of the free creatures of the world."

"That indeed makes no sense," agreed Erundil, pausing and pondering all that he now had to consider. "But tell me, Mataput, if Ulohendel was speaking of the eliants in this poem, why is this only the first time that these words are being recited to me? Are not all of my people's poems kept safe in the Great Hall of Poems? Tell me then where I can find this lost poem of Ulohendel so that I can ponder all of these sayings of his before my very eyes."

Mataput sighed to himself. "It pains me to say that this poem has likely been lost, Erundil," he confessed. "But I promise you that Orieant and I would never deceive you, and when I say that I watched Ulohendel write these very words which I spoke to you, you can rest assured that I am telling you the truth. Though I cannot remember what book he wrote these words in, I assume that it was recorded in the lost and great book of wisdom which we are searching for."

Erundil's stubborn face remained full of unbelief. "Until I see those words before my own eyes and the context behind it, I will refuse to believe that Ulohendel was referring to the eliants," he obstinately said. "For who can save a group of creatures whose fate was sealed when they chose to follow the Dark Lord in his rebellion? Should I care for creatures who have fought numerous battles against my people? And shall anyone dwelling within the circles of this world be able to deliver just one corrupted creature from their condition, let alone an entire group of them?"

"The King of Watendelle has the power to deliver the eliants from the shadow of darkness," responded Mataput, with a glimmer of hope shining sharply in his eyes. "When writing the words of this poem, Ulohendel foresaw the day when the great king coming in the days after his departure would set sail to the land of Canlodar to bring freedom to the eliants. If your revered forefather pitied them, would it be right for you not to show pity toward them, Erundil? Will you not show the eliants mercy, Erundil, so that a stench of evil residing in this world can forever be eradicated?"

Erundil bowed his head, breathing heavily as the full weight of Mataput's words came crashing on his head. "Pity and mercy are qualities that a king must possess in at least the smallest measure," he said. "But those qualities have always been meant to be directed toward our people first, and I do not see how I can show that to creatures who have willingly chosen to submit themselves to a shameful ideology and being that is in direct opposition to what my people believe and hold dear to. I know that you mean well in all you say, and you and Orieant have filled my mind along with the minds of everyone in this company with profound and wise revelations. But what you have asked me to do is beyond my understanding and for that I am unwilling to attempt to set the eliants free, nor am I willing to entertain the thought that they can turn to that which is good. And since we are speaking of the eliants, should we not also wonder about the wuzlirs, hzarves, and goblins, and consider whether or not they too can be saved from corruption? I cannot see any reason to believe what you are saying, Mataput."

"What you have said regarding the other corrupted creatures of this world is a good point, Erundil," said Mataput. "As far as I know, all hope for their redemption is likely unattainable, but who other than Jangart himself can say that for certain? Yet what I can see with my own eyes as Jangart has revealed to me through the writings of Ulohendel is that hope remains for the salvation of the eliants. For you, Erundil, are the King of Watendelle, the King of the Gamdars! And I will not stop urging you to change your mind about the eliants, because I know that you hold the high position as the king over your people, a people whose rich history is full of mighty kings, bold soldiers, talented musicians, and loremasters of wisdom. And because your people are full of such awe-inspiring splendor and brilliance, it would be in the best interest of this world if you were willing to spread your glory for another group of creatures to turn from their ways and embrace the way of light. For Ulohendel wrote that the eliants would answer to the King of Watendelle, who would possess the key to set them free."

Erundil shook his head in amazement at Mataput's persisting words. "I must honor your determination to prove me wrong, Mataput," he said, with a proud look now coming onto his face. "And I am glad that while trying to make me change my mind about the eliants, you also rightfully mentioned that I am the king over my great people, as I would argue that we are the mightiest and wisest ones of all the free creatures of Jangart. But when before has a king of my people ever been able to free corrupted creatures from the influence of the Dark Lord? And besides, where is this key that can supposedly set the eliants free?"

Mataput smiled at Erundil. "Are you forgetting something, Erundil?" he asked. "Because I am sure that you have read what Ulohendel wrote when he said: '*The hand of the king frees the lost.*' And as the king, you shall have the power to free the eliants by your hand. And I know it is hard for you to believe that they can be saved because of their corruption and the harm that they brought to your people long ago. But for too long have they sat alone in the darkness with no one to help free them with a lending hand. And if we can help show them the truth, why should we allow the Dark Lord any chance to keep them in deception?"

Erundil stared at Mataput for a moment, thinking deeply to himself before responding to the volvier. "I do not agree with allowing the Dark Lord any opportunity to further impose himself than what he has already done," he said. "But I am afraid that the damage that has been done cannot be reversed. The hand of the king does indeed free the lost, but I find no reason to believe that the eliants are lost. They decided long ago to follow in the path of the enemy, which led them to battle against my people. Their minds have been corrupted by the Dark Lord's shadow, and for that reason, they are not innocent. And even if they have not fought for the enemy for quite some time, they are still not ignorant of his devices. So why would I hold onto blind and foolish hope by going all the way to the land of Canlodar only to be ambushed and humiliated by the eliants? I wonder if they are deceiving us by not fighting on the Dark Lord's side to make it seem as though they serve no one, only to later launch a surprise attack on us that would bring lasting destruction to all that remains fair in this world."

Mataput breathed a heavy sigh to himself, looking on at Erundil with a disappointed expression on his face. "So be it, Erundil," he said. "I will allow you to hold onto your opinion. But know and understand this, that one day the hand of the king will free the lost just as Ulohendel prophesied. And though that day may not come during your reign as king, Erundil, it will still come to pass," he then turned his attention toward Erundil's sons who were the only ones among the company still paying attention to the gamdar and volvier's discussion. "If you are not willing to change your mind, Erundil, then I wonder what your sons' opinions are. So I will ask you, Lelhond, Prince of Watendelle, what do you have to say in regards to this matter? Will you be the king as prophesied by your forefather to free the eliants from their corruption?"

Lelhond turned toward his father before bringing his attention to Mataput and answering him. "I can't help but believe that my father is right in expressing his doubts," he said "It is hard to see how hope still exists for creatures who willingly chose to embrace the way of darkness. And if I were to be king, I also cannot see how I would find the motivation led alone a sign of confirmation to set sail to the land of Canlodar to deliver salvation to the eliants."

A look of hopelessness covered Mataput's face, and turning to Orieant the two of them could only shake their heads in displeasure. "Well I suppose that Orieant and I will have to wait for some more time before Ulohendel's prophecy comes to pass," he said. "Unless of course any of you are willing to change your mind and see that these words will eventually come to pass despite your stubbornness. Whether it takes a year or a thousand years for these words to be fulfilled, the eliants shall come to freedom one day, and with each second that passes we get closer to see that day coming."

"And as long as I live, I shall continue to object to that day ever coming," remarked Erundil, before turning his back on Mataput and walking away.

Mataput said nothing, convinced that no words of his would be able to alter Erundil's mindset. He desperately wished that Erundil would realize the scope of the power he possessed to free the eliants from their bondage, yet he knew that the proud gamdar would only provide more reasons in offering an alternative explanation. And so he and Orieant watched on in disappointment as Erundil and his sons rejected their words and walked away from the two of them, not wishing to open their minds to new ideas. Yet hope remained in their hearts that one day the King of Watendelle would fulfill the great prophecy of Ulohendel. And deep within their hearts, they sensed that the day would come sooner than they imagined.

The rest of the company had drifted off while Mataput had spoken with Erundil, with Huminli and Glophi walking around the caves and fixing their attention on the many images and drawings that filled the cave walls. Steven and Peter meanwhile had not walked as far as the smalves but had still examined the many drawings of eliants and endless unreadable writings that met their gaze in almost every direction. As they focused their attention on specific drawings, they could see many more images of other creatures, with some appearing to be wild and large beasts, and others harmless and small insects. Not one blank spot resided on the cave walls, and the company didn't blink their eyes one time as they couldn't help but stand in amazement at all that their sight could bear.

But as they continued gazing in wonder at the many images and writings of the cave, they hadn't realized that the smalves had drifted too far away, and then as if lightning had struck them, Mataput and Orieant were the first ones that became aware that Huminli and Glophi were missing.

They immediately alerted the rest of the company that the smalves couldn't be seen anywhere in sight, and they all began to frantically search the cave for them. They looked for any trace of the smalves that they could find, as just a hint of footsteps would rekindle their relief. But nothing but a flat surface without even a scratch of marks could be observed and nothing but the sound of their hurried footsteps could be heard throughout the cave.

Growing slightly worried, Mataput called out to the smalves in the hope of an answer. "Humiregardophi! Where are you two?" he called out, with his echoing voice being the only answer.

The rest of the company followed suit in shouting out for the two smalves, but again no answer followed other than their echoing cries. They continued searching through the cave in every direction to no avail, and sensing that they were going nowhere with their pursuits, they all sat on the ground and shook their gloomy faces.

But among them who had doubts that the smalves were lost was Erundil, who had a faint grin on his face. "I'm telling you that those smalves must be playing games with us," he said. "After all it's the smalves that have proven to us that that's all they are known for, and so I won't be surprised when those two troublemakers suddenly appear before us after they had fooled us. Come, let's not bury our heads in hopelessness because before we know it, we will all find ourselves laughing in amazement at how worried we were for them."

The company took no comfort in Erundil's words and instead ignored him, with many of them having their heads buried to the ground, while others looked on at him with cold eyes of despair. But shaking his head, Erundil stood up and began walking through the cave, with no sense of fear seemingly in his mind. He casually strolled across the ground and occasionally changed the direction he was facing to search for the smalves, yet he had no concern for them as he believed that they were only hiding from the company.

He soon stopped walking around and came back to the rest of the company. "I can't find them," he said. "But I assure you that those smalves are playing good tricks on us, and all they're doing is creating unnecessary trouble for us."

"No, Huminli and Glophi are not joking around this time," assured Orieant. "I know that they enjoy having fun, but I can sense that they have unintentionally lost track of us. Whether they have drifted too far away from us in this cave or whether they are entirely somewhere else, all I know is that they are not hiding from us and we must continue to look for them."

"So let's continue searching for them," remarked Peter, springing up to his feet. "Much time has already passed and the evening must be fast approaching now. I would hate for the two of them to be lost and fear that they would never be able to find us soon. I'm going to look for them and hopefully, our worries will be gone sooner rather than later."

With that, Peter went off in searching for Huminli and Glophi, covering the distance of the cave as best he could by examining the ground, touching the walls, and searching for every minor detail he could find. The rest of the company stood up as well but instead opted to watch the boy on in the hopes that he would deliver good news to them. The bright light that illuminated the cave was a great help for Peter, but still, no sign of the smalves could be seen anywhere throughout that place.

For many minutes he searched in every direction of the cave he could, but not being able to see even the faintest footsteps of the smalves, he eventually gave up and returned to the company.

"I can't find them anywhere," he miserably said, with his head bowed to the ground. "But I know that they have to be here somewhere, even though I can barely see any traces of them."

Peter slouched to the ground in dejection as the company could only offer him their limited comforting words. They all silently sat on the ground, worn out and without any hope of finding Huminli or Glophi anytime soon. They stared into the distance with worrying thoughts beginning to flood their minds, and they started recalling the memories of the time they spent with the smalves. They desperately hoped that they could enjoy the stories and playful jokes of the smalves once more, but the sweetness of the memories grew more bitter in their minds as they wondered if they would ever see their faces again. Even Erundil shook his head in shock as the expression on his face grew ever more concerned for Huminli and Glophi. Yet throughout their anxious thoughts, the company believed that they would see the smalves again, as most of them had only known Huminli and Glophi for a week and they knew that their already close friendship with them had to continue to grow. But at the present moment, it seemed that their relationship with their new friends would suddenly be ripped away from their grasp.

Eventually, Erundil rose to his feet while the company looked on at him with despairing looks on their faces. "I admit that I am very concerned for the smalves, but we can't just be sitting here and doing nothing this whole time," he said. "At the moment, the smalves are lost and unless they reveal to us that they were either fooling us or had lost track of us by wandering into some other place, then I am afraid that we may have to forget about them and continue in our journey. But in the meantime, I suggest that we should at least walk around and talk with each other and maybe we might find at least some hints as to where the two of them went."

"That sounds like a good idea to me," remarked Steven. "But I don't agree with just leaving Huminli and Glophi behind. Why should we give up hope of finding them so easily?"

"I don't mean that we should give up looking for them, Steven," responded Erundil. "But all I know is that if we had the choice of either finding the lost book of Ulohendel or finding the smalves, then I'm sure you and everyone here would make the same choice as me. But I agree, let's not give up hope of finding them before we have thoroughly covered every part of this cave."

At once, the gamdar started walking slowly through the caves, searching through and touching every piece of the walls. The rest of the company rose slowly to their feet, silently strolling past the images and writings on the walls, filled with hopelessness that they wouldn't be finding the smalves anytime soon. No seasoned words of comfort could restore their joy, and their tired faces were worn out by how challenging their journey had already been and by the fear of how more difficult it would become.

They each individually searched for the smalves in this way for some time, wondering when a spark of hope would light up their faces in joy. But for the time being, a heavy cloud of sorrow consumed their hearts as they now knew their journey had taken an unexpected turn for the worse, and they knew not in which direction this newfound challenge would take them to.

But then suddenly, amidst everyone's feeling of weariness and despair, Peter's eyes lit up with fresh hope. Staring into the distance with widened eyes, it seemed as though he had discovered something that he and the company had missed out on the whole time.

"Look over there!" he cried, pointing to a small opening in the far distance toward the right. "How have we completely missed seeing that small space? Surely the smalves must have peeled away over there and lost their way. That explains why I felt like there was still much more space that we needed to search for them!"

The mood of the company was instantly changed as Peter's observation brought them a sudden and unexpected rejuvenation of hope. Their broken hearts face immediately strengthened and repaired with a foundation of joy and they were comforted in knowing that there was still a much larger area for them to search for the smalves and perhaps find them.

Yet even despite the company's change in mood, Mataput and Orieant remained unfazed and when Peter began walking in the direction of the small opening, Mataput quickly stopped him from progressing any further. "No, don't go any further, Peter," he said placing his hand on Peter's shoulder. "I sense that it would be wise for us to remain where we are."

Peter looked on at Mataput with a bewildered expression on his face. "I don't understand why you are worried, Mataput," he said. "This is the only place that we haven't searched and yet you think it wouldn't be wise for us to go there? What if Huminli and Glophi are lost there and we didn't manage to search for them in that area?"

Mataput sighed to himself and released his hand from Peter's shoulder. "All that you have said is completely logical, Peter," he said. "And I know how brave of a young boy you are as you have proved to me and everyone else that you are not afraid of any unexpected danger. But you must know that Orieant and I have traveled through this land numerous times to know when evil may be lurking in the shadows. And I can feel such a heavy change in the air in that direction that I fear that if we go in that small opening, it will lead to a dangerous path where we will all have to remain strong to resist whatever presence may reside there."

"I can sense that presence of evil as well," chimed in Orieant. "I can't exactly configure whether or not a physical being resides there in that opening, but whatever the case may be I can smell a foul stench lying in that place which will present us with an even worse challenge if we encounter it."

"But why should we not at least go there just to see if Huminli and Glophi are lost there?" asked Peter. "Will we just sit here in fear wondering what presence of evil resides there while we let our friends suffer all by themselves in that evil place? As far as I am here with this company, we will never leave our behind like that."

Even with the company's fearful faces, faint smiles came across all of their faces as they listened to Peter. "You know what, you are proving me wrong, Peter," remarked Orieant. "Your loyalty and bravery have continued to amaze and inspire me in ways I would've never imagined, and I can already see how much of a great leader you are on your way to becoming. But at the same time, I fear that we may be walking into a trap if we go that way. But if you want to go in that direction, then every single one of us will be willing to follow you. Mataput and I would not be fulfilling our purpose by letting you go through that opening without helping you. All of us will stick by your side and whatever danger may come, we will deal with it together."

"I concur," said Mataput in agreement with Orieant. "The purpose of this company was for each of us to remain by one another's side in every choice we make, and so it would be wrong of us to end that now. If Peter is brave enough to go through that opening, then we all must follow his lead."

The hearts of the company were overtaken with courage, and they were greatly encouraged as they witnessed Peter's bravery. Though they remained wary of the possible presence of evil that resided in the opening, from that moment onward they were filled with a resurgent feeling of confidence that they would find the smalves.

A broad smile covered Erundil who was particularly impressed with Peter. "This boy has indeed shown us what it means to be brave," he remarked. "From rescuing Steven as he tumbled down the snowy paths of this mountain, to being the first one willing to go through an unknown and dangerous passage, he has inspired all of us to take bold risks for the benefit of this company. So if he is willing to go through that passage, then I will join him."

"And I will also join him as well," commented Lelhond. "Why should we let the presence of danger threaten us from at least seeing if we can attempt to rescue Huminli and Glophi?"

"We should not let it scare us away," said Peter, with no signs of fear on his face. "So it is time for us to let our words match with our actions.

Let us fear no evil and go on and see what may lurk through that passage. Are we all ready to go?"

The company all voiced their approval of Peter, and the proudest to see Peter's courage was Steven. "Count me in, Peter," he said. "Wherever you lead us I trust that your bravery will only lead us to more hope and joy. You have already proven your faithfulness to myself and this company, and so it would be foolish of us to let you go on by yourself."

The company agreed with Steven and with everyone willing to follow Peter, the young boy began walking in the direction of the small opening. Directly behind him was Steven, with the volviers following directly behind him, and Erundil with his three sons at the rear of the group. They inched their way ever so closer to the small opening, unsure of how they would feel or what they would encounter once they came to it.

But in time they came to the small opening, and suddenly the bright light which has illuminated the whole cave flickered and grew dim before almost all of its light vanished. Ahead of them, the company could faintly see a long and narrow passage, but they didn't know what was there as the area surrounding it was pitch black. And before they knew it, the company found themselves cowering in shock and fear at the sudden and unexpected disappearance of the cave's light, with all of them hardly being able to see each other let alone themselves. They placed their hands on the dark walls around them, inspecting to see where they were.

"What just happened?" asked Steven, blinking his eyes and placing his hands on whatever solid surface he could find. "Where has the light gone and why do I feel so uncomfortable in this dark space?"

"Because evil lurks down the passage ahead of us," responded Orieant. "Light and darkness have no fellowship with each other, and because this company was able to illuminate these caves by our purity and goodness, the darkness cannot stand that. So the light has gone out but we have no choice but to go down this narrow and dark passage as I sense that there is still light at the end of the road."

"Well let us go then," said Peter taking Orieant's words to heart, though he could sense a slight tingle of anxiety itching at his heart. "If Huminli and Glophi possibly went down that way, what is stopping us from doing the same?"

"Peter is right," remarked Lelhond. "If Huminli and Glophi were able to spread their light down this evil and dark passage, then we should be willing to do the same with no hesitation. We are the light that stands opposed to the darkness of the enemy, and we do not need to fear any malicious attacks brought by the enemy because our aura of goodness and light will surely overcome the darkness."

"Well said my son," said Erundil with a smile. "And since we know that darkness and light have no fellowship with one another, then we must be determined to use our light to expel any darkness that stands in our way."

"All of you have spoken well," said Orieant. "So let us waste no time spreading our light down this dark passage to find Huminli and Glophi."

With that Peter set off again, this time walking even more slowly than before, while touching the walls that bordered the path. The company all closely followed him from behind, carefully taking their steps to make sure they didn't crash into each other in the dark area. As they walked on the space grew more narrow and tight, and the ground grew rockier which made them nearly trip before, but they all managed to keep their balance and continue their way through the dark place.

They continued moving steadily in this way for the next half hour, and despite how dark and challenging the narrow passage was for them, they managed to endure it with little trouble. But at that moment, a horrible stench flew in their direction and as they continued walking the smell only continued to get worse. Covering their noses, the terrible smell seemed to blanket the air, and along with its foul scent was a sense of dark corruption that seemed to have once thrived in the dark passage that the company found itself walking through. Being unable to handle the unpleasant stench, the company stopped walking to breathe and cough out the terrible smell.

"What is that awful smell?" asked Steven while coughing. "I can even sense an evil stirring in the air, though I can't figure out what it exactly is."

"Evil once resided in this passage," responded Mataput. "I assume that the melondairs must've gone through this way on numerous occasions, and since those eliants were loyal to the Dark Lord at the time, the presence of corruption ran through this dark passage, spreading across the air to create this foul stench."

"But there is no need to fear," said Peter, not wishing the company to back out from the challenge they had already set out to achieve. "Are we not the light that can overcome the presence of darkness that tries to pursue us? Why should we then allow this smell to stop us from advancing to rescue Huminli and Glophi?"

Despite Peter's words, Steven grew increasingly wary of the evil presence that began to take its toll on him. "I don't know, Peter," he said with a slightly quivering voice. "There is a great manifestation of evil roaming across the air, and I don't think that it's going to go away any time soon. I don't know if I can carry on this way, and I'm doubting that Huminli and Glophi were able to go through this passage."

"Oh come on, Steven," responded Peter, with the tone of his voice disappointed with Steven. "Have we not expressed our desire to stay with each other in every step we take throughout this journey? Why should we break that promise so early then just because we have been presented with a challenge? I know that you can continue because when I witnessed you boldly leading myself and the rest of the people on Earth away from King Maguspra and his spies and after you brought us to our new homes, I knew that I could trust you to make the necessary decisions to lead us to success. Why do you want to give up so easily then if you have already proven how capable you are to display brave exploits?"

Steven thought deeply to himself for some time, before a small smile came onto his face. "You have reminded me of something that I nearly forgot about, Peter," he admitted. "I have been so worried of the dangers we would face in this quest, that I have failed to realize the many challenges I have already faced. And so for your sake, Peter, you who have been such a brave and great friend of mine, I will continue through this passage."

The company breathed sighs of relief, glad to hear that Steven was willing to continue. And so they continued their journey through the dark passage, with the smell in the air continuing to plague them with every step they took. But they found a newfound strength in their bones to motivate themselves, and being led by Peter they were filled with confidence.

Another half hour passed with the company still slowly making their way through the passage, with the way seeming to be an endless dark road that they would have to endure for hours upon hours. Many of them were growing restless, but fixing their attention on rescuing Huminli and Glophi they remained hopeful that there would be light at the end of the road. And to their amazement, as time progressed it seemed as though a layer of darkness began to steadily vanish away, with the terrible scent in the air also starting to become more bearable. The company was now able to uncover their hands from their noses, breathing the air again while also being able to faintly see the walls that stood to their side.

As the heavy darkness slowly began to diminish in its intensity, the company started quickening its pace, with the most relieved of them being Steven, who was glad he had listened to Peter urging him to continue. The path that the company found themselves on was more visible and they could see each other's eyes now. With encouraged hearts and smiles covering their faces, they awaited the sight when they would see the smalves at the end of the passage.

Several more minutes passed, and by now the curtains of light were slowly rolled back with a dim flickering light beginning to make its appearance while the darkness faded into the distance. The company could faintly see each other's faces, and now that they could see everything that was around them, they started smiling and laughing out of relief and encouragement. They knew that the darkness and presence of evil had been forced to go away by the light they brought, and as they continued walking they started speaking with one another.

"Well what did Orieant say?" asked Erundil, from the very back of the group. "Light and darkness have no fellowship together, and once we determined to boldly make our way through this passage, the darkness had no choice but to get away from our sight and to go back to where it came from."

"That is right indeed," remarked Lelhond. "And as far as I'm concerned, no further darkness can stand in our way as long as Peter the Brave leads us!"

Peter couldn't help but blush out of embarrassment, but from the broad smile on his face, it was quite clear how grateful he was for Lelhond's praise of him. And being unable to hold back his own words of praise for the young boy, Steven placed his hand on Peter's shoulder to express his gratitude for him.

"Peter, Peter," he said, with a wide and joyful smile. "Where would we be without Peter the Brave? I certainly wouldn't have had the boldness to come this way, without you convincing me to go through this passage. You have never ceased to amaze me with the tremendous boldness you display daily, and I am more than thankful that I can continue to listen to you and find the motivation to endure whatever challenges come my way."

Peter could no longer keep silent as his smiling face grew red. "Oh please stop, Steven," he laughed. "I am no braver than you have proven yourself to be and I know that I wouldn't be here today if you hadn't chosen to become my friend. I have learned many things from your leadership which has helped me in making brave choices."

"And we could all say the same thing about you, Peter," chimed in Karandil. "Even I as a soldier have learned many things from your bravery."

"That is right," remarked Forandor. "Our people have shown how brave we are throughout our long history, but Peter has proven to be just as brave as our heroes of old. Amidst the presence of darkness and the uninviting danger, he has boldly commanded us to fear nothing and directly go through the challenges we face. He is indeed Peter the Brave and though he may be young, he is mature well beyond his years."

Peter could only smile as he listened to the way everyone was impressed by his bravery. "I am very grateful for all of your kind words, but if it wasn't for any of you being in my life I wouldn't be as brave as I am today," he said, trying to direct the center of attention away from himself. "The ones who have influenced me in ways beyond my understanding have been Steven, Mataput, and Orieant, whose leadership and wisdom have made me the person I am right now in such a short time. If it wasn't for them, I wouldn't be here leading you through this passage, so please give them the much-needed attention that they deserve as well."

"We don't need any attention, Peter," responded Orieant. "For Mataput and I, our purpose has been to help and guide this company on this journey, and while doing that we have had instances where we have had to make brave decisions. And you have proven that you are willing to step up to that challenge, and for that reason, it would only be right for us to admire and celebrate you."

Peter could only shake his head with a wide smile on his face, and with Steven rubbing his hand on his friend's shoulder, Peter's heart was warmed by how loved he felt by the entire company. Allowing this to fuel his desire to find Huminli and Glophi, he once again led the company through the passage, and as they went on for the next few minutes, every last inch of darkness had completely passed away, as the bright light once again illuminated the passage that the company walked on. They all celebrated in astonishment how the darkness had vanished, and they were even more amazed that the horrible smell in the air was now a memory of the past.

Filled with a fire of energy that was restored to them unexpectedly, the company nurtured this motivation by walking freely and without fear of the presence of danger. Steven couldn't help but whisper in Peter's ear how thankful he was for the young boy sticking with him even in his doubts, to which Peter simply responded that Steven would convince him to do the same as well. The rest of the company smiled in admiration at the young boy who led them through the passage, and with the light now shining brightly and clearly in the space they were in, to many of them it seemed as though Peter was sparkling as a flashing star.

Some more time passed as the company followed Peter with no thoughts of worry, and eventually, they came to the end of the passage as they found themselves standing at the entrance of a small opening with an even brighter light shining through it. They stood in silence for a moment, wondering what their next step would be.

But as they each imagined what would lay beyond that opening, Peter suddenly went through the space, disappearing through the gap shining with an intense glowing light. For a brief moment, the company tried calling him back, not knowing what they would encounter through the opening. But they were unable to bring him back, as he had vanished through the unrelenting bright light, losing track of the rest of the company. And so not wishing to be separated from the one who had led them through the passage, they decided to follow in his lead once more.

And then, just as they crossed through the small opening and found themselves squinting their eyes from the brightness of the space they were in, they immediately recognized Peter's voice in the far distance.

"This place is incredible!" he said. "What are you all waiting for? Come quickly and allow yourselves to gaze in amazement at this wonderful place"

The company sprung to action upon hearing Peter, filled with eager expectation that their mouths would drop to the ground once they had a clear look at where they were. And so with no hesitation, they started walking in the direction of where Peter's voice came from, and as they neared where the boy was, the bright light started to grow dim and at that very moment they saw what Peter was talking about.

14

The Awakening of Kolmaug

ONCE THEIR EYES WERE open and they could see in clarity, their mouths did indeed drop to the ground as they expected, as they were filled with awe at what lay all around them. A vast cave sparkling with all sorts of gems, materials, and rock structures met their eyes, being far more splendid than the cave they had come from. A large pond could also be seen in the distance with glittering waterfalls shining in the bright light. Narrow stairs beyond this location also led to more spaces within the caves, seemingly filled with even more riches and materials. The company stood in amazement for some time, overwhelmed by all the treasures and materials they observed.

At last, they saw Peter, who was far into the distance gazing at the treasures and riches for himself. "Isn't this place amazing?" he asked once he saw the company. "Look at all the gold and gems over here; there seems to be an endless supply of them! And just when I thought it couldn't have gotten any better, there happen to be stairs in the distance leading to an area filled with even more riches and treasures!"

He was about to walk in that direction with the company following him, but just at that moment, Glophi sprung out of nowhere, standing on the narrow stairs. "Welcome, my precious servants, to Huminli and I's caves of wonder!" he said, in a mood of jest. "Come and have a look at these wonderful treasures, and perhaps you can take some for yourselves in the journey."

Immediately afterward, Huminli came to his side. "Yes, welcome and welcome!" he happily said. "We will not hinder you from sharing in these magnificent treasures and riches! So what are you all waiting for? Come here and allow your eyes to feast on these spectacular sights!"

The company laughed out of relief and joy that they had finally found the smalves. They felt as though a heavy burden on them had been slowly lifted off their shoulders, and a warming sensation of delight filled their hearts.

"How did you two manage to make it here through the dark passage?" asked Steven. "We were quite worried for your safety and we were even more fearful when we had to suffer through that passage, not knowing if you would have been able to endure that dark and evil road."

"Ah, my good servants," said Glophi, still in a joking mood. "Glophi and I over here are masters of these caves, and no passage of darkness would be able to stop us from rightfully dwelling in these caves as its rightful lords. And besides, we knew that you would eventually find the passage and discover us here."

The company shook their heads in amazement at how relaxed and untroubled the smalves seemed to be, but Erundil remained frustrated by their attitude. "You troublemakers," he muttered while grumbling to himself. "We were really worried for you two, and here you are enjoying yourselves and acting as though the passage you went through wasn't difficult in any way. You should be grateful that we were so determined to find you, as you two would have been stuck here for who knows how long. You are very lucky and you shouldn't be acting as careless as you are now."

"They're only joking around," said Peter, trying to lighten the mood. "And besides, we all should be grateful that we are here together in these caves, safe from any present danger we could have encountered. But what is this place anyway? I have never seen an area with so much gold, gems, and other materials and treasures before."

Everyone stood silently for some time, soaking in the richness of the cave and wondering how and why the place was so opulent. Yet none of them knew how this was the case, none except for the gamdars.

"I know what this place is now," remarked Mataput, placing his hand on his chin while examining the cave. "I was at first not familiar with this place, but after seeing the many treasures and rich materials that fill this place, I now know where we are standing. These are the caves of Omron Rahndu, which means, '*The Place of Sparkling Rain*,' and it is here where the melondairs stored many of their precious gems, materials, and treasures, much of which was given as a reward for their efforts during the days of the Great Sea War by the Dark Lord himself. If you remember, Orieant stated that the melondairs wanted to build a magnificent kingdom within these vast caves, and so they filled this area along with others with many stores of riches. They took great pride in these caves and they were the ones who named them Omron Rahndu, for they believed that everything including the waterfalls within these caverns could glisten and sparkle with brilliance if they set their heart to do it. They very nearly achieved this goal, as they mined and built many things here with their materials that helped make nearly everything from the waterfalls and ponds, to the rock structures and walls glitter with bright lights. But before they could fill these halls with their ultimate dream of what it should look like, they soon perished from the bitter weather of these mountains, with the freezing wind and piles of snow finding a way inside here and trapping them to their deaths."

The company listened in fascination to Mataput, and walking through the cave and observing the many treasures and riches they could see, they couldn't help but smile in amazement. Endless supplies of gold, precious gems, and diamonds shimmered throughout the cave, with its beauty appearing even more spectacular by the glittering lights that seemed to shine in every direction. Most interested in what they saw were Huminli and Glophi who couldn't resist the urge to pick up and hold many items that piqued their curiosity.

The company quietly went about their business by gazing at everything they could, but while they were all gathered in the same place Steven went off into a section of the cave where many old manuscripts written in strange letters of some distant tongue were gathered together in great piles. He stared in fascination at these many manuscripts and wondered what the writings meant. But one such manuscript caught his eye above all the others, for as he flipped through the pages of this one many images of eliants riding on tall ships across the sea covered each page. But in the middle of one of the ships, he looked closer as he was engrossed in the image of a strange and large creature.

Staring at the creature he could see that its appearance was that of a sea turtle, though it was no ordinary turtle as its gigantic size made all of the giant eliants seem like grasshoppers as compared to it. Its mouth was open with what seemed to be sharp fangs on the corners of its teeth, and growing from the top of its large shell was a long tail whose end seemed to have some sort of sharp stinger. Its particularly long neck frightened Steven, but what bewildered him was that as he picked up the manuscript and allowed the light to reflect through the book, the whole body of the turtle seemed to be covered in a rainbow of colors.

Steven placed the manuscript down, standing silently to himself in both perplexion and fascination at what he had just seen. Then seeing the company walking around and observing the many other items that filled the cave, he called them to see what he had just witnessed himself.

"You all should come over here!" he shouted, calling the company over. "There's an image of a strange and particularly large turtle with a group of eliants on a ship, and I don't know what to think of it! Maybe Mataput or Orieant can explain what it means."

He picked up the manuscript again, staring at the image of the sea turtle with a puzzled expression on his face. Meanwhile, the company came over to Steven with Huminli and Glophi dashing their way to him as they were greatly intrigued by what he described. As they all came to Steven, he showed them the image on the page of the ancient manuscript, and as they stared at the image of the turtle their eyes widened in bafflement.

Not only were they filled with curiosity at the strange drawing of the turtle, but its gigantic size made some of them slightly frightened. They wondered who the creature was, and turning to Mataput and Orieant they awaited to see if the volviers would provide them with an answer. But to their shock, as they looked at the volviers they noticed that a nervous expression covered both of their faces, and they seemed to be even more fearful than the rest of the company was. Orieant motioned for Steven to hand the manuscript over, and once he took a close-up look at the giant turtle, his mouth seemed to open ever so slightly.

The company was bewildered by seeing how worried the volviers seemed to be, and Steven brought the matter up. "Is everything fine with you two?" he asked. "Why are you more frightened by this turtle than the rest of us are?"

Orieant muttered a few inaudible words to himself before speaking clearly. "Seeing this image I have been reminded that this cave is dangerous," he said. "We have to get away as far as we can from this place. It's not safe for us to be here right now."

The company was left even more confused by this, and they laughed as they saw Mataput nod his head in agreement with Orieant.

"Why exactly do we have to escape from this place?" asked Huminli. "Just a moment ago we were all enjoying ourselves just by looking at the many treasures of this cave, but now it is a perilous place somehow. And it seems as though you two only became worried once you saw this image of this weird turtle."

Orieant sighed to himself. "You are right, Huminli," he confessed. "Once I saw the image of this sea turtle, a sudden chilling sensation of fear came to my heart, and the reason for that is because Mataput and I are certain that we know who this creature truly is. This turtle is no ordinary turtle, for if I am not mistaken this turtle is the same one who caused much havoc and destruction during the Great Sea War. She was a mighty beast used by the melondairs and with her enormous size and venomous sting, she struck great fear in the hearts of every gamdar. And she was so adored by the melondairs during the time that she fought for them that they named her Kolmaug, which in their tongue means, '*The Master Sea Warrior*.' She was hailed as a mighty hero among the melondairs and if it wasn't for her presence during that war, they would have had a much more difficult time in battling the gamdars."

The company stared intently at Orieant, and some of them felt a cold shudder run through their bones as they listened to him. "Where did she come from?" asked Glophi, while the rest of the company stared in silence at the image of Kolmaug in the manuscript. "And why is she so gigantic and abnormal in her appearance?"

"None know for certain where she came from," responded Orieant.

"But the first time that she appeared within this world was soon after the end of the War of Great Alliances. For many years she spent her time hiding in the land of the Dark Lord before he sent her to the land of Canlodar to aid the eliants in the Great Sea War. It is not known whether she was always so large or if the Dark Lord had turned her into such an enormous beast, but what is known is that during the time she dwelt in the land of Nangorid, she was personally trained by the enemy to bring much damage against the gamdars. Not only was she a terrific swimmer who could overthrow ships under the sea, but she was also incredibly dangerous as she could fight on land, and had a venomous stinger on her shell that would be used to strike and instantly kill many gamdars if they came into contact with her."

The company grew uneasy as they listened to Orieant and even Peter started shaking in fright. "What happened to her after the war?" he asked, still staring at Orieant with widened and alarmed eyes.

"She must have perished long ago," remarked Orieant. "Because ever since the melondairs came to these mountains, Kolmaug has vanished from all sight. She either perished in the sea during the days of the Great Sea War or even in these caves when the bitter weather of Lehu Shalank inflicted death on every single eliant who dwelled in these halls. But it has also been said among the eliants and even some wuzlirs that her spirit still lives on, supposedly hiding and roaming around to seek an opportunity to return to life as a ghost."

Chills went down the spines of the company as they heard this, and some of their faces turned pale as they listened to the mere mention of a ghost. Yet many questions still arose in their minds about Kolmaug, and the one who doubted this tale the most was Erundil, who was confused as to how her spirit still endured even after death.

"But how can these things be?" he asked with a slight chuckle. "Has it not been said by many of my people's loremasters and wise figures that the spirits of the dead roam their graves to provide comfort with the rest of the dead? How then can someone resurrect from the dead and dwell among the living? Even Ulohendel recorded in many of his books and poems preserved in our Great Hall of Poems that one can't be raised from the dead."

"I hear you, Erundil," said Mataput, wishing to provide his insight.

"But if I may enlighten you, I think it is important for you to know that even Ulohendel didn't perfectly know all things. There are many secret things that even the wisest figures in the history of this world have not been able to comprehend. These strange matters belong only to Jangart, and even he has not been willing to share them with Orieant and me, believing that it is only appropriate for himself to know. But there is a day coming when Jangart will reveal the hidden revelations that only he knows, and when those things are made manifest for all to plainly see, then we will understand his will and purpose to a more completed end."

"I hear what you are saying," replied Erundil. "And I understand that there are certain things that only Jangart himself rightfully knows. But I am still having a difficult time piecing these matters together, as only recently have I learned that many strange things exist and function in this world."

"That is true," said Mataput. "And even Orieant and I can hardly fathom many of the things that have been revealed to us, and I can only imagine how I would react in the day when all things will be made manifest for all creation to know. But strange things do move and breathe in this world, and though you may be only learning them for the first time, that does not make them any less true than they are. For the truth is sometimes harder to believe than a lie, but we must be willing to believe in it, or else we will be heavily disappointed if we fall prey to either disbelief or deception."

"All I can do is trust that you and Orieant will never lie to any of us," said Erundil. "I will still have a hard time believing in these many strange things, but perhaps it is not too strange for you and Orieant, as you two have seen far more odd things."

The company continued staring at the image of Kolmaug with many questions still running through their minds, and they were especially intrigued at the possibility of her spirit still finding a way to endure and dwell among the living. But as they thought about this their attention was brought back to the location where they found themselves standing, and they didn't grow tired of how vast and impressive the riches, gems, and materials of the cave were. They wondered if the melondairs had gathered all of the precious gemstones of the world in these caves, and a rush of excitement filled their hearts as they allowed their eyes to take in all they could. So thrilled were Huminli and Glophi that they ran toward the riches and dived into the cups, rings, jewels, diamonds, and other precious materials there were. Peter followed them as he too also dived into the endless materials, being unable to contain himself from enjoying the moment.

The three of them laughed and played joyfully together, swimming through the many materials and jewels, and playfully throwing the many cups, rings, and diamonds in the air. The rest of the company could only shake their heads with smiles on their faces, with Steven's smile being the broadest. Seeing how happy he was, Peter called out to Steven to join him and the smalves in having fun.

"Come over here, Steven!" he said, calling out to him. "This is so incredible and you don't want to miss out on any of the action!"

"No, no, Peter," responded Steven, preferring to watch Peter and the smalves have fun. "I am too old to participate in these childish games, but go ahead and continue to enjoy yourself with Huminli and Glophi."

"Oh come on Steven," said Peter, with a disappointed expression on his face. "I know that this quest is extremely serious and that we will have difficult times, but this is the one time when you will be able to have some fun. Why would you want to let this moment come and go? You better come over here before Huminli, Glophi, and I will have to drag you over here."

Steven chuckled to himself still refusing to move an inch, but seeing the way that Peter was staring at him, he could sense that at any moment the boy would force him to join him along with the smalves. Even Huminli and Glophi stopped messing around with the treasures and items of riches, eagerly awaiting Steven to join them in the fun. The rest of the company even nodded their heads in agreement with Peter when Steven turned toward them, urging the man on to spend some time truly laughing and relaxing his body. And so shaking his head with a broad smile covering his face, Steven walked in the direction where Peter, Huminli, and Glophi were, and before he knew it Peter came over to him and tugging at his shirt, he cheerfully pushed him into the stacks of treasures.

After being pushed into the treasures, Steven expected Peter to help him up, but to his amazement, the young boy started wrestling with him, and even the smalves joined in the playfulness as well. The four of them burst out in laughter and a great joyful light covered Steven's face, with this experience bringing back fond memories of his days growing up in the village of Frosh when he wrestled and played fun games with his siblings. Eventually, the four of them grew tired and stopped playing, being exhausted from all their wrestling and desiring just a sip of water.

"Ah, now that was unexpectedly fun," said Steven, while lying on the piles of treasures with a broad smile on his satisfied face. "You were right, Peter, in saying that I was missing out on some fun. I'm glad that you forced me over here so that I could enjoy this time."

"Well I'm usually right when I tell you to trust me, Steven," responded Peter with a laugh. "But seriously, I knew that you would have a great time playing with Huminli, Glophi, and I, as we didn't want to let this fun time just pass us by. Now in the meantime, I could really use them water to quench my dry throat."

The four of them stood up from where they were lying down and walking over into the distance they brought their attention to the waterfall that poured down huge streams of water into the large pond. Coming to the brink of the pond, they buried their faces in the water, chugging down as much liquid as they could while also washing their sweaty faces. They were pleasantly surprised by how fresh the water was, and they took out their bottles to fill them with more water for when they journeyed on.

Having drunk enough water Peter burped and wiped off the drops on his face. "Ah, that was nice and fresh water," he said. "A delightful filling of water is just what I needed to quench my dry thirst."

"Same here," said Glophi. "We smalves love freshwater, sometimes just as much as our food. But even despite how satisfying this water is, nothing beats our healing soup as it not only heals those that are sick, but it's also a pleasantly delicious meal for anyone to enjoy."

"But all we need for now is this freshwater," remarked Huminli, as he buried his face in the pond and continued drinking more water. "A fresh and endless supply of water is just fine with me right now. But let's make sure that none of us drink this entire pond before everyone else can fill their bottles with more water."

They continued talking and laughing with each other, with Huminli and Glophi sharing funny stories that made Steven and Peter laugh uncontrollably. The rest of the company could see them from a far distance and smiles were on their faces as they were glad to see how joyful the four of them were, especially Steven. Meanwhile, Steven, Peter, and the smalves didn't notice the volviers and gamdars looking on at them, but once they met their gaze, the four of them agreed to go back and meet up with the rest of the company."

They started walking in the direction where the volviers and gamdars were, but as they were making their way there, Huminli suddenly stopped dead in his tracks. Staring at the ground, his eyes were drawn to a strange object that he couldn't help but resist picking up and grasping into his hand.

"What are you holding, Huminli?" asked Glophi, upon noticing his brother holding the object. "I want to see what it looks like."

Steven and Peter also urged Huminli to show them what he was holding, and so uncovering his clenched fist, Huminli showed the three of them what he had.

In his hand was a small golden cup with a golden saucer covering it, and for some strange reason all four of them found that they were instantly enthralled by the sight of it, as this was no cup they had ever seen before. It had a unique shape to it, as it was molded in almost the form of an ear, with a tiny handle on its right side. As Huminli turned the cup around, they observed that there was a clear and strange type of writing on it, with the writing being blue and filled with bizarre and interlacing characters that they had never seen before. The writing seemed to be of some distant tongue spoken of in the ancient past, possibly that of the eliants they assumed.

They stared at the golden cup and the writing on it for several minutes, filled with wonder at what all of it could possibly mean. They were especially surprised by how different this writing seemed to be than the writing that was covered on the walls and written in the manuscripts. They wondered if this was indeed a creation of the eliants, or if it belonged to an entirely different kind of creature.

"What is this?" asked Huminli, holding the cup aloft his head to see the writing even more clearly in the bright light. "What type of creature could this strange writing system belong to?"

"I don't know," responded Steven, closely staring at the cup as many questions lingered through his mind. "But perhaps Mataput and Orieant know, as they have shown us just how much they know about these things."

"That's a good point," said Huminli. "Let's go to them then and ask if they know what this writing on this cup could mean."

The four of them slowly made their way back to the volviers and gamdars, with their eyes still drawn to the unique golden as they walked. They quietly discussed among themselves what they thought the writing meant, but they knew that their guesses were far more accurate. But they continued spewing theories to one another which only further confused them. Eventually, they made their way to the volviers and gamdars who all had smiles on their faces. But as Mataput and Orieant saw the golden cup which Huminli held in his hand, their happy looks were immediately turned to concern.

"We found this cup with a strange type of writing on it," said Huminli as he showed them the golden cup. "We don't know what it means and perhaps it's something trivial that we don't have to worry about, but we couldn't help but wonder what it could mean. So we have come here to bring it to you and we imagined that with both of your vast knowledge, you would also be able to uncover what the meaning behind this could be."

"Let me take a closer look at it," said Mataput, with a sense of uneasiness growing in his mind.

Huminli handed the cup to Mataput who closely examined every single spot of it, trying to see if he could find anything to explain what it meant. He held it tightly in his hand as though he were trying to feel the weight of the cup, and even Orieant came close to have a good look of the cup. The two of them focused their attention on the strange writing on the back of the golden cup, and they spent a long time pondering what it could mean. The company silently watched the volviers as they inspected the object, wondering what they would have to reveal to them. But for the time being, Mataput and Orieant's expressions remained unchanged as they continued staring and examining the object.

But then suddenly, Mataput's eyebrows rose to the top of his forehead, as though a wind of shock had just sparked his body. He raised his face to the sky and shook his head in disbelief and started mumbling inaudible words to himself. Everyone else stared at him in confusion, wondering what it was he had discovered.

And then, as though all had been made clear to him, Orieant's mouth dropped to the ground as he too was stunned by what he had seen. It seemed to the company that his face grew pale and he too began mumbling words to himself that were too quiet for the company to piece together what he could be saying. Puzzled expressions covered the company's faces, and some of them were growing concerned for the volviers as it seemed as though they were starting to lose their minds.

"What is going on?" asked Peter, with a troubled look on his face. "Is there a serious problem that explains why you two are so fearful?"

The volviers stopped mumbling words to themselves and casting their eyes away from the golden cup, they looked on at Peter and the rest of the company with wide eyes and pale faces.

"We cannot stay here," said Mataput, while breathing heavily. "I have seen that great memories of an evil stir within this golden cup. We have no choice but to escape from these caves now and make our way to safety."

Orieant agreed with Mataput and the two of them started urging the company to follow them and make haste away from the caves. But the company was bewildered by how fearful the volviers were, having almost never seen this sudden behavior come from them.

"Will you at least tell us what you saw?" asked Huminli. "Were you able to understand what was said about the writing on the cup?"

"There is no time for that," responded Orieant. "The more time we spend talking the more we put ourselves in danger. We must make our way away from these caves as quickly as we can, and that starts with going down the dark passage that we came from. The presence of harm is stirring in this place and if we are not careful, we will find ourselves trapped."

"I certainly don't want to be trapped, but I won't go on unless you tell me plainly what is going on," protested Huminli. "At least tell us what it was that you saw about this cup and then perhaps we will see why we must make haste."

While listening to Huminli, Erundil shook his head in annoyance and rose in defense of the volviers. "Have you not heard what Mataput and Orieant have said?" he frustratingly asked. "Evil has been awakened by your discovery of this golden cup, and even though you are innocent in trying to trap us in these caves, your finding has still brought a curse to us."

The company stood frozen for a moment, shocked by Erundil's harsh words. But before anyone could respond, Lelhond stood in defiance of his father to defend Huminli. "It is not the smalf's fault if we face danger, father," he said. "And he makes a good point as well. If we are going to hurriedly escape from this place not knowing where our next destination will be, then we should at least know the true gravity of the situation we are facing. Why should we remain unaware of what this presence of evil truly is that we want to flee from?"

The company remained silent, agreeing with Lelhond and looking on at Mataput and Orieant with hopeful eyes that the volviers would fully explain themselves to the company. The volviers sighed to themselves, but nonetheless, they eventually gave in to the company's plea for a full explanation.

"Very well then, I will tell you what Mataput and I have seen," said Orieant. "But understand that once I explain this to you, we must be on our way as the precious time of safety is ticking away from our grasp. But the letters you saw on this cup are of a secret ancient language that was likely invented by one of the leaders of the melondairs in order for them to communicate with the wuzlirs. It is no longer spoken today as the eliants have lost all contact with the outside world, and the Dark Lord has forced the wuzlirs to utterly forget about the invented language as he has been burning with exasperation in the way that the eliants have not heeded his call for them to fight on his side. But regardless, because of the vast wisdom given to Mataput and me by Jangart in being able to interpret all kinds of languages and tongues, we were able to understand what was written on the back of this cup. I shall not utter these words as they were written in this ancient language, as I fear that a long and rested shadow of darkness may spring forth from wherever it's hiding.

But I will instead translate it for all of you to understand and in that way, we should remain safe as its words should not have a major effect on us."

The company gazed at Orieant with their whole attention, with many of them shaking in fear of the unexpected. Then speaking in a commanding voice, chilly shudders ran through the bones of the company as they listened to Orieant:

A place of comfort for the roaming spirit to rest,
In our caves of gold where we shall all die.
Deep in the darkness for her power to manifest,
A place of dominion for her soul to lie.

The place of riches to rouse her slumber,
Where she passes into the shadow with her lidless eye.
In the cup of gold with its cover,
A place of dominion for her soul to lie.

He paused for a moment, closing his eyes and sighing to himself before speaking again. "If what the melondairs wrote on this cup was true, then my worst fear has come to pass. For it is likely that Kolmaug herself, that giant sea turtle who fought loyally in battle after battle on their side during the Great Sea War, is still lurking in the shadows of these caves in the form of a ghost, and it might very well be that she finds herself stuck in this golden cup."

The company gasped in shock at this revelation, with a sharp stinging pain seeming to have struck their hearts. They shook their heads in disbelief, yet a sense of heavy fear covered their faces as a thick veil, knowing that what Orieant said had to be true. Many of them twitched and shuddered in terror, and Huminli nearly dropped the cup to the ground as he wondered if a giant sea turtle ghost would suddenly appear out of the object.

Yet doubt still consumed his heart. "But how can these things be?" he asked. "It is not natural for such a large ghost to be trapped in a small golden cup as this, so how can we believe in something that we have never seen before?"

"There are many things that you haven't seen or known, yet they have now been made manifest to you," responded Orieant. "This matter is the same case, and you cannot forget that when Mataput and I have reminded you that strange matters exist in the world, we have always told the truth regarding that. There are many things that all of you have discovered on this quest for the first time, so this should be no different. But enough with talking and debating, for if the writing on this golden cup proves to be true, then we risk being trapped in these caves by the ghost of Kolmaug. So we must not waste any more time and instead give us a headstart so that if peril comes to us, then we will be able to escape it."

Mataput agreed with Orieant, with an urgent desire to leave glowing on his face. "Yes, there is no more time to waste," he said. "Huminli, give me the cup you are holding and everyone else can follow Orieant and I."

Huminli stared at the cup for a moment, as though he was enthralled by it before he handed it over to Mataput. Immediately, Mataput grabbed the cup, and he with Orieant turned toward the narrow tunnel in their rush to escape and the company closely followed them from behind. They didn't dare to turn or look back, deciding that they would altogether forget about the gold, gems, diamonds, treasures, and other riches that their eyes had been dazzled by in the sparkling and rich light of the caves.

Now as the company neared the entrance of the tunnel, Mataput dropped the golden cup over to the side and ordered nobody else to touch it. Agreeing to this, the volviers entered the dark passage and led the company away from the caves of Omron Rahndu. The cup rolled a few times before eventually stopping without a scratch on it, or a hint of the saucer being opened, as it remained tightly attached to the cup. Breathing sighs of relief that they were finally leaving the cup behind, the company followed Mataput and Orieant, allowing their minds to be free from the worry of Kolmaug roaming in the object, all save for Huminli and Glophi.

For they were unwilling to let go of the overwhelming desire to look upon the golden cup and enjoy the riches of the caves which they had been the ones who had discovered and thus justly earned the right to spend more time in. And so they lingered behind, gazing with wide eyes at the object while everyone else heeded them not, as they were too bothered to even notice that the smalves had fallen behind. The smalves stood still for quite some time, being entranced by the bright golden light that reflected against the cup, and being unable to contain himself, Huminli found himself leaning over to pick up the cup, where he held it for a long time as he and his brother took a long stare at it.

A dominating temptation to just stay behind in the caves filled the hearts of the smalves as they longed gazed in a rush of thrilling excitement at the golden cup. And then, along with the desire to stay in the caves, a new urge as though a compelling voice was playing in their heads filled their minds, and that was to not only gaze at the golden cup, but to open the saucer which closed it. As though they had just discovered this new desire of theirs, their eyes widened in a rush of curiosity and their mouths began to droll as a luring enchantment took control of their entire beings as a vast shadow that they had been deceived into believing to be a shining light. This one desire to open the cup now took precedence in their thoughts, and nothing else seemed to matter to them in that instance.

And so they found themselves helplessly unable to stop their hands from acting on that desire. Huminli made the first move, moving his hand ever so slowly to the top of the saucer before he eventually smothered his hand over it with his fat and hairy hand. And then being urged by his brother Glophi to act on both of their wishes, he made his move and steadily began to remove the saucer from the golden cup.

But at that very moment, sensing as though a flash of lightning had struck them, Mataput and Orieant, being far ahead of where the smalves had lingered behind, suddenly turned around with enlarged eyes. As if a clear vision had just flashed before them, their entire bodies seemed to drop in tremendous astonishment which soon morphed into an overwhelming shock of horror. A sharp and terrible fear stung their hearts, so much so that Mataput cried aloud in alarm. The gamdars along with Steven and Peter immediately turned around in fright, wondering what terrible thing must have happened to have caused so much dread in the volviers. And as they turned around, to their own amazement it was as though a keen sense of sight had been magically placed on them, and seeing Huminli and Glophi holding the opened golden cup with broad smiles on their faces caused their hearts to be pierced to the very core.

Steven and Peter nearly collapsed to the ground in terror, while the gamdars cried out in desperation and started running back in that direction to urge the smalves with every bit of convincing screaming they could to immediately close the cup and leave it far behind.

"No! Shut the cup quickly!" they cried collectively, with Erundil shouting in the loudest voice above everyone else. They followed the volviers as they all ran in the opposite direction, determined to do whatever they could in their strength to stop the smalves from bringing terrible danger to them, even if it meant dropping every bit of energy they had remaining.

But it was too late. Even as they sprinted and made their way back to the entrance of the dark passage, the crushing desire of the smalves had proved too great with the damage already being done. Huminli had removed the saucer from the cup with his brother Glophi encouraging him by his side, and there was no escaping from what they had done. The company froze for a moment, with a tremendous feeling of disbelief gripping their hearts to the point that they had no strength to speak or even move. They were heavily disappointed by what the smalves had done, yet they found no energy to cry in grief, rather finding themselves standing as still statues with pale faces covered with horrified expressions.

While they stood frozen, surging darkness passed over the cave as a mighty breath of wind, and even in that area where the light had shone brightest and reflected the many precious materials and treasures that had fascinated the company, that heavy darkness spread to the beautiful lights of that cave and brought a heavy dimness that soon turned to pitch-black darkness.

The company still didn't move, but now they were trembling at what had just happened, and how things had turned terribly for the worst. But then, to their brief surprise and relief, a light came. For a moment, they almost wanted to smile at the appearance of the light, believing that it had once again defeated the darkness that seemed to have almost consumed them in that short instance. But very soon they realized that the light was not good. As they turned toward Huminli, their eyes widened with alarm as they realized what was coming out of the golden cup he held. Once the smalf saw this, he shrieked aloud in pure terror and dropped the cup to the ground, while he and everyone else found themselves unable to do anything but slowly move backward while cowering over in fear. The light was incredibly bright, but almost in a switch the light grew incredibly dim, and as it did, a figure began to form and appear in clear out of the cup.

There before them in the form of a bodiless ghost was a large figure, a gigantic beast in height, weight, and length, in what was the shape of a sea turtle. Though the beastly ghost didn't possess a tangible body, beneath the dimmed white light of its ghostly shape could be seen the reflection of a rainbow of colors was reflected all around its bodiless figure. Growing from its iron shell was a long and sharp tail, similar to the one that the company had seen in the image of Kolmaug in the ancient manuscript, yet far more large and terrifying than they could have ever imagined, especially considering how lethal the tip of its stinger seemed to be. As the beast hovered in the dark air, it remained still for some time, glaring at the company through its huge and piercing eyes. Then it suddenly collapsed to the ground, and once it did, it opened its mouth, revealing sharp and terrible fangs that grew on its teeth. As though this didn't have the required effect it wished it would have on the company, the beast suddenly let out an ear-piercing and earth-shaking roar, far louder and more terrifying than that of a mighty lion.

The company collapsed to the ground and covered their ears in dismay at the terrible roar of the beast. But bringing everyone to their feet, Mataput and Orieant shouted in such strong voices that the company had never heard coming out of their mouths before.

"Kolamug has been awakened!" they cried in unison. "Her ghost has been raised to life to torment us! We must flee from her!"

The volviers immediately made their way to the dark tunnel, while the company followed them from close behind in their escape through the passage. As they ran, many of them cried out in dismay, especially Erundil who was particularly frustrated with the smalves.

"The smalves have cursed us!" he cried in despair. "They have discovered these caves to only bring us here to curse and trap us! Oh, would it be that I could see their true intentions so that their wicked actions would be brought down on their heads and pain tenfold in full!"

"We are all going to die!" cried Steven, breathing heavily while he ran and having no strength to hold onto hope.

"We are not going to die," said Mataput, trying to calm the company down. "And neither have Huminli and Glophi purposely tried to trap us here as Erundil thinks. I will let none of you give up or blame others for this troubling situation we are now encountering. Take courage all of you and follow Orieant and me through this tunnel!"

Despite their immense fear, the company listened to Mataput and followed the volviers through the dark passage. But the tunnel remained pitch black, and they knew not in which direction they were running, except that they could faintly see the outline of the volviers in front of them. But Kolmaug remained just behind them, breathing a dark wind of malice from their back. She growled in brooding anger as she crawled her way slowly in the direction where the company was running.

The company had a slight advantage over the beast, and it seemed as though she was unable to run because of some heavy limp. But the company was not naive enough to take any chances, and they continued running as fast as they could through the heavy darkness of the passage so that they could reach the exit far ahead of the beast. A vast array of blackness hovered in the tense air, and the company started to seriously sweat from the hot and stuffy tunnel.

But then suddenly, far ahead of humans, gamdars, and smalves, two gleaming white lights shone in the darkness, and for a moment the eight of them covered their eyes from the light. But as they slowly opened their eyelids, they learned that the bright lights were the volviers themselves, whose entire bodies were glowing with a brilliant illumination of light. At this sight, Kolmaug seemed to stumble from behind the company, and let out almost a choking sound as if the terrible lights had struck her. But the beast soon recovered, and though she remained far behind the company, they could now see clearly that she would not give up on chasing them.

For a moment, the company couldn't help but gaze in amazement at the brilliant light that reflected from Mataput and Orieant. And seeing now that Kolmaug was far behind them now, they felt greatly relieved and took a moment to catch their breath and speak with each other.

Although all of them had relieved smiles on their faces, Erundil had a wrathful expression on his face as he brought his attention to Huminli and Glophi. "Why don't we leave the smalves behind?" he asked, with a growing shadow of anger coming on his face. "We shouldn't even be here, yet it was because of their own curiosity that this disaster has been brought upon us! Let them pay for what their actions deserve as I fear that more danger may come to us if we don't part ways with them."

The company gasped and shook their heads in great shock at what Erundil said, and they immediately opposed him with his son, Lelhond responding to him. "No, father, what you are saying is wrong," he said. "It would be cruel of us to leave the smalves behind just because of a mistake that they made. Who are we to decide to make such a choice to depart from them forever? The purpose of this company was for the ten of us to stick close by each other's side in every moment, and though this great danger has been brought to us, further and even more terrible things would befall us if we made such a foolish decision."

The angry expression still covered Erundil's face though he said nothing in response to his son. And before anyone could comment anything, Mataput quickly ordered the company to continue their escape through the passage.

"As long as this company is together, Huminli and Glophi will always be with us," he said. "But we have no time to waste, as Kolmaug is still behind us though she has taken a big tumble. But let's get on our way before further trouble comes to us!"

Immediately the company stopped speaking with one another, and springing to action they followed the light of the volviers and continued their escape through the tunnel. All of them ran through the narrow passage with all of the remaining burst of energy they contained, refusing to look back as the volviers continued urging them to look forward. But they grew increasingly worried as they could hear the silent grumblings of Kolmaug edging closer to them, with the sound of her crawling growing stronger in its intensity as she steadily preyed on them.

But the company refused to allow the beast to intimidate them, instead focusing on Mataput and Orieant while they led them, and taking great comfort in the hope that their light brought to them. Yet their hearts were also beating fast, and their legs even started trembling while they ran, as they could hear the music of Kolmaug slowly mounting on them. But the volviers were determined to not allow the beast to trouble the company, and desperately urged the company to trust in the two of them.

"Do not look back!" they would shout every once in a while. "Continue straight on for if you look behind, Kolmaug will only desire to trample us even more!"

The company heeded this warning, obeying Mataput and Orieant as they continued running as fast as they could, not daring to tempt the beast by turning around for even the slightest and quickest of glances. Yet they couldn't ignore the sound of her crawling shell growing ever so closer to them as they narrowly made their escape through that tunnel. It seemed that with each passing step, the beast could practically jump onto them, even though she was a lot farther back behind them than they felt. But a great presence of terror surrounded them as a cloud of darkness while they ran, though they refused to allow this to let them stop or even worse, give up. Mataput and Orieant continued leading them courageously and never stopped commanding the company to take courage and fear nothing. And seeing how bold the volviers were, the company refused to even allow the smallest hint of difficulty to make them disappoint the volviers in any way. They knew that they had to endure this trial for the prize on the other side would be their increased trust and confidence in each other. And so with all of these thoughts racing through their minds, a great morale boost came upon the company, and even as they ran smiles of resilience spread across their faces.

With swords in their hands, they adamantly refused to give up as they didn't stop running with all the strength they had. They went on for another mile through the narrow tunnel as the volviers continued encouraging them, though it seemed that hours were passing while Kolmaug chased them. But none of them wanted to allow this challenge to change their minds, and seeing how confident the volviers were, Peter followed their lead, and coming just behind them he also offered his words of encouragement for the rest of the company.

"Let us not give up!" he shouted, while continuing to look straight forward. "Never forget that we are the light that stands courageously amid the shadow of darkness, and this wicked beast following us shall surely not defeat us while we continue holding onto hope!"

At that moment, the words of Peter seemed to fill the company's hearts with a newfound burst of energy which made them run with even more pace and intensity. Their purpose of being a light in the darkness filled them with even more hope that they would escape in the end, no matter how much the beast would try to catch or even torment them. Their hearts were racing faster than they had ever felt in their whole lives, yet a deep pull of confidence filled their hearts and minds as they sprinted through that tunnel.

And as they ran it seemed to them that the sound of Kolmaug's crawling and quiet grumbling grew even more silent before its sound diminished so much that it grew incredibly faint to the point where they could barely even hear her. A dark shadow as it felt passed away from them, and all they could see was the light of the volviers ahead of them, and they knew that they were so close to reaching the end. Yet even in their relief, Mataput and Orieant reminded them that they had yet to reach their destination.

"Do not stop!" cried Mataput. "Let us not stop or look back in the false belief of victory! We still have work to do, and we can celebrate once we reach the end of this passage and shut this beast behind in the dark abyss!"

The company took Mataput's words to heart, hoping and believing that they would make it in the end and escape from Kolmaug's presence for good. They refused to take a rest until the beast ceased lurking behind them, yet they couldn't hide the excitement that covered their faces, as they knew that they were nearing the exit of the tunnel. Knowing this, the thought of collapsing to the ground and resting for a while consumed their thoughts, and they all started motivating each other with this realization, even as the remaining strength they had began to slowly wane.

"My sons, we are almost reaching the end of our long road!" said Erundil, trying to encourage his three sons even with his heavy breathing while he ran. "We are almost there my dear boys and we will soon be able to proclaim with boldness that we escaped from the clutches of Kolmaug and trapped that ghostly beast in these cursed caves!"

"Yes father!" responded Lelhond, with his spirits being lifted by his father's words. "Let us not give up now for we have come too far for us not to celebrate escaping this challenge!"

They continued on for some more time, fending off each other's words of encouragement that were spread around. Coming to a sudden sharp right turn they followed the light of the volviers, maneuvering their way through the tight space and continued running. By now they had been running for what felt like almost an hour of time, yet their encouraging words seemed to breathe fresh life into their bodies.

Yet as time passed, they started to feel the effects of the endless running on their bodies. Their feet began to ache in soreness, and endless drips of sweat came pouring down their faces and covering every part of their bodies. Stuck in the narrow space of the tunnel, the air grew muffled and by now they were struggling and gasping for air as they ran. Their hearts were beating even more rapidly now. They couldn't deny that they were now exhausted, and as the constant running started to take a tear from their bodies, they all grew completely silent. But they refused to acknowledge how tired they were to each other nor did they want to even show it in the slightest way. Lingering at the very back of the company were Huminli and Glophi who though being particularly filled with fatigue, still refused to give up, as they didn't want to bring any more harm to the company.

But as anyone fought the mental and physical battle that came crashing at them as a brick of walls, Steven was the one who started to falter. Not only was he physically exhausted, but his mind was filled with discouraging thoughts. Every time and again he began stumbling over as his legs started shaking, causing him to run far slower which caused him to drift just behind the smalves. He couldn't help but ponder thoughts of giving up or at least taking a brief rest, and though he quickly brushed these thoughts aside, he couldn't resist them as they grew stronger inside of his head. But he also thought of how disappointed the company would be in seeing him do this, especially Peter who continued to motivate him. Yet the temptation to just fall down and take a rest was too strong for him, and he couldn't take it anymore. He had to stop running.

And so he suddenly came to a sharp stop and threw his body onto the ground, lying flat on his back and breathing deep breaths both to circulate air in his body and to release the relief he wanted to. He had no strength left in his body to say anything, and for a few seconds, he just lay there, almost like a dead man with no one realizing what had just happened. But immediately after, Huminli and Glophi noticed what had happened, and turning around their eyes widened with horror as they saw Steven lying on the ground. They were beyond shocked and they cried out to the rest of the company for them to stop and help Steven.

"Mataput! Orieant! Steven has collapsed!" cried Glophi. "He has fallen to the ground and is breathing heavily! He needs our help!"

He and Huminli continued crying out in desperation for the company to stop and turn around, and hearing what the two of them said, Peter was the first one to turn around and dash toward Steven and the smalves. Following suit, Mataput and Orieant with deep sighs turned around and came to Steven, with Erundil and his sons closely following the volviers from behind.

Coming to Steven, Mataput placed his hand on Steven's exhausted face. "He is fine, but his face is cold," he said, with Peter immediately breathing a sigh of relief. "But we cannot let him lie here. Though I cannot see her, I sense that Kolmaug will come upon us at any moment. So we must pick him up and continue on."

Mataput slowly raised Steven's body from the ground and as he placed him steadily on the ground while Steven's legs staggered and trembled, he was surprised to see that Steven was eventually able to stand firm with his own strength. The company was greatly encouraged to see this, but they knew that they had no more time to waste.

"It is good to see that Steven is doing well, but now we must carry on," said Orieant, as he urged the company to follow him and Mataput through the passage.

But for some reason Steven stood silently for a while, staring ahead into the distance with no strength left in his body to continue. Standing as a statue he didn't move an inch, even as Peter shook him and tried motivating him to follow Mataput and Orieant, saying that they were almost at the end of the tunnel.

"Come on, Steven!" he cried, shaking his arm though Steven made no response to him. "We are almost there, Steven, and in just a little while longer we will be able to take a rest. But that time is not yet, so please don't give up now just before the end!"

But no matter how hard the boy tried to convince Steven to continue on, the weary man remained unflinching in his desire to rest at that moment. He stood frozen as though he were paralyzed with fear and weakness, and turning around, Mataput and Orieant were greatly disappointed to see Steven standing still. For the two of them deeply believed that Steven had enough remaining strength to muster one last push of energy to run down the passage as they neared the end of the tunnel. And so they along with everyone pleaded with Steven to continue, but no amount of desperate cries of theirs would have any effect on Steven.

So with no choice left, Mataput and Orieant turned around and tried to force Steven forward, tugging at his shirt and trying to pull him along the passage. But with the strength left in his body, Steven managed to resist them. In response, the volviers tried to pick him up and carry him across the tunnel, but with desperation, Steven evaded their grasp even as they tried to tightly hold him.

Managing to escape from the volviers, Steven fell facedown to the ground and lay there flat on his stomach for some time. When Mataput and Orieant tried to pick Steven up again, he again escaped from them, wildly flapping his arms and even starting to run backward in the direction from where they came. The company looked on in horror at the sight of Steven running away from them, and tears streamed down Peter's face as he desperately ran on to try and catch his friend. And finally, though Steven ran with all the speed he possessed, Peter managed to outpace him, and grabbing onto his shirt he stopped his friend dead in his tracks.

The two of them collapsed to the ground, with the rest of the company catching up to them. Steven finally gave up once his friend had caught up to him, deciding that he had gone too far and that it was in the company's best interests that he trudged along to the end of the tunnel. The company was beyond glad to see Steven not trying to resist them anymore, but Mataput and Orieant still grabbed ahold of him and dragged him forward, with huge expressions of disappointment covering their faces. Seeing this, Steven deeply regretted his foolish actions and wasted no time in being honest with them.

"I heavily grieved but what I have done, and I would like to apologize for what I have done," he said to the volviers, not daring to look at them in the eyes. "I was foolish to run away from you, and I hope I have not brought any more danger to all of us."

"I am afraid that the damage has already been done, Steven," responded Orieant, looking at Steven with slight irritation. But even as he looked at the helpless man, a rush of pity sprung in his heart and his hard face softened. "But I do not want you to let this weigh heavily on your mind, Steven," he continued. "You are forgiven, and though you are foolish for what you have chosen to do, I am glad that you have wholeheartedly acknowledged your error. But now let us put the past behind us and focus on what is ahead of us, which is making our way to the end of this passage."

"Yes, it is good for us to focus on reaching that goal," agreed Steven. "And I promise you that I will run as fast as I can until I reach the very end of this passage."

"Are you sure, Steven?" asked Orieant. "I do not doubt your resolve, but if you need help we will be willing to carry you if you are too exhausted to continue walking or running."

"I am sure," responded Steven, turning toward Peter, whose face seemed to shine with gladness over what Steven said. "And I promise you that I will do everything I can to not give up again and make the same mistake again. And even if I am too tired to continue, I will not attempt to abandon you as I did, and will instead fight and endure until the very end."

"Very well then," said Orieant with a bright smile on his face. "I will not hinder Mr. Loubre from doing as he wishes. If he promises to be strong enough to continue, then who am I to reject that or doubt his promise? Let us go on then for our course is almost complete."

Seeing the change that came over Steven, the company sensed a fresh refilling of energy filling their very own bones, as though Steven's strength to overcome his weakness had been spread to them. They were greatly pleased and encouraged to see how bold he was, and they all patted him on the back, with Peter giving his good friend a long and warm hug. Turning to what lay ahead of them, they soaked in the bright lights of the volviers, allowing the truth of their words to fill them with hope knowing that they were the lights of the world, who with enough bravery could overcome any darkness they faces. And so once again they prepared to set out again through the tunnel, determining to reach the other side of their hopes.

Yet with even all the motivation they had gained, they all came to a sharp stop once the sudden realization of what was behind them was made clear once again. A vibrating roar resonated throughout the walls around the tunnel, and covering their ears they were that the presence of danger had discovered them again. And if that wasn't worse enough, they could hear the slow sound of a beast crawling toward them, seeming to be a mere meters away from them. They all froze and slowly turned around, constantly blinking their eyes to see what would appear from the shadows before them.

And what they saw made them nearly collapse to the ground in the shock of what was before them. Kolmaug had finally come. That terrible beast with her piercing eyes that seemed to flare up with sparks of fire within them, had come back with a vengeance, viciously roaring in the company's presence and flashing her deadly sharp fangs. The company was devastated that she had caught up to them, and they were taken off guard as they had completely forgotten about her in the time that passed. As they stood face to face with the beastly ghost, she seemed to be smiling at them, as though she were glad to finally have the chance to destroy them all for good. She started to wildly swing the tail on her shell in the air, sparking great fear in the company as they knew not how deadly that singer was. They stumbled back, beyond aghast to see the gigantic and terrible presence of Kolmaug before them in all her fury and strength.

Once they stood on their feet, none of them moved an inch with what felt like an electric shock running through their bodies, making them utterly helpless and paralyzed in front of Kolmaug. But then suddenly, Huminli and Glophi being unable to take in the fear anymore, cried out in dismay and nearly collapsed to the ground. But Mataput and Orieant immediately held them up and urged them to remain strong.

"Hold your ground!" said Mataput. "The time for us to battle this beast has come upon us, so draw your weapons, be brave, and strike her if we have to!"

Mataput and Orieant drew out their swords, tall and sharp ones that glimmered brightly as the light reflected from them. They held their weapons tightly in their hands and held them outstretched toward Kolmaug, as a warning of how sharp its tip was. For a moment, Kolmaug didn't move, and the company wondered if fear had been struck in her cold heart. But then she snapped out of her shock and issued forth a thunderous roar that resonated through the company's ears as a loud trumpet. Their legs trembled in terrible fear at the might of Kolmaug now made manifest to them, but following the lead of the volviers they too drew out the swords from their backpacks, and some of them even threatened to strike Kolmaug.

"We are not afraid to strike you!" cried out Peter. "If you dare to attack us, then you better be prepared for us to attack you even harder!"

In response to this, Kolmaug let out a blaring roar, one so loud that the ground even started shaking. It even seemed as though she was leaving even in the midst of her anger, and seeing how unconcerned the beast was by their words the company couldn't help but tremble in fear as they stood in front of her.

But they refused to give up, and following Peter's lead, Lelhond too wished to send a message to the beast. "We are not afraid of you!" he cried, staring at Kolmaug with an unrelenting resolve to stand with courage. "Your laughs and roars have no power over us for we are the ones who are the light standing in the presence of darkness, and we are the ones who hold the authority over you, you cursed beast of shadow! Come here and we will strike you so hard that you will have no choice but to go back to the darkness from whence you came!"

With Lelhond's last words, Kolmaug suddenly sprung into the air, with such terrible wrath that hot smoke came from her nostrils. Her gigantic figure covered the whole tunnel in a vast cloud of heavy darkness, and for a moment it seemed as though the lights of the volviers had been eradicated by the darkness. Terrible and mighty was she in that instance, with her sharp fangs and hateful eyes striking unimaginable terror in the hearts of the company. She made her first move, with the desire to destroy them all with one strike.

But the company was not going to go out without a fight, and they narrowly managed to escape her spring by brushing themselves to the side. Crashing to the flat ground, Kolmaug's tremendous weight vibrated through the air with a loud boom. And for that short moment that she lay on the ground, light returned to the tunnel, for the volviers stood on their feet having evaded the darkness.

But Kolmaug just as quickly came to her feet, and being uncharacteristically annoyed she let out a ferocious roar of vexation, and came rushing toward the company at terrible speed. As she came to them, she held out her large flippers with what appeared to be curling claws growing along their edges. The company held its breath, holding onto its weapons as they closed their eyes and hoped for the best.

And then suddenly, to their great amazement, Mataput and Orieant as flashes of lightning sprung out of nowhere and with great strength managed to stab Kolmaug's side with their swords as the beast mounted upon the company. Immediately upon being stabbed by their sharp swords, the beast let out a hideous scream of heavy pain and fell backward, rolling over the ground with her massive weight. Yet even in her pain, she managed to come to her feet again, and with steaming wrathful eyes she slowly made her way to the company once more.

Though she crawled towards the company, the enraged look on her face could not be hidden as the company, though holding their weapons, stood terrified and knew not what to do if she attacked them again. The beast's eyes were fixed on them all, but as she came closer to them, the company soon realized that her attention had been moved to Steven, as her face was glowering directly at him. Crawling toward the weak man, she panted heavily in his direction, while Steven couldn't help but embrace the horrible rush of terror that filled his body. He felt like collapsing to the ground and conceding to the wrath of the beast, and he started fidgeting with his sword while his heart raced and knees uncontrollably shook.

But Peter, upon seeing the terror that was in Steven's eyes while Kolmaug prepared her attack on his friend, stepped forward in front of Steven. Pointing his sword toward the beast, he spoke in a commanding voice at her.

"Don't you dare touch him!" he said, staring at Kolmaug with a fire in his eyes. "For if you don't take me seriously you will face the wrath of Peter! But I wouldn't mind if you were to experience my wrath, for it would be rightfully deserved. So come here, you cursed beast, and see what light looks like in darkness."

Kolmaug gave out a hideous grunt as she couldn't dare listen to Peter, and coals of fire grew in her bulging eyes. Peter gulped in fear of her, yet still held his sword in his hand, and immediately after he once again threatened her and even started mocking her to her very face. Mataput and Orieant urged him to keep silent and not rouse Kolmaug to anger anymore, yet he refused to listen to them and only continued making the beast angrier with each passing second.

Eventually, however, Peter took the volviers' advice and ceased mocking Kolmaug and instead opted to glare at her, while she too glared at him. The two of them stood face to face for some time, staring at each other as Kolamug's domineering presence cast a shadow of darkness over Peter. Yet even with her terrifying appearance and glaring eyes, Peter stood as still as a statue as he held out his sword toward her, with the beast not moving either. The rest of the company held their ground, not wishing for Kolmaug to bring her attention to them, but also being ready to defend Peter if she made her move.

But once again, annoyed by the silence of the beast, Peter laughed once more and continued to mock Kolmaug. "Ah, I see now," he said, throwing his hands in the air. "The old beast has no courage and is only one of big talk, but no action. Come here then if you are willing to make the first move, only for me to chop your head off!"

Immediately, Mataput stepped forward and stood next to Peter. "Peter, you must stop with all the talking and mocking," he whispered. "It is not wise to threaten this beast, as she is capable of doing terrible things that would leave lasting scars on this company. So instead of taunting her, let us hold our ground, stand side by side, and wait for what she does."

"But what if she overwhelms when she makes her move?" asked Peter in response. "What power will we have then to stand our ground? Why should we wait for her to attack and hurt us?"

"If we stand our ground, I promise you that we will be able to attack her back," responded Mataput. "But we must be careful not to poke this beast any more than we have already done. If she attacks us, then we will attack her even stronger, so do not worry Peter, for there are ten of us who are ready and armed with weapons."

Peter sighed to himself but gave up trying to argue with the volvier. "You are right," he said. "Who am I to know any better than you? I will not taunt this beast anymore for the safety of this company."

With one last glare at the beast, he chuckled silently to himself and backed away from her presence. Mataput too turned his back on Kolmaug and made his way back to the rest of the company who stood a good distance from the beast. But as they all turned their backs away, they had completely forgotten that one man was now left vulnerable in the hands of the beast, one whom Peter had initially tried to protect.

Steven was left alone by himself, with all his attention of him having been completely lost while the company had been focused on Kolmaug. He stood now as a helpless and weak man in the presence of this ancient and mighty beast of many tales, not knowing what his next move would be. And seizing her opportunity, Kolmaug let out a great guttural roar at Steven, and filled with the anger of Peter's taunting words just a moment ago she came mounting towards Steven at a terrible speed, with her presence casting a large shadow over him.

Immediately, the company was made aware of their horrible mistake, and turning around their first instinct was to run to try and save Steven. But seeing how far they were from him, they knew that it was too late as their speed would be no match for the beast. None of them knew what to do, and even the volviers stood frozen, wondering how Steven would be saved. But coming to Steven's rescue were Erundil, Lelhond, and Karandil, who doing what they felt was their only choice pulled out the bows and arrows they had packed in their backpacks and started firing them at the beast.

They managed to pierce Kolmaug's side with their arrows, but with all her momentum the beast had managed to wrap her great tail between Steven's chest and neck. Steven rolled over to the side, avoiding the full weight of the beast crashing upon him. Letting out a horrifying cry of pain, Kolmaug recoiled back and fumbling over her face was punched to the ground, with her whole body lying flat there as one who is dead. With no sign of movement in the beast, the company celebrated for joy that a heavy blow had been inflicted on her.

But even as the beast lay on the ground non-motionless, Steven was gasping for air, and holding onto the right side of his chest, the company could see that he was in great pain. Seeing this their eyes widened with shock and they rushed to help him.

Peter was the first to come to Steven, and he held his friend's hand tightly. "Are you all right, Steven?" he asked, panting with fear as he couldn't bear to see Steven so badly hurt.

Steven didn't answer and instead looked into Peter's eyes with a great cloud of gloominess swelling in his eyes. His face was as still as a statue, and noticing this, Peter's eyes started to water and he held onto his friend's hand even more tightly.

"Steven, what's going on?" he exclaimed, with his voice shaking with desperation. "Why aren't you speaking to me? You feel so weak and you are not moving either!" He turned to the rest of the company. "Will one of you help Steven? Can you not see that he is not doing well and is clutching onto his chest?"

Orieant crouched down to take a look at Steven, placing his hand on the spot where he was holding onto his chest. After examining him for some time, a bolt of lightning as it felt had struck his body, and he started shaking his head in disbelief as his eyes were covered in horror. The company was confused as to what was going on, and concern festered among them.

"What is the matter?" asked Peter, looking on at Orieant with great worry. "What terrible thing have you discovered?"

Orieant sighed to himself, and the company could see a single tear that streamed down his right eye onto his cheek. "Steven has been stabbed by Kolmaug," he said, with an audible shaking in his voice. He bowed his head to the ground.

Peter collapsed to the ground in horror and disbelief. "But how is this possible?" he cried. "How could Steven have been stabbed by her? It didn't even seem like he was hurt when she attacked him. But if Steven has been stabbed, will he die now? Oh, the things I would do for that thought to not even brush against my mind! Please, tell me the truth, Orieant, why does this terrible thing have to inflict us even after we defeated this beast?"

Orieant went over to Peter and embraced the hurting boy. "Keep your peace, Peter," he said, placing his hand on the boy's chin. "I stand assured in saying that Steven will be fine; this is only a challenge that he will have to endure. But when Kolmaug wrapped her tail around Steven, the stinger which is on the tip of it must have pierced his chest and infected him. For that tail is no ordinary tail as it is extremely poisonous."

"Can we treat him then?" asked Peter, still crying and gasping. "If his chest is now infected with poison, let's give him as much medicine and rest as he needs! We will all take a break from our journey to ensure that Steven is fine and ready before we go again."

"We will give Steven the proper treatment he needs," assured Orieant. "But first, we must escape from this tunnel and go back to the haven of the cave we came from, for I fear that though this sleeping monster has been struck, she is still waiting for the opportune time to awaken. The caves of Omron Rahndu have brought much peril and evil things to this company, so it would be most wise for us to escape from even the slightest hint of its shadow altogether."

"I understand, but why can't we just quickly treat him here?" asked Peter. "Kolmaug is likely dead now and besides, even if she is alive, she is likely too wounded to cause any worse damage than she already has."

"This company has come too far for us to take any risks, Peter, no matter how sensible they may seem to be," responded Orieant. "And do not be so presumptuous with your words, for it is not that easy to kill this beast, as the spirit of Kolmaug is always lurking and looking around to cause trouble. If we are not careful, then we risk being trapped by her again and so we must make our way away from this passage and go back to the other cave. From there we will provide Steven with the medicine and rest he needs, but for now, let us focus on escaping from this evil place."

"Then let us go on then," suddenly interjected Erundil, growing with impatience. "Let us escape from this evil place and we will provide Steven with the appropriate gamdarian medicine that will surely heal him from the pain in his chest."

Huminli hastily jumped in to offer his help for Steven. "I am glad to see that there is plenty of medicine to treat Steven, but it is for this very reason that my brother and I packed our healing soup," he said. "The healing soup of my people will surely cure Steven of any pain in his chest and renew his strength."

"Yes, and our healing soup is not only appetizing in taste but also capable of healing all sorts of wounds," added Glophi. "And it's the same soup that our ancestors used during the days of the War of Great Alliances to heal the soldiers of all the free creatures of the world, even including battle horses and other animals used to fight. I suggest that once we escape from here, we let Steven drink some of our soup."

The company felt that was a good idea, and many of them thanked the smalves for offering their help. But to everyone's shock, great frustration toward the smalves could be seen on Erundil's face, which he didn't hide.

"No!" he exclaimed, shaking his head. "You two have caused much danger and evil within this company, and now you claim to want to help Steven? I am beginning to wonder if you have ulterior motives which you managed to hide in your innocence. But if that is the case then I refuse to be blind to the truth, and I am willing to defend Steven from you trying to kill him with your poisonous soup!"

The company gasped in horror at what was said, and Huminli and Glophi took heavy steps backward, touching their hearts as though a large weight of bricks had been cast toward them.

Mataput and Orieant looked on at Erundil with great anger. "That is enough, Erundil!" said Orieant in a commanding voice. "Yes, we know that Huminli and Glophi made a foolish mistake in awakening Kolmaug, but who are you to claim that they have put poison in their healing soup? Were not Mataput and I alive during the days of the War of Great Alliances, and was it, not us who saw with our own eyes the healing soup of the smalves that healed many soldiers of the free creatures, particularly your people the gamdars? So we must be willing to help Steven in any way possible, even if the way it goes is against your wishes."

"Let us at least give Steven our own medicine first," responded Erundil. "That way we will give him something stable, before risking him with this supposed healing soup of the smalves."

"Very well then, have it your way," said Orieant, not wishing to argue anymore with Erundil. "We will first treat Steven using your medicine, but if he does not make any progress in the next few days, then we must let him drink the healing soup of the smalves."

"Fine," said Erundil, with visible irritation on his face. "But do not be quick to blame me if anything bad happens to Steven if he is forced to drink this soup."

"Nothing bad will happen, and you will see that, Erundil, if you have faith in the smalves," said Orieant, with a slight smile on his face as he looked upon Erundil. "But I have a feeling that the day will come when you will fully embrace them, and trusting them you will be free from the stubbornness that has held you bound all these years. Yes, I have foreseen that day coming soon with my own eyes."

Erundil shook his head, not wishing to entertain what Orieant said. Yet, he couldn't deny the wisdom of the volviers and he feared that what Orieant said would come true. But he swiftly brought his attention away from that and fixed his eyes back on Steven, who was still holding onto the right side of his chest.

Orieant went down again to place his hand on Steven, but as he went down, he heard the slightest rustle of movement behind him, and he immediately became alerted that Kolmaug, even as she lay on the ground was still likely alive.

"We must make our way away from here," he said, immediately standing up. "At any moment Kolmaug will awaken and if we waste more time we risk being trapped in this dark place."

Suddenly, even as Orieant said that Steven began breathing heavily and to the surprise of those around him he began speaking. "What is going on?" he asked, speaking weakly and slowly turning his head to look at the company. "Where am I right now? Did Kolmaug manage to catch up to us?"

The company was overjoyed to hear Steven speak and see him move, though the awareness of Kolmaug being awake still weighed heavily on their minds. Orieant once again crouched down to Steven, with a smile covering his face.

"I am glad to see you moving and speaking, Steven," he said. "And yes, Kolmaug, unfortunately, managed to catch up to us. Not only that, but the stinger on the tip of her tail stabbed you in the chest, which caused you not to move or speak for several minutes. But things could have been worse for you if Erundil, Lelhond, and Karandil had not fired their arrows and also stabbed Kolmaug's side."

Steven's eyes widened as he listened to Orieant. "How was she able to stab me?" he asked, filled with deep shock.

"She attacked you, Steven, and while wrapping you with her poisonous tail, she managed to strike you on the chest," responded Orieant. "But do not worry, I can see that she was only able to brush you with the slightest part of her tail. Anything else and we could be looking at a far bleaker picture. We will provide you with medicine, but first, we must escape from this place as Kolmaug is still alive, though she is silently recovering from her wound."

Steven could feel his strength beginning to falter as he shuddered. "I am sorry, but I just feel so weak," he said slowly. "I don't think I have the strength to reach the end of this place."

"Oh no, I can see that you have enough strength to endure, Steven," said Orieant, and bringing Steven to his feet, the man was able to stand up by himself though he still clutched onto his chest."

To his astonishment, Steven sensed a spark of a rekindling of strength flowing through his body, and though he remained in pain, he felt that he could give one last push. "I can continue," he said. "I feel that I can give one last push, but I will need a good and long rest once we make our way through here."

"And you will get that rest," said Orieant. "But for now let us focus on reaching the end of this tunnel."

With that, Mataput and Orieant lead the way again, going on a slow jogging pace with the company following them from behind. Steven ran on with them, though he held onto his chest and was at the very back of the group. Peter came to his side, helping his friend and continuing to encourage him to press on forward. Every while and again the company glanced back to see if Kolmaug was following them, but to their knowledge she was still lying on the ground, with only the slightest rustles of movement being the sign that she was not dead. But once they had made their way far enough from her, the beast could neither be seen nor heard, but they continued to jog, not wishing to slow down and risk her catching up to them. They journeyed their way through both smooth and rocky levels of ground down the narrow passageway, with the bright lights of the volviers continuing to guide them. The air grew stuffy in the tunnel, but with the volviers urging them forward, they were encouraged that they were nearing the end of the passage. They continued in this way for many more minutes, jogging at times and other times speed walking. But knowing that the unexpected could happen, they refused to ever stop as they dreamed of seeing the end of the passage.

But then suddenly, even as their confidence had grown, a trace of faint footsteps in the distance could be heard coming up behind them. Looking behind, Steven caught from the corner of his eye the tip of a long tail growing from a shell. Seeing this he suddenly gasped in shock and felt as though a sharp jap of pain had struck the same spot of his chest where Kolmaug had stabbed him.

"She is coming! Kolmaug is coming!" he cried, coming to a sudden halt as he held on to his chest. "The beast is coming for us, and yet I thought we were miles ahead of her! How will we escape from this now?"

His strength greatly waned and failed him at that moment, with thoughts of utterly giving up starting to plague his mind. Yet Peter remained by his side, and as long as he was with his friend he would not let that happen. As the young boy placed his hand on Steven's shoulder, he reminded him of how far they had come in their journey.

"Now is not the time to give up, Steven," he said. "There is still hope that we can escape from this evil place. We are almost there, we just need to press on a little further."

Grabbing ahold of Steven's hand, the young boy pushed him forward to continue running and not look back. At that moment, Steven's weakness passed away from his body, and looking into Peter's eyes that urged him to continue, he felt a spark of strength reenter his body. Though he still held onto his chest and ran the slowest out of everyone else, Peter remained close by his side, slowing down his own pace to run alongside and motivate his friend.

But Kolmaug mounted upon them and filled with an unimaginable level of fury she craved and desired to see the light of the company extinguished by every meter of darkness she covered. Coming toward them with great wrath, she drew ever nearer to them with every step she took, but looking forward the company could see small traces of the end of the tunnel just ahead of them. Their hearts began beating rapidly, as they knew that they were a mere minutes away from escaping from Kolmaug's grasp, though they knew that the beast would not give up in pursuing them.

Turning around to see where the rest of the company was behind him, Mataput noticed that Steven and Peter were far behind everyone else. "Do not stop running!" he said. "We are almost at the end of the tunnel!"

"Do not worry!" replied Peter. "Steven is just a little tired which is why he is running slower than everyone else. But I promise that we will not stop running!"

"Good, I am glad to hear that," said Mataput. "But just make sure that you don't fall too far behind us. We are almost at the end, and it would be a terrible thing if Kolmaug managed to catch up to us."

Suddenly, Steven's body shook and awoke, as though he had responded to Mataput's suggestion of Kolmaug catching up to the company. He sensed a tingling sensation flowing through his body and a strong resolve not to fail filled his mind.

"I promise to not give up," he said softly yet assuredly. "I can even see the end of this tunnel ahead of me, and I can't see how Kolmaug will manage to cover much ground to catch up to us."

From behind, the company could hear the rough grunting laugh of Kolmaug responding to Steven, but Steven at that moment felt no fear, and took great confidence knowing that the end was in plain sight. But Kolmaug still fixed her eyes on him and was not ready to give up in launching one last attack upon him and the company.

Seeing the confidence that covered Steven's face, Lelhond joined in offering his own words of encouragement. "You speak wisely, Steven, for I too cannot see how Kolmaug will catch up to us," he said. "So continue to hold onto your confidence, knowing that there is nothing that you need to worry about. And even if she does manage to attack us, then all ten of us will confront and fight her, not fearing her wicked laughter or deceiving roar."

"Indeed we will not think twice of confronting her, for that beast is no match for us," added Huminli. "And behold! Just as Steven observed, the end of the tunnel can be seen just ahead! We are probably only a few hundred meters away from reaching the end!"

What Huminli said was true, for as the company had been running for so long through the narrow tunnel they now recognized that they were indeed a mere hundreds of meters away from reaching the small opening they had come from. Yet with each step they took near the end of their long road, Kolmaug remained ever determined to cast a shadow of fear about them and desired to eventually trap them once they neared the very end. Some of them shuddered with fear as they ran, sensing the beast closely watching and following them from behind as a keen hawk. And for a brief moment, some of them, especially Steven felt a strong desire to just turn around and look one last time to see how close Kolmaug was to them. But they immediately cast this desire away from their minds, especially as it seemed that Mataput had read their thoughts.

"Do not look behind you!" he cried in a loud and commanding voice. "We are almost near the end and there is no need to give this beast even the sniff of a reason to try and overpower us! We are right where we need to be so remain patient, and now that in just a few minutes we will be able to celebrate having escaped from the wrath of Kolmaug."

The company breathed sighs of relief in response to Mataput's comments, and fixing their eyes on his and Orieant's light leading them, they continued running through the tunnel, even as the small opening signaling the end of their race loomed larger with the distance they covered. And though the sound of Kolmaug's rushing feet and angry grunting grew louder as she intensified her fury against them, they remained one step ahead of her.

And then, at last, the company finally made their way to the end of the long and difficult passage, now standing within touching distance of the small opening right in their faces. The first ones to cross over were Mataput and Orieant, and soon after the gamdars and smalves made their way over the opening. But the final two to come had lingered far behind the company, and even as Steven and Peter neared the opening, the rest of the company's eyes widened in dread as they could see that right on their tail was Kolmaug, only a short distance away from them and breathing heavily as her shadow surrounded them.

Seeing them near the end, the company urged Steven and Peter on, encouraging them b how close they were to reaching the finish. As Steven and Peter ran it seemed as though their faces shone with bright lights even as Kolmaug's ghost of many colors grew darker and more hideous as her wrath burned heavily against them. And with one last display of her anger, she garnered the strength to let out a thunderous roar, one so loud that it bellowed right through the path of the two humans. For a brief moment, the two of them stopped, being weakened by both the shock and fear of how close the beast was behind them. But with the company continuing to encourage them, they felt strengthened enough to ignore their worries and trust in what lay ahead of them.

And so with one final push, Steven and Peter managed to plunge themselves into the opening where the rest of the company was. But even as they crossed over, Steven felt a heavy presence close behind him, desperately grabbing ahold of his shirt. The hand that touched him twisted him backward, and as he saw what was behind him, Steven shrieked in horror as he realized that Kolmaug had finally caught up and was grasping him tightly.

The company gasped in horror at seeing this, and immediately the gamdars and volviers began to rapidly fire arrows at Kolmaug. But their desperation seemed to not affect the relentless beast, and even as Steven cried out and pleaded for help, she only continued to hideously laugh and scratch and claw at him. She roared in anger at his face, and picking him up she started carrying him down the way they had come from in the tunnel, away from the company as they could only stare at this in disbelief.

But at that moment, even as hope seemed to slip away from the company's grasp, Mataput and Orieant stepped up and chased Kolmaug down the narrow tunnel, and brought forth their bright light to stop the beast in her tracks. And Kolmaug couldn't help but turn around to meet the volviers, and seeing the glory that surrounded the two of them, a bitter hate ran through her bones and she suddenly mounted toward them while she carried Steven, with a fiery flame of wrath in her eyes.

The rest of the company peered through the small opening, with some of them covering their eyes and only fearing for the worst.

Yet even as Kolmaug's inevitable attack would come upon them, something very strange happened in that instant. Even as the beast leaped into the air with Steven in her grasp, in the split second that followed, Mataput and Orieant outstretched their arms, and behold! A great and awesome blinding light as the sun in its full strength covered their faces and entire bodies. This bright light could not be compared to the previous light theirs which they had used to lead the company through the dark tunnel, as this radiance shone a thousand times brighter than that other light. Even as the company had blinked and witnessed this stunning sight, it was made obvious to them that they had seen just a facet of the great glory of the mighty volviers, the once great spirit beings of Jangart when they once dwelled in the heaven above the heavens, Starlight. They appeared before all who beheld them as glorious stars, undimmed in their radiance and splendor. Steven looked up at them in awe, feeling a sudden sense of unworthiness to even be in their presence.

And as though the sudden revelation of this previously unseen and unexpecting light had put a dagger through her heart and struck her blind, Kolmaug suddenly flew back even as she had jumped in the air just a few seconds ago, letting out a hideous and terrible cry of deep shock and pain. The wrath that she had allowed to build up in her ghostly form had suddenly passed away from her as the wind, and any desire to attack the volviers had vanished from her mind. Falling in weakness, Steven managed to easily slip away from her grasp, and with no strength left in her, she had no choice but to crawl and slide away down the dark and narrow tunnel.

Steven meanwhile, ran toward the rest of the company, who were relieved to see him well and safe. He crossed over to the other side of the opening, with the volviers also making their way over as well. But even as the company turned their backs away from Kolmaug, Mataput, and Orieant still faced the beast, and holding their ground, they stared down at Kolmaug even as it seemed as though she would forever be lost in the darkness far from their glorious presence. But in that instant, the sudden realization that her appetite still hadn't been full possessed the beast's mind, and she began to slowly turn around, perhaps to see if she could just have the slightest of opportunities to leave one last unforgettable memory for the company.

But even as she began to turn around to face the company, Mataput and Orieant spoke together in commanding voices. “Go back to the darkness!” they said, in deep voices that rumbled like thunder.

Immediately, Kolmaug let out one last terrible shrieking cry, and as though a spirit now possessed her, she tumbled backward down the dark and narrow tunnel at an uncontrollable speed. Even as her echoing cries grew fainter, her dark and colossal figure also grew smaller until the last sight of her shadow disappeared.

As soon as any traces of the beast had gone away, the sound of a deep rumbling was heard while the gathering of a great number of rocks echoed throughout the tunnel and soon crashed onto the ground on the other side of where the company stood. The rocks gathered together in one location, and they completely covered what was once the small opening leading to the tunnel. The passage was now permanently blocked, with what appeared to be a sturdy wall prohibiting the entrance to it. The volviers had sent Kolmaug back into the darkness, with what appeared to be no way out.

15

The Bitter Mountains

FOR A MOMENT THE company stood frozen, trying to process all that they had just witnessed. They all couldn't help but gaze in awe at the volviers, not only for the great power they had displayed but also because of the glorious light that radiated from them, making them shine almost as the sun itself. Then they looked in each other's direction, not saying a word though their astonished faces proved that their hearts were now filled with newfound deference for Mataput and Orieant.

Amidst their silence, Mataput and Orieant walked forth to the company, and as they came the glorious lights that shone all around them slowly vanished away. Very soon they now appeared as the old and insignificant men that they appeared to the outside world, cloaked in their regular gray cloaks. But even as they returned to their normal state, the company did not forget the awesome and great power and glory that they had just witnessed being displayed in the volviers.

The company couldn't stop blinking their eyes, amazed that the glory they had just seen had now passed away. Filled with awe, Peter managed to speak to the volviers. "How, how did that just happen?" he asked, stammering even as he spoke. "How did you two turn into such glorious beings, and repel Kolmaug away by your bright light?"

The company echoed Peter's question, wondering how the volviers had transformed themselves into such awesome beings and managed to utterly destroy Kolmaug in an instant. Steven was particularly the most amazed by all he saw, blinking and pinching his eyes to make sure he wasn't dreaming. But he realized that the volviers had indeed turned into glorious bright lights and had sent Kolmaug back into the darkness, he couldn't resist bowing his head to the ground and going down on one knee, as if he were in a posture to worship them.

Mataput and Orieant, however, swiftly discouraged him from doing that. "No, no, Steven," said Mataput. "Do not do that, for though we allow people to respect us, we are not worthy to be worshipped. Only Jangart is worthy of your true devotion and deep admiration."

They brought Steven to his feet, who still stared at them with both wonder and amazement. "But seriously, how were you able to do what you just did?" he asked, with him and the company still desiring to hear answers to their questions. "How were you able to turn into such glorious lights that seemed to shine as the sun, and then on the other hand turn back into your normal appearance as an old man? Even the lights that you manifested yourselves as when leading us through the dark passage, and also protecting me, Peter, and our people from Moneshob, Londriel, and the wuzlirs cannot be compared to this light that you displayed. For this light was far more bright, splendid, and unparalleled in its intensity. Tell me how you did that because I didn't know you two could display such awesome power like that."

Steven continued rambling on, asking more questions and staring in amazement at the volviers as he did. Mataput and Orieant remained still and silent, looking intently at him with smiles on their faces as they listened to all of his questions. The company also listened closely to Steven, echoing his many questions as well.

At last, growing tired of the company's questions and concerns, Mataput responded to all that went through their minds. "As you all know, Orieant and I are volviers, the great protectors and helpers of the free creatures of the world," he said. "Our purpose is to lead, guide, and protect all of you, so that you may have hope in standing against the dark things of this world devised by the secret purposes of the Dark Lord. Yet before we entered the circle of the world, as you all already know, we were once the great spirits beings of Jangart, with our glory, power, and light being reflections of Jangart's own splendid and unimaginable greatness. That which you have witnessed in us today, as awesome as it may appear to be, cannot be compared to the splendid light and majesty that we once possessed. But what you have seen just now is a small fraction of the light, glory, and power that we once had, which Jangart permitted us to have once we took the shape of old men so that in times of trouble we could protect and rescue you."

The company, but especially Steven stood astounded by all they heard, with the image of the glorious light and authority they had seen in Mataput and Orieant still fresh on their minds. The company stood silent, but being unable to help himself Steven was filled with even more questions for the volviers.

"So why can't you two just manifest yourselves in that power all of the time?" he asked. "Because if you can do that, then nothing will be able to stand in our way, and any attack of the enemy would only be forced to go back from where it came from, as you did with Kolmaug. And if this was only a fraction of all of the glory you have, then why can't you use your full glory to repel any danger that comes our way?"

Orieant this time responded to Steven. "Because we are no longer the spirit beings of Jangart," he said. "We are now the volviers, the great helpers of the free world, and our being is now tied to the circle of this world, as our purpose is to now bring hope to the free creatures of the world. When we left Starlight we lost our names and our positions of power, with a veil being cast over our light and glory, making us unable to fully use the power and authority we once had. And it is good that things are this way, because the light we once had was the very light that radiated from the presence of Jangart himself, and no creature who lives in the condition of this fallen world and sees the glory of Jangart can live. Yet a portion of our power and glory remains, and in times of danger we can display it to protect all of you."

"Well I am grateful for all that you have done to protect us," said Steven. "And if it wasn't for the power that you two have, who knows what Kolmaug would have done after she grabbed ahold of me? Yet you two ensured that I didn't have to worry about this, and I can now instead look back on this with relief."

"I am glad to hear that you are relieved, Steven," said Orieant. "But see to it that you do not fear, for Mataput and I are always here to defend this company, as this is what the end of our long road has come to."

A broad smile covered Steven's face as he looked upon Orieant and

Mataput with a sense of wonder and reverence. At that very moment, it seemed as though all the darkness and despair he had felt when Kolmaug had him in her grasp had vanished away because of the light and hope that the volviers brought to rescue him. A sweet and calming wind of peace, as it felt, came down upon him, filling him with comfort and rest beyond measure. At that moment, as though all had been made plain to him, he realized that he had nothing to fear, neither pain, danger, sorrow, or even death. Everything would be fine and nothing would be able to take away the joy and peace that he was experiencing all because of the mighty yet partial revelation of the glory and power Mataput and Orieant had revealed in themselves. He felt confident enough to travel through the land of Nangorid with no sign of fear in his heart.

Yet even with all of this confident assurance building up in Steven, a sharp pain suddenly pierced his chest. Crying out in pain he was reminded of the place where Kolmaug had stung him, and the feeling of fear and despair returned to his mind.

"Ah!" he cried, falling to his knees and clutching onto his chest as he breathed heavily. "I am in severe pain!"

The company swiftly rushed to him, with their sense of peace and confidence quickly vanishing as they saw Steven on the ground and crying out in pain.

"We must give Steven our healing soup," remarked Huminli, looking on at the man with a disturbed expression on his face. "It is obvious that he has been left severely wounded by Kolmaug's deadly sting, but I am sure that our soup will heal him of his discomfort in no time."

"Your soup will only do more harm to him!" suddenly lashed out Erundil in response. "If Steven needs medicine, then we will treat him with the gamdarian medicine of my people, not with this poison that you smalves call healing soup. Have you not seen how much danger you and your brother have brought to us? Why should we be willing to allow anything else dangerous befall us?"

"Enough Erundil!" said Orieant in a commanding voice, and immediately Erundil along with the company fell silent as they turned their attention to the volvier. "How many times do I have to tell you the same thing? I gave you my word earlier that we would first give Steven some gamdarian medicine, but if he doesn't get better within the next few days, then we will have to give him the healing soup of the smalves. And if their soup is what works, would you hinder him from drinking just a few drops of their soup if it meant that he could evade the shadow of death?"

Cold and fearful shudders ran through the company's bones at the mere mention of death. They trembled at the slight possibility of Steven's condition deteriorating so quickly that they would need to do anything so that he could escape death. They worried, wondering how badly Steven would be feeling if he didn't get better in the coming days.

"Steven will not die," eventually said Erundil. "My people's medicine can be trusted as it has proven time and time again that it can help those who are injured and weak to not only recover but to be restored to an even better state than they were before. He will need time, but I am confident that he will be just as healthy as he was before Kolmaug stung him."

"Very well then, give him your medicine then," said Orieant. "We are all willing to give Steven time to rest and recover but know that if he only seems to grow worse in these coming days, then other ideas will have to take precedence."

And so with a begrudging voice of agreement to this, Erundil went over to Steven and after asking him to sit down, he lifted Steven's cloak to see where his wound was. He immediately gasped in shock upon seeing Steven's wound on his chest, where on the right side was a giant black rash with a tiny red mark on the center of it. The black wound seemed to be spreading throughout his whole chest and even seemed to be spreading toward the left side of his body. The rest of the company came close together to see Steven's wound, and upon seeing it, they too gasped in disgust at the giant wound.

"Oh no!" exclaimed Peter. "Now I see why you are so hurt! I never imagined that a wound could look so painful, and look, it already seems to be spreading throughout your whole body!"

"Do not worry, Peter," said Erundil in response to the boy. "My people's medicine will heal Steven from his pain and very soon his wound will disappear."

"I sure hope it does," said Peter hopefully, yet deep within his heart was a strong feeling of doubt and concern.

Amidst the company's great worry, Erundil reached into his backpack and pulled out a small jar, opening it up and dipping his hand into it. A foamy white cream covered his fingers once he took out his hand from the jar, and placing the cream right on the center of Steven's wound, he began rubbing it in circles around his chest.

While Erundil rubbed the cream on his wound, an unpleasant and even sharp pain came onto his chest. The cream itself was surprisingly warm, but in that moment Steven felt as though a sword had pierced through his chest. Crying out in pain for some time, Peter tried to intervene and help his friend, but Mataput and Orieant held him back and after telling him that all would go well, the boy retreated and silently watched Erundil as the gamdar continued rubbing the cream on Steven's wound. Over time, Steven felt the sharp pain of the cream slowly leave him, and a comforting warmth soon began to fill his body and mind.

At last, after Erundil had finished rubbing the cream on Steven's wound, he let the cream dissolve for the next few minutes before covering his chest with his cloak. By now Steven felt a good deal better, though he could still feel the slight twitch of an occasional moment of pain in his chest. But feeling much better, he was ready to stand up and let the company know how he was feeling, but Erundil swiftly prevented him from standing to his feet.

"Sit down, Steven, I am not finished yet," he said. "I must also give you the healing leaves of my people to eat, and so you must remain seated for the next few minutes, before feeling how you are."

Steven obeyed Erundil and remained seated as the king continued to treat him. The gamdar once again reached into his backpack and took out one mere green leaf from it. Ripping a small and seemingly insignificant piece from the leaf, he brought it to Steven with his hand outstretched.

"Eat," he said. "This leaf will taste as sweet as honey, but it will be sour once it enters your body. Nonetheless, it will bring restoration of strength and relief to your body, and your wound will stop spreading."

Steven once again obeyed Erundil and taking the small green leaf from his hand, he brought it to his mouth and ate. And indeed, once he began chewing on the leaf it was pleasantly sweet, more so than even the sweetest drop of honey. He savored every chew of that satisfactory leaf, closing his eyes and eating in pure delight and peace. But as he ate and swallowed the leaf, Steven felt a sudden sour taste enter his mouth and eventually go deep into his stomach. He immediately opened his eyes and began wildly wagging his tongue, hoping that the bitter taste would leave his mouth and stomach.

Erundil laughed as he watched Steven complain about the bitter taste. "It is fine, Steven," he said. "The bitter taste will soon go away, but it is for your benefit that it tastes very sour because for you to be healed, the taste must be like that."

Yet Steven couldn't take the bitter taste anymore and soon began to desire for some water so that the sour leaf would soon leave his mouth. He almost stood up to go to his backpack and find his water bottle, but Erundil again stopped him.

"Wait, Steven," he said, to which Steven sighed to himself, believing that he would be sitting down all day. "The final thing you need to complete your recovery process is the healing leaves that my sons brought. Once you eat those, then we will be finished and you may be able to stand up."

As Erundil called out to his three sons, they likewise did the same as their father by each taking out a small leaf from their backpacks. Lelhond took out a yellow leaf, Karandil took out a red leaf, and Forandor took out an orange leaf, with all three of them breaking a small piece from each of their leaves. They came to Steven holding the pieces in their hands as Steven looked on at them with fascination.

"These healing leaves that my sons are holding come from the forest of Palororen," said Erundil. "Eat them, and they too will be as sweet as honey, but will then turn sour and bitter once you chew and swallow them. But after a while, the bitterness will soon disappear and you shall be healed from your wound in the coming days and weeks."

Steven first took the yellow leaf from Lelhond and ate, and it too was sweet at first but turned bitter just as Erundil had said. Once he finished eating the leaf, he ate Karandil's red leaf, and after that, he ate Forandor's orange leaf. They also were sweet, but as he chewed the leaf pieces they turned sour and their bitter taste was even more unpleasant to him than Erundil's lead was. But he had finally managed to swallow the leaf pieces and once they had entered his body he desperately hoped that he could drink some water to get rid of the horrible sour feeling.

"Now that I've eaten your healing leaves, can I now stand up and drink some water?" he asked, looking on at Erundil.

Erundil looked at Steven with a straight face for some time, before the crack of a smile broke out on his face. "Yes, Steven, we are now finished and so you may stand up and hydrate yourself to see how you are feeling now," he said, allowing Steven to do as he pleased.

A broad smile instantly came on Steven's face and standing up, he rushed over to his backpack and taking out his water bottle, chugged down some water. Almost immediately he felt the bitter taste of the healing leaves leave his mouth and stomach, and he felt much more refreshed. Though occasional sharp pains came to his chest every while and again, he still felt a great deal better and believed that the cream and healing leaves of the gamdars had helped tremendously. With the company watching him, they could see that he felt much better, and Peter came to his friend to speak with him.

"How do you feel, Steven?" he asked, looking at Steven with hopeful eyes. "Has the medicine of the gamdars worked?"

"I feel better," responded Steven. "The medicine has certainly affected me, but I can still feel the wound in my chest, gnawing at me every while and again. But the pain has been alleviated and I hope that it will be gone very soon," he then turned to Erundil with a smile of gratitude on his face. "But regardless, none of this would be possible without Erundil's efforts to provide me with this special gamdarian medicine. Thank you for offering me help and for reducing the pain in my wound. I am sure that in no time this wound will go and these occasional sharp pains I feel will be no more."

"That is right, Steven," responded Erundil. "I am glad to see the confidence you have knowing that everything will be fine. Just give the medicine some time to work, and in the next few days maybe even within hours, the occasional pain that you feel will drastically decrease, and your wound will begin to disappear."

"Well I like to hear that," remarked Peter with great relief. "I was so worried about you, Steven, and I thought that your wound would spread throughout your whole body, resulting in your pain becoming unbearable. But I am glad to hear that things will only get better, not worse, and that the wound will soon be gone before we even know it."

"Yes, and we all hope that Steven's wound goes away quickly," chimed in Orieant. "But let us not forget, that if he continues to feel the occasional and sudden pain in his chest, and if his wound doesn't make any signs of disappearing within the next few days, then we will have to allow Steven to try and drink some of the healing soup of the smalves. But for now, let us wait and see how this medicine works on him."

"Yes, let us first wait with patience and see how he progresses," immediately responded Erundil. "The medicine will heal him in no time, we just need to wait as you said yourself, and very soon changes will become evident."

"That is what we all wish for," said Orieant, looking on at Erundil suspiciously knowing that the gamdar was still unwilling to let Steven drink of the healing soup of the smalves if it came to that.

The company fell silent, staring at each other and hoping in their hearts that the medicine of the gamdars would heal Steven in no time. Meanwhile, deep within their hearts the smalves secretly hoped that they would still have the opportunity to treat Steven with their healing soup to prove their value to Erundil. Yet they still desired to see Steven swiftly healed and restored to his former condition, and they felt assured that everything would go smoothly. Most relieved of the company was Peter, who especially took comfort that the gamdarian medicine would work wonders for his friend. Mataput and Orieant hoped for the best for Steven, yet in their hearts they felt convinced that some other road would lead Steven to experience true healing one that was blurry and they were unsure of. Yet they kept these thoughts to themselves and despite this unknown feeling, they believed that all would go well.

Amid the long silence among the company, Lelhond spoke up and revealed what had been on his mind. "So what now?" he asked, looking toward the volviers. "Is it still safe for us to be in these caves, or should we journey away from here to bring safety among ourselves? Yet the night has already come, as I can through these small cracks that the sky is dark outside."

"We are safe here," responded Mataput. "Orieant and I sent Kolmaug back into the darkness down that long and dark passage, and no presence of evil will cause us trouble here. We will rest here for the night, and in the morning we will continue in our journey through the mountains of Lehu Shalank."

"The morning, why the morning?" asked Steven, groaning in displeasure. "If this place is truly safe, why can we not wait here a bit longer for the next couple of days so that we can all rest and recover, and so that my wound can heal?"

"We have not journeyed through the land of Nangorid to rest and by doing so potentially bring danger upon us, Steven," responded Mataput sternly. "Nor did we come here to sit and hide in caves instead of making our way closer to accomplishing the goal of our quest. Our purpose has always been to be on the move and find the lost book of Ulohendel, and to do that we must do that as quickly as we can. There will be times for us to rest and recover, and if your wound grows worse as we journey through these mountains tomorrow, then we can make short stops and rest for a while in these caves. But for now, we will rest here for the night, and in the morning we will continue our journey because we have no time to waste now."

Although he remained slightly displeased, Steven conceded to Mataput and mentally prepared himself ahead of the company's continued journey through the mountains in the morning. "Fine," he said, with a sigh. "You and Orieant have proven to know what is best, and so I am willing to continue in our journey tomorrow morning."

"Good," replied Mataput. "But before you think about tomorrow, you will need to let your body and mind rest tonight so that you are strengthened for the morning."

"Speaking of being strengthened," chimed in Glophi. "That reminds me, since it is now the evening, we should be having something to eat to give our bodies energy for tomorrow. I'm starving after all that running we did to escape from Kolmaug, and I know that tomorrow will only continue to be difficult as we trek through that horrible snow and freezing wind."

"I'm starving too," remarked Huminli, with his stomach rumbling. "I guess that means now is a good time to eat, after all, when a smalf's stomach growls, it's always the right time to have a good meal."

"You two always seem to remind us whenever it's time to eat," laughed Mataput. "But you are right, after all of the running and fighting we did for hours throughout our time in these caves, it would not be a bad idea to eat a meal together and replenish our bodies."

"Then let us make a fire to gather together and eat," said Lelhond. "Though it may not be a formal dinner as my people are used to, we are still able to adapt to whatever situation we find ourselves in. And besides, after a long and difficult day as today was, I wouldn't mind sharing a nice meal."

"Neither would I," agreed Erundil. "Let us do everything you have suggested, my son, and we will share many more stories and enjoy fellowship with one another before we sleep for the night and travel again in the morning."

Agreeing to this, the company went throughout the cave and gathered as many sticks and rocks as they could find and heaped them together in a pile. Eventually, as the gamdars worked to start the fire, a spark came forth, and beginning to spread a giant and warm fire was created. The company huddled together, warming themselves by the fire and taking out the food they had in their backpacks they began to eat. Though it was a plain and simple dinner, they enjoyed the time they had to relax and sit down with each other. But as they ate the bread, meat, and vegetables that were in their backpacks, they noticed that their food supply was gradually dwindling. They still had enough food to last for many more weeks, but they wondered what would happen if they ran out of food, and if there would be any food to hunt for in the evil land they were in. But they brushed these thoughts away, knowing that they wouldn't have to worry about starving and lacking food any time soon.

After they had finished eating, the company talked among one another, sharing numerous stories of their people and respected homes, and expressing their amazement at how unique it was that they had all managed to cross paths with each other on their journey through Nangorid. Mataput and Orieant described how this was no coincidence, and how it was rather part of the plan of Jangart all along to bring the free creatures of the world together to unite and aid one another in a stand against the growing darkness of the world. The company took these words to heart and continued expressing their hopes for what lay ahead of them.

Along with that, they confessed their tiredness and expressed their wishes to be over with the quest as soon as possible, to go back home in peace and security. They desired to go back to their families and friends, having brought back the lost book of Ulohendel that Steven would use to rule righteously over his people on Earth. They wondered how much longer they would have to spend in this corrupted land of the enemy, and they desperately wished that the quest would be worth their effort and time. Erundil desired to see his wife and daughter, while the smalves couldn't stop thinking about their friends, family, and delicious food back in their homeland of Laouli. Steven and Peter set their minds on the people by the coast just outside of Fozturia, picturing the many eager faces who had inherited the rich land and were excited to see the wisdom in which Steven would rule over them.

The company continued sharing all that was on their minds, not hindering anything that was on their hearts. Yet as Lelhond spoke with all his heart, the company noticed that something deep within his heart was troubling him, as he would often stare into the distance with bleak eyes. As they listened to him mumbling something under his breath, they could piece together that he was talking about someone in Watendelle that he missed. He seemed to be talking about someone whom he loved, yet it didn't seem to be about his mother, sister, or even one of his close friends. He seemed to be speaking of someone who he wasn't able to spend time with, which filled him with heavy regret. Eventually, upon noticing that Lelhond was acting differently with the concern and regret that covered the gamdar's face, his brother Karandil asked him what was going on.

"Are you fine, Lelhond?" he asked, looking on at his brother with concern. "You keep on mumbling about someone that you miss back home. Is it mother that you miss, or perhaps one of your close friends?"

"It is neither," quietly responded Lelhond. "I am thinking of one whom I love, though I never seem to be able to express my love openly to her."

Suddenly, Karandil along with his brother Forandor and father

Erundil understood what and who it was that Lelhond was talking about. Erundil rolled his eyes in irritation toward his son.

"My son, why are you still dreaming about Nahelion?" he asked, with a stern expression on his face. "Though she is the daughter of my chief advisor, Olindule, she and her father are of the Fuendil kindred, while we are of the Xinlar kindred. And you know that the law of our kingdom says that it is for our benefit that different kindreds do not mingle blood with each other."

"What you say is true, but that law is only a suggestion, not a command, father," protested Lelhond. "And besides, our blood has been mingled in the past before, and though it has scarcely been done since then, it still has happened numerous times throughout our history. And I have always been close to Nahelion since childhood, but I have never gotten the chance to proclaim my close affection for her."

"Our blood has only been mingled when it needed to be done," responded Erundil. "And besides, even if Nahelion wished to marry you, her father Olindule will not hand her in marriage with you, for he too knows that the blood between our kindreds should not be mingled. Not to mention that he has never held you in high esteem, ever since you mocked him in your youth."

Lelhond shook his head in annoyance. "Those were in the days of the past when I was young and still learning," he said. "I have moved on from that and have matured significantly in the years that have followed. I am sure that Olindule knows that."

"He may or may not know that," said Erundil. "But in either case, he will not permit you to marry his daughter, and neither will I. But I am more than willing to let you marry anyone of our Xinlar kindred, as that is the kindred of the line of the Kings of Watendelle."

The company listened in fascination to Erundil and Lelhond's conversation, with the humans and smalves especially looking on at them with both curiosity and confusion. They wondered why it was forbidden for different kindreds among the gamdars to intermarry with each other, and they couldn't stop scratching their heads at Erundil's explanations of why Lelhond couldn't marry his love.

Eventually, Glophi decided to intervene and asked Lelhond what was going on between him and his father. "Who exactly is Nahelion?" he asked. "Please, tell me more about this love of yours, Lelhond, and why it is that you can't marry her."

Lelhond sighed to himself, and for a moment he seemed to wander in a drowsy trance. But soon after he opened his mouth, and began to softly sing to himself which happened to be loud enough for the company to hear him. The words he sang were at first faint, but slowly became clearer as he continued. As the company listened they were amazed by how sweet Lelhond's voice was, and the song seemed to be one full of beauty, joy, and sadness, that was directed toward his love Nahelion:

The leaves were rich, and the forest shone,
As the birds sang and the beasts danced.
My first meeting with you all alone,
Was one of enchantment, where to you my eyes glanced.
Your hair in the sun shone like gold,
Just as Gonyardu, the fair and immortal one.
I came up to you as one who is bold,
But before I could declare my love, you were gone.

Yet in days to come, my eyes met yours again,
And you came forth clad in gold.
Your face shone even in the rain,
And your hand I desired to hold.
Your voice rang clearer than the birds of the sky,
And your laughter fell like drops of crystals.
You appeared to me as a star ready to fly,
And because of your glory, I considered us as equals.

This time you did not leave my sight,
And you grew to be a companion of mine.
You alone were my great delight,
And as moments passed you seemed to shine.
Yet my meeting with you remained short,
For your household wanted no part with me.

I could not be your consort,
For my heart's desire was hindered to be free.

In sadness did my meeting with you depart,
As the sunny day passed into the starry night.
Again we were forced to remain apart,
And we were forbidden to see each other's sight.
Yet many times we met in secret,
Where I desired to proclaim my love for you.
But in those times I was forced to hide in the closet,
Before your household could bring charges against me anew.

And so I brought these tidings to my household,
But they too rejected my desire for love.
The sunny days with you turned to bitter cold,
As my desires were covered in a glove.
The air grew gloomy and the forests turned gray,
As our misfortune took over our joy.
Our households made us stray,
From our true joyful day.

He fell silent with a grim expression on his face and eyes filled with heavy sorrow. The company became as silent as graves, with the sound of the wind outside the cave gently brushing against the rocks of the cave. Erundil shook his head and stared at his son with cold and hardened eyes and a stern expression on his face. Karandil and Forandor both seemed to be shocked by what Lelhond had sung about, while Mataput and Orieant looked on with no sign of emotion on their faces. Meanwhile, Steven, Peter, and the smalves had puzzled faces as they tried to interpret everything that Lelhond had sung about.

At last, Erundil broke the silence and spoke in response to his son. His eyebrows were raised and his face hardened even more in astonishment at what he heard coming from Lelhond's mouth. "My son, it is not good for you to feel this way," he sternly said. "How can you speak such words against your household, and the household of Olindule, my chief advisor? You must let go of your wishes and realize that it is not your place to marry Nahelion. For she belongs to her kindred while we belong to our kindred."

Lelhond seemed to be growing impatient as he listened to his father. "But this is my life and I have the right to make the choice I desire, father," he objected. "Will you deny your firstborn son the one thing that he greatly desires?"

Erundil's eyes suddenly flashed with light as he clenched his hands. The company could feel the tension growing between the two gamdars. "As your father, I must discern when your desire is against what is right!" he said, with the sound of his voice rising. "And this desire of yours, my son, is not right. But Lelhond, you are my son and all that you have is a reward for the many good things you have done in your life. You are the second in command of the army of Watendelle, you are a mighty soldier in your own right, you are learned in the lore and wisdom of our people's history, and all that you lay your hands on not only enriches yourself to succeed but also all those around you as well. I have given you all that your heart has desired and I have withheld nothing from you, yet this one desire of yours, I cannot grant you it as I fear it would divide our very own people, something that has never happened in our long history."

A heavily strained expression covered Lelhond's face as it seemed as though he had been struck by a crushing weight of disappointment as he listened to his father. He looked on at his father with hopeless and bleak eyes, yet even as he considered what his father said he soon began to understand where he was coming from. "I hear you, father," he said. "And I have never considered the terrible repercussions that could come to our people by something that splits opinion as this does. A civil war is something that our people have never thought about, as it is unheard of and even laughed at ever happening among us since we are so united. But I suppose that in your wisdom you have looked ahead, and perceived that even just a supposedly innocent seed could lead to much sorrow and destruction. I can now see why this is something that you are fiercely against, yet I still cannot deny this burning desire that is setting my heart on fire. And if you are thinking of the damage that this desire of mine could bring to our people, why should you not also consider the change and success that this could to us? If I were to spend the rest of my life with Nahelion is it not also equally likely that the relationship between our kindreds becomes even stronger, so much so that things that we would normally despise in the past would now intrigue and fill us with great joy?"

Erundil pondered his son's words, even nodding his head in amazement at his display of knowledge. "I am glad that you understand where I am coming from, my son," he responded. "But again concerning your wish, you know the laws of our people, and I do not want you to act as though you are ignorant of them now. Our people do not change with the times, as we are faithful to the laws that have filled us with wisdom and joy. And besides, there are many gamdarian women among our kindred that you can marry, and I know that your joy would be fulfilled in the same way."

Sensing that he was going nowhere in his conversation with his father, Lelhond sighed to himself and fell silent, staring far off into the distance. The rest of the company watched on, seeing if Erundil would say anything more, but the gamdar instead remained silent, with no word or action happening among the company for quite some time.

Eventually, Mataput broke the silence to express his desire for Erundil and Lelhond to remain united with each other despite their opposing views. "Erundil and Lelhond," he said, with the two gamdars immediately bringing their attention to the volvier. "You two are the King and Prince of Watendelle, and if you remain divided then not only will your family be split between two ways, but so will your people. I will not instruct you, Erundil, on what you should do regarding Lelhond's desire to marry Nahelion, for that is not my part to judge. But what I will say is that you must not let seeds of bitterness or division grow in any way, for it will only signal a slow downfall for your kingdom."

The company gulped in fear as they listened to Mataput, but they hoped that this warning would bring Erundil and Lelhond close together. And in that moment it seemed as though their hope would come to pass, as Erundil looked on at his son with what seemed to be a smile on the corner of his face. Lelhond looked on at his father with a sense of newfound respect toward him, and as the two of them came close together, they whispered words in their native Tuntish tongue to each other. Though the company couldn't hear or understand what they said, as they turned their attention to Forandor and Karandil, the two gamdars seemed to be able to hear the faintest of words that their brother and father spoke, and with smiles of relief on their faces it became apparent to the company that Erundil and Lelhond had seemingly put their differences aside and reconciled themselves to each other.

The company breathed heavy sighs of relief at this sight, glad to see that Erundil and Lelhond were back together and not arguing over what they disagreed with. And so the company continued talking and joking among themselves, with joyful faces hiding any sign of tension they had experienced just a few moments before. But amidst their talking, they started to grow tired, and seeing the pitch-black sky outside of the cave they knew that it was the right time to sleep for the night.

"What a day this has been," remarked Huminli, yawning while he spoke. "I'm exhausted after this long day of running and evading danger. Maybe it would be a good idea to rest now and prepare for the morning."

"Yes, for once the smalf is right," agreed Erundil. "Let us rest here for the night before we continue our journey first thing tomorrow morning. We need as much sleep so that our minds and bodies are at rest for this long journey."

"I sure need plenty of rest," said Steven, with his eyes beginning to twitch in tiredness. "After such a difficult day as today, a good night's rest for the body and mind is much needed and appreciated."

The company agreed to this and being worn out from the long day of running and fighting, they were ready to rest and allow their minds and bodies to be at peace for the next few hours. They eventually ceased speaking to each other and gathering large rocks scattered throughout the caves, they laid their heads on them and covered themselves with the extra cloaks in their backpacks for warmth. Before they knew it they soon passed out into a deep sleep, with all knowledge of the arduous day passing away from their minds.

The next morning, the company suddenly woke up to the blaring noise of the wind screaming and blasting its way through the open cracks of the cave from outside. It brought a chilly presence inside the cave, with not even the company's cloaks providing them with much warmth. The wind flew through the cave at great speed, blasting small rocks aside and even slightly moving the larger ones that the company laid their heads on. The company immediately stood up, wondering how the wind had managed to come inside the cave.

Glophi was the last to stand up, slowly staggering to his feet as he scratched his head and shivered while listening to the sound of the chilling wind that unleashed its power inside the cave. "How is the wind managing to come in here?" he asked, with chattering teeth. "Is there another cave that we can go to where the wind won't manage to enter and make us so cold?"

Orieant turned his attention to the small opening that led outside of the cave. And he noticed that the great wind had managed to storm its way through that opening. He could see that the sky was quite bright, and even though no snow was coming down, great piles still covered the ground. He stared at this sight for some time before turning to Glophi.

"No, the wind is only spreading to every cave that there is," he said. "But don't worry, we will not stay here any longer. Once we are ready we will continue on our journey through these mountains as it is already the morning time with the sun shining brightly. But it will still be very cold and windy outside, perhaps even more so than it was yesterday. We may stop in some caves along the way, but we must make sure that we cover these many openings with rocks so that the wind can't blast its way inside. Nonetheless, our short stops will be quick as we must cover much distance through these mountains before we begin the next stage of our quest which will be our journey through the deserted wildernesses of Nangorid, where it should be much quieter and warmer in that region."

Huminli's eyes suddenly lit up in eager anticipation of what Orieant said. "Well I can't wait before we reach that next stage of our journey," he said. "Going to a region that is much warmer than this mountainous region full of intense cold, freezing wind, and endless piles of snow sounds like an excellent idea to me! When shall we begin going in that direction?"

"Whenever everyone is ready we will start going," responded Orieant. "And so are we all ready to continue in our journey, or does anyone need more time to rest?"

"I'm ready," responded Steven, rubbing his cold hands to keep himself warm. "I can't stand this cold weather and not even a fire would be able to completely remove this chilling wind. We should be on our way before we freeze to death in these caves just as the melondairs did."

"Do not worry, we will not freeze to death in here," laughed Orieant. "But if we are ready to go, then let us make sure that we pack all that we brought with us and not forget anything, as we will certainly never come back to this place, not even in a thousand years."

"I wouldn't even dare to sniff this place in ten thousand years," remarked Huminli. "It seems that we are all ready to leave, so let us not waste any more time."

Immediately, the smalf gathered his backpack and started walking in the direction of the opening that led outside of the cave. Glophi quickly ran up to his brother, he too wishing to leave the caves as soon as possible.

Upon seeing the smalves eagerly making up their minds to leave the place where they were gathered, the company also hastened their pace and gathered their items and backpacks to follow the smalves to the opening. As they made their way there they could see the sun shining brightly in the clear sky, though the weather was anything but warm as the wind roared with all its might through the air. But they were glad to finally catch a breath of fresh air after staying in the stuffy cave the day before. Yet before anyone could step outside, Mataput and Orieant swiftly came to the front of the group and stopped them.

"Do not forget that the wind outside is very chilly and blowing at great speed," warned Mataput. "All of you should wait and follow and Orieant and I before you get lost when the wind takes you wherever it chooses to."

Instantly, the company made way for Mataput and Orieant to lead them, and seeing that they were all ready, the volviers made their way through the opening as the company followed them from behind.

Almost immediately after they had crossed their way through the opening and stepped outside onto the snow, a viciously powerful and chilly gust of wind came flashing in the company's direction. Surprised by how powerful the wind was, the company stumbled over and nearly fell to the snowy ground before they quickly regained their balance. They found themselves standing on high snow that was halfway between their ankles and knees, and they shivered as they could feel the cold sensation of the ice and the snow brushing against their legs. No snow came down from the sky as there was not a single cloud in the sky, but a great amount covered the ground where they stood, with no rocky or solid ground within sight of the path they were on. The mountains were completely drenched in piles of snow and the company could see great icicles growing within the sides of the mountains. The air was devastatingly cold and the company could feel the chilly wind making its way through their cloaks and even enter their very bones, or so they thought. But they all stood miserably by each other's side, shocked by the horrible weather conditions they would have to endure.

Huminli grumbled to himself, standing miserably under the bitter cold. "I can't believe that I forgot how terrible the weather was outside," he said. "And before we know it, all of these piles of snow will grow to be just as tall as us! Ugh! Why did we ever choose to make our journey through these bitter mountains?"

"Going through these mountainous paths was the best way for us to go, Huminli, whether the ground was covered in snow or not," responded Mataput. "The path we have set out upon is the path we must trek, and besides, the Dark Lord's slaves will have a difficult time in tracking us through these bitter mountains, which will only be to our safety and benefit. So take courage, my friend! In a little while longer we would have completely traveled through these mountains and we would have received our reward for enduring this momentary challenge."

"Journeying somewhere warmer on a flat surface would have still been my preference," said Huminli, continuing to complain. "But I suppose that this path will do, as we will soon reach the end of these mountains. It looks like the weather should be our only challenge."

"It should indeed be our only challenge," remarked Mataput. "But how will we manage to endure that challenge if we remain standing here in this cold? Come, let us make our way through these snowy paths so that once we have passed the test we can boldly proclaim that we endured these bitter mountains!"

"Now that sounds like music to my ears!" excitedly said Huminli. And with that, he cast away his miserable face, and smiling with courage he began to walk through the winding path covered in deep snow.

Glophi caught up with his brother, while Mataput and Orieant led them with smiles on their faces, glad to see a change in Huminli's attitude. The rest of the company also changed their minds, and with eager expectation, they too began walking down the winding snowy path, trudging their way slowly through the deep snow, while shaking their heads in amazement at the volviers who easily glided down the snow. Yet they slowed down their pace so that the rest of the company could closely follow them from behind, as the wind blew heavily in their faces. But with the company gathered close together, they all walked in a single file with Mataput and Orieant leading the way, Huminli and Glophi behind the volviers, Steven and Peter in touching distance from the smalves, and the gamdars holding their ground from the back of the group.

The sun continued to shine brightly in the sky but it only further deceived the company as the weather was the opposite of being warm. But still, they trudged their way through the heavy snow, trying their best to ignore the terrible weather conditions that plagued them. They made their way carefully through the winding and snowy path, knowing that ice was packed deep inside the snow. Meanwhile, the wind continued to scream in their faces, forcing them to walk even more slowly and even crouch down at times to prevent themselves from falling over.

Time began to swiftly pass, with the company by now having walked through the snow-trodden path for nearly an hour. Yet it didn't seem to them that they had covered much distance, as they were forced to walk extremely slower than they did the previous day because of the chilly speed of the wind that blew in their direction. The wind had grown in its intensity and even with their gray cloaks that were supposed to keep them warm, the company felt as though their bones were beginning to freeze. Their legs ached as they walked on the heavy snow and winding path, and their mood grew more weary and gloomy in the time that passed.

The company grew more tiresome as they climbed their way through the difficult winding path covered in snow. As he went on, Steven was made aware of his wound as occasionally he would feel sharp moments of pain inflict his chest. He would briefly clutch onto his chest before releasing his hand when the pain would go away, but as this kept going on for some time, he eventually couldn't take it anymore. Coming to a sudden halt he went over to the side of the path and sat down on the snow with his back against the mountainside. He exhaled deep breaths to himself and closed his eyes, wishing for the pain to be gone permanently.

The company immediately stopped walking and made their way back to Steven with deep concern on their faces. "Is everything fine, Steven?" asked Peter, being the first to come to his friend's help.

Steven sighed to himself and slowly opened his eyes. "I can feel the pain returning to my chest," he said wearily. "It's as though sharp daggers are striking my wound for brief seconds before quickly going away." He fell silent, grimacing in heavy pain as the sharp aching feeling inflicted his body, causing him to clutch onto his chest once more while breathing heavily and hoping for the pain to go away again.

Peter could say nothing and instead looked on with wide eyes and a pain-filled expression on his face as he couldn't bear to witness Steven in the condition he was in. "What should we do?" he asked, turning toward the company behind him. "Maybe we should take a break before we continue climbing up this path. Steven is aching in terrible pain right now."

"We should give him more of my people's medicine," suggested Erundil. "Each morning we should put more of the cream on his wound and let him eat more pieces of the healing leaves so that these occasional instances of pain will be completely gone."

Erundil reached into his bag to gather some more of his packed medicine to treat Steven, but Orieant swiftly prevented him from treating Steven. "No, Erundil," he said. "Treating Steven with too much medicine can be to his detriment. What he needs right now is rest, but we cannot rest here under this bitter cold with the wind blowing in our faces. We should see another cave within the next half hour to an hour where we can stop there and take a rest before we continue." He went over to Steven and brought him up to his feet. "Come on, Steven, we will find you a cave where you can take as long a rest as you need before we go again on our journey."

"I would rather stay here to rest," protested Steven. "Even just half an hour feels like a much longer time than it has ever felt because of how miserable these snowy and winding paths are."

"But the time will pass away before you know it, Steven," remarked

Peter, trying to encourage Steven. "We just need to walk a little further up these paths and then we find a cave that will be much warmer than it is outside here with this cold wind and snow."

Steven sighed to himself and shook his head, but seeing how desperate everyone was for him to go on a little further, he finally gave in. "Fine," he said. "I am willing to go on a little further under these miserable weather conditions and even under my pain, in the hope of finding a warm cave to rest and recover."

Smiles came on the company's faces, and they immediately set out again, climbing up the narrow winding path as meticulously and slowly as possible. Peter held onto Steven's arm as the two of them walked together, with Peter giving his friend as much support and words of encouragement as he deemed the weary man would need. And even with the terrible wind blowing in their faces, they still boldly followed the lead of the volviers. They walked on for several more minutes, though the time felt like hours, and occasionally Steven would clutch onto his chest, with the moments of pain still managing to inflict him. But he endured, hoping that the sight of a cave would appear in the corner of his eye so that he could finally enter it and collapse onto the ground, receiving the rest and treatment he needed. More time began to steadily pass as the company walked through the deep piles of snow covering the winding path, yet no sign of a cave appeared. And the temperature grew even more cold and bitter as the minutes passed, with the wind growing more cruel in its power, though the sky remained bright and clear.

But then suddenly, clouds began to take shape in the sky as the sun's light grew dim. And even while this happened, small flakes of snow came falling softly from the sky, and as the minutes passed the snow started to gradually increase in its amount when before they knew it, great amounts of snow came crashing down upon the company. They were caught off guard by this sudden change in the weather, forcing them to hasten their walking as they knew they had to find a safe dwelling to shield them.

Yet even as the snow came down, something else caught their attention which made them stop dead in their tracks. As they hurried their pace through the winding and snowy path, with all of their attention fixed on the snow that now covered them, suddenly, from the corner of their eyes they noticed that heavy rocks mixed with snow near the top of the mountain were beginning to fall on them. Upon seeing this, they immediately dodged to the side of the path and cast their backs on the mountainside to avoid the heavy and snowy rocks from falling on them.

But more rocks mixed with snow continued to rain down from the mountaintop, some being massive and others quite small. The company was overtaken by shock and fear at the terrible sight of the snowy rocks flying down upon them at lightning speed, and Steven covered his eyes in dismay, stunned by the sudden turn of events that had gone against the company. Unable to endure this anymore he fell to the ground and covered his head with his hands, trying to avoid the snowy rocks from falling on him, while the rest of the company cast their backs against a rocky wall against the mountainside.

"Oh what a terrible disaster that has fallen upon us!" cried Steven. "Right when we were hoping to see a cave these snowy rocks have chosen to have other ideas!"

Peter rushed over to Steven's side and pulled him up from the snowy ground. "Well you can't just sit there and do nothing, Steven," he told his friend while bringing him to his feet. "Getting your head smashed by these rocks while talking will sure do wonders to shut your mouth, though I would hate to see that happen."

Peter brought Steven over to the mountainside where the company stood as still as they possibly could, with their backs against the wall and their hands grabbing onto any solid thing they could find so that they could keep their balance against the high-intensity wind. They watched on anxiously as more snowy rocks continued flying down from the mountain peak, having to narrowly escape from them at times. They continued to dodge the rocks, all the while trying to remain calm and collected, but terrible fear gripped their hearts as they knew that more rocks would only continue to rain down upon them. A large rock almost collapsed on Huminli, if it was not for his brother Glophi quickly warning him to evade the danger. Huminli swiftly jumped to the side, digging his head and body into the snowy ground on the winding path.

Huminli came up from out of the snow, with his gray cloak almost entirely drenched in white icy crystals. Meanwhile, along with the snowy rocks, more snow continued to rain down from the sky, which completely covered his hair in a white snowball. He quickly made his way back to where the company was, making his way back beside his brother as the two of them looked around hopelessly, wondering why this sudden change in weather and events had overtaken them. Huminli could feel his legs and feet growing numb from the icy cold snow, and the freezing weather had destroyed any confidence he had in reaching a warmer region away from the bitter mountains. But worst of all, even more so than the weather and snow, was that more snowy rocks continued to fall from the mountain peak, and they only seemed to be growing heavier and larger as time passed.

"What has happened?" cried out Huminli, while dodging yet another rock that threatened to fall on him. "Why has the weather suddenly become so unbearable and why are these snowy rocks raining down upon us without any signs of stopping?"

"This place is known as the bitter mountains for a reason, Huminli," responded Mataput, with he and Orieant seemingly not concerned by the falling snowy rocks, much to the company's astonishment. "But there is no need to fear, for even though the weather has suddenly turned against us, I expected this to happen sooner rather than later. And the only reason why these rocks are falling from the peaks of the mountains is because of the terrible force in which this wind is moving."

"But that doesn't encourage me at all!" exclaimed Huminli. "That only makes me feel even more miserable because what if the wind decides to increase its force so much so that this entire mountain collapses on us? What will we do then?"

"The mountain will not collapse on us, Huminli," reassured Mataput. "Do not let your mind wander to imaginations that will only cause you to walk in fear. The only way that the mountain could fall on us, would be if the Dark Lord himself were to command it to do so, but he doesn't know that we are here. So it is up to us to walk boldly under these less-than-ideal conditions and endure this weather a little longer, and before we know it we will have no cause to worry about this again. So take courage! Once the coast is clear we will continue our journey without fear of falling rocks."

Huminli felt a good deal better after listening to Mataput's encouraging words, yet he still couldn't shake off the feeling of fear that was in his eyes as he looked hesitantly at the falling snowy rocks. He and the rest of the company were shaking because of the cold, with the wind and snow showing no signs of stopping or even slowing down. They waited for several more minutes, continuing to avoid more snowy rocks while hoping that they could finally go on in their journey.

Finally, it seemed that their wishes would soon be answered as the wind started to slowly die down in its intensity while fewer and even lighter rocks came down from the mountain peak. Though the weather conditions were still very difficult to endure as snow continued raining down from the sky and the chilly frost hung in the air, the company felt a resurgence of hope fill their cold and dreary bodies. Even Mataput and Orieant's eyes seemed to light up, as they perceived that it would soon be safe for them to continue their way through the winding and snowy path.

Yet their confidence would be short-lived. For in that very moment, distinct and strange noises could be heard far into the distance ahead of them. The company gazed up at the sky in response to the strange sounds, and as they cast their heads upward, they gasped in shock as they saw what looked like vast shapes as great dark shadows seeming to cover the bright sky in dark clouds. They were greatly confused at the odd sight and for a moment, the fear of snowy rocks falling on them and the misery of the freezing weather suddenly vanished from their memory, as their full attention was now brought to the unusual sight in the sky. As they looked, the shadows seemed to be growing near to them, and they were indeed as they soon noticed that they were flying at lightning speed toward them.

Then the sounds grew distinct and became clearer to them, and they soon made out the noise of a loud flapping, as though massive birds were hastening their way to them. The shadows grew nearer with the sound of flapping growing increasingly louder, and then, as the shapes of the shadows grew closer, the company suddenly understood what was going on. They discovered that the shapes of the shadows were that of winged figures, gigantic in size and terrible in their might and presence of dread. Then came the sound of hideous screeching noises, and at this very moment, the company became greatly alarmed. Spirits, as it seemed of dreadful fear, consumed their trembling hearts, and they cried aloud in horror at the sight of overwhelming darkness covering the slightest spark of light they had. But they now understood perfectly what was going on and who had come to take away their hope and torment them. The matis had come.

At once, Mataput and Orieant sprang to action, diving themselves into the nearest pile of snow they could find. "Hide yourselves in the snow!" shouted Orieant, urging the rest of the company to follow suit in their direction. "The winged spies of the Dark Lord have returned! Hide before you are caught in plain sight!"

Immediately, the company took heed to Orieant's warning and looked for piles of snow that were large enough and they dove into them to hide from the matis. Steven staggered his way to a pile of snow nearby, feeling overwhelmed by all that was happening around him. He sensed another pinch of sharp pain gnawing at his wound, and seeing the deep pain his friend was in, Peter quickly grabbed ahold of him and the two of them hid next to each other in a pile of snow.

As they hid in the snow, the company could still hear the noise of terrible screeching flying high above their heads. Even though their heads and bodies were buried deeply beneath the snow, they still had to cover their ears, as the excruciating sound rang loudly inside their ears. But then the sound instantly disappeared out of nowhere, and the noise of the wings of the matis seemed to grow silent for a moment, as if they had stopped in the middle of their air, waiting for their chance to pounce upon the company.

Yet eventually, the screeching sound returned while the tumult of flapping wings rang noisily throughout the sky. The matis soon passed over where the company hid and went on with a different errand of theirs.

Sensing that the winged creatures had left, the volviers were the first ones to pop out from the snow. "The matis have left," remarked Orieant, helping the rest of the company stand to their feet. "There is no need to fear, for the coast is now clear for us to continue walking."

Steven came up out of the snow, clutching onto his chest. "I can't continue," he said wearily. "I don't think I have the strength to continue walking. I don't even care if we are a few minutes away from a cave. I simply can't carry on. We shouldn't carry on." His words were slow and each breath he took was difficult, and in the blink of an eye, he suddenly collapsed to the ground.

Peter rushed to his side while the rest of the company looked on at Steven with troubled expressions covering their faces. Erundil stared at Steven for a moment, with a sense of sympathy growing in his eyes for the man in pain. He then turned toward Mataput and Orieant while the two of them cast their attention on Steven as well.

"I believe that Steven is right," he said. "We should by no means continue in this path that we are currently on, for what if more matis and other servants of the Dark Lord are still spying on us and happen to capture us because of our foolishness? And let us not forget about this weather, as it is only growing even colder with the snow and wind showing no signs of slowing down. My feet are drenched with snow and ice mixed and all we are going to do is kill ourselves under these terrible conditions if we do not turn aside from this path."

"I agree," said Huminli, shivering in the cold. "It doesn't look like we will see a cave anytime soon, so I think we should turn back and start descending these mountains."

The company agreed with Erundil and Huminli, who were so frantic by the fear and coldness they felt that they became worried that they could die either because of the terrible weather or from the attacks of the enemy. They were all willing to turn around, even Peter, who couldn't bear seeing the condition that Steven was in. They were suffering because of the cold, and as far as they were concerned, they were on the same page. Yet Mataput and Orieant sighed to themselves as they saw the complaining and misery that consumed the company's hearts, and they were disappointed to see them willing to give up so easily.

"I admit that I thought all of you still had enough strength left inside to endure this difficulty," said Mataput, with his disappointment obvious in his eyes. "I don't understand why all of you are willing to give up so easily, and you, Peter, I thought that you would be the one encouraging us to continue."

"I would've continued, but this cold weather is becoming almost unbearable to endure," confessed Peter. "And just look at Steven, he is lying on the ground in complete despair, and it would be unfair to force him to continue when he is clearly in deep pain."

Mataput stared at Steven for some time as he lay on the ground, with pity for the man growing in his heart and being visible on his face. "I understand that you are going through a lot, especially you, Steven," he said. "But I know that you can overcome this difficulty, and you can trust me when I say that these circumstances will not destroy you. But you along with everyone else must be willing to endure this great plague before we find a cave to truly rest and find protection from this brutally cold weather."

"Caves will not save us from this trouble though," remarked Lelhond. "And besides, if we didn't expect the winged spies of the enemy to roam the sky and cause us to fear, what is stopping them from continuing to search this region and possibly find us?"

"You are not wrong in what you say, Lelhond," responded Mataput. "We are not expecting caves to keep us safe forever nor are we ignorant enough to believe that we will not face any more challenges. But when we do encounter danger as we already have, we have no choice but to hide either in caves or in the snow, as we were forced to do. And if hiding in the snow means protecting not only our lives but the secrecy of our quest, then perhaps the snow can prove to be our friend and not our bitter and cold enemy."

"Perhaps so, but I don't want to walk through any more paths covered in snow," grumbled Glophi, growing increasingly weary and cold as each minute passed. "I'm starting to feel like my feet will freeze if we travel any more through these snowy paths, and this cold is not making me feel any better either. Please, why don't you let us turn back around?"

"Even if we do turn around, we will be walking through these same snowy paths for several more hours," responded Mataput. "And the cave that we came from is about an hour away from us."

The company grumbled to themselves as they heard this from Mataput, completely forgetting how long they had already walked. They sighed to themselves as they realized they would have to endure many more hours if they were to descend from the mountain, and they pondered what they would do now. They felt as though they were in a terrible prison, trapped and knowing that whatever next move they made would only be a difficult path to take.

But suddenly, amid their state of dejection, Forandor noticed something in the distance behind them. As he looked closer, his eyes suddenly flickered with light and the expression on his face changed. Karandil noticed the change in his brother and wondered what he had seen or discovered.

"What is it, Forandor?" he asked. "Do you bring tidings of hope in this moment of despair?"

"I do, though very much unexpectedly," responded Forandor, pausing momentarily as he turned around and stared at what he had seen. "There is another path in the distance behind us," he continued. "The path appears to be quite steep, but I think that we should be able to manage it, and perhaps going in this direction will allow us to descend this mountain in a far shorter time."

The company immediately turned their attention to what lay behind them, and after searching for the path that Forandor talked about, their faces suddenly lit up with excitement. They could see another path towards the left of the mountains and on the lower level of the winding path they had walked on. Though it was quite steep, it was covered in far less snow, to which they all rejoiced at this sight and desperately desired to go in this direction.

"Please Mataput and Orieant!" pleaded Huminli, falling to his knees in front of the volviers. "Allow us to go in this direction rather than continuing in the direction that we're currently on. Will you allow us just this one thing?"

Mataput and Orieant help to feel pitiful for Huminli and the company, as they observed the desperation that covered their faces. Yet, the two of them had worrisome glances on their faces, as if they knew something troubling that was hidden from the company.

"I am sorry, but it would not be wise for us to go down that way," responded Mataput amid Huminli's begging words. "For even though that way will allow us to descend these mountains in a short time, that path will lead us down a dangerous and dark place. It will lead us southward and not westward, and it will bring us to a valley through the deserted city of Tuwanor."

The company instantly fell silent, with chills of fright running down their bones. But suddenly, amid everyone's fear, Steven stood up from where he was lying in pain, much to the company's relief and amazement.

His eyes lit up at the mention of the city of Tuwanor. "Is this the same city that you talked about when we first entered this land?" he asked.

"Yes it is, Steven," responded Mataput. "And just as I explained before, it is the same city where Raleshob, the most powerful wuzlir to have ever lived once dwelled and ruled for many long years. It is he who led the Dark Lord's army in the War of Great Alliances, and on behalf of his master, he committed many terrible acts of darkness against the gamdars, being rewarded for every evil act he enacted. But long ago that city of perpetual fear and darkness was destroyed, and only fragments of its once-firm foundations now remain. Many wuzlirs fled from the city amidst its destruction, and it is now believed to be completely deserted. Yet the city is still full of the memories of great evil, and it is not a place where anyone should desire to go, as its malicious nature has never gone to sleep in all the centuries that have passed."

The company's faces became covered with terror by all they heard, especially the gamdars, who shuddered with fear. Yet even despite his fear, Erundil's face suddenly became emboldened by pride as he thought to himself for a while.

"Why should we be afraid of the deserted city?" he asked. "Was it not destroyed long ago by the might of my people's great army, and is it not said that only one living descendant of Raleshob exists today? I say that we should boldly go on that path which leads us through the deserted city because no power of darkness can hinder our light."

"I am glad to see your boldness, Erundil, but I wouldn't dare go that way unless we had no other choice," responded Mataput, with grave concern on his and Orieant's face. "And I will warn you, don't let your confidence turn into proud ignorance because I do not wish for you to be caught unexpectedly by the vast evil that still resides in that empty city. And as I mentioned that direction will only lead us southward instead of westward, and our journey to the region of Parsuglin to find the lost book of Ulohendel in the tower of Wuzinch Torgol would be delayed by many days and possibly even weeks because we should have gone westward. It would be unwise to take that path, and you can trust me when I warn you of the dangers and consequences going down that road will entail."

"Maybe it would be unwise, but it would still be a courageous choice to make just as you command us to be," responded Erundil, with a wide grin toward Mataput at the volviers. "Now what do you, my sons, have to say about all of this?" he asked, turning toward his sons. "Should we go down the path leading us away from these bitter mountains in quicker time to travel through the deserted city of Tuwanor, or should we suffer under these terrible weather conditions, that only seem to grow worse with every passing day?"

"I think that we should travel through the deserted city," responded Lelhond. "It is not that I want to disregard the wisdom of Mataput and Orieant, but I am struggling to understand why we should fear journeying through a city that has been deserted for many centuries."

"We certainly should not walk by fear," remarked Orieant. "Nor are we saying that we should allow the enemy to scare us from taking risks. But even despite that, we should not be so eager to throw away the wisdom we have learned over time, just because of a momentary difficulty."

"But this momentary difficulty has done serious damage to us physically and mentally, especially to Steven," responded Lelhond. "And not only that, but it seems as though the enemy is searching throughout these mountains to try and discover if anything strange is going on in his land. Perhaps if we took this path to descend this mountain, we wouldn't have to worry about any servants of the Dark Lord potentially finding us."

"Perhaps we won't have to worry about that," said Orieant. "But that remains a large risk, and it would be safer for us to continue in the direction in which we have set out to tread."

"It may be safer, but I think we should go on that other path," suddenly interrupted Peter. "It is good to be brave, but I feel that it would be harsh for us to continue traveling through this terrible cold up here in these mountains. A valley where it is much warmer and easier to travel through sounds like a much better prospect."

"I couldn't agree more," chimed in Steven, smiling gladly toward Peter. "Finally, for once this boy agrees with me," but as he was reminded of his wound, his smile quickly faded and he clutched onto his chest for a brief moment. "I can still feel the sharp pain of the wound on my chest, and I believe that the weather is making it even worse. Please, at least for my sake, let us go down these mountains on the path that will lead us to a warmer place, where the wind and snow won't hurt my wound."

As Mataput and Orieant listened to Steven and saw him still being tormented by the pain of his wound, they felt a newfound sense of sympathy for him. Sighing to themselves, they finally conceded to the wishes of the company even though they felt that everyone would regret their choice in time to come.

"Very well then," said Orieant. "For the sake of Steven and your morale, we will go on the steep path leading us down these mountains and into the valley southward through the deserted city of Tuwanor."

Suddenly, the company erupted into celebration as Huminli and Glophi jumped up and down and everyone else sighed in relief. They could hardly believe that Mataput and Orieant had granted their wish, and they couldn't stop thanking the volviers.

"Thank you, thank you, thank you!" exclaimed Glophi, while he constantly jumped up and down. "You don't know how much this means to us!"

The company couldn't stop smiling with relief and gratitude, yet Mataput and Orieant were anything but gleeful. "Just remember that Mataput and I are doing this for your sake," warned Orieant. "And do not forget that this path will make our journey through the land of Nangorid much longer than what we would have originally expected. We now have to be even stronger mentally and physically, because even though we should find more food and water on our journey, we will still have to eat and drink in moderation now."

"I'm fine with that!" said Glophi, still bouncing with excitement. "Huminli and I could do with a little less food if that means we can go in another direction other than these bitter mountains."

"Very well then," said Orieant, gazing intently at Glophi and the company. "Let us go on then, but do not forget all that Mataput and I have warned you about."

And with that, Orieant and Mataput turned around in the direction behind them and began leading the eager and excited company down the winding path from whence they came, into a new and steep path leading to another way. The company followed along with a resurgence of hope and joy burning inside them, while the volviers led them with hearts and faces filled with concern.

16

A New Direction

THE COMPANY CLOSELY FOLLOWED the volviers from behind, unable to hide the growing excitement that they felt. Broad smiles covered their faces and they couldn't wait to start descending the mountains. Steven felt a resurgence of strength that entered his body, though the slight tingling pain of his wound still bothered him from time to time. Meanwhile, as the company made their way to the steep path that would lead them down the mountains, they first went through the winding and snowy path for several minutes, enduring the fierce wind blasting in their faces as more snow continued pouring down from the sky. Yet even despite the terrible weather still inflicting pain on them, they paid no attention to this struggle as they knew that they would very soon escape from its tormenting presence.

Eventually, they finally came to the steep path that they had so desperately wanted to go on when they first caught sight of it. Making their way to the path they couldn't stop smiling at how far less covered in snow it was, with its rocky ground visible to them. Bits of ice still grew along the side of the path, but it seemed to be melting in the bright sunlight.

Excited, the company began to descend their way down the path, but it was quite steep and with the wind blowing quite strongly near the side, they slowly made their way down the path, staggering as they carefully came down. As they slowed their pace, they were all able to make their way down the steep path, except for Steven, who seemed to fumble and shake with every step he took."

As his feet stumbled on the path, he clutched onto his chest once again, feeling sudden pain return to his wound. "Can someone help me?" he asked, with his legs shaking. "I'm afraid that I'm going to tumble over, and nobody would be able to save me if it happened."

Peter immediately rushed up to Steven and held the man's right hand. Huminli came to the other side and held his left hand, and the two of them helped Steven keep his balance and slowly walked by his side to give him the extra bit of support he needed to walk down the steep path. Mataput and Orieant turned around, with pleased smiles on their faces in seeing Peter and Huminli helping Steven. Yet they remained concerned over his overall wellbeing, and whether or not going down the steep path would make his health even worse.

"Do you still believe that it is good for you to go down this path, Steven?" asked Orieant. "I can see how much you are struggling, and indeed, if you or anyone else were to tumble over and fall down this mountain, it would be nearly impossible for any of us to save you, because of how steep this path is."

Steven immediately responded to Orieant. "We have already made our choice," he said without wavering. "We have already said that we don't want to endure the terror of these mountains ever again, and we are willing to go down this steep path if it means we can be free from this place. I for one want to escape from these bitter mountains as soon as possible, as this horrible weather will only make my wound even worse."

The company echoed Steven's statement and continued expressing their desire to go down the steep path. "Very well then, you have made your choice," responded Orieant, ceasing to try and change the company's mind about going down the path they were on. "We will continue to go down in this direction, to make our way from these mountains and to the deserted city of Tuwanor."

"That sounds good to me," remarked Steven, with his eyes set forward. And with his final word, Mataput and Orieant once again led the company down the steep path, while Peter and Huminli continued to hold onto Steven as they supported him.

The company continued in this way for the next hour or so, walking as steadily as they could down the steep path. But as time progressed, their legs and feet gradually ached in pain, and their excitement had cooled off with their smiles slowly fading.

Suddenly, Glophi stopped walking and leaned over, placing his hands on his knees. “I think we should take just a brief rest,” he said, breathing heavily. “Maybe we should’ve gone in another direction that is not so steep as this path is.”

Mataput, however, was having none of it. “Were you not jumping up and down with excitement when Orieant and I allowed you to go down this way?” he asked, with a stern expression on his face. “You have made your decision and it is final, and there is no time to go in any other direction. And why would we take a rest here on this steep path with the wind blowing in our faces and around us?”

Mataput walked away with visible frustration on his face, while Glophi shrank down in embarrassment for having made his comment, and Erundil made sure that his shame wouldn’t go away any time soon. “You better not make us look bad now, smalf,” he said, whispering in Glophi’s ear. “If you or your brother decide to go in another direction, then I would be fine with that, but don’t you dare try and drag the rest of us in the way of your foolishness.”

He moved away from the smalf, looking down at him in disdain as he continued walking down the steep path. Glophi felt even more ashamed by what he said, and he stood still by himself for a moment as the company continued walking on. Even his brother Huminli continued walking ahead of him, with him, Peter, and Steven not seeing how embarrassed Glophi was or seeing what Erundil had whispered to him.

However, one member of the company had noticed the shame that covered Glophi’s face and had seen Erundil whisper something in his ear. Coming to Glophi’s side, Lelhond placed his hand on the smalf’s shoulder and spoke with him. “There is no need to feel ashamed, Glophi,” he said, with a genuine smile on his face. “I’m even starting to feel a tingling of pain in my feet, but trust me, we are nearing the surface and very soon we will be able to take a long rest.”

A smile came on the smalf’s face as his eyes gazed at Lelhond with a sense of deep appreciation for the gamdar’s understanding. Seeing how much better he felt, Lelhond then urged Glophi to continue walking down the steep path, and so the two of them walked together at the very back of the group and talked with each other.

"I can't thank you enough, Lelhond," said Glophi as the two of them walked along. "Your level of understanding means so much to me," he smiled at Lelhond, but then paused for a moment, with his smile suddenly fading away.

Lelhond could see that something was visibly disturbing him, yet Glophi said nothing. A concerned look came on the gamdar's face as he wondered what was going on with the smalf. "What is it, Glophi?" he asked. "What is bothering you?"

Glophi sighed to himself, with a look of shame coming onto his face once again. "I'm just wondering whether or not Mataput and Orieant think poorly of me now," he confessed. "Because I don't understand why Mataput would lash out at me like that, and he seemed to be frustrated with me too."

Lelhond nearly laughed aloud in response to Glophi. "No, no, Glophi," he said. "Mataput and Orieant think very highly of you and your brother. Why would they have been so adamant about bringing you and your brother on this journey if they thought poorly of you? And Mataput wasn't lashing out at you, he was instead making a firm statement to all of us that because we collectively made our choice to go in this direction, it would be wrong of us to try and turn our backs on that choice. We must be faithful to our word, and that is what Mataput was trying to teach all of us at that moment. He is not angry with you, Glophi, instead he was trying to strengthen your inner resolve even more because he knows how important you are to this company."

A small smile came on Glophi's face and his mood suddenly changed. His face shone as his shame was slowly cast away from his mind. "Thank you again, Lelhond, for your encouraging and truthful words," he said. "You are proving to be a very good friend, and perhaps your leading will help mend the strife between your people and mine."

"Perhaps so," said Lelhond, with a smile. "But I am sure that one day my people's eyes will be opened and they will see the good that is found in the smalves, including my father who will change his mind about your kind."

The two of them continued walking side by side with each other and talked away in a long and deep conversation. They shared their many hopes and concerns, not withholding anything that had been placed on their hearts. Lelhond spoke of many stories and lessons he had learned in his life and even pulled out his sword from his backpack to show Glophi some helpful tricks to use if he ever found himself in danger. Glophi talked about the simplicity of his life and shared tales of the great adventures of his great grandfather Berry Frauttins, and about how many of his traits had been passed down to him and his brother. Lelhond could sense that Glophi was trying to impress him with his many stories, but the gamdar still listened to the smalf with a broad smile on his face. And as they talked, they seemed to be growing into very close friends who couldn't stop sharing everything that was on their minds.

The company could hear Lelhond and Glophi talking with each other even from where they were far ahead of the two of them, and they wondered why they had suddenly grown so close. Erundil even turned around to walk by his son's side while Glophi walked together on the other side of Lelhond.

"My son, is everything fine?" he asked, in a whispered voice to Lelhond. "Why are you talking so closely to the smalf as if you two have been friends for years?"

"His name is Glophi, father," sharply responded Lelhond. "And yes, everything is fine, because he is a very admirable smalf, which I hope you will begin to see yourself. And to your point, I wouldn't mind us becoming friends because of how eager he is to help us on this quest."

"Friends?" said Erundil in a loud and sneering voice, before he quickly lowered his voice level in a whisper to his son. "Why would you choose to become friends with a smalf? I understand that you said earlier at the council you would always be by the side of the smalves to help them in times of danger, but to now be a friend of theirs is a drastic change from what you originally promised. I must tell you the truth, my son, in that there is nothing to gain in being friends with a small little creature, who has no strength or wisdom to be compared to our people. I sense that there is everything to lose in being close to them, as that could be a signal of your downfall."

Lelhond shook his head in shock at his father's words. "I am worried that you are beginning to act hysterical, father," he said. "Have you not discovered by now what the purpose of our journey is? Our goal is not only to bring back the lost book of Ulohendel for the whole of humanity to be led in the direction of freedom, but it is also for the free creatures of the world to bring friendship among each other, which includes the smalves. And if we fail to build our relationship with the smalves, then this journey will either fail or be in vain even if we do succeed."

"This quest will not fail, nor will it be in vain," confidently responded Erundil. "But we do not need to stoop our level down so much just to allow the smalves a chance to prove themselves, which they have failed in doing so miserably. Rather, you and I along with your brothers can succeed by our strength and wisdom, with Mataput and Orieant leading us, and even Steven and Peter helping us. But I am beginning to regret this choice of mine to bitterly concede to the wishes of everyone around me to allow the smalves to join us on this most important quest. Have you not seen, Lelhond? They have brought great evil to this company through their foolishness by awakening Kolmaug from her slumber, and as a result, Steven now has a deadly wound on his chest. And who knows what level of peril they may bring to the rest of our journey? My son, why not reverse your stance on them, with you, your brothers, your sister, and your mother being just as you once were, distrusting of the smalves as you now see firsthand how foolish and dangerous they are?"

Lelhond felt a sting strike against his side as he listened to his father's negative whispers against the smalves. He felt greatly hurt to be hearing these words but was reminded that not too long ago he once held the same stance on the smalves in the same manner as his father. And he was also reminded that most of the gamdars in Watendelle also held the same view, including many of his friends and fellow soldiers of the gamdarian army. But he still couldn't help but feel guilt and pity for the smalves who he believed didn't deserve this unnecessary hate. And knowing that he once was not afraid to express his distrust and hate of the smalves, made him all the more determined to defend them and teach whoever he could to reconsider their negative towards the people group.

"I will not change my stance, father," he eventually said in a whisper to his father. "And I am confident that Karandil, Forandor, Glowren, and mother would not be willing to turn aside from the truth which has set them free from unnecessary bitterness."

Erundil chuckled to himself. "We will see about that," he said. "But you will see very soon that these smalves will lead us into even more disastrous situations, which hopefully will change you and your brothers' minds about them."

Lelhond fell silent, not wishing to hear any more of his father or allow the conversation to grow more bitter and tense. But Glophi could sense the tension growing between Erundil and Lelhond, and though he could barely hear them speaking because of their whispering words, by just looking at the expression on Erundil's face he could see that the gamdar didn't have good things to say about him or his brother.

He tapped Lelhond on the shoulder. "Is everything between you and your father?" he asked, eyeballing Erundil. "Is he saying anything nasty about me or my brother?"

At this question, Erundil suddenly glared at Glophi with piercing eyes. "And why are you barging into my son and I's conversation?" he asked, with a wry smile. "I see that you and your brother are always trying to stir discord and trouble with this company, which is what exactly you are trying to do with me now. But I tell you, the trouble that you cause will eventually come back around and fall on your head if you continue doing this."

Glophi suddenly came across to Erundil and stood in front of him with a fire in his eyes. "How long will you continue saying such nasty things against my brother and me?" he asked. "When will you learn to let go of your pride and unnecessary hostility against us and learn to trust us, just as Lelhond, Karandil, and Forandor have demonstrated the ability to do so? You claim that we are stirring trouble that will come back on our heads, well guess what? If you continue stirring up division and even more hate for this company, then you will pay tenfold for all that you've done."

The wry smile on Erundil's face suddenly faded as he looked on at the smalf with a flash of anger glowing in his eyes. Lelhond immediately held onto Glophi's arm and separated the two of them from allowing their tension to boil over. "Easy now, that is enough between you two," he said, trying to act as a peacemaker. "We need to learn to trust each other rather than fighting at the slightest differences."

"But your father does not trust me or my brother!" protested Glophi. "And yet my brother and I have trusted him throughout this journey. And I'm not afraid of saying that if he continues acting like this, then I wouldn't be surprised to see his words and seeds of hate fall back on his head. And I wouldn't mind seeing that, for just as my great grandfather Berry said, '*Seeds of hate will always produce bitter thorns.*'"

"Who cares about what your or your great grandfather Berry has to say?" said Erundil, with a look of contempt on his face. "Those words will certainly not affect me, although they may come back to bite you."

Erundil walked away from Glophi, looking down at him with a proud expression covering his face. But with the tension finally boiling over, Glophi immediately came over to him, not willing to allow the gamdar to have the final say.

"You better be careful with what you say old gamdar!" he shouted, standing up on his tiptoes to get right in Erundil's face. "Your words may come back to haunt you and I wouldn't feel bad for you if that were the case!"

Lelhond came running to the two of them. "Enough!" he said, separating the two of them once again. "Did I not already make myself clear? We cannot continue going on like this, as it's not right to speak such evil things against one another. We all have one goal in mind, and we must focus on that no matter what our own opinions may be."

Glophi withdrew from Erundil, hoping that no one else had heard his argument with the gamdar. But the damage had already been done, as the rest of the company had stopped walking as they became aware of the tension that was boiling from behind them.

"Is everything all right?" asked Mataput, turning around toward Erundil, Lelhond, and Glophi. "Why am I hearing Erundil and Glophi speaking such negative things against each other? Are we not all in one accord regarding the purpose of our quest?"

"He started it!" cried Glophi, pointing at Erundil. "He was the one who started resorting to saying such nasty things against me! Is that not true, Lelhond?"

"Yes, it's true," admitted Lelhond. "But at the same time, Glophi, we cannot continue fighting one another and looking to spread the blame. We must put aside our differences and learn to work together if we wish to succeed in this journey."

"Very true, Lelhond," remarked Mataput. "Your words ring true indeed, for all that you have said is the true purpose of our quest. And if Erundil and Glophi can find a way to get along, then this journey would be much easier. But for our journey to go much smoother than it already has you, Erundil, must choose to cast away your bitterness towards the smalves, and in doing so you will have gained tremendous respect and admiration not only from Orieant and me, but also from your sons, your daughter, your wife, and the people of your kingdom. You will have the power to change the hearts of your people concerning their attitude towards the smalves, and you will restore the goodness and dignity of the land of Watendelle."

Erundil stared straight ahead into the distance and said nothing in response to Mataput, passing Lelhond and Glophi as he walked on forward. Mataput and Orieant turned forward as well and continued leading the company through the steep path, with Lelhond and Glophi both sighing to themselves as they continued walking.

The company toiled on for some more time down the long and steep rocky path, and over time, the wind slowly died down with the snow only coming down in small flakes. Peter and Huminli fell behind at the back of the company, going at a slow pace to provide Steven with the support he needed. Every while and again, they would take very brief rests whether their feet ached or if Steven felt a sharp sting in his chest.

But eventually, as a couple of hours passed, the company could see the huge progress they had made in descending the mountain. Their spirits were lifted as they knew that very soon they would be completely away from the bitter mountains once and for all. And as another half hour passed, the company could now practically see the bottom of the mountains from where they were.

And finally, taking one more step the company came to a stop as they had now reached the bottom of the mountain. They found themselves staring at a wide valley surrounding them, and all they could do was breathe a deep sigh of relief that they had finally reached the bottom of the mountains and could now take a good long rest. Steven collapsed to the ground in exhaustion and lay on the ground for some time on his back. The rest of the company had small smiles on their faces, as they looked on the great and bitter mountains of Lehu Shalank to their side, knowing that they had finally escaped from its horrible presence.

The weather was calm, and though it was still cold with small flakes of snow falling every while and again, it still didn't compare to the terrible blizzard they had endured in the mountains. The sun was shining high and brightly in the sky, with hardly any clouds visible. The company stood silently for a moment, greatly relieved that they had finally escaped from the bitter mountains.

However, as they stared at the sight of the valley, they learned that the region wouldn't instantly provide them with much comfort. Even as the sun was shining, the valley remained quite bleak with brown grass covering the ground, and only a few scattered trees and plants being seen far ahead into the distance. As far as the company could see, there were no clear paths visible in the valley, which caused the company's mood to change once more with a sense of gloominess filling their hearts.

"We are here at last," remarked Mataput, breaking the long silence as the company gazed into every direction of the valley. "This is the region that you all wished to journey through, so I thought you would be more excited than you are now."

Steven stood up from where he lay. "Where are we?" he asked, rubbing his eyes. "This valley seems so lifeless, and it seems as though no other living creatures reside in this place."

"Yes," said Huminli, agreeing with Steven. "I hardly see any trees or plants, and the grass is not even partially green. And even with the bright sun shining high above us, it seems to only be exposing the bleakness of this valley. There's absolutely nothing in this place to give us a sense of comfort or happiness."

"Before you all start complaining, understand that this is the direction you chose to go through," responded Mataput. "After all, this is the way that will lead us to the deserted city of Tuwanor just as you asked, and what were you expecting to see? A beautiful valley teeming with life displayed in flowers, trees, and plants? I am sorry, but we are in the land of Nangorid, which is a miserable and dark place because of the presence of the Dark Lord which is reflected in every region of his domain."

"I guess you are right, Mataput," said Steven with a sigh. "We are here because this is the direction that we all wanted to go through. But you still haven't answered my question. Where are we, or more specifically, what is this place called?"

"We are in the Himarshish Valley, which means the lifeless valley," responded Mataput. "This is the region south of the mountains of Lehu Shalank, which means we will now begin traveling southward in a circular loop, rather than going westward in a straight line through Nangorid. As I said earlier, this path will prolong our journey much further through the deserted city of Tuwanor, but Orieant and I only agreed to go this way for your sake."

"That means it would not be right for us to blame anyone," said Peter. "Because we collectively chose to go this way, and that means the idea of turning around to go through the mountains and find a shortcut is long gone."

"Regardless, I wouldn't go through those mountains again even if we arrived at the Dark Lord's tower the very next day," commented Erundil. "It is indeed an idea long gone, and so we must be determined to go through this new way."

"But before we go again, I think we should take a rest," said Huminli. "Descending that steep mountain path was not an easy task, and I could feel a slight bit of pain in my feet. And besides, I'm quite hungry too, since we haven't eaten in hours."

"Then let us take a brief rest and eat a meal before we continue again," said Orieant. "We will need the extra bit of energy and nourishment for the next stage of our journey."

The company found a place to sit down on the brown grass and opened up their backpacks to dig through the remaining food they had. They still had a decent amount of food left which was enough to last them several more weeks, but as Huminli and Glophi opened up their bags, their eyes suddenly lit up with shock. As they turned their attention to the rest of the company and saw the food they had remaining, they discovered that they had far less than everyone else. They still had plenty of fruits and vegetables left to last for a few more weeks, but they had a meager amount of meat and bread, which would likely only last them for another week or so.

They tried hiding this from the company, but upon noticing the amount of food they had and seeing the embarrassment that was on their faces, Orieant spoke to them. "How is it that you two have far less food than us?" he asked.

Huminli and Glophi said nothing at first, but being prompted by the company to reveal the truth, Glophi eventually responded. "Perhaps we ate some food in secret," he confessed, with his face fixed to the ground in embarrassment as he wished not to see Orieant's glinting eyes. "I am sorry, but Huminli and I just couldn't help ourselves during the long and tiring journey through the mountains. And so, at times we fell to the back of the group and ate some food quietly, while you led the way in front."

Glophi looked up again, expecting to see Orieant's eyes steaming with wrath. But to his surprise, he saw that the volvier had a peculiar smile on his face, as he chuckled to himself.

"You two make me laugh," remarked Orieant, smiling at Glophi and Huminli. "Do not worry, I am not angry at you, but I would've preferred if you had privately told Mataput and me how hungry and tired you were, before deciding that."

"I was afraid that you and Mataput would've gotten mad at us," suddenly broke in Huminli. "After all, you told us to eat this food in moderation as it wouldn't last us the entire journey."

"I did say that," said Orieant. "But Mataput and I wouldn't have gotten mad at you, since we know that you smalves love food. But all should be fine, as though there are hardly any living things in this valley, we may still find some fruits growing on the scattered plants and trees that reside in this land, along with some animals roaming around that we can hunt for. But if we don't manage to find any of that, then we may have to share some of our food amongst each other."

"But even with that, Orieant and I are not concerned about the amount of food we have left," commented Mataput. "Because as we pass through the deserted city of Tuwanor, not only is there a land full of fruits and animals that we can gather and hint, but therein lies in secret, the land of Lundarin, the hidden realm of Gonyardu. Orieant and I have known the Lady Gonyardu for many thousands of years, and if our food supply does indeed prove to be quite scarce, then we can pass through there and even spend a short time there if we need to. For Lundarin is a haven, a forested region that was established by the Golden Lady many thousands of years ago, intended to be a place of refuge and recovery for the many soldiers of the free creatures, especially for the gamdars as they fought during the days of the many wars and battles happening throughout the land of Nangorid. It is a wide forested region, remarkable in its beauty, and very reminiscent of Watendelle, even more remarkable is that the region is protected from the Dark Lord and his slaves, as they are unable to enter the region since it is protected by the Girdle of Gonyardu. It is a land rich in various types of trees, plants, flowers, and fruits, and we will surely find the protection, rest, peace, joy, and nourishment that we would ever need in the land of Lundarin if the need ever drove us to go there."

Huminli and Glophi suddenly lit up with fascination and encouragement as they listened to Mataput, and they wished to see this secret region called Lundarin. Steven and Peter were also filled with curiosity and wished to visit the place along the way of their journey.

But most fascinated of everyone were the gamdars, as they were far more excited to hear about Lundarin than the rest of the company. Their eyes lit up with overwhelming joy, and it seemed to everyone around them that they had heard of this place before.

"Lundarin?" remarked Lelhond, as if he was remembering some distant place of his memory. "Will we be going to Lundarin? The place where many tales have been told and many songs have been sung of Gonyardu the Fair? Oh, how I would wish to see the rich and colorful trees and witness the life of all the wonderful animals and creatures that dwell in that colorful land! And how I would wish to see Gonyardu herself, the Golden Lady, the one whom Nahelion resembles!"

"And how I would wish to see my fellow people!" said Erundil, in a strong voice full of joy. "How I would wish to see what happened to the many gamdars who stayed behind in Lundarin, a place of protection even in the land of Nangorid itself. I have heard many stories of my people who dwell in this land, but I would wish to see and hear from them myself."

The rest of the company listened and watched in fascination as the gamdars expressed their happiness over Lundarin and Gonyardu. They were especially surprised to hear that many gamdars lived in the land, rather than in their homeland in Watendelle.

"There are gamdars who live in Lundarin?" asked Peter, puzzled with amazement. "I never would've imagined that gamdars would choose to live here in the land of Nangorid, even despite being in an area protected from the Dark Lord and his slaves."

"Yes, many gamdars dwell in Lundarin," responded Karandil. "I have heard many stories and tales of our soldiers who throughout the many long years of war and hardship, found the Forest of Peace which resulted in many of them bringing their wives and children with them to live there permanently. They were filled with awe at the glory and beauty of Lundarin and were enchanted by Gonyardu. And so it is believed in my homeland of Watendelle, that many thousands and even tens of thousands of gamdars live in Lundarin."

"Why would they be so amazed by Lundarin though?" asked Peter in response. "Isn't Watendelle so glorious and amazing in beauty? Why would they leave the home that they've known for so long and live in a land which though being protected, is still right in the middle of the land of the enemy?"

"None know for certain," responded Karandil. "But it is said that they were so enchanted by Gonyardu's beauty and light, and filled with an incomprehensible array of joy and peace that they had never experienced before, that they refused to leave Lundarin, and brought many more of their friends and family to dwell with them in the land."

"Who is Gonyardu then?" asked Peter, still filled with many questions. "And why would the gamdars be so enchanted by her beauty and glory?"

Suddenly, at the mention of Gonyardu, Forandor turned to Peter with a broad smile on his shining face. "There are many reasons why our people were enchanted by Gonyardu and her glorious realm," he said. "But there remain other reasons that we still don't know of. But of what we do know, many of the reasons are recorded in our tales and sung proudly in our songs, and what we do know, I will sing to you."

Then, with his still face shining with joy as the brightness of the sun shimmered around him, Forandor began to sing a song, in his sweet and beautiful voice:

A lady of light from days of old,
Has endured like a bright star in the night.
Her raiment sparkles purer than gold,
And none can resist her shining eyesight.

A lady of glory and endurance she has always been,
Even with evil mounting outside her reflection.
Yet she has chosen to not rule as a queen,
Gathering the weary to her realm for their protection.

Our people found the fair land,
Even amid their wandering from the battlefield.
They were drawn by the Golden Lady's hand,
And she brought them to a special land revealed.

There they stood enchanted by her fairness,
And by the fairness of her home.
They found a shelter to protect them from darkness,
And land to freely roam.

They found a land whose trees glittered with every color,
And whose gardens produced every kind of fruit.
There they were clothed with honor,
And sown to produce strong roots.

A wind of peace fell on them,
And they were reminded of their land.
Yet they wished not to depart from the hidden gem,
Where the fruits and flowers never grow bland.

They chose to remain with the Fair Lady,
With many others brought to the unseen forest.
There their faces never ceased to be happy,
When they found a place to rest.

They had no use for a sword or helm,
Nor did they find any purpose in armor,
For they found peace in the fair realm,
In Lundarin, the hidden gem of color.

Forandor fell silent, with the eyes of the company fixed on him. After some time, he spoke again and explained what the song meant. "The song explains why the gamdars refused to leave Lundarin," he explained. "They found a land of such incredible beauty and peace which they had never seen before, that it brought them an exceeding feeling of joy and rest which they would have never experienced if they returned home to Watendelle. They looked into the very eyes of Gonyardu and found a powerful and strange, yet compassionate and loving figure who provided them with refuge and life. Even if they tried to leave the peace, joy, and bliss that covered the land of Lundarin, they wouldn't have been able as they knew that there was no other place in this world that could compare to that land. And so they refused to return to the land they had known, choosing to lay down their weapons for war and instead live a life of peace, free from battles against the enemy which would only increase their sorrow and death."

A bewildered look came on Erundil's face as he listened to his son explain all of this. "That was a strange choice of theirs," he remarked. "To choose to let go of the life you have always known, and to no longer have any desire for war and rightful revenge on all the damage the Dark Lord and his slaves have caused to our people greatly confuses me. Our people have always been renowned for our readiness for battle, but strangely, these gamdars chose to stray away from that path. But whatever they saw in Lundarin or the light of Gonyardu's face, surely led them to make this decision, to which I hold no bitterness against them. Yet I still wonder why they chose to go down this way, as I'm sure they must have still seen their fellow people fighting in many battles throughout this land."

"Or maybe they weren't able to see what was going on outside of Lundarin," suggested Karandil. "And maybe that is the case for them to this very day, where perhaps the Girdle of Gonyardu has protected them from the outside world so much so that they can't see what happens outside of the protected land they are in."

"No," suddenly interrupted Orieant. "Though that is an interesting suggestion, Karandil, it remains an incorrect one. The gamdars living in Lundarin are still able to see the outside world, including all that happens in the realm of the enemy, and the memory of their homes in Watendelle and of their fellow people still rings deep in their memory. But they have chosen to stay in Lundarin with Gonyardu, knowing that this choice would result in them never seeing their homeland again."

"So why would they still choose to stay in Lundarin knowing this reality?" asked Karandil. "If they are indeed still able to see the suffering and sorrow that their fellow people have endured in Nangorid, why then would they be unwilling to lend any help? I understand that they were enchanted by the beauty of Lundarin and of Gonyardu, but that has still not answered my questions."

"Perhaps Gonyardu had many wise things which she revealed to them," responded Orieant. "Things that even Mataput and I don't know of, and neither Dulanmidir himself despite all of the hidden and awesome things which the gorlinto has made manifest to him. Perhaps the Lady of Lundarin had shown them visions of the final defeat of the Dark Lord and of all evil for that matter, which would have ensured that they had no reason to ever return to the outside world. But even despite all of these possibilities, it is likely that they were simply filled with tremendous awe at the beauty, wonder, and glory of Gonyardu and her fair realm of Lundarin. None know for certain what the truth of this matter is, but I for one can assure you that Lundarin is far more beautiful than anything that has ever been seen before in this physical world. And only Starlight, where Jangart sits upon his mighty and uplifted throne, is more beautiful and glorious than Lundarin."

The company fell silent at this as they listened to Orieant with amazement at all he said. They ceased asking any more questions, as they felt no desire to question the volviers regarding the land of Lundarin, and perceiving that the company had no desire to speak anymore, Mataput broke the silence.

"We can speak of Lundarin later," he said. "There is no point in exhausting our minds by wondering many things about Gonyardu and of the gamdars who stayed there and live there to this day. Perhaps we may not need to go to Lundarin, as it was only a suggestion that I brought up after seeing that Huminli and Glophi's food supply was lower than the rest of ours. But do not be anxious about anything, instead allow your minds to rest and focus on the journey ahead of us."

The company spent several more minutes finishing up their meals and resting in the short time they had. And before long they all stood up, with Mataput and Orieant leading them away from where they sat as they continued their journey southward through the bleak valley. The air remained quite cold, but no snow could be seen coming down from the sky, and all about them there lay a bare and wide valley covered in heavy brown grass.

They continued in this way for some time, but eventually, the company noticed that there were no paths they were walking on, and as far as they could see, no routes existed in the Himarshish Valley.

"Which paths will we be taking?" asked Glophi. "Or are there no paths in this bleak and lifeless land?"

"We will not be going on any paths because there are none, just as you have correctly observed," answered Mataput.

"Then how will we reach our destination in the deserted city?" asked Glophi. "Will we just be traveling in circles through this endless valley before eventually losing our way since we will not know where we are going or when we will see a change in the landscape?"

"Do not worry, Glophi," responded Mataput with a smile on his face. "Orieant and I know where we are leading you through. We will not be traveling in circles through the Himarshish Valley, and though there are no visible paths in this region, this valley will still lead us through the deserted city of Tuwanor. In a few days, you will see a change in the landscape would have arrived at the deserted city by then."

"Good," remarked a relieved Glophi. "Because I don't think I would have been able to endure going through this lifeless and boring place for longer than a few days. I can't wait to see a change in this landscape and atmosphere."

"I am glad to see how eager you are to get going, Glophi, but I would advise you not to be so excited," warned Mataput. "The city of Tuwanor is still located within this valley and it is a very evil place, more so than where we are now, though there are hardly any creatures living within this place or in the deserted city. There are only scattered statues, buildings, and walls throughout the deserted city that will shelter us, but will not give us much comfort or relief. So do not expect to be seeing many trees, gardens, or things of natural beauty within the next stage of our journey, but I would advise you to be ready to face anything that may come our way."

Glophi sighed to himself but accepted all that Mataput had said, and after that, he spoke no more and continued following the lead of the volviers.

As the company walked on, Steven felt as though the pain from the wound on his chest was slowly vanishing away. He hardly felt any moments of sharp pain, and he was easily able to walk by himself without the support of others. He felt greatly strengthened and recharged, as did the rest of the company, and though the land all about them was bleak, their moods weren't as depressing as the landscape as they looked forward to the next stage of their journey.

They walked through nothing but brown grass, at times through low and flat areas of land and at other times through high hilly regions of the valley. The sun shone as bright as ever throughout that long afternoon, but it didn't provide much warmth to the company and instead acted as only a bright light in the sky amidst the chilly air. Oftentimes the company wondered in which direction they were going in, as the whole valley seemed to only lead in the same direction. But they trusted that Mataput and Orieant would lead them in the correct direction, and knowing this they didn't have any cause to ask the volviers any questions.

They continued in this direction for the next ten miles, as the hours seemed to pass by the quickest they had ever experienced in their journey so far. To their surprise, they didn't feel like taking a rest any time soon, as they were confident that they could walk on for another couple of hours before the sky grew dark and evening time approached. And so they marched on, continuing to make their way through the same boring and uninviting valley, as Mataput and Orieant led them. Not once as they walked did Steven feel any pain in his chest, though a small white mark could still be seen where Kolmaug had stung him. For the most part, the company's mood was positive, even though they hardly spoke to each other in the time that passed.

By the time they had walked for another five or so miles, the sky had begun to grow dark as the bright sun began to glow red and dark as it sunk slowly behind the clouds. A few lone stars could be seen shining in the darkening sky, as by now it was around eight or nine o'clock with the day slowly fading away. The company felt it was the right time to stop their journey, as they were worn out from all the walking they did. But they were quite proud of themselves for walking for five or six hours without having to take a rest.

Mataput and Orieant led the company over in the direction of a few scattered trees, where they started a small fire and gathered together in a group, gazing at the few bright stars in the night sky as they finally took a long and deserved rest.

"The light of day has gone and the dark of night is now upon us," remarked Orieant. "We have done well to travel for around fifteen miles on our journey through the Himarshish Valley, and if we continue covering distance like this in the coming days, then we will arrive at the deserted city in a very short time."

"That's good to hear," said Erundil. "And after we arrive at the deserted city, we will travel through it in no time."

"And perhaps after that, we can stop in Lundarin," added Lelhond. "To see Gonyardu the Fair and my fellow people that dwell in the Forest of Life would be a wonderful gift beyond my sweetest dreams. And maybe we will receive many gifts from the Golden Lady and many more things to aid us in our quest."

"Maybe," said Orieant. "But let us not imagine those things yet, we do not know what tomorrow may bring, so instead we must focus on what we have in store for us at this moment right now."

"You are right," responded Lelhond with a silent sigh. "And speaking of focusing on the moment, I think now is the right time for dinner, as I'm sure that Huminli and Glophi are starving just as the rest of us are."

"You haven't failed to read our minds, Lelhond!" said Huminli with a bright smile. "A big and satisfactory dinner after a long day of walking doesn't sound like a bad idea to me!"

"It is far from a bad idea, which means we will now eat," said Orieant with a laugh. "But do not ignore me, Huminli and Glophi, when I say that you two shouldn't eat too much tonight, as we want a good supply of food left for us on our journey. But I'm not too concerned about our food running out, and who knows, maybe we might even find some animals here in this lifeless place to hunt and eat!"

Just as the words slipped from Orieant's mouth, ahead into the far distance could be seen two large chickens walking briskly through the land. They were ordinary chickens, ones that Steven and Peter had seen many times before in their homeland, where many farms filled their villages. The birds were white with a few black streaks on different spots of their bodies, and they also had red faces with bright orange beaks. The company silently stared at the chickens for some time in amazement that life existed in the bleak valley they were in.

"Well what are you all doing staring at the chickens?" laughed Mataput, amidst the company's silence. "You won't catch two birds just by staring at them, nor will you likely have a better chance of finding food to eat in this land! Go on and hunt them since you don't have weapons in your backpacks for nothing!"

The company stared at each other for a moment, as if debating among themselves in their minds about who would hunt the chickens. Eventually, Lelhond and Karandil stood up to their feet, and taking out their bows and arrows, they swiftly went ahead into the distance and eyed their targets closely. At once, Lelhond fired his bow and struck the bird's side, resulting in the large bird crying out in a loud croak before it collapsed to the ground. Karandil immediately followed suit and fired his arrow at the other chicken, yet the bird didn't fall and instead staggered to the ground for some time. Once he fired another arrow, the bird finally collapsed to the ground, and the two brothers ran after the targets that they had killed and carried the large birds back to the company.

"Well that was quick!" remarked Huminli, as the brothers came to the company seated by the fire. "You two were easily able to hunt those chickens for sure!"

"Yes, and as you could see, I was able to kill it in one shot unlike, not in two," said Lelhond, in an innocent taunt towards his brother.

"Regardless, I still killed it," replied Karandil, in a more serious tone than his brother. "And we will certainly be taking full advantage of eating these two chickens tonight."

"And that's all that matters," remarked Mataput. "There is no need to complain over who killed the chicken in one shot or two, as we will still eat our meal and celebrate that we were able to find two chickens to hunt and eat in this otherwise lifeless land. After our meal tonight, we will have plenty of food remaining afterward, which we will divide amongst ourselves for the rest of our journey. But Huminli and Glophi will receive the most remaining food, as they have the least remaining food in their packs."

"Yes!" shouted Huminli and Glophi together, excited to be receiving the most remaining chicken once they and the company finished eating. The rest of the company could only laugh at the smalves, except for Erundil who watched and listened on with an irritated face.

"But how are we going to eat these chickens with no salt or spices?" asked Peter. "We have fire to cook the chicken, but I'm afraid that it's just going to be bland pieces of chicken that we'll be eating tonight and in the days to come. I have no salt or spices in my bag, as I only have food, weapons, and extra cloaks stored in here."

"And I'm afraid that I have no spices either," remarked Steven. "I wouldn't mind eating a fresh chicken if only we had good spices to cook it with, but at least the meat stored in our backpacks has some salt and spices already in it. But does anyone happen to have any spices we can use to make these chickens tasty?"

Mataput and Orieant hadn't thought of bringing spices on the journey, and neither did the gamdars. The company became silent for some time and stared at each other as if they were waiting to see if anyone had brought anything to spice their food during the journey. And after some time of silent waiting, Huminli and Glophi spoke up.

"Do not worry, we are going to have a merry meal tonight!" excitedly said Huminli. He and his brother both reached into their backpacks and took out small bottles containing salt and other herbs and spices within them. They also took out two large cooking pots from their bags to cook the chickens in.

"We knew that we couldn't forget to bring these spices and pots with us on this journey," said Glophi. "Here in these small bottles are sprinkles of salt along with many of our herbs and spices that we grow on our farms in our homeland of Laouli. We always bring spices with us wherever we go, as we don't know when they will come in handy. But if we ever need to use them, we ensure that we never miss out on a merry and good meal!"

"I must confess that you smalves have done very well," admitted Erundil. "I can't believe that my sons and I forgot to bring our spices with us, but I'm glad that at least someone remembered to pack them."

The rest of the company had broad smiles on their faces and felt relieved because of the smalves. "You two have saved us," remarked Orieant. "Even Mataput and I didn't think of bringing salt and spices with us, but looking back at it, enjoying our food on this journey is quite important. And you two have ensured that our meals will remain tasty, even if we have to hunt for our food at times."

"And thank goodness for that!" remarked Peter, full of joy and satisfaction in the moment. "We will indeed be having a merry meal tonight as you said, Glophi, so go ahead and spice the chicken for us, so that we can enjoy the wonderfully cooked meal that you and Huminli have ensured we can have!"

At once, Huminli and Glophi grabbed the two large chickens that Lelhond and Karandil had hunted and put them in their large pots. Their pots were just large enough to fit the two chickens, being quite wide and deep, and they poured a bit of water from their bottles on the chickens to wash them and then sprinkled some of their spices, herbs, and salt throughout the chicken. They mixed the ingredients with their hands, closed the pot, and began to shake it all around, after this, they placed their pots with the chickens just above the fire so that they could cook the birds. The company found themselves staring at the smalves in amazement at their cooking and felt greatly pleased just by smelling the sweet aroma of all the spices mixed in the chickens.

Even as the company waited for the chickens to be fully cooked,

Huminli and Glophi didn't fail to keep the company entertained. At times they would balance the cooking pots on their heads, which made the company scratch their heads and wonder how they could do that, especially since the pots were hot after hovering over the fire. Other times they danced and celebrated, sharing many stories of the secrets of their wonderful cooking.

In one instance, they broke off into a song of celebration, which prompted the rest of the company to also dance and celebrate with them. It was a song of the joys of food and cooking, and the company listened on with fascination to Huminli and Glophi. And even as the smalves sang to the company, they all stood up and danced to the tune:

Come and see the roasting of the chicken,
And don't forget to witness the skill of our cooks!
From spices and herbs and everything in between,
Our food will hook you on longer than books!

Don't be shy and neglect our food,
For we don't care if you eat our plate!
It is better than anything you call good,
Our food which you and I celebrate!

The smell of our spiced fish is fresher than fruits,
And is a cause for endless dancing!
For we find our herbs even in our deepest roots,
And mix it in pots with our food boiling!

Don't stop celebrating and singing,
This is a reason to be happy!
Our special skill sends you running,
And fails to stop you from acting crazy!

As they danced along to the song, the company felt an incredible thrill of happiness just by looking and listening to the smalves. They couldn't help but sing and celebrate together, everyone except for Erundil.

He had a small smile on the corner of his face as he was glad to see his sons so joyful, yet he couldn't bring himself to let go of the bitterness he still held in his heart toward Huminli and Glophi. But of all his sons, Lelhond was the most enthusiastic and seemed to be dancing as if he were possessed by awesome craziness. Forandor danced more calmly and maturely, while Karandil danced with a broad smile on his face. Even Mataput and Orieant danced slowly with smiles on their faces, while Peter danced at a far faster and more energetic rate.

Steven danced calmly with a smile on his face, experiencing such an incredible amount of joy and peace that he hadn't felt in quite some time. He couldn't help himself from smiling and laughing while Huminli and Glophi continued to entertain him and the rest of the company. And as he danced, all memory of the pain of his wound disappeared from his mind, and it became some distant thing which even though it had tormented him, was now gone forever.

The company continued dancing for many several more minutes, which felt like hours to Erundil as he silently watched them all. But eventually, Huminli and Glophi suddenly stopped singing, dancing, and entertaining the company, and removing the lids from their pots they dug their heads into the pot and smelled the cooked chickens for themselves.

As they smelled it, their faces seemed to be filled with an overwhelming sense of satisfaction and pride in what they had cooked.

"Well the chickens certainly smell like what we are used to!" said Huminli. "I can already sense that it will be incredibly delightful to our taste buds, and so the rest of you should have a smell of it for yourselves."

At once, the company went over to Huminli and Glophi to have a smell of the cooked chicken for themselves, and their faces were instantly changed because of how pleased they felt by the smell of the food. Even Erundil stood up from where he sat and smelled the chicken for himself, and was surprised by how well the smalves had cooked it.

"The chickens certainly do smell very delightful," remarked Peter. "And I'm sure that it tastes even better! And so we should enjoy our merry meal right now!"

Peter, Huminli, and Glophi immediately got ready to dive into the chickens for themselves, with their faces filled with delight at the sight and smell of the cooked meat. However, before they could dig in and eat,

Mataput and Orieant quickly stopped them so that they wouldn't finish all the food before the rest of the company had a chance to eat.

"Wait, wait," said Mataput, stepping in front of Peter and the smalves to slow them down. "Before the three of you finish both of the chickens on your own, we must first divide it among ourselves. Did Huminli and Glophi happen to pack any knives with which we can use to divide the chicken up?"

"Yes we did," responded Glophi, and at once he and Huminli reached into their backpacks and took out two large knives that would be used to divide up the chicken.

Mataput and Orieant took the knives from them and began to cut up the chicken into evenly sized pieces. Peter, Huminli, and Glophi watched on impatiently while the volviers divided up the two chickens, and were ready to pounce once they had the chance to eat their meal. And eventually, after a few minutes of waiting, Mataput and Orieant gave the two large knives back to Huminli and Glophi after they had finished dividing up the chickens.

Before Peter or the smalves could grab onto any of the chicken pieces, Orieant spoke to the company. "We will each have five pieces of chicken for our meal tonight," he said. "That way we will have plenty enough pieces left for us on the rest of the journey. And as we agreed, Huminli and Glophi will be receiving the most remaining pieces of chicken since they have the least amount of food left in their backpacks."

Before Orieant had finished saying his last few words, Peter, Huminli, and Glophi, grabbed their five pieces of chicken and started eating away at them. The rest of the company waited for Orieant to finish speaking before grabbing their five pieces of chicken and eating them. Upon tasting the cooked meat, the company was greatly amazed by how well-spiced it was, especially Peter, who was impressed by how well and tasty Huminli and Glophi had made the chickens.

"This food is really good!" he exclaimed, even while he chewed on a mouthful of chicken. "This is the best chicken I've ever tasted, and I don't think anyone in this world could make better chicken than what Huminli and Glophi have cooked!"

"I can only agree," said Steven, with his face lighting up with pure delight while he ate some of his chicken pieces. "I don't know about the rest of you, but just like Peter said, this is some of the best chicken that I've ever tasted in my whole life! I can't imagine being able to cook so brilliantly as Huminli and Glophi have done, yet it seems as though this is a common occurrence for the two of them."

"I appreciate your kind words," responded Huminli. "Glophi and I have been taught to cook well ever since we were young smalves, and it's something that our people have always learned to do, and we greatly enjoy doing these things! I'm glad to see that you enjoy our cooked food, as I sure enjoy it myself!"

"I enjoy good food, and I can confirm that this is better than I could have ever imagined," remarked Lelhond. "Ever since I tasted your crumpo soup, I knew that you two along with all of your people are incredible cooks. I wouldn't mind learning a thing or two about cooking from you two, as I'm sure my people could use this to make our dinner feasts even more enjoyable."

"We'll teach you some time for sure, Lelhond," responded Huminli. "And for that matter, we would be more than open to teaching Karandil and Forandor, and even to Erundil if he's open to it."

"We'll show you sometime how we spice and cook our food," said Glophi. "Perhaps we'll be lucky and find another pair of chickens or other animals for that matter to hunt and cook!"

The company finished eating their last piece of chicken before Mataput and Orieant divided up the remaining meat they had left. There was still a decent amount of food left that would add to their remaining food supply, and as promised, the smalves received the most remaining pieces of chicken while the rest of the company received a lesser, but substantial amount nonetheless.

By now the sky was pitch black and the pale moon could be seen shining high overhead, with a few stars gathered around it. The company could sense they were growing tired, with even Huminli and Glophi starting to yawn despite all the dancing and singing they had done just earlier.

"Well, it's been a long day," eventually said Orieant, noticing the company growing tired. "And we will need as much rest as we can get before the morning dawns. So now should be a good time to sleep before we continue in this direction to the deserted city of Tuwanor. Tomorrow and the next few days are going to be long and weary days with lots of walking, far more than we managed to do today. But a good amount of rest will certainly give us enough strength and energy we need to press on."

"Regardless, long and weary days don't sound quite fun," said Steven, in a dreary tone. "But you're right in saying, Orieant, that we should be going to sleep now, though it was a merry meal and a fun time of dancing and singing that we got to enjoy tonight."

Orieant looked longingly at Steven as if some thought had suddenly sprung into his mind. "That reminds me, Steven," he said, staring at his chest. "We haven't had a look at your wound in a long time, yet in all this time, I haven't seen you complain about it one time. Is the wound beginning to disappear and is the pain of it healing?"

"Yes, it is disappearing and healing," responded Steven, lifting his cloak to show his company to the wound. They all took a good look at it and could only see a small white mark where he had been stabbed in his chest, that seemed to have significantly faded away.

Peter was glad to see that Steven's wound had almost completely gone. "Before we know it, that white mark won't be on your chest anymore," he excitedly said. "At least we have one less thing to worry about on our journey now."

"Though I wish that were the case, it's still too early to say that for certain," responded Mataput. "Steven's wound is healing at a good and fast rate, but it's still visible on his chest even though Steven doesn't feel the pain anymore. But you are correct in saying that we don't have to worry about it, at least not as much as we did before. But let's not spend our night talking about this, we must go to sleep as we have a long day tomorrow."

With that, the company put out the fire and they each found a place to lie on the ground. They covered themselves with their blankets and dozed off into a light sleep.

The next morning they were roused by the voices of Mataput and Orieant. It must've been a little after dawn, but the sky was still relatively dark and the sun couldn't be seen. Yet, the volviers had woken up early and had to shake the rest of the company up from their sleep.

"Why are we up so early?" asked Huminli, in a sluggish tone, wishing to get more sleep. "The sun has not even risen yet and I can barely even open my eyes."

"I know, Huminli," said Mataput. "But we must be on our way now if we want to make any significant progress in these next few days. If we wake up as late as we have been lately, then it will take us at least a week to get to the city of Tuwanor. And did Orieant not say yesterday that these next few days would be long and weary ones?"

Mataput picked Huminli up from where he was lying down, as the smalf was not too eager to get up so early. Orieant did the same with Glophi, while the gamdars and humans managed to bring themselves to their feet. After having a brief breakfast, the company got ready to depart for more traveling on their journey.

"The landscape today will be pretty much the same as yesterday," remarked Mataput, with the company gathered around him and Orieant. "But I hope that we can travel for at least twenty-five miles today, as that will bring us closer to the hilly region of this valley, which I assume we will begin to see tomorrow. We will still take a few stops here and there today, as needed, but we must prepare ourselves for a long day of journeying today."

And so off they went, continuing their journey down the valley with only a few scattered trees to their side. There was of course still no visible path seen in the distance, as they continued to travel through long and dry brown grass. After a few minutes had passed since they went off, high ahead in the sky could be seen the pale reflection of the sun shining proudly.

The day went on much the same as the previous day had gone, with the company only seeing a few scattered trees and bushes as hardly any forms of life could be seen around them. The land was identical to what they had seen the day before, and the company could've sworn that they were traveling in circles. However, they tried to remain positive and continued to trust Mataput and Orieant as the volviers led them.

Yet the hours of traveling they endured seemed to be the longest they had experienced so far on their journey, as the long time dragged on slowly through the early morning. No sound of any living creatures roaming around the valley could be heard, with the slight breeze of the wind being the only thing to alert their ears.

"Well this is quite a dull morning," remarked Glophi, gazing at the wide and boring land all around him. "This for sure is going to be a long and boring day."

"It will be a long day, but a couple of hours have already passed," said Mataput. "Our day has only begun, and we still have many more miles to walk. But do not worry, Glophi, for very soon you will not be seeing this land.

"I sure hope so, because I can't bear fixing my eyes on this boring place," muttered Glophi to himself.

The company walked for at least another five miles before briefly resting under a tree. They ate some of the food in their backpacks, including the leftover chicken from the night before, and soon after that, they got ready to continue walking.

The rest of the morning and afternoon happened to be much the same, as the lifeless land didn't provide the company with much excitement. The company was for the most part in a cheerless mood and didn't talk much to each other, and not a single trace of fruit could be seen on the shaggy bushes or the skinny trees that were scattered throughout the wide valley. They had to manage with the remaining water left in their bottles, as not even a drop of water was seen throughout the dry land.

However, the hours soon passed rather quickly for the company to their great relief. They made another quick stop to rest and recharge before they set out again, and by now it was late in the afternoon as the morning had seemed to vanish just before their very eyes.

"I reckon that we have walked for around fifteen miles now," said Mataput. "At this rate, we will probably be nearly thirty miles just before the end of the day. We are doing very good as we are almost a little over halfway through our journey today, and so we just need to continue walking while only taking a few brief stops and rests."

"I can't wait until the evening sets in," remarked Huminli. "We've already done quite a lot of walking today, and a good long rest and sleep at the end of the day will do me well."

"That will come in due time," assured Mataput. "But for now, let us focus on what is ahead of us as we have plenty of more walking to do!"

The company managed to follow Mataput and Orieant as they walked for some more time, though their legs were beginning to grow heavy and tired. They hoped that a sign would come in the sky that it would start growing dark and that the night would soon come as a signal that they could have a good night's sleep. But for the time being, the sky was still bright in the afternoon and they had to manage trudging through the valley for the rest of the long day.

But they managed to endure the long afternoon hours before the sky grew dark, with the smallest stars beginning to twinkle in the sky. Another hour or so passed and the sun sank far into the sky as the day grew old, with the night knocking on the door. They had made a little over thirty miles of progress during the day, and they came to a stop to sleep for the night before they would continue their journey in the morning.

The company woke up the next morning, ready to endure another day of tiring walking. It was still fairly early in the morning, but they hadn't been roused to wake up by Mataput and Orieant like the day before.

"Why didn't you wake me up so early like you did yesterday morning?" asked Huminli to Mataput.

"Because we made a lot of progress yesterday," replied Mataput. "We walked more miles than I would've expected us to, so I was willing to let you all sleep in a little bit more so that you could be fully energized for this day."

"But regardless, we still have a long day ahead of us," said Orieant. "So once all of you have breakfast, we should prepare to be on our way at once."

Once they had eaten breakfast, the company got ready to depart again for another long day of traveling. The sun had risen by now, but it wasn't shining as high and bright as it was the day before. It was a bit of a gray morning with a few misty clouds covering the sky, with the sky not helping with the company's already dreary moods. The wind seemed to pick up a little more in its intensity, sending a slight tingling chill through the air. Everyone prepared themselves for the day that lay ahead, and once they were ready they followed Mataput and Orieant.

All that morning there wasn't a single change in the landscape, as ahead of them the company could see an endless array of the low valley covered in brown grass. It was slightly foggy in the early morning, but once a couple of hours had passed, it had cleared. The morning soon passed into early afternoon when they took a brief rest to have some food, and soon after they got ready again to continue journeying.

They journeyed hard through the rest of the day, only taking a few breaks whenever their legs or feet grew tired. The day seemed to go on forever, but they managed to endure the long day and once evening time came, they came to a stop with some of them collapsing to the ground out of exhaustion. They were fatigued from their long journey, and it seemed to them that they hadn't made much progress. They were growing frustrated, especially Erundil who had noticed that the landscape hadn't changed that much since they had entered the valley.

"We have been walking for three days now, yet not a change has been seen in this valley," he complained. "How many more days will we be walking through this dreary place? If I had known that the way through this land would be like this, then I wouldn't have ever left the path leading us through the mountains. In that case, it would have taken us far less time to travel through the mountains, than traveling through this lifeless place which is taking us ages to go through."

"But you wanted to go in this direction rather than through the mountains," responded Orieant. "And we have already traveled for days now, so it is far too late to turn back and go in the opposite direction."

"I know," said Erundil. "But in what direction are you and Mataput leading us? Endless areas of valleys that will take us many more days to walk through? We haven't even seen a single path throughout our journey through this region, and I'm beginning to think we are walking in circles."

Erundil expected a response from the volviers, but suddenly Peter stepped in and offered his own words. "Orieant and Mataput know where they are leading us," he remarked. "Did they not say that they have traveled through this land before? And have you ever stepped foot in the land of Nangorid before we started our journey, Mr. Erundil? Why then are you saying we're walking in circles when none of us have ever seen this valley before?"

Erundil looked away, realizing he was wrong but refusing to admit so. Lelhond swiftly came to his father's side to speak with him privately. "Mataput and Orieant know what they are doing, father," he said. "Why then should we doubt them after seeing the good and success that they have brought to us?"

"I hear and understand you, Lelhond," responded Erundil. "They have indeed brought us much good on this journey, and I would never choose to deviate from what they say. Yet, I also have the right to hold my opinion, and by my observations, I can't determine whether or not leading us through this direction will be to our benefit."

"Yet we decided to travel in this direction," replied Lelhond. "The volviers would have brought us through the mountains if it wasn't for our decision to go in the other direction. But I do not have any regrets about going down this way, since the mountains of Lehu Shalank were simply too bitter and cold to endure. But let us not dwell in the past, as we should instead focus on what is ahead of us just as Mataput and Orieant always say. And very soon we will accomplish our ultimate goal of finding the lost golden book of our forefather, Ulohendel."

A smile came across Erundil's face. "We will indeed accomplish our goal," he confidently said. "And you are right, we must focus on what is ahead of us, otherwise we will not go very far in our journey."

Lelhond was pleased to see his father's spirits lifted, and though they didn't know it, Mataput and Orieant had overheard their conversation and had broad smiles covering their faces. And once the sky grew pitch black, the company prepared to sleep for the night, while dreaming of what the next day would have in store for them.

The fourth day began much the same as the previous days had gone, with the landscape not changing much. The air was clear all around the company, and it wasn't as gray of a morning as it was the previous day, though there were still many clouds filling the sky as the sun hid behind them. The company prepared itself for another dull day and was in no mood for any joking around.

Once they started walking, the morning proved to be another dull one as they had expected. However, to their delight, the hours passed by rather quickly, and before they knew it, the time was around noon. Coming to a stop they ate a quick meal, before continuing in their journey as they were ready for the afternoon to pass just as swiftly as the morning had proven. They didn't expect to see any changes in the landscape so they prepared themselves for another boring afternoon.

However, they had not even walked for half an hour when suddenly they noticed a change in the broad look of the landscape. To their great surprise and delight, they looked ahead and saw the shape of hills in the distance, with the grass seeming to be much greener with what seemed to be plenty more trees and plants filling the land with berries and other kinds of fruits growing on them. Their spirits were suddenly lifted at this sight, and their walking pace drastically increased.

"Oh, finally we have seen a change in the landscape," said Steven with great relief. "I can see many hills ahead of me, and the grass is much greener."

"And look! There seem to be berries and other fruits growing on the trees and plants," observed Peter.

The company stared ahead into the distance, greatly amazed to see such a vast change in landscape. They felt as though their dreariness had been lifted off their shoulders, and great relief which they hadn't felt in quite a while fell upon them. Most relieved was Erundil, who gazed into the distance with a light seeming to glow in his eyes. He couldn't hide the relief he was experiencing, as it covered his whole face.

The company swiftly went at once to the land ahead of them, with their burdens of weariness lifted off their minds and hearts. Some of them even picked up their pace and seemed to be jogging instead of walking, while the others quickened their pace to keep along. Huminli and Glophi went on ahead of the group, leading them to the hilly land ahead in the distance. A sudden joy had seemed to overflow into the hearts of the company, with the feeling of dreariness seemingly a thing of the recent past.

They came at last to the hilly region and found an abundance in the number of trees, plants, and bushes around them. It seemed to them that the entire land had been showered with rain, as the grass was teeming with the greenness of life. They found many fruits growing on the trees and plants, including apples, berries, and grapes, and there were even a few small water springs scattered throughout the region, which the company took full advantage of by filling their water bottles with water and drinking as much as they could.

They gathered as much fruit as they could, stuffing them into their backpacks. Most joyful of everyone were Huminli and Glophi, who couldn't believe the amount of fruit they would be able to gather and eat.

"I never would've thought that we would see such greenness and freshness teeming in this region!" exclaimed Glophi. "This has been an incredible surprise!"

"Yes, it is a pleasant surprise," remarked Lelhond. "And so we should gather as much fruit as we can because we do not know when we will find a plethora of provisions in this wild land."

The company rested under a large tree filled with all sorts of fruits and ate the fruit that they had gathered for themselves. They gazed around at the vast land that teemed with green hills and fruits, and they were amazed to see such a change in the landscape, from walking through a dry and dreary valley to now gazing at rich and green hills filled with trees and fruits. And as Lelhond pondered this difference, a confused look came on his face.

"Why is this land overflowing with richness in terms of its landscape and the many trees and plants filling it?" he asked, observing the trees, plants, and fruits that populated the hilly land. "How is it that just behind us this same valley was covered in dry brown grass, and now here we are standing amid green hills with trees and plants bearing every fruit we could ever imagine? It is as if we left the land of Nangorid and returned to my homeland of Watendelle."

"I presume that it must be of the doing of Gonyardu," responded Orieant. "She has the power to sprinkle the land outside of Lundarin with her precious spark that causes trees, plants, and fruits to grow in richness and abundance even in the dreary Himarshish Valley of the land of the enemy."

"But why would she choose to do that?" asked Lelhond. "What benefit would there be in providing this land with her blessing?"

"I guess that she knows that we are traveling through here," answered Orieant. "She is very wise and so she likely knows and understands that we have had to endure tremendous weariness and challenges already in the early stages of our quest. And so she has likely provided us with rich grasslands, trees, and fruits to aid us on our journey so that we can finish strong until the very end. And just based on the number of fruits that we have found here, it looks like we might not need to stop in Lundarin to find rest and provisions."

"I still would've liked to see Lundarin for myself," remarked Lelhond, with slight disappointment. "It would have been an honor to see the Lady of Lundarin herself alongside my people who dwell in her realm. I would have enjoyed resting under the great trees of Lundarin and experiencing the beauty and bliss of the rich land," he sighed and fell silent.

"Perhaps one day you might go to Lundarin, Lelhond," said Orieant, coming to Lelhond's side to comfort him. "And who knows? Maybe we might still make a stop there, even in our journey. But we should at least be grateful for this rich land that Gonyardu has showered us with her blessing and beauty. Let us rest and eat here for a while before we continue again in the wild as we might not find a place like this again in a while."

A smile came to Lelhond's face as he listened to Orieant, while the rest of the company continued eating and gazing at the rich land that they found themselves in. They soaked in every moment they could enjoy, and rested in peace for as long as they would be allowed to.

But after a little over half an hour had passed, the time came for them to continue their journey, and though they wished to rest where they were and stay there for the rest of the day, they knew they had to continue walking. Yet Huminli and Glophi were unwilling to leave and wanted to enjoy more fruit and rest for a longer time. Mataput and Orieant had to drag the smalves to their feet so that they could continue going on, and once everyone was ready, the company got ready to depart and continue their journey through the land ahead of them.

As they traveled, the number of large trees filled with fruits along with the number of healthy plants and bushes began to slowly dwindle in count. The greenness of the grass on the hills also began to change color, growing more brown as they went on, and after another hour had passed, the land had almost completely changed as the hills grew more scarce and hardly anything teeming with life could be seen. The feeling of gloominess returned to the company as they stared at the dismal land that surrounded them. Turning around they caught a glimpse of the land full of rich green hills that they had left behind, and some of them began to regret leaving the place behind so quickly.

"Look, I can see the green hills and rich trees filled with fruits behind us," said Peter, as he turned around.

"Why did we ever leave that place so soon?" asked Huminli, looking at the land behind him with regret. "Why did we think it was a good idea to spend only a short time there when we experienced such great peace and life that we haven't enjoyed since traveling through this land? Gonyardu did bless and shower us with rest, peace, and joy, and I wish we would've stayed there even longer to enjoy all that she rewarded us with."

"I enjoyed the time of rest myself," remarked Mataput. "And it was indeed a pleasant surprise, one that I enjoyed a lot. But we still have other things that we must prioritize in our journey, and we must continue to focus on the goal that made us set out on this quest in the first place. Many more surprises are still yet to come, and so perhaps we might find another place to rest in peace and joy even longer than we just did."

"I sure hope we will have more surprises," remarked Huminli, as he looked behind him one last time before taking Mataput's advice and continuing to focus on the company's goal that was ahead of them and not behind.

The rest of them fixed their eyes ahead as well, focusing on the dreary valley land that now surrounded them. The rest of the afternoon proved to be a boring one, a sudden change to the brightness and peacefulness of the hilly region where they had come from. They wished that Gonyardu would shower more of her blessings on the land so that the dry grass would flourish and that more trees and fruits would surround them. Most of all, however, they wished to see animals as they were tired of being the only creatures journeying through the colorless valley.

At last, as the afternoon waned and the sky grew dark with the evening appearing, Mataput and Orieant led the company over to the side where they sat near a few bushes. It appeared to many of them that they were done traveling for the day, which surprised them as it was only around six o'clock and they usually would've walked for at least another couple of hours before coming to a complete stop from their journey.

"Why have we stopped walking?" asked Steven, turning toward

the volviers. "It may be evening time, but it's still quite bright and I would've thought that you two would want us to make more progress on our journey."

"We have done enough walking for today," responded Mataput. "If we were to go on we would have arrived at the borders of the city of Tuwanor. We should wait until tomorrow before we go on."

"Finally, it's about time that we've arrived at the deserted city," said Erundil, with great relief.

"Yes, it is about time," said Mataput. "But let us not get too excited as the deserted city is still a place of great evil, even though it may be evil that arose from the ancient past. I can sense that there is an evil presence that resides in that place, though I'm not certain what that is specifically."

Shudders ran through the bones of the company at the mention of an evil presence dwelling in the deserted city. Erundil, however, shook off the fear and sat confidently. "We will not fear any presence of evil or danger in the deserted city," he said. "For darkness cannot endure the light, no matter how hard it may try to."

"You are right, Erundil," said Orieant. "Nonetheless, let us make sure that we remain vigilant so that we don't do anything foolish to awaken the evil that dwells there."

The company fell silent, although the volviers could see the fear that covered their eyes, even with Erundil who tried to hide his worry. They were beginning to have some doubts about traveling in the direction where they had chosen to, though they said nothing about it knowing that they couldn't alter their decision.

"Regardless of what Mataput and I have said of the deserted city, none of you should walk in fear," said Orieant, observing the fear and worry that was on their faces. "We will be safe if we remain together, and whatever happens we will defend ourselves and expel the darkness with our light."

The company took Orieant's words of encouragement to heart, though they remained worried and anxious over what the next day would have in store for them. But they didn't have any more time to express their worries about this as the night sky soon came over them, which meant they could now sleep for the night in the valley, though thoughts of fear and uncertainty continued to plague their minds.

17

The Deserted City

THE NEXT MORNING, THE company woke up a little after the first light of dawn, with many of them having slept uneasily during the night as their worries and anxious thoughts only continued to grow worse. They found that sleeping was not doing much to help them, and so they were forced to get up early so they could spend some time to think to themselves and relax their minds.

Great anxiety surrounded the entire group, and Mataput and Orieant could sense it even while they were sleeping. And when they all woke up, the volviers saw the terror that covered the company's faces as many of them paced back and forth to try and relax.

Eventually, Mataput got their attention and gathered the company together to speak with them regarding their fear. "I can see the fear on your faces," he said, observing their faces. "It is the same fear that Orieant spoke of yesterday, and even just listening to the sound of your restlessness as you all tried sleeping last night, I knew that you were still quite anxious. But why is that? Just yesterday Erundil was speaking about how the darkness cannot endure the light, and that is true. Are we not the light of the world? And yet I can see deep roots of fear in your eyes, even in yours, Erundil."

"I am not afraid of anything or anyone," confidently responded Erundil. "I just feel a bit uneasy at your descriptions of how the city of Tuwanor is a place of great evil, even with no inhabitants dwelling there."

"Then you are afraid," remarked Mataput, examining Erundil with piercing eyes that seemed to reveal even his darkest secrets. "There is no need to deceive yourself and say you are not afraid when it is clear that you are. Orieant and I are not here to punish you for your fears, but we are here to encourage you to overcome them."

"Well I am not feeling too encouraged myself," muttered Erundil, while Mataput could see the growing irritation on his face. The rest of the company continued shuddering with fear and felt tension building up in their bones.

"All of you should take a moment to eat and think to yourselves," said Orieant, still seeing the fear that possessed everyone. "It is not good to continue on our journey right now if you are not mentally ready, so take a moment to yourselves, and once you are ready we will get ready to depart from this place."

The company took Orieant's words to heart and took out some food from their backpacks to give them the energy they needed for the day. They all sat together in a circle, staring at the far distance behind and ahead of them, seeing nothing but a wide valley covered with brown grass. They tried calming their minds, but nothing they tried worked and they only continued to feel worse and tenser. They said nothing to each other as they were in no mood to share what was on their minds.

But once they had finished eating, many of them stood up to walk by themselves and try to cool their minds. Steven and Peter sat alone by each other, saying nothing and instead staring at the distance around them. Eventually, however, Steven turned to Peter to speak with him privately, revealing all that was on his mind to his friend.

"You know, Peter, I must confess that I'm feeling quite worried," he said. "Even though I didn't say it in front of Mataput and Orieant, I feel as though something bad is going to happen as we travel through the city of Tuwanor."

A concerned and slightly confused look came on Peter's face. "Why do you say that?" he asked. "I will admit, I'm feeling a bit uneasy, but we should trust Mataput and Orieant when they say that everything will be fine no matter what danger we face. We have each other, Steven and everyone in this group has many strengths to accompany us toward success and victory."

"I suppose you're right, Peter," responded Steven in an unconvincing manner. "By I still feel a bit off, if you know what I mean. I feel quite uncomfortable even though we haven't had much danger in our journey so far, apart from the matis and the terrible snow blizzard on the mountains of Lehu Shalank. I don't feel too good, Peter, and I'm worried about that."

"Is it your wound?" asked Peter, staring at Steven's chest with worry in his eyes. "I thought it was almost completely gone, and that you weren't experiencing much pain anymore."

"No, it's not the wound," answered Steven, lifting his shirt to reveal only the tiniest mark on his chest that was hardly visible. Peter breathed a sigh of relief at this. "I haven't felt any pain in my chest for days now, but the way I'm feeling right now is almost as bad as I felt when the wound still stung in my chest. Yet this isn't physical pain, but some other heavy pain that I can't quite describe."

"You'll be fine, Steven," said Peter. "Once we start walking and pass through the deserted city, I'm sure that you'll be feeling much better."

A small smile came on Steven's face, though he still felt some doubts slowly creeping into his heart. He said nothing else and stared ahead into the distance, though Peter still looked at him with concern covering his face.

Another half hour passed before the company gathered together and got ready for the next stage of their journey. They felt slightly better, though doubt and fear still weighed heavily on their hearts and minds. Nonetheless, they got ready to depart and started walking in the direction ahead of them before suddenly realizing that Glophi was standing still by himself, refusing to go.

Lelhond came to his side, wrapping his arm around Glophi's back and trying to encourage the smalf. "Everything is fine, Glophi," he said with a warm smile on his face. "All will be well because you have me and everyone else to walk by your side and support you in everything we face."

Lelhond offered his hand to the smalf, prompting him to walk along with the company, to which Glophi gladly took Lelhond's hand with a smile on his face. The smalf began to walk with confidence as he and Lelhond walked together hand in hand, with Mataput and Orieant each having big smiles on their faces as they watched the two of them. After a few minutes of walking, Lelhond let go of his hand while Glophi was still by his side, as the smalf now felt far better and assured.

It was a little after seven in the morning when the company departed that day, to make their way through the deserted city of Tuwanor. It was a cloudy morning, with the sun only deciding to peek through the clouds at certain times. It looked as if a storm would be coming soon though not a single drop of rain fell on their heads. Mataput and Orieant led the way, walking with confidence and without fear as the rest of the company walked behind them with troubled hearts and anxious looks covering their faces.

No change was visible in the land ahead, behind, or to the side of them, with the same look of the dry valley covered in brown grass with a few scattered trees and bushes covering the barren land around them. The land did nothing to ease their anxiety, nor did the dark and cloudy sky, though some of them felt a bit better as they received some fresh air as they went along on their journey. The wind blew gently against their faces, providing a cool air that satisfied them at times. Yet, they wouldn't feel satisfied for long as the realization of where they were heading continued to weigh heavily on their minds.

Hours soon passed in the early morning before noon fast approached, and as far as the eye could see, no change appeared yet in the land. Mataput and Orieant kept reminding the company that they were nearing Tuwanor, but not even the remains of a gate or an opening could be seen welcoming them to the deserted city. They walked for many more miles, taking only a couple of quick rests in the long morning hours that passed. They wondered when they would, at last, come to the deserted city, or at least see a change in the landscape as they came to the borders of the city. However, as the early afternoon soon came, no signs of a change in the landscape could be observed. And as the time continued to pass, now a little after one o'clock, none of them imagined that they would see any changes in the land in the next few hours ahead of them.

However, even as they thought about this, a sudden difference in the ground was made manifest to them. As they walked on, they began to notice that the dry ground covered in brown grass started to grow rockier. The more they went on, the more the ground grew rockier, before it began to thin out and grow in a long narrow line ahead of them. They soon realized that they were walking on a road, or at least the remains of one.

They were greatly fascinated by this sudden change and wondered why some road had suddenly appeared out of nowhere. As they observed the road they also noticed the remains of some rocks and stones dug into the ground of the brown grass. They wondered where they were, and what the road and many other remains could mean.

"Where are we?" asked Huminli, observing the road and the many rocks and stone remains around him. "And why are we now suddenly walking on a rocky road when this entire time we saw nothing else but brown grass covering this valley?"

"This is the Revanyil Road," revealed Orieant. "This is the road built by the wuzlirs many thousands of years ago, leading to the deserted city of Tuwanor. The remains of this road signify that we are nearing the entrance of the deserted city."

The company was slightly relieved to hear that they were nearing the deserted city, though they still felt anxious thinking about what lay ahead of them. They nervously continued to walk through the rocky road, staring at and observing the rock and stone remains that surrounded them. As they looked on, they saw that some of the remains were larger than others and looked as if they were once part of individual structures of their own. What remained of them, however, were remains of the ancient past, worn down by time and war.

"What are those rocks and stones off to the side?" asked Karandil, unable to ignore what was around him. "They seem to be remains of statues or other pieces of architecture, though I doubt the wuzlirs during this ancient time were as skilled as my people."

"They are just as you said, Karandil," responded Mataput. "Many of these rocks and stones you see were once part of statues, tombs, pillars, and buildings built by the wuzlirs. They were meant to be intimidating objects and structures whose purpose was to strike a sense of great fear and respect for those who entered the now-deserted city of Tuwanor. But in the days of the War of Great Alliances and the many other wars to follow it, many of these pieces of architecture were destroyed by the gamdars and turned to rubble, just as you see right now. Thus it came to pass that this road was abandoned as it no longer was a source of pride for the wuzlirs, but rather a source of embarrassment that the gamdars had destroyed their many successful and greatest works. And the Dark Lord was not happy with his slaves for allowing their bitterest enemies in the gamdars to do all of this to them."

"Let him remain unhappy!" suddenly blurted out Erundil. "And let his slaves continue to feel embarrassed! We gamdars did a noble thing in destroying the evil works of the wuzlirs, so why should we care about their feelings? I wouldn't mind destroying any more of their works that remain in the deserted city."

"Don't speak such things so loudly without caution, Erundil," warned Mataput. "We are on the borders of the deserted city and it is dangerous to mock and threaten the wuzlirs so loudly. You could do that in Watendelle, but not where we are right now."

"But why should we fear the Dark Lord and the wuzlirs?" asked Lelhond. "Did you not say earlier today that we had nothing to fear after you had observed our anxious faces? So because of you and Orieant, I will heed your words and not fear anything that the Dark Lord or his slaves try to intimidate us with."

Erundil nodded his head in agreement with his son, and a look of confidence came to his face. Mataput, however, shook his head, even though he was glad to hear Lelhond speak with such confidence.

"I am glad to hear your confidence, Lelhond," he said. "And I also appreciate you, Erundil, for not giving into the fear which the enemy has long tried to instill in our hearts. But you must understand that the city of Tuwanor was once the greatest work of the wuzlirs, apart from their construction of the tower of Wuzinch Torgol, where the Dark Lord himself resides. Nonetheless, the city of Tuwanor was an intimidating and evil stronghold that showcased the terrible works of the wuzlirs at the height of their wisdom and might. And it remains an evil place, with a dark presence that still lurks in the shadows even though it has long been deserted in the years that have passed."

"I wonder why an evil presence still dwells there," remarked Forandor. "If it has long been deserted why then is it such a terrible place to go to?"

"Because the spirit of Raleshob lives on," answered Orieant. "Not his actual spirit of course, but his actions and doings live on through his descendants, even now in his last living descendant, Moneshob, who is the commander of the army of wuzlirs. All of what made Raleshob so dangerous, intimidating, and deceptive, lived on through his descendants. From his flaming sword to his deep and seductive voice, these things have never been gifted by the Dark Lord to the other wuzlirs, but only to Raleshob and his line. And while his line lives on, the city of Tuwanor remains evil and dangerous."

The company fell silent at what Orieant explained and they felt too weak or fearful to even say anything. Yet as he thought about what the volvier had mentioned, a realization suddenly came to Steven's mind.

"Wait, so the same Moneshob who deceived me and the people and attacked us, is the last living descendant of Raleshob?" he asked, stunned over everything he had heard. "I can't believe what I'm hearing! But that would make sense as to why he was able to deceive us so easily, as his fair voice along with the deceptive wonders he performed like his flaming sword convinced us that we could trust in him. But I wonder why the rest of the wuzlirs who attacked us had ugly voices and regular swords when compared to him."

"Yes, it is him," responded Orieant. "Long ago when the Dark Lord Natugura made Raleshob the King of Tuwanor, he gave him special powers such as deception by using his fair voice and giving him a flaming sword, while the rest of the wuzlirs weren't rewarded with these powers. But the Dark Lord also allowed Raleshob's entire line to have these powers, so that Tuwanor could thrive and their kings deceive and destroy anyone who came in their way. They used these gifts to their advantage, even managing to deceive and trap many gamdars by making them believe they were on their side. Most notably, Huyanshob, the fourth King of Tuwanor, managed to deceive hundreds of gamdars and tortured them in ways that I will not speak of. And Moneshob nearly did the same to you and the people by his words of deception and almost leading all of you to your dooms."

Steven walked silently with his mouth wide open, along with Peter, Huminli, and Glophi, as they were all shocked to hear this from Orieant. Even the gamdars listened with astonishing looks on their faces, as even though they had an idea of this before, they had never heard of such a detailed explanation of the situation as to what Orieant had revealed to them. However, small looks of disgust began to grow on the gamdars' faces, at the mention of the kings of Tuwanor deceiving many gamdars and even torturing them. They wondered exactly what had been done and wanted an answer for this.

"I can't believe all that I'm hearing," remarked Erundil, amidst everyone's silent shock. "But I'm most shocked to hear that the accursed kings of Tuwanor had managed to deceive and even torture my fellow people. Tell me, Orieant, what did they do to the gamdars, and by what means did they torture my people?"

"It is a grievous tale," responded Orieant. "I understand your concern, Erundil, but trust me, you do not want to know what they did to your people."

"But as the King of Watendelle, I should know," replied Erundil. "And my sons and I are desperate to know what terrible things the wuzlirs did to our people. Please, Orieant, you don't need to tell a long tale, but at least give us an honest description of what happened to our people so that we may know the truth."

Orieant said nothing at first, but as he turned and looked into the eyes of Erundil and his sons, and saw their desperation for an answer, he couldn't help but present them with what they desired. And so sighing to himself, he gave the gamdars the answer they sought for.

"As I said before, it is a grievous tale and one that will be difficult to contain," he said. "Nonetheless, if you want the truth then I will give you the truth and hide nothing from you as that is what you seek. In the days of Raleshob, the first King of Tuwanor, the wuzlirs were busy at work and building many things throughout the deserted city. At the center of Tuwanor was a large and imposing temple, round in shape, blacker than the darkest shade of color, and covered with frightening images of the Dark Lord and his slaves. Now at the top of the temple were sharp and spiky stones spread around it like a great circular ring, and in the middle of the ring were stacks of wood. And it came to pass that this temple became known as the Temple of Natugura, where the wuzlirs would worship the Dark Lord and pay homage to him by bringing gifts and other valuable items out of respect for him.

"But things wouldn't stop there, because as time progressed it came into the heart of the Dark Lord to demand more terrible offerings from his servants. He soon began to demand that the kings of Tuwanor use their skill of deception and cunningness that he had gifted them with, to deceive and capture many groups of gamdars. The wuzlirs would hold these captured gamdars in chains and lock them in the most terrible prisons, yet this would not satisfy the Dark Lord for he desired to smell the smoke of burned bodies offered to him in his temple. He ordered these wuzlirs to sacrifice the gamdars for him as it would greatly satisfy him, and so the wuzlirs obeyed their master and offered the Dark Lord these gamdars as burned offerings for him. They lit them on fire on the wood atop the temple, and it is said that the cries of their torment and smell of their burned bodies came to the Dark Lord in his tower and he was greatly pleased at this."

Orieant fell silent and immediately regretted that he had shared this with the gamdars and company. The gamdars along with the entire company stopped walking, with their bodies trembling with such great fear and sorrow that they had never felt in their lives. The gamdars especially felt angered as well to hear how the Dark Lord had demanded those terrible sacrifices from the wuzlirs. Erundil wished to go to war against the wuzlirs just because of the horrible things that they had done to the gamdars.

"It is a grim and sad tale," remarked Orieant, amidst the company's silence and mixed emotions. "I am sorry for sharing it with you all, even though Erundil and his sons wished to hear it."

"No, it was important to learn about the truth regarding this terrible matter," responded Lelhond. "It was important to learn what the terrible fate of our people was, and I never would've imagined that such a thing so terrible could've ever happened to our people. But at least the city of evil has since been left deserted, never to be populated again with evil creatures who did such unimaginable dark deeds against my people."

"I take comfort in knowing that," remarked Erundil. "I am glad that the evil city of Tuwanor is now deserted and destroyed, never again to be feared as a city booming with innumerable transgressions against our people," he suddenly fell silent and thought of something to himself. "But now that I'm thinking," he continued. "How is it possible that this city full of great evil was deserted? I can understand that my people destroyed it by their power and bravery, but I never would've imagined that the wuzlirs would be so terrified of us that they would flee from their city, though it greatly pleases me to think of that."

Mataput smiled at Erundil. "I'm sure that you already know this, Erundil," he said. "But the gamdars are brave and bold creatures, so much so that even the wuzlirs have feared them at times. The gamdars destroyed their city out of vengeance for their evil acts, and I'm sure that the wuzlirs feared what they would do to them out of their righteous anger. And so they likely fled from your people out of such vast fear that they have hardly ever experienced before."

A smile came on Erundil's face. "Well, that is good to hear," he said. "And I wouldn't mind bringing more vengeance upon the wuzlirs, for the many other transgressions that they've committed against my people. I would love to go to war against them sometime, though the time to do that may not be now as we have our quest to worry about. But regardless, I still desire for that day of justice to come."

"Justice will prevail one day, Erundil," said Mataput. "But there is no need to worry or wish for that day to come by your liking or at your own time, for that is only for Jangart to decide. What we must do is succeed in the purpose of our journey, and maybe a time will come when your wish comes true."

As Mataput spoke, Erundil and his sons, along with the rest of the company, grew encouraged and their feeling of sorrow began to slowly fade away. Though they were sad to imagine how terribly the gamdars sacrificed in the Temple of Natugura suffered, they still felt encouraged that the source of pride for the wuzlirs had been destroyed and that the evil creatures had been repaid for their evil.

They walked along the road for just under another hour, before they stopped by the side to have a short rest and meal. They sat quietly to themselves for some time, but as Peter looked around at the many rock and stone remains of the destroyed city, he wondered how exactly the gamdars had managed to attack and destroy the once strong and seemingly impenetrable city. He understood that the gamdars must have been courageous during that time to destroy the city of the wuzlirs, but he had a hard time grasping the fact that the wuzlirs themselves would flee from their city, especially after the gamdars had destroyed it.

Unable to hold onto this thought to himself, Peter presented his question to Mataput and Orieant. "I understand that the wuzlirs fled from their city out of fear of the gamdars after they destroyed it," he said. "But how exactly did the gamdars manage to destroy the city? The city itself must've been well armed with plenty of wuzlirs, so how could they have broken through and humiliated the armies of the wuzlirs in their stronghold?"

"My people destroyed the evil city because of how militarily strong we are," responded Erundil, unaware that Peter's question wasn't directed at him. "What Mataput said earlier is the truth, that my people are brave and bold which means that we are resolutely unwilling to surrender to any presence of darkness. We came to their city with vengeance, and nothing could stand in our way."

"I understand that," replied Peter. "But still, there must have either been some well-thought-out strategy from the gamdars or some heavy weakness from the wuzlirs that led to their city being destroyed. After all, nobody's army or home ground gets wiped out because of luck as there are always reasons behind them being permanently damaged. Sure, the gamdars are the bravest and boldest creatures that I know of, but from my experience, the wuzlirs look quite dangerous themselves. They don't look or seem like the creatures to back down from any shadow of trouble, just as I would imagine that the gamdars would stand in the face of danger with boldness. So I wonder what skills other than bravery and boldness aided the gamdars in destroying the city of the wuzlirs."

"Well, you are one wise boy," remarked Orieant, impressed with what Peter said. "There were many other factors that contributed to the downfall of Tuwanor. Just as Erundil said, the bravery of the gamdars was crucial, along with their skill and organization in battle. But, one thing that must also be understood is that the gamdars managed to destroy the deserted city in a time when the wuzlirs were divided, which proved to be the main reason as to why their city was destroyed."

"Oh really?" said Peter, surprised to hear that a time existed when the wuzlirs were once divided. "Please enlighten me to this reality, Orieant, because I find it strange that the wuzlirs were once divided in their history."

"I wish to know as well," remarked Erundil, shocked himself to hear this. "In all my life, I have never heard of the wuzlirs ever being divided, as I always thought those abominable creatures would have always been of one accord under their master."

"They have always been of like mind when it comes to submitting to the will of the Dark Lord," responded Orieant to Erundil. "But to answer your question, Peter," he continued, now shifting his attention to Peter. "You must understand that unity is the best defense for any kingdom, city, or civilization to possess. Without unity, everything that any creature has ever known runs into the risk of being shattered and destroyed, as was the case for the wuzlirs."

"So why would the wuzlirs be divided then if unity is so important?" asked Steven, who had been silently pondering over what Orieant said. "Unity is important, as I've firsthand seen the consequences of division in my homeland of Fozturia. But how can the wuzlirs still be standing today if they were once divided? And are they still divided today?"

"No, they are not divided today," answered Orieant. "And that is the reason why they are still so mighty and terrifying today, even though they are not as powerful as they once were. To tell you the truth, there was a time when the city of Tuwanor still stood with their kings ruling and during that time the wuzlirs were divided into two groups. Some were rich and born into special places of honor as a result of their families being close to the kings of Tuwanor, with these wuzlirs being loyal to the kings of Tuwanor which rewarded them with even more special privileges and honors from the kings. But some were jealous of the kings of Tuwanor as they were indignant that they received special powers from the Dark Lord, such as their fair voices, flaming swords, and great riches. They wanted these for themselves, but since they weren't as rich or born into families that were known by the kings of Tuwanor, they were instead treated with disdain.

"As a result of their poor treatment, these wuzlirs grew increasingly divided from the other privileged wuzlirs. They looked on at them with jealousy, while the other group looked down on them with scorn, even their kings. This growing conflict reached its climax when under Yoreshob, the eighth and final King of Tuwanor, the jealous wuzlirs began to silently plan to stir a rebellion against the king and his supporters. They planned to seize control of the city for themselves so that they could forcefully have the glory, power, and riches that the kings and privileged wuzlirs had enjoyed for so long. However, before they could do that, the gamdars took advantage of this growing division and weakness of the wuzlirs by besieging the city for many weeks before they attacked and destroyed the stronghold.

"The wuzlirs were completely caught off guard by this and because of their division and weakness, they had no power whatsoever to even try and defeat the gamdars. And so they all fled from the city of Tuwanor while the gamdars burned and destroyed the place, with some of them fleeing to the mountains, others to forests, and even others hiding in the deserts and wastelands of Nangorid. And so the city of the wuzlirs was destroyed, and the Dark Lord punished them for not only being divided amongst themselves but also for fleeing from their city instead of fighting back against the gamdars. And so to this day, the wuzlirs remain scattered throughout the land of Nangorid, but their master has made sure that they are not divided amongst each other, and he has continued to train them in armies, making sure that the descendants of the kings of Tuwanor are the ones leading them in battle."

"Wow, I never would've thought that a group of wuzlirs would be willing to rebel against their people and kings," remarked Steven. "And I can't help but observe how this sounds similar to what was happening in my own home in Fozturia. At least the Resistants and I didn't try and plan a rebellion against Maguspra and his elites and supporters, yet I'm beginning to wonder if our division is a good thing. Moneshob nearly led me and the Resistants astray, and if he succeeded, who knows how much more damage the Dark Lord could've brought to Fozturia and the other kingdoms of the Earth? Shouldn't we have tried to reconcile with Maguspra and unite as Fozturians, and that way the Dark Lord wouldn't have been able to take advantage of our division, just as he tried to?"

"No," suddenly responded Peter. "If I may be allowed to offer my opinion, I think it was good that you led us away from the hand of Maguspra. Because I imagine that even if we tried to reconcile with him, he would've instead punished us for all we did rather than listening to our voices. And besides, once we find this lost book of wisdom on this quest, then you will be an example for all the kingdoms of the Earth on how to reign righteously with justice. And as a result, their kings will also reign with righteousness and justice once you share the book with them. Only then will we be united not only as Fozturians, but as humans, and on that day there shall finally be no more wars, battles, or divisions amongst ourselves, as we all become part of the free creatures of the world just like the gamdars and smalves are."

The company listened on with amazement at Peter's wise words, with Steven now reminded of what the purpose of his and the company's quest through the land of Nangorid was all about, and of the many benefits that would result from their journey. The rest of the company too shook their heads in agreement with Peter and many of them became eager to see all of humanity unite as the free creatures of the world.

"Peter is right," remarked Mataput. "And as for what you said, Steven, though your idea sounds good in all actuality it wouldn't work. It was your destiny to lead a group of people with a like mind of yours to escape from Maguspra, and having those people of the same opinion as you would make it that much easier to mend their hearts once they are introduced to the wisdom and transforming power found in the lost book of Ulohendel."

"That sounds very good," responded Steven. "And I understand the vast importance of what our quest entails, but for some reason, I'm beginning to have doubts about the whole idea of this book transforming myself and every person on the Earth. How is it that a book written thousands of years ago can have the power to change every single human from a corrupted to a non-corrupted creature? I for one find it impossible that Maguspra would be willing to turn from his ways and embrace a change in his heart no matter how much he reads from the lost book of Ulohendel."

As Steven expressed his doubts and concerns, the company became silent as most of them were shocked to hear all of this coming from his mouth, with the most surprised being Peter as he never imagined that Steven would say or even think of such things. The boy's first thought was to try and respond to his friend with reassuring words, yet he found himself unable to think of anything satisfactory to come up with. Even Mataput and Orieant remained mute and sat still as they listened to

Steven reveal his uncertainty about whether or not the lost book would even bring the change that the company hoped and believed it would.

They sat silently there for some time, unable to respond to Steven after listening to his honest admission. But even as they thought to themselves for some time, Lelhond suddenly stood up and sat beside Steven. Placing his hand on the man's shoulder, he tried to grab Steven's attention while the rest of the company stared at him to see what he would say.

"Listen, Steven, your doubts are understandable," he said. "And I must confess that I've even had some doubts over these past few days, regarding whether or not my ancestor's written words would be able to change the hearts of men. But I've also been reminded of late that the words Ulohendel wrote weren't just mere words, but supernatural words that contained the power to transform the minds and hearts of individuals. Why else would the Dark Lord have ordered his slaves to steal the book and lock it in his tower so that no one would have access to it? And why would my people be so grieved once it was stolen, if they were just regular ordinary words that possessed no authority? I could be wrong, but I believe that Ulohendel's words must have been inspired by Jangart himself, and I think that my ancestor saw things that no other gamdar has ever seen before, which inspired him with every word he wrote in that book. And I am confident that the words of his great book can change the heart of every human, which includes yours, Peter's, and even Maguspra's."

The slightest of smiles flashed across the corner of Steven's face and he sensed a warm sensation of comfort and assurance filling his body and mind. The rest of the company sat in silence, marveling over Lelhond's wise and supportive words, and even they felt a resurgence of confidence flowing through their veins.

Erundil came over to his son with a warm smile on his face. "You have reminded all of us about very important matters, Lelhond," he said. "And I can imagine that Ulohendel is looking down on you with great pride and joy to hear his descendant say such wise things."

"Ulohendel is surely thinking of wonderful things of you, Lelhond," chimed in Mataput. "And all that you said is correct, mainly being that the lost book of Ulohendel has tremendous power to transform the hearts of men, even that of the evilest ones. I am not sure if Jangart himself inspired the words that Ulohendel wrote, but what I do know is that they were special words that he wrote."

"They were indeed special words," remarked Orieant. "And I hope we can all agree that the purpose of our journey is not in vain nor will it ever be so. I hope you believe in that truth, Steven, but I am glad that you expressed your doubts and concerns with us. Yet now after hearing all that Lelhond has said, do you have faith that the lost book of Ulohendel will change not only your heart but the hearts of all men?"

Steven's smile slowly faded and he stared at the ground for a moment, before looking up and seeing the eyes of the company fixed on him. He sat silently for a while, listening to the two opposing voices in his head trying to convince him of their point of view. He felt a mixed rush of emotions, some of hope and doubt, others of joy and fear, yet as he stared at the many faces of the gamdars, smalves, and volviers around him, he noticed a genuine compassion and support that filled their faces. And as he stared into Peter's face, he could sense a hope beyond measure that beamed through the young boy's eyes. As he gazed into his smiling face, he could see a boy filled with the courage and belief that everything would be fine, and so a smile returned to Steven's face, this time a broad expression of hope and joy.

"Yes, I believe that with all my heart," he eventually said with bold confidence. "All of you have reminded me of the purpose of our journey and why we will succeed because of that motivation. I'm glad to be surrounded by you all, as you have provided me with so much hope and support."

The company was relieved to see Steven's confidence restored, and most pleased of all was his friend Peter. "I'm glad to see your faith strengthened, Steven," said the boy, with his face lit with joy and relief. "We all have our moments of doubt and worry, but we must not lose faith because without faith our quest will either fail or be in vain."

"And without faith, our very lives would be meaningless," added Mataput. "And you, Steven, have been chosen by Jangart himself even before you were born for this very purpose; to find the lost book of Ulohendel and save the world of men. Our quest for the deliverance of humanity will not be in vain as long as we stay together no matter what we face or how we feel in certain moments of this quest."

"That is right," remarked Erundil, feeling a resurgence of hope and strength as well. "You, Orieant, and even Peter always seem to give us words of encouragement when we need it most."

"That is because we are always here for each other," said Mataput, looking around at the many faces of the company. He couldn't help but smile with satisfaction that everyone involved in the quest was perfect for the role they had been assigned, even without many of them knowing exactly what it was.

As the company sat there for some time, Steven reflected on Mataput's words on how he had been chosen by Jangart to fulfill his very purpose in life. And though he felt slightly overwhelmed by the thought of it, at the same time, an even greater overwhelming sense of support and faith that he experienced just by being with those around him, warmed and strengthened his often weary heart.

The company rested for some more time by the side of the road, with Steven continuing to ponder everything they had shared while imagining how he would feel when they completed their quest. He tried picturing the joy that would fill his heart when he finally reached the end of his journey, and he knew that the mission he was embarking on was the most important thing he would ever do in his life, which only motivated him all the more to triumph in his most important journey.

Yet, even as he thought of the end of his long journey, he imagined the many more difficult and troubling times he would experience. He thought of the danger that he would possibly encounter, dangers that would possibly be the worst he would ever experience in his life. He thought of the evil world that he was now in, and wondered what more darkness his eyes would gaze at in the deserted city. A brief cloud of anxiety flooded his mind, but just like the passing wind, it quickly vanished away from his thought since he knew that because he was supported, hope would always win in the end no matter what presence of evil would choose to encamp around him.

Several more minutes passed and no one among the company spoke a word. They all sat silently for some time, thinking to themselves and resting, but then suddenly, a look of curiosity came on Glophi's face as a thought sprung to his mind.

He turned his attention to the volviers. "When do you think that we will arrive at the deserted city?" he asked. "How much longer will we have to walk on this old boring road before we finally arrive at our destination."

"Not much longer," replied Orieant. "Right now, I reckon that it's a little after two o'clock. But we should be continuing to walk on this road as we have had a longer than necessary rest. We should arrive at the remains of the city gate in the next few hours if we start now."

"Well, I'm ready to go," remarked Glophi, growing excited. "This is the moment we've all been waiting for, so I'm more than ready to get going."

The smalf sprung to his feet from where he sat, eager to get going on in the journey. The rest of the company stood up as well, feeling relaxed from their much-needed rest, and they at once followed Mataput and Orieant on the road, continuing their way southward toward the deserted city of Tuwanor.

The afternoon hours passed rather slowly as the company trekked their way down the stone road. The sky was still filled with clouds, though the sun began to peer through the sky more so than it did in the morning. There was more light from the sun that shone in little pockets of the land around them, but the air remained mostly gray and dark, with the small light of the sun not enough to completely brighten up the land.

As they walked the road began to curve on each side, going in a zigzag pattern. The road seemed to be growing more sturdy as the rock remains soon turned into solid stone patterns in the ground. The rocks and stones in the grass along the side soon started to disappear, as the only thing of minor interest now was the change in the road. The long hours proved to be quite boring, with hardly anyone in the company speaking to one another as nothing proved to spark their interest.

But after a couple of hours had passed, the company noticed a strange sight that lay ahead of them. As they journeyed through the valley on the road, tall gray pillars of stone suddenly surrounded them on each side of the road, with many of the pillars being connected in pairs and overhanging together by a long triangular-shaped piece of stone. As they observed the pillars they observed some form of writing near the bottom of the stone works, though they were written in a strange alien language, unknown by all of them.

Their interests were sparked by these strange pillars, though that feeling would soon change. As they walked along the road, staring at the large pillars, they felt a strange uneasy feeling stirring in their bones as if they could sense that they were now entering a place of great evil and wickedness which they had no business in going through. And just as this unsettling sensation came over them, the sky instantly grew darker and the gray clouds seemed to swarm and grow tighter together. Just then, small but profound drops of rain fell from the sky, and the raindrops seemed to have a certain feeling of intensity to them as if a foul presence was stored within their meager drops.

The company put their hoods on, immediately feeling glad and thankful that they had warm cloaks with hoods. Yet, even with their head coverings on they could still feel the strange and foul presence surrounding them as it came down on them in the form of little raindrops. The air around them seemed to be filled with a loathsome spirit as well, and the strange pillars that they saw gave them a slight sense of fear.

Steven suddenly froze and collapsed to the ground, feeling heavy weakness and terror from the top of his head to the toes of his feet. The company immediately stopped walking and brought Steven up to his feet.

"Are you fine, Steven?" asked Peter. "You just collapsed to the ground out of nowhere and your eyes almost seem to be popping out from your face."

Steven staggered to his feet, with a cloud of anxiety covering his face. "I don't know," he said. "I just felt so weak when I saw these strange-looking pillars and the air along with the rain seemed to be filled with an overwhelming foul presence."

"I understand what you're saying and I can feel it too," remarked Peter. He gazed around at the wide distance around him, observing the pillars and the foul presence of the air. "I felt quite uneasy myself when I saw these weird pillars, and the feeling only grew worse when the rain came down. Does anyone else feel the same way as us?"

Erundil looked around him, sniffing the air with a distasteful look on his face. "Yes, I feel the same way as you two," he responded. "And I can smell an ugly scent in the air as if the ugliness and darkness of the wuzlirs still live on in this place."

"The smell is quite repulsive," remarked Lelhond, covering his nose from the terrible aroma of the air. He turned toward Mataput and Orieant. "Do you know what that is exactly?" he asked. "What is this horrible smell in the air?"

"And what about the strange pillars around us?" asked Huminli. "They look so weird and frightening."

"The terrible smell and foul presence flowing through the air is from the wuzlirs that dwelled here long ago," answered Mataput. "We are nearing the gates of the city of Tuwanor. The endless miles of pillars you see were built by the wuzlirs as a way to honor their kings and the Dark Lord. The words written on the bottom must be some terrible curse on the gamdars or something to glorify their master. But I admit that I know nothing about the language of the wuzlirs and I would rather choose not to know."

"So would I," said Erundil. "And I know that whatever curses they might try to instill in us will never succeed."

"Yes, that is right," agreed Forandor. "But we should probably start walking now as I have a feeling that this rain will only get worse. A strange presence is stored within its drops, as though this rain itself was of the making of the Dark Lord himself."

"Don't speak such things, Forandor," warned Orieant. "For that is not true since only Jangart has the power to control the weather, not the Dark Lord. And even if he did have the power that Jangart did and this was indeed of his making, then he would have found where we are right now. But I am confident that he is unaware of where we are if I can say such a thing with boldness."

"I believe that you are right, Orieant," said Lelhond. "And there is no harm in saying what you truly believe is on your heart since you and Mataput have proven to be far wiser than the rest of us combined."

Just as they were talking, a rumble of thunder vibrated through the sky as a downpour of rain suddenly came down. The company shivered from the cold raindrops and they knew that it was the right time to continue on their journey.

"Now is the time for us to get going," said Orieant. "You were right, Forandor, the rain has shown that it will only get worse. Let us go quickly since there are a few scattered buildings in the city where we should be able to find shelter from the rain."

The company wasted no time in starting to walk, all the while they continued to shudder from the massively cold raindrops that came pouring down from the sky. They picked up their pace, hoping to find shelter as soon as possible. The darkness of the approaching city was now of little concern to them, as their only wish was to go through the city gates and find protection from the cold raindrops and loathsome presence of the air.

They trudged their way through the stone road, as the heavy rain continued to splash on their protected heads. Their cloaks were soaked with water and surrounding them were large puddles of water. They painstakingly walked around the large puddles, not wishing for their shoes or socks to be immersed in cold water. The smell of the air only got worse with the strange and foul feeling that had surrounded them only growing stronger. Still, they managed to endure these dreadful conditions, as they desperately hoped for just the slightest bit of shelter.

About half an hour passed before the company came at last to a wide stone wall painted in black, with a round shape and massive black spikes growing near the top of the structure. The company stared at the massive wall for a moment, with what seemed like a frightening shadow suddenly passing over them. Everywhere they looked, they could see nothing but the colossal shape of the terrifying presence of the stone barrier. No gate could be seen, neither was the faintest of openings visible to them.

Huminli punched the wall, hoping that at least a part of it would crumble to provide an opening for the company to enter. Yet, as he did this, he immediately exclaimed in pain, grabbing onto the knuckles of his hand.

"Do not do that, Huminli," said Mataput, seeing the smalf crying in pain. "Though this wall is thousands of years old, it has stood the test of time and remains sturdy even despite the long years that have passed since this city was deserted. There is no need to hurt yourself for nothing."

"Then what are we going to do?" complained Huminli. "Stand here in this soaking rain while not even the smallest hint of an entrance is visible to us? Are we going to sleep here in these wet and terrible weather conditions?"

"No, Huminli," responded Mataput with a smile. "Orieant and I never would have brought all of you here if there was not a way to enter."

Huminli mumbled something under his breath and sighed to himself, doubting that the company would ever be able to enter the city with the massive black walls blocking them. But just as he thought this, Mataput and Orieant stepped closer to the wall and outstretched their arms toward it. Then as they brought their arms down, a great cracking sound could be heard as numerous black stones collapsed from the wide wall. Before their very eyes, the company saw a large opening provided for them to enter the city. They stood paralyzed in shock over what they had witnessed, with Huminli staring at the volviers with widened eyes and a gaping mouth.

"Why did I ever doubt you two?" he remarked, stunned and filled with instant regret. "I am sorry for complaining about our situation, as I don't know how I could have ever forgotten of the great power that you two have."

"One cannot so easily forget the great power of the volviers," remarked Erundil, briefly staring at Huminli with slanted eyes. "After everything that you have witnessed them do and say, how can you choose to lack faith? I would have never doubted Mataput and Orieant even if we had waited here for hours."

Huminli rolled his eyes in annoyance while Mataput shook his head. "There is no need to condemn Huminli, Erundil," said the volvier. "And do not speak so confidently in yourself as you have also had moments where your faith has been tested."

"My fault," said Erundil, with an unchanged expression on his face. "But let us go on and enter through this opening. This rain is freezing and I can see large buildings along the side of a wide road inside, so we should find a place to shelter ourselves from outside."

He immediately went forward through the opening, giving Huminli a look of scorn from the corner of his eye with a large grin on his face. The rest of the company followed Erundil as they made their way through the opening that the volviers had made. Once each person had passed through, they stood silently in wonder at the scope and size of the city. They found themselves standing on what seemed to be a long ramp, covered in brown and black stones, and all around them were huge buildings, some of brown color others of darker grays or blacks, built within great hillsides. They had a certain frightening presence to them, which was only further exemplified by the massive statues depicting what looked like ancient wuzlirian figures or even other terrifying creatures.

They tried soaking in everything their eyes could see, but certain statues and buildings gave them such a dreadful feeling that they tried looking away from them at times. They all silently stood in place, not moving a muscle or dimming their alarmed widened eyes.

Eventually, Orieant broke the long silence that hovered over the company. "Well, we are here at last in the deserted city of Tuwanor," he said, observing all that lay ahead of him and also noticing how the company remained frozen out of fear. "There are many buildings around us and yet all of you are just standing still and doing nothing. Let us go and find a place of shelter before we are caught off guard again."

Nobody stirred to move at first, but eventually, they managed to get over their fears and began to move down the long stone ramp. They walked slowly, anxiously following Mataput and Orieant while staring at everything that met their eyes. The size and dark presence of the city gave them chills, and they didn't sense much comfort in going inside a seemingly terrifying building. Still, they reluctantly followed the volviers out of the desire to find a place to shelter them from the rain that continued to lash down upon them.

Eventually, they came down the long ramp and found themselves walking on a flat and dry ground covered in dirt with some patches of brown grass. By now it was a little after six and the sky began to darken as the night fast approached. As they walked on the flat ground, they became even more frightened at the sight of the many large and fearsome buildings that surrounded them. They were all mainly of a dark gray or blackish color, built with strong stones to last for many years. Some were triangular shaped, others round, while others seemed to be formed in a sort of zigzag fashion. And while some still looked well-grounded and strong, many others looked like they would collapse at any moment.

Nonetheless, every structure had a frightening aura to it, and some form of writing seemed to be on many of the buildings.

Mataput and Orieant led the company in the direction of one specific black building, with a rounded shape and many tall pillars built within it. On top of the building was what appeared to be a large stone dome, and there were many small openings all along the side walls with painted images of some kind of figure. It appeared to be a tomb of some sort, and it looked very well-built and imposing in its size and architectural design. The company nervously made their way in this direction, wondering what would lay in store for them.

Suddenly, as they made their way over, a rumble of thunder vibrated through the valley and a bright white spark of lightning illuminated the darkening sky. The rain came storming down with even more ferocity, and a powerful wind swiftly made its way through the air.

Mataput and Orieant immediately started to run in pursuit of the shelter they had found. "Quick, to our right is a tomb that will shield us from this rain and lightning!" shouted Mataput. "We must go on quickly now and not stop, so follow us!"

As if a switch had gone off in their minds, the company swiftly snapped from walking in a leisurely manner and started running as they followed the volviers in the direction of the tomb. More lightning continued to flash across the sky, as the wind came flying in their direction. Great fear consumed them, and they wished not to be caught in the wrath of the weather. They ran as if they were being chased by fire while covering their heads from any potential lightning strikes.

But at last, they made their way to the tomb and ran up a long step of stairs to hurry inside. Just as they made it in, a great boom of thunder vibrated through the sky and ground, which made them all collapse to the ground and huddle together in a tight corner. Bright white lights continued to shine in the sky, while the rain showed no signs of slowing down. But the sturdy wall and roof of the temple protected the company as they sat together shuddering with fear. They were relieved to find safety, but the sound of the pouring rain and rumbling thunder didn't provide them with much comfort. It continued in this way for the next few minutes, as the company could only stare at the terrible weather outside.

But in that moment there came a sudden silence, as the sound of thunder vanished away with no signs of lightning appearing in the sky. Even the rain slowed down, though it still poured down from the sky. The company breathed a sigh of relief and felt somewhat relaxed now, as Mataput and Orieant stood up with the others remaining seated. Some of them still felt an uneasy sensation running through their bones, which was not aided by the fact that everything around them was dark, meaning that they could hardly see one another.

"We are here at last," remarked Orieant, walking over to one of the side openings and peering outside at the pouring rain. "I do not know why the weather has drastically changed against us, but regardless, I am glad that we are at least safe in here."

"Where are we?" asked Steven, with his teeth chattering with coldness. "I don't feel any better here than when we were outside in the pouring rain with the lightning flashing in the sky. I can feel something strange inside this place, but I can't quite make out what it is exactly."

"Heck, I've been feeling something strange ever since we came near the gates of this city," said Glophi. "And I don't like it one bit. This place is only making things worse and the darkness in this tomb or building isn't helping things either."

Just then, bright sparks of light came reflecting inside, which were in the form of two large torches that Mataput and Orieant picked up and brought near to the company. The torches allowed the company to not only see each other but also observe all that was around them. They found that they were sitting near a large stone coffin, with images and writings on it, and as they looked in the corners around them, they found even more coffins and even scattered statues of different kinds of creatures and figures. The tomb that they found themselves in was rather large and spacious, and they found themselves surrounded by well-built thick stone walls. The ground where they sat was wide and dusty, built with all sorts of rocks and stones. The company was in an endlessly long and wide hall, in a tomb built and crafted by the wuzlirs long ago.

They gazed all around them, not knowing how to feel or respond. Eventually, Orieant spoke and revealed where they were. "We are in one of the tombs that the wuzlirs built long ago," he remarked. "This place was never meant to be cozy, but it has the best bit of shelter that we will find in this city. In the meantime, we can rest here for the night before leaving tomorrow morning, when hopefully the weather will be much better."

"Good, I can't wait to leave this place tomorrow because I'm already soaking wet, and having to spend the night in this dark and spooky place doesn't sound too friendly," complained Glophi, who nervously stared at the many statues and coffins around him, feeling a great deal of uncertainty.

One such statue that sparked both his curiosity and fear was around ten feet in height and seemed to depict a winged creature of some sort. The creature had scales all over its body along with fanged teeth, and on its head was what looked like the remains of a stone crown. It appeared to have a level of authority to it, and Glophi didn't appreciate the look of it.

"What's that?" he asked, pointing toward the statue. "It looks like the depiction of a mati, yet it has a crown on its head."

"That's because it is a mati," responded Mataput, stepping closer to the statue and examining it as he stared longingly at the figure. "The statue depicts Hoshlog, the King of the Matis during the days of the War of Great Alliances. He was the largest mati to ever live, and it is said that the flapping of his wings could be heard from one end of Nangorid to the other. He caused much devastation in the air and wherever he landed on the ground, and during his time, the matis gathered together in their full number here in the deserted city. There must have been at least hundreds of them at that time, but now I doubt if there are even more than a dozen."

"Well, I hope there are no more than a dozen matis that exist today," said Glophi. "These statues are giving me the creeps just by looking at them, and this particular statue of Hoshlog is giving me real chills in my bones. I don't like his sharp fangs, nor do his outspread wings give me much comfort. And just look at his terrifying face!"

Glophi cowered into a small corner, hiding his face from the statue. Mataput came over to him, placing his hand on his shoulder and looking deeply into the smalf's eyes.

"There is no need to fear, Glophi," he said, trying to comfort the smalf. "We are all here together in this tomb, and this statue won't come to life and attack you, nor will any of the other statues here. Tomorrow morning we will immediately depart from this place, as we are only here in this tomb because it's providing us with the best protection from the storm outside."

Glophi straightened his posture with a smile coming to his face as he listened to Mataput. Most of the fear he felt passed from his mind and Huminli came to sit by his side and wrap his arms around his brother.

"We will be fine, Glophi," he said, smiling at his brother. "Though these statues gave me fearful shudders, knowing that we are all gathered together in one safe spot, provides me with much comfort."

"It provides me with comfort too, Huminli," replied Glophi. "I feel a lot better now, and I'm glad that we won't have to worry about seeing this sight for much longer."

The company sat there silently for a while, waiting for the evening to pass swiftly. But time moved anything but swiftly, as mere minutes felt like endless hours. They tried to entertain themselves, staring at the walls, statues, and coffins around them, but these only sparked fear in them again. They tried talking to each other, with the smalves sharing jokes and stories, but this did nothing to amuse them. All they wished was for a couple more boring hours to pass so that they could go to rest and wake up for a new day. And so they spent more time sitting silently among themselves, staring off into the distance and waiting as time passed.

Eventually, after an hour had passed, or possibly even long minutes that felt like hours, Steven stood up to his feet. Stretching his arms and body, he at once began walking in the direction of his right down the long and empty hall.

Orieant immediately stood up, wondering what Steven was doing. "Where are you going, Steven?" he asked.

"I just want to walk around," responded Steven. "I don't want to just sit around here in this corner and stare off into space. If I am going to stare off into space, then I should at least get up and see if anything is interesting to observe."

"But nothing is interesting about this place," said Peter. "Just sit here, Steven, and tomorrow morning we'll be able to leave here."

"No, let him go, Peter," remarked Orieant, much to Peter's shock.

"Just make sure that you do not leave this building, Steven. We are safe and protected in this place and there is no reason to unnecessarily get lost in that space without any of us knowing where you are. And here," he said, handing Steven one of the torches that he and Mataput had picked up. "Take this torch so that you are not lost in the darkness."

Steven took the torch. "Don't worry, I'm not going to leave this building and go outside," he said. "I'm just going to look around and see if anything sparks my interest, but I'll let you know if anything is fascinating enough to bring you out of your boredom."

"Go then, Steven," said Orieant. "Though I doubt that you will find anything fascinating in this tomb, I will allow you to do what it is you desire."

And so Steven continued to make his way through the long and wide hall, using his torch to light his way as he touched and observed the walls, statues, and coffins around him. He was amazed by how strong they were, even after the long years of erosion and weathering that had taken place. He was impressed by how skillful the wuzlirs were in building and crafts, though he still felt disgusted by all the evil acts had committed under the Dark Lord's authority. He continued walking through the hall, examining and processing all that his eyes beheld.

He soon came to a regular-sized stone door that was left open, and through the door, he saw a wide and empty room that didn't seem to have anything within it. Yet, a strange feeling of curiosity struck him, and he desired to enter the room, though nothing appeared to be of much interest. And so he slowly made his way into the room, using his torch to light his way through the opening.

He found himself in what looked like a wide chamber, larger than what he had imagined it to be. The walls were old and dusty, and hanging down from the ceiling were many interlacing cobwebs. The ground itself was covered in dust and dirt, and the air was tightly compact, giving Steven slight difficulty in breathing. The room was unattractive and old, yet Steven still explored it to see if he would find anything alluring.

Just as he was wandering through the dusty old chamber, Steven found something tucked away in a small corner. His eyebrows lifted with curiosity and he quickly made his way to see what it was. He came and found hiding in the corner a small brown box that was halfway opened, and immediately, a feeling of doubt and uncertainty seized control of him, but it suddenly went away as he made his way closer to the box. He now felt a strong impulse to see what was in the box, though the feeling of suspicion still lingered on, creeping its way slowly and deeply into his heart. But he again quickly brushed aside any feelings of worry and suspicion, and eager to see what was hiding in the box, he brought his hand to it and lifted the top of it.

He beheld a small and seemingly insignificant black ball lying in the treasure box, one that was perfectly round with everything about it seeming to be perfect. Steven stared at the object for a moment, which turned into multiple moments, and even longer than that. He couldn't stop staring at the ball, and to his amazement he found himself starting to drool over the sight of the object. He felt like he was being hypnotized by a power beyond his reckoning, which he tried to shake off, but was unable to. He tried looking in the other direction but found himself powerless to even try and free his mind from the obsession with the ball. He attempted to muster all his strength to leave the ball behind, but he still found himself without the ability to go away from its sight. And so he gave up, and reaching over he picked up the ball which he continued to stare at as it fit perfectly in the palm of his hand.

Just then, wild imaginations began to run freely through his mind, and as he gazed at the ball, a broad smile spread across his face and he suddenly began to laugh hysterically, in a slightly devilish manner. He felt an uncontrollable urge to have the ball all for himself, and to never lose sight of it. He felt so enamored by the ball, that everything else in his mind went blank, and for a split second, he completely forgot about the company, where he was, or even what his name was. As if a great power was bewitching him, he dared not depart his gaze from the ball nor put it back in the box. For what seemed like endless hours in Steven's mind, he tightly held onto the ball in his hand, not letting go of it.

Then suddenly he sprung back into time, as he could hear a voice though he couldn't tell whether it came from an outside source or in his mind. He turned around and found Peter standing off in the distance and loudly calling his name.

"Steven! Steven!" he called. "Is everything fine with you?"

Steven hastily put the ball in his backpack, wildly moving his body with high tension covering his face. He reopened and closed the zippers on his backpack, doing it in such a delicate manner as if he feared that his bag would rip open and his ball fall. Peter watched him with confusion, wondering what madness had come over him.

"Steven, I've been calling your name for a while now," he said. "You were holding something in your hand that I couldn't quite see and once you saw me you immediately put it away as if you were trying to hide something from me. And even now you still haven't responded to me. Is everything fine?"

"Yes, yes, I mean, well, yes, there's nothing to worry about...yes," hastily said Steven, nodding his head while not even looking at Peter. A cloud of anxiety covered his face, which only further added more confusion for Peter.

Peter stared at him for a second with bewilderment, before shaking his head and turning around. "Well, you should probably come back with me to sit with the rest of the group," he said. "I think you've had plenty of time for yourself."

"Yes, haha, you're right, Peter," said Steven, laughing nervously and anxiously. He opened his backpack one last time and gave a quick glimpse to make sure his ball, as he now thought of it, was still in there before making his way outside of the large room. He followed Peter through the long halls of the tomb back to where the rest of the company was. As he walked behind his friend, he couldn't stop sweating and shaking with nervousness as he hoped that Peter wouldn't discover what he had found, or tell anyone else about it, especially the volviers.

The two of them soon made their way back to the small corner of the long hall where everyone else sat silently. Mataput and Orieant were the only ones standing up, with relief covering their faces once they saw Steven and Peter walking back to them.

"Thank goodness you're fine, Steven," said Orieant, with the concern on his face disappearing, tough disappointment could be heard in the tone of his voice. "We were worried for you and had to send Peter to make sure nothing worrying happened to you. But please, next time make sure you get back here much sooner as we don't want to be worrying about you for nothing."

"Yes, that's my fault. I promise not to do that next time," said Steven, looking all over the place nervously and fidgeting even as he spoke. Everyone stared at him with bewildered faces, especially Peter and the volviers who were growing increasingly concerned for him.

Even Lelhond was perplexed by Steven's change of personality and attitude, and couldn't help but think he was hiding something. "Is everything fine, Steven?" he asked. "You've been acting quite strange with us ever since you came back from wherever you went. Did you see something strange that's been affecting you in acting like this?"

"Oh, no no," quickly replied Steven with a nervous laugh. "I didn't see anything weird or strange. I just went for a short walk around this tomb and now I'm back here. Is there anything strange about that?"

"No, nothing is strange about that," slowly said Lelhond as he observed Steven's face and movements. "But the strange thing is that Peter had to come find you, and ever since then, you've been acting differently than you normally are. I hope there's nothing bad going on with you, so please tell us if there's ever anything concerning you. We are all here together which means that none of us should ever feel alone."

"Nothing is concerning me," said Steven, trying to appear normal to Lelhond and the company. "I must have just wandered off by myself for too long, but nothing strange is going on with me, contrary to what you believe. There's no reason for any of you to be worried about me. Just let me go! Please, leave me alone!"

His voice suddenly grew louder with frustration, and he was breathing heavily as he seemed to be deeply offended by something. Everyone couldn't help but stare at him out of disbelief at his sudden change in tone. Upon seeing everyone staring at him, Steven quickly went away from their sight, sitting by himself in a small corner, with his back to their sight. Peter, feeling greatly grieved tried going over to talk with his friend, but was immediately stopped by Mataput.

"No Peter," said the volvier in a soft voice. "Leave Steven alone, as I deem it is best that we leave him alone to think to himself. With whatever he's going through, it seems wise to let him be by himself so that we don't add any more trouble to his mind."

"But he's not acting like himself," protested Peter. "He's never been like this and yet now after wandering through these halls for so long, he's now acting in this strange manner. Whatever he saw, I just hope it hasn't affected his mind."

Mataput looked in Steven's direction, watching over the man with heavy concern on his face. He turned toward Peter once again. "Do you know if he discovered something wherever he staggered to?" he asked. "Was there anything unusual that you might have seen?"

Peter thought to himself for some time, deep in thought as he tried to remember and piece together all that Steven had said and done when he found him. Suddenly, his face lit up as his memory became clear.

"Yes, I remember that he held something in his hand," he recalled. "I couldn't see it, but it appeared to be some sort of object that he quickly hid in his backpack once he saw me. From then on, he's been acting strangely, as if he's worried or anxious about that object."

Mataput placed his hand on his chin, processing all that Peter had said. "Well, that is interesting," he said, before pausing for a long moment and not saying anything.

"Should we do anything then?" asked Peter, observing Mataput's silence. "Should we find out plainly what it is that he's hiding from us?"

Mataput said nothing at first, instead looking on at Steven as if he were examining all the different possible outcomes that would result from their interrogation of him. "No," he said, after the long pause. "We should not do that. Let's leave him alone by himself tonight and hope that he's feeling better by tomorrow morning."

"And what if he's not?" questioned Peter. "What if he's still feeling and acting the same way that he is now?"

"Then that would be a cause for concern," admitted Mataput. "Nonetheless, we shouldn't hope for the worst, instead we must have faith that Steven will come to his senses tomorrow morning and that whatever he's feeling will soon pass away from his mind. Let us continue hoping for his freedom from whatever is plaguing him right now."

Peter's face didn't change, with a cloud of uncertainty still covering his face. He dropped his head to the ground and sighed to himself. Mataput placed his hand on Peter's shoulder, with the young boy lifting his eyes to look at the volvier.

"I promise you, Peter, that you will have your friend back," he said. "Whatever he is going through is only a shadow that must eventually pass away. He will not remain the way he is forever, and I am certain of that. But you must not worry about him, just let your mind and body rest tonight so that tomorrow morning you will be refreshed and we can all accurately assess how he is doing."

The faintest of smiles flashed on Peter's face, and even though images of concern and confusion still preoccupied his mind, he now felt a great deal better from Mataput's reassuring words. He looked one more time at Steven, seeing only the back of his head as he sat far away from the company. Peter sighed to himself one last time, before turning back to where the rest of the company was gathered together.

Meanwhile, Steven continued sitting by himself far away from the sight of the company. He stared at the walls that lay ahead of him for some time, observing its writings and many engraved images. He opened up his backpack and making sure no one could see him, he took out the small black ball he had found. A smile came on his face as he stared at it for some time, with sensations of relief and comfort filling his heart. Yet, even as he experienced the momentary happiness that came from the ball, he also regretted that he had spoken with such frustration against Lelhond. He knew that the company was worried about him, especially Peter, and at that moment he felt a sudden urge to go over and apologize to them. But he swiftly brushed the feeling aside and shifted his focus from the company back to the small ball that he grasped in his hand.

The rest of the company sat huddled together in their corner, talking among themselves. They mainly spoke of Steven, sharing their fears and worries about him, though Mataput and Orieant did the best they could to provide calmness and comfort to the company. And so even with their deep concerns for Steven, they managed to remain where they were while they allowed Steven to think and relax for himself without feeling the need to constantly examine or talk to him.

Another half hour passed and by now it was time to rest for the night. The rain outside had calmed down tremendously in the time that had passed, with only a small drizzle of drops falling from the sky. The sound of the wind had also pacified, with only a chill breeze making its way through the air. It was around nine or ten o'clock by now, and only the half moon and twinkling of a few meager stars provided light in the pitch-black sky. Yet even though the night was now upon them, the company found themselves restless and unable to bring themselves to pass out deep into the night.

However, this was not the case for Steven, as once he began yawning, he slowly curled himself into a ball and shut his eyes. He soon passed out into a deep sleep, forgetting everything that had happened during the long day.

Meanwhile, everyone else lay on their backs with wide-opened eyes, staring at the ceilings above and the walls around them. They were unable to close their eyes and failed to embrace the sense of tiredness that usually led them to fall asleep. They were concerned with many things, chief among them being the way that Steven had been acting. They found themselves unable to brush aside these worries of theirs, and for the next few minutes, they accepted these thoughts that ran rampant through their minds.

It remained this way for the next half hour or so, with nothing changing. Everyone tried covering their ears from the sound of Steven's snoring, while they couldn't even bring themselves to a half-asleep state. They wondered when the drowsiness would come over their bodies and lead them to a deep slumber, but all they could do was think and imagine all kinds of different matters with wide-awakened eyes.

But then suddenly, the great roaring of a harsh noise shook their entire bodies with terror. The company immediately froze in shock at what had happened, while Steven remained deep in his sleep as everyone else was lying down paralyzed with awful dread. The terrible noise soon died away, giving them a moment to process what had just happened.

Yet just as swiftly, the noise came again and with it this time came the rumbling of a deep stirring in the ground as if a mighty earthquake had just occurred. This time the company stood up, with Huminli and Glophi screaming in horror.

Even Steven suddenly sprung up to his feet, looking up, down, and to his side as he feared that some wicked creature had come to torment him and the company. The sound of the blaring rumbling continued to blast through the ground, with small cracks beginning to form within the ground where the company stood.

They ran from where they were, with Steven following them from behind, unbeknownst to them. They suddenly stopped dead in their tracks with the small cracks in the ground beginning to form in a large ring around them. They tried hanging themselves to the walls around them, but even the hard stones within them began to crack and crumble. The smalves continued crying in horror, while everyone else either screamed or acted wildly out of terror.

"We are stranded!" screamed Huminli, jumping to the side to avoid another crack in the ground. Tears began to swell all over his face. "There's no hope in surviving this!"

"We are all going to die!" cried Erundil, holding on to his sons. "I didn't imagine that our quest would end like this! What are we going to do?"

"We must hold onto hope!" urged Lelhond. "Our journey doesn't end here, for we will find a way to escape from this place!"

"Look!" said Peter, pointing out a smooth part of the ground that led to the doors. "Over there is a path for us to escape from this place! If we want to survive, then we should be on our way!"

"Hold on!" said Mataput. "Let us first make sure that Steven is with us because we cannot leave this building without him! Are you with us Steven?"

"Yes, I am here!" shouted a loud voice, from behind. The company turned around and their faces were immediately covered in shock and relief to see that Steven was with them the whole time.

"Good!" remarked Mataput with a sigh of relief. "Follow Orieant and me as we make our way of escape, and whatever you do, make sure that none of you are separated from the group!"

With that, the company started dashing toward the exit doors, springing over the cracks of the ground as Mataput and Orieant led them, holding the same two torches in their hands to light the way. Even as they sprinted, the walls began to crumble and the structure of the building itself began to collapse. They ducked and dodged away from numerous stones flying in their direction, and remained close to each other even as they ran.

They reached the exits of the doors, fleeing as far as they could from the impending collapse of the building. They managed to survive with one final push, with Steven being the last to make his way through the doors, only narrowly escaping the collapsing stone structure with a large jump. The ground had stopped rumbling and shaking, with the company breathing a sigh of relief at this. Yet they had no time to waste, as to their shock, they discovered that more buildings were collapsing around them, and would trap them if they came to a halt.

"Quick, we must flee from this city!" cried Orieant, with him and Mataput darting in the direction that the company had entered the city from, lightning the path with their torches for the rest of them to follow.

As the company ran, they found that the road seemed to suddenly grow weaker and less sturdy. Some of the stones began to disintegrate, with many of them almost collapsing as they made their escape from the scene. Still, they pushed themselves with the remaining might they had, using every last bit of energy that was contained in their bodies.

But just then, a terrible screeching sound came vibrating through the sky, with what sounded like the racing of hoofs dashing towards them. The screeching noises grew louder as they ran, with what felt like an approaching army gaining ground on the company.

The company screamed in horror at the terrible sounds that plagued them, with Mataput and Orieant suddenly turning to the right to cut across the road in a different direction from where they had entered the city.

"What is happening?" cried Karandil, quickening his pace to make his way closer to the volviers who were at the front of the pack. "And where are you two taking us to?"

"We are under attack," said Mataput. "As there is a large number of wuzlirs riding on horses and fast approaching us. They are coming in our direction, so follow us as we try to flee from their wrath!"

The company cried in disbelief that they were being chased by a group of wuzlirs. "Now I'm convinced that we are all going to die!" cried Steven. "I never should've agreed to go on this quest as my life is now going to end!"

"Your life will not end now," sharply answered back Peter. "Do not say such things, Steven, because we are all on this journey together. Now is not the right time to think about giving up!"

The company quickened its speed as the imminent advance of the wuzlirs grew ever so close to their presence. Their hearts were beating with rapid intensity, so fast that they felt as though they would fall outside of their chests at any moment. An overwhelming weight of fear seized control over their bodies, filling them with such frantic distress that they thought of collapsing. Still, they endured the fear that consumed them and tried pushing on, even as the clarity of their minds began to fail them.

As they ran, the road grew paved as hard stones began to slowly wear away, and before long they found themselves running on a dirt road, mixed with grassy weeds and roots. Surrounding them were buildings, tombs, walls, domes, and other structures that continued to collapse. They dodged the showering debris fizzing towards them at every side, while meanwhile, the sound of the terrible screeching noises grew increasingly louder as did the trotting hoofs galloping their way across the ground.

Suddenly, there came a great boom that seemed to strike its way into the sky and down to the earth. Just then a blinding light flashed through the pitch black of the night, and there before their eyes, the company saw the shapes of dark figures riding on what appeared to be galloping horses. They came racing at the company from every side, carrying tall sharp swords in their hands that seemed to be dipped in a red tinge at its tip. The figures slowly and steadily crept their way toward the company, covered in a terrible black darkness far darker than the shadow of the night. The company abruptly stopped dead in their tracks, overcome by sudden alarm and terror at the number of wuzlirs that suddenly appeared before them.

Soon the group of wuzlirs surrounded the company in a large circle, with what seemed to be at least twenty of them. Along with their sharp swords and dark bodies, they also carried a vicious and ugly presence that stifled the fresh air. They pressed closer toward the company while pointing their sharp swords in their faces, and as they gathered close together, the creatures seemed to be speaking or even laughing in a hideous speech that burned the ears of the company.

The wuzlirs continued to slowly compress the space of the company, yet they showed no signs of attacking or striking them. The company stood trembling as their space became enclosed, disgusted and fearful by the oozing presence of hate and darkness that surrounded the creatures who came close to them.

But just then Lelhond pulled out his sword and without hesitation, pointed it toward the wuzlirs. "Back off you accursed beasts!" he cried. "Back off, for you will not succeed in your evil desires!"

The rest of the company followed suit in displaying Lelhond's boldness, pulling out their swords and other weapons. Erundil drew out his bow and arrows, aiming it towards the wuzlirs, while Mataput an Orieant didn't take out any of their weapons and instead pointed their torches in the sky, preventing the wuzlirs from getting any closer to the company. Peter drew out his sword and pointed it toward the wuzlirs, while Steven stood frozen as he was stricken by terror.

"If you attack us, then I will have to do the same as well!" shouted Peter. "Make one move, and this sword will strike your hearts!"

Orieant swiftly went forward to stand in front of the young boy. "Do not attack Peter," he ordered. "One wrong move and it could prove disastrous for all of us."

The group of wuzlirs watched on while laughing at the trembling company in a cruel and ugly manner. One of them, which seemed to be larger than the rest, dismounted from his horse and stood staring at Peter for a moment, examining him from head to toe.

"And who are you?" he asked, in a foul way that stirred heavy uneasiness in the company's hearts. He then suddenly laughed aloud in a devilish manner. "Foolish boy, I care not for your fake display of strength. You may think you are a bold man of strength, but all I see is a careless and pretending weakling."

Peter said and did nothing, feeling an overwhelming cloud of numbness that covered his body. He was weak and knew that he was powerless to try and attack the group of wuzlirs.

But just then, the wuzlir who had mocked him suddenly turned his gaze toward Steven, watching him silently as he observed the man trembling with his sword in his hand. The creature turned toward the other wuzlirs gathered around, with the group of them whispering and talking amongst themselves.

"Now who is this weak man?" asked the wuzlir. "He is a strange one, for unlike the others he seems to show no regard in trying to hide his fear."

The wuzlirs spoke together, laughing and hissing in hideous

collective voices. One of them whispered his response in the ear of the wuzlir who presented the question.

"He's the one whom the Grand Master reported to us about," he said. "He's the so-called special man who's stolen something valuable from our master."

The large wuzlir dramatically stepped back, as if stricken by shock. He then turned toward Steven, staring at him with intense hate through his dark mask, before crying aloud in a foreign and harsh shout, seemingly urging his fellow wuzlirs to attack the helpless man.

Just then one of the wuzlirs dismounted from his horse and charged toward Steven, pointing his sharp sword at the man. He overshadowed the powerless man as a black cloud blocking out all hope of light, and all Steven could do was let out a terrible cry, while he clutched onto his chest. Immediately, Erundil rose in defense of Steven and fired an arrow from his bow which struck the back of the wuzlir. The wuzlir cried out in a terrible guttural shout, before getting onto his horse and escaping through the night.

This prompted the other wuzlirs to attack as well, some of them jumping off their horses, while others charged toward the company on their horses. Peter immediately stepped in front of Steven, preventing the wuzlirs from attacking him while he lay on the ground in heavy pain. Huminli and Glophi ran headlong into the wuzlirs ready to strike them, while Karandil and Forandor fired some of their arrows with Lelhond holding out his sword ready to strike any wuzlir that dared to attack them.

"Hold your ground!" cried Mataput and Orieant, with the company expecting the wuzlirs to attack, though they only seemed focused on attacking Steven, with another one of them charging towards the besieged man.

Peter managed to strike one of the horses of a wuzlir with his sword, causing the rider to swerve off his steed. More wuzlirs came charging toward Steven, grunting in harsh voices and cursing the man with great bitterness and anger. The gamdars fired more of their arrows, but the wuzlirs and their horses only continued to plunge their way through the crowd as they came headlong toward Steven.

But then suddenly, a blinding light came reflecting from the middle of the company, which separated them from the group of wuzlirs. Some of the wuzlirs collapsed from their horses in shock at the light, while others stumbled and crashed to the ground. The company looked staggered to their knees, before standing up and seeing that Mataput and Orieant had used some of their awesome power in resistance against the wuzlirs. For a brief moment, they saw Mataput and Orieant's bodies covered in such bright light that they were unable to see their shining faces. But rather than being with the company, the volviers were separated from them and right in front of the wuzlirs.

As they came to their feet, the wuzlirs noticed that they surrounded the volviers in a large ring. As if they were in disbelief of their fortune, they froze for a moment before laughing aloud and managing to grab ahold of Mataput and Orieant, chaining their hands and ankles and tying the two of them to their horses.

Placed on the horses of the wuzlirs, the light of the volviers dimmed before completely vanishing in the darkness of the night. As the two of them were led away in chains, the company observed that they looked weak and tired, as though they had used all of their strength to separate the company from the group of wuzlirs. Filled with horror and disbelief, the company didn't know what to do in that split moment, finding themselves only gazing at the volviers with opened mouths while they remained unable to utter words to express the despair they felt.

Suddenly, the wuzlirs dashed off with the captured volviers chained on their horses. And as though lightning had struck them, the company snapped out of their trance and shouted in collective voices as they ran to try and save Mataput and Orieant.

"No! Mataput! Orieant!" cried Huminli, with he and the rest of the company sprinting toward the wuzlirs on their horses in the hopes of rescuing the volviers. Yet to their surprise, the volviers instead ordered them to flee in the other direction.

"No, you must flee for your lives!" shouted Mataput. "Go in the direction that we led you to and do not stop running until you escape from this evil city which has awakened from its long slumber!"

With his final order, Mataput along with Orieant cast their heads toward the ground, closing their eyes as the wuzlirs carried them away.

The company obeyed Mataput's orders and immediately turned in the other direction, fleeing from the city. Yet Huminli still tried running after the wuzlirs to save the volviers but was swiftly carried away by Erundil in the other direction. Steven was still lying on the ground, continuing to shout and cry in pain, with Lelhond managing to hastily pick him up, though he gasped in horror as he saw that his chest was stained with blood.

"Steven is losing blood!" said the gamdar, alerting the company to the news. "I don't know how much worse it will get, but we must run as fast as we have ever managed to if we want to save his life!"

Peter cried out in shock at this revelation, suddenly coming to a halt. "We have to stop and treat him," he said. "He's going to die if we don't help him!"

But just then, they were reminded of the noise of galloping horses, which seemed to be coming toward them. And indeed, as they turned around the company saw that some of the wuzlirs had turned around and were now charging at them.

"No, we are being attacked by these wuzlirs behind us!" said Erundil. "Just continue carrying him, Lelhond, as we have no choice but to flee from this place."

Peter and the company at once continued running, as they saw the group of wuzlirs charging toward them. Steven was growing weary, and his eyes slowly began to close as he began saying things in an inaudible slurred voice.

Erundil led the company on, cutting through sharp turns as the wuzlirs continued to chase them from behind. The blood on Steven's chest spread throughout his body, staining his clothes, while tears streamed from Lelhond's eyes as he carried the weak and dying man. Turning around, Erundil noticed that the wuzlirs had covered ground swiftly and were now just a few mere feet away from the company.

"We have to quicken our pace if we wish to escape from the wuzlirs!" he shouted. "They are right behind us and are making ground at a terrible pace!"

The company ran on, hoping that they would have the remaining speed and energy to escape from the wrathful hands of the slaves of the enemy. But the wuzlirs proved to be too quick, and with every gallop of their horses, they seemed ready to pounce on the company at any moment.

But just as all hope seemed to be lost, there came a voice ringing from behind the company. The sound of galloping soon stopped, and all that could be heard was the sweet singing of a woman, with her voice like the musical tune of birds humming in a colorful garden on a bright summer day. The company stopped and turning around saw a bright golden light, with the wuzlirs so afraid of the light that they slowly backed away from its presence. Then coming forth from the light, with the sweet musical melody of the voice the company had heard, there also came a strong and commanding voice that flowed from the mouth of the woman.

"Be gone you accursed slaves of the dark enemy!" she cried, with her voice strong and authoritative, though there was a sweet calming ring to it.

At once, the wuzlirs wasted no time, and crying in loud screeching noises fled from the woman of light. Once the wuzlirs had left, the light started shrinking and coming forth came from it came the figure of a remarkably beautiful woman. The company gazed at her in wonder and was filled with awe just to be in her presence.

A radiant golden light seemed to surround the woman, with her face shining brightly. She was clothed in a long golden dress with long flowing golden hair coming down almost to her waist. She was extremely tall, even slightly taller than the gamdars, and appeared to be ageless as if she had lived through long forgotten ancient times. Yet, her face was clear, and her skin light and fair as a young woman. Though she held no sword or weapon of any kind, she appeared to be some being of great power, for within her was contained a fire of supernatural power, far beyond what anyone among the company had ever seen or imagined. The gamdars fell to their knees, while Peter and the smalves stood gazing at her in wonder.

"*Ar aumelie imbolar Gonyardu,*" suddenly said Lelhond, speaking in his native tongue as he gazed at the woman in wonder and respect.

The woman came forth to Lelhond, whispering something into his ear, before grabbing ahold of Steven and carrying him on her back. She then turned her attention toward the rest of the company and spoke to them.

"Do not be worried, for I am a friend of yours," she said, in a soft and sweet voice. "In my land, you will find rest for your weary souls and comfort for your anxious minds. Follow me and your eyes will be opened to the many beautiful things that exist in this troubling world."

She lifted her hand to the night sky with all immediately becoming silent in the air. A great stillness hovered above the heads of the company with the foul feeling of the air suddenly vanishing away. She gazed into the eyes of the company, with a bright smile covering her gleaming face.

Peter stared at her in wonder, though he remained worried for Steven. "Will my friend be fine?" he asked. "It doesn't look like he's moving at all, and I fear that he may die."

He started to weep bitterly as he looked into the helpless face of his friend. The woman came toward Peter, placing her hand on his shoulder.

"Steven will be fine," she said. "Follow me and you will find a land where no sickness or disease can enter through its hidden walls. Painful death is not a thing in the golden land, and only those who choose to lay down their lives may pass away in peace."

Even as she spoke, Peter gazed at her in growing admiration. He wiped the tears from his eyes as he felt a warm sense of comfort that filled his heart as he listened to her calming words. The woman led the company through the deserted city, with a great number of destroyed and collapsed buildings and other structures surrounding them. Even as she moved, she didn't seem to walk, but rather to effortlessly glide across the ground. The company noticed that she wasn't fearing shoes or sandals, but was barefoot with a clear and bright light shining on her feet.

"Who are you?" asked Glophi, gazing at her in amazement. "And what about Mataput and Orieant? I hope that they will be able to fight back against those wuzlirs who captured them."

"Do not worry about them," she said, in such a soothing voice that all fear was immediately lifted from Glophi's heart. "Mataput and Orieant knew what they were doing in saving you from the wuzlirs, even at their own expense. And even now I trust that there is a purpose behind their deeds. Now as for who I am, that will have to wait for the moment. But first let me take you to my home, where thousands of weary travelers have found rest and peace beyond anything they have dreamed of."

The company said nothing but instead listened to her with growing fascination. They followed her through the deserted and further destroyed city, wondering where she would lead them. Yet Erundil and his sons had smiles covering their faces as they already knew who she was.

18

Refuge in Lundarin

STEVEN AWOKE FROM A soft bed, covered in a mattress made of golden and green leaves. He embraced the warm glowing sensation of the sun's bright light which shone on his face, with a soft wind flowing through the room he was in. He gazed at the window to his right and beheld a wide valley covered in endless forests of golden, red, orange, yellow, and green trees. He saw splendid gardens and flowers growing in wide lands, along with great tree houses, beautiful and incredibly exotic beyond anything he had ever seen before. Many long rivers with a clear blue color ran their course through the vast land, with walls of green and other colorful flowers and plants surrounding them. He felt such incredible peace in his body, mind, and soul which he had never experienced before in his life, and was so well rested that he wondered if he had slept for many days.

He gazed around at the room he was in and discovered that it was quite spacious with the bright sunlight shining through the many windows along the walls. He stared at the walls and saw that they were overlaid with pure gold and covering them were many carved images of creatures and figures, most of whom looked like the appearance of gamdars. One such carved image depicted a beautiful ageless woman that looked like a human, yet she seemed to have great power, almost supernatural power beyond anything that a mere human could ever possess. On the golden walls and golden ceiling were also splendid leaves and flowers of all sorts of colors that shone brightly from the rays of the sunlight, with golden glimmers of light reflected throughout the room. He soaked himself in the beauty of the room for some time, looking around at the many elegant things that met his gaze.

Suddenly, the door in the room opened with the door itself covered in beautiful flowers and plants, with writing on it that looked like that of the language of the gamdars. Coming through the door was Peter, who came dashing towards Steven with tears of joy welling in his eyes as soon as he saw his friend awake.

"Steven! Steven! You are awake!" he exclaimed, giving Steven a big warm hug with his tears splashing in every direction.

Steven was confused, wondering where he was and why Peter was so excited to see him. Even more strange was the clothing that Peter wore, with Steven observing that instead of wearing the gray cloaks they had journeyed in, the boy was now clothed in what looked like a long green robe, covered with green and red leaves. It looked quite royal and beautiful, and it reminded Steven of the clothing of the gamdars.

Peter at once left the room, calling in a loud voice for others to enter the room. Steven remained lying on his bed, observing the room that he found himself in, before soon realizing that he too was clothed in a robe similar to Peter's though his was mainly red, along with green and red leaves. He touched the robe, amazed by how soft and light it was and also by how remarkably comfortable and beautiful it was to look upon.

Looking out into the many windows again, he saw a vast number of gamdars populated throughout the land. Some were old, others young, but they were all clothed in the same similar clothing that he was wearing. A light and joy was covering their faces which was so magnetic that Steven could tangibly sense it from the room. He felt a soft warmth which comforted him, though he remained confused as to why there were so many gamdars in the land he was in and why they looked so different from the ones he saw in Watendelle.

Immediately after he thought of this, there came the sound of many footsteps climbing numerous steps, before the doors flung open. There before him, Steven saw his many other friends with Huminli and Glophi dashing toward him, while Erundil, Lelhond, Karandil, and Forandor looked on at him with joyful faces. He was amazed by the change in everyone's clothes and appearances, especially of the gamdars.

For the gamdars no longer looked like weary travelers on a long journey, but rather as the high and glorious figures they had always been. Erundil was clothed in a golden robe covered in green and golden leaves, and on his head was what appeared to be a small crown of golden leaves. He looked refreshed and full of happiness, with a sparkling light shining on his face, the same light and glory that Steven had seen on the gamdar's face when he first met him in the kingdom of Watendelle.

Lelhond and his two brothers were likewise clothed similarly, with the only difference being the color of their robes. They looked mighty and glorious in their unique manner, just as Steven had pictured them before their quest had begun. Even Huminli and Glophi looked different in their clothing, as they were each clothed in brown robes covered in green leaves. Steven felt overjoyed beyond imagination to see them and hugged each one of them from his bed.

"We are glad to see you awake Steven," said Erundil, with a bright smile on his face. "You were unconscious for three whole days, and we were worried that you would never wake up. But you have gladly proven us wrong, and much credit has to go to Huminli and Glophi, as these two intelligent smalves have shown why they have always been so useful for this company."

Steven was surprised to see Erundil's change of attitude toward the smalves, observing that not even the slightest hint of grumpiness could be seen on his face, as rather his appearance was one of joy as he softly smiled from ear to ear.

"What did Huminli and Glophi do?" asked Steven. "And why are you so fond of the smalves now? What happened that you changed from viewing them negatively to now gladly celebrating their contributions to this group?"

"A lot happened in the time you were asleep, Steven," admitted Erundil. "The Lady Gonyardu managed to lead us here in her fair land of Lundarin after you had been stabbed by a wuzlir's sword in the same spot where Kolmaug had stung you with lots of blood gushing out from your chest. Huminli and Glophi insisted on using their special healing soup to help you recover, to which I firmly stood against the idea. But after talking privately with Gonyardu and allowing her freeing and enlightening words to give me a new perspective on many different matters, she managed to soften my opinion of the smalves. She opened my eyes and I finally saw how the smalves were incredibly impressive and great sources of help to our company, which I was not able to see for the longest time because of the bitterness I held against their people for too long of a time. I talked with my sons and along with their wise words, I saw the error of my ways and thinking, to which I repented and allowed Gonyardu to heal and repair my heart. In the end, Huminli and Glophi managed to feed you with their healing soup while you were unconscious, and slowly over time, your wound started to disappear. And now you are completely awake and healed, all because the two of them have proven yet again that they are tremendous sources of help for us."

Erundil paused for a moment, looking toward Huminli and Glophi with a warm smile on his face. Steven was amazed to hear the honesty that came from Erundil and was glad that he had changed his mind regarding the smalves.

"That is amazing to hear," said Steven. "But I'm still confused as to how I'm even here and why I'm clothed in this robe. And who is this Gonyardu that you keep referring to?"

Just then, a beautiful and tall woman, probably eight feet in height came through the door and approached Steven. She was clothed in a long golden dress with a bright shining light that covered her body and face. Steven gazed at her in awe for a moment, struck by not only her beauty but of the power that she seemed to possess.

As if answering his question, Gonyardu spoke to Steven. "You are in Lundarin, Steven," she revealed, speaking in almost a sweet musical voice. "I am Gonyardu, the Lady of Lundarin, and I lead you here into my realm to find rest, healing, and peace of mind. All those who come to this land, find healing in their weary bodies and mind, and it already seems that you are finding restoration in this land of light."

"I am," remarked Steven, though he looked around as if something troubled him. "But where is Mataput and Orieant? I wish to see them, and I have much I want to share with them. They have been such great mentors and friends of mine throughout the past few weeks, and also to everyone else on our important quest."

Gonyardu sighed to herself. "I am afraid that Mataput and Orieant are not here," she said sadly. "While using all of their strength and power to save you and the company, they were captured and taken as prisoners by the wuzlirs. Where those creatures carried them off, I cannot say, but I sense that they are still thriving and thinking of you, Steven. And perhaps they will manage to escape and rejoin with you all on your quest."

Steven gasped in horror at this revelation, but then slowly began to piece together all that had happened while the wuzlirs had attacked them. His memory returned to his mind and he recalled the sharp piercing of the sword that had struck him, and briefly remembered the bright golden light of Gonyardu coming to save them. He then remembered that the volviers had mentioned Lundarin and Gonyardu while they were journeying through the valley and that the gamdars, especially Lelhond were aware of the place and her name. He now understood why he had seen so many gamdars from his window, as he recalled how Mataput and Orieant had told them that many gamdars had come to live permanently in Lundarin, wishing to find peace and refuge in the land.

"Oh, so it is you that came to save us!" he said to Gonyardu. "I can remember a bright golden light that came to save us after Mataput and Orieant had been captured and chained by the wuzlirs, but I couldn't distinctly see your face. I remember on our journey how Mataput and Orieant mentioned that you and your realm of Lundarin was a place of great beauty which was a refuge to find rest and peace, where many gamdars had come to live permanently. But I think that this passed away from my memory after I went unconscious since I was confused as to where I was when I woke up."

"Yes, that was me," remarked Gonyardu. "And indeed, you did forget about everything that Mataput and Orieant had said about me and my realm of Lundarin. You nearly died, Steven, but the healing soup of Huminli and Glophi helped raise you to life again, as did the medicine of not only Erundil and his sons but of the many gamdars that dwell here in this land, along with my little touches. Yet I suspect that there are more reasons as to why you are alive, Steven, as it wasn't just because of the smalves or gamdars or even of myself, that you are alive and healed. Steven, you must understand that you were raised for such a time as this, and nothing can ever change that truth. You have a destiny beyond anything you could ever imagine, and that destiny of yours shall be fulfilled very soon."

Steven felt greatly comforted by Gonyardu's words, and her bright glimmering face warmed his heart. Yet he still couldn't shake off the shadow of sadness that he experienced knowing that Mataput and Orieant were no longer with the company. He worried for the safety of the volviers, yet just by listening to Gonyardu, confidence and assuredness were renewed in his heart as he knew that everything would end up fine and that the volviers would return to the company one day.

He gazed at Gonyardu for a while, finding himself unable to do anything but stare at her in wonder. He was comforted and joyous just by being in her presence and thought of nothing else in his life except for her goodness and light. Yet he wondered who this mighty being exactly was, as he observed that she wasn't just an ordinary powerful woman, but rather looked like some great supernatural being, taking on human form just as Mataput and Orieant had done.

"But who are you exactly?" he asked, continuing to gaze at Gonyardu. "Where did you come from before you dwelled in and ruled over your land?"

Gonyardu suddenly laughed, though it was a beautiful and sweet laugh with a delightful ring to it. "That is a good question, Steven," she said. "But I am afraid that not even I know the true answer to that question. What I do know for certain is that I once lived somewhere else before I came to Lundarin, though that place was likely not even within the sphere of this world. But I once had a different name and form than how you see me now. But the more I ponder on and long for the past, the more I realize that my life goes back to the ancient days of old, which my mind has many pictured as a sweet fading dream that passes from your memory once you awake from your calming slumber."

She sighed to herself, while Steven and everyone else stared at her with curiosity at everything she had said. Then as they all gazed at her, Gonyardu began to hum something in a low voice before the words became clear to the ears of all who heard her. Her voice was the most magnificent thing that Steven had ever listened to, with a charming and comforting breeze that seemed to come forth even from her mouth as she sang. Everyone silently listened to her delightful voice, with a growing golden light seeming to grow within her clear blue eyes even as she sang:

Through lands unknown and worlds remote,
Down sloping gardens and dark forests.
I came at last to the end of the road
And found a land of endless harvests.

I sing of golden leaves and purple flowers,
Of endless glades of green and clear golden hazes.
Into Malah Ardmillia I discovered my long-forgotten powers
And found a new life, away from the darkness.

In this land, I must abide,
Even with the dark borders of evil around me.
Yet the dark enemy cannot break inside,
This protected land, where I am free.

Come unto me all you that suffer,
And find shelter in this hidden land.
Hide yourselves under my tree houses for cover,
Where you shall not fear falling but shall stand.

Come unto me all you that are ill,
Into a world where no disease is free to be loose.
All those who flee from the outside world's evil
Can lay down their lives here, whenever they choose.

Her pleasant melodious voice ceased, with everyone in the room gazing at her in amazement. It seemed as though the color of her golden dress grew lighter with what appeared to be a radiant white light showering upon her. Steven felt an overwhelming sense of joy and relief while she sang, as though the weight of all his challenges and anxieties had been lifted from his shoulders. He couldn't stop thanking Gonyardu in his mind for welcoming him into her wonderful realm of Lundarin with such incredible hospitality, yet he found himself unable to utter any words to express his gratitude for her. But he stared at her, a broad smile spread across Gonyardu's face. And as though she had read his mind, she outstretched her right hand toward the man and closed her eyes as she spoke to him.

"May your worries and troubles pass from your memory in the name of Zomladil," she said, in such a soothing voice that relaxed not only Steven but everyone standing around him.

Yet Steven immediately became confused at what Gonyardu had meant when she said, 'in the name of Zomladil,' as he wondered what it could mean. "Excuse me, but who is Zomladil?" he asked, directing his attention to Gonyardu. "Is he or she some other powerful and ancient being like you are?"

Gonyardu simply smiled at Steven in such a way as if she knew that he knew who Zomladil was. Steven waited for an answer from her, but before she could even open her mouth, Lelhond spoke up.

"Zomladil is another name that my people use instead of Jangart," he explained. "The name Zomladil is believed to be the true name of Jangart, which Ulohendel discovered in a vision that was divinely granted to him. In our native tongue of Tuntish, the name means, 'One of Eternity.' We do not name any gamdars using that name, as it only belongs to Jangart, the only being who has existed throughout eternity. We hardly utter that name since it is so holy and possibly even dangerous to say with the evil that corrupts this world, but I suppose that it is ordinary for those in Lundarin to boldly proclaim that great name without fear."

"Yes, all that you say is correct, Lelhond, son of Erundil and Prince of Watendelle," said Gonyardu, glancing at Lelhond with a sparkling light in her clear blue eyes. "It may be dangerous to utter the name of Zomladil in the land of Nangorid and possibly even in the kingdom of Watendelle, but here in Lundarin, there is no reason to fear. Here in this precious land is found protection from the darkness that corrupts this old and weary world, where the blessings of Zomladil shower upon all those who honor him."

The company listened to the wisdom of Gonyardu in amazement, especially Karandil and Forandor who who had never imagined how significant the true name of Jangart was.

"I am blessed to hear this from you, Gonyardu, the fair and golden lady of Lundarin," said Karandil. "I pray that I am among those who honor Jangart, the one true king of the world."

"And so do I," remarked Forandor. "Yet all I can only hope is that he will be gracious enough to shower his blessings upon me."

"Hope?" said Gonyardu, as if the word itself surprised her. "Why hope when you already have full assurance of the truth? There is no need to worry, for all of you standing inside this room honor Zomladil. And because of that, he has shown mercy upon you all, in gracing you with the opportunity to redeem the world of men. And especially beloved of Zomladil are the two men standing in the midst of us," she said, now looking into the eyes of Steven and Peter. "You two are among the few humans on Earth that respect, honor, and love Zomladil, and because of that, your quest has been blessed and guided by his hand."

All those who listened to her were overwhelmed with joy and felt greatly honored to be loved by such a high and glorious being as Jangart. Steven and Peter were especially overwhelmed, experiencing a range of emotions that made them want to cry out in happiness.

Steven silently gazed at Gonyardu for a moment, before quickly casting his attention away from her when she locked eyes with him again. A bewildered look came on Gonyardu's face while she smiled at him as if she knew that he was hiding something from her.

"Do not fear, Steven," she said. "Here in Lundarin, there is no reason to worry, so tell me all that is on your mind and reveal any questions that you have for me."

Steven looked up at her, taking comfort in her words. "I was just wondering how you know so much about Jangart, even though you haven't seen him?" he asked. "Or perhaps I'm wrong and you have seen him yourself."

Gonyardu looked intently into Steven's eyes for a moment, as if she was thoughtfully examining his deepest questions and worries. He sensed that she was able to perceive something in him which made him feel uncomfortable for the time being. But as he continued to gaze into her comforting and bright face, he felt peace in knowing that he could trust her even if his deepest secrets were made manifest to her.

As the look of anxiety was removed from Steven's face, Gonyardu spoke in response to him. "There are many things that you know about Zomladil, Steven, even though you have never seen him," she said. "Everyone standing in this room, from the smallest smalf to the tallest gamdar knows something about who Zomladil is or what he is like. But as for me, though the earliest chapters of my life are but a passing memory from my ancient mind, I know that there are things I have seen in this world or even beyond this world, that none of you could ever dream about. Perhaps I was blessed with deep revelations of the spirit world where the Eternal One resides and rules, or perhaps I have seen visions of bright stars outside the borders of this world that are more real than even my life right now. Yet, I am not concerned about those things, for whatever my past was, it will have nothing to do with who I am right now. Though I would love to know what my name once was, or what my appearance was like, or even what the world was like in its younger days, I have no choice but to remain the way I am today, as Gonyardu, the Lady of Lundarin."

Steven fell silent, stricken with awe at the poetic grandeur and importance of what Gonyardu had said. Even the slightest hints of doubt which had been tingling in his heart, left him in that moment, and he no longer had the desire to question her anymore.

"Well, I guess that sums everything up," remarked Glophi, himself amazed by all Gonyardu said. "It's quite obvious that Gonyardu can be trusted, and whoever says otherwise is a fool in my book."

"Yes, and my book must be the same as yours then, Glophi," laughed Erundil. "For the Lady of Lundarin is unlike any being that I have ever met before in my life, save only the volviers. With her is a joy and peace that one can never truly experience within their soul and body, even in their homeland. I am glad that we are here in Lundarin, to find refuge and rest in the house of Gonyardu."

"I wish we could stay here forever," added Peter. "Though I know that it isn't even in the slightest bit of possibility for us to do that. But the more that I think about it, even though I know that our journey has only started, I can't help but wonder how we will succeed on our quest without Mataput and Orieant guiding and leading us. Who will be the leader of this company now?"

"I shall be," quickly responded Erundil. "Not only because I am the

King of Watendelle or that I wish to have the final say on matters, but it is because I wish to make amends for my many wrongs which I have especially committed against Huminli, Glophi, and the smalves as a whole. Throughout my life, I have said many terrible things regarding the smalves, and when my entire family decided to change their views on them, I should have done the same. Yet I remained stubborn in my ways and refused to surrender my pride, but since losing Mataput and Orieant and coming here to Lundarin where I have received the chance to speak with Gonyardu, she has purified my heart and mind and has replaced my hardheartedness and pride with love and humility. And for that, I am grateful to the Lady of Lundarin, and wish to fill the void of the volviers, as best I can."

The company stood in amazement at Erundil, especially Huminli and Glophi who were still so unused to seeing such a change in his attitude towards them and their people. With his change of mind came also a change of appearance, as he looked greatly refreshed as his slowly graying beard became darker in color and several years of age seemed to be taken away from his body. Most proud of him were his three sons, who were grateful beyond measure that their father had finally changed and seen the error of his thinking. But they were most thankful to Gonyardu, who had enlightened him in seeing the truth.

Gonyardu shook her head in approval of what Erundil had said. "Good, that is what the King of Watendelle should say," she said. "And you, Erundil, are the one who has been chosen to lead this company once the time comes for you to depart from my land. Yet I deem that you shall not lead them for long, as I suspect that you are called to lead others for other deeds and matters that will come in due time."

A shocked expression came on Erundil's face. "What do you mean?" he asked. "I hope that nothing worse than what we have already dealt with will fall upon this company."

"No, Erundil," said Gonyardu, shaking her head. "There is nothing to fear. But I have many other matters to share with you and everyone in this room which I decided to reserve until Steven awoke from his unconscious state."

"So why don't we talk about it now then?" asked Steven. "We are all gathered here together so I don't see why we can't talk about it now."

"No, we can't talk about it now," responded Gonyardu. "Now is not the appointed time for that. But first, you must spend some more time resting and once you are ready every one of you shall come with me to Malah Ardmillia, the chief city of Lundarin. There we shall gather with the many gamdars who dwell in my land and hold counsel together as many things can only be discussed in the heart of Lundarin."

"Fair enough," said Steven, conceding to Gonyardu. "I suppose we should depart from this room, as it gives us a chance to see firsthand the beauty of this land."

And so with one last smile toward Steven, Gonyardu turned her back and headed toward the door, with the rest of the company following her while Steven lay in bed. She opened the door, with the bright sunlight illuminating the room and the sound of many birds chirping in the colorful and delightful land of Lundarin. After the company said their goodbyes to Steven, she let them go down the stairs of the tree house, and once they had all climbed their way down, she too got ready to go down the stairs, beginning to close the door.

However, Steven quickly stopped her. "How will I find all of you when I'm fully rested?" he asked.

Gonyardu smiled, opening the door. "We will be here, Steven, don't worry," she said, and with that she shut the door behind her, gliding down the stairs of the tree house.

19

Discussions in Malah Ardmillia

STEVEN SAT IN HIS bed for some time, processing all that he had just experienced and talked about with Gonyardu and the company. He wondered what the city of Malah Ardmillia was like, and what important things Gonyardu would discuss with him there. His thoughts then turned toward the company, as he thought of Peter, Huminli, and Glophi and the joy and playfulness that they brought to his heart, and of Erundil and his sons, with the stability and protection that he felt in their presence. And no matter how painful it was for him to dwell on, his thoughts would always return to Mataput and Orieant. He thought about what Gonyardu had said about the volviers and how they had used up their remaining strength to save him and the company. He felt beyond grateful and forever in debt toward them, with tears running down his face as he pictured their wise faces which had already begun to slowly dwindle from his memory. He knew that he could never forget about them, and assured himself that he and the company would be rejoined with them again to complete their quest.

After about an hour of thinking to himself and resting, Steven got out of bed and was about to walk to the door before he suddenly stopped dead in his tracks. Hidden underneath the bed he could see the corner of his brown backpack. His mind was reminded of the black ball he had found in the deserted city of Tuwanor, and he immediately opened up his bag to pull the object out.

He gazed at the ball for a while, staring in wonder at its shape and beauty. All other thoughts of the volviers, the company, Gonyardu, and even of Lundarin left his mind for that brief moment. His mind was now entirely focused on the object he beheld, with nothing else able to disturb him. A wide grin ran across his face as he continued staring at it for endless minutes as it seemed, yet all thought of time passed from his memory.

Just then there came a loud knock on the door, and Steven immediately grabbed his bag and stuck the ball inside. "Yes, come in!" he said after he had hidden the ball inside his backpack.

Coming through the door was a gamdar clothed in a light brown robe with green and brown leaves covering it. He was a rather tall gamdar and quite slim as well, with a healthy appearance. His long hair was a beautiful sparkling silver color, and his eyes and face were so bright that it seemed to Steven that he had traveled to the sun itself and stared at it. He had a dignified yet gracious look on his face and appeared to be a powerful figure of noteworthy honor. He appeared neither old nor young but seemed to be a wise and experienced gamdar who had lived for many long years in life. Steven found himself unable to say a word to the gamdar and instead chose to stare at him in silence for some time.

The gamdar eventually broke the silence. "Hello, Steven, I am Hiladar," he said, greeting Steven with a warm smile. "I was sent here to see if you are ready to join the rest of your company in walking with Gonyardu over to the city of Malah Ardmillia."

"Yes…I'm ready," responded Steven, rather uncomfortably as he tried to hide any sight of the black ball in his backpack. "But why do they want me to come now? Gonyardu told me to rest saying that whenever I was ready I could just come outside and gather together with them."

"Your friend, Peter, wanted to show you something," said Hiladar. "I assume he wants you to come now because of how awe-struck he has been of the land of Lundarin. Many of your fellow companions have never seen or experienced such a beautiful place as this in their lives before, with only Watendelle, the home of the gamdars worthy enough to be compared to this beautiful and glorious land."

"Yes, this land is truly remarkable," remarked Steven. "And that reminds me of what Gonyardu, Mataput, and Orieant all said about that gamdars who dwell here. Are you one of those gamdars who came to live here permanently?"

"Not me myself, but yes, my ancestors came here many years ago to live here permanently," responded Hiladar. "I have been told that they came here upon hearing the rumors of a golden land even more beautiful than that of Watendelle where no stain or mark of evil or sorrow could ever touch it. My family was amazed upon hearing this revelation, especially because Lundarin is right here in the land of Nangorid, which is the stronghold of the Dark Lord. Nonetheless, they chose to come here and dwell in this land. Over time my family line grew more powerful before we eventually became among those who were the advisors of Gonyardu. And I happen to be the chief advisor of Gonyardu, and have held that title for many years."

"Wow, that's amazing," said Steven. "I knew that you must have been very important just by looking at your face and clothing, but I'm even more amazed to learn that Gonyardu has advisors. How could such a mighty being need advisors around her, when she knows just about everything?"

"She doesn't know everything, Steven, only Zomladil does," responded Hiladar. "And that is an important truth to grasp, one that Gonyardu has tried to implant into our hearts. And though the Lady of Lundarin is wiser than anybody I have met in my life, save maybe Mataput and Orieant, she is still incredibly humble and knows the importance of having wise helpers around her to advise her in the choices she makes. We help scout the land and regions of Nangorid to identify if there might be any dangers or issues that we should be aware of. And we also go out to bring more gamdars and other creatures that might need refuge in Lundarin. Gonyardu hardly ever leaves her fair realm, and when she came to save you, it had been a long time since she felt the need to save a group of travelers."

"So, she must have known who we were and how important our quest was," remarked Steven. "I'm still blown away by her incredible knowledge and wisdom."

"Yes, it is quite remarkable," said Hiladar. "And even more remarkable is this land which she discovered and made into a glorious and beautiful domain. I am convinced that there is nothing in this world as beautiful as Lundarin, and I am grateful for every day I get to spend in this peaceful land."

"Well, I can't wait to see the land for myself," said Steven, growing rather excited with everything that Hiladar was saying about Lundarin. "I need to gaze at this place for a while, and just soak in the beauty of this land."

"Then come follow me," said Hiladar, motioning to Steven to follow him outside. "Gonyardu and the rest of your friends are sitting outside by a table with many other gamdars as well. So come and I will lead you to them."

Hiladar began walking over to the door, but before following the gamdar, Steven made sure to bring his backpack with him, not wishing to leave his discovered ball behind in the room. Hiladar opened the door and instantly the warm and glorious light of the sun shone upon their faces. Steven held his breath in awe of the wonderful sights that met his gaze outside, and the two of them began walking down the many steps of the tree house.

As they came down the stairs and stood upon a wide array of rich green grass with many tall and colorful trees surrounding them, a great plethora of birds suddenly came flocking towards them, each with their own color and unique feather patterns. The birds were all singing in unison together, and Steven couldn't help but notice the slightest of smiles on each of their little faces. He also observed how Hiladar seemed to be carefully choosing his steps as if he were following the birds in a particular direction.

"Are the birds leading us somewhere?" asked Steven, who couldn't help but mention this curious observation of his.

"Yes, they are," responded Hiladar. "The creatures that dwell in Lundarin, from the smallest and seemingly insignificant insect to the flying bird, and even to the wisest gamdar, are all connected in such a way that cannot be found anywhere else in the world. All who dwell here have a common purpose, and that is to serve one another and spread more light, love, and beauty to this rich land. And one of the ways that the birds contribute to serving others is by leading the creatures that live here into the very presence of Gonyardu."

"Wow, that is incredible," said Steven, finding himself unable to describe his amazement in any other words, instead choosing to dwell on the amazing revelations and ways of life that were revealed to him in the land of Lundarin.

The two of them walked on for some time through the wide and rich forests of Lundarin, with the sun shining brightly overhead in the sky and seeming to provide the slightest bit of a remarkable golden color that filled the clear blue sky. Steven stared at this stunning sight for some time, unable to keep his eyes away from the beautiful color of the heavens.

Eventually, he managed to cast his attention away from the sky and into the direction of where he was walking. He found himself now striding onto a smooth brown path with a hint of a golden color coming from the light of the sun. On each side of the path were flowers and plants that covered the grass, each with its rainbow of colors and unique shapes. He again stared in silent wonder at the nature of Lundarin, in awe of its unsurpassed beauty.

They walked on for a few more minutes, following the birds as they sang their delightful chorus of music to them. As he walked, Steven closed his eyes, soaking in the clear sounds that illuminated his eardrums, and the reflection of the sun's light that provided warmth to his body. He soon opened his eyes once more, to see what else would catch his attention.

Just as he reopened his eyes, he noticed that they were soon approaching the sight of a long river. He was immediately struck by its incredible length and size, seemingly going on forever without even the slightest sense of the extent of its end. But as he came closer to it, he was now struck by its beauty, mainly due to its distinctive hue. For though the color of the river was a strong and distinguishing blue, golden sparkles were seemingly much more substantial than just reflections of the sunlight covering the water. And as he came right to the bank of the river to peer over and observe it, he finally observed a clear and yet solid golden texture to the river, that must have been a physical substance that gave the river its color.

As he was examining the strange yet intriguing sight of the river, Steven heard a voice that was calling his name. He instantly recognized that it was Peter's voice and as he watched the birds flying over to his left, he found Peter along with the gamdars, smalves, and Gonyardu, all sitting together at a large blue table, with strong and tall trees providing them with shade.

He rushed over to them, with Hiladar now following him from behind. He found an open brown chair and sat next to Peter, before gazing around at the wide land covered with endless beautiful trees, plants, flowers, rivers, and animals. He sat there to himself for a moment, absorbing the beauty that surrounded him, while those seated at the table with him noticed a growing light of joy that illuminated his face.

"I can see that you are enjoying yourself, Steven," remarked Lelhond, noticing the joy and peace that covered the man's face. "I'm glad to see you like this, especially after how much you have suffered in these past couple of weeks."

"Yes, I sense such inner rest and bliss that could only be found here in Lundarin," said Steven. "This place is beyond anything I could have ever imagined, even with all the descriptions Mataput and Orieant gave us while journeying through the land of Nangorid. I can't believe all that my eyes have seen already this morning, and everything just feels like a remarkable and perfect dream, yet it seems to be too real for it to only be a sweet fading dream."

"It's more real than anything in this world, Steven," remarked Peter. "That's what Gonyardu has been reminding us of this whole time, as we have learned that here in the land of Lundarin, time moves slowly without fear of imminent seasons and concern for the outside world. Yet, this provides us with something that is nearest to our hearts, a peace that cannot be found anywhere else. And for that, Lundarin is truly more real than even our very lives in our homeland."

"Very well said, Peter," remarked Gonyardu. "Now would you be willing to give your friend some of the water from the river? He is correct in saying that he feels at rest now, but he still needs refreshment and strength after all he has been through on your journey."

"Oh, no, I'm fine," quickly responded Steven. "I don't feel like eating or drinking anything right now, as I would rather just gaze at the beautiful nature of your land."

"Trust me, Steven," insisted Gonyardu. "The water that flows through the Flurien River throughout the land of Lundarin is unlike any water you have ever tasted. It has special properties to it, properties to strengthen, refresh, and give peace to all those who drink its liquid. You will need to drink it, Steven, if you want strength and peace to continue on your journey. Though you feel rested and at peace now, once you continue your quest, you will want to return to my land even though you will not be able to then. You will need extra bursts of strength and refreshment than you think you need to thrive in the rest of the time you travel through the land of Nangorid."

"Okay, I will drink some of the water then," conceded Steven. "Let's see how special this water is and if it provides me with much nourishment."

Peter at once went down to the bank of the river, holding a small brown cup in his hand before he scooped some of the water into the cup and brought it to the table, handing it over to Steven. Steven stared at the water for a moment, fascinated again by its texture and color that he had seen from afar when gazing at the river from a distance. But now that he could see it up close for himself, he noticed small little things in the water that he hadn't noticed before. What appeared to be small bubbles flowed through the water and its slight golden hue became even more distinct now.

He put his mouth to the cup and with everyone's eyes watching him, he took a sip of the water and set his cup down. But as he set his cup down, he immediately picked it up again, amazed by what he had just tasted. The liquid was quite cool and he felt it wash his bones as it digested through his stomach. There was a certain sweetness to it, almost like the taste of honey, but it was only a faint taste with the rest of the liquid tasting like normal clear water. Yet, he knew that it couldn't have been normal water because of how refreshing it was, and in that moment, he already began to feel strengthened as any remaining aches and pains in his body began to slowly vanish away.

He hurriedly took more sips of the water, but the small sips soon turned into large gulps and before he knew it Steven found himself chugging the cup of water. But before he could finish the cup, Gonyardu quickly intervened.

"No, no, Steven," she said while laughing. "You don't need to finish the entire cup, as a few sips are enough to energize you whenever you are tired or weak."

"But it's so good!" exclaimed Steven with excitement. "I could drink entire jugs of this water without even stopping to catch my breath!"

"That would not be a wise decision, Steven," warned Gonyardu with the slightest expression of a stern look on the corner of her face. "Too much of this water can lead you to becoming unusually energetic or sometimes drowsy. I have seen many of the gamdars and animals who live here act in strange ways when drinking too much of this water, and besides, when you do return to go on your journey, I will not have jugs to give to each person since you will not have enough space to carry it with you. And so you will have to carefully manage how much of this water you drink, and only consume it when it proves necessary."

Steven put his head down, ashamed at what he had done and said, feeling that he had dishonored Gonyardu by acting so wildly. He was too embarrassed to even look at her or his other companions in the face, but as he eventually lifted his head again, he found Gonyardu looking upon him with a warm smile of compassion.

"Do not be embarrassed, Steven," she said, sensing the shame and regret that he felt. "You only did what you deemed to be right, but I am glad to see that you were willing to drink the water because if you did not, your eyes would not have been enlightened to this source of energy, strength, and refreshment that can only be offered in Lundarin."

Steven gazed at her, surprised and grateful for the compassion and love that she lent to him. He was again unable to utter any words, but a wide smile covered his face as he listened to her comforting words.

For several more minutes, the company talked with one another, sharing the joy, peace, relief, completion, and other feelings they experienced in Lundarin even without Mataput and Orieant with them. They shared their many questions with Gonyardu and Hiladar, who amazed the company with their wise words. The company felt as though they could talk forever with them, without needing any nourishment or rest.

But in due course, Lelhond interrupted their many conversations upon noticing that they had been talking for quite some time. "My lady Gonyardu, I hate to interrupt the joyous conversations that we are all having, but should we not be on our way to the glorious city of Malah Ardmillia, the chief city of Lundarin?" he asked.

"Yes, and I am glad that you have reminded me, Lelhond," responded Gonyardu. "And now that all of you are well rested and in good spirits, now would be the appointed time for you to gather together with me and my many advisors and counselors to discuss the latest news that very much concerns you and your journey."

"What is the latest news?" asked Erundil, confused by what Gonyardu meant. "Is there something wrong that's going on that we should know about?"

"We will discuss these matters only in Malah Ardmillia," said Gonyardu. "These things are not meant to be discussed here, but rather in the city where my advisors and counselors are gathered together to make the wisest decisions."

"I am more than ready to head to Malah Ardmillia then," remarked Erundil. "Since the days of my childhood, I have heard many stories regarding the great meetings and discussions that take place there on how to combat the evil of the outside world. I cannot wait to see your glorious chief city for myself."

"Me too," chimed in Huminli. "I'm anxious to see what matters we will be discussing, but I just hope they don't scare me or anything."

"My dear Huminli, you do not need to fear anything in Lundarin," said Gonyardu, looking upon Huminli with a radiance of compassion and love surrounding her. "All that we will discuss will be meaningful and important, and some things might be heavy and tough to take, but that should not fill your heart with worry. For if you hold on to the hope, peace, and courage found here in this land, then nothing, not even the power of darkness can stand against you nor take away that which resides with you."

Huminli felt a warm and calming sense of peace and stability fill his heart as he listened attentively to Gonyardu, with her reassuring words giving him great confidence that everything would end up for his good.

"You speak wisely my lady," said Erundil. "And you, Huminli," he said now directing his attention to the smalf. "I hope that you take her words to heart and grasp them tightly, refusing to ever let them go. May they be a guide for you in all situations of your life, of your brother Glophi's life, and the lives of all the smalves of the land of Laouli."

As he spoke, Huminli and those around him continued to sense and discover a new Erundil, one filled with compassion and love not only for his sons and fellow gamdars but also for the smalves that he had once considered his enemies. Huminli and Glophi couldn't help but smile astounded and grateful over the gamdar's change in attitude over the past few days in Lundarin, and Gonyardu was especially touched to see Erundil's conversion from hate and bitterness to love and friendship with the smalves.

"Good, I am glad to see the changes that are stirring throughout all of your hearts and souls," remarked Gonyardu, looking around at those seated at the table with satisfaction. "You are at peace with yourselves, and it pleases me to see that. And so, I now know for certain that you are ready to go with me to the city of Malah Ardmillia."

She at once stood up from her seat, prompting the rest of the company to also stand up as they were ready to follow Gonyardu to the chief city of Lundarin. They made their way through grasslands covered in beautiful flowers and through forests of gigantic, colorful trees. All around them, they could see tree houses of all different types of shapes and sizes, and along the way, they saw many gamdars, especially children dancing and playing in the forests alongside the many unique animals and creatures that populated them. An unspeakable joy could be seen on their shining on their faces, and as Gonyardu passed through, the gamdars and even the animals bowed their heads to her. Yet it was not out of fear that they bowed their heads to her, but rather out of respect and pure joy for the many good things she had brought to their lives.

Also along the way were many gamdars either playing musical instruments or singing, with their singing and music being extremely pleasant to all who heard them, with their faces also seeming to be illuminated by the delight in which they played their music. Those who were in the chorus of singers sang in the native Tuntish language of the gamdars, and as they listened carefully to the words, Erundil and his sons stood in awe at all they heard. And though Steven, Peter, and the smalves couldn't understand a word they sang, the four of them still felt an overwhelming sense of peace that filled their hearts and lifted their spirits.

Peter turned toward Gonyardu, filled with wonder at the sight of the many gamdarian singers. "What are they singing about?" he asked. "I feel such incredible delight just hearing them, but I would also love to know what they are saying."

"They are singing about many things regarding the land of Lundarin," answered Gonyardu. "They are singing of the wholeness that one experiences in the land of no blemish, and of the restoration of one's heart just by looking around at the nature and atmosphere that fills this place. One is unable to fear in this land since there is no cause for anxiety, as peace and joy are the realities of this land, and for that reason, the gamdars, animals, and all creatures can sing for joy and celebrate the goodness found in the land of Lundarin."

"All that you say is true, Lady Gonyardu," remarked Peter. "I felt the peace, joy, and restoration that you described even though I didn't understand a word that the gamdars were singing of. But I wonder, how are you able to discern and accurately describe all that I am feeling in the deepest parts of my mind and heart?"

"There are matters that even the very wise cannot comprehend, Peter," responded Gonyardu. "And perhaps lest I be filled with hubris, Zomladil gave me this gift without my full understanding of how and why I have it. But do not worry about me, rather focus on yourselves so that you may know the part that you play in Zomladil's grand stage."

Peter gazed at Gonyardu for some time out of wonder for her wise words, but he soon found himself processing all that she had said and thinking of his own life and what role he had in the world. For a moment, he was filled with a sense of humility, thinking of himself as not all that important compared to a wise and ancient being like Gonyardu. But as her words began to stir and resonate within his heart, he understood that he was important, not because of what he had done, but merely because of the grace of Jangart in using his life to make a difference in the world. He thought of the quest he was on and the power it had to change the entire world of humanity, and he knew that he had an incredible role to play in the affairs of the world, which was all because of Jangart's grand plan.

As they continued walking, Peter couldn't help but feel an overwhelming sense of gratefulness for Jangart. But he kept his feelings to himself, holding it closely to his heart. Yet even though he assumed that no one else knew what he was feeling in his heart, the faintest of senses came to his mind, as though Gonyardu was nodding her head in approval of all that he was feeling and thinking of.

But for now, all that the company was thinking about was the pleasant scenery that covered the land of Lundarin. An endless plethora of trees and flowers met their gazes and didn't fail to leave them open-mouthed, with the sun continuing to shine in all its afternoon strength, giving the clouds a sort of golden color. Yet rather than feeling as though they were being burned by the sun, they instead felt a calm and delightful warmth that filled their bodies. The silent passing wind provided a sweet-sounding rustle in the tree leaves, as they swayed from side to side on the branches of their trees. Nothing unusual or repulsive could be seen as they passed through wide havens of unharmed land.

An hour or even more must have passed as they walked, yet to all of them, it seemed to be mere minutes. They felt as though they could stroll through the land of Lundarin forever, without stopping to take a break. The river seemed to go on forever and ever, leading up to the chief city of Lundarin. Hardly any sweat appeared on their bodies, even as the sun shone proudly in the bright blue sky.

But soon there came a change in the land. The sight of large and colorful trees began to slowly vanish from sight, and they soon found themselves in a wide field of flowers and plants. The path they were walking on began to climb up, and they saw the river running its course from down below. As they climbed up they soon found themselves standing aloft on a large hill, covered in clean-cut green grass and spread throughout it was a rainbow of colorful flowers, plants, and bushes. Small butterflies fluttered through the air, along with many creeping insects of all shapes and sizes. They walked for a while through this hilly region, before they came across the sight of a long canopy of overhanging trees.

The company eventually came to the canopy and started walking through the mini forest that was atop the hill. The trees were tiny compared to the ones they had previously seen, yet the sight of them still didn't fail to amaze the company. All of the leaves of the trees, except for a handful were golden in color with hints of silver, and before they knew it, the company found themselves longingly staring in awe at the trees, having never seen ones of this color before. Even Erundil and his sons who had grown up seeing the golden tree of Palororen in their homeland of Watendelle, knew that these remarkable trees could not be compared to anything they had ever seen in their lives. They passed peacefully under this canopy of overhanging trees for several more minutes, with the golden light of the sun peeking through the trees to provide wonderful glimmers of light.

"What is this place?" asked Lelhond, overwhelmed by all his eyes saw at the moment. "I have never seen such a sight as this before; a small forest with overhanging trees of golden and silver leaves. Who could ever dream of something like this?"

"We can all dream of sights like these," remarked Hiladar. "The only question is if we can conjure them up so that they become realities in our lives."

"I cannot do what you say," responded Lelhond. "As I have never seen such unique and beautiful trees like these in my life. And speaking of this sight, why are these types of trees only found here on top of this hill and not in all the other places of Lundarin, where many wider forests with taller trees can be observed?"

"Because this is the border leading into Malah Ardmillia," answered Hiladar. "And it is only in Malah Ardmillia where the great Dahroon trees of Lundarin can grow since it is the one place where the dahroon seeds are found."

"Ah yes," said Erundil, as if recalling some distant memory from his mind. "Long have I heard tales of the great Dahroon trees that grow in fruition within the chief city of Lundarin. I have always wondered what these golden and silver trees were like, and how large they were."

"I have always thought that the golden tree of Palororen was an example of what the Dahroon trees were like," remarked Forandor. "And in my ignorance of the outside world, I once thought that nothing could compare to its enormous height and golden leaves, yet the leaves of these trees are more golden than even the great golden tree of Palororen itself. But at the same time, these trees are quite small compared to the golden tree of the kings, as I thought that they would have been much larger than this."

"They are very large though," said Hiladar. "The only reason why you are unable to see the golden and silver towers that grow in this land is because we have not arrived at the city of Malah Ardmillia just yet. But once we reach there, you will see great myriads of Dahroon trees that continue to grow with each passing day, reaching into the heavens."

"When will we be privileged to witness this sight then?" asked Karandil. "I yearn to tell my friends and fellow soldiers in Watendelle that our eyes have seen the mighty Dahroon trees of Malah Ardmillia."

"And we will have to let Aradulin and Glowren know as well," remarked Erundil. "You know how much they love trees and nature, I just wish that they were here with us to cast their gaze upon what we have been richly rewarded to see."

"Well, if you want to see the fullness of the Dahroon trees for yourselves then come here," said Gonyardu, and turning around, Erundil and his sons noticed that everyone else was standing at a distance by a small opening, with a glimmer of golden light shining through.

"Through this opening lays the chief city of Lundarin, Malah Ardmillia," said Hiladar. "Do you wish to go through or would you rather spend this time talking of a place that lies right here before your sight?"

"I will go through," said Erundil. "I apologize, as my sons and I spent too much time talking and asking questions that we didn't even see this opening. Please, may we go through?"

Hiladar gave no response but instead smiled at Erundil before he turned his back and followed Gonyardu as they passed through the opening. Erundil and his sons rushed over to walk behind Gonyardu and Hiladar, with Steven, Peter, Huminli, and Glophi all following from the back of the group. The golden light of the opening grew stronger as they walked, and they could sense themselves slowly descending the hill. Then the veil of the golden light was lifted from their sight, and all seemed to turn into puffed smoke. They immediately covered their eyes from the shock of the sudden change, but soon after everything returned to its original and normal state, they removed their hands from their eyes and finally saw it. Malah Ardmillia.

The city of Malah Ardmillia was unlike anything they had ever seen before. It was set before them in such a refined combination of the natural world and the beautiful architecture and craftsmanship of the gamdars who dwelled there. As they came down to the bottom of the hill, they stood in speechless awe, gazing at the vast Dahroon trees that seemed to have no end of their highest peaks. The leaves were gloriously arrayed in a rich and colorful gold and silver hue, and there seemed to be a crystal twinkling light that shined throughout the trees.

The great and long Flurien River of Lundarin ran its course through the grasslands and forests, with sparkling lights glimmering throughout its rich blue and hinted golden color. A sweet and moist scent was in the air, presumably coming from the delightful smell and presence of the river itself. Many gamdars, mostly children or young adults, were gliding through the smooth-flowing current of the river on small blue ships, crafted and carved in the shapes of swans. Many gems and crystals sparkled throughout the ships, and a great flock of swans, geese, and ducks relaxing in the river seemed to be drawn to the remarkable boats.

The company noticed that the river led to a steep spring, where it provided water for the trees, grasslands, flowers, and plants that covered the land. But just ahead of the spring, they noticed a most unusual yet remarkable sight, where a long bridge lay ahead though it seemed to be made of the leaves of the Dahroon trees themselves. The bridge led to a row of silver stairs that sparkled in the sunlight, and there were a great number of stairs, perhaps many dozens where at the top of them lay a glorious sight.

There before the company's eyes was a structure of some sort, though they couldn't quite make out what it exactly was. They observed a circular type of building that was built in such a way that it sprung round and round in a sort of endless winding spiral road. There seemed to be no end to the great spiral, but to their amazement, they saw that it led to a high and pointed peak, shaped almost like a slim tower. The material of the building was most amazing, seemingly made of a mix of silver glass, stone, and hints of gold. Yet they couldn't properly observe the building itself because of how sheltered it was from the Dahroon trees that protected it like a vast wall. In that moment, the company found themselves in the presence of greatness, and their only response was to humbly consider themselves as insignificant in the sight of such a unique and fascinating piece of architecture.

Many gamdars could be seen populating the spiral streets of the building, either working or minding their own business. Gonyardu and Hiladar led the company in the direction of this structure with broad smiles covering their faces.

"There lies Adun-Parantu," said Gonyardu, pointing toward the structure. "There we shall hold our important meeting with my many other advisors."

Steven gazed in growing admiration at the building, wondering what it exactly was. "Is that a tower, or a palace, or even perhaps a mini city within a city itself?" he asked, trying to piece together all he could to find out what it might be. "I have never seen such an incredible sight like this before. And look at the mighty Dahroon trees that shelter it; standing tall like great statues that surround a city!"

"It is up to you to decide what you want it to be," said Gonyardu, with a smile toward Steven. "Even if you find it to be as dear as a home, I will gladly accept that since it is a place where deep secrets are revealed and where many long-forgotten things are preserved."

"Ah yes, the great tower of Adun-Parantu, the Sight of Preservation as it is known in the common language," remarked Forandor, staring in wonder at the sight of the building. "I have always known it as a tower, yet now that you bring that point up my fair lady, it offers a new perspective to me of what it may truly be. I have heard many tales of this sight in my days growing up as a young gamdar, and many of the songs of Adun-Parantu remain dear to my heart," he began humming a tune to himself, before opening up his mouth and singing a brief part of an old rhyme:

Books of lore and scrolls of old,
Long believed to have passed from sight,
Held in safe keeping in soft folds,
In the hands of Gonyardu's pure hands of white.

Halls of wisdom uncovering truths untold,
Of our people and honor we lose,
Found in the forests of gold,
And locked away in the tower of Adun-Parantu.

"Long have I wondered of the many important things that my people have lost," said Forandor. "And now my wish has come true, as I will finally go to the place that I have heard mentioned in so many of our songs."

"If you wish to find objects and truths of your people, then I am afraid that you will end up disappointed," said Hiladar in response to Forandor. "For that is not the purpose of your coming to Adun-Parantu, rather you and the company are here to discuss many important matters with Gonyardu, myself, and her many advisors. Is that not so, my fair lady?"

Gonyardu paused for a moment, looking at Hiladar and then at the curious eyes of the company. "There is nothing to hide, Hiladar," she said at length. "If there are things the gamdars or even humans and smalves want to discover, then let it be zo. Adun-Parantu is not only a locked tower but also an open haven for many troubled souls to discover and learn the truth."

Hiladar's face suddenly swelled up in shock, but he refused to argue with Gonyardu, knowing that what she had said was true and because of that all he could do was agree with her. And so he kept silent, not wishing to hinder the company from whatever it was they were seeking.

The company remained silent for a while as they neared Adun-Parantu, but at length, Glophi broke the silence. "I must say, Forandor, that song of yours sounded delightful to my ears," he remarked. "And I imagine that it's even more beautiful in the language of your people."

"It is," said Erundil, before Forandor could even respond. "Come, Glophi, I will teach you the full song in our native language, and I promise that you will never regret learning it."

Glophi immediately went over to Erundil with excitement, and the two of them walked side by side, as the gamdar taught the smalf all the words of the song in his native language. The rest of the company observed Glophi trying to sing the words in the native language of the gamdars, though he didn't seem to be doing quite the best.

"No, not quite, Glophi, but you're almost there," said Erundil with a warm smile. "More learning and practice will help you in learning these words."

"But I want to learn it now!" said Glophi, growing rather frustrated at himself. "Why am I unable to understand it?"

"Don't blame yourself, Glophi," said Erundil, placing his hand on the smalf's shoulder. "We won't always grasp everything that we learn for the very first time, so patience and persistence are very important when trying to learn new things. In time you will understand how to sing this song in our native language, and very soon I imagine that you will be able to sing even more songs in our tongue than I can myself! But do not worry, Glophi, let time do its work, while you do the work that only you can do."

A cheerful look was restored to Glophi's face, and he felt reassured and confident again just by looking into Erundil's eyes and seeing his genuine care for him. He was amazed and grateful to see his change of attitude toward him and his brother and wished that Mataput and Orieant would've been there to witness it for themselves.

For the rest of the time that they walked, Erundil and Glophi spent time talking with each other, as Erundil taught the smalf all he could regarding his native language. Wide smiles covered both of their faces, as they laughed together with great joy that filled their hearts.

The company passed through the great Dahroon trees and gardens of Malah Ardmillia, soon making their way onto the bridge covered in golden and silver leaves. They nervously and slowly walked across it, to ensure that it wasn't flimsy in any way, however, Gonyardu and Hiladar, walked confidently across the bridge, not seeming to worry about their safety.

"Do not fear," said Gonyardu, seeing the anxiety that covered the company's faces as they made their way across the bridge. "Though it may not seem to be sturdy, this bridge was made with my intervention, and no power within this world, not even the power of the Dark Lord will be able to tear it down."

The company took Gonyardu's words to heart and soon found themselves confidently strolling their way through the bridge. Once they made their way across, they breathed sighs of relief before soon starting to make their way up the seemingly endless steps of sparkling silver steps. On each side of the steps were strong silver railings, along with faces of what looked like gamdars built within them. Many golden and silver leaves were scattered throughout the railings as well, crisscrossing each other in a very beautiful and meticulous pattern. The company stopped in fascination at this sight but continued going up the stairs upon seeing how many more were left to climb.

They finally reached the top, after walking for what seemed like many minutes. Huminli hunched over, breathing heavily and putting his hands on his knees, with Glophi coming over to his side, laughing at the sight of his brother struggling.

"How are you already this tired?" he asked, laughing at his brother. "The steps weren't even that many, and yet look how finished you are!"

"That's enough, Glophi," said Huminli, not in the mood for his brother's jest. "And don't lie to yourself either, I couldn't even count how many dozens of steps there were. And I know you couldn't either."

"I bet if I tried counting I could tell you the answer," responded Glophi. "But that doesn't even matter. You're the only one out of all of us who's tired after walking a few steps."

Glophi continued laughing at Huminli, and his brother was soon about to reply to him again before Erundil stepped in front of them both.

"That's enough you too," he said calmly, with a smile on his face. "I don't want any division between us, even though I assume that it's only because of brotherly love that you too are arguing. But look ahead of you," he pointed straight ahead, where winding streets filled with gamdars, statues, and Dahroon trees could be seen. "Isn't that a wonderful sight to behold?"

At once, Huminli and Glophi along with the rest of the company spent some time gazing at the ring of streets, trees, statues, and gamdars that filled the streets surrounding the great tower of Adun-Parantu. They observed the gamdars that were there, with all of them seeming to be busy at work; either building, writing, discussing, or walking in the direction of someplace. It seemed to be a very lively and busy place, as compared to the calm locations that were found throughout the rest of Lundarin. Regardless, the company still felt welcomed and at peace as they gazed in every direction, feeling the sense of peace and refuge that could be found throughout the land of Lundarin.

"Wow, everything here is amazing," remarked Steven, gazing at the wonderful sight. "Where are we going to go now?"

"We are going to go inside Adun-Parantu," answered Gonyardu. "These are only the streets that surround the great structure. Our purpose is to go inside the building where we shall gather together in the great hall along with my many other gamdarian advisors to hold our important meeting."

The company followed Gonyardu and Hiladar with the two of them leading them through the circling streets surrounding the great tower of Adun-Parantu. Many things of beauty were laid before their eyes, from great statues and carvings of luxurious pieces of architecture displaying the might of the gamdars to the beauty and refinement found in the natural world containing the many trees, flowers, and plants found throughout the gardens and forests of Lundarin. They continued observing many more gamdars, all wearing the same clothing as the company, though theirs was mainly covered in the golden and silver leaves of the Dahroon trees. Upon seeing Gonyardu, all of the gamdars immediately stopped doing their work and greeted her.

They continued their way through the streets of stone, going up many levels until they came to a vast courtyard of white marble. There before their eyes was the great tower of Adun-Parantu itself, a great and mighty fortress made of silver glass, stone, gold, and even hints of sapphire that sparkled throughout the structure. The tower itself looped round and round until its top reached a high and sharp point in the clouds of the sky. The company gazed in wonder at this sight and were even more fascinated to see what lay inside.

Gonyardu and Hiladar led them over to the doors of the tower, which were as white as the stars of the night sky, yet had sparkling gems of sapphire scattered throughout. On each side of the door stood two gamdarian guards, though they had no armor on. They carried a sword and shield in each hand, and stared straight ahead into the distance, paying no heed to Gonyardu. Also on each side of the door was a single

Dahroon tree, the tallest and strongest one that the company had seen yet, with its top reaching the very peak of the tower itself, and its bottom seeming to be as strong as iron. Just in front of the door was also a large fountain, and at its center was a small marble statue depicting a group of gamdars each holding books and scrolls.

The company made its way to the door, which remained closed. But as Gonyardu came in touching distance with it, the door opened in and of itself, with no force needed to open it. The company stood in amazement at this and followed Gonyardu as she led them inside.

They gazed in awe at all their eyes saw, with their attention first brought to the ceiling, which was shaped like a wide dome, covered in endlessly colorful paintings and images, depicting many figures and important events. Many statues there were, made of all sorts of unique materials from stones, sapphires, rubies, gold, and silver. The floor itself seemed to be made of silver glass, and the company could see their reflections on the ground. Many rooms there were, and in them could be seen many gamdars either talking with one another, writing, building, or painting. But whatever they did, a joyful light could be seen sparkling on their faces with no signs of stress or tiredness. Hanging throughout the marble walls were white banners depicting the great Dahroon trees of Malah Ardmillia, and throughout the great hall, many flowers and plants could be seen, some of which could be found covering the stone pillars.

After they had seen all of this, Gonyardu led the company to a stairway of silver glass, with railings covered in plants, flowers, and bushes. They climbed their way up the many stairs, with many windows that covered the walls on their side. As they climbed up, there seemed to be a growing light that shone in their direction, as if they were going so high up that the light of the sun grew in its strength. They climbed for many steps, which the steps leading to the streets of the structure itself couldn't even be compared to. There seemed to be no end to their walking, and the growing light grew in its intensity and strength. As more time passed they began to grow increasingly concerned, feeling as though there would be no end to their walking. They felt like bringing their concern to Gonyardu's attention and wondered when they would finally reach their destination.

But just as they were on the brink of giving up, they finally reached the top of the stairway. There before them lay a long hall of white marble, and along the walls were windows that shone with the light of the sun, as well as large gems and jewels that sparkled with phenomenal radiant lights themselves. For a moment, the company covered their eyes with their hands, as they had not expected to be met with the incredible brightness of the hall. But as they lifted their hands from their eyes, the light seemed to grow somewhat dim and they were able to observe the hall in full.

Many paintings and statues filled the great hall, and a large furnace just lay ahead of them. Above the furnace, the company observed one such painting in particular that provided them with much fascination. It depicted a figure seated on a high and lofty throne, and just above his head was a circle of stars, shaping what looked like a crown placed on his head. His figure could be seen, and he seemed to be shaped like a man, having on a pure white robe sparkling with many crystals and gems. His right hand was stretched out, and in it was a great ball, with what looked like a rich country of trees, grasslands, mountains, and even animals populating the land. His hands and feet were covered in white unfading light, and all around his presence were rays of shining light. But in the painting, his face could not be seen. A bright light, covered his whole face so that not even any features could be seen on it, with this greatly intriguing the company as they wondered who this mighty figure could be.

"Who is that?" asked Erundil, gazing at the painting in awe and even in a sense of reverence. "And what is he holding in his hand?"

"It is a painting depicting Zomladil," answered Gonyardu. "The Eternal One unbounded from the fate of the world. He is holding his very own creation in the palm of his hand, as it is believed that the entire world is held within his tight grasp."

"Why can't we see his face?" asked Steven. "I can only imagine how glorious his face would be if the light wasn't blocking his appearance."

"None have ever seen his face," responded Gonyardu. "Save maybe Mataput, Orieant, and Natugura, who were once the great spirit beings of Zomladil many ages ago. But even their previous lives are far distant memories to them; much like an ancient period to them. They are now bound to the lives they live in this world."

The company continued gazing in wonder at the painting, thinking, and processing all that Gonyardu had said. And after they had taken their eyes off the wonderful creation, they noticed that about three dozen or so gamdars were gathered together at a large glass table, each seated in golden chairs. They were all dressed in outfits covered in golden and silver leaves and had fair and noble faces just like Hiladar. There was a power and strength that seemed to be contained within them, and the company could feel that they were among the most important advisors of Gonyardu.

But as soon as the advisors saw Gonyardu, most of them left the room and went down the stairway that the company came up from, while about a dozen of them stayed where they were in their seats. Gonyardu and Hiladar led the company over to the gamdarian advisors, where they found a seat in the remaining open golden chairs there were. At their spots were glasses and plates, and near the center of the table were large baskets of bread, fruits, and vegetables, along with a large vase of water.

After the company was seated, one of the gamdars greeted Gonyardu and Hiladar. "It is a pleasure to see you two here," he said, before turning toward the company. "Please make yourselves comfortable here, and have some food to eat and water to drink."

The company took some of the bread, fruits, and vegetables placed them on their plates, and poured some water into their glasses. They were amazed at the taste of the food, as there was a certain sweet texture to it, being far unique to anything they had eaten before. The water was ordinary, not taken from the Flurien River, but it remained cool and fresh enough to quench their thirst.

Once they had settled in, Hiladar spoke to everyone seated at the table. "Gathered together here in the tower of Adun-Parantu and the city of Malah Ardmillia, are the gamdars, humans, and smalves who were led on a quest by the volviers to bring back the lost book of Ulohendel," he said, presenting the eight of them to the many gamdarian advisors sitting around the table. "Erundil King of Watendelle, his three sons, Steven, the hope of the humans, his friend Peter, and the two smalf brothers Huminli and Glophi, were each chosen by Mataput and Orieant to embark on their quest that would change the fate of not only humanity but of the entire world. Unfortunately, Mataput and Orieant, the great helpers and protectors of the freedom of the world, were captured by a group of wuzlirs and taken away from this company. Thankfully, those whom you see now were saved by Gonyardu and brought to this land to recover and rest from their weary bodies and minds.

"And so we along with Gonyardu all imagined that your troubles would be lifted away from your hearts as you rested in the land of Lundarin, which originally seemed to be the case. But just a couple of days ago, while all of you had just gotten here, Orubinar, who is sitting over there," he said pointing to a gamdarian advisor of Gonyardu on his right, "came to us and reported a most remarkable discovery he had made while standing on the borders of this land. An army of tens of thousands of gamdarian soldiers of Watendelle, riding on their battle horses and carrying their swords, shields, arrows, spears, and war banners with them, came to Orubinar, wishing to speak with Gonyardu. They were offered to come into the land of Lundarin, but they refused to do so, explaining that they were on their quest and that their purpose was not to come to Lundarin," he paused, with everyone staring at him in bewilderment and excitement. "That is about everything regarding this tale that I know of," he concluded. "The Lady Gonyardu may now share what the purpose in their coming to the land of Nangorid was."

Before Gonyardu could speak, Erundil objected. "All that you have said, Hiladar, is strange news to me," he said. "Why would my soldiers decide to come to Nangorid without me or my sons' command? What would motivate them to do such a thing? I am not angry, but rather surprised that they came here, and even more, confused at what the purpose of their coming was. We are currently in a time of peace, and we have not had any wars for many decades now, so what is going on?"

"Before Lady Gonyardu speaks, I would like to say something," remarked Orubinar, with all attention now fixed on him. "Though I do not know the true purpose of this riddle, which we will soon find out the meaning from Lady Gonyardu, what I do know is that the soldiers looked greatly concerned and desperate. Many of them were worn out from long traveling and it seemed as though they were following a certain group of people. But when I asked them why they had come, they said that they could only share it with the Lady Gonyardu."

"What could be the meaning of this?" whispered Erundil to himself, shaking his head as his surprise and confusion soon turned into growing concern.

Everyone else sitting at the table remained silent, staring at each other with mixed faces of confusion, shock, excitement, and worry. Many of them now grew concerned for the gamdarian soldiers and wondered if they were safe, with even many of Gonyardu's tightening with tension, eagerness, and worry to hear what the lady would have to say.

Amidst the deafening silence of the room, with everyone feeling a mix of emotions and with many questions racing through their minds, Gonyardu explained everything that had transpired.

"I will tell you all that I know of," she said, with everyone's attention now entirely focused on her. "It was for this purpose that I gathered you together in Adun-Parantu, to discuss many important matters that the gamdarian soldiers shared with me. And after you have heard all that you must know, we will collectively make our final decision on what to do. But you must promise me that you will not fear or distress after I share these matters with you. Can you promise me that?"

Everyone remained silent at first, wondering why Gonyardu urged them to make such a promise. But as they looked into her sharp blue eyes and the glory that radiated throughout her presence, they couldn't resist obeying her command.

"Yes, we promise," they said in collective voices, though they remained worried about what she would reveal to them.

"Good," responded Gonyardu after hearing their promise. "I will now share all that was revealed to me, yet I will warn you that I and even the soldiers do not know the true meaning of all that has transpired. Nonetheless, I will share what they told me with you all," she paused, gazing into everyone's eyes that remained fixed on her. And then with a deep breath, she told them the long tale in full.

"It all began when Orubinar, came to me the day after this company had arrived in my land," she said, speaking in a clear and refined voice. "He explained how he had seen a large army of gamdarian soldiers gathered together just outside the border of Lundarin. And so I asked him what they wanted or what news they brought to me, but he said that they wished to speak with me alone, for they had many unprecedented tales to explain. I was bewildered by this, and even my wisdom was unable to interpret what their concern was, so I speedily came to the border of this land, wondering what was going on.

"And sure enough, there before my eyes an army of gamdarian soldiers, clad in their heavy golden and green armor, wearing strong helms, and carrying broad shields along with sharp swords, spears, arrows, and war banners. Their faces were grim and hardened, and many of them looked concerned or even terrified. But once they looked into my eyes, it seemed as though a great burden of weariness and fear had left them, and they could now share everything with me in full as they understood it, without fear of anything or anyone.

"I asked them what their purpose in journeying through the land of Nangorid was and if war was inevitable. They all looked at each other for a moment, as if wondering who would respond to me. But eventually, Bardulil, the army's captain and leader in place of King Erundil and Prince Lelhond's absence, spoke up and withheld nothing from me. He said that a couple of weeks ago, soon after the company had departed the Earth to journey through the land of the enemy, Dulanmidir, who seldom leaves his home in the Palororen forest, had come to the great palace of the king wishing to speak with the Queen Regent Aradulin. There the two of them spoke in private, where Dulanmidir revealed to Aradulin all that he had discovered.

"He shared with her that while lounging in his home, he noticed a strange sight in his gorlinto. It was lit all around in a great rim of blue fire, yet as he grew closer to the object, it seemed to grow larger and expand as though he were entering a vision. Suddenly, in what he described as an out-of-body experience, he was taken to the land of Nangorid where he saw the company journeying through the land. Everything seemed to be going fine at first, but as he looked ahead to where they would soon pass through, he saw a mighty and terrible presence of evil that awaited them. He did not know where specifically it was located, or what the evil exactly was, but he knew that they would encounter it at some stage of their quest. To his surprise, they encountered the evil presence but seemed to be completely unaware of it. But very soon as time passed, he witnessed the evil have devastating effects on them, with disaster after disaster befalling them. He described trying to warn them in the vision to avoid going in the direction of the evil presence, but they were unable to hear, see, or sense him. Then at once, the vision ended, and he was sent back to his home, lying on the ground in horror at what he had just seen.

"Upon hearing this revelation from him, Aradulin almost collapsed to the ground, fearing for what evil would befall the company, and especially for her husband and sons. Dulanmidir claimed that there was a rising danger fast approaching the company, though he did not fully know what it was. He suggested that the army of gamdarian soldiers be sent to track the company and reach them just in time to provide support. Aradulin at first objected to Dulanmidir's wish, not wishing to waste any valuable lives of soldiers in a time when there was no war. But Dulanmidir eventually managed to convince her, and her chief advisor Olindule, warning them that this new rising danger was beyond anything ever seen in Nangorid and that the entire company's lives were in severe danger.

"And so, a great number of gamdarian soldiers reaching into the thirty thousand were sent to the land of the Dark Lord, on a mission to catch up with the company and warn them of all Dulanmidir had seen in his vision. Unfortunately, they narrowly missed out on getting to them in time, yet they remain here outside the border of my land, ready to meet up with the company once they depart Lundarin. This is the end of the tale, and I must admit that it is alarming news to me. I am unable to interpret it, but we must make a wise decision."

Everyone seated at the table from the gamdarian advisors to the company, gasped in horror at everything Gonyardu had shared and felt as though the air had been sucked out of the room. They felt as though their hearts had been shattered, and they wondered, especially in the company of eight, what rising danger or evil they had encountered in their journey.

"Are we all going to die?" cried out Huminli in horror. "Our lives are now in dangerous peril, so what are we going to do?"

"We will be fine," responded Erundil, wishing to comfort the young smalf, though he was greatly fearful. "Yet this is a dire situation that we find ourselves in, and we have no choice but to depart at once to where my army is and speak with them. Evil is following us, and I fear for their safety."

"Do not fear," said Gonyardu, wishing to calm down those seated in the room. "I have provided a girdle for them where they will not be harmed while they await your arrival. But please understand that we cannot afford to make hasty and ill-planned decisions, as now is not the time for that. We must calm down and make wise choices, for I deem that your very lives depend on it."

"Yet now I fear even more for Mataput and Orieant," remarked Lelhond. "I can only hope that they are fine wherever the wuzlirs took them, and I wonder exactly what this evil that is following us could be."

"Have faith, Lelhond," assured Gonyardu. "Wherever the volviers are, I sense that their strength, courage, and wisdom are still very high. They will be fine, but as for you, we must now decide what to do with these grievous tidings. I do not know what this evil is, whether it is a person, object, or spirit, but what I do know is that we must make a wise decision on what to do. You must not fear or despair, for if you do so, then all hope will already be lost."

Everyone became silent, not knowing how to respond or what to think now. They desperately wished that what Gonyardu had shared was untrue, but they knew that no lie could come forth from her mouth. They all stared at each other as if trying to imagine what each one of them was thinking.

Peter looked deeply into Steven's eyes and saw a look of not only terror but also concealment on his face. Just then he suddenly remembered how back at the deserted city of Tuwanor he had noticed a change in Steven after he had discovered something there. And he was reminded of how Steven tried to hide it, not wishing to share any details with the company. But Peter knew that he had to share this with everyone at the table, especially after he observed how worried Steven was compared to everyone else. He hoped that Gonyardu or even her advisors would have an answer for his worries.

He looked in Gonyardu's direction and broke the long silence. "I have something I would like to say," he said.

"Go ahead, Peter," responded Gonyardu. "Share all that has been laid on your heart, and be free of any heavy burdens you may have."

Peter sighed to himself, with everyone peering at him with wide and curious eyes. Once he had finally let go of his fears he began to speak, sharing everything that he had experienced and withholding nothing from those around him.

"I cannot lie when I say that I've been noticing a change in Steven as of late," he remarked, with everyone suddenly looking at him with even more keen eyes, with Steven feeling a sudden sense of alarm. "Perhaps it's because he was stung by Kolmaug in those evil caves of the bitter mountains, or maybe because he was stabbed by the wuzlirs which left him unconscious for a few days. But there must be something more to his change in attitude than just being stabbed a few times. Just a few days ago when we were journeying through the deserted city of Tuwanor, I briefly noticed the outline of some object which Steven held. Right when he saw me, he quickly hid it in his backpack, as if he was scared that I would see what it was. When I brought this to his attention, he suddenly lashed out at me, before soon coming to his senses. But I've still seen the same kind of worry and unusual anxiety on his face since this occurred, and though I do not know exactly what all of this means, I fear that this new rising danger may somehow be connected to whatever Steven saw or touched in Tuwanor."

The boy fell silent, leaving everyone stunned at the table. Steven slumped back into his chair, not wishing to look into Peter's face, with his body beginning to slightly shake and his hand inching closer and closer to his backpack.

"Well this is certainly remarkable news," said one of the advisors of Gonyardu seated. "I wonder indeed if this new rising evil that Dulanmidir saw in his vision is connected somehow to whatever Steven saw or even currently possesses."

"Perhaps we should have a look inside his backpack," suggested Peter. "Because as far as I know, this certain object that Steven discovered is still in his bag."

With no prompting, Peter stood up from his seat and walked toward Steven. No one else made a move and instead watched how the situation would unfold. Steven, however, swiftly grabbed his backpack and hid it under the table, refusing to let Peter even touch it.

"I just want to help you, Steven," said Peter. "It is for our good that we make sure that what you have isn't endangering us."

"No!" cried Steven, in a sharp voice, staring into Peter's eyes with a growing cloud of anxiety, as drips of sweat poured down his forehead. His hands and feet were now violently shaking, and he became ever more defensive of himself.

"Please, Steven, I am just trying to help you," urged Peter, who refused to stop trying to convince Steven to give up his bag. "I am your friend, and so you can trust me. I want to help you we all want to help you. It's not been good the way you've been acting lately, as you were never like this before."

He placed his hand on Steven's shoulder, trying to assure him that he was only trying to aid him. "Get away from me!" shouted Steven, slapping Peter's hand off his shoulder. His voice was now rumbling with fiery wrath, and his eyes were bulging with vexation as his hands were clenched tightly in balls of rock. "I do not want your help nor do I need it! Save your pity to yourselves and let me be!"

Peter looked on in horror at his friend, shocked and devastated at the sudden change he had just witnessed. He turned his back away from him, heading back to his seat with his head down, as drops of tears soon streamed down his face before he placed his hands over his face. Erundil came over to him, placing his hand on his back and whispering words of encouragement to him. Everyone soon came around Peter, one by one as they each assured him that he was doing the right thing. Steven soon calmed down, regretting that he had lashed out at his friend, yet refusing to apologize to him.

Amidst the moment of shock and sudden change in atmosphere, Gonyardu managed to garner everyone's attention. "Peter, what you did was right," she said, trying to comfort the boy once more, whose tears only continued to flow down his face. "You are brave for what you did, and I appreciate the insight that we now have. As for Steven, I can see that you are grieving and in a difficult situation, but whatever it is you are going through, I can only encourage you to be free of it. Whether that means letting go of whatever object is in your bag or moving on from the past, we cannot continue to have any more divisions within this company. You already had some strife with Erundil and the smalves, which I am glad to see has now been resolved. But I do not wish for this to become another one of those divisions within your group. Do you understand me?"

Steven remained silent for a while, before finally giving in. "Yes, I understand," he said quietly, staring off into space.

"So what are we going to do now?" asked Lelhond. "We have found ourselves in a really difficult spot, but an old proverb of ours says that there is always hope when a choice is made."

"That is right, Lelhond," remarked Gonyardu. "But the key is making sure the choice we make is the right one. Whether this rising danger is following you or even if you have already encountered it, the best thing you can do is to gather together and make a choice."

"So what do you think we should do then, Lady Gonyardu?" asked Erundil. "My wisdom is not even worth comparing to yours, or even to your advisors, so surely you know what is best for us."

"I can give you my advice, but ultimately this quest lies in your hands," responded Gonyardu. "I deem that it would be best for you to first spend some more time resting and healing here in this land before you depart for the outside world. But it would be wise in my eyes that after spending some more time to heal and strengthen, to meet up with the gamdarian soldiers and join them on your journey. I do not know what you would want to do from there, for this quest is yours, not mine, but all of you, even including my advisors must make a collective decision and present it before me. I will leave this room, and once you have made a wise decision that you all agree with, you may call me and I will weigh it out to see if it is indeed a wise one."

At once, Gonyardu stood up from her seat and entered one of the side doors, closing the door behind her. Everyone else left sitting at the table discussed at once together, debating on what their next step would be. They spent many long minutes debating, arguing, and disagreeing about what their next move should be, as they each had their own opinions. An hour soon passed, yet they seemed to be no closer to agreeing when they had first begun speaking with one another.

But eventually, mainly due to Erundil's display of leadership and mediation, they finally struck an agreement and were united in their final decision. Once they agreed, Hiladar went over to the door where Gonyardu was, knocking on it and letting her know that they were ready to share with her what they had decided.

Gonyardu came forth from the door, gazing into every one of their eyes as she made her way to her seat. They all stared right back at her as she sat down, smiling and resting assured in their final decision.

"Well, it took you over an hour and a half to come to a decision," remarked Gonyardu, with a smile. "But I am glad that you managed to strike an agreement with each other, and I can't help but admire that all of you look satisfied with your decision, and so I sense that it was a wise choice that you made. So tell me then, what have you decided upon?"

For a moment they all looked at each other, wondering who would present their idea to her. But Erundil soon managed to step in and straightening his posture he looked into Gonyardu's eyes and explained all that they had agreed to do.

"We spent much time arguing with each other because of our differing opinions," he began saying. "But after much meaningful discussion, we have agreed that once we meet up with the soldiers of Watendelle, we will journey together with them as far as we can. And if war calls us to stand and fight, then we shall battle with them against the enemy. Yet not all of us will go to war with our fellow soldiers if war were to be our fate, as we understand that the main purpose of our journey is to find the lost book of Ulohendel and bring it back for Steven, Peter, and the humans to use to live changed lives of freedom. And so, we have agreed that if we are going to go to war, then we will have no choice but to split up. It will be myself, Lelhond, and Karandil who will go with the gamdarian soldiers to battle, while Steven, Peter, Huminli, Glophi, and Forandor will remain behind to complete our quest. We hope that we will not have to make this decision, but we are prepared to do so if we have no other choice."

Gonyardu gazed into each one of the company's eyes, evaluating if they were all truly on the same page with what Erundil shared. After processing everything that Erundil shared and observing the contentment that covered everyone's faces, she simply nodded her head in approval.

"That is a wise decision," she said. "I am glad that you are willing to go along with the gamdarian soldiers for as long as possible, even to war itself if you are called upon to go to battle. I am also pleased that you understand that your quest has not ended and that you must still complete it. I too hope that you will be able to go with the soldiers for as long as possible, but the entire purpose of your journey is to travel in stealth and with as few numbers as possible. Perhaps you going to war with the gamdarian soldiers will provide a shield and distraction for Steven, Peter, Huminli, Glophi, and Forandor to journey through the land of Nangorid. I approve of your idea, yet I have one question. Tell me, why is it, Forandor, that you will travel with the humans and smalves instead of the gamdars if you would be going to war? Will it not be a sad and bitter parting to leave your father and brothers?"

"It was a tough decision we made, but ultimately we believe it to be the best one to make," answered Forandor. "I have never been the soldier type within my family, as I instead have always enjoyed listening to and playing music, as well as reading and studying many books of knowledge and lore. But I will still go with Steven, Peter, Huminli, and Glophi as they journey to find the lost book of Ulohendel, to provide protection and support for them. We have made our decision, and it is one that I will proudly stand by."

At that moment it seemed as though that Forandor suddenly grew tall and strong, just like his soldier brothers Lelhond and Karandil. Yet the dignified grace and elegance that he always possessed remained within him. Everyone there looked on at him with satisfaction, especially his father and brothers who sat smiling proudly at him.

Gonyardu smiled and gazed at Forandor for some time, and it seemed to all those there that her mouth began to slowly open and a white light glimmered through the faint sight of her teeth. She soon spoke in response to the gamdar.

"So be it," she said at last. "I am amazed at the decision that all of you have agreed to, but it looks as though you are all happy with the decision, even you Steven."

Steven was caught off guard by her sudden attention to him, yet Gonyardu appeared to be right, for he no longer looked as angry and worn out as he had a couple of hours ago. "Yes, I am feeling much better," he responded. "I believe that our decision will prove to be wise and effective, and during the time we were talking, Peter and I were able to resolve our differences, and I apologized to him for my sudden change in attitude toward him. We have united once again with one another."

Peter nodded his head and smiled toward Steven, with no trace of any remaining bitterness on his face. Gonyardu observed in silent approval. "Good, all looks very good with you all," she said. "You are united in your purpose, and even if something unexpected happens to thwart your plans, wisdom will remain your constant guide. May Zomladil continue to bless you with abundant wisdom, strength, love, and joy as you embark on the next chapter of your journey. But for now, you may stay for some more time in my land, to fully heal and recover from any weariness and troubling memories plaguing your minds."

"I will certainly need more rest," remarked Steven. "But I'm glad that I feel much better now."

"Yes, I think that a few more days, or even up to another week of rest in Lundarin will be for the betterment of our quest," said Erundil. "In the coming days, we will have more time to think, ponder, and rest on the decision we have made. And once we are ready to depart, we will have no regrets lying in the back of our heads."

"I agree," said Lelhond. "There is no fault to be found in all you said, and I know that I need more time to spend in this land of my dreams, and once we are ready, I will be glad to join together with my fellow brothers. Does anyone oppose what we say?"

No one opposed what Erundil and Lelhond said, and instead voiced their agreement with them. Everyone from the smallest and curious smalf to the tallest and wisest gamdar seated together at the table was all in one accord with one another, and all Gonyardu could do was smile and admire this remarkable sight, having nothing else to say to them.

"This is a sight of beauty," she remarked, with a beam of light sparkling through her joyful face. "Never before have I seen a group of individuals so united in their purpose, and not even the harmony displayed in the groups of gamdars that came into my land after suffering through the pains of war could ever compare to yours. And even more amazing is that you are made up of gamdars, humans, and smalves, with gamdars and smalves not even meant to have close fellowship with one another, yet you have managed to tear down that dividing wall. I have nothing else to say to you, other than may blessing and honor be bestowed upon you all. Well done! Our discussion and debate in Malah Ardmillia has come to an end, and you may now follow me as I lead you back to where we came from."

Gonyardu stood up from her seat, with such a joy and light on her face, combined with the glory of her golden dress and hair, that all who looked upon her in that moment, had to cover their eyes for a brief while, feeling unworthy to receive such high praise from a glorious being as her. Yet as Gonyardu looked into every one of the company's eyes, they perceived a humbleness that covered her heart and a sense of wonder that possessed her. They now understood that the fair and glorious Lady of Lundarin was filled with humility by them, making her greatly honored to be in their presence. And so they all stood up from their seats, humbled and honored to be loved and admired by Gonyardu herself.

Looking outside the windows they saw the sky growing dark as evening was now upon them, yet the golden and silver leaves of the trees seemed to be radiating bright lights throughout the land, just as the moon illuminates the night sky. They beheld the sight in astonishment and wonder but soon made their way down the many long stairs overlaid in silver glass. Peace now covered and protected them, and though many great concerns and troubles were laid ahead of their quest, they remained confident that all would be fine.

20

Joyful Partings

THE COMPANY DEPARTED FROM the chief city of Malah Ardmillia, experiencing peace and assurance even though their situation remained grim. They followed Gonyardu through the rich hills, forests, and paths through the land, making their way back to where they were staying in Lundarin. The red sun grew dimmer as the evening wore on before it completely vanished from sight with the sky becoming pitch black. Yet to their delight and astonishment, bright lights led them along the way, and not only did the shining light of the moon give them a sight to see, but also the glimmering gems of the tree leaves and the sparkling presence of Gonyardu led them through the way. Though the walk took several hours, they hardly felt that minutes had passed as the beauty of Lundarin and Gonyardu kept them occupied the entire time.

They each climbed their way to their tree houses, wishing one another a peaceful sleep as they covered themselves in the warm and soft beds and mattresses that Gonyardu had provided them with. In all their wandering throughout the land of Nangorid, they had never slept in real beds, and even as they slept they continued to thank Gonyardu in their dreams that she had provided them with such a luxury. They slept peacefully that night, unbothered by the problems of the world.

The days to come would be much the same with shining lights of peace and joy reflecting from their faces. They spent most of their time resting and delighting in the joys of nature, even washing and cleaning themselves in sparkling clean pools and showers found throughout the land. Once a day they would gather together and speak in a group with Gonyardu, sharing all that was on their minds and how they felt. They delighted themselves in hearing her clear refined voice, and soaking in the beauty of her singing and of the music of the many gamdars of the land. They observed the flying birds and creeping beasts of the forests and fields, who at times would dance in blades of grass covered in rainbows of flowers and plants. All this time the thought of departing Lundarin was not even an afterthought to the company, and they began to wonder what eternity in this land would be like.

Yet these thoughts wouldn't last for too long, for just as quickly as these thoughts came to their mind, so did the thoughts of the outside world's evil and of all that they had discussed in the council of Malah Ardmillia. The days began to wane faster, and though they still experienced joy and rest, feelings of discontentment slowly began to seize their hearts. They started to think of Mataput and Orieant, and what ways they could find them. Their thoughts naturally turned to the gamdarian soldiers as well, picturing what they were doing as they waited for the company to join them. Troubling thoughts of uneasiness soon took control of their minds, and they felt that time was slowly chipping away from their grasp.

Thus after another week or so had passed since they held their council meeting in Malah Ardmillia, the company gathered together to share and discuss their many thoughts. They were surprised by how similar they felt but took it as a sign that their time to depart Lundarin was fast approaching. They understood that the next stage of their journey would soon begin, and it would be better to start it sooner rather than later. They talked with each other for a long while, before striking an agreement on what they would do from there.

And so, on an unusually chilly but sunny morning, as the leaves rustled in a slightly uneasy manner, the company made their way to the forest where they found Gonyardu gazing into the sky and pacing back and forth through the glade. Her eyes were closed and she seemed to be muttering inaudible words under her breath, possibly speaking in a strange and unheard-of language. The company walked steadily to her, ready to announce their desire to depart from her land.

"My Fair Lady, it has been an honor to have been so blessed in your land," said Erundil, standing close by her side, though Gonyardu still didn't open up her eyes and instead continued muttering words under her breath. Erundil continued speaking. "But I think it is the appropriate time to announce our intention and share all that has been laid on our hearts. If you may, we would like you to hear what we have to say."

Gonyardu opened her eyes, and the company saw sparkling rainbows of color that glimmered in her eyes. She examined every one of them, with a serious tone on her face, before she broke out into a broad smile.

"Yes, I know all that it is you wish to tell me," she said. "How you wish to depart my land and continue in the next stage of your quest. And I agree that the appointed time to do that has arrived for all of you, and so you now must rise and make a choice to alter the spreading tide that wishes to bring evil and destruction to this fair world. But you are right to believe that your time of parting has come."

"How did you know that this was what we were thinking about?" asked Peter, stunned that Gonyardu had figured this out.

"That is not for you to know," responded Gonyardu with a smile, before pausing for a moment and sighing to herself before speaking again. "But I have gone to war for each of you, determined that the will of the Dark Lord shall not prevail against you. I have petitioned Zomladil that he protect and guide you all at this point of your lives, for the Dark Lord and his evil servants desire to destroy you. But I have a full assurance that you shall complete your task in the end and that the mighty volviers, Mataput and Orieant, will still have a part to play in shaping this world for the better."

The company stood dazed for a moment, amazed that Gonyardu had spent much time fighting for them. Gratefulness for her wisdom and love took control of their hearts, but they naturally wondered what evil they would soon encounter on their quest. And they began to picture in their minds what the Dark Lord would try and throw at them.

"I am in awe of you, my Fair Lady," confessed Lelhond, bowing his knee and face to the ground in front of Gonyardu. "Yet I am worried about what we will now face in our journey, and what vile things the Dark Lord will try to throw our way. But I have faith in all that you say."

Gonyardu softly placed her hand on Lelhond's chin, lifting him from the ground, while Lelhond and the company gazed at her in wonder and veneration. But Gonyardu simply laughed as she saw them staring at her, and speaking in a clear and musical voice she eased their worries.

"Lelhond, you do not need to bow to me," she said. "I am not worthy of such respect, no matter how much you may think I am. But there is one who is worthy of it all, and he interacts in each of your lives even in the most seemingly insignificant matters. And because he does, you all do not need to fear or worry. Though the world may stand against you and all hope seems to be lost, know that there is one who always defends you and gives you hope in your direst time of need. Difficult times will come, for there is a presence of evil rising just as Dulanmidir saw in his vision, but this evil will have no choice but to back away and hide for good once the light of this world comes against it. You will soon begin traveling again as the light of the world, and nothing shall be able to extinguish your flaming spark. The light of my land shall always be a cause of remembrance for you and a source of hope and joy even in the darkest tunnels of your quest."

The company soaked their minds and hearts under Gonyardu's words of hope for a while, even seeing sudden flashes of her guiding hand leading them through their journey. They stood courageously, not fearing any evil plan that the dark enemy would try to throw against them. They said nothing to one another for some time, instead choosing to gaze at the glory of Gonyardu and the beauty of her land which both gave them strength.

Soon, Peter interrupted the silence of the group. "So when are we going to depart?" he asked. "Though I love this land and Gonyardu, my confidence and hope have been significantly raised just by hearing from the Fair Lady today. I am sure that nothing will be able to stand against us anymore."

Gonyardu smiled and laughed in response to Peter's confidence. "Your faith is a sight to admire, Peter," she said. "All of you will surely be safe wherever you venture next. The time of your departure has come, but before you go I must give you my final blessings so that you are strengthened even more before you continue on your quest. Come, all of you, and follow me before I send you out from my land."

The company followed Gonyardu as she led them through the wide forest, and they each gazed in enchantment at the many animals and creatures that filled the area of trees. They were soon led onto a path with a wide plain of grass surrounding them with flowers, plants, and colorful trees filling the land. They could faintly hear a combination of the sound of cascading waterfalls and a large number of gamdars singing in the distance, though they knew not where it came from. Gonyardu continued to lead them, and as they walked the sound of the beautiful music grew louder and far more splendid than anything they had ever heard before. Tingling sensations began to stream down their bones and they soon found themselves almost dancing along to the music.

They soon found out where the music was coming from. Ahead of them they saw several waterfalls emptying into a large body of water which seemed to be a pond, yet had the same color and texture as the Flurien River. Around the pond were spacious gardens filled with plants, flowers, and bushes of every array of colors, with many small creatures crawling and playing around them. Beside the waterfalls were large silver stones, and standing on them were gamdarian men, women, and even children, all holding silver harps and singing together in collective voices. There appeared to be hundreds of them in total, and their singing grew in power and majesty as they saw Gonyardu and the company approaching them. Large and colorful trees were scattered around this place as well, bearing many unique fruits on their branches. The company could do nothing but gaze in admiration at the fair sight.

"Before you leave, I must gift you with final blessings and wonders," said Gonyardu to the company.

The company stared at her as she made her way up the silver stones where many of the gamdars stood. About half a dozen of the gamdars stopped their music and followed Gonyardu as she made her way to the garden. She and the gamdars soon disappeared from everyone's sight, and the voices of the gamdars suddenly grew silent in response. The company was bewildered by this, and Huminli and Glophi thought about trying to find her, but they were quickly stopped by Steven, who grabbed ahold of their arms.

"No, let's wait for her," he said cautiously. "I think she wants us to wait for her, and besides, she did say that she would bless us one last time before we left, and I assume that's what she's going to do right now."

The smalves listened to Steven and restrained themselves by standing still. The company waited patiently for a few more minutes before Gonyardu and the gamdars returned. Immediately the voices of the gamdars grew louder once more and as they saw what she and the other gamdars carried, there seemed to be growing wonder and pride that came out from their voices. The company tried to look and see what Gonyardu and the gamdars carried but found that it was all covered by blankets covered in leaves. Gonyardu and the gamdars made their way to the company, placing all that they carried onto the grass. The company stood silently, without moving an inch.

Suddenly, Gonyardu and the gamdars stooped down and uncovered the blankets, revealing everything there was. There before their eyes, the company observed the many gifts that were laid across the ground. They saw thick armor overlaid with green and gold, with an image of a golden tree placed on the center of its chest armor. They also saw golden helms, shields, swords, and arrows that went along with the armor, and besides the armor, they also saw many other smaller and plainer swords and arrows that still looked sharp and effective. There was a basket filled with pieces of bread and another basket with distinctive fruits and vegetables, bottles seeming to contain a decent amount of water, and several gray cloaks that looked similar to the ones they had on their journey.

Immediately, Erundil and his three sons gasped in joy and amazement at what they saw. The rest of the company was filled with wonder as well but were not as dramatic as the four gamdars were. Erundil and his sons broke out in celebration, dancing and singing in their native Tuntish tongue, while the rest of the company looked at them in confusion, wondering why they were so excited.

"Is everything fine?" asked Steven, staring at Erundil and his sons in astonishment at their sudden joy. "Is there something that we don't know that explains why you four are so excited?"

"No," responded Erundil. "The rest of you do not have any reason to be as joyful as we are, but the reason why our hearts are filled with joy is that the armor and weapons you see laid on the grass, are the armor and

The company then brought their attention to the other gifts that were on the grass; the cloaks, food, bottles, and other weapons there were, and they imagined how it would serve them on their journey. They listened to Gonyardu as she explained the importance of the gifts to them.

"The rest of the gifts that you see will either be for some of you or all of you," she said. "The gray cloaks have been specifically designed by the gamdars of my land for warmth and protection, but it also contains a relative softness to their material. They are only for Steven, Peter, Huminli, Glophi, and Forandor, because Erundil, Lelhond, and Karandil will not need for them. The smallest swords and arrows are for the smalves, the medium-sized ones for Steven and Peter, and the largest ones for Forandor. They have been intricately crafted by my gamdars, and though they may look much plainer and simpler than the swords and weapons wielded by the gamdarian soldiers, they remain very sharp and useful. The rest of the gifts are for all of you and they include the bread that you see, which I solely baked. Just a few bites will give you enough strength you need to continue in your journey, while fruits and vegetables are tasty and have enough sugar to give you the needed energy to go on. And last of all, the bottles are filled with water from the Flurien River, and just a few sips will last you almost an entire day. These are all the gifts I have blessed you with, and they will give you the much-needed provisions that you desire on your long quest."

The company thanked Gonyardu many times for her generosity and immediately went to collect some of the gifts for themselves. They divided the food amongst themselves, each putting an equal amount into their backpacks. There were three cloaks for each of them, besides Erundil and his sons, and the rest of them put on their cloaks, keeping the clothes that they had worn in Lundarin as memories of their time spent in the land of bliss.

"My lady, thank you for your tremendous generosity," said Forandor, comforting himself in his new gray cloak. "Your bountiful giving and blessing have been more than we could ever hope for, and I know that it will serve us well in our journey."

"I have only given you what you need," remarked Gonyardu. "You will need it for your journey, for I deem that this next stage of travels will be one full of perils and dangers, yet I know that you shall come out of the fire unscathed. But these gifts shall serve you for the time being, and possibly for a much longer time."

Forandor gulped to himself but encouraged himself in Gonyardu's reassuring and hopeful words, while the company looked at each other and nodded their heads in agreement that all would go well.

And then to everyone's amazement, Erundil moved forward in the direction of many of the gamdars standing and singing on the silver stones, before finding an open stone to stand on. To all that beheld him, he appeared as a commanding and glorious figure, an image that even his sons had never seen in him before. For a sudden moment, as if a concealed revelation had suddenly flashed itself in an open disclosure before them, they imagined that Ulohendel had come back to life to share his words of wisdom with them. The gamdars stopped their singing, and all eyes were drawn toward the King of Watendelle.

Then speaking in a clear voice, he revealed everything which had been placed on his heart. "This company has gone through trying times," he said. "From losing Mataput and Orieant to the captivity of the wuzlirs, to Steven being wounded in the chest on two different occasions, we have certainly not been spared from the wrath of the Dark Lord. And during this time, my heart remained bitter toward Huminli and Glophi, for they were smalves and I believed that all smalves were purposely seeking to help bring the downfall of my people. As King of Watendelle, I wished to lead and protect my people in safety and prosperity, and I was convinced that the smalves stood against that, even though I considered them insignificant and weak. Yet even the hardest of hearts can be softened and the unrelenting mind can be transformed, just as mine was. I have been redeemed from my wrong way of thinking, and my life has completely changed. I no longer am the stubborn and hard-hearted king I once was, but I am first and foremost the leader of this company, and if I cannot guide and be an example to this company, then I cannot lead my people as King of Watendelle. And for that, I am determined to lead this company into the ways of success and righteousness to whatever end is laid in store for us. May Zomladil bless us!"

Erundil stepped away from the silver stone, with the sun shining on his face and royal armor. All that gazed at him found themselves staring at him in awe of his glory, even the gamdars which stood on the silver stones. Then they remembered the words that he had spoken, all that he had revealed to them, and how his heart and mind had been completely changed.

They all broke out into a loud eruption of praise, crying and singing in mighty collective voices to celebrate the life of Erundil. "The King of Watendelle has spoken and he has revealed all that has been placed on his heart!" they cried in loud voices. "May he be blessed and may Zomladil bless him!"

Such an eruption of celebration had never before been heard in the land of Lundarin since the days the first gamdars had discovered Gonyardu and the hidden land. Everyone from Gonyardu and the singing gamdars, to the company and even the roaming animals of the garden bowed their knee to the King of Watendelle. They saw in him a majesty never before seen since the days of Ulohendel the Wise, and they humbled themselves in full confidence of Erundil. The celebration went on for a while, but they soon quieted themselves down as Gonyardu spoke to them for the final time in their presence.

"I am now more than confident that all will go well for you," she said, smiling in pure delight at them, especially for Erundil. "The King of Watendelle has shown why he is the leader of both this company and his kingdom of gamdars. May he and his family be blessed, and may the smalves and humans of this company be blessed and strengthened beyond anything they could ever reckon. Come, the time of your departure has come, and I will send you away from my land to go down the Partua River and meet with the gamdarian soldiers waiting for you."

Gonyardu then entered the vast garden surrounding the waterfalls, as the company followed her. The singing gamdars continued their music and singing, honoring the company one final time before they were led away from their sight. Gonyardu led them through the vast garden, and they observed how even the animals and many other creatures removed themselves from their way, allowing them to walk without coming in contact with them. Then, at last, they came to a narrow opening, and removing the bush which blocked them, Gonyardu led them away from the garden.

They passed from the garden, and found themselves along a river bank, with two decent-sized boats lying along the side of the river. They were both blue and carved in the shapes of swans, shaped identically to the same ships the company had seen in Malah Ardmillia. The company soon discovered their shoes were drenched in the water that soaked the grass, with a change also in the atmosphere as though the peace of the land of Lundarin had now departed from them.

"Here at last, along the Partua River comes our parting," said Gonyardu. "Yet our parting shall not be one of sorrow, but one of joy. For your quest has only begun, and much happiness is still in store for you. You must now depart from my land, and return to the outside world."

The hearts of the company were heavy at this final farewell from Gonyardu, yet they knew that it was the right decision to make. Tears streamed down Huminli's cheek, as the thought of never seeing Gonyardu again grieved him.

But Gonyardu came forth to Huminli, and placing her hand on his chin, the smalf looked up to her. "Do not worry or despair, my dear Huminli," she said, comforting him. "Though it may seem to be a bitter parting at this present moment, this shall not be the last time you look upon the face of Gonyardu. And I can see that the memory of me and my land shall remain dear to your heart."

A faint smile came on the corner of Huminli's face, and his faith was once again restored. The company made their way onto the two boats, with Erundil, Lelhond, Huminli, and Glophi entering one, and Karandil, Forandor, Steven, and Peter entering the other. And then with heavy hearts, they began to slowly paddle their way down the river, departing the land of Lundarin for good.

"Farewell my Lady," said Lelhond as Gonyardu watched the company. "It has been an honor to spend this blessed time in your land."

"Farewell, Lelhond," replied Gonyardu, outstretching her hand in an almost welcoming posture. "You are forever permitted to enter my land, in whatever season of life you may find yourself in."

The rest of the company said their final goodbyes to Gonyardu, who likewise said her final goodbyes to each one of them. They took her final words to heart and waving one last time, they set their sights on the long river and land that lay ahead of them.

But the company couldn't help themselves but turn around a few times as they went down the river, finding Gonyardu still standing alone by the side of the riverbank, smiling as she watched them go on. Then there came a clear voice like the sound of rushing water which came from behind, and looking back they saw that Gonyardu's arms were outstretched as she sang a song. Yet as the words became clear to them, they knew that it wasn't just any song she sang, for they interpreted that the words she sang appeared to be a prayer to Jangart. Her voice grew louder and more beautiful even as they paddled farther from her. Such a beautiful and marvelous voice had never before been heard in the history of the world, and not even the collective voices of the gamdarian choirs of Lundarin could compare to the singular voice of Gonyardu. The company listened closely to the words she sang, delighting themselves one last time as they slowly drifted away from her presence:

May he be a constant light,
May his presence always shine.
May the darkest night have a star sparkling bright,
And may his plans triumph and not mine.

Oh, may Zomladil be a shield unto you,
And an anchor to hold your feet on.
For his words are always true,
Causing none of his children to mourn.

May they be blessed with a showering of his favor,
And be shown his mercy and kindness,
Oh would Zomladil not waver,
From exhibiting his glorious brightness.

May the plans of the enemy not prevail against them,
And his love be a constant guide.
For Zomladil is more precious than the most valuable gem,
And none can stand before him in pride.

Oh, would Zomladil pour out his faithfulness,
And bless you beyond measure.
For even the world's joyfulness,
Cannot compare to his great pleasure.

The company closed their eyes in peaceful rest even as Gonyardu spoke for the final time to them in her song of prayer, with a calming wind surrounding them. They turned around for the last time but found that Gonyardu had vanished from their sight, returning to her land. All that lay behind them was an array of bushes, covering the land of Lundarin, and at that moment, they seemed to notice an invisible power that shielded them from re-entering the land of Lundarin. They now cast their attention straight ahead, holding onto the memories of Gonyardu and of her land, and focusing on what now lay ahead of them.

"We have now left the land of Lundarin," remarked Erundil. "And we must now travel through the land of Nangorid. May we forever treasure the blessings and favor shown to us by the Lady Gonyardu, and may it be a constant guide and reminder to us, even to the very end of our days."

"May it be!" responded the company collectively, and they continued paddling their boats up the river.

As the company went on, the change in the atmosphere they had previously noticed continued to grow and change, with a tide of stifling darkness seeming to pass through them in the cool breeze of the wind. The sun grew dimmer with clouds appearing in the sky and the weather dropping suddenly, yet the company was not cold, for their cloaks kept them warm, and even the armor of Erundil, Lelhond, and Karandil was found useful to provide them with warmth. The growing evil surrounding them troubled the company, but they knew that it was to be expected, granted that they were now in the middle of the land of the Dark Lord.

They traveled downstream in their boats for the next couple of hours, without any sounds of creatures crawling by the banks or the wings of birds flying above in the sky. All was silent, and their hearts grew heavy as they thought about the life that existed in Lundarin.

"I already miss the nature of Lundarin," remarked Lelhond in a soft voice, as though he were in some distant and sweet dream. "I miss not only the great number of gamdars that dwelt there, but also the birds that populated the skies, the animals and creatures that roamed in gardens and forests, and of the trees, plants, and flowers that blossomed with life. And now we find ourselves in the lifeless and dark land of Nangorid," he sighed to himself, pondering everything the company had left behind in the land of life.

"I miss Lundarin too," said Peter. "But we have made our choice to depart from that land and continue on our journey. And if we managed to survive for weeks in this evil land, then surely we could survive for many more weeks, maybe even months if we had to."

"Peter is right," agreed Erundil. "Though I sympathize with my son, the time to move on was laid on our hearts in Lundarin. And we all made the collective decision that it was right to depart, and besides, though memories may not be the same as things we experienced, they are still a source of great joy and remembrance."

"I guess you two are both right," softly said Lelhond, now feeling a bit encouraged, though he was still left picturing the beauty of Lundarin. "Even I agreed that our time to leave had come. We have some business to do, and I am ready for it."

"I am ready to get the business done as well," remarked Glophi. "And I don't want anything to prevent us from succeeding at what is next in line for us."

"Then let us hold onto the memories of the past and walk with confidence into the future," said Erundil. "Let us not give into fear or despair, but rather let us be filled with hope as we plan to succeed in this next stage of our journey."

The company agreed to this, and for the rest of the boat ride they sat silently to themselves, focusing on what lay ahead of them. Another hour or so passed, and they could see that the river was coming to an end. Very soon, the river's delta stopped their boat, and they jumped out and stepped onto the grass. All that they could see in every direction was a vast plain of grassland, going on for endless miles upon miles. They wondered how they would start and which direction they would go in.

"What now?" asked Steven. "All that I see is an endless plain of grass that could go on for an eternity."

The company looked all around them, wondering which way would be the best to trek. But as they looked on, Erundil saw something far up northward that immediately caught his attention.

"Look!" he said, pointing in the northward direction. "There are hills up there, with bushes and a few lone trees. We should probably go up there."

"But how do we know that it's the right way?" asked Karandil. "What if it's some trap devised by the enemy?"

"It cannot be a trap, Karandil," responded Erundil. "And besides, the eight of us will fight whatever battle that comes against us. I have a feeling that we will find the gamdarian soldiers up there, so come and let us go on to see if our luck has any bearing!"

Erundil set out in this direction and began walking toward the hilly region, with the rest of the company following him cautiously. Though they had their doubts, they had just enough confidence in Erundil that he knew what he was doing, especially in the glorious way that he had been revealed to them just before they left the land of Lundarin. And so, they walked in this direction for the next couple of hours, making their way closer to the hilly region. Over time they grew hungry and weary, as the afternoon now proudly dawned upon them.

"When will we take a break?" asked Huminli, arduously taking each step. "I am tired and hungry and could use a short rest."

"It will only be a little while longer before we will enter the hills," responded Erundil. "Just look at how close we are, and once we get there, we will take a much-needed rest. Also, it will be much better to protect ourselves in that area rather than making ourselves vulnerable in the open."

Huminli mumbled something to himself but went on anyway, with the rest of the company deciding to go on as well. Over the next half hour of walking, they inched their way closer to the hills, even as hunger and tiredness took control of their bodies.

But at last, they climbed their way up the hills, and finding some bushes and trees to rest under, they took out their food and munched on some fruits, vegetables, and a couple of bites of bread. They felt greatly nourished and filled by the food and also took a couple of sips of the water provided to them by Gonyardu, which instantly strengthed them and reminded them of the peace that existed in fullness from the land of Lundarin. They also took some sips from the water in the bottles that they had remaining.

After they had had their share of a short meal, they spent some time resting and relaxing amongst themselves, unconcerned by their long journey at the present moment. Even the smalves' eyes began to flutter, as sleep tried to naturally take them. They rested for over half an hour and would've gone on even longer as nobody spoke a word of interruption to each other.

But just as they felt the peace of rest returning to them, something terrible immediately alarmed their attention. Loud footsteps could be heard coming from the bushes in the distance, and collective growling sounds hovered over the air. Then springing forth from the bushes came five large black bears, snarling their bared teeth at the company and showing off their razor-sharp claws.

The company immediately awoke from their rest and sprung to their feet. "Bears! Bears are here!" exclaimed Karandil at the first sight of the terrifying black bears. "I knew that something wasn't right in this area!"

The company swiftly grabbed their weapons, standing still with shaking knees as the bears approached them. Lelhond fired an arrow in haste, but it badly missed hitting any of the bears. One of the bears leaped towards the company, but they collectively managed to quickly dodge to the side, with the bear collapsing to the ground in a loud thumping noise. But it picked itself up immediately again, with the other bears gaining speed as they charged at the company. Many more arrows were fired, but they too failed to hit their target, and with the bears charging toward them at full speed, they hoped that a miracle would come just in time to save them.

But just then, coming from the bushes in the opposite direction, there came dozens of arrows flying at lightning speed across the air, striking down all five bears at once. Another set of arrows rained forth, which confirmed all the bears as mortally wounded. The company stood anxiously, amazed that they had just been saved, but fearful of who had fired the arrows. But then coming forth from the bushes, they saw who it was that had saved them.

A vast number of green battle horses, ten thousand upon ten thousand came forth from the bushes and placed upon them were stern-faced gamdarian soldiers, strong in build and handsome in appearance. They each had the same type of armor that Erundil and his two sons had on, and carried the same weapons, with some of them carrying spears instead of swords. Between one to two dozen of them carried war banners; white and green flags with golden trees at their center. The company noticed that with the soldiers were three horses without riders, presumably for Erundil, Lelhond, and Karandil. Steven and the smalves instantly recognized that one of the battle horses was Linfast, the king's battle horse, whom they had been introduced to during their stay in the kingdom of Watendelle. Seeing the soldiers, Erundil and his sons, including Forandor went forth to greet them with great delight. Meanwhile, Steven, Peter, Huminli, and Glophi simply stared at them in wonder for both their imposing strength and the dignity with which they conducted themselves.

Immediately as Erundil and his sons approached them, every one of the soldiers stepped off from their horses, and went on one knee, bowing their heads to the ground. They then placed all of their weapons in their hands, outstretching them toward the four gamdars. Then crying out in powerful collective voices, they honored Erundil.

"Hail Erundil, King of Watendelle!" they cried aloud, as they remained on one knee with bowed heads for some time, before eventually standing up from the ground and boeing one last time in front of Erundil.

Erundil smiled and looked deeply into the eyes of his soldiers. "It is an honor to see all of you again," he said. "I have missed you for quite some time and wondered what you were all up to, but I am glad to see that you are doing well."

The soldiers smiled toward Erundil and placed their hands on their hearts out of respect for him. They then slowly started to back away, before one of the gamdars, taller and more physically imposing than the rest approached Erundil. His face was covered with long years of experience, yet his arms and shoulders were just as strong and broad as they were from the full vigor of his younger days. A meager smile was on the corner of his face, yet all that looked upon him could see that he had gone through grim times throughout his time in the world. He came forth to Erundil, and the two of them spoke face to face and alone with each other, with all eyes cast on them.

"Bardulil, it is good to see you," said Erundil, placing his hand on the soldier's shoulder. "I appreciate all the work you have done in my absence. What news do you bring to us?"

Bardulil's face grew hard. "I bring ill news, my king," he confessed. "I spoke with Lady Gonyardu a couple of weeks ago, and I assume that she told you this, but if you do not know, war is now upon us. Dulanmidir sent us here to find and warn you regarding this rising danger that he saw in his vision. This evil has either been following you or has been with you all along in your quest, and it is for this very purpose that we were sent to the land of Nangorid."

"Yes, I know all it is that you say," responded Erundil with a sigh. "Gonyardu revealed all of this to us in our discussion in Malah Ardmillia, and since then we have decided to go along with you in our quest, and if in due time we must separate, then we are prepared to do so."

"My king, the time to separate is now," revealed Bardulil. "Just two days ago, I saw thousands if not tens of thousands of wuzlirs mounted upon black battle horses mobilizing for war ahead in the valley to the southeast. Your quest lies to the west, but these wuzlirs are going in another direction, and they seem to be going in the direction of the Earth, ready to land an assault upon the humans. We must not let them do this, my king. We must meet them in battle and fight, which means that your company must separate."

Erundil sighed to himself but shook his head in agreement with Bardulil. "We have prepared long enough for this day to come," he said. "And I suppose that time is now upon us," he turned toward the company, who each had tears welling in their eyes.

Huminli and Glophi ran over to Erundil and hugged him. "But you can't leave us now, Mr. Erundil!" insisted Glophi. "Let us at least go on for a few days together, and then maybe I will be willing to depart from you, Lelhond, and Karandil. But I can't bear to do it now."

Erundil smiled at Glophi, embracing him and his brother Huminli tightly. Meanwhile, the gamdarian soldiers looked on in confusion at the sight, especially Bardulil whose face was covered in intense disgust.

"With all due respect, my king, what are these smalves doing here?" he asked. "And what are you doing embracing those creatures?" He stared at them for a while with a hard face and menacing eyes.

"They are part of my company," responded Erundil, with a smile. "I know it may not make sense to you, but I have seen the light. I have seen the good that the smalves bring to the world, and my hate and bitterness have been forced to go away from my heart."

Bewilderment covered Bardulil and the gamdarian soldiers' faces, and they could only shake their heads in astonishment. "Never would I have imagined these words to be coming from your mouth, my king," said Bardulil. "Do your sons have these same views of yours now?"

"Yes, we do," replied Lelhond. "For our unnecessary hate was exposed to us, and now our hardened hearts have been softened. I wish for your heart to be softened as well."

"I do not need your empty words of advice," snarled Bardulil, with his hate for the smalves now made manifest for all to see. "Neither do I need to change my way of thinking, unlike you."

"Everyone, let's calm down now," intervened Erundil. "There is no need for us to argue and boil our tempers against one another. We don't want any division within our army, especially now that we will enter into battle against the enemy."

The gamdars fell silent, shrinking back in response to Erundil's command. Erundil then whispered into Huminli and Glophi's ears. "I am sorry for that, my dear smalves," he said to them. "I hope that you two are feeling fine, but please, don't take what Bardulil said personally."

"It's fine, Mr. Erundil," responded Glophi with a smile. "I am confident that Mr. Bardulil can change for the better just like you did."

A smile came to Erundil's face in response to Glophi, and all he did was ponder on what the smalf said. "Are we ready or not?" asked Bardulil, growing impatient with the delay.

"Yes, but first let me and my two older sons say our final goodbyes to my younger son and also to my new friends," replied Erundil, with Bardulil immediately jumping onto his horse and waiting for Erundil and his sons to say their final farewells to the rest of the company.

And so it was that Steven, Peter, and Forandor gathered together with Erundil, along with his two older sons as well as Huminli and Glophi. For many long minutes, there was much weeping among the company, though broad smiles of joy covered each of their faces. Once they had left one another's presence, it was only Forandor with his father and two brothers who stood alone together. For some time, the four gamdars spoke in their native Tuntish language, and many tears that had never before been seen coming from the eyes of gamdars came from all four of their eyes. There was much talking and hugging among the family, but once they had finally collected and controlled their emotions, Forandor left them as Erundil, Lelhond, and Karandil jumped onto their green battle horses.

But before they left, Forandor called out to his father one last time. "Father, in which direction shall I lead the company?" he asked.

"In the direction, we have been going," responded Erundil. "Lead them on as straight as you can, going westward through the land of Nangorid. Meanwhile, we will go in the southeast direction to go to war against the wuzlirs."

"I wish you the best, father!" said Forandor. "May Zomladil bless you greatly, and farewell until I see you again!"

"Farewell, my dear son!" replied Erundil, with such a broad smile that had not been seen on his face in a long time. "I love you deeply, and cannot wait to hear from you on how you led the company to victory!"

Forandor then turned toward his brothers, with great joy covering his face as he saw them seated on their battle horses and clad in their thick golden and green armor. Tremendous pride for his siblings took control of his heart, and he felt grateful that he could call them brothers.

"Farewell, Lelhond and Karandil! I love you both with all my heart," he said to them, with a tear falling onto his cheek.

"Farewell Forandor! We love you too!" replied Lelhond and Karandil together, with bright lights reflecting off of their wide smiles.

Then with that, Erundil stirred Linfast to gallop, and with one last wave, he said his final goodbye to Forandor, Steven, Peter, Huminli, and Glophi, and led the army of gamdarian soldiers down the hill and into the vast valley. Yet as they rode on, the company of five could hear the mighty voice of Erundil singing or crying as they galloped downhill.

The company soon understood that he was leading a battle cry as he led his army, and they all listened silently and could just faintly hear what he cried aloud:

Stand up ye sons of Watendelle!
Courage and strength are now most needed!
Unto victory, we ride into the enemy's field,
And stand proudly against his wicked schemes!
Fear no darkness as you ride on,
For we ride unto victory!

With that, there was a loud eruption of collective cries, with great trumpets and horns blasting across the air as the soldiers of Watendelle shouted for joy and pure passion. The company watched that day as the army of gamdarian soldiers rode towards the field of battle, silently standing as they observed the bravery that filled their hearts. The afternoon sun shone on them as they rode on, and the grass reflected glitters of gold. They rode on with great ferocity like that of a rushing wind, and the sound of their horses' galloping hooves was that of a mighty noise of thunder rumbling across the ground. The company watched in awe as Erundil, Lelhond, and Karandil rode on for war, with broad smiles on the faces of the gamdars even as they went head-on toward the enemy.

Milton Keynes UK
Ingram Content Group UK Ltd.
UKHW020731271123
433341UK00020B/1699

9 781665 7511